TRAVELER
OF THE CENTURY

TRAVELER
OF THE CENTURY

ANDRÉS NEUMAN

TRANSLATED FROM THE SPANISH BY

NICK CAISTOR AND LORENZA GARCIA

FARRAR, STRAUS AND GIROUX

NEW YORK

Farrar, Straus and Giroux
18 West 18th Street, New York 10011

Distributed in Canada by D&M Publishers, Inc.
Printed in the United States of America
Originally published in 2009 by Santillana Ediciones Generales, Spain,
as *El viajero del siglo*
English translation originally published in 2012 by Pushkin Press,
Great Britain, as *Traveller of the Century*
Published in the United States by Farrar, Straus and Giroux
First American edition, 2012

Library of Congress Cataloging-in-Publication Data
Neuman, Andrés, 1977–
[Viajero del siglo. English]
Traveler of the century / Andrés Neuman : translated from the Spanish
by Nick Caistor and Lorenza Garcia. — 1st American ed.
    p. cm.
ISBN 978-0-374-11939-3 (alk. paper)
I. Caistor, Nick.   II. Garcia, Lorenza.   III. Title.

PQ6664.E478 V5213 2012
863'.64—dc23

2011047016

www.fsgbooks.com

1   3   5   7   9   10   8   6   4   2

To the memory of my mother, which echoes and echoes.
To my father and brother, who listen to it with me.

Strange old organ grinder,
Should I stay with you?
Will you churn out a tune
To the sound of my singing?

Wilhelm Müller / Franz Schubert

Europe, dragging your tattered rags,
Will you come one day, will your day come?

Adolfo Casais Monteiro

Trees have roots and I have legs.

George Steiner

Wandernburg: moving city sit. approx. between ancient states of Saxony and Prussia. Cap. of ancient principality of same name. Lat. N and long. E indeterminate due to shifting co-ord. [...] Hydro. R. Nulte non-navigable. Econ. activity wheat-growing and text. ind. [...] Despite accounts of chroniclers and travellers, precise loc. unknown.

CONTENTS

The Light Here Is Ancient   1

Almost a Heart   147

The Great Handle   293

Sombre Chords   451

The Wind Is Useful   535

THE LIGHT HERE

IS ANCIENT

A -ARE YO-UU C-COLD? THE coachman shouted, his voice fragmented by the jolting of the coach. I-I'm f-fine, th-ank yo-uu, replied Hans, teeth chattering.

The coach lamps flickered as the horses sped along the road. Mud flew up from the wheels. The axles twisted in every pothole, and seemed about to snap. Their cheeks puffing, the horses blew clouds from their nostrils. An opaque moon was rolling above the horizon.

For some time now Wandernburg had been visible in the distance, to the south. And yet, thought Hans, as often happens at the end of an exhausting day, the small city seemed to be moving in step with them, and getting no nearer. The sky above the carriage was heavy. With each crack of the coachman's whip the cold grew bolder, pressing against every outline. I-s the-ere mu-mu-ch f-f-urther t-oo g-oo? asked Hans, sticking his head out of the window. He had to repeat the question twice before the coachman heard him above the din and shouted, pointing with his whip: A-as yo-uu ca-an s-eee! Hans was uncertain whether this meant they were only a few minutes away or that it was impossible to tell. Since he was the only remaining passenger and had no one to talk to, he closed his eyes.

When he opened them again he saw a stone wall and an arched gateway. As they drew closer, Hans sensed something odd about the thickness of the wall, as if it were a warning about how hard it would be to leave rather than to enter. By the dim light of the coach lantern he could make out the shapes of the first buildings, the round-cut tiles like fish scales on some of the rooftops, the needle spires, the ornaments shaped like vertebrae. He had the impression he was arriving in a place that had just been evacuated, where the clatter of hooves and the wheels jolting on the cobblestones were producing too loud an echo. Everything was so still, it seemed as though someone was spying on them with bated breath. The carriage turned a corner, and the horses' gallop was suddenly muted—they were now on a beaten earth track. They went down Old Cauldron Street. Hans caught sight of an iron sign swinging in the breeze. He told the coachman to stop.

The man climbed down from his perch. When he reached the ground, he looked puzzled. He took a few steps, peered down at his feet, smiled uncertainly. He patted the lead horse's neck and whispered some words of thanks in its ear. The animal replied with a snort. Hans helped him untie the ropes from the luggage rack, pull back the wet canvas, then unload his case and a big trunk with handles on it. What have you got in there, a dead body? complained the coachman, dropping the chest to the ground and rubbing his hands. Not one dead body, Hans said with a smile, several. The man laughed abruptly, although a twitch of alarm flitted across his face. Will you be spending the night here too? asked Hans. No, the coachman explained, I'm going on to Wittenberg. I know a good place to sleep there, and there's a family who have to get to Leipzig. Then, looking askance at the creaking inn sign, he added: Are you sure you wouldn't like to ride on a little farther? Thanks, replied Hans, but this is fine. I need some rest. As you wish, sir, as you wish, said the coachman, clearing his throat several times. Hans paid him, refused the coins he offered in change, and bade him farewell. Behind his back he heard the crack of a whip, the creak of wood, and the thud of hooves moving off.

It was only when he was on his own outside the inn that he noticed a shooting pain in his back, sensed his muscles tremble and heard a pounding in his ears. He could still feel the jolting coach—the lights seemed to waver, the stones to be shifting. Hans rubbed his eyes. The windows of the inn were steamed up, making it impossible for him to see inside. He knocked on the door, where a Christmas wreath still hung. No one came. He tried the frozen handle, then pushed the door open. He saw a corridor lit by oil lamps suspended from hooks. The warmth drew Hans in. From the far end of the corridor came the crackle of an open fire. He struggled to drag the case and trunk inside. He stood beneath one of the lanterns, trying to warm up. With a start, he saw Herr Zeit staring at him from behind the reception desk. I was on my way to let you in, Herr Zeit said. The innkeeper moved extremely slowly, as if he were trapped between the counter and the wall. He had a huge, barrel-shaped belly, and smelt of musty fabric. Where have you come from? he asked. I've come from Berlin, said Hans, not that it really matters. It matters to me, young sir, Herr Zeit cut in, not suspecting that Hans had meant something else. How many nights do you intend to stay? Just one, I suppose, said Hans, I'm not sure yet. Well, when you've decided, please let me know, said the innkeeper, we need to be sure which rooms will be available.

Herr Zeit searched for a candlestick, then led Hans down the corridor and up a flight of stairs. As Hans watched the rotund figure heaving himself up each step, he was afraid he might come crashing down on top of him. The entire inn smelt of burning oil, the sulphur from the lamp wicks, and a mixture of sweat and soap. They reached the first-floor landing and carried on up. Hans was surprised to see that all the rooms appeared unoccupied. On the second floor, Herr Zeit paused at a door with the number seven chalked on it. Recovering his breath, he declared proudly: This is our best room. He took a battered ring laden with keys out of his pocket, and after several attempts and muttered curses, they entered the room.

Candlestick in hand, Herr Zeit ploughed his way through the darkness over to the window. When he opened the shutters, there was the sound of creaking wood and a cloud of dust flew up. Rather than illuminating the room, the feeble light from outside seemed to seep into the darkness like a gas. It gets quite sunny in the mornings, Herr Zeit explained, because it faces east. Hans screwed up his eyes to examine the room. He could make out a table and two chairs. A camp bed with a pile of folded woollen blankets on it. A zinc bathtub, a rusty chamber pot, a washbasin on a stand, a water jug. A brick-and-stone chimney piece with a ledge that seemed too narrow to accommodate any objects (Only rooms three and seven have a hearth, Herr Zeit announced) and beside it were several tools: a small shovel, a poker, a pair of blackened tongs, an almost bald brush. In the fireplace lay two charred logs. On the wall opposite the door, between table and tub, Hans's attention was drawn to a small painting that looked to him like a watercolour, although he could not see it properly. One more thing, Herr Zeit concluded solemnly, taking the lamp over to the table and sliding his hand along the surface. It's pure oak. Hans stroked the table contentedly. He glanced at the candlesticks with their tallow candles, and at the rusty oil lamp. I'll take it, he said. He was immediately aware of Herr Zeit helping him out of his frock coat and hanging it on one of the nails in the wall beside the door—the coat stand.

Wife! the innkeeper bellowed, as if he had just woken up. Wife, come up here! We have a guest! Instantly there was a sound of footsteps on the stairs. A broad-beamed woman appeared in the doorway, wearing skirts and an apron with a huge pouch over her bosom. Unlike her husband, Frau Zeit moved swiftly and efficiently. In a trice she had changed the bed sheets for a slightly less yellowing set, given the room a cursory sweep, and vanished downstairs again to fill the water jug. When she reappeared with it, Hans drank greedily, almost without pausing for breath. Will you bring his luggage up? Herr Zeit asked. His wife sighed. Her husband decided the sigh meant she would, and so, after nodding to Hans, he in turn disappeared down the stairs.

Lying on his back on the bed, Hans could feel with his toes how rough the sheets were. Closing his eyes, he thought he could hear scratching sounds from beneath the floorboards. He drifted off to sleep, letting all his cares slide away, and said to himself: Tomorrow I'll gather my things and move elsewhere. If he had examined the ceiling closely with a candle, he would have seen the huge cobwebs between the beams. Hidden among them, a spider watched over Hans's sleep, thread by thread.

He woke up late, his stomach empty. A warm sun was dancing over the table, flowing down the chairs like syrup. Hans washed in the handbasin, opened his case, and dressed. Then he went over to the small painting and confirmed that it was indeed a watercolour. The frame seemed to him rather too ornate. When he took it down to examine it more closely, he discovered a tiny mirror on the back. He hung it up again, this time with the mirror facing towards him. He filled the basin with the water left in the jug, broke off a piece of soap, rummaged for his shaving brush, his razor and his colognes. He whistled while he shaved, unaware of what it was he was whistling.

On his way downstairs he ran into Herr Zeit, who was climbing the steps laboriously one by one. He was carrying a small notebook, and asked Hans to pay for the night's lodging before breakfast. It's a house rule, he said. Hans went back into his room and came out with the exact sum, plus a one-groschen tip, which he gave to the innkeeper with a wry smile. Down on the ground floor Hans had a look around. At the far end of the corridor he could see a large dining room with a blazing hearth and a big cooking pot over the fire. Opposite it was a sofa, which, as Hans quickly discovered, sank in the middle as soon as you sat on it. On the other side of the corridor was a door, which he imagined must lead to the Zeits' apartment. Next to the door stood a Christmas tree that was so exquisitely decorated he could scarcely believe either of them could have been responsible for it. Out the back of the inn he discovered a courtyard with latrines and a well. He made use of one of the latrines, and returned feeling much better. A raft of smells caught his attention. He strode towards it and found Frau Zeit chopping chard in the kitchen. Hams, strings of sausages and sides of bacon hung like silent sentinels. A pot was boiling on the stove. Row upon row of frying pans, serving spoons, cauldrons and saucepans refracted the morning in whorls of light. You're late, sit down, Frau Zeit ordered, without looking up from her chopping. Hans did as he was told. We usually serve breakfast in the dining room, she went on, but I can't leave the fire now, so you'd best have it in here. On the board were laid vegetables, a basted joint of meat, the rippled skins of potatoes. A tap was dripping into a sink full of dirty dishes. Underneath were piled baskets of firewood, coal and slack. Farther off, stacked among a jumble of pitchers and jars were small sacks of beans, rice, flour, semolina. Frau Zeit dried her hands on her apron. In one swift movement she sliced through a fresh loaf, and spread jam on it. Placing a bowl in front of Hans, she filled it with ewe's milk, then poured coffee in until it slopped over the sides. Will you be wanting eggs? she asked.

Recalling how desolate Wandernburg had seemed the night before, Hans was surprised at the hustle and bustle in the streets when he went out after breakfast. Although all the activity seemed somehow restrained, Hans had to accept the evidence that people did indeed live in the city. He wandered aimlessly around. Occasionally, he thought he had lost his way in the narrow, steep streets, at other times he realised he had walked in a circle. He discovered that the coachmen of Wandernburg avoided slowing down so as not to pull on their horses' mouths, and only gave him a few seconds to jump out of their way. As he walked, he noticed lace curtains being drawn aside, then closing again. When Hans tried to smile courteously in the direction of some of these windows, the shadows immediately withdrew. Snowflakes threatened to turn the air white, but were quickly engulfed in mist. Even the pigeons fluttering above his head seemed to crane their necks to look at him. Bewildered by the winding streets, his feet sore from the cobblestones, Hans paused in the market square for a rest.

The market square was the place where all the streets of Wandernburg converged, the centre of its map. At one end was the town hall, with its red-tiled roof and pointed turrets. At the opposite end stood the Tower of the Wind. Seen from the pavement, its most prominent feature was the square clock face sprinkling the time over the square below. Yet from the top of the tower, even more impressive was the arrow on its weathervane, which quivered and groaned as it twisted this way and that.

In addition to the stalls selling food, peasants came to the market square from the surrounding region, their carts laden with produce. Others turned up hoping to be taken on as day labourers in the fields. For some reason Hans could not understand, the traders peddled their wares almost in whispers, and haggling was carried out in hushed tones. He bought some fruit at a stall. He strolled on again, amusing himself by counting the number of lace curtains that twitched as he went past. When he raised his eyes to look up at the Tower of the Wind, he realised he had missed the afternoon coach. Resigning himself to the fact, he walked round in circles three or four times more until he found himself back in Old Cauldron Street. Night had fallen like a curtain.

Walking along the streets of Wandernburg after dark, passing mouldy arches and isolated street lamps, Hans experienced the same sensations as when he had first arrived. He could see that the city's inhabitants went home early, almost scuttling back to their houses for safety. Their place was taken by cats and dogs, disporting themselves as they pleased, gnawing at any scraps of food they could find in the streets. As he was entering the inn and reflecting that the Christmas wreath had disappeared, Hans heard the cry of a nightwatchman. He was coming round the street corner, wearing a hood, and carrying a long pole with a dim light on the tip:

> *Time to go home, everyone!*
> *The church bell has chimed six,*
> *Watch over your fire and your lamps,*
> *Praise be to God! All praise!*

Herr Zeit seemed surprised to see him, as if he had been expecting his guest to vanish into thin air without warning. Everything in the inn was as quiet as before, although as he passed by the kitchen Hans counted six dirty plates piled up next to the sink, from which he deduced there were four other guests. His calculation turned out to be wrong, however, because as he headed for the staircase a slender figure emerged from the door to the Zeits' apartment bearing a Christmas tree and a box of candles. This is my daughter, Lisa, said Frau Zeit in a hurried introduction as she scurried down the corridor. Still wedged between the counter and the wall, Herr Zeit himself noted the ensuing silence and shouted: Lisa! Say hello to the gentleman! Lisa smiled mischievously at Hans, calmly shrugged her shoulders and went back inside without saying a word.

The Zeits had had seven children. Three were now married; two had died of the measles. Still living with them were Lisa, the eldest, and Thomas, a boisterous child who wasted no time in bursting into the dining room where Hans was eating dumplings with bread and butter. Who are you? asked Thomas. I'm Hans, said Hans, to which Thomas replied: Then I don't know who you are. With that he stole a dumpling, wheeled round, and disappeared down the corridor.

When he heard Hans's footsteps going upstairs, the innkeeper struggled to prise his belly free and came to ask if he were planning to leave the next day. Hans had already decided he was, but Herr Zeit's insistence made him feel as if he were being turned out, and so in order to contradict him he said he did not know. The innkeeper seemed extraordinarily pleased at this reply, going so far as to ask Hans whether he needed anything for his room. Hans said he did not, and thanked him. When Herr Zeit still stood there, Hans added in a friendly tone that apart from the market square, the streets of Wandernburg seemed to him rather dark, and he mentioned the gas lighting used in Berlin or London. We don't need all that light here, declared Herr Zeit, hitching up his trousers, we have good eyesight and regular habits. We go out by day and at night we sleep. We go to bed early, and get up early. What do we want gas for?

Lying on his back in bed again, Hans yawned, tiredness mingling with bewilderment. He promised himself: Tomorrow I'll gather my things and move on.

The night barked and meowed.

Atop the Tower of the Wind, piercing the mists, the weathervane seemed about to fly off its hinges.

After another stroll over the frosty ground, Hans had the strange feeling that the city's layout somehow shifted while everyone was asleep. How could he lose his bearings so completely? It was beyond him—the tavern he had lunched at the day before was on the opposite corner from where he remembered it, the clangs from the smithy, which should have been on the right as he turned the corner, surprised him by coming from the left, the sloping street that went down now went steeply up, a passageway he remembered walking through which should have opened onto an avenue was a dead end. Feeling his pride as a seasoned traveler challenged, Hans booked a seat on the next coach for Dessau, and then resolved to familiarise himself with the maze of streets through which he was wandering. And yet, no sooner had he congratulated himself on two or three successes than he realised to his dismay he was lost again. The only easy place to find was the market square, which he kept going back to in order to get his bearings. Killing time before his coach left, trying hard to memorise the city's cardinal points, he was standing in the square like a sundial, his thin shadow cast over the cobblestones, when he saw the organ grinder arrive.

Moving laboriously yet gracefully, as though as he shuffled along he imagined he was dancing, the grizzled organ grinder came into the square pulling his barrel organ, leaving its track in the fresh snow. With him was a black-haired dog. With an innate sense of rhythm, the dog always kept the same distance from its master, respecting his every pause, stagger, change of pace. The old man was dressed after a fashion in a threadbare-looking dark overcoat and a translucent cape. He came to a halt on one side of the square. Slowly and carefully, he spread out his things, as though miming what he was going to do later. Once installed, he untied the battered umbrella fastened to the cart handle. He opened it and placed it on top of his instrument to protect it from the flurry of snow. This gesture touched Hans, who stood waiting for the organ grinder to play a tune.

The old man was in no hurry, or he enjoyed dawdling. Beneath his beard Hans saw him smile knowingly at his dog, which gazed up at him, its triangular ears pricked. The barrel organ was of modest size—sitting on the cart, it barely reached the organ grinder's waist, obliging him to stoop even lower to play it. The cart was painted green and orange. The wooden wheels had once been red. Enclosed by a metal hoop barely holding them together, they were not round but a more uneven shape, like the years they had spent rolling. The front of the organ had once been decorated with a naive landscape of a tree-lined river.

Hans never felt nostalgia for anything: he preferred to think about his next journey. And yet, when the organ grinder began to play, something touched the edge of something. When he heard the barrel organ's metallic past, Hans sensed that someone else, some past self, was trembling inside him. Following the melody as if it were words streaming on the wind, Hans experienced something unusual—he was aware of what he was feeling, he could see himself being moved. He was listening because the barrel organ was playing, the barrel organ was playing because he was listening. Hans had the impression that the organ grinder was not so much playing as trying to remember. With an airy hand, his fingers stiff with cold, he turned the handle. As he did so the dog's tail, the square, the weathervane, the light, noon itself, went spinning round and round, and as soon as the tune was approaching the end, the organ grinder's timekeeping hand created not so much a pause, or even a silence, more a slight tear in a fabric, before turning the handle again, so that the music started up once more, and everything carried on spinning round, and it was no longer cold.

Coming back down to earth, Hans found it odd that no one else seemed to notice the barrel-organ music. Used to it, or in too much of a hurry, everyone walked by without even looking. Finally, a small boy stopped in front of the organ grinder. The old man said hello with a smile to which he responded shyly. Two huge shoes planted themselves behind the boy's loose shoelaces; a voice leant over saying: Don't look at the man, can't you see the way he's dressed? Don't bother him, come along now, come along. In front of the old man was a shiny dish into which people would occasionally drop small copper coins. Hans noticed that those showing this consideration did not stop to listen to the music either, but left the money as if they were giving it to a beggar. This did not seem to spoil the organ grinder's concentration, or the rhythm of his hand.

At first, Hans was content to watch him. After a while, as though waking up from a dream, he realised that he too was part of the scene. He walked over noiselessly, and, in an attempt to show his appreciation, bent over to leave an offering that was twice as much as what was already in the dish. At this, for the first time since he had arrived, the organ grinder straightened up. He smiled openly at Hans with an expression of calm content, then carried on playing, unperturbed. Hans assumed the old man had not interrupted his playing because he knew he was enjoying the music. More matter-of-factly, the organ grinder's dog appeared to think this called for some sort of formal recognition—he squinted as though the sun had just come out, opened his jaws very wide and unfurled his long pink tongue.

When the organ grinder took a break, Hans decided to talk to him. They stood for a while conversing, the falling snow soaking their clothes. They discussed the cold, the colour of Wandernburg's trees, the differences between the mazurka and the cracovienne. Hans found the organ grinder's polite manners charming, and the organ grinder appreciated the deep timbre of Hans's voice. Hans looked at the clock on the Tower of the Wind and calculated that he had an hour left before going back to the inn to fetch his luggage and wait for the coach. He invited the organ grinder for a drink at one of the taverns in the square. The organ grinder accepted with a nod and added: In that case I must introduce you two. He asked Hans's name, then said: Franz, this is Herr Hans, Herr Hans, this is my dog, Franz.

To Hans it seemed that the organ grinder followed him as if he had been expecting him that morning. On their way to the tavern, the old man stopped to greet a couple of beggars. He exchanged a few friendly words that revealed he knew them, and as he took his leave he handed them half the money from his dish, then calmly carried on walking. Do you always do that? Hans asked, gesturing towards the beggars. Do what? said the organ grinder. You mean the money? No, no, I couldn't afford to. I shared what you gave me today so that you know I'm accepting your invitation not out of self-interest, but because I like you.

When they reached the door of the Central Tavern, the old man ordered Franz to wait outside. Bringing the barrel organ with them, they went inside, Hans first, then the organ grinder. The Central Tavern was crammed to the rafters. The stoves, the oven and the tobacco smoke created a blanket of heat that smothered voices, breathing and smells. The smokers blew out spirals like ribcages—a smoke animal devoured the patrons. Hans pulled a face. Doing their best to protect the barrel organ, they managed with difficulty to make a tiny space for themselves at the bar. The organ grinder had a dreamy smile on his face. Less relaxed, Hans resembled a prince watching a carnival. They ordered two wheat beers, and, elbow-to-elbow, raised their glasses in a toast before resuming their conversation. Hans said he had not seen the old man the previous day. The organ grinder explained that in wintertime he went to the square every morning, but never in the afternoons because it was too cold. Hans still had the feeling that they had missed out the main topic, that they were both talking as though they had already said the things that in fact had not even been mentioned. They ordered two more beers, followed by another two. That's good, the old man said, his whiskers covered in froth. Through the bottom of his glass, Hans's smile was lopsided.

A coachman came here asking for you, Herr Zeit declared. He waited a few minutes then stomped off angrily. Herr Zeit added thoughtfully, as if he had reached this conclusion after a great deal of effort: It's Tuesday already! Playing along with him, Hans replied: Quite right, it's Tuesday. Herr Zeit seemed satisfied and asked whether he planned to stay more nights. Hans paused, genuinely unsure this time, and said: I don't think so. I really must get to Dessau. Then, since he was feeling quite merry, he added: Although you never know.

Ensconced on the sofa in the dining room, her face glowing orange in front of the fire, Frau Zeit was darning a pair of enormous socks: Hans wondered whether they belonged to her or her husband. When she saw him come in, she stood up. She told him his supper was ready and asked him not to make any noise because the children had just gone to bed. Almost at once, Thomas contradicted her by bursting through the door clutching a handful of lead soldiers. Colliding with his mother, he stopped dead, a pale skinny leg flailing in mid-air. And as swiftly as he had arrived he turned tail and ran. A door slammed in the Zeits' apartment. Instantly, a shrill adolescent voice screamed out Thomas's name, followed by some other protests they could not hear. The little scallywag, the landlady muttered under her breath.

Lying in bed, mouth half-open as though waiting for a drip to fall from the ceiling, Hans listened to his own thoughts: Tomorrow for sure, at the very latest the day after, I'll gather my things and leave. As he drifted into oblivion he thought he heard light footsteps padding down the corridor and pausing outside his room. He even imagined he could hear someone breathing nervously on the other side of the door. But he could not be sure. Perhaps it was his own breathing, growing gradually deeper, his own breathing, his own, his.

Hans had gone to the market square to find the organ grinder. He had discovered him in the same place, in the same position. On seeing him, the old man had gestured to his dog and Franz had gone to greet him, tail wagging from side to side like a metronome. They had shared a lunch of warm soup, hard sheep's cheese, bread with liver pâté and several beers. The organ grinder had finished his day's work and now they were strolling together along the River Walk towards High Gate, where Wandernburg ended and the countryside began. After objecting to Hans paying for his lunch, the old man had insisted on inviting him to his house for tea.

They walked side by side, waiting for each other whenever the organ grinder stopped pushing the cart to catch his breath, Hans lagged behind to peer into a side street or Franz paused to lift his leg here and there. By the way, asked Hans, what's your name? Well, the old man replied, switching to a less formal way of addressing him, as if they were already firm friends, it's an ugly name and since I seldom use it I hardly remember what it is. Just call me organ grinder—that's the best name for me. And what's yours? (Hans, said Hans.) I know that, but what's your surname? (Hans, repeated Hans, laughing.) Well, what does it matter, eh? Hey, Franz, will you stop pissing on every stone please? We have a guest for tea today, behave yourself, it's getting dark and we're not home yet, good, that's what I like to see.

They walked through High Gate, continuing along a narrower earthen track. The countryside opened out before them, smooth and white. For the first time, Hans saw the vastness of the U-shaped plain to the south-east of Wandernburg. In the distance he glimpsed the hedges of crop fields, the pastures for the farm animals, the sown cornfields lying in frozen expectancy. At the end of the path he could make out a wooden footbridge, the ribbon of the river, and beyond it a pinewood and rocky outcrops. Surprised at not seeing any houses, Hans wondered where the old man was taking him. Sensing Hans's thoughts, and at the same time adding to his bewilderment, the organ grinder set down his cart for a moment, took him by the arm and said: We're almost there.

Hans calculated that they had walked more than half a league from the market square. Had he been able to climb the rocks behind the pinewoods, he would have had a panorama of the whole of the surrounding countryside and the city. He would have been able to observe the highway along which he had traveled on the first night, as it skirted the eastern edge of the city—at that very moment, several coaches were making their way north to Berlin, or south to Leipzig. On the far side, to the west of the plain, the air was stirred by the sails of the windmills around the textile mill with its brick chimney stack polluting the atmosphere. In the hedged fields, a few peasants were dotted about, carrying out the first hoeing of the year, slowly scratching at the soil. And snaking through it all, a silent witness, ran the River Nulte. Too shallow for boats, the Nulte was an anaemic river. Its waters seemed worn out, resigned to their fate. Bordered by two rows of poplars, the Nulte trickled through the valley as though in search of help. Looked at from the top of the hill, it was a loop of water flattened by the wind. Less a river than the memory of a river. Wandernburg's river.

They crossed the tiny wooden footbridge over the Nulte. The pinewood and the stony outcrop seemed to be the only things ahead of them. Hans did not dare ask where they were going, partly out of politeness and partly because, wherever they were going, he had enjoyed discovering the outskirts of the city. They walked through the pinewood almost in a straight line. The wind hummed in the branches, the organ grinder whistled to echo the sound, and Franz echoed his master's whistles with barks. When they had reached the first rocks, Hans said to himself that the only possibility left was for them to go through the rock.

And, to his astonishment, that was what they did.

The organ grinder stopped in front of a cave and began unloading his cart. Franz ran inside and trotted out with a morsel of herring in his mouth. Hans's first thought was that this must be some mistake. On second thoughts, it struck him as altogether wonderful. And that nobody in a long while had surprised him as much as this old man. The organ grinder, who was smiling at him again, welcomed him with a sweep of his arm and said: Make yourself at home. Hans responded with a theatrical bow, stepping back a few paces in order to get a better view of the cave's setting. On close inspection, and ignoring the fact that it bore no resemblance to a house, the cave could not have been better situated. There were enough pine trees surrounding it to soften the effects of the wind or the rain, without making it inaccessible. It was close to a bend in the River Nulte, and thus guaranteed a source of water. Unlike other barren, muddy areas at the foot of the hill, the entrance to the cave was blessed with a thick patch of grass. As though concurring with Hans, the organ grinder said: Of all the caves and grottos in the hill, this is the cosiest. As he stooped to enter, Hans discovered that, although undeniably damp, the cave was warmer than he had expected. The old man lit some tinder and tallow candles. By their light, the organ grinder took Hans on a tour of the cave, showing him every nook and cranny as if it were a palace. One of the great advantages to this dwelling is the lack of doors, he began, which means Franz and I can enjoy the view from our beds. As you see the walls aren't exactly smooth, but the irregularities break the monotony and create an interesting play of light, and what light! (The old man raised his voice, wheeling round with surprising agility—the candle he was carrying traced a faint circle on the walls, sputtered, but stayed alight.) Besides, how can I put it, they provide plenty of opportunity to enjoy some privacy or sheltered sleep. The reason I mention privacy (the organ grinder whispered, winking) is because Franz is a bit nosey, he always wants to know what I'm doing, sometimes it feels like he's the owner of the house. Anyway, sshh! I didn't say a word, let's carry on! Here we have the back of the cave, which, as you can see, is simple, but notice how still, how quiet it is, all you can hear are the leaves. Ah, and as for the acoustics, the echoes are amazing, when I play the barrel organ in here it feels as if you've downed a bottle of wine in one.

Hans listened to the organ grinder spellbound. Although he found the damp, the gloom and the dirtiness of the cave uncomfortable, he thought it would be an excellent idea to spend the evening or even the night there. The old man lit a fire with some broom, dry grass and newspaper. Franz had been down to the river to drink and had come back shivering, his fur standing on end, the flecks on his paws a little paler. When he saw the fire, he trotted over to it, almost singeing his tail. Hans burst out laughing. The organ grinder passed him a demijohn of wine he kept in a corner. Only then, in the glow of the fire the old man had lit, could Hans appreciate the entire cave and study its odd furnishings. A few bits of clothing hung from a rope stretched across the entrance. Beneath the rope, the sharp point of the umbrella was embedded in the ground. Next to the umbrella were two pairs of shoes, one almost in tatters, stuffed with balls of paper. Lined up against the wall in order of size stood a row of earthenware cups, some plates, empty bottles with corks in them, tin pitchers. In one corner lay a straw pallet, and on top of it a heap of sheets and scraps of filthy wool. Scattered around the mattress like a ruined dressing table lay bowls, small wooden boxes and pieces of soap. A bunch of newspapers was hanging between two rock ledges. At the back of the cave was a pile of shoeboxes filled with pins, screws and various pieces of equipment and tools necessary for repairing the barrel organ. Spectacularly out of place in the midst of all this lay the immaculate rug the instrument sat on. There was not a single book in sight.

There were two temperatures in the cave now. Within a half-yard radius of the fire, the air was warming up, caressing their skin. An inch beyond that, the room was freezing, lending a hard outline to everything. Franz appeared to be asleep, or intent on getting warm. Rubbing his hands together, Hans puffed into them. He pulled down his liberty beret, wound his scarf twice more round his neck, turned up the collar of his frock coat. He gazed at the organ grinder's threadbare overcoat, its baggy seams and worn buttons. Aren't you cold in that? said Hans. Well, it's seen better days, the old man replied. But it brings back good memories, and they keep us warm, too, don't they?

The fire shrank slowly.

A few days after meeting the organ grinder, Hans was still intending to leave Wandernburg at any moment. And yet, without really knowing why, he kept putting off his departure. One of the things that most captivated Hans about his new acquaintance, besides the way he played his instrument, was his relationship with his dog. Franz was a Hovawart with a broad forehead, an alert muzzle and a bushy, restless tail. He was as sparing with his barks as if they were coins. The old man would let Franz guide him through the countryside; he would talk to him and whistle tunes from the barrel organ to lull him to sleep. Franz seemed to have a remarkable ear for music, and would growl if the old man stopped in mid-tune. Occasionally they would look at one another knowingly, as though they could both hear some inaudible sound.

Without giving away too much, Hans had explained to the old man that he was a sort of traveler, who journeyed from place to place, stopping off at unfamiliar destinations to discover what they were like, then moving on when he grew bored, felt the urge to travel again or found something better to do elsewhere. A few days earlier, Hans had suggested to the organ grinder that he accompany him to Dessau. The old man, who never asked questions Hans did not seem happy to answer, proposed he stay on another week and keep him company before leaving.

Hans usually woke up late, later anyway than the handful of other guests who, to judge by the leftover food, the footsteps on the stair and the sound of doors opening and closing, were also staying at the inn. He would eat his breakfast under the watchful eye of Frau Zeit, whose furious prowess with the kitchen knives would have woken him, or he would go out for a bite to eat at the Central Tavern. There he would read for a while, have a coffee, or more precisely two coffees, and after that would go to meet the organ grinder. He would listen to him play, watch him turn the handle and let his memory spin round in circles. To its rhythm, he would think of all the places he had visited, about the future journeys he would make, about people he did not always wish to remember. Some days, when the hands on the Tower of the Wind said it was time to go, Hans would accompany the organ grinder home. They would leave the city centre, stroll along River Walk and through High Gate, follow the narrow earthen path to the footbridge, cross the babbling waters of the River Nulte, and traverse the pinewood until they reached the rocky outcrop. On other days, Hans would pass by the cave later, and the organ grinder would welcome him with an open demijohn and a blazing fire. They would pass the time drinking wine, talking, listening to the river. After the first few nights, Hans lost his fear of the path and grew used to going back to the inn on foot. Franz would accompany him part of the way, only turning back when the lights of High Gate came into view. Herr Zeit would get out of bed to unbolt the door for him, fat cheeks furrowed, grunting and cursing to himself, snoring in his slippers. Hans made his way upstairs, wondering how much longer he could put up with the rickety old bed.

The Zeit family would rise at first light, when Hans had only been asleep a few hours. Herr Zeit made them gather round while he read a short passage from the Bible, then the four of them ate breakfast in their apartment. Afterwards, they would each go off to fulfil their different duties. Herr Zeit would take up his position behind the reception desk, spreading the newspaper over his formidable belly as though it were a lectern, and there he would stay until shortly before midday, when he went out to settle a few bills and other payments. He would stop off on the way home to drink a few beers and listen to the local gossip, which he maintained was part of his job. In the meantime, Frau Zeit would tackle a long list of chores that included cooking, fetching firewood, doing the ironing and cleaning the rooms, and ended after supper with a last bit of darning in front of the fire. Then the frown would fade from her brow; she would cast off her apron and parade around the bedroom in the flannel gown she insisted on calling her kimono, swaying her hips with a mixture of sadness and faded charm.

Thomas's sister Lisa would take him to school. Besides being constantly on the move and never finishing his homework, the boy had a habit that infuriated his sister—he was fond of easing his stomach by letting out little explosions. Each time he did so, Lisa would march out of the bedroom they shared and fetch their mother, who would come and give him a scolding. While Frau Zeit bawled him out and threatened punishment, Thomas would begin again. So, amid giggles and explosions, explosions and giggles, Thomas would finish dressing. He came home every day for lunch, and attended Bible class twice a week. Lisa did not go to school, even though she had always been a more hard-working pupil than her brother. After dropping him off, Lisa would return to help at the inn, shop for groceries in the market square or wash linen in the Nulte. In winter this was the hardest chore, because the washerwomen had to search for stretches that were not iced over. Lisa was tall for her age and quite thin, although in the past year she had begun to fill out, a fact of which she was proud and faintly uneasy. Her skin was smooth and downy, except for her hands—in contrast to the softness of her neck or shoulders, Lisa's hands were coarse. Her knuckles were red, her fingers chapped, the skin above her wrists raw from the freezing water. Hans noticed this one morning when he wanted to take a hot bath. Lisa was ferrying pans of boiling water up and down the stairs to fill the tub. He suddenly found himself staring at her hands, but she snatched them away, ashamed, and concealed them behind her back. Abashed, Hans tried to distract the girl by engaging her in conversation. Lisa seemed to go along with the ploy, and for the first time since his arrival uttered more than a few words to him. Hans was surprised at how knowledgeable and self-assured she was, although at first she had seemed so timid. When the bathtub was almost full to overflowing, Hans turned to open his case and had the impression Lisa was lingering in the room. As soon as he heard the door close, he felt foolish for even having entertained such a thought.

Worried about the frugality of the organ grinder's meals, which consisted mainly of boiled potatoes, salted herring, sardines or hard-boiled eggs, Hans would take with him to the cave a little meat, a wheel of sheep's cheese or some of Frau Zeit's sausages. The organ grinder accepted these delicacies, but the moment Hans left, fed them to Franz. When Hans discovered his ruse, the old man explained that, although grateful for his generosity, he had promised himself many years ago he would only live off what his barrel organ could provide, which was why he played it in the first place. Hans finally managed to win him over him by persuading him they were simply dining together. One evening, as they were both tucking in to a piece of larded beef and a bowl of rice with vegetables, Hans asked him whether he ever felt lonely in the cave. How can I feel lonely, replied the organ grinder, chewing his beef, when I have Franz watching over me? Isn't that right, my boy? (Franz trotted over and licked his hand, using the opportunity to help himself to a small chunk of beef.) Besides, my friends come to see me. (Who are they? asked Hans.) You'll meet them soon enough, you'll meet them soon enough (the organ grinder topped up his glass), I expect they'll show up tomorrow or the day after.

Sure enough, a couple of days later, Hans found two other guests at the cave when he arrived—Reichardt and Lamberg. Nobody knew Reichardt's exact age, but it was obvious he was at least twice as old as Lamberg. Reichardt scraped a living as a hired field hand. He would offer his services to hoe, plough, sow or do a few days' work on seasonal tasks. He lived crowded together with his fellow labourers on church lands about twenty minutes from the cave. Reichardt was one of those men whose once relatively youthful appearance makes them look even older as they age; their lean bodies betraying more starkly the ravages of time. He suffered from stiff joints, and his hairless skin was cracked and blotchy from the sun. Half his teeth were missing. Reichardt took pleasure in using swear words; he preferred them to the actual subject of a conversation. That evening, when he saw Hans arrive, he greeted him by saying: Shit, so you're the fellow who comes from who-knows-where. Pleased to meet you, replied Hans. You don't say? Reichardt replied with a guffaw. Shit, organ grinder, he's even daintier than you said he was!

Beside him sat Lamberg, as always listening and saying nothing. Unlike Reichardt, who would frequently stop by the cave, Lamberg went there mainly on Saturday evenings or on Sundays, which was his day off. He had been working in Wandernburg's textile mill since he was twelve. He shared a room in the houses built around the mill, the rent being deducted from his wages. His muscles were always clenched, as if he were permanently suffering from cramp. The fumes from the mill meant his eyes were always bloodshot. Everything he looked at seemed to turn red, to burn. Lamberg was a man of few words. He never raised his voice. He rarely disagreed with the person he was talking to. He simply fixed them with his eyes, red like two glowing pistons.

Franz did not seem to trust the two men equally—he showed a playful familiarity towards Reichardt, whom he kept licking and who he wanted to rub his tummy, while from time to time he would sniff at Lamberg's legs suspiciously, as though he were still not quite used to his smell. Sitting across from them as the wine was passed around, Hans noticed the two men's different way of getting drunk. Reichardt was an experienced drinker—he waved his glass about a lot, but only occasionally lifted it to his lips. He remained relatively alert in his drunkenness, like a gambler waiting for his fellow players to become completely intoxicated. There was a youthful impetuosity to Lamberg's thirst. Although, Hans reflected, perhaps Lamberg's aim was to find the quickest route to unconsciousness, and this was why he drank as though he were swallowing not only the alcohol but also all the words he never spoke.

At the start of the evening, Hans felt that he would prefer to be alone with the organ grinder to be able to talk to him peacefully as was their custom. And yet, as the hours went by, Hans noticed that Reichardt began swearing at him more affectionately, and Lamberg clapped him on the back more gently. Hans descended from proud aloofness to comic verbosity. He regaled them with tales of his travels, some unbelievable yet true, others plausible but invented. Then he described the inn, the way Frau Zeit filleted fish, Thomas's little explosions and Lisa screaming his name. When Hans swayed from side to side trying to imitate Herr Zeit, for the first time Lamberg let out a long guffaw, then seemed amazed at himself and sucked his laugh up again like a noodle.

Amid the tobacco fumes and the heat from the stoves, a city councillor had made his way over to say good day to him. Hans found this doubly baffling—he had never seen the man before, and besides, it was evening. The councillor had planted his elbows on the bar and beamed at him with a friendliness that was tainted with something. Hans had tilted his head back to take some sips from his beer. But the councillor was still there, and he had not come over simply to wish him good day.

After a few polite phrases, abounding with the words "*gnä-diger Herr*", "esteemed visitor", "honourable gentleman", the councillor looked at him differently, as though focusing a lens, and Hans knew he was about to say what he had come to say. We're delighted to welcome you here among us, the council-lor began, Wandernburg is a city that appreciates tourists, for you are a tourist aren't you? (More or less, replied Hans.) And, as I say, tourists are most welcome here, you'll soon see how hospitable we Wandernburgers are (I've already noticed, Hans observed), marvellous, marvellous, yes, most welcome indeed, let me tell you. If you don't mind me asking, are you from around here, from these parts? Are you planning to stay long? (I'm just passing through, Hans replied tersely, and, no, I'm not from these parts.) Aha. I see. (The councillor snapped his fingers to order two more beers. The waiter hurried over to serve them.) Well, my dear sir, it's a pleasure to converse with a man of the world like you, we welcome visitors who are men of the world. Doubtless you'll think me inquisitive, and if so I beg your pardon. I simply like to know what's going on, you know, curiosity, my friend! Such an important quality! And so, forgive me, but when I came in I couldn't help noticing your attire (my attire? Hans said, pretending to be surprised), yes, that's right, your attire, and as I did so, I said to myself: Our visitor is undoubtedly a refined gentleman, and, as I said before, nothing makes us happier. And then I said to myself: But isn't it a little daring? (A little daring? Hans said, realising the best way to respond to the man's cross-examination was by repeating his questions with a quizzical look.) Daring, precisely, I see we understand one another! And so it occurred to me, and you will see I have your best interests at heart, to suggest that, as far as you are able and naturally without any obligation, you should abstain from offending the sensibilities of the authorities. (The councillor beamed at Hans again and gestured at his traditional German dress, frowned upon by the post-restoration regime.) I'm referring of course (he added hurriedly, in order not to give Hans time to echo his last words) to the use of certain garments, in particular your beret. (My beret? said Hans. The councillor frowned.) Yes, indeed, your beret. Of your own free will, I repeat (I see, said Hans, you're too kind, my free will and I are most grateful for your advice), good, very good.

Before taking his leave, perhaps by way of compensating for the negative effect of his observations, or to carry on observing Hans, the councillor invited him to a reception that same evening organised by the city council to commemorate a local hero. All the best families in Wandernburg will be there, the councillor said, you know, cultured people such as journalists and merchants. And distinguished visitors, he added as though illuminated by a sudden inspiration. Hans thought the best way to avoid suspicion and to enjoy himself would be to go. He accepted, mimicking the councillor's pompous manner. When he was alone, he walked out into the market square and glanced up at the clock on the Tower of the Wind. He calculated that he had just enough time to return to the inn, take a bath and change his clothes.

To his disappointment, Hans noticed nothing extraordinary

during the soirée. Beyond the tedium, the evening was sadly uneventful. The inside of the town hall was like all other town halls—a mixture of grandeur and gypsum. The councillor had come over to greet him with a theatrical show of friendliness, and had introduced him to Mayor Ratztrinker. Excellency, he had declared, it is my pleasure to introduce you to ... Mayor Ratztrinker, who had a beaky nose and a shiny little moustache, had shaken his hand without so much as looking at him, then moved on to greet someone else. Looking down from the chandeliers, the reception hall resembled a dance floor where curved topcoats mingled with pointed shoulder capes, flashes of coloured cravats, and lights reflecting faintly off polished shoes. Hans had changed out of his frock coat buttoned to the neck, his tight breeches, knotted scarf and beret, and was wearing a waistcoat and tails, which suited him well, although he detested them.

After making polite conversation yet speaking to no one, Hans had backed himself into a corner and was waiting for the most appropriate moment to leave. It was there he made the chance acquaintance of a gentleman with bushy moustaches and an amber pipe, who was on his way back from the bathroom. When two strangers remark on the tediousness of a party, they enjoy themselves together—something similar happened between Hans and Herr Gottlieb, who claimed he was exhausted even as he went on dipping his moustaches in glasses of wine, like some hairy bird drinking at the edge of a fountain. With no one more interesting to talk to, Hans gratefully accepted his company, and managed to be more or less witty. Herr Gottlieb was the widowed father of a well-to-do family, and, as he told Hans, he had been a tea importer and a textile merchant, businesses from which, at his age, he had now retired. His moustaches had quivered when he uttered the words *at my age*, and Hans had felt sympathy for him. The informal tone of their conversation seemed to amuse

Herr Gottlieb. After three glasses of wine and as many jokes, he decided Hans was a strange but agreeable enough young fellow, and in a sudden burst of enthusiasm invited him to his house for tea the following afternoon. Hans said he would be delighted, and the two men parted clinking glasses. The light from the chandelier floated down and drowned in the wine.

When Hans turned round, he stepped on the councillor's foot. Are you enjoying the evening, my good man? the councillor smiled, rubbing his shoe on his trouser leg like a heron.

The Gottlieb house was a few yards from the market square, on a corner of Stag Street. The entrance boasted two stout front doors. The wider one on the left had a bronze knocker in the shape of a roaring lion's head, and opened onto a vaulted corridor leading to the coach house. The door on the right had a swallow-shaped knocker and provided access to the stairs and the courtyard. Hans tapped on the door with the swallow-shaped knocker. At first it seemed no one was going to let him in. As Hans clasped the swallow's wings to knock a second time, he heard footsteps hurrying down the stairs. They drew nearer, slowing before they stopped on the other side of the door. Hans found himself staring at Bertold's lip.

Herr Gottlieb's valet, Bertold, had a small scar that split his lip in two, creating the impression that he was always about to say something. The scar moved, and Bertold said good afternoon to Hans. We used to have a doorman, the servant explained apologetically, tugging on his sleeves, but ... They climbed the stone staircase, fitted with a burgundy-red carpet and brass stair rods. The banister was a twisting geometrical figure, topped off with an oak handrail. When they reached the first floor they stopped. This was the main part of the house, where the Gottliebs resided. Had they carried on climbing the staircase, Hans would have seen how it changed, grew narrower, shed its carpet, how the steps were made of creaking wood and the fake marble wall coverings replaced with whitewash. The servants' quarters were on the second floor. The cook and her daughter slept in the attic room on the third floor.

They crossed a freezing hallway and went down a long corridor that felt as draughty as a bridge. The ceilings were so high they were almost invisible. At the far end, Herr Gottlieb's magnificent whiskers parted slightly. Come in, come in, he said, puffing on his pipe. Thank you, Bertold, you may go. Welcome to my humble abode, this way, this way, we'll sit in the drawing room.

When they reached the main drawing room, Hans was able to study the recent course of history in its hotchpotch of styles: the Empire furnishings, the rather provincial insistence on classical motifs, the discreet capitals and pilasters, the pompous symmetry, the proliferation of cubes. Almost every piece of furniture, which Hans took to be made of mahogany, was decorated with excessively ornate gilt-bronze mounts typical of all those countries aspiring to be like the French. Other adornments had been added, mostly in Louis XVIII style, in a vain effort to conceal the fact that time had passed; the more modern furniture showed a different kind of sobriety, a metamorphosis, as though they were insects mutating unimaginably slowly towards rounded forms and paler woods (poplar, Hans suspected, or perhaps ash or cherry wood), as though the battles, treaties, freshly spilt blood and new round of armistices had undermined mahogany's traditional stronghold, besieging it with inlays of amaranth and ebony, overwhelming it with rosettes, lilies, less weighty, more carefree crowns. While Herr Gottlieb pointed him to a chair opposite a low table, Hans remarked from the infrequent touches of Biedermeier that the owner of the house was not at his most prosperous. There was only the occasional homely touch, such as an overwhelmingly Germanic sideboard or an oval side table devoid of triumphant angles and made of simple young walnut or birch. This house, concluded Hans, has tried to find peace and failed.

As they waited for the tea to arrive they talked of business (Herr Gottlieb spoke, Hans listened), and travel (Hans spoke, Herr Gottlieb listened), of matters as harmless as they were trivial. Herr Gottlieb was an experienced host—he had the gift of allowing his guests to feel at ease while not neglecting them for a single moment. Observing that Hans kept glancing towards the bay windows, he stood up and invited him to admire the view. The windows overlooked a balcony that ran along the whole of the front of the house to the corner of Stag Street. Leaning out to the left, half of the market square and the sentry-like silhouette of the Tower of the Wind were visible. Looked at from the opposite direction, from a tiny window in the tower, the Gottliebs' balcony was a thin line suspended in mid-air, and Hans's figure a vague dot on the house front. Suddenly, Hans heard the chink of teacups behind him, then Herr Gottlieb giving orders, and finally his raised voice calling Sophie.

Sophie Gottlieb's skirts swished in the corridor. The rustling sound made Hans vaguely uneasy. A few seconds later, Sophie's figure stepped from the dim corridor into the brightness of the drawing room. My child, Herr Gottlieb announced, let me introduce you to Herr Hans, who is visiting our city. My dear Herr Hans, this is my daughter, Sophie. Sophie greeted him, raising an eyebrow. Hans was overwhelmed by a sudden urge to praise her or to run away as fast as he could. Lost for words, he remarked awkwardly: I didn't think you'd be so young, Fräulein Gottlieb. My dear sir, she replied coolly, surely you'd agree that youth is an accidental virtue. Hans felt terribly foolish and sat down again.

Hans had misjudged the tone, lost the thread of the argument. Sophie's polite yet ironic response to another of his remarks, the kind of ill-judged quip men make when they are too eager to impress a woman, obliged him to take a different approach. Fortunately, Elsa, Sophie's maid, came over to serve the tea. Hans, Herr Gottlieb and his daughter began the customary exchange of polite chitchat. Sophie scarcely took part, and yet Hans had the impression that she was the one determining its rhythm. Hans was impressed not only by the perceptiveness of Sophie's comments, but by the way she spoke—she seemed to be selecting each word carefully and articulating, almost singing her sentences. As he listened to her voice, he swung from tone to meaning, meaning to tone, trying to keep his balance. He tried several times to impress her with one of his observations, but he seemed unable to ruffle the calm aloofness of Sophie Gottlieb, who, in spite of herself, could not help noticing Hans's long locks, and the way he kept brushing them from his brow as he spoke.

Something else surprised Hans as he sipped his tea—Sophie's hands. Not so much their appearance, although they were unusually long, but her way of touching things, caressing surfaces, probing them with her fingertips. Whatever she touched, whether her teacup, the edge of the table, or a fold in her dress, Sophie's hands appeared to determine its significance, to interpret every object. Observing her stealthy, darting fingers, Hans thought he understood Sophie's manner more adequately, and he concluded that her seeming aloofness came from a deep-seated mistrust, a need to examine everything. This reflection offered Hans some relief, and he felt able to embark upon a subtle offensive. Herr Gottlieb continued to be interested in what he had to say, and Hans realised that the best way of communicating with Sophie was through the answers he gave her father. He stopped trying to impress her, made sure she knew he was no longer observing her, and focused instead on showing off his spontaneity and ingenuity as best he could to her father, who moved his whiskers up and down in approval. This different line of attack appeared partially successful, for Sophie gestured to Elsa to draw back the curtains fully. The quality of the light changed, and Hans had the impression that the sun's last rays were offering him another chance. Sophie stroked her teacup thoughtfully. She slipped her forefinger out of the handle, and placed the cup delicately on its saucer. Then she picked up a fan lying on the table. While he was making Herr Gottlieb laugh, Hans heard Sophie's fan splay out like a pack of cards shuffling fortunes.

The fan opened, moved to and fro, contracted, snapped shut. One moment it was a-flutter, the next motionless. It made little twirls, revealing then suddenly concealing Sophie's mouth. Hans was quick to see that regardless of her silence Sophie's fan was responding to every word he uttered. Trying not to lose the thread of his conversation with Herr Gottlieb, he concentrated on deciphering the movements of her fan out of the corner of his eye. As long as the meanderings and digressions typical of a first visit went on, Sophie flapped her fan disdainfully. Once these opening sallies had finished, Herr Gottlieb sought to steer the conversation onto a terrain that Sophie secretly found te-diously masculine—the rather crude exchange of achievements and supposed exploits through which two newly acquainted men become friends. Sophie found herself hoping that Hans, if he was as clever as he seemed to think he was, would swiftly find a way of manoeuvring their talk away from this banal topic. However, her father was determined, and she watched their young guest struggle in vain to find a way of changing the subject without appearing rude. Sophie flipped the fan into her other hand. Alarmed, Hans redoubled his efforts, but only succeeded in strengthening Herr Gottlieb's belief that they both found the subject equally enthralling. Sophie slowly began retracting her fan. She appeared to have stopped listening and was gazing towards the windows. Hans realised time was running out, and, in a desperate lunge, made an unexpected connection between the matter to which Herr Gottlieb kept stubbornly referring, and something completely unrelated. Herr Gottlieb looked bewildered, as though the ice he was skating on had suddenly disappeared. Hans hastened to assuage his doubts with a torrent of arguments that justified the arbitrary association and finally succeeded in pacifying him, bouncing back and forth between the original and the new theme like a ball gradually losing height, slowly moving further and further away from the original topic until he was ensconced in the new one, which was far more likely to be in tune with Sophie's interests. The folding stopped; the fan remained half open; Sophie's head tilted towards the table. The discussions that followed were accompanied by a series of placid undulations from the fan, whose leisurely movement gave the pleasing impression that the conversation was taking the right direction. In a sudden fit of excitement, with a deft thrust Hans invited Sophie to abandon her position as spectator and join in the lively debate he was having with her father. Sophie was not prepared to yield this much terrain, yet the rim of her fan lowered an inch. Emboldened by these minor victories, Hans got carried away and made some impertinent remark—the fan snapped shut, tracing an emphatic 'no' in the air. Hans retreated, qualifying his remark with exemplary sophistry to such an extent it seemed he had meant the exact opposite, while not allowing his face to betray the slightest sign of distress. Sophie pressed the ribs of the fan against her lips, faintly mistrustful but plainly interested. This time Hans bided his time, listened patiently to Herr Gottlieb, and chose the precise moment in which to place a few apposite remarks that forced Sophie to raise her fan abruptly in order to conceal a conspiratorial blush. Then the flapping grew faster, and Hans knew the fan was on his side. Savouring a delicious feeling of confidence, Hans allowed himself to venture onto a slippery slope that might have descended into vulgarity (the fan, Sophie's breathing, even her blinking stopped) had he not performed a swift verbal pirouette, alleviating with a dose of irony a remark which might otherwise have seemed conceited. When Sophie raised a slender, compliant hand to her cheek in order to train a perfectly trained curl, Hans sighed inwardly and felt a sweetness course through his body.

The fan episode had lasted scarcely a few minutes, yet to Hans it had felt like an eternity. Once it was over, Sophie joined in the conversation again with seeming normality, continuing to make her terse, perceptive observations. Herr Gottlieb encouraged her participation, and the three ended up chuckling merrily. After their second cup of tea, before she rose from the low table, Sophie looked straight at Hans, stroking the ribs of the fan with the tip of her forefinger.

As the formal farewells began, Hans saw Sophie's movements disappear before his eyes, as though sucked into a whirlpool, and all he could hear was the hum of the house. Hans shuddered, suddenly afraid of having appeared too distant, or of not having paid enough attention to what Herr Gottlieb had been saying. And yet his host beamed contentedly, saw him to the door without ringing for Bertold, and kept saying what a pleasure his visit had been: A real pleasure, Herr Hans, such an agreeable afternoon, don't you agree? I'm so glad you liked the tea, we get it straight from India, you know, that's the secret, it's been a real pleasure, my friend, and don't forget to come round and say goodbye if you leave soon, of course, farewell for now, thank you, you're too kind, the same to you.

Out in the fresh air, Hans began to walk without any idea where he was going, feeling terrible, wonderful.

In the drawing room, Elsa had begun lighting the candles and Bertold was attending to the fire. Smoke emanating from his pipe and whiskers, Herr Gottlieb looked out of the windows, pensive. A likeable young man, he concluded. Bah, Sophie murmured clutching her fan tightly.

Look who's here, Franz! cried the organ grinder when he saw Hans's sleepy head peering inside the cave. Franz ran up to him and hung on his jacket. We were beginning to miss you, the organ grinder admitted. Hunched over the open lid of his instrument, spanner in hand, the old man was checking its interior. Spread out on a newspaper were two cylinders studded with pins, some coiled strings, and a shoebox full of tools. Hans went closer to the organ. At first it looked as if the pins were scattered like tiny insects over the barrels, but on closer inspection he saw they were placed with great precision. He saw the hammers at rest, the lines of three screws to which the strings were fastened.

These pins here, the organ grinder began explaining, turn with the handle and push up the hammers. There are thirty-four hammers in all, and they strike the strings. The low notes are on the left of the barrel, the high notes on the right. Each pin is a note, and each cluster of pins is a tune. You put a tune on the cylinder by punching holes in these parchments, you see, then stretching them round the barrel and banging the pins into the holes. But here's the secret—the pins vary slightly in length and width, making the notes longer or shorter, enhancing or muting them. Each pin is a mystery. Not a note exactly, the promise of a note. The strings wear out, naturally, and sometimes one of them needs replacing. That's a real problem because they are expensive. I buy them second-hand from Herr Ricordi at the music shop. I knock on the door and give him whatever I have in my dish. The strings have to be tightened with this device here, you see? Yesterday I was playing a pavane and, oh! the B-flats were terrible.

How many tunes are there on each barrel? asked Hans. That depends, replied the organ grinder, these aren't very big, eight apiece. I change them from time to time, or depending on who's listening—no one wants slow tunes in summer, people like lively dances. Now that it's winter on the other hand, people feel more introspective and are glad to hear classical tunes, especially when it rains. Don't ask me why, but people prefer slow music when it rains, and they are generous (is what they give you enough to live on? Hans wanted to know), well, we manage, I live frugally, and Franz doesn't need much either. Sometimes I get asked to play at a dance if people can't afford an orchestra. Saturdays are good days because people give a lot of parties (what about Sundays? said Hans), Sundays it depends, if people leave church feeling repentant, they leave me something. People are more generous when they feel guilty. In any case, I don't let it worry me too much, I enjoy playing, I enjoy being in the square, especially in spring. I hope you'll be here to see spring in Wandernburg.

When the organ grinder had finished tuning the strings and closed the lid, Hans could not help caressing the handle. May I? he asked. Of course, the old man smiled, only be careful, you have to turn the handle as if, I don't know, as if someone were turning you, no, not so fast, relax your arm, that's better, now let's choose a tune, shall we? You see this small handle here? To change tunes you have to push it in slightly or pull it out, oh dear! Let go, I'll do it. What do you prefer, a polonaise, a minuet? A minuet is better, it's easier to follow the rhythm, go ahead, stop! Not that way, Hans, you'll break it, you have to turn it clockwise! Slowly, let's see?

Hans was surprised by how easy and at the same time awkward it was to play the barrel organ. Sometimes the handle would speed up, and other times it would drag. He was unable to make it turn twice at the same speed, and the music came out warped, misshapen, a hiccupping travesty. The organ grinder chuckled and exclaimed: What do you say, Franz, do you like it? The dog made an exception and gave several barks: Hans took this as a bad sign. When the tune had finished, Hans accidentally turned the handle the wrong way before the barrel had finished rotating. There was a crack. The organ grinder looked solemn, moved Hans's hand aside, and opened the lid in silence. He checked both ends of the barrel, took the handle off, replaced it. I think we should leave it for now, he puffed. I understand, Hans said, forgive my clumsiness. Oh, it's nothing, the organ grinder said more calmly, it's been playing up lately, I think the changes in temperature affect it. They don't make them like this any more, the new ones have bellows and pipes, this one is irreplaceable, superior quality, made in Italy. Italian? said Hans, where did you get it from? Ah, said the organ grinder, that's an old story. Hans said nothing—he simply perched on the edge of a rock, elbows resting on his knees, chin in his hands. Franz went over and lay down at his feet.

How strange, the old man said, I've just realised I've never told this to anyone. A Neapolitan friend I had many years ago built this barrel organ, Michele Bacigalupo, may he rest in peace. Michele was fiercely proud of this instrument, and when he was asked to play at a dance, he always took it with him because he claimed it had the merriest sound of all. He made his living with it, until one evening, while he was playing a tarantella, a young man was stabbed for refusing to let his fiancée dance with another man. All of a sudden, there was a scrum of men fighting each other rather than helping the victim. When she realised her fiancé was bleeding to death, the poor girl screamed and threw herself off the roof. When he saw the girl fall, the young man who had stabbed her fiancé leapt after her. It seems the rest of them were too busy brawling to notice any of this. And do you know what Michele did? He carried on playing! The poor man was so petrified he started up the tarantella again and again. From that moment on, the villagers became superstitious about the barrel organ—the families of the victims claimed it was cursed. No one wanted to dance to its music any more and Michele could no longer play it in public. Years later, I met Michele and began as an apprentice in his workshop. He taught me to play the barrel organ, to appreciate its sound, and to repair it, and then one day he gave it to me. He told me he couldn't bear the fact that no one listened to it any more, and he knew it would be safe with me. I painted it, varnished it and promised him I would never make it play a tarantella (and have you kept your promise all these years? Hans broke in), my dear boy, how can you even ask? Tarantellas are not to be taken lightly.

And that's how this creature ended up with me, the organ grinder said, caressing the wooden box. And do you know what? That was my last trip, I was a very young man in those days, but I've never been out of Wandernburg since. (And those landscapes on the sides, said Hans, did you paint them yourself?) Oh, they're nothing much, only what you see from the cave in spring, I painted them so it would get used to the breeze from our river, which is as small and melodious as the organ itself is (some credit should go to the hand, shouldn't it? Hans said with a smile, you saw what a mess I made of it), well, it's not so difficult, it's a question of having the right touch, touch is the important thing. (Hans, who was toying with the idea of bringing a notebook with him to the cave, persisted: Tell me more.) My dear fellow, you talk like a detective! (Almost, said Hans, I'm a traveler.) Well, this is how I see it—every tune tells a tale, nearly always a sad one. When I turn the handle I imagine I'm the hero of that tale and I try to feel at one with its melody. But at the same time it's as if I'm pretending, do you see? No, not pretending, let's say that even as I'm getting carried away I have to think about the end of the tune, because I know how it ends, of course, but maybe the people listening don't, or if they do they've forgotten. That's what I mean by touch. When it works nobody notices, but when it doesn't everyone can hear. (So, for you the barrel organ is a box that tells stories, said Hans.) Yes, exactly! Goodness, what a way you have of putting things, playing the barrel organ is like telling stories around the fire, like you the other night. The tune is already written on the barrel and it may seem like it's all done for you, a lot of people think you just turn the handle and think of something else. But for me it's the intention that counts, just turning the handle isn't the same thing as really applying yourself, do you see? The wood also suffers, or is grateful. When I was young, because I was young once like you, I heard many organ grinders play, and I can assure you no two tunes ever sounded the same, even on the same instrument. That's how it is, isn't it? The less love you put into things the more they resemble one another. The same goes for stories, everyone knows them by heart, but when someone tells them with love, I don't know, they seem new. Well, that's what I think, anyway.

The organ grinder lowered his head and began dusting his barrel organ. Hans thought to himself: Where did this fellow spring from?

Light snow had begun to fall outside. The old man finished tuning his instrument. Excuse me, he said, I'll be back. He went out into the snow and lowered his trousers, unembarrassed. A slow light shone through the leafless poplar trees bordering the river, entangling itself in their branches before filtering through the other side and onto the organ grinder's scrawny buttocks. Hans stared at the old man's urine melting a hole in the snow, his meagre excrement. Common or garden shit, plain old shit, shitty shit.

How beautiful you look this morning, daughter, said Herr Gottlieb, taking Sophie by the arm as they stepped into St Nicholas's Church. Thank you, Father, Sophie smiled, there's still hope I'll return to normal by the afternoon.

The parishioners had formed a queue along Archway, opposite the entrance to the church. St Nicholas's Church was set back from the market square, shielded by a small park with some wooden benches. The church was Wandernburg's oldest and most peculiar building. Looked at from nearby, from where the parishioners were now gathered, the most striking thing about it was its brown brickwork, which looked like it had been baked by the sun. Besides its main portal, which fanned out into pointed arches within arches, it had numerous side doors shaped like keyholes. Stepping back a few yards and examining it as a whole, what most stood out were the church's asymmetrical steeples. One ended in a sharp point like a gigantic pencil, the other, more rounded, housed a toneless bell in a tower with such narrow openings that the wind could barely pass through. And yet what most bewildered Hans was the facade slanting perceptibly towards him, as though it were about to topple forward.

Since his visit to Herr Gottlieb's house, Hans had continued to be friendly towards him. What worried Hans was that, despite greeting him warmly and stopping to chat with him when they met in the street, Herr Gottlieb had not extended him another formal invitation to the house. For the moment he was content to drop vague comments such as "How nice it was to see you" or "Let's hope we bump into one another again", courtesies too casual to justify Hans's turning up at the house unannounced. Hans therefore had been discreetly loitering in Stag Street for days, hoping to force a meeting with Sophie. He had succeeded on a couple of occasions, but she had seemed rather enigmatic. Although she answered him with unswerving abruptness, the way she looked at him made him tremble inside. She never drew out their conversations, nor laughed at his jokes, and yet when she stopped to talk to him she stood at a distance that would have aroused Hans's suspicions had he not felt so unsure of himself. Determined to keep trying, and having learnt that Sophie accompanied her father to Sunday matins at St Nicholas's Church, Hans had risen early that timidly bright Sunday, in order to go to Mass. When Frau Zeit had caught sight of him in the kitchen at eight o'clock, she had frozen, knife in mid-air, her mouth gaping wide like the cod she was about to fillet.

As he entered the church Hans had felt more like an outsider than ever. Firstly because it had been years since he attended Mass. And secondly because no sooner had he set foot in the dark interior than he felt himself the object of everyone's scrutiny. The young girls peered at him curiously from their pews; the older men frowned as he walked by. Hat off, snapped one woman. Without realising it, Hans had walked into St Nicholas's Church wearing his beret and looking as though he were a tourist. The church smelt of candle wax, oil and incense. Hans advanced along the central nave. A few faces looked familiar, although he was not sure where he had seen them before. He scoured the congregation, but could not see Sophie, despite having thought he recognised her from a distance. The far end of the nave was almost in darkness, the heavy stained-glass windows letting in only a trickle of light, a fine white dusting. As the liturgy had not yet begun, Hans kept walking towards the front pews. When he reached the end of the murmuring voices he had a clearer view of the high altar with its imposing crucifix, a pair of three-branched candelabra on either side, four altar candles and a grim altarpiece adorned with acanthus leaves. The altarpiece was decorated with two angels seemingly struggling to hold up an oval, perhaps because on top was a chubby third angel clinging on as though suffering an attack

of vertigo. To the left of the oval was a snake coiled around
a stick and to the right a thorny creeper entwined in a tree. It
would only have been possible to see from quite high up, from
over the plump little shoulder of the third angel, for example,
how close in fact Hans was to Sophie, to predict the moment
when he would catch sight of her, and even to appreciate how
kind fate had been to provide a vacant seat in the opposite pew,
on the men's side.

   Theoretically, the central aisle and the strip of light running
along it separated the two sexes. In practice, this division only
stimulated everyone's interest, giving rise to a series of coded
exchanges. As Hans searched for a seat, he glimpsed gestures,
winks, handkerchiefs, messages, sighs, grimaces, frowns, nods,
half-smiles, fans, fluttering eyelashes. The diversion was abruptly
cut short by the booming first chord rising from the organ,
whose grandiose prow towered above the main entrance. The
congregation stood up as one. The boys' choir began to chant
a slow, high note. Various figures emerged from the shadows
and circulated among the pews collecting alms for the parish. At
that moment, an altar boy, a slightly cross-eyed censer-bearer,
and a deacon who shuffled along knees bent, filed out, followed
by Father Pigherzog, parish priest of St Nicholas's and head
of the Catholic Church in the principality of Wandernburg in
the absence of the archbishop. Hans sat down on the first available seat in the nearest pew. The holy procession approached
the altar, the four men kneeled before the tabernacle, and
Hans squeezed himself in between two stout men. Father
Pigherzog kissed the altar and made the sign of the cross.
Hans cleared his throat, and one of the men looked askance
at him. The boy swung his censer to and fro over the altar,
and Father Pigherzog began intoning the Introit and the Ky-
rie. There! There she is! Hans realised with a start. And there
indeed was Sophie, serene and graceful, as though sitting for

a profile portrait, her eyes fixed somewhere above the altar.

Father Pigherzog sang the Gloria with great gusto, and the choir responded. Sophie maintained the slyly flirtatious attitude of a young woman pretending to have no idea someone was staring at her. *Dominus vobiscum*, Father Pigherzog chanted. *Et cum spiritu tuo*, the congregation responded as one. Hans could not tell whether Sophie was listening attentively or if her thoughts were entirely elsewhere.

While Herr Gottlieb exchanged pleasantries with a few acquaintances outside the church, Father Pigherzog, now in his cassock and cape, had gone over to talk to Sophie. He clasped the young woman's hand in his—Sophie's slender hands had always fascinated the priest, who considered them particularly apt for prayer. Do you remember when you used to come to confession, child? Father Pigherzog mused. And look at you now, it is one of God's miracles how time passes through our souls, look at you, you're a grown woman now, but why do you no longer come to confession, my child? For years I've been asking myself, why did you stop? Father, Sophie replied, trying out of the corner of her eye to determine how long Herr Gottlieb might be taken up with his acquaintances, you know how time flies, and a young woman in my situation has many duties to perform! It is precisely your situation, my child, the priest declared, which requires your constant communion with the word of Our Lord. As you yourself put it, Father, Sophie retorted, with the same acuity as your holiness always shows—time passes through our souls, and that is why they change. You always were a gifted child, said Father Pigherzog, with a good mind, but one which, how should I say, is apt to be unfocused, your curiosity is boundless, so that you end up filling your head with too many facts and becoming sidetracked from the most important fact of all. You explain things so admirably, Father, said Sophie, that you leave me with nothing to add.

Child, child, the priest lamented, why don't you at least come to pray from time to time? You see, venerable father, she said, if you'll allow me to be sincere, and, given that in the sight of God's house it is only right that I should be as sincere as you are in your own mission, at the moment I feel no need of prayer in order to commune with my conscience. Father Pigherzog took a deep breath as he tried to follow Sophie's reply. When he thought he had fully understood its meaning, one which Sophie attempted to soften by gazing at the priest with exemplary innocence, he stammered: Listen to me, child, those ideas are making you lose your way, your soul is in peril, but I can help you, if only you'd allow me. I appreciate your concern, said Sophie, and beg you to forgive my ramblings, but it sometimes seems to me that a dogged insistence on faith conceals an exaggerated need to be right. And I doubt everything, Father, and am too weak to bear so much conviction. Hail Mary, full of grace! Father Pigherzog crossed himself. I know you don't really believe that, you enjoy confrontation, but deep down you are penitent. Perhaps you are right, Father, said Sophie, preparing to walk over to Herr Gottlieb. Listen, my child, said the priest, moving closer to her, I know something is tormenting you, and when you come here on Sundays, even if it is only on Sundays, I see you sitting in the pews with that faraway look in your eyes, don't think I haven't noticed, and I see your confusion is looking for a way to repent. Must we be getting home, then? Sophie exclaimed, craning her neck towards Herr Gottlieb, who had not uttered a word. I suggest, said Father Pigherzog, taking her by the arm, that we continue this conversation, we can talk for as long as you wish, it will unburden you and help you see things more clearly. I don't know how to thank you, Father, said Sophie, evasively. Will you come, child? the priest insisted. Will you? Will you who are so fond of reading refuse to study a few passages of the Scriptures with me? I am unworthy of your generosity, said Sophie, and, since you invite me to do so, I must confess that of late I have become interested in religious writings of which your holiness would disapprove. Such as? queried Father Pigherzog. Such as, she replied, *The Catechism of Reason* by Pastor Schleiermacher, who, with all due respect, Father, seems to be the only theologian to have noticed that we women, besides being sinners, also make up half the world's population at the very least. At the very least? echoed Father Pigherzog, astonished. Sophie! Herr Gottlieb finally called out. Shall we go, Sophie? Father Pigherzog stepped back, and said, Have no fear, child, I know these ideas of yours are transient acts of rebellion. May God be with you, my child. I shall continue to pray for you.

On their way home, Herr Gottlieb and his daughter crossed the market square. All of a sudden, Sophie stopped in her tracks, let go of her father's arm and walked down one side of the square, drawn by the gentle, weary strains of the old instrument she had noticed more than once when out strolling. The organ grinder was rolling out a mazurka, raising a grizzled eyebrow at every third beat. Hans, who was opposite the organ grinder and beaming with contentment as he stood flanked by two melodies, observed Sophie observing. In fact, he had been watching her since they had left church, but her conversation with Father Pigherzog had gone on too long for him to find an excuse or a posture that would enable him to linger in the background for the chance to greet her. And so he had given up and gone to the square to see the organ grinder. The moment he had stopped trying to find Sophie, here she was walking towards him, nodding her head gaily. Hans nodded back in silence, and, following the slow rhythm of the mazurka, gazed with impunity at her pale neck, her fingers clasped behind her back.

Yes, yes, Hans told him, she stopped just opposite you. (I remember a young woman approaching, said the organ grinder, and I noticed you were very interested, but I can't remember her face, what did she look like?) Ah, so you suffer from the same problem? (What problem is that?) You can't visualise Sophie's face either? You might think this odd, and it's hard to explain, but when I try to imagine her, all I see are her hands. I see her hands and I hear her voice. That's all, no features. I can't remember her. Yet it's impossible for me to forget her. (I see, that's too bad.) It's strange what happens to me when I think of her, I'm alone, out walking, and all of a sudden I see a blurred image of Sophie, and I have to stop, you see, to stare into the distance, as if in my memory tiny brushstrokes, flashes of Sophie's face, were becoming jumbled up, and I had to untangle them in order not to lose them. But just as I'm about to make the pieces fit into a whole, to glimpse her face, something slips away, eludes me, and then I feel the urgent need to see her again so that I can store her up in my memory once more. What do you think that means? (I think it means you're going to have to stay a little longer in Wandernburg, said the organ grinder, grinning.)

Before long Reichardt arrived, followed shortly afterwards by Lamberg. Each of them was carrying a bottle wrapped in newspaper. It was close to sunset, and a sudden wave of cold had descended on the afternoon. Reichardt slumped to the ground and said: Shit, old man, are you a fakir or what? Come on, get that fire going! Good afternoon all, said Lamberg, his bloodshot eyes kindling the flames. He paused, then said to Hans: I saw you in church this morning. You, in church? Reichardt spluttered. Hey, old man, your friend here's gone all pious on us! Hans went there to meet a young woman, the organ grinder remarked calmly. I thought as much, said Reichardt, you scoundrel! He forgot to take his beret off, Lamberg told them. Oh, so you noticed, smiled Hans. Yes, replied Lamberg, the girls were pointing at you. And did they laugh at him? asked Reichardt. I don't know, replied Lamberg, I think they liked him. Let's drink to your beret! cried Reichardt. Hear, hear, agreed the organ grinder.

An hour later, the cold was so severe that the fire no longer warmed them, and rubbing their hands and legs did not help. Every time they opened their mouths, vapour came out. The wind entered the mouth of the cave and seeped into the cracks, through the gaps in their clothing, and under their nails. Hans's fingers felt hollow. Lamberg clenched his jaw. Franz swished his tail like a child attempting to shake frost off its rattle. The organ grinder had curled up under his blankets and was smiling peacefully. Shivering from cold, Reichardt suddenly burst into fits of laughter. His whole body shook, he laughed as only those about to freeze can laugh, he let out a puff of steam and began yelling: Butler, the stove, light the damned stove, will you? The organ grinder fell back laughing and cracked his head on a rock. Seeing this, Reichardt jabbed a finger at him before dissolving in a fit of vapoury coughing. Hans pointed at them both and doubled up with laughter. When he saw the other three unable to stop laughing, Lamberg could not help but join in. Say something, Franz! say something! Reichardt roared, his gums stained with red wine.

The fire was dying down. The bottles were empty. Do you hear? whispered the organ grinder. Do you hear it? (All I can hear are my guts, said Reichardt, haven't you got anything else?) Hush, there, in among the branches. (What is it, organ grinder? asked Hans.) They're talking to each other! (I can hear noises, said Lamberg.) They aren't noises, they are the voices of the wind. (What are you on about? said Reichardt.) It's the wind, the wind talking. Franz and the organ grinder listened closely, narrowing their eyes. All I hear is silence, old man,

Reichardt insisted. There's no such thing as silence, the organ grinder replied, and he went on listening to the night, head tilted to one side. I don't know why you're doing that, old man, said Reichardt. The wind is useful, snorted the organ grinder.

After a week of calculated meetings and assiduous courtesies, Hans achieved his aim and began to pay visits to the Gottlieb residence. Herr Gottlieb would receive him in front of the marble fireplace in the drawing room, smoking his amber pipe. On the mantelpiece stood a row of indolent statuettes that seemed about to topple into the hearth. During his visits, Hans had the chance to study the paintings hanging on the walls more closely—besides a few dusty family portraits, a couple of poor copies of Titian, one or two gloomy still lifes and some dreadful hunting scenes, his attention was drawn to a painting of a figure, seen from behind, walking through a snow-covered forest, lost or perhaps leaving, with a crow perched on a nearby tree trunk.

Herr Gottlieb had a habit of bursting out laughing, almost invariably because of something his daughter said. It was an admiring and at the same time nervous laugh, the laugh men put on when they are listening to an intelligent woman who is much younger than them. Whenever Herr Gottlieb gave one of his guffaws he looked down at the tips of his whiskers, as though surprised at how bushy they were. Hans would spend more time taking tea with him than with Sophie, who would often go out to the dressmaker's with Elsa, or to go over musical scores at a friend's house, or to return a social call. Only when he was able to keep Herr Gottlieb talking until the late afternoon did Hans manage to see her and exchange a few words. Sophie was oddly reserved—she seemed intent on avoiding serious conversation or remaining alone with him, but her gaze still had a dizzying effect on Hans. When he was out of luck and left the house early, he would go straight to the market square to accompany the organ grinder back to his cave.

Although Herr Gottlieb had little in common with Hans, he seemed to have found in him the perfect interlocutor. Herr Gottlieb was one of those men who in shying away from intimate conversations show an obvious need for them. Hans sensed that Herr Gottlieb misunderstood his questions yet gave Hans the answers he wanted to hear. And so, after some trivial remark about the beauty of the house, his host seemed to think he was referring to Sophie, and let slip some of his concerns about his daughter. Hans refrained from setting him straight and began listening eagerly. Her mother having died during birth, Herr Gottlieb, who also had a married son living in Dresden, had always been Sophie's sole guardian. He had brought her up with that mixture of over-protectiveness and panic that is the lot of the youngest members of a family. Herr Gottlieb was undoubtedly proud of his daughter, and yet, perhaps for that very reason, he was also plagued with anxieties. As you have seen for yourself, said Herr Gottlieb, Sophie is an extraordinary young woman (Hans tried not to agree too heartily), but I've always feared that with her character and her high expectations it will be hard for her to find a good husband, you see? Perhaps you are worrying unnecessarily, ventured Hans, your daughter seems like a fascinating young woman with a forceful personality (Hans immediately thought: I shouldn't have said *fascinating*), that is, she is a distinguished young woman, and I'm sure she is perfectly. Herr Gottlieb cut across him: If my daughter persists in being so fascinating and strong-willed, she'll end up with a string of suitors but no husband.

Before Hans had a chance to reply, Herr Gottlieb added: That is why it is imperative that her marriage to Rudi Wilderhaus should take place at the earliest opportunity.

Hans did not respond straight away, as if he had only perceived

an echo of what Herr Gottlieb had said and was still waiting
to hear his voice. Immediately afterwards he felt something
like a blow to the forehead. I beg your pardon? What? Hans
stammered, and fate provided another convenient misappre-
hension—Herr Gottlieb assumed Hans was interested in Rudi
Wilderhaus. Just so, replied Herr Gottlieb, none other than
the Wilderhauses, if you please, and do you know something?
They are in fact very friendly, much more friendly than they are
reputed to be, and, naturally, awfully sophisticated (Naturally,
said Hans, who hadn't the slightest idea who they were), but
above all, generous. Only a few weeks ago the Wilderhauses
were here in this very room, well, in the dining room to be precise, and his parents formally asked for my daughter's hand in
marriage, and I, can you imagine, good God, a Wilderhaus! (I
can imagine! exclaimed Hans crossing his legs abruptly) Well,
I played hard to get, as is only natural, and after that we settled on the earliest possible date, in October, at the end of the
summer. Even so, I confess …

At that moment they heard footsteps and voices at the end
of the corridor that led from the hallway to the drawing room.
Hans heard the familiar rustle of Sophie's skirts. Herr Gottlieb
stopped in mid-sentence, his face breaking into an expectant
smile, which he maintained until his daughter appeared in the
doorway.

Why does she look at me like that, if she's engaged to whatever
his name is? Hans wondered. He could think of one reason that
was both simple and logical, but dismissed it as too optimistic.
That afternoon, Sophie seemed particularly attentive to what
he was saying, and kept giving Hans quizzical looks, as though
she had guessed why his face was frozen in an expression of disappointment. During his conversation with Sophie, which had
taken on a far more intimate tone than on previous occasions,
Hans noticed how, progressively and perhaps foolishly, his hope

began to feel renewed. He promised himself he would not examine this feeling, but allow it to carry him along like an object
borne on the wind. And so, when Sophie declared he would
be welcome company (welcome company, Hans savoured the
words, mmm, "welcome company") at her salon, he accepted
without hesitation. Sophie Gottlieb held her salon on Fridays
at teatime, and at them her guests would discuss wide-ranging
questions of literature, philosophy and politics. The only virtue
of our humble salon, Sophie went on, is that anyone can say
what they like. Apart, should I say, from my good father, with his
sense of propriety. (Sophie smiled disarmingly at Herr Gottlieb.)
Our only rule is that people be sincere in their opinions, which
believe me, Herr Hans, is nothing short of a miracle in a city
like this. Guests are free to come and go as they please. No two
afternoons are the same, some are incredibly stimulating, others
more predictable. As we are in no hurry, these gatherings usually
go on until quite late. I understand that for this reason alone, my
dear Herr Hans, you would make an ideal member of our circle.
(Hans could not help feeling a frisson of pleasure at Sophie's
small gesture of connivance.) We have tea and refreshments,
and we serve an aperitif with a few canapés, we do not exactly
go hungry. Occasionally we play music or perform impromptu
readings from Lessing, Shakespeare or Molière, depending on
how the mood takes us. We are relatively at ease in one another's
company—there are only eight or nine regular members, including my father and myself. In short, it is a pleasant way to spend
the afternoon, so, if you have nothing better to do this Friday …
or are you perhaps leaving before then? Me, leaving? said Hans,
sitting bolt upright in his chair. Not at all, not at all.

Accustomed to the dense quiet of the Gottlieb residence, Hans
was surprised to find the drawing room so abuzz the following
Friday. While Bertold took his coat and walked away touching

the scar on his lip, Hans's first impression was of a concerto of murmurings with teacups as percussion. The main group was seated on chairs and armchairs around the low table. There was also a man standing over by the windows, wearing a thoughtful expression, and in a corner two other people were engaged in a more private conversation. Sophie sat to the right of the marble fireplace, or rather brushed the chair with the lace of her skirts, always about to stand up. With calm alacrity she would rise to her feet to serve tea, attend to one of her guests or walk about the room like someone overseeing the different functionings of a loom. She was the discreet hub of the circle, the mediator who listened, suggested, commented, forged links, smoothed out differences and elicited responses, constantly proffering pertinent remarks or stimulating questions. Hans gazed at her in admiration. Sophie looked so radiant, happy and self-assured in her movements that he was unable to stir from the doorway but stood for some minutes just watching her, until she herself went up to him—There's no need to be shy!—and ushered him into the centre of the room.

She introduced him one by one to all the members of the salon except for Rudi Wilderhaus, who was absent that afternoon. Firstly to Professor Mietter, Doctor of Philology, Honorary Member of the Berlin Society of the German Language and the Berlin Academy of Science, Emeritus Professor of the University of Berlin. Wandernburg's very own cultural luminary, he had contributed to several editions of the Gottingen *Almanac of the Muses* and published a poem or a literary column in the Sunday edition of the local paper, the *Thunderer*. Professor Mietter's mouth was set in a slight grimace, as though he had just bitten on a peppercorn. He wore dark blue and sported an unfashionable white ringleted wig on his bald pate. Hans was struck by the professor's air of unruffled solemnity amid the gaiety around him, as if he did not so much disapprove of it as consider it the result of flawed reasoning or a methodological error. Opposite him, teacup suspended mid-way between saucer and mouth, sat the wary Herr Levin, a merchant with a penchant for theosophy. Herr Levin avoided the eyes of his interlocutors, appearing to focus instead on their eyebrows. A man of few and perplexing words, quite the opposite of Professor Mietter, Herr Levin had the awkward manner of someone trying to appear irreproachable even in repose. Next to him sat his wife, the mouse-like Frau Levin, who was in the habit of speaking only when her husband did, either to echo what he said, to agree with him, or very occasionally to call him to order. Next, Hans was introduced to Frau Pietzine, for many years a widow, and a fervent devotee of Father Pigherzog's sermons and of gemstones from Brazil. Frau Pietzine, who usually had a piece of embroidery in her lap which she would work on as she spoke, closed her eyelids as she allowed Hans to kiss her hand. He gazed at her yellow feather boa, her diamond ring, the strings of pearls that plunged like fingers into the pinkish skin of her cleavage.

Lastly, Sophie paused in front of the gentleman Hans had noticed standing beside the windows. My dear Herr Hans, she said, it is my pleasure to introduce you to Herr *Urquiho, Álvaro de Urquiho*. Urquijo, the man corrected her, Urquijo, my dear Mademoiselle. Of course, *Urquixo!* laughed Sophie, excuse my ignorance. Hans pronounced his name properly. Álvaro de Urquijo bobbed his head, sweeping the room with his eyes as if to say "Welcome to *this*". Hans noticed the hint of irony in his gesture and felt an instant liking for him. He confirmed that Urquijo's German was flawless, although imbued with an accent that gave it an impassioned quality. Our dear Herr Ur, er, Álvaro, said Sophie, however much he might regret the fact, is now a true Wandernburger. Believe me, my dear Mademoiselle, smiled Álvaro, one of the few reasons I do not regret becoming a Wandernburger is that you should consider me such. My dear friend, Sophie retorted, raising a shoulder towards her chin, you must not be so subtle in your flattery, remember you are a Wandernburger now. Álvaro gave a loud chortle and refrained from replying, conceding the point to his hostess. Sophie took her leave with a swift gesture, and went to attend to Frau Pietzine, who was clutching her needlework with a look of boredom on her face.

The afternoon slipped by pleasantly. Under the auspices of Sophie, who facilitated occasional exchanges between them, Hans was able to study the other members of her salon more closely. Each time he was asked what he did for a living, Hans replied that he traveled, he traveled and he translated. Some understood from this that he was an interpreter, others a diplomat, still others that he was on holiday. And yet everyone responded politely: Oh, I see. The conversations ebbed and flowed. Sophie circulated from one to another, aided by Elsa and Berthold. Herr Gottlieb, slightly removed from the centre of the gathering, his whiskers curled around his pipe, sat in silence observing the proceedings ironically, sceptical of whatever was being discussed, but proud of his daughter's easy grace. Whenever she spoke, he smiled benignly like a person who believes they know the person to whom they are listening very well. Sophie on the other hand glanced at him out of the corner of her eye, and gave him the opposite kind of smile—that of someone who believes the person listening to them hasn't a clue about their beliefs. Herr Gottlieb seemed to pay most attention to Professor Mietter, often agreeing with what he said. Contrary to what he had initially thought, Hans had to confess that the professor was extremely knowledgeable. Despite his tedious way of holding forth, he advanced his arguments in a rigorous and impeccably orderly fashion, without his wig shifting an inch. Professor Mietter is almost unassailable, thought

Hans—he either uses simple logic to put forward his views or else imposes them thanks to his listeners' inertia, since in order to refute his opinions it is necessary to break down each of his erudite arguments, which he erects like firewalls. Although Hans was careful not to contradict him during that first meeting, he knew that if they met regularly they were destined to clash. For his part, Professor Mietter treated him with a studied politeness that Hans found almost aggressive. Whenever the professor listened to Hans's opinions, so at odds with his own, he would raise his teacup cautiously to his lips, as though not wanting to steam up his spectacles.

Hans thought Bertold was following Elsa around, or that Elsa was trying to avoid Bertold, or both. Despite her attentiveness, Hans sensed a rebelliousness in Elsa—her gaze was more direct than was usual among servants, as though behind her silence there was defiance. Although they had both been employed at the Gottlieb residence for roughly the same length of time, Bertold seemed to be part of the furniture, whereas Elsa gave the impression of just passing through. Bertold attended the guests obligingly, Elsa did so grudgingly. My dear! Frau Pietzine suddenly called out to her. My dear, go to the kitchen and ask if there are any meringues left, yes, thank you, dear, and so, darling Sophie, will you not delight us today with your piano playing? Really? Oh, I'm so disappointed! The piano when it is well played is so, so, I just adore the piano, don't you think, Herr Hans, that our beloved Sophie ought perhaps to, well, to play a little welcoming piece in your honour? I think if we all insist, what do you mean you refuse! Oh don't make us plead, child! Really? Next week, you say? That's a promise? Very well, very well, but remember you've given your word! It's my age, you see, Herr Hans, at my age music moves one so!

Whenever Frau Pietzine referred to her age, she would make a dramatic pause and wait for a fellow guest to pay her a compliment. Still unaware of this, Hans was not forthcoming with any praise. Frau Pietzine lifted her chin, blinked three times in succession and turned around to join in the conversation between Herr Levin and Álvaro. Hans edged closer to Álvaro, hoping to renew at the first opportunity the discussion they had left off previously. As soon as he exchanged a few ideas with Herr Levin, Hans had the impression he was far too condescending towards him really to agree with anything he said. He suspected Herr Levin of concurring with everyone not out of modesty, but because he was secretly sure of quite the opposite but was not prepared to argue about it. He also thought Frau Levin behaved towards her husband in the same way he did to the others. As for the Spanish guest, Álvaro, Hans was able to confirm what he had suspected—he was different from the others, not because he was a foreigner but because of some dissenting convictions that aroused Hans's interest. Álvaro seemed willing to satisfy his curiosity—when Professor Mietter launched into one of his monologues, Álvaro would catch Hans's eye, and a flicker of amusement would appear on Álvaro's lips, which turned into a frank smile when Hans responded.

That afternoon Hans made these and other observations. And yet they all turned on the same axis, like threads around a bobbin—the focus, the real reason for his visit to the Gottlieb Salon, was beyond a doubt his desire to be close to Sophie. She spoke to him now and then, although their conversations never ran on, and it was always Sophie who broke them off on some pretext or other. So it seemed to Hans at any rate. Was it shyness? Or pride? Perhaps he was behaving inappropriately. Or possibly his conversation bored her. But if so then why had she invited him? That afternoon, Hans agonised over the meaning of Sophie's gestures, conferring on each too much significance, veering constantly between enthusiasm and disappointment, sudden delight and petty resentment.

For her part Sophie had the impression that Hans, seemingly with impeccable courtesy yet with a certain underlying impertinence, had spent the entire afternoon creating small points of intimacy between them during their conversations. Sophie refused to tolerate this attitude for a number of reasons. Firstly, she had endless things to attend to during these gatherings, and was not about to neglect her duties in order to please anyone. Secondly, Hans was a newcomer, and should not expect any preferential treatment—this would be unreasonable and unfair on the others. Thirdly, she was of course a recently betrothed woman and her father was keeping an eagle eye on her from behind the veil of his pipe smoke. Finally, without knowing why, Sophie realised with annoyance that whenever she spoke to Hans her mind began to wander and she had inconvenient thoughts quite unrelated to the salon.

Even so, Sophie told herself as she swished her skirts from one end of the room to the other, these slight objections were not enough of a reason to stop inviting Hans to the salon—she could not deny that his contributions, more frequent as the hours went by, were original and slightly provocative, and would enhance the debates. And this was the only thing, Sophie kept saying to herself, the only thing that persuaded her Hans should be allowed to keep coming.

I don't know what it is about this city, Hans said, handing the bowl of rice back to the organ grinder, it's as if it won't let me leave. The organ grinder chewed, nodded his head and tugged on his beard. First you appeared, Hans said, and then her, there's always some reason for me to delay my journey. Sometimes it feels as if I've just arrived in Wandernburg; other days I wake up with the sensation of having lived here all my life. When I go out I look at the coaches and say to myself: Go on, climb aboard, it's very simple, you've done it a thousand times. Yet I let them go by, and I don't understand what's happening to me. Why, yesterday Herr Zeit didn't even ask me when I was leaving as he does every night. I paused as we crossed on the stairs, but instead he looked at me and said, See you in the morning. It felt terrible. I hate knowing the future. I could hardly sleep for thinking about it. How many days have I been here? To begin with I knew exactly how many, but now I couldn't say for sure. (Why does that worry you? the organ grinder said, what's wrong with staying here?) I don't know, I suppose I'm afraid of carrying on seeing Sophie and then having to leave, it would be worse, maybe I should continue my travels while there's still time. (But isn't that what love is, the old man said, being happy to stay?) I'm not sure, organ grinder, I've always thought of love as pure movement, a sort of journey. (But if love itself is a journey, the old man argued, why would you need to leave?) Good question, well, for example, in order to come back, in order to be sure you're in the right place. How can you know that if you've never left it? (That's how I know I love Wandernburg, replied the organ grinder, because I don't want to leave.) All right, all right, but what about people? Does the same rule apply to people? For me there's no greater joy than being reunited with a friend I've not seen for a long time. What I mean is, we also go back to places because we love them, don't you think? And loving someone can be like a homecoming (being older, I think that love, love of places, people or things, is about harmony, and harmony for me is to be at rest, to observe what's around me, being happy to be where I am, and, well, that's why I always play in the market square, because I can't imagine a better place), places and things stay the same, but people change, we change. (My dear Hans, places are constantly changing, haven't you noticed the branches, the river?) No one notices those things, organ grinder, everyone walks around without seeing, they become accustomed, accustomed to their houses, their jobs, their loved ones, and in the end they convince themselves that this is their life, there can be no other, it's just a habit (that's true, although love can be a habit, too, can't it? Loving someone could be, I don't know, like living inside that person), I think I'm getting drunk, Hans sighed, slumping back onto the pallet. The organ grinder stood up. I think we need a third opinion, he announced with a grin. He poked his head out of the cave and proclaimed: What do you think, Franz? But Franz did not bark, and went on lifting his leg calmly against a pine tree. The organ grinder looked at Hans, who sat head in hand. Come on, the old man said, cheer up. What would you like to hear, a waltz or a minuet?

Herr Zeit saw the dark lines under Hans's eyes and cleared his throat. Good morning, he said, it's Friday already! Yes, Hans replied, without much enthusiasm. But then immediately thought: Friday! and remembered the salon was that afternoon. He pulled himself together, instinctively tidied his hair, and felt a sudden rush of tenderness towards the innkeeper's rippling belly. Do you know something, Herr Zeit? he said, to make conversation. I was wondering the other day why there aren't more guests at the inn. Are you unhappy with the service? said Herr Zeit apparently offended. I didn't mean that at all, Hans explained hurriedly, I'm simply surprised the inn is so empty. There's nothing strange about it, Frau Zeit's voice chimed in from behind. Hans wheeled round and saw her walking towards them, carrying a pile of logs. It's the same every year, she said, in winter we have next to no guests, but in spring and particularly in summer, we get so busy we even have to hire a couple of servants to attend to all the guests. Herr Zeit scratched his belly. If you stay on until the season begins, you'll see for yourself, said the innkeeper. I was also wondering, Hans added, where I might send a telegram from. I haven't seen any telegraph offices. There aren't any in Wandernburg, replied Herr Zeit, we don't need them. When we have something to say to each other we do it in person. When we want to send a letter, we wait for the postman and we give it to him. We're simple folk. And proud of it.

Lisa! Are you bringing that laundry in or what? yelled Frau Zeit. Lisa came in from the backyard carrying a basket full of stiff linen. She had an annoyed look on her face and her hair was speckled with snow. When she saw Hans in the passageway, she dropped the basket on the floor as though it didn't belong to her, and pulled down her jersey, which filled out slightly. Here it is, Mother, she said looking at Hans. Good morning, Lisa, he said. Good morning, she beamed. Is it very cold outside? he enquired. A little, she said. Noticing that Hans was holding a cup, Lisa said: Is there any coffee left, mother? Later, Frau Zeit replied, first go and fetch the groceries, it's getting late. Lisa sighed. Well, she said, I'll see you later, I suppose. Yes, see you later, he nodded. When Lisa closed the door, Hans, Herr Zeit and his wife all remained silent. Lisa raised the lapels of her coat round her face. She grinned.

The whole of Old Cauldron Street, the windows, rooftops, as well as the surrounding roads and country paths, had almost disappeared beneath the snow. Above Wandernburg, across the floor of the sky, came the sound of furniture being shifted.

Professor Mietter's wig glowed in the firelight from the marble hearth as he talked with Herr Gottlieb. Frau Pietzine embroidered, listening in to their conversation. Herr Levin and Frau Levin exchanged discreet smiles. Álvaro was chatting to Hans and gesticulating wildly. Standing to one side of the fireplace, next to her father's chair, Sophie threaded conversations together, making them circulate around the room. Hans was content—owing to an unavoidable engagement with a count new to the region Rudi Wilderhaus had been unable to attend the salon that afternoon either. Hans had been seated next to Sophie, so that in order to see her face when she was sitting down he was obliged to turn his head. As a newcomer, Hans was, or felt he was, too conspicuous to dare make any suspicious movements. And so, by shifting his chair slightly each time he rose to his feet or sat up straight, he contrived to move within visual range of the large round mirror hanging on the wall opposite the fireplace. Thanks to this he became accustomed to studying Sophie's movements and gestures without seeming indiscreet. Hans did not know whether she had noticed his optical manoeuvre, although the intricate poses she began adopting in her chair made him think as much.

I for one, asserted Herr Gottlieb, consider the introduction of a customs union unwise. Just think, my friends, of the terrible competition it would unleash, and who knows whether the small shopkeepers would end up being driven to the wall, not to mention all the family businesses people have worked so hard to build up. On the contrary, Herr Gottlieb, argued Herr Levin, a customs union would stimulate the market, businesses would prosper and trade would increase (as would commissions, eh? Professor Mietter remarked sardonically), ahem, I am merely hazarding a guess. I wouldn't be so sure, replied Herr Gottlieb, some broker might come here tomorrow from, I don't know, from Maguncia, for instance, and take over all your business! I think we should stay as we are, things can always get worse, believe me, I have seen it happen. Well, said Herr Levin, if it's a division of labour we are talking about, perhaps Mr Smith is not so mistaken when he suggests that each country should specialise in what it is naturally disposed to produce (naturally? What does naturally mean? said Álvaro), well, according to its conditions, climate, tradition and so forth, and, yes, be able to trade its produce freely with other countries, ahem, that's the idea. And an interesting one, Herr Levin, Hans spoke up, although in order to talk of free trade we must first consider who would preside over this specialised or natural form of production, or whatever we want to call it. For if there were only a handful of owners it follows they would become the country's true masters and would be the ones who decided the rules of the game, and the conditions in which everyone lived. Smith's theories are capable of enriching a state and impoverishing its workers. Before free trade I think other measures are needed, such as agrarian reform, the dismantling of the large estates and a more just distribution of land. This would not mean simply freeing trade but breaking down the real barriers, beginning with the socio-economic ones. Oh, said Professor Mietter, I suppose you are going to start quoting Saint-Simon? Not exactly, Herr Professor, Hans retorted, although I don't see any reason why not. Workers cannot be entirely reliant on their masters, the state should not exactly control, but intervene up to a certain point, in order to guarantee certain basic rights. Naturally, said Professor Mietter, we need a powerful state to show us the way, a state like the ones Napoleon or Robespierre wanted! That is not what I meant, Hans said, a redistribution of wealth does not have to end in a reign of terror. (And who can guarantee it will not lead to such extremes? asked the professor. Who will control the state?) Well then professor, are we to leave control of the factories in God's hands? Ahem, interrupted Herr Levin, to get back to Smith ... I agree with the customs union, Hans interrupted him, aware he was probably talking too much, but only as a first step. With all due respect, Herr Levin, free trade among nations would be the least of it, important, of course, but not essential (and what would be essential, if you do not mind telling us? asked Professor Mietter), well, in my view the essential thing would be a common foreign policy. Completely

different from the Holy Alliance of course, which is simply designed to protect the monarchies. I am speaking of parliamentary
rather than military union, of a Europe that would think like
one country, a society made up of citizens, not a collection of
trading partners. Granted, the first thing would be to do away
with some of its borders. After that, why not continue with
customs unions? Why not think of the German union as part
of a continental whole? Professor Mietter's mouth formed into
an "O" as though he were sipping a cocktail. How ingenious of
you! he said, and who exactly would we unite with, Herr Hans?
With the French who invaded us? With the English who have
monopolised industry? Or with the Spaniards, who are as likely
to crown the same king twice as they are to proclaim an illegal
republic? Let's be realistic! Let's stop dreaming! In any event,
Hans shrugged, I consider it a dream worth having. Flights of
fancy, indeed, Herr Levin reflected, although …

Sophie clasped her hands together smiling discreetly, and said:
In principle I concur with Herr Hans's dream. Herr Gottlieb's
eyes narrowed. He lit his pipe, and appeared to set his thoughts
on fire. Don't exaggerate, Professor, said Álvaro (don't exaggerate about what? asked Professor Mietter), about Spain (ah, said
the professor). Would anyone like some more pastries? Sophie
said, standing up and evading Hans in the round mirror.

For a while Hans's mind strayed from the discussion. When
he went back to it, Álvaro was speaking. Spain? he was saying,
well, that depends, I was in the habit of reading Jovellanos and
Olavide. My dear man, Professor Mietter said, with genuine
interest (although Hans, still unable to distinguish the nuances
of his voice, thought he was being ironic), I'm afraid we do
not know who those two might be. Then it will be my honour
to enlighten you, said Álvaro (and now Hans was unsure if he
meant it ironically), and don't worry, Professor, we Spaniards
are used to it—my country boasts few thinkers, the few we have

are rather good at it, and abroad everyone thinks we have no thinkers at all. Olavide was a courageous man, too much of a Voltairean to be a Sevillian, or too much of a Sevillian to carry out a French-style revolution. Scarcely anyone read him then and now they read him even less. Jovellanos on the other hand became quite well-known. He was a learned man although, shall we say, not without his contradictions. His vocation as a priest compromised his reformist tendencies, if you see what I mean. Naturally, he was too intelligent not to offend many people. Where I come from, dear friends, even moderate liberals end up in exile. A change of monarch was enough to send Jovellanos from the Madrid court to the Asturian mines, and from there to a prison where he was allowed to swim in the sea under guard, without ever really changing his cautious opinions (how interesting! exclaimed Frau Pietzine. It reminds me of a novel I read recently. My dear, Sophie said, stroking her arm, do tell us about it later) until at the last he died of pneumonia. I would even go so far as to say, my friends, that in Spain it is well nigh impossible to be a liberal and not to die of pneumonia. To Hans's surprise, Professor Mietter took a notebook from his pocket, jotted down a few words and said: And in your estimation, Herr *Urquiho*, what is *Hovellanos*'s best work? *Urquijo*, Álvaro said, smiling. His best work? That is hard to say. In my view Jovellanos's greatest achievement was to make Spain understand that the way its people play, amuse themselves and fight bulls depends on the way they live, work and are governed. Ah, I see, Mietter said, glancing up from his notebook, a product of the French Enlightenment. Álvaro sighed: A genuine one, yes. Hans sensed he was holding something back and asked: But? Pleased by his intuitive response, Álvaro nodded at him as he replied: Only that he took Communion every fortnight! (Hans glanced at Herr Gottlieb and stifled a laugh.) There it is, the Spanish Enlightenment was a melancholy joke.

Seeing her mollify Professor Mietter with praise as she smiled enthusiastically, Hans began to suspect Sophie's silence was strategic rather than a result of her having no opinions. Perhaps she enjoyed the passion of their debates. Perhaps she encouraged them by avoiding interrupting their ripostes while keeping the professor as happy as possible. This woman will reduce me to a nervous wreck, thought Hans. But, *mein Herr*, said Professor Mietter, straightening his spectacles, order in Europe is absolutely essential; I need hardly remind you of all the wars and invasions we have endured. Professor, replied Hans giving a sidelong glance in the mirror, there will never be order in Europe without a just order in every country. Is it not worth at least giving a thought to the fact that the constitutions imposed on us by our invaders have given us greater freedoms than our own?

At that moment, there was an interplay of glances—in the round mirror Hans saw Herr Gottlieb turn to look at him, while at the same instant he saw Sophie trying to catch his eye in the glass to signal to him he should look round. Hans wheeled just in time to say: I beg you to excuse my vehemence, sir. Herr Gottlieb shook his head, as though declining to issue any judgement. My dear Monsieur Hans, Sophie broke in, my father is respectful of everyone's opinion and appreciates the freedom with which we express ourselves in this salon. It is one of the things I most admire about him, is it not, dear Papa? Herr Gottlieb smoothed his whiskers in a gesture of modesty, took his daughter's hand and settled back in his armchair. This, ahem, commented Herr Levin with unexpected archness, is precisely what I was saying, *laissez faire, laissez passer*. Everybody laughed as one. An invisible cog appeared to be released and began turning once more. In the mirror, Hans saw Sophie raise her eyebrows.

Gnädiger Herr Hans, resumed Professor Mietter, will you tell us why you detest Metternich so much? Because he has a big nose, replied Hans. Sophie was unable to stifle a giggle. Then she glanced at her father, looked away and hurried off to fetch some more cake, taking Elsa with her. Álvaro joined in: His Majesty Friedrich Wilhelm is also rather well endowed in the snout department—perhaps that explains why he is able to ferret out anything that whiffs of republicanism. Professor Mietter, who had an amazing ability to remain all the more calm when he seemed about to lose his temper, responded in a patronising voice: Who does not aspire to *liberté et fraternité? Sans rancune bien sûr, mais qui ne les voudrait pas?* Why, Our Saviour himself preached them! Frankly, gentlemen, you astonish me with the old-fashionedness of your newfangled ideas. Remember, Herr Gottlieb chimed in, raising his forefinger and poking his whiskers out from behind his armchair like a beaver popping up its head, remember what happened after the storming of the Bastille. My dear Monsieur, replied Hans, with the way things are in France now, it would be no surprise if they storm it again. Professor Mietter gave an abrupt laugh. I see you possess *l'esprit moqueur*, Hans added. As they looked one another in the eye, each was forced to concede that the other spoke French with an impeccable Parisian accent. Just then, Sophie re-emerged from the corridor. The flurry of her skirts stopped at the fireplace. Herr Hans, my dear young friend, Professor Mietter went on in a more mellifluous tone, let us be reasonable, consider where the Revolution has brought us, as our dear Herr Gottlieb pointed out, and tell us—is this justice? Does it herald a new era? Chopping off heads? Going from one absolutism to another even greater absolutism? Overthrowing kings in order to crown emperors? Explain to us how this is meant to be our famous *liberté*? I have no idea, replied Hans, but believe me I know how *not* to achieve it. By abolishing constitutions and outlawing the freedom of the press, for example. In France, Álvaro added, they were promised a revolution, and all they got was an insurrection. A true revolution would be quite different. Yes, but what, said Herr Levin, appearing to come to life, what would it be? I imagine, said Hans, it would be totally different, something that would change us before it changed our governments. At least in France, Álvaro said mockingly, governments start revolutions, here it is left to the philosophers. If we look at the meaning of the word in Latin it is quite clear, declared Professor Mietter, *revolution* means a turning back. It simply repeats itself. And I fear, gentlemen, that what you call freedom is merely historical impatience. Impatience, Professor, is the cornerstone of freedom, said Álvaro. Or not, ventured Herr Levin. Why not? Frau Pietzine intervened unexpectedly. Monsieur Hans? enquired Sophie. I would prefer, said Hans with a grin, not to lose my patience.

Cutting through the silence, Sophie suddenly said: And what about you, Madame Levin? Frau Levin looked up at her in horror. Me? she stammered, What about me? My dear friend, said Sophie, you are as quiet as a mouse! I am asking about your political views, if that is not too impertinent a question, she added, gazing at Herr Levin and fluttering her eyelashes enchantingly. To tell the truth, said Frau Levin reaching up to touch her chignon, I do not have any political views to speak of. Do you mean, Madame, said Álvaro, that you never think about politics, or that you find the subject tedious? Herr Levin said: Political discussions bore my wife because she never thinks about such matters. Monsieur Levin, sighed Sophie, you do have a way of breaking the silence!

Steam from their refreshments mingled with the smoke from Herr Gottlieb's pipe. Elsa and Bertold lit candles. Bertold whispered something in Elsa's ear; she shook her head. In the candlelight, Professor Mietter's features took on a faintly heroic air. And in my view, said the professor, far from considering Bonaparte's demise and the defeat of his armies as the end of an aberration, the French see it as the beginning of a magnificent rebirth. French politicians are embittered and behave with a kind of offended innocence. I am not sure whether this will help them restore the nation or whether the nation will overthrow them a second time. Remembering too much is humiliating, yet if they pretend to be suffering from amnesia they will never understand how they got where they are. What you say is very true, said Hans, although we Germans would do well to remember this happened to us once and it could happen again. Quite so, said Professor Mietter, the traitors who aligned themselves with Bonaparte and now hope to unite us with Prussia are essentially doing just that, disregarding history and, why not say it, cultural differences. Esteemed Professor, Herr Levin said, are people so very different from one another? Is it necessary to dwell upon our divisions rather than? Take note, Professor Mietter interrupted, do those of you who speak blissfully of harmony, of a brotherhood of nations and who knows what else besides, believe the differences between people will disappear if you ignore them? Historical differences must be studied (but not inflated, interjected Hans), studied, Herr Hans, taken into account one by one so as to create realistic borders, not in order to play at recklessly suppressing them or moving them around willy-nilly. This is how Europe is behaving, as though we had all agreed to rush ahead without looking back. Allow me to point out, moreover, that under the old regime, our dukedoms, principalities and cities enjoyed greater freedom and autonomy. True, Hans retorted, straightening up in his chair, they had so much autonomy they never stopped fighting over who should rule. Gentlemen, declared Álvaro, this reminds me of Spain in the Middle Ages. Is that such a bad thing? asked Frau Pietzine, curious about the Middle Ages or about Álvaro de Urquijo. Not bad, he replied, far worse. I adore Spain! Frau Pietzine sighed, such a warm country! My dear Madame, said Álvaro, have no fear, you will get to know it better. Herr Hans, Professor

Mietter went on, what puzzles me is that you speak a great deal about individual freedoms yet resist the idea of nationalism as an expression of a people's individuality. That remains to be seen, said Hans, sometimes I think nationalism is another way of suppressing the individual. Ahem, an interesting thought, asserted Herr Levin. I am simply saying, the professor insisted, that if Prussia had done everything in its power to stop the advance of the Revolution, the French would never have invaded us. And I am telling you, Hans retorted, that we merely chose the wrong kind of invasion; we should have allowed ourselves to be invaded by French ideas, not the French army.

Seeing Professor Mietter take a deep breath in order to reply, Sophie held out a plate of warm sago to him and said: Monsieur Hans, please tell us more. Yes, Hans went on, we were betrayed and humiliated by Napoleon. Yet today we Germans rule ourselves and, oddly enough, having expelled the invaders it is our own government that oppresses us, is it not? My dear Monsieur Hans, interjected Herr Gottlieb, you must take into account that for twenty long years we have endured the humiliation of watching French troops march by, install themselves along the Rhine, cross Thuringia, capture Dresden—incidentally, my child, has your brother written to you? He hasn't? And yet he complains we never go to see him! Anyway, where was I? Oh yes, the troops, they occupied Berlin and even Vienna, my dear Monsieur Hans, Prussia was nearly obliterated, how could you not expect a violent reaction? Let us not forget, my dear Monsieur Gottlieb, said Hans, that it was our very own princes who. I haven't forgotten, Herr Gottlieb interrupted, I haven't forgotten, still, I sincerely hope that one day the Prussians will avenge all those outrages. Don't say that, Father, protested Sophie. *Voilà ma pensée*, declared Herr Gottlieb, raising his arms aloft and sinking from view behind the wings of his armchair. We are quite capable of bringing about the destruction of Europe ourselves, without any help from Napoleon, said

Hans pensively. Indeed, I have just come from Berlin, Monsieur, and can I assure you I do not care one bit for the young people's eagerness for war. I wish our politics were more English and we had fewer Prussian policemen. Don't be frivolous, retorted Professor Mietter irately, those policemen are there to defend both you and me. They have never even addressed me, Hans said sarcastically. Messieurs, Sophie intervened, Messieurs, calm yourselves, there is still some tea left and it would be a shame to waste it. Elsa, dear, would you …

In the round mirror, Hans saw Sophie talking to Herr Levin, and he turned his attention to them. Monsieur Levin, Sophie said, you look rather pensive, tell us, what opinion do you have of our favourite monster? Ahem, said Herr Levin, none in particular, that is, well. Let us admit that among other things, ahem, worthy of mention, he introduced a certain civic equality, did he not? We quite understand, interrupted Professor Mietter with a scowl, I wonder what the Torah has to say about civic equality? My dear Professor, Sophie urged, that is not a joking matter. Then Álvaro said: Since we are on the subject, what does our charming hostess think of the matter? Hear, hear, agreed Professor Mietter, we are all dying to know. My dear, you are surrounded! declared Frau Pietzine. Herr Gottlieb's whiskers bristled with anticipation. Frau Levin stopped sipping her tea. Hans glanced back at the mirror, eyes open wide. What I think, Messieurs, Sophie began, and I am aware that compared to you all I am an ignoramus when it comes to politics, is that the failures of a revolution needn't make us regress historically. Perhaps I go too far in my conjectures, but you have all read *Lucinde* have you not? And do you not consider this slim volume a legitimate product of revolutionary aspirations? My dear Mademoiselle, said Professor Mietter, that book is not about politics at all! *Lieber* Professor, Sophie smiled, shrugging her shoulders delightfully in order to soften their disagreement, indulge me for a moment, and let us pretend that it is, that *Lucinde* is a deeply political novel, because it speaks not of matters of state but of people's lives, the new intimacy of people's lives. Can there be any greater revolution than that of social behaviour? Professor Mietter sighed: What bores the Schlegel brothers are. And how stupid their railings against Protestant rationalism. The younger brother has proved to be as insignificant as his aphorisms. And as for his elder brother, the poor man can think of nothing more interesting than to translate Shakespeare. But Hans, overwhelmed, had turned away from the mirror. So, you are an admirer of Schlegel, Mademoiselle? he asked in a hushed voice. Not of Schlegel himself, replied Sophie, well, that depends. I adore his novel, the world he evokes. You have no idea, Hans whispered, how profoundly we agree. Sophie lowered her gaze and began shifting the teacups around. Moreover, Sophie went on, seeing that her father and Professor Mietter had begun a separate conversation, I think Schlegel has become like Schiller—he is terrified of the present. In fact, if those two had their way I would be too busy trying on dresses even to discuss their work. My dear friends, Herr Gottlieb suddenly announced, standing up, I hope you enjoy the remainder of the evening. Then he walked over to the clock on the wall, which said ten o'clock sharp. He wound it up as he did every evening at the same time. He gave a nod and retired to bed.

A while later, realising he should not be the last to leave, Hans rose from his chair. Bertold went to fetch his hat and coat. Hans bowed to the other guests, his eyes remaining fixed on Professor Mietter. Sophie, who seemed more spirited since her father's departure, went over to say goodbye. Mademoiselle Gottlieb, said Hans, please do not think I am being polite when I say that, thanks to you, I have enjoyed a delightful evening. It was very kind of you to ask me to your salon, and I hope my outspokenness will not result in me being exiled. On the contrary, my dear Monsieur Hans, Sophie replied, it is I who must thank you. Today's discussion was one of the most lively and interesting we have had, and I suspect this is partly due to your presence. Your sympathy overwhelms me, Hans said, overstepping the mark with his flirtatiousness. Have no fear, Sophie retorted, putting him in his place, next Friday I shall be more disagreeable and less indulgent. Mademoiselle Gottlieb, said Hans, clearing his throat. (Yes? she asked abruptly.) If you will allow me, I would like, well, I would like to applaud your brilliant comments on Schlegel and *Lucinde*. Why, thank you, Monsieur Hans, Sophie smiled and rubbed one side of her hand with the other, you will have noticed that, while I try not to contradict my guests, when asked what I think of Napoleon, I am hard pressed to agree with the restorationists. Nevertheless, my dear friend (when he heard the word *friend* Hans's heart skipped a beat), if I may be so bold as to clarify something concerning the French Revolution (please, do go ahead, said he), I assume we both defended it this evening because of our loyalty to certain convictions, but in order to remain true to my own beliefs I must remind you of something you did not mention. Of the many things for which we could reproach the Jacobins, one is their horror at French women demanding the right to participate in public life. This is why I said that we need an intimate revolution as well as political change. I hope you agree with me that the natural outcome of such a revolution, were it conducted properly, would be a change in public functions, allowing us women to aspire to parliament as well as needlework, although I assure you I have nothing against needlework, on the contrary I find it quite relaxing. In short, my dear Hans, I trust you do not think me fanciful, and I hope next Friday you will come up with an interesting response. Bertold! Bertold! There you are! I was beginning to think you'd run off with the gentleman's overcoat! Goodnight, and take care, Hans, it is dark on the stairs. Goodbye, thank you, goodbye, goodbye.

As he made his way in a daze towards the front door of the Gottlieb residence, Hans heard his name being called from the staircase and stopped. Álvaro's eyes flashed as he passed between two patches of darkness. My dear Hans, he said clapping him on the back, don't you think the night is too young for two gentlemen such as us to go home?

Tramping across frozen mud and dried urine, they left Stag Street behind them. The flickering gas lamps lent the market square an intermittent presence—its luminosity fluctuated the way an instrument changes chords, the gradient of the deserted cobblestones rose and fell, the ornate fountain vanished for an instant then reappeared, the Tower of the Wind became smudged. Álvaro and Hans crossed the square listening to the sound of their own footsteps. Hans was still struck by the contrast between day and night, between the colourful fruit and the yellow darkness, the throng of passers-by and this icy silence. He reflected that one of the two squares, the daytime or nighttime one, was like a mirage. Gazing up, he saw St Nicholas's lopsided towers, its slanting silhouette. Álvaro stared at it and said: One of these days it is bound to topple over.

Unlike in the surrounding countryside where night falls slowly, day ends abruptly in Wandernburg, with the same alarming swiftness as that with which the shutters swing shut on the windows. The evening light is sucked away as down a drain. Then the few passers-by begin tripping over barrels outside taverns, all the carriage gear, kerbstones, loose logs, household waste. Beside each doorway bags of refuse decompose, while drawn by the stench dogs and cats gather round eating as the flies buzz overhead.

Looked at from the sky, the city is like a candle floating on water. At its centre, the wick, is the gaslit glow of the market square. Beyond the square, darkness gains ground in an ever-widening circle. Threads of light spread out like a pattern of nerves along the remaining streets. Rising from the walls like pale creepers, the oil lamps scarcely illuminate the ground beneath them. Night in Wandernburg is not as black as a wolf's mouth—it is what the avid wolf devours.

For a while now, on certain nights, in the streets bordering the square, avoiding the nightwatchmen, standing in the shadows, merging with the walls, someone has been waiting. Along Wool Alley, in narrow Prayer Street or at the end of Our Saviour's Alley, breathing silently, dressed in a dark flowing cape and black-brimmed hat, wearing snugly fitting gloves, arms thrust into pockets, clutching a knife in one hand and a mask and a piece of rope in the other, lurking on street corners, this someone is alert to every footstep, to the slightest sound.

And on this night, as on every night, near to the poorly lit streets where this someone is waiting, at times only a stone's throw away, the nightwatchmen pass by with their lanterns dangling on the end of poles, and each hour on the hour remove their hats, blow their horns and cry out:

Time to go home, everyone!
The church bell has chimed eight,
Watch over your fire and your lamps,
Praise be to God! All praise!

And the drifting market square with its frozen weathervane. And beyond, the lopsided towers of St Nicholas's, the pointed steeple puncturing the edge of the moon, which goes on seeping liquid.

The drinkers crowded at the bar and sat round scratched pine tables. Hans glanced about the room, eyes darting from tankard to tankard, and was surprised when he recognised a familiar face. But isn't that? he asked. Isn't he? (You mean that fellow over there? Álvaro said.) Yes, the one with the shiny waistcoat, drinking a toast with the other two, isn't that? (The mayor? Álvaro finished his sentence for him. Yes, why? Do you know him?) No, well, someone introduced me to him at a reception a few weeks ago. (Oh, you were there, too! What a pity we didn't meet then.) Yes, it was a crashing bore, what do you suppose he's doing here at this time of night? (There's nothing unusual about it, Mayor Ratztrinker is very fond of the Central Tavern and of his beer, he always claims his aim in life is to serve the townspeople, so I imagine drinking with them until dawn is the best way of getting to know them.)

Álvaro ordered a lager. Hans preferred wheat beer. Standing side by side in the steamy warmth, the two men soon confirmed that their fellow feeling in the salon had been no accident. Now that he was on his own, Álvaro spoke at length and openly, showing a passion he concealed when in company. Like all people with a lively temperament he possessed the twin qualities of anger and tenderness. Both were evident in his excitability when he spoke. Álvaro was drawn to Hans's quiet conviction, the feeling that he knew more than he was saying. He was intrigued by Hans's way of both being and not being there, that polite frontier from which he listened with an air of being about to turn away. They spoke in a manner two men rarely succeeded in doing—without interrupting or competing with one another. Amid laughs and long draughts of his beer, glancing sideways at the mayor, Álvaro told Hans about Wandernburg's amazing history.

In actual fact, Álvaro said, it's impossible to pinpoint the exact location of Wandernburg on any map, because it has changed places all the time. It shifts so much between regions it has become all but invisible. As this area has always been under Saxony or Prussia without either being the absolute ruler, Wandernburg developed almost exclusively as a result of land owned by the Catholic Church. From the start, the Church agreed to a few families in the region exploiting it, among them the Ratztrinkers, who own the mills and a large part of the textile industry, and the Wilderhauses. (The Wilderhauses? Hans started, the ones? …) Yes, the family of Sophie's fiancé Rudi, apparently the Wilderhauses are direct descendants of the original princes of Wandernburg, why are you pulling that face? Seriously, they say Rudi and his brothers and sisters are the nephews and nieces of a great-great-grandson of one such prince. Besides owning a great deal of land, the Wilderhauses have relatives in the Prussian army and others in the civil service in Berlin. The fact is that these old families swore that, providing the Church gave them a part of its land, they would never accede to the demands of the Protestant princes, Saxon or Prussian. That land continues to provide their descendants with a substantial income, a divine third of which they hand over to the Church. (Very clever, said Hans, but why weren't they invaded? Why did the Protestant princes tolerate this resistance?) Probably because there was little to gain from an invasion. The landowners around here have always been highly productive as well as competent managers. I don't think anyone else would obtain such a high yield from this amount of land and livestock, which is scarcely worth going to war over. Who do you think received until recently one of the two remaining thirds of profit? The reigning Saxon prince, of course. So you see everyone came out winning—no one needed to invade anyone and there was scarcely even any need for legal wrangling. The Church held on to its property in the heart of heretic country. The Saxon princes avoided further embroilment in border conflicts and problems with the Catholic princes, and gained a certain reputation for clemency, which they used to their advantage when it suited them. And the Wandernburg oligarchs were safe from harm so long as they paid taxes to both sides, do you see? (Perfectly, said Hans. Where did you learn all this?) Business, my friend, you've no idea what you can learn when doing business (I'm still amazed you're a businessman, you don't talk like one), hold on, hold on, keep in mind two things: *la primera*, my dear Hans, is that not all businessmen are as stupid as businessmen seem, and number two, my friend, is a tale that begins in England and which I'll tell you another day.

And how do you get along with all these families? asked Hans. Oh, marvellously! replied Álvaro. I secretly despise them and they pretend not to be watching me. In fact, we're being watched at this very moment, *pues que les den bien por el culo*! (Come again? said Hans. I didn't catch that.) Nothing, it doesn't matter. We smile at one another and do business together. I'm aware that some families have tried to find other distributors for their cloths. But we are the cheapest, and so for the moment they are better off putting up with me to be able to do business with my English partners. (And why aren't you in England?) Well, the reply is a sad story that I'll also leave for another day. The fact is they need our London distributors. After Napoleon's defeat and the end of the blockade, they had no English contacts here in Wandernburg, and they saw in my partners a chance to expand their market. They are hardly in a position to choose; this is a tiny region, far from the Atlantic, which does little trade with the North Sea or Baltic ports. Quite simply they need us. Be patient, Herr Mayor! murmured Álvaro, raising his tankard towards Ratztrinker's table. The mayor, who was out of earshot, responded with a grimace.

One thing I fail to understand, said Hans, is why the Church owned land in this region? What was a Catholic principality doing in Protestant territory? This city becomes more baffling by the minute. Yes, said Álvaro, it surprised me at first, too. You see, during the Thirty Years' War these lands were virtually on the border between Saxony and Brandenburg, you might say they were Saxon by the skin of their teeth. The Catholic army invaded the region and used it as an enclave to disrupt the enemy communications. Thus, inadvertently, Wandernburg became a bastion of the Catholic League at the heart of the Protestant Union. At the Peace of Westphalia it was declared an ecclesiastical principality, waiter, two more tankards, what do you mean no! Never say no to the last round, no, I insist, you can pay next time, or don't you intend to visit another tavern with me? What was I saying? Yes, and this became the Principality of Wandernburg, which is still its official name. Remember that in Westphalia princes were free to choose the religion of their state, a deplorable decision, I know. And it seems the ruling prince here at the time was a Catholic. Apparently, in order to save the city from destruction, his parents collaborated with the Counter-Reformation troops. That is how Wandernburg came to be, and still is, Catholic (very interesting, said Hans, I'd never heard that story, I didn't even know Wandernburg was an ecclesiastical principality, I've traveled past it a few times, but), I'm sure you have, like everyone else, I came here for very different reasons, otherwise I'd never, well, let's leave that for another day. Yes, and still more strange—the situation has remained almost unchanged in two centuries. This was only a small region, surrounded by enemies and one of hundreds of states scattered throughout Germany, and the reunification of the empire was never going to be determined by a few hectares. (And what about Napoleon? Didn't everything change under the French?) That's the interesting thing! Since Saxony sided with Napoleon, his troops carried out a peaceful occupation of Wandernburg, through which they passed unimpeded on their way to and from the Prussian front. In return for services rendered, Napoleon's brother decided to respect the Catholic authority in Wandernburg. But when the emperor was overthrown, Prussia occupied part of Saxony, and Wandernburg ended up a few miles inside Prussian territory. Once again it became a border territory, only on the other side this time. And so, my friend, a toast! We're Prussians now, *coño*! and should declare it from the rooftops. Let's become inflamed with Prussian zeal! (And clinking tankards with that foreigner, Hans felt at home in Wandernburg for the first time.)

Álvaro laughed: Now it's Prussia which receives its share of the tribute, and that's why it respects Wandernburg's exceptional status. The Wildherhauses, Ratztrinkers and other landowners continue to declare themselves Catholics, and as defenders of the Church uphold its many privileges, while at the same time declaring themselves tolerant, interdenominational and Prussian before the King of Prussia, as vehemently as they once claimed they were Saxons, supporters of the French or what have you. This is why some descendants of exiled Lutheran families have returned, like Professor Mietter. Prior to the Congress of Vienna the authorities and the press would never have treated a man like the professor with such respect, but now it is politically advantageous (I don't suppose Saxony will stand by and do nothing, Hans said), well, Saxony has made no moves as yet, I imagine they don't expect the borders established at Vienna to hold for very long either, the way nothing does in Germany. That, I guarantee, would be no problem for the Wandernburg authorities. They would simply throw themselves into the arms of the corresponding Saxon prince, bemoan the atrocious torments they suffered at the hands of his Prussian enemy, declare a public holiday and receive the new prince with true Saxon pomp and ceremony. And so it will be evermore, until this land falls into the sea or Germany is unified. And for now neither event seems likely. I hope I haven't bored you with my disquisition!

(*Disquisition*? Where did you get that word from?) Well, in all modesty, I also know the word *homily*. (You sound like a Saxon grandmother!) So, as you see, Wandernburg's borders change from one day to the next (aha, Hans said, jokingly, maybe that's why I get lost whenever I walk around it. Álvaro looked at him, suddenly serious), so I'm not the only one, you also have the feeling sometimes that (that what? That the streets … move?) Yes, yes! I've always been too embarrassed to mention this to anyone, but I often leave home well in advance in case something changes place unexpectedly. And I thought I was the only one! Your health!

The alcohol was beginning to slur Hans's speech. He put a hand on Álvaro's shoulder. Er, sorrry, he said to Álvaro, 'd'I step on your toe? Paardon me, y'know, ev' sin' we beggan talkin' I been m-meanin t'ask you how ccome you spea' ssuch good Sherman? Álvaro slumped suddenly. That, he replied, is the story I didn't want to tell you. I was married for many years to a German woman. Ulrike. She was born about three leagues from here. She loved this place. The scenery. The customs. I don't know. Those were her childhood memories. That's why we came to live here. Ulrike. Many years. Who could possibly leave now?

Hans contemplated the frothy remains on the rim of his beer mug, the hollow ears of the handles, all the things one looks at when everything has been said. Then he whispered, When? Two years ago, said Álvaro. Of tuberculosis.

Álvaro and Hans drank up their beers. The waiters were wiping down the tables with the reproachful air they have when it is time to close. Hey, Hans stammered, aren't there a lot of wwidowed people in Wwandernburg? Sophie's father, Fffrau Pietzzzine, Proffessor Mietter even, perhaps. It's no coincidence, Álvaro replied, border cities are soothing, they make you think there's another world nearby, I don't know how to describe it. Travelers come here, people who have lost their way or were headed somewhere else, lone wolves. And they all end up staying here, Hans. You'll get used to it. I don' thin' sso, said Hans, I'm p-passing through. You'll get used to it, Álvaro repeated, I've been passing through here for over ten years now.

Hans was perched on his trunk, legs apart, trying not to drip water onto his bare feet, shaving in front of the mirror he had placed on the floor, the washbasin on one side and on the other a towel draped over the back of a chair. He liked this way of shaving, leaning as though over a tiny pond, because he felt it helped him to think—when you get up, especially if you are a night owl, your brain needs a bit of a shake-up. Sometimes it feels as if there aren't enough hours in the day, Hans reflected. He had woken up in good spirits and eager to carry out all the tasks he had set himself. He would finish the book he was halfway through over lunch, go to see the organ grinder and suggest they dine together, meet Álvaro for coffee then follow Sophie a little, if, as on other occasions, he managed to bump into her out strolling with a friend, emerging from a shop with Elsa or on her way to pay someone a visit. Sitting clutching the razor, face streaked with foam, still only half-dressed, Hans had the impression all this could be done in a trice.

His reverie was interrupted by shouts from downstairs. Considering the day officially started, Hans dried his face, replaced the watercolour on its hook, got a splinter in his foot, pulled it out cursing, finished dressing, and went out into the corridor. The shouts continued. Lisa was trying to get into the kitchen, while her mother and the suspended hams blocked the way. I don't care what you say, Frau Zeit exclaimed, you can't fool me, there's at least fifteen or ten groschen missing. Mother, Lisa argued, can't you see I bought an extra pound of beef as well as more tomatoes? Of course I can see, Frau Zeit retorted, and I'm wondering who asked you to buy all those tomatoes, the meat doesn't matter, what's left over can be salted, but who do you think is going to eat a whole basketful of tomatoes? And anyway, a pound of meat couldn't cost that much, do you think I'm stupid? Mother, replied Lisa, I told you the prices went up this morning by one loth in seven. We'll see about that! her mother protested. I'll go to the market myself tomorrow, and I warn you. Do as you please, Lisa interrupted her mother in turn, if you don't believe me you can go and see for yourself tomorrow and the day after, and every day if you want. I'm not interested in the butcher or in tomatoes or in arguing with you. But child, Frau Zeit replied, seizing Lisa by the wrists, even if it's true, don't you see what things cost? When will you learn? If they put the price up overnight you have to haggle like the rest of us, do you hear? Haggle! And stop giving yourself such airs and graces.

Lisa was about to respond when she glimpsed Hans, who was standing motionless in the corridor, listening. She turned away at once, pretending she hadn't seen him. Hans's curiosity got the better of his embarrassment and he stood there without moving. Lisa went on countering her mother's admonishments with short, sharp ripostes. Notwithstanding her maternal authority, Frau Zeit was getting the worst of the argument. The two women shifted position, so that they were almost facing Hans. In the glow of copper and tin from the kitchen, he could see the creases spread over Frau Zeit's face each time she raised her voice. And the scars, blotches and cuts on Lisa's hands as she gesticulated. For an instant the contrast in their silhouettes, beauty and posture was lost, so that to Hans they became one and the same woman at two different moments, two identical women of different ages. Then he walked away from the kitchen.

Hans had to wait until Thomas burst in before he was able to recapture the light-heartedness he had felt when he got up. It was impossible to resist the boy's tireless enthusiasm, his instinctive breed of optimism. Thomas said good morning to Hans absent-mindedly, asked him whether he liked elks, snatched his cup of coffee and hid it behind the couch, spun round in circles, arms akimbo, one leg in the air, and pelted down the corridor. Hans got to his feet, at which Thomas, thinking he was about to give chase, tore up the staircase. Not wishing to disappoint the child, Hans raced after him, pretending to be an angry ogre and bellowing for his cup of coffee, which he had already retrieved from the floor. When Thomas reached the end of the corridor on the second floor and was thrust up against the window, he turned to face his persecutor, his face suddenly so contorted, his eyes filled with such dread that for a split second Hans really believed himself an ogre. He was about to ruffle the boy's hair so as to reassure him, when Thomas burst out laughing, and Hans realised the boy was the better actor. Taken aback, he glanced out of the window and noticed it was raining.

Thomas, you rascal! roared Frau Zeit with the redoubled rage of one who has scolded their other child to no avail. Thomas, I told you to come down at once and finish your homework! For the love of God, you haven't even done the first exercise! They ought to start opening the school on Saturdays! Oh, and you can forget about going tobogganing! The boy looked at Hans, regained his composure, then shrugged as though acknowledging their game was over. Head sunk on his chest, he walked towards the staircase. The two of them went down in silence. When they had reached the bottom of the stairs, Thomas let out two small explosions. Furious, his father strode out from behind the counter, grabbed his son by the ear and dragged him down the passageway towards their apartment. When he returned, flustered, he said to Hans: As you can see, we're just like any other family. Of course, Hans replied, don't worry. The innkeeper plunged his hand into the pocket of his sagging trousers and said: By the way, since you are staying on, and in view of your, well, your late-night habits, I'm giving you this bunch of keys. Please don't lose it. And always take it with you when you go out at night.

Midday was drowning. Umbrellas vied for space on the narrow pavement. Hans's boots splashed in the puddles distorting his footsteps. Throwing up a spray of muddy water, carriages drove past him like a temptation. In the market square, the vendors were packing up their stalls. Hans glimpsed the organ grinder in his usual spot, hunched over, absorbed in the music, making the square turn. Drops of water dripped from his beard, sticking out from beneath his hood. Seeing him there, serene, Hans reconciled himself to the gloomy day—so long as the old man continued at the heart of Wandernburg, the city would be in order. As always, Franz was the first to sense his arrival—he pricked up his black ears, lifted his head from the floor, stretched his legs and shook his coat.

How goes your day? Hans enquired, squeezing Franz's muzzle while the dog squirmed. Beautiful, replied the old man, have you noticed the way the mist sparkles? The mist? No, Hans confessed, I haven't. It's been changing colour all morning, the organ grinder went on. Do you like the mist? Me? Hans said, surprised, not especially, I don't think. Franz and I enjoy it, don't we, old rascal? the organ grinder said. And your public? Hans asked, gesturing to the dish in a fit of pragmatism he felt rather ashamed of. I mean, did you have much of one? Not many, replied the organ grinder, enough to pay for supper, you will come won't you? Hans nodded, wondering whether to offer to buy the wine, for the old man usually took offence if he suspected Hans brought food to the cave in an attempt to stock him up rather than as a mark of courtesy. The old man went on: Lamberg says he'll stop by for a while after supper. That boy worries me, he works himself half to death in the factory and he doesn't laugh much, it's a bad sign when someone drinks a lot and doesn't laugh. Let's try to cheer him up tonight, shall we? You can recount your travels to him, I'll play a lively tune, and with a bit of luck Reichardt will tell a few dirty jokes. And you, rascal, have you been practising any new barks?

Fearing the weather might worsen, Hans went to talk to a coachman about taking him as far as the bridge that evening. The coachman told him the carriages had all been full that day and he couldn't promise him a seat in one with a top. Hans said in that case he would reserve a seat in a tilbury without a top and would bring an umbrella. The coachman hemmed and hawed, then said he wasn't sure there were any seats available in a tilbury either. Hans gazed at him fixedly, sighed, and handed him a couple of coins. The coachman immediately remembered a possible vacancy in the last carriage.

On his way back to the inn, where he was planning to read for a while, Hans strolled along the broad, acacia-lined pavements of King's Parade, where the carriages rolled along with their polished wheels, sturdy horses and liveried coachmen. Among the calèches with folding tops, the gleaming landaus and the elegant cabriolets, Hans could not help remarking a carriage drawn by two white horses speeding along at a ceremonial trot. It took Hans a moment to transfer his gaze from the outside to the inside of the carriage—he started when he made out Sophie's profile shrinking back from the rain, and next to her the outline of a hat. Sophie jerked her head away from the window and Hans heard a voice asking if she were feeling well.

The carriage turned off King's Parade. At the end of Border Street, a figure was walking towards Archway. As the coach passed the figure turned around—Father Pigherzog, wearing a shovel hat and a cloak on top of his cassock, folded his umbrella and bowed in greeting. Inside the red velvet-lined cabin, Sophie remained motionless while her companion straightened up in order to return the gesture. *Guten Tag, mein lieber* Herr Wilderhaus! cried Father Pigherzog, his head revolving as the coach rolled by. And then he added, a little too late perhaps: God bless you! As the priest opened up his umbrella again, his hat fell onto the ground and got muddy. Annoyed, he walked up Archway clasping it between thumb and finger.

The sacristan was polishing the holy vessels. Peace be with you, my son, said Father Pigherzog as he entered the sacristy. The sacristan helped him off with his cloak, left his hat to soak in water and finished arranging the relics. How did the collection go, my son? asked the priest. The sacristan handed him the small metal box they referred to as the vessel of the divine will. God be with you, Father Pigherzog said, you may go now.

When he was alone, Father Pigherzog glanced about the sacristy and sighed. He looked up at the clock and sat down beside one of the lamps, transferring one of the piles of books on the table to his lap. He put the book of sacraments and the *Misal Romano* back. He pored over Pius V's catechism for a moment, slipped a bookmark between its pages and placed it with the others. A large volume entitled *Notes on the State of Souls* remained in his lap. In it Father Pigherzog took note of various matters relating to Church business: details of each family's practice and observance of Easter rituals; his personal impressions of parishioners, including brief reports about them; comments on and consequences of the weekly liturgy; shortages and possible requirements of the parish, as well as any significant contributions or donations; and lastly a section in which he wrote less frequently, addressed to "Your Excellency" and concerning the "Balance of the quarterly accounts of the lands given in concession by the Holy Mother Church", which the priest would check before copying out the figures and posting them to the Archbishop. All of this Father Pigherzog would do in his neat script, dividing the subjects under headings.

He opened the *Notes on the State of Souls* at the most recent entry and browsed his comments. He took his quill, leisurely dipped it in the ink pot, wrote out the date and began his task.

... who I am concerned about is Frau H J de Pietzine, whose trials and tribulations we have remarked upon on previous occasions. A host of fears confound her conscience and darken her soul, the salvation of which will depend in large part upon her willingness to embrace penitence, the exercise of which she is inclined to observe with far less enthusiasm than the act of prayer. A woman of faith and family condition should not make an exhibition of herself by attending frivolous social gatherings of every kind. Address this tendency at next confessionals.

... as is clear from the previous entry, the excellent Herr Wilderhaus, the younger, whose nobility and generosity towards this humble parish we profoundly appreciate, has made an understandable choice, attendant upon certain of Fräulein Gottlieb's virtues, virtues which, dare I say, in recent years have been unbecomingly eclipsed by xxxxxx a degree of rebelliousness and frivolity. Nothing, I hasten to add, which marriage, domestic bliss and the duties of motherhood cannot redress. Send sacristan to Wilderhaus Hall with a fresh letter on the parish's headed paper thanking them again for their pious donation. Suggest to Herr Gottlieb a private interview with his daughter.

... having thus abandoned her catechism classes. Her renunciation of past heresies is no less praiseworthy, although it remains to be seen whether this is permanent. The case of her husband is far more arduous, A N Levin, who not only refuses to renounce his xxxxxx Semitic profanation and Arian deviance, but confounds his wife with spurious theosophies ranging from an adoptionism that blasphemes against the indivisible essence of the Father and the Son, to an adulterated hotchpotch of pre-Nicene Christology and Brahmin pantheism. From what I have gathered thus far, his wife was on the point of being persuaded

by this pantheistic argument. It was necessary for me to explain to her that such a system leads to spiritual indifference, for if God were equally present in all things, it would make no difference if we paid attention to clouds and rocks or the Holy Spirit. I was obliged to remind her that not everything is God but that God is everything. Keep Frau Levin on her guard. Also request that she consult her husband about the transactions on the following pages.

… with unheard-of impudence. Attempt to find out in the corresponding Bible class. Upbraid the teacher in question.

… of these encouraging signs. Taking his work as an example, devote Sunday's collective prayer to the supremacy of self-denial.

… not to mention gluttony. Give him a final warning under penalty of banishment from dining hall.

… impure thoughts of an alarmingly frequent and xxxxxx vivid nature. Insist upon penitence. Speak to his tutors.

… collected in our vessel of the divine will, which has had such a blessed impact on our humble parish and on the absolution of souls, I find myself duty bound to inform you that this amount diminished by seventeen per cent last month from an average of half a thaler per parishioner to the current eight groschen per parishioner at Sunday Mass, amounting to an overall reduction in our revenue of fifteen louis or twenty-two ducats. I therefore beseechingly implore Your Excellency to consider and find a way of compensating for this loss, if only in small part. Lastly, owing to a reduction in productivity, the tithes are to remain unchanged until the third quarter, at which time they will be increased to three and a quarter thalers per taxpaying peasant. I hereby attest to the above, and, as your humble servant, await Your Excellency's next visit in order that I may kiss your hands, discuss these matters in person and celebrate a pontifical Mass in all its solemnity and beauty.

I'm so glad you brought up Fichte, Monsieur Hans (Sophie remarked, stroking the inside of her teacup handle, almost introducing her finger into it, then pulling it back again, while

Hans watched, becoming increasingly troubled), because if I remember rightly last Friday none of us mentioned him during our debate about this country. Professor Mietter, so do you not think (she said, changing the tone and direction of her voice, her fingers wandering from the handle to the outside of her teacup, caressing its rippled surface as though she were reading Braille) that it might be appropriate to consider him for a moment? My dear young man (Professor Mietter, who had hitherto been dominating the conversation, addressed Hans with his fingers firmly clasped in front of him), I notice you show an interest in certain philosophers, may I ask what you have studied? (Sophie took her hands away from the teacup and they hung there for a moment, like ears.) Me? Philosophy (Hans replied, but not before hesitating and rubbing his hands together in what Sophie interpreted as a gesture of unease). Ah, philosophy (said Professor Mietter unclasping his fingers and leaving them pointing upwards), how interesting, and where exactly did you study? At Jena (Hans replied, hesitating once more, placing his hands on his thighs as if to say: That's all).

From what I know of Fichte (said Herr Gottlieb without taking his pipe out of his mouth) I agree with his ideas about Germany, although I have heard he was virtually an atheist. Father (said Sophie, bringing her hands closer together), what an interesting ring the word *virtually* has! For Fichte, the "I" (observed Herr Levin, whose hands were usually motionless, as though bound together) is a divine category. In my view (said Hans, smoothing his trousers, perhaps in order to soften his disagreement with a gesture of false modesty), no "I" can be divine, except, of course, if it believes itself partly to be He. (Sophie's forefinger moved back to the inside of the cup handle.) Ah, but (Herr Levin reflected, pointing to an imaginary spot on the table) the most important thing would be the We that is beneath this He. My dear (said Frau Pietzine, dropping her needlework), may I have a little more cake?

At the beginning of the session, Sophie had announced that Rudi Wilderhaus had just sent her a message in which he asked all the other guests to excuse his absence and promised he would be there without fail the following Friday. Hans had deduced that this was therefore his last chance to impress Sophie before her fiancé arrived on the scene. And so he threw himself into the debate about Fichte. I am quite drawn, he said, to his ideas on the individual, but his theory of Germany leaves me cold. If each of us were a country, then every people would be a country made up of countries, would it not? But surely no individual, however sacred he thinks himself, can embody a country or express its fundamental nature. (Tell us, protested Herr Levin, do Bach and Beethoven not represent our nation in the most favourable light? Ah, touché! Professor Mietter exclaimed, trying to look amused but sounding piqued. But Hans was talking only for Sophie now.) No, I don't mean that. If a poet or musician succeeds in personifying a country's sensibility it will always be coincidental, a historical phenomenon rather than a metaphysical one. Or do you really believe Bach composed from his Germanness? This is precisely why I am suspicious of Fichte. How can he espouse a radical form of subjectivity and from it construct an entire nation? I wonder what the devil he means when he speaks of the German ideal? Who exemplifies it? And who is incompatible with it? In his discourses, he explains how German uniqueness was a result of migration, while the other Teutonic tribes stayed in their places of origin. What amazes me is that Fichte acknowledges this and then has the audacity to assert that resettlement wasn't really so significant, and that ethnic characteristics predominate over place, etc etc. You yourself, Professor (Hans was speaking almost without drawing breath, and the professor, unable to find a natural break in his rapid monologue, turned away as though he had not heard his name) have traveled and are therefore aware of how outward changes give rise to inwards ones. History shows that peoples are as changeable as rivers. Fichte describes them as if they were made of marble, solid blocks that can be moved or chiselled but remain essentially unchanged. He underestimates the importance of the mixing of the Germanic lineage with the conquered peoples, and as if that weren't enough he insinuates that all our problems, our age-old problems, aren't really German, but foreign. What nonsense! What is he trying to tell us? Whom is he suggesting we flee from in order to avoid contamination? (Herr Levin coughed twice.) I have learnt everything I know from traveling, that is, from associating with foreigners. Very well, let us suppose Fichte's intention was to restore our faith in ourselves after the French occupation or whatever. Much obliged to you Herr Fichte for having renewed our Germanic spirit, but now our optimism has been restored, let us discover common principles not Germanic tribes.

Hans finally fell silent, like the others. It only lasted a moment. Sophie had difficulty concealing the impression Hans's words had made on her. And in particular she was unable to work out whether this impression had been philosophical or of some other nature quite unrelated to Fichte. But at once the habitual noises, voices and gestures resumed as a teaspoon clinked against a cup, someone asked for sugar, and someone else stood up and asked to use the water closet.

Rubbing his knuckles, Álvaro argued that Germany was the only country in Europe where the Enlightenment and feudalism had been equally influential. He went on to say that in his opinion (and Professor Mietter considered this idea too republican) the nature of German government was directly at odds with German thought. And this contradiction explained why the Germans were so bold in their thinking and so submissive in their obedience. The professor returned to Fichte. He argued that precisely because of Germany's feudal roots, the only way forward was to find a cornerstone upon which to build a united Germany, and this cornerstone could only be Prussia. At this point, Frau Pietzine (to everyone's amazement) stopped embroidering and quoted Fichte. The quotation was not philosophical, but it was Fichte, and it referred to the physical education of German youth. Ah, gymnastics! Hans tried to sound ironical. That great manifestation of culture! Professor Mietter defended physical discipline as an expression of spiritual control. Indeed, I myself exercise every morning (he confessed with a flash of coquetry). And rest assured, my dear Professor, Sophie said, you look splendid, you are quite right to keep yourself in shape, take no notice of Monsieur Hans. *Vielen Dank, mein liebes Fräulein,* Professor Mietter replied contentedly, the thing is some people think they are going to stay young for ever.

The topics alternated between the trivial and the lofty. However, each time they went back to discussing philosophy, neither Professor Mietter nor Hans was prepared to yield an inch. The professor leant back in his chair and folded his legs, as if to make clear he had experience and calm on his side, while Hans had nothing but unease and uncertainty. Hans leant forward in his chair and straightened up, as if to suggest that strength and conviction were his, while the professor could offer only cynicism and world-weariness. As the two men continued debating, Herr Gottlieb's whiskers vanished behind plumes of pipe smoke. Herr Levin would tentatively take sides depending on the topic, and then contradict himself. Frau Levin did not say a word, but watched Hans in a vaguely hostile way. Álvaro scarcely spoke, but when he did it was nearly always to back Hans, either because he agreed with him or because the professor's authority irritated him. He was surprised to see Elsa the maid stop tapping her foot and give the appearance of listening intently. Sophie quoted authors, books, ideas, then withdrew discreetly, making a great effort not to seem to take either of their sides, so that both men felt they could respond freely. And yet their opinions overwhelmed her, and a few times she was tempted to take the floor and challenge them both. Some afternoons, thought Sophie, pouring the tea, one feels the urge to behave in an unladylike way.

If I had to choose a national discourse, said Hans, then I would opt for Herder, who says that without history we are nothing a priori, don't you agree? A country ought not to ask what it is, but when and why. Professor Mietter responded by comparing Kant and Fichte's ideas of nationhood in order to show that, rather than betraying Kant, Fichte had taken his argument a step further. Hans said that in contrast to his views on Fichte, he liked Kant better when he spoke of countries rather than individuals. Every society, said Hans, needs order, and Kant proposes a very intelligent one. Yet every citizen also needs a measure of chaos, which Kant refuses. In my view, a free nation would be, let us say, a group of chaotic elements that respects the order containing them. In my view, Professor Mietter retorted, Fichte's national aspiration is invaluable in the present situation (and what situation is that, Professor? asked Hans), you know full well. Germany cannot go on choosing between foreign occupation or disintegration. It is time we took a step forward and decided our own fate. (But our fate, Hans argued, also depends on that of the other European countries, you cannot define any nation without redefining the continent.) Are you saying this because of your Napoleon, *gnädiger* Hans? (No, Hans parried, your Holy Alliance!)

Sophie felt excited and troubled in equal measure—this was the first time she had seen a guest seriously stand up to the professor, and she could not bring herself to intervene since she knew she would be incapable of expressing some of Hans's ideas as eloquently herself, partly owing to her father's presence, but also because of her neutral role as host. This neutrality was beginning to strike her as suspect, and the greater her misgivings, the more her slender hands moved hither and thither, the more she devoted herself to passing round the canapés, jellies, pastries and hot chocolate. In the meantime, surprised that Sophie did not censure Hans's impertinences, Professor Mietter continued to argue without growing angry, and indeed hoping she did not do so, in order that he could go on refuting them.

My dear friend, the professor said, should I remind you that without strong nations there can be no satisfactory international law? And I, my dear Professor, said Hans, must insist that I cannot help feeling much more like a citizen of Kant's Europe than of Fichte's Germany. Your feelings are your own affair, said the professor, the fact is that federal republicanism did not bring peace to Europe, only power struggles. Quite the contrary, Hans retorted, we have had wars when federalism failed. Kant envisaged a society of free states, which is incompatible with imperialism. The problem is each European treaty is a signature on the next war. Europe, my dear young man, said Professor Mietter, is founded on a common religion; that is the only basis for lasting unity. Do you not see that denying that is counter-productive? It surprises me (Álvaro declared, trying to tear his eyes away from Elsa's ankle) to hear a Lutheran speak in this way. I am a Lutheran, Professor Mietter bridled, but first and foremost I am a Christian, a Christian and a German. Gentlemen, ahem, Herr Levin ventured, if you will allow me, it is trade, not morality, that guarantees unity, that is, if Europe traded more it could not allow itself to go to war, you see, no, not so much cake, please, that's enough, thank you. Agreed, said Hans, but such changes cannot take place independently of a common political policy, for if we over-emphasise the identity of every nation, there will continue to be wars to decide who controls the markets. It is also possible to educate the economy, wouldn't you agree? Yes, replied Herr Levin, not forgetting that education depends on the economy. Economic wisdom, Professor Mietter insisted, forms part of nation building, and there Fichte hit the nail right on the head. Kant hit the nail on the head, Hans replied, when he wrote *Lasting Peace*. That's a good one! (said the professor, devouring a canapé, without clarifying whether he meant the canapé or Kant.) For your information, young man, the utopia of peace was invented over five hundred years ago by a man named Dante. But Dante thought peace depended on a political elite, Hans objected, almost exactly like what we have today! Kant thought law should be the guarantor of peace, a law established by a union of equal states. Entrusting peace to a handful of leaders is to legitimise despotism. Ahem, my belief (Herr Levin asserted, evading the caress his wife tried to give him by way of a warning) is that we occasionally get caught up in abstraction, that is, with all due respect, don't you think peace is related to wealth? But that, Hans nodded, also takes us onto moral ground, for unless wealth is shared there will never be peace—poverty is a potential cause of conflict. Hear, hear! said Álvaro. Gentlemen, please, Professor Mietter sighed, let us not be ingenuous. Peace and war seek to achieve the same aim, which is to decide who rules, only the former does so by different means we like to think of as peaceful. That's all there is to it. Ahem, perhaps, Herr Levin demurred, there is another reality to war, which is that the cost often outweighs its benefits, even for the victor, so that an impartial evaluation of the cost of war should be enough for us to renounce it.

Gentlemen, said Herr Gottlieb rising from his seat, please feel free to continue. I have a few matters to attend to in my study. This has been a most stimulating evening, as always.

Hans had the impression that as he said the word *stimulating* Herr Gottlieb had looked at him. Herr Gottlieb wound up the clock, which said ten o'clock sharp. He gestured to Bertold to light the candles, kissed his daughter on the forehead, bowed

in a way that sent his whiskers flying, and vanished down the
corridor. Finding herself alone with her guests, Sophie took a
deep breath—now she could speak her mind without having
to worry so much. Just when she was getting ready to join in
the debate, Frau Pietzine intercepted her to take her leave as
well, grasping her by the hands and whispering a few words
no one else could hear. Sophie nodded, glancing sideways at
the group made up of Professor Mietter, Hans, Álvaro and the
Levins. No sooner had Elsa fetched Frau Pietzine's blue scarf
and ribboned bonnet than Sophie hastened to sit down again.
To her dismay, the others were no longer discussing politics
but had moved on to Schopenhauer.

No, it hasn't enjoyed much success, Herr Levin was saying,
although I found the book interesting, or at least different. This
fellow Schopenhauer can't be all bad, Álvaro jested, if he has
translated Gracián he must speak Spanish, which is quite good
coming from a German. Bah! said Professor Mietter dismiss-
ively, mere plagiaries of Eastern religions, these people cannot
replace God, so they go searching for answers in Buddhism. I
like Schopenhauer, said Hans, because he loathes Hegel. But
don't you find all that despair rather tragic? retorted Herr Levin.
Perhaps, Hans replied, but he also lends himself to an optimistic
reading. We can admit the idea of free will, while refusing to
accept that it must always lead to suffering. That would mean
we are condemned to try to be happy, would it not? And yet,
gentlemen, the professor objected ...

And so the gentlemen of the salon went on spouting their
opinions endlessly, their lips quivering in the candlelight, as
though the glow of the flames breathed life into their arguments.
Sophie listened with a mixture of concentration and exasperation—she appreciated the things they said and detested what
they left out. She glanced at the silent Frau Levin, clutching her
husband's shoulder, knowing he enjoyed the fact that she was

listening to him. Sophie imagined them going home, strolling in search of a cab, she leaning on her husband's arm, he bending slightly towards her, and saying: Are you all right, my dear? Are you warm enough? Or declaring: Ahem, what an interesting discussion about Schopenhauer! Waiting for her to say, Yes it had been most interesting and how brilliant his observations had been, even though she did not know much about it, at which Herr Levin would straighten up, grip her arm more tightly, and explain to her who Schopenhauer was, where he taught, what works he had published, It's really quite simple, you know, my dear, and he would proceed to tell her everything he had not had the opportunity to say in the salon, once more listened to and listening to the sound of his own voice.

Sophie wrung her hands like someone screwing up a piece of paper.

What about you, my dear? she asked Frau Levin all of a sudden. Have you nothing to say? Frau Levin looked bewildered. My wife, Herr Levin spoke for her, ahem, my wife agrees with me. What a happy coincidence! Sophie exclaimed. He's right, Frau Levin said in a faint voice, I agree with him. Sophie bit her lip.

What about you Mademoiselle? Hans said provocatively, staring intently at her lip.

Me? replied Sophie crooking her wrist level with her chest. Why, learned gentlemen, I feel honoured simply to be listening to you, for nothing delights us women more than to witness such a show of wisdom, isn't that so, my dears? Why, we could spend days on end admiring this virile exchange of opinions. Yet, lo and behold, in full flow, you question a novice like me about Schopenhauer! and I must admit to feeling embarrassed, as the mere question bestows on me a value of which I am unworthy. And so, *meine Herren*, I beg your indulgence as well as your pardon for my poor knowledge of the subject, but you know what scant attention we women give to the great thinkers. Having said all of which, I shall venture upon this difficult topic in order to state that, as far as I can see, which undoubtedly is not very far, Herr Schopenhauer is decidedly one of the most wretched authors I have ever had the opportunity of misinterpreting. I must admit it is only recently I have had the temerity to read his book, but he seemed rather muddled on the subject of women, insisting we devote ourselves to housework or gardening, but never to improving our minds by reading literature, much less thinking about politics. And therein, gentlemen, lies a paradox, because in order for his ideas to thrive, that is, in order for his doctrine to be heeded, Schopenhauer would do better to recommend all of us women to make a thorough study of philosophical works, in particular his own. Despite my limitations as a theorist, it seems to me the greatest philosophers of our day are bedevilled by a contradiction—they all seek to establish new systems of thought, yet they all think the same way about women. Do you not find that terribly amusing, gentlemen? I am sure there are more palm hearts if anyone is hungry.

They had arranged to meet at midday in the Central Tavern. Álvaro was waiting for him, elbows resting on the bar, one foot on the rail, in the pose of a good horseman. Hans staggered into the tavern half-an-hour late. Good afternoon, welcome back to the world, Álvaro said, more entertained than annoyed when he saw the dark circles under Hans's eyes. I'm sorry, said Hans, I went to the cave last night, then back to the inn where I stayed up reading. What time is it? What! said Álvaro, astonished. Do you mean to tell me you don't wear a watch? The fact is, I don't see any point in watches, said Hans, they never give me the time I want. Well, Álvaro smiled, this is what is known as a cultural exchange—I resemble a German and you a Spaniard.

My ancestors, Álvaro said, munching, came from Vizcaya. I was born in Guipúzcoa, but I'm Andalusian by adoption. I was brought up in Granada, do you know it? Yes, it's beautiful, that's where I spent my childhood, my father found a job at the Hospital Real and we stayed there. I think everyone should see two things before they die—the Generalife in springtime and Plaza Bib-Rambla in the morning. You should see the señoras of the city dressed up to the nines to go to the fishmonger, and their husbands out strolling with that bad-tempered yet in the end likeable air. Sometimes when I open my eyes in the morning I still think I'm in Granada. I don't suppose you know where you are when you wake up, I imagine, well, perhaps you will one day. I've never made any friends like the ones I had in Granada. It's a melancholy city, too, and in that way it resembles Wandernburg—the people are proud of their melancholy. Apart from the first few years here, with Ulrike, I tell you I've never felt as happy as I did back then. Maybe it was because I was younger, but everything seemed on the verge of happening. In fact the whole of Spain's fate was about to be decided—we would either be invaded by foreign troops, or a traitorous king would be restored to the throne, or we would proclaim a republic. The days of the Cádiz Cortes were exhilarating, I take it you've heard of that? I'm sorry, but you Germans don't give a … about Spanish politics! and well, things in my country came so close to being so different! As it was, I decided to go into exile when King Ferdinand swept back into power and tore up our constitution, reinstated the Inquisition and began executing people. Was I forced to leave? Yes and no. Admittedly, people were being spied on, driven from their jobs and arrested left, right and centre. But the main reason I left was that I was disillusioned, do you understand? They had taken over the country we'd been fighting for, we had won only to lose. So that even before we left many of us felt we were no longer living in our own country.

Yes, please, another two over here, your health! When

Napoleon's lot arrived, I confess I felt peculiar. Yes, they had invaded our country, and yet they brought with them a culture we admired and laws we wanted. Did it make sense to fight for a rotten, medieval state? Hadn't we always been independent without being free? Finally, I enrolled and spent a few months fighting in Andalusia and Extremadura. Then I was billeted at the garrisons in Madrid and Guadalajara, together with militiamen from all over Spain. And I swear, Hans, it was listening to the discussions, seeing my compatriots' points of view that made me consider deserting more than once. But, *coño*, this was my country, after all! My idea was to receive the enemy, to learn as much from him as I could before driving him out and carrying on the revolution without him. I joined the guerrillas with one eye on the revolutionary juntas and the constitutional assembly, which were what most interested me. And I couldn't help wondering where the hell the fatherland was, what exactly were we fighting for? Did I find out? Ah, that's a good point. It may sound strange, but from talking to the other militiamen I realised it was our childhood memories we were fighting for.

During the occupation, the thing that most, another? Steady on, all right, but only if you're paying, I'm joking, what most upset me was seeing the way the priests supported us, the scoundrels were terrified Spain would end up like France! I can still remember the loathsome lessons they preached around the parishes. "What are you my child? A Spaniard by the grace of God. What are the French? Once Christians, now heretics. Of what is Napoleon born? Of sin. Is it a sin to kill a Frenchman? No, Father, heaven is our reward for killing one of those heretic dogs." They weren't patriots, they had an instinct for survival (patriotism is precisely that, said Hans), don't be a cynic. I was unable to sleep at night and was assailed by doubts. What if we were fighting the wrong enemy? What if by fighting for Spain we were actually fighting against Spain, like the supporters of the French we so despised? Who was betraying the country more? I don't want to bore you. The fact is, after the restoration I finally fled Spain. I roamed half of Europe until I arrived in Somers Town. On my first stroll around London I emptied out my pockets and realised all I had was one duro, do you know how much a duro is worth? Not enough to change into pounds, or should I say shillings. And so I walked as far as the Thames, gazed into its depths and tossed my coin into the water. (You threw it away? Hans asked, surprised. Why?) My dear friend, a gentleman like me could hardly come to a great city with that little money! I preferred to start from scratch than to manage on a paltry sum. I made contact with the Spanish community, for a while I lived off loans, and I took on a few of those jobs that are wretched to do and interesting to talk about. I was a nightwatchman, a waiter, a fish gutter, a groom at a racing stable, a framer's assistant and a replacement teacher at a fencing school. (Are you that good a swordsman?) No, which explains why I was only the replacement! Finally, almost by chance, I entered the textile business. I had a stroke of luck, I invested my savings and they doubled. A friend and I made some more favourable investments, and that's when I decided to take the risk and begin working exclusively in that industry. And I picked the right moment. Various relatives of mine joined the business, and a few years ago we set up a wholesale company trading between Germany and England. We operate in London, Liverpool, Bremen, Hamburg, and in Saxony and the surrounding area, which I am in charge of. I can't say I enjoy what I do, but it gives me a good income and well, you know, you reach an age, a rather pitiful age if you like, when income becomes more important than enjoyment. And then of course there was Ulrike.

(Pass the meatballs, said Hans. And did you never return to Spain?) No, yes, well, I went back after the 1818 amnesty. To see what things were like, I suppose. But I found the atmosphere disturbing, so I went straight back to London. That was when I met Ulrike, on a business trip to Germany. It was so, so … It was like a, a revelation. Unique. (Here, have a drink, said Hans.) She was from this part of the world, she was longing to come back here, so we moved to Wandernburg. One of the things that most pains me is the thought that Ulrike never got to know Spain, I was never able to show her the places I grew up in. No. We had plans to go there, we would often talk about it, we always used to say: "One of these days", "This summer at the very latest", you know the kind of thing. And then the Hundred Thousand Sons of Saint Louis arrived, and the Holy Alliance, may the devil take it, which made it impossible to go anywhere, and politics, the constitution and my relatives all went to hell. That was when the remaining members of my family went into exile in England. You and I come from wretched countries, Hans. Both were invaded by Napoleon and ruled by his brother, both fought for their freedom and regressed once they had attained it. Spain is my home, but not today's Spain, the Spain of my dreams. A republican, cosmopolitan Spain. The more Spain asserts its Spanishness, the less Spanish it becomes. I suppose all countries are like that, aren't they? Vague entities that guide us (I don't know, Hans said, I don't think countries guide us, I think we move around because of people, and they can be from anywhere), yes, but many of the people we love we meet in our own country, not another one. (We move around because of languages, Hans went on, which we learn, or, like you said, because of memories. But what if memories move around, too? What if your memories all come from different times and places? Which are truly yours? That's my problem, that's what my problem is.) Hey, are you feeling all right?

Their shoulders began to fold like umbrellas. The Central Tavern had been filling up with other customers, the smoke and the smell of fried food floated up to the ceiling, mouths munched, laughed and drank. Having lost the relative privacy they had been enjoying at the bar, Álvaro and Hans began to feel a little out of place—the surrounding merriment seemed to mock their solemnity. What are they all laughing at? said Álvaro. Nothing in particular, replied Hans, people are the same everywhere—they laugh because they're eating. Aren't we simply a couple of sad sacks? Álvaro suggested. That's another way of putting it, said Hans. They both burst out laughing, and in doing so their talkativeness came back. They spoke of the Wandernburgers' strange manners, which combined surliness with an almost fanatical observance of etiquette. When I first arrived in Wandernburg, Hans told him, I didn't have a clue how to behave. People here scarcely smile at you or lend you a hand, yet they have half a dozen ways of bowing and a limitless repertoire of greetings. That is, of course, assuming they manage to recognise one another through the accursed fog. How do they manage to flirt when they can't even see one another? How do they reproduce? I suspect, said Álvaro, that they only couple during the summer months. Here, Hans went on, a man can hold on to his hat for a whole hour if his host doesn't invite him to put it down. The ladies keep theirs on so as not to have to ask permission to go to the water closet to tidy their hair. You never know whether to sit down, bob your head, bow or tuck in your backside. In short, concluded Álvaro, they insist on manners because they are so uncouth.

Hans saw five unusually well-dressed, or prodigiously badly dressed, men enter the tavern. What most struck him was that despite the place being packed to the rafters, a waiter elbowed his way across the room and turfed a group of young people from a table. Once it had been cleared and given a good wipe, the five men ceremoniously ensconced themselves, as though they had just walked into an assembly hall rather than a tavern reeking of smoked sausage. Three of them crammed shiny fat cigars into their mouths. The waiter brought over five tankards of stout and a bowl of strawberries. Álvaro explained to Hans that these men were Herr Gelding and his associates, owners of the Wandernburg textile mill. That's where Lamberg works, Hans remarked. Is that the fellow your organ grinder introduced me to the other day? said Álvaro. I don't envy him working for them. And there's no avoiding them, because all the businessmen, industrialists, contractors, brokers and bankers in this city are related to one another. They stick close together. Intermarry. Cohabit. Reproduce. Look out for each other's interests. And they're forever guzzling beer. And this great family spends its time employing the members of another great family, that of the lawyers, doctors, notaries, architects and civil servants. If you added the two together you'd have the entire wealth of the local middle class, with a bit of loose change to spare. Some of which might belong to Herr Gottlieb. But not much. You might say this city's economy is based on organised incest. I see you know them well, Hans chuckled. I know them *too* well, nodded Álvaro, and the worst of it is that as soon as they see me, we'll be obliged to go over and pay our respects. Because, among other things, I make my living by selling what they produce.

Five minutes later, Álvaro and Hans were sitting at the table with Herr Gelding and his associates. Hans was surprised at the exaggerated politeness with which Álvaro spoke to them, marshalling his accent, masticating his voice, imbuing it with a military air completely at odds with the singsong Spanish lilt he had when he spoke to Hans. Herr Gelding immediately launched into the question of his payments, which Álvaro responded to by quoting figures, prices and dates from memory.

What vexes me, Herr Gelding said, sucking on his cigar, the corners of his mouth stained with strawberry juice, is this culture of self-pity, this constant griping despite improving conditions. Although you have to hand it to the scoundrels, conditions have improved because of their griping! No, I'm not denying certain things aren't negotiable, I can even understand day labourers wanting, shall we say, guarantees of longer-term employment. What I'm saying, gentlemen, as God is my judge, is that I work longer hours than they do in order to keep production up. And as is only natural, I demand no less of a commitment from my workers. People rail against flexible hiring practices, yet such practices have seen this accursed city grow by seven per cent in each of the past twenty years, perfect, congratulations, yours is an excellent guild, but do you know what, gentlemen, can you guess what happens when you give in and make an employee permanent? Ah, surprise, surprise, he stops working so hard! Look, work takes work. They'll be asking us to turn off the machines next so they can take an afternoon nap! Upon my soul, gentlemen, I don't know what the world is coming to. Take the machine operators, for instance. The machine operators start work half-an-hour later because it takes time for the boilers to warm up. Very good, I accept that, that's the way boilers work, someone stokes them up and then you come along afterwards. Ah, yet they still find reasons to complain! Isn't that enough to, well, isn't it? Those damned machine operators get up later than I do, and they work a twelve-hour day. And what does that mean, gentlemen? Unless I've lost the ability to count, it means they work half a day, half a day, and the other half they have off. Is that enough to exhaust a man? Is it a reason to start making demands? Or do they expect to have more time off than at work? In my day, gentlemen, in my day! What would these operators think of the hours my father put in, my good father, may God keep him in His glory, who never complained in his life, and who built up a factory all on his own! Oh, no more strawberries, what a shame. My father knew how to, but what's the use. This is no way to build a nation, or anything else for that matter!

Encouraged by Hans's frowns, Álvaro cleared his throat and said: My dear Herr Gelding, you will have noticed that your workers spend most of their time off sleeping. Herr Gelding stared at him, cigar drooping, mouth open in astonishment. He looked more puzzled than offended, as though Álvaro hadn't understood what he had been saying. Ah, but Herr *Urquiho*, replied Herr Gelding, we mustn't interfere, no, a worker must be free to do as he pleases in his time off, without any meddling from me, of course! I don't know how they run things in your country, but rest assured, one of the rules in my company is complete freedom of the workers outside the workplace. I imagine we agree on that!

The knocking on his door finally forced him out of bed. A few bands of light filtering through the drawn shutters crept towards Hans's cold feet. He pulled on the first thing he could find on the chair, shuffled over to the door and opened it, still trying to unglue his eyelids—smiling, Lisa handed him a mauve sheet of paper. Hans meant to thank her, although he gave a yawn that sounded like *hanyeu*. He took the letter from Lisa's chafed fingers and closed the door.

In the dim light filtering through the shutters, Hans glimpsed the name on the card accompanying the letter—Sophie Gottlieb.

He jumped up, went to the washbasin to splash water on his face, opened the shutters, and sat down by the window. The card was printed on stiff paper and had a thin raised edge. The inscription was an unusual orange-grey colour that suggested solemnity and a hint of coquetry. Despite his eagerness, Hans paused before opening the letter, enjoying the uncertainty, savouring this moment of heightened expectation, lest what followed should be a disappointment. Sophie's swift, resolute, slightly sprawling pen strokes caught his attention—this was a feline hand rather than the writing of a young lady. There was no heading or greeting.

I have been thinking, in odd moments, about the arguments you put forward at last Friday's meeting. And, although I will not try to hide the fact that some of what you said jarred with me a little, or perhaps what jarred was your tone (why are you in the habit of making what is intelligent seem a challenge, and what is logical appear conceited?), I must confess I also found it interesting, and even to some extent original.

"Interesting"! "To some extent"! Hans glanced for a moment at the sun pouring through the window, delighting in Sophie's sense of pride. He knew that whatever she went on to say, he was going to enjoy her letter.

For this reason, my dear Herr Hans, providing you are willing and can find no better way to spend your time, it would give me great pleasure to have the opportunity to speak to you outside the salon, which you may have observed requires me to share my attention and even to employ the ruses of a hostess, as I am sure you have perceived.

This fleeting complicity with him, "as I am sure you have perceived", made his breath quicken. So, she admitted perceiving that he had perceived! *What* exactly they had both perceived remained to be seen. But if Sophie thought she could get away with this disclosure without any consequences, she was mistaken—Hans was willing to cling to her words as to a branch in mid plunge.

Therefore, if you have time, my father and I would be delighted to receive you at our house tomorrow afternoon at a half past four. I trust I am not importuning you with a fresh engagement—it appears you are a tireless reader, and tireless readers have little time for socialising. Kindly reply

at your leisure during the course of the day.
  Affectionately,
                    Sophie G

Hans was aware of an omission in her aloof and rather abrupt ending, the subtle omission of a conventional, and, in this case, he thought, extraordinarily significant word—*yours*. If Sophie had not finished her letter with the usual polite phrase *yours affectionately*, perhaps her coy omission of that possessive revealed a sensual fear that could not be entirely ingenuous. Could it? Or couldn't it? Was he imagining things? Was he making a fool of himself by being overly susceptible? Was he reading too much into it? Was he being too clever by half? Was he once more inadvertently confusing intelligence with conceit?

He was rescued from this confusion by the postscript, which looked as if it had been jotted down as an afterthought, and revealed an uneasy hesitancy:

PS I will also take the liberty of asking you to refrain from appearing before my father in the beret and broad-collared shirt I have seen you wearing in your walks around the city. Without wishing to deny my sympathies for the political connotations of such attire, I am sure you appreciate its inappropriateness in a household as traditional as mine. The more formally you dress the better. Thank you in advance for complying with these tiresome rules of etiquette. I shall do my utmost to reward your goodwill with canapés and sweetmeats. S G

And Sophie's last words were sweet, sweet her very last word.

Hans was beside himself with joy and anticipation. What should he reply? And how long should he wait before doing so? What clothes was he to wear the following day? He stood up, sat down again, got to his feet again. He felt a wave of happiness, had a violent erection and then could barely control his emotions. He realised he must first read Sophie's letter in a calmer state. He made himself wait a few minutes, looked out of the window at the heads, hats and feet moving up and down Old Cauldron Street, while he let the letter cool down. He read her opening admonishments over and over. He smiled at Sophie's gentle rebuke, which revealed her nature as surely as they alluded to him. He studied the dissembling nature of her invitation, her winning disdain, the charming piquancy of her complicity. He pondered the abrupt ending, trying to gauge how much of it was due to aloofness and how much to prudence. And to finish off he savoured the marvellous appeal in the postscript, which was Sophie's way of saying that she too noticed him in the street. Hans picked up his quill and dipped it into the ink pot.

When he had written his reply, he avoided rereading it so as not to repent of some of the liberties he had taken in the midst of his euphoria. He took a deep breath, signed his name and folded the piece of paper. He finished dressing and went downstairs to give it to Lisa, taking the opportunity to ask who had delivered the letter and whether they had said anything. From Lisa's description he knew that Elsa was the messenger. She said that she had said nothing worth mentioning, although, in Lisa's opinion, she had been rather abrupt, and had even cast a disapproving eye over the inside of the inn. And that (Lisa did not say as much, but Hans deduced it, amused) both she and her mother believed Elsa was the author of the mauve letter. Lisa stared with a mixture of envy and longing at the paper Hans gave her. For a moment he thought Lisa was being inquisitive as she puzzled over the names of the sender and the addressee. He immediately felt a flash of shame—Lisa was not reading, she was wishing she could. She raised her eyes and studied Hans's face, as if to show him she at least knew how to read his thoughts. Lisa's adolescent beauty suddenly became firmer, as if anticipating the future. Hans did not know what to say or how to apologise. She seemed content with her brief intimidating flash—her features softened, she looked like a young girl again, and she said: I'll deliver it right away, sir. Hans felt humbled by the word *sir*.

Hans was sipping vegetable broth in the dining room when he saw Elsa's hat appear in the doorway. He invited her to sit down, and was surprised when she accepted. After a moment of awkward silence, he smiled: Well? Elsa's leg was pumping up and down once more, as though working an imaginary pedal. Do you have a message for me? Hans asked, without realising he was not looking her in the eye but watching her leg go up and down. Elsa stopped moving it abruptly. She handed him a letter. It's from Fräulein Gottlieb, she said. This seemed to Hans so obvious that there must be more to it. I see, he ventured, trying to draw her out further. She gave it to me an hour ago, Elsa said, and asked me to deliver it here at the inn. I see, he nodded, with growing anticipation. I couldn't come until now, Elsa said. That's all right, said Hans, I'm grateful to you for bringing it. There's no need, she said, I'm doing my duty. (I wonder what she means, thought Hans. Did she bring me the letter willingly despite being obliged to, or, on the contrary, would she not have brought it unless she'd been forced to? Hans was so nervous he was lost in his conjectures. Perhaps Elsa hadn't meant either of these things. Perhaps her mind was elsewhere or she had simply wanted to rest for a moment on the sofa. But in that case why was she still there?) Elsa continued: Fräulein Gottlieb told me you needn't reply, unless you wish to. (And what was he to make of this? Should he refrain from replying, did Sophie's new missive imply some kind of interlude? Or was Sophie's caveat an invitation to carry on with their communication, like the gestures she had made with her fan? Thinking wasn't easy after a generous serving of vegetable soup.)

Elsa left Hans with the impression she hadn't managed to say everything she wanted, or hadn't wished to tell him everything she should have. She had been inscrutable yet polite, avoiding his questions without refusing to answer them. After poring over Sophie's letter, Hans felt none the wiser—in evasive, flawless grammar, Sophie expressed her delight at the news of his attendance the following afternoon; she mentioned some trivial detail about the meeting; above all (and this was almost the only thing he noticed in her letter) she seemed to have tempered the tone of her previous communication, rebuffing his flattery with cautious irony. Reluctantly, Hans realised he could spend the entire day trying to decipher hidden meanings, but no amount of effort would put an end to the waiting nor to the feverish turmoil he was beginning to fear would accompany his every movement from now on.

As the light began to fade, Hans, the organ grinder and Franz crossed the city together. The little orange-and-green cart juddered over the cobblestones and the beaten earth. Hans marvelled at the way the old man calmly pushed his instrument almost two miles every day to and from the square. It also amazed him that the organ grinder never wavered when he reached a bend or crossing or fork in the road. Hans had been there for at least a month and a half and had so far failed to take the same route more than twice in a row—he would always reach his destination, but never without some modification along the way. Hans now suspected that rather than secretly shifting position, Wandernburg rotated suddenly like a sunflower turning to follow the sun.

The mud from the day before had begun to dry. Patches of melting frost gave off a slight mist. A stench of churned earth and urine wafted up from the ground. The grey city walls were stained with moisture and the remains of the day.

Hans contemplated the age-old grime, the clotted neglect of Wandernburg to which he was still unaccustomed. The organ grinder sighed, and, placing a skinny hand on his shoulder, declared: Isn't Wandernburg pretty! Hans looked at him with astonishment. Pretty? he said. Don't you find it a little dirty, gloomy, small? Of course, said the organ grinder, but also very pretty! Don't you like it? That's a shame. No, please don't apologise, there's no need be so formal! I understand, it's normal. Perhaps you'll like it better when you get to know it. What I like about Wandernburg is you. You, Álvaro, Sophie. It's the people, don't you think, who make a place beautiful? You're right, said the organ grinder, but for me it's also, how can I explain? These alleyways never cease to amaze me, I never tire of looking at them because, Franz! Leave those horses alone! Come here you rascal! When that dog is hungry he thinks everyone's his friend and is going to give him a bone instead of a kick. Where was I? Ah yes, to me these streets are, how can I put it, they're so old that they seem new. What nonsense I talk! They fascinate me. Tell me, said Hans, what fascinates you? What exactly do you like about them? Nothing, everything, the organ grinder said, the square for instance, even though I've been playing there for years, every day I find it more interesting. I used to be afraid I'd grow bored with it, you know, that I'd have had enough of the square, but now the more I look at it, the less I seem to know it. If you could see the tower in summer compared to when it snows! It looks as if, as if it's made of a different substance. And the market, the fruit, the colours, you never know what each new crop will bring, this winter, for instance, Franz! Watch out! Come here! Or what can I say, I like it when they start lighting the street lamps, have you noticed? I like watching the way people change without realising it, they keep walking by, the men's hair thins, the women grow stout, the children grow up, new ones appear. It saddens me to hear young people say they don't like this city, it's good they are curious and think of other places, but wouldn't it be good if they were also curious about where they are from, because perhaps they haven't looked closely enough. They're young. They still see things as either beautiful or ugly. Do you know I enjoy talking to you, Hans. I never talk this much to anyone.

Far away in the meadows, sheep were finishing giving suck to their lambs, who clung to their teats as to a last ray of light. The wool of night was quickly being woven.

Reichardt and Lamberg had been the first to arrive, and were now sharing a bottle of wine and some stale bread. Álvaro had turned up a little later. At Hans's request he had begun to drop by the cave from time to time, and, also at Hans's request, on these occasions would bring with him a generous helping of food that his cook had prepared. Since he had been widowed, Álvaro lived alone in his house on the edge of the city, not far from the textile mill. He usually went everywhere on horseback. Once he was in the city he would leave his mount at a stable and either take carriages or walk. Álvaro sat bolt upright on his horse, heels flush with the animal's flank, arms relaxed, almost down by his side. Seeing him ride one had the impression that his lively steed was at one with him, rather than obeying the tug of the reins. Álvaro never stayed very late at the cave. At a given hour, he would glance at his pocket watch, bid the others good night, and climb back on his horse.

Unusually for him, Álvaro arrived at the cave looking dishevelled. His hair was tousled and his cheeks flushed, as if he had washed his face after some strenuous effort. Sorry I'm late, he muttered, sitting down in front of the fire, I had a disastrous tilbury ride. First we almost turned over, then one of the wheels got stuck and I had to get out and push while the driver whipped the horse. The brute beat him so hard I feared the poor creature might not make it! It seemed to Hans his friend was explaining too much for the informality of the cave. He recalled his walk there earlier with the organ grinder, the state of the road, and remarked casually: How odd your tilbury should get stuck in the mud, it was almost dry this afternoon. That's as may be, Álvaro replied abruptly, but the part we went along was muddy!

Their appetites sated and sharing the warmth of the fire, they struck up a friendly banter. Álvaro appeared to have regained his composure, and began joining in, having a laugh with Hans whenever he could, nudging him and patting him on the back. Their conversations gradually grew muddled. But before making them inebriated, the wine had granted them a couple of hours of clear-headedness. Then Álvaro had asked Hans something no one had ever asked him before: You're always threatening to go to Dessau, he said, what exactly is it you have to do there? Herr Lyotard is expecting me, Hans replied solemnly. And who might he be? Álvaro enquired. I'll tell you another time, said Hans, winking at him. Hey, Álvaro asked, and what about Berlin, don't you ever think of going back there? No, said Hans, what would be the point? I may have good memories of it, but can I go back and find them? I may go there again but I could never go back. Going back is impossible. That's why I prefer new places. And before Berlin, the organ grinder said curiously, where were you? A long way away, replied Hans. But, my dear boy, the old man said, folding one of Franz's ears as if it were a handkerchief, why do you travel so much? Let's just say, Hans replied, that I'm unable to live any other way. I think if you know where you're going and what you're going to do, you're likely to end up not knowing who you are. My work is to translate, and I can do that anywhere. I try not to make plans, and to let fate decide. For instance, a few weeks ago I left Berlin. I was thinking of going to Dessau and decided to stop off here for the night, and now look—by chance I am still here, enjoying talking to you. Things don't happen by chance, said the organ grinder, we help them along, and if they turn out badly we blame chance. I'm sure you know why you're still here, and I'm delighted you are! And when you leave you'll know why you did so as well. Hey, you two professors! Reichardt groaned. If you carry on philosophising I'm going to fall asleep!

No, no, Lamberg suddenly declared, narrowing his eyes, Hans is right. I'm never sure why I stay here. I don't know what I'm doing at the mill or where I might go next. I'm the same as Hans, but I don't move.

The fire and Lamberg's eyes competed, sparking off one another.

I can't help it, Hans went on, when I stay in one place for a long time I notice I don't see so well, as if I were losing my eyesight. Things begin to look like one big blur, and nothing amazes me any more. On the other hand, when I travel everything is a mystery, even before I arrive. For instance, I love going by stagecoach and observing my fellow travelers, I invent lives for them, speculate about why they are leaving or arriving somewhere. I wonder whether something will happen that will bring us together or whether we'll never meet again, which is more likely. And, since it is almost certain we'll never meet again, it occurs to me this intimacy is unique, that we could remain silent or declare ourselves, you know the kind of thing; for example, I look at one of the ladies and think: I could tell her right now "I love you"; I could say "Madam, I want you to know I care", and there would be one chance in a thousand that instead of looking at me as though I had lost my mind, she'd say "Thank you" or smile at me (my eye! said Reichardt. The lady would slap you in the face for being so forward), yes, of course, but she might also ask "Do you mean it?" or confess "It's been twenty years since anyone said that to me", do you see? What I mean is it thrills me to think that this is the only time I will ever meet the passengers in this stagecoach. And when

I see how quiet, how serious they are, I can't help wondering what they're thinking as they look at me, what they must feel, what their secrets are, how much they suffer, whom they love. It's the same with books, you see mounds of them in bookshops and you want to read them all, or at least to have a taste of them. You think you could be missing out on something important, you see them and they intrigue you, they tempt you, they tell you how insignificant your life is and how tremendous it could be. Everyone's life, Álvaro declaimed in a comic voice, is both insignificant and tremendous. How young you are, Hans, said the organ grinder. Not nearly as young as I look, Hans replied with a grin. And such a flirt! Álvaro added. Hans hit him on the head with a twig. Álvaro pulled Hans's beret down over his face and jumped on top of him. They rolled around the floor, laughing aloud, while Franz joined in excitedly, looking for a chance to enter the fray.

I see mysteries everywhere, too, the organ grinder said pensively, only, like I was telling you today, I see them without having to leave the square. I compare what I see with what I saw yesterday, and I tell you, it's never the same. I look around and I see if one of the fruit stalls is missing or if someone is late for church or if a couple have had a quarrel or if a child is sick. Do you think I'd notice if I hadn't been to the square so many times? I'd feel giddy if I traveled as much as you do, I'd have no time to concentrate. You think it's so wonderful, Reichardt said mockingly, because you get mesmerised just looking at the view. I'm almost as old as you. (Which of you is older? Hans asked, amused.) That's a rude question, whippersnapper! Can't you see with your own eyes? He is, he is, look at my arms, feel! My problem is I get bored. I'm not so curious any more, as if places had aged like me. I mean, everything's the same, but diminished.

Hans looked at Reichardt, drained his glass and said: What

you just said is brilliant. "Everything's the same, but diminished."
I don't think you realise how brilliant, damn it. I'll realise
whatever you like, as long as you pass the bottle, Reichardt
retorted. In short, said Álvaro, there seem to be two types of
people, wouldn't you say? Those who always leave and those
who always stay put. Well, and there are also those of us
who first leave and then stay put. The way I see it, the organ
grinder asserted, is this—there are those who want to stay
put and those who want to leave. All right, said Álvaro, but
wanting to leave and leaving aren't the same thing. Take me,
for example, I've wanted to leave Wandernburg ever since,
well, it doesn't matter, for a long time now, yet look, I'm still
here. Thinking of leaving is one thing, but actually doing it
is another. My dear man, the organ grinder said, am I not
always on the move? But you're different, said Hans. (No, no,
said the organ grinder, letting Franz lick the palm of his hand,
we're just like everyone else aren't we, boy?) You know where
your home is, you've found your place, but apart from a few
exceptions like you (and Franz, the organ grinder said, don't
forget Franz), seriously, though, I think that in order to know
where we want to be we have to travel to different places, get
to know things, people, learn new words (is that traveling or
running away? the organ grinder asked), that's a good question,
let me think, well—it's both, traveling can also be running
away, but that's not a bad thing. And running away isn't the
same as looking ahead either.

Lamberg spoke once more: I've always dreamt of running
away to America. To America or any place where you can start
afresh. I'd like to start afresh.

Lamberg went quiet and gazed into the fire as if attempting
to read a map in the flames.

The organ grinder's bony fingers played along Franz's flank
as the dog began to fall asleep. I've hardly traveled at all,

he said, and honestly, Hans, I admire all the things you've seen. When I was young I was afraid to travel. I thought it might lead me astray. Lead you astray? said Hans, puzzled. Yes, explained the organ grinder, I thought it might lead me into thinking my life was different, but that this illusion would last only as long as I went on traveling. I don't know, Álvaro reflected, leaving or staying, perhaps that's a simplistic way to look at it. In fact, it's impossible to be fully in one place or to leave it completely. Those who stay could always have left or could leave at any moment, and those who have left could have stayed or could always come back. Doesn't virtually everyone live like that, on the frontier between leaving and staying? Then you'd feel at home in a port city, like Hamburg, Hans said. I had a home once and lost it, sighed Álvaro. I've just remembered an Arabic proverb, Hans said, placing a hand on Álvaro's shoulder—he who follows a path becomes the path. What the hell does that mean? said Reichardt. I don't know, Hans grinned, proverbs are ambiguous things. The best path is a winding path, declared Álvaro. Is that another proverb? Reichardt asked, belching. No, replied Álvaro, I just made that up. The best path, Reichardt ventured, is the one that leads to the sea. I haven't seen the sea in thirty years! The best path, suggested the organ grinder, is the one that leads you to the point of departure.

For me the best path, Lamberg spoke again, would be the one that makes me forget the point of departure.

The organ grinder thought this over. He was about to respond when Lamberg leapt to his feet, brushed off his corduroy jacket and wool breeches. I have to go, he said, gazing at the dying embers. It's late and I'm working tomorrow. Thanks for the supper. The organ grinder stood up laboriously and offered him a last swig of wine. The four others said goodbye without getting up. Before stepping through the cave mouth, Lamberg turned and said to Hans: I'm going to think about what you said. With that he vanished into the night.

And why can't you have another home? the organ grinder asked. It's too late for that now, Álvaro stammered, half out of sorrow, half in his cups. Aren't you happy here? said the organ grinder. I never wanted to come here, Álvaro protested. So why don't you leave? Reichardt asked. Because I don't know how to, Álvaro replied. The best thing to be, said Hans, would be a foreigner. A foreigner from where? the organ grinder said. Just a foreigner, Hans shrugged. I ask because the ones I know are all different, said the old man. Some never adapt to the place they live in because they aren't accepted. Others just don't want to belong. And others are like Álvaro, who could be from anywhere. You speak like Chrétien de Troyes, Hans said in astonishment. Like who? asked the organ grinder. An early French poet, Hans replied, who said something extraordinary: He who believes his birthplace to be his homeland suffers. He who believes all places could be his homeland suffers less. And he who knows that no place can be his homeland is invincible. Wait a minute, Reichardt protested, now you're complicating things. What has some long-dead Frenchman got to do with anything? I was born in Wandernburg, this is my home and I couldn't live anywhere else, and that's that. Yes, Reichardt, said Hans, but tell me, what makes you so sure? How do you know your home is here and not in another place? I just do, damn it, snapped Reichardt. How could I not know? I feel part of the place, I'm a Saxon and a German. But Wandernburg is Prussian now, argued Hans, so why do you feel Saxon and not Prussian? Why do you feel German and not Teutonic, for example? This place has been Saxon, Prussian, half-French, practically Austrian, and who knows what it will be tomorrow. Isn't it pure chance? Borders shift around like flocks of sheep, countries shrink, break apart, grow bigger; empires are born and die. The only thing we can be sure of is our lives, and we can live them anywhere. You just like to complicate things, Reichardt sighed. I think you're both right, the organ grinder said. It's true, Hans, our life is the only sure thing we have. But that's precisely why I know I'm from here, from this cave, this river, this barrel organ, they are my home, my belongings, all that I have. Fair enough, said Hans, but you could be playing your barrel organ anywhere. If it were anywhere but here, the organ grinder smiled, we would never even have met.

Now there were only three of them. Reichardt had gone to sleep it off. The wine was almost finished, and Álvaro's speech had become punctuated by slurred *s*s and exotic *j*s. Hans reflected that Álvaro's German improved as his pronunciation worsened, as though being drunk brought his foreignness to the fore once and for all, and the patent impossibility of adapting completely to another language made him more careful, more confident. His mouth dry, his tongue loosened, Álvaro was entering his last half-hour of clear-headedness. He scrutinised almost every word the other two uttered, rolling them round on his tongue with a puzzled expression, savouring them as though they had only just been invented. *Gemütlichkeit?* Álvaro repeated. Amazing, isn't it? And so difficult—*Gemütlichkeit* … First it compresses your lips, look, as if you were whistling, *Gemü* … but then suddenly, eh, suddenly you have to smile, how funny! *Tlich* … but, I'll be damned, the joy doesn't last long before there's a kick to the palate, *keit*, there *keit!* and your jaw is left hanging … Hans, who had been listening with amusement, and contorting his lips along with Álvaro, asked how he would translate the word into Spanish. I'm not sure, Álvaro frowned, that depends, let me see, the problem of course is that you can say the word *Gemütlichkeit* to mean, to mean simply *cosy*, or *blissful*, can't you? Bah, but that's nonsense because it can also mean what you were saying, *Gemütlichkeit*, that is, oh I can hardly talk any more, the, the pleasure of being, of being where you are, the joy of staying, of having a home, can't it? That's what you were saying and that's what I don't have. That, said Hans, is what no German can find. Oh, but do you know what? Álvaro went on, taking no notice of Hans, I've thought of another word, one, one that's the opposite of the other one, and, well, actually it's not Castilian, its Galician, but every Spaniard knows this word, it's very pretty, listen to the sound, it's funny—*morriña*. When he heard how musical the word was, the organ grinder clapped and shook with laughter. He insisted Álvaro repeat it six times in a row, attempting to say it himself and chuckling each time he heard it. Suddenly exhilarated, Álvaro explained that *morriña* was a kind of nostalgia for the homeland, a far-away feeling of sadness that was somehow sweet. And that to be republican and Spanish was like suffering from *morriña*, a bittersweet feeling, an honour and a sorrow. A sorrow that comes and goes, the sorrow of sailors, said Álvaro, but we all have something of the sailor in us.

Somewhat incoherently and between hiccups, Hans told them the Tibetans referred to man as "he who migrates", because of his need to break his chains. The organ grinder, apparently still sober, replied pointing to the pinewood: I have no chains, if anything a few roots. Yes, well, of course, Hans stammered, of course, well, yes, but what the Tibetans mean is that things like chains and roots hinder our movement, and to travel is to overcome these limitations to free ourselves from our bodily ties, do you understand? Álvaro, my friend, you understand what I'm saying don't you? Certainly, comrade! Álvaro exclaimed. Let's overcome our *morriña*, our nostalgia and our *Gemüt* … *Gemütlichkeit!* Lads, the old man smiled, I'm too advanced in years to overcome my bodily ties, if anything I'm trying to preserve them. As for nostalgia, well, isn't nostalgia a way of traveling? Hans's hiccups suddenly stopped, he contemplated the organ grinder and said: Álvaro, listen! If we took this fellow to Jena, more than one professor would be out of a job! Are you listening, Álvaro? Alas, no, Álvaro spluttered, I'm not listening to you or to myself any more.

Álvaro was dozing, open-mouthed, on the straw pallet. He had burbled a few slurred words in a foreign tongue. Hans was grinning idiotically, eyelids half-closed. The organ grinder covered him, then pulled an old blanket over himself. You're quite right, Hans murmured all of a sudden. No, replied the organ grinder, you're the one who's right. Then we agree, said Hans, half nodding off. They remained silent for a while, watching the moist light of dawn arrive. The pine trees slowly emerged and the river began to appear as they looked from the cave.

The light here is ancient, said the organ grinder, it finds it hard to come out, doesn't it?

What captivity, Hans whispered, what weakness.

Or what peace, the old man sighed, what repose.

And that Friday it happened—that Friday, at last, shortly after the meeting had begun, the scar on Bertold's upper lip wrinkled solemnly as he announced Rudi Wilderhaus's arrival at the Gottlieb salon. Herr Wilderhaus, intoned Bertold. Struggling to overcome a pang of jealousy, Hans had to admit he had grown used to hearing about Sophie's fiancé and to acting as though he did not really exist, as if ignoring him were enough to prevent his existence. The salon-goers stood up as one. Herr Gottlieb went over to the doorway to greet his guest. In the round mirror, Hans saw Sophie pull up the neckline of her dress and turn her back on him.

The two pairs of footsteps grew louder as they walked down the corridor—those of Elsa light and nervous, those of Rudi dawdling and squeaking. The squeaking noises came from the guest's patent-leather shoes, which as they drew nearer seemed to resonate through the room before they finally arrived, gleaming, and came to a halt in front of Herr Gottlieb. Rudi Wilderhaus was taller than Hans would have liked. He wore a velvet frock coat, which Bertold gingerly helped him out of, gold epaulettes, a waistcoat with two rows of jewel-studded buttons, snug white breeches with braid down the side and silk knee-length stockings. His sleeves were tapered at the wrist. Rudi Wilderhaus's starched collar gave the impression of offering up his robust head, adorned with an impeccable crimped wig, on a plate. *Gnädiger, gnädiger Herr!* exclaimed Herr Gottlieb, bowing and seizing his wrists. The ladies bobbed slightly at the knee, while the gentlemen (including Hans, who felt like a complete fool) tilted forward. Rudi Wilderhaus moved towards Sophie, took one of her slender gloved hands, brushed it with his lips and announced: *Meine Dame ...*

Once Hans had been introduced to him, he was aware of three things. Firstly, Rudi used powder on his face as well as a touch of rouge. Secondly, his clothes were freshly perfumed, giving off an overly pungent whiff of lemon. Thirdly, Rudi Wilderhaus spoke with his shoulders raised, as though his muscles were holding aloft his words, which for the moment were utterly prosaic. To Hans's surprise Rudi greeted him, if not cordially, then at least with a measure of respect he had shown neither the Levins nor Frau Pietzine. I was told the salon had acquired a new member, said Rudi. I'm delighted you could join. You have already seen what a pleasure it is to be welcomed into this household. Our dear Herr Gottlieb and my beloved Sophie are undeniably model hosts.

Our dear and my beloved, Hans ruminated. *Our dear and my beloved.*

Owing to his numerous other engagements, Sophie explained to Hans as they all sat down again, Herr Wilderhaus is not always able to honour us with his presence. Indeed, today he must leave before the end of the evening, but he will keep us

company until eight o'clock. You will only take tea? Pray do
not be so abstemious, my dear Herr Wilderhaus, you must at
least try a spoonful of jelly, or I shall be most put out! Elsa,
please, that's more like it, you see how I must cajole him into
even trying a mouthful! Just before you arrived, my dear Herr
Wilderhaus, we were discussing the fascinating differences
between Germany, France and Spain, the latter thanks to the
observations of Herr *Urquiho*, no, forgive me, *Urquixo*, is that
right? Well, anyway, that was the subject of our discussion. I
see, Rudi replied, trying to sound interested, good, very good.

Why does she insist on addressing him *my dear Herr Wilderhaus*?
thought Hans. Isn't such politeness a trifle artificial? Isn't it
overly formal? Isn't it inappropriate for someone who? Could
it mean that? Why am I being so foolish? Why am I building up
my hopes? Why can't I gather my thoughts? Why? Why? Why?

Professor Mietter was holding forth: Grossly oversimplifying,
we may argue, then, that the French regard external objects as the
driving force for their ideas, whereas we Germans regard them
as a stimulus for our impressions. Granted, here in Germany we
tend to converse about matters that would be better off written
about in books. However, the French make a far worse error by
writing on subjects that are only worthwhile in conversation. I
would argue that first and foremost the French write in order
to be admired, in the same way we Germans write in order to
think, or the English write in order to be understood. Do you
really think so, Professor? said Frau Pietzine. But the French are
so elegant! *Ils sont si conscients du charme!* Frankly, dear Madame,
said Professor Mietter, the two values can scarcely be … Ahem,
Herr Levin interrupted, I don't see why there is any need to
choose? Every aesthetic, the professor declared, is founded on
choice. Well, yes, of course, Herr Levin conceded, still, I am
not entirely sure. My dear Professor, Sophie intervened, if I
may say so, in my opinion we Germans would benefit from a

touch of frivolity. As you so rightly point out, every aesthetic is doubtless based on choice. Yet, surely we may also decide on the mix, since an aesthetic is made up of concepts, abstractions, objects and anecdotes, wouldn't you agree? Hmm, Professor Mietter admitted grudgingly. (Hans made sure Rudi was not watching him and gazed at the tiny pores on Sophie's arm, wishing he could run his tongue over them.) And what in your opinion should we think of the French, Rudi? asked Sophie (*Rudi*! Hans cursed. Now she's calling him *Rudi*! Although this time she didn't say *dear*. Why am I being so ridiculous?) Me? Rudi jumped, raising his shoulders. Why, I concur with you entirely on the matter, my dear. (He uses the formal "you", Hans noted, I wonder if he does that when they're alone?) What I mean is, there is no difference between our two ways of thinking. None at all? Sophie persisted, come now, don't be bashful, I am inviting you to disagree. That is not the reason, Rudi smiled, it is simply that you speak like an angel. Then, Sophie jested, you do not question the existence of angels either? My dear Mademoiselle, Rudi replied, not when I see you, I confess.

(Ugh! Hans bit his lip.)

And what is wrong with austerity? said Professor Mietter. Is it not nobler than the spirit of decorativeness? My dear Professor, ventured Sophie, would it not be more just to refer to it as the spirit of sociability? Here in Germany we keep everything to ourselves, we hide it. In France everything is on display. Here we are naturally unsociable, or so we believe, and we end up seeming awkward. How right you are, said Frau Pietzine, there's no denying it. I was in Paris a few years ago and, well, it was another world, my dear. Those dresses. Those restaurants. Those parties. Upon my word! Let me tell you, my dear, a French corpse enjoys himself more than any living German! Germany, said Herr Levin enigmatically, is the kitchen of Europe and France is its stomach. Sociability notwithstanding, Professor

Mietter resumed, the French read less. Professor, Sophie said, I hesitate to contradict someone as well-informed as you, but what if instead of reading less the French read in a different way? Perhaps the French read in order to discuss books with others, whereas we Germans consider books as companions, a kind of refuge? The difference is more profound, Mademoiselle, Professor Mietter asserted. The problem with the French is that not only do they read for others, they also write only for others, for their audience. A German author creates his own audience, he moulds it, he makes demands on it. A French author is content simply to please his audience, to give it what it expects. Behold your French sociability, *et je ne vous en dis pas plus*! Professor, Hans remarked tetchily, is it not simply that in France there is more of an audience than here? Paris boasts more theatres and bookshops than Berlin. There is scarcely any audience here for artists to please or despise. Perhaps that is why we console ourselves with the idea that our authors are more scrupulous, independent and so forth. In Paris, my dear Monsieur, said Professor Mietter, what prevails is easy success and popular appeal. Berlin values loftiness and personality, do you not see the difference? You said it yourself, Hans retorted. In both cases there is a pre-existing pattern. Paris values one approach, while Berlin gives prestige to another. In both cases the author is seeking approval from his audience. Some seek the plaudits of the well-read, who fortunately abound in France, others the plaudits of critics and professors, who, in Germany, are the only people who read. Neither of the two alternatives is more or less sociable or self-seeking than the other. I see no difference in the nobility of their intentions. Monsieur Hans, if that is indeed the case (Sophie said as if colluding, inclining her head towards him while smiling disarmingly at Professor Mietter), how would you suggest bringing the two countries' readerships closer together?

Hans, who had given this matter much thought, was about to answer Sophie, when a more mischievous idea occurred to him. He placed his teacup and saucer on the low table, made as if Rudi had just tried to catch his eye, and said in a very loud voice: Please, Monsieur Wilderhaus, let us hear what you have to say.

Rudi, who for the past half-hour had done nothing but take snuff and respond with the words "of course, of course" to each of Sophie's ideas, sat bolt upright in his chair and raised an eyebrow. He shot Hans a black look, which he avoided, closely examining the trays of sweetmeats. Rudi noticed that his beloved was watching him with anticipation, and realised he must give some meaningful answer. Not to save face in front of the other guests, whose opinion he did not care a damn about, not even for the sake of his honour, which depended on far loftier values than these literary trifles. No—he must do so for Sophie's sake. And perhaps to teach a lesson to this impertinent young upstart who was not even wearing gloves. Rudi brushed a few grains of tobacco from his waistcoat, cleared his throat, raised his shoulders and declared: Paris may outstrip us in printing presses and theatres, but it has none of the nobility and uprightness of Berlin and never will.

The discussion went on as before. Only now Hans was smirking, and the snuff spilt out of Rudi's snuffbox.

Yes indeed, my friends, Frau Pietzine was saying, for me there is no better entertainment than reading. Is there anything more amusing and absorbing than a novel? (I see you are much *entertained* by reading, dear Madame, Professor Mietter said, sarcastically.) Just so, Professor, just so! Culture has always been a great solace to me. I am forever telling my children, as I did their deceased father, may God keep him in His glory—nothing is equal to a book, nothing will teach you as much, it doesn't matter what you read, just read! But you know how young people are these days, they are only interested in their friends, their games, their dances. (But are we sure? Herr Levin said. Ahem, are we sure it does not matter *what* we read?) Well, books cannot be bad, can they? (With all due respect, Álvaro said, I think the idea is an ingenuous one, of course there are mediocre, futile, even harmful books, in the same way there are atrocious plays and worthless paintings.) Well, I don't know, viewed in that light … I agree with Monsieur *Urquiho*'s appraisal, said Professor Mietter. Readers should be educated to reject inferior books. There is nothing terrible about that. I ask myself why we revere anything in print, however nonsensical. (But who decides? protested Hans. Who decides which books are nonsensical? The critics? The press? The universities?) Oh, please don't start telling us that all opinions are relative, let's show some nerve, someone has to have the courage to (I am not suggesting, interrupted Hans, that all opinions are equally worthy, yours, for instance, Professor, are far more authoritative than mine, what I am wondering is who is responsible for deciding where a work sits in the literary hierarchy, the existence of which I do not deny), very well, *Herr* Hans, if you do not consider it an impertinence on my part, I suggest a rather simple equation—the responsibility should lie with the philologist rather than the grocer, and the literary critic rather than the goatherd. Does that seem to you like a good place to start? Or should we discuss the matter first with the craftsmen's guild? (Professor, said Sophie, isn't your tea growing cold?) Thank you, my dear, in a moment. (We needn't consult them, retorted Hans, but I assure you if a philologist were to spend even half-an-hour examining the life of a craftsman, it would transform his literary opinions.) Yes, my dear, a little more please, it has gone cold.

One contemporary novelist, Professor Mietter went on, has suggested that the novel, yes, with sugar, please, the modern novel mirrors our customs, that ideas are irrelevant and only observation matters, and everything that happens in life is worth writing about. An interesting notion, and one that accounts for the prevailing bad taste, wouldn't you agree? Any arrant nonsense or folly is worth relating simply because it *happened*. This idea, said Sophie, of the modern novel as a mirror is much bandied about these days, but what if we ourselves were the mirrors? I mean, what if we, the readers, were a reflection of the customs and events narrated in the novel? This, Hans concurred, seems to me a far more attractive idea, it means each reader becomes a kind of book. My dear, said Rudi, hastening to show his appreciation and seizing her hand, it's brilliant, I completely agree. The idea, Álvaro remarked, was already invented by Cervantes.

When the salon-goers began discussing Spain, Rudi glanced at the clock, stood up and said: If you will excuse me … Herr Gottlieb rose to his feet, and the other guests immediately followed suit. Elsa started towards the hallway, but Sophie restrained her with a gesture and went to fetch Rudi's hat and cape herself. Rudi took the opportunity to say: This confounded dinner I have to attend is quite untimely. Believe me, I have found these discussions absolutely captivating. It has been a pleasure, *meine Damen und Herren*, a veritable pleasure. We shall meet again soon, perhaps this coming Friday. And now, with your kind permission …

Hans had to admit that the moment Rudi moved from the realm of debate into that of gestures, manners and pleasantries, he exuded an extraordinary self-assurance. Waiting there, solid, radiant, statuesque, Rudi Wilderhaus gave the impression of being able to stand still for an hour without feeling the slightest discomfort. When Sophie came back with his hat and cape, Herr Gottlieb walked over and whispered a few words to them which made his whiskers soften, and the three of them disappeared into the corridor. Hans stared after them until all that remained were wisps of pipe smoke drifting up in the air, the squeak of patent-leather shoes and the rustle of fabric. The guests glanced at one another, suddenly self-conscious, and the *Indeeds*, *Anyways*, *Do-you-sees* and *What-an-agreeable-evenings* ricocheted around the room. Then they fell silent, helping themselves from the trays Elsa was passing around. Professor Mietter began leafing through a book next to one of the candelabras. Álvaro winked at Hans, as if to say "We'll talk later". Amid all this silence, Hans was surprised by the sudden fit of loquaciousness that overcame the usually taciturn Frau Levin—she was talking rapidly into her husband's ear without pausing for breath, gesticulating furiously, while he nodded, gazing down at the floor. Hans strained to hear what Frau Levin was saying, but only managed to make out the odd word here and there. One of them drew his attention and made him a little uneasy—he thought it was his name.

When Sophie re-entered the room, the guests came to life and once more the place was filled with laughter and voices. Sophie asked Bertold to light extra candles and Elsa to tell Petra, the cook, to serve some bowls of chicken broth. Then she went to sit down and the salon-goers gathered around the low table. Hans thought to himself that without a doubt Sophie possessed the sublime gift of movement—nothing around her remained still or unresponsive. Just then, Herr Gottlieb also came back, flopped into his armchair and sat twirling his whiskers round a plump finger. Although the conversation went on as before, Hans noticed that Sophie was avoiding his gaze in the round mirror. Far from unsettling him, Hans interpreted this sudden reticence as a good sign—this was the first time her fiancé and he had been together with her.

So you also know Spain, Monsieur Hans? Frau Pietzine said excitedly. I can't imagine how you have found the time to visit so many different countries! There's really nothing to it, my dear Madame Pietzine, Hans replied, it is simply a question of sitting in coaches and on boats. Judging from the numerous voyages you have described to us, Professor Mietter said sardonically, I suppose you must have spent your entire life traveling. Yes, in a way, I have, replied Hans, refusing to rise to the bait, and burying his nose in his teacup. In an attempt to ease the tension, Sophie turned to Álvaro and said: My dear friend, perhaps you would like to tell us a few things about today's literature in your own country. I am not sure there is much literature of *today*, Álvaro grinned. We are still catching up with the Enlightenment. Take Moratín, for example, does the name ring a bell? I am not surprised, he crossed the Alps and half of Germany without learning anything about *Sturm und Drang*. To be fair, Frau Pietzine chipped in, being *à la page* is not everything, is it? You cannot deny the allure of the Spanish villages, the charm of the common people, their festive spirit, their. Madame, Álvaro cut in, do not remind me! I have heard, said Herr Gottlieb, plucking his pipe from between his teeth, that religious fervour is purer than it is here, more heartfelt (father, sighed Sophie). And the music, Professor Mietter added, the music emanates from a different source, from the people themselves, from the very heart of their traditions and …

Álvaro listened to his Germanic fellow salon-goers with a sad smile on his lips.

My friends, my dear friends, Álvaro said, taking a deep breath, I can assure you I have never in all my life come across as many Gypsies, guitars and pretty maids as I have in the paintings of English artists or the journals of German adventurers. As you see, my country is so extraordinary that half the poets in Europe, or Romantics as they are now known, write about Spain, while we Spaniards learn about ourselves from reading them. We write little. We prefer to be written about. And what horrors! The young men of Madrid seducing women with song! Young lasses killing each other or themselves because they are hot-headed Mediterraneans! Workmen idling on balconies, preferably in Andalusia! Religious bigots, working-class women from Lavapiés built like Amazons, enchanted inns, antiquated carriages! Well, the latter are real enough. I understand the appeal of such folklore, provided it relates to a foreign country.

A silence descended over the room, as though they had all been watching a soap bubble float to the floor.

At ten o'clock sharp, Herr Gottlieb heaved himself out of his chair. He went to wind up the clock and said goodnight to his guests.

In view of the rather gloomy atmosphere hanging over the gathering, Sophie suggested they devote the rest of the evening to music and performance, an idea warmly received by everyone, in particular Professor Mietter, who would occasionally accompany her in a Mozart or Haydn duet, and even the odd sonata by Boccherini (the *even* was Professor Mietter's word). Sophie sat at the piano and Elsa fetched the professor's cello case. Before the music began, Elsa was able to sit down for the first time since the beginning of the soirée, and for the first time, too, she appeared completely attentive. She ground a few crumbs into the carpet with the toe of her shoe—the crumbs turned to dust with the first stroke of Professor Mietter's bow. Hans could not take his eyes off Sophie's supple, tapping fingers.

The duet proceeded peacefully, disrupted only by abrupt nods from Professor Mietter, to which Sophie responded with discreet half smiles. When they had finished and been applauded by their fellow salon-goers, Sophie insisted Frau Pietzine come to the piano. Flattered by her entreaties, Frau Pietzine duly resisted, and then, just as Sophie appeared to back down, agreed, blushing theatrically. There was further applause—Frau Pietzine's necklace came away from her bosom and swung in mid-air for a moment. Then she turned to the piano, and with a clatter of rings and bracelets began to sing excruciatingly.

What did you think? asked the flushed Frau Pietzine. With

great astuteness, Sophie answered: Your playing was excellent. In an attempt to rouse Frau Levin from her stupor, Sophie suggested she and Frau Pietzine play a piece for four hands. Everyone declared this an excellent idea, and their implorings ended in a burst of applause when the flustered Frau Levin rose from her seat, glancing around her as though surprised to find herself on her feet. She made her timorous way towards the piano. Frau Pietzine's generous hips slid along the stool. Backs straight, shoulders tensed, the two women tackled Beethoven with more ardour than was seemly. Contrary to Hans's expectations, Frau Levin was an excellent pianist, disguising her companion's mistakes and compensating for her missed notes. During the recital, Herr Levin's eyes remained fixed on the piano stool, not quite on his wife's skirts.

The soirée ended just before midnight with a selection of the classics. Frau Pietzine requested Molière, Álvaro suggested Calderón and Professor Mietter demanded Shakespeare. Herr Levin came up with Confucius, but there was no book by Confucius in the house. Hans asked for nothing and was content to study the down on Sophie's arms, which changed shape, colour and (he assumed) taste according to the candlelight. Sophie was unanimously elected to recite the chosen passages. Hans was very curious to listen to her, because not only did it enable him to gaze at her with impunity, but he also had the idea that from listening to someone read aloud it was possible to read their erotic inflections. What Hans did not know was that Sophie shared his opinion. This was why Hans's looks, digressions, slips of the tongue and hesitations made her uneasy, but more than that, if she were honest, they disturbed her.

Hans felt that, although Sophie's voice was not beautiful, she modulated it perfectly, achieving a convincing tone without being strained, avoiding sounding on the one hand bland and on the other affected, maintaining a controlled delivery, her lips slightly pursed, deliberately threading together the inflections, lingering on the more emphatic ones and skimming over the softer ones, alternating between the long and the short sounds with a rocking movement, modifying the punctuation to suit her breathing rather than any grammatical requirements, savouring each pause without drawing it out. In short, being sensual, not in order to please her audience, but for her own enjoyment. Hans thought: This is terrible. He half-closed his eyes and in his imagination tried to enter Sophie's throat, to float inside it, to be part of her air. The air undulating in her neck like warm liquid. She recites as though she were drinking tea, thought Hans. The comparison struck him as ludicrous, and his mouth felt suddenly dry. Moistening his lips with his tongue he realised he had become distracted from the texts again. Sophie must have partly been able to read Hans's thoughts, for when she had finished the last but one paragraph, she fell silent, closed the book on her forefinger marking the page, passed it to Hans and said: My dear Monsieur, pray give us the pleasure of hearing you recite the final passage. With that, she smoothed the creases in her dress, daintily crossed her leg and settled back in her chair, gazing at Hans and smiling provocatively. Suddenly she fixed her eyes on the succulent bulge of Hans's throat, a nest of words. Go ahead, said Sophie, savouring the thought, we're listening.

Standing beside the door, neither was able to utter the last word. All the other guests had gone and both Sophie and Hans had bade them farewell one by one without moving, behaving as though they had already taken leave of one another yet postponing their goodbye indefinitely. A gentle breeze seemed to be blowing between them, making them quiver. For want of kissing her violently and putting a stop to the unbearable tension, Hans vented his frustration by being aggressive and referring to her at every opportunity as *Frau*. *Fräulein*, corrected Sophie,

I am still Fräulein. But you'll soon be married, protested Hans. Yes, she retorted, as you say, soon, but not yet.

They remained silent, almost touching, dismayed by their own aggressiveness, until Sophie added: Don't be impatient, I will invite you to the wedding.

As the days slipped by, they continued to observe the same courtesies when addressing one another, each echoing the other's formal tone, yet imbuing these identical utterances with a note of impatience that was increasingly playful and ambiguous. On the surface nothing was happening. Both kept their composure in their own particular way: Sophie disguised her hot flushes with displays of aloofness, while Hans repressed his desire with theoretical expositions and literary quotations. Sophie derived strength from the heat of the debates themselves, from the analytical distance she forced herself to assume when communicating with him. Hans succeeded in appearing calm when he focused on a theme, losing himself in his argument. On Fridays at midnight when the salon was over, the two of them would talk for a while in the corridor as though on the point of parting, without really parting. They sought to do this in full view of Elsa or Bertold, as if making it clear they had no need to hide everything they needed to hide. After the arrival of Sophie's first letter, they began taking tea together at her house. On those afternoons, Herr Gottlieb would emerge from his study to sit with them and the three would converse amicably. Herr Gottlieb welcomed Hans as warmly as ever, although less effusively. Hans was his daughter's friend now, and he was obliged to withdraw a little in order not to seem like an interfering father, and above all so as to be able to watch over her from a distance. Herr Gottlieb was only too aware of his daughter's tempestuous nature. He knew that any opposition or outright prohibition was enough to make her persist in disobeying him with an obstinacy he sometimes found alarming. And so the most sensible thing to do was to let her have her own way and to stay alert.

Had Hans been capable of thinking about it objectively, he would have understood why Sophie's behaviour towards him was so erratic. When they were face to face, gazing excitedly into each other's eyes, she was confrontational. Yet when another guest criticised his point of view she would discreetly leap to his defence. But these signs remained relatively invisible to anyone else. In part because the language of gestures is not transparent like a piece of glass but reflective like a mirror. And in part because each had their own reasons for interpreting them in their own way.

Besides his habit of not taking part in any of the discussions, with the result that he didn't feel they concerned him in the slightest, Rudi Wilderhaus felt too certain of his position, his status, his betrothal, to be at all concerned. Or rather he *was obliged not to* be concerned, for if he had been that would have meant lowering himself to the level of an unknown stranger with no social standing. Professor Mietter appeared to find nothing odd either in Sophie's discreet and constant solidarity towards Hans, since (as he himself could testify from his first months at the salon) she was an attentive hostess, whose rule it was to indulge new members in order to make certain they stayed. For this reason the salon had begun with three or four regular members, and now boasted double that number. Moreover, in the professor's view, Fräulein Gottlieb's passionate and somewhat stormy nature was behind her tendency to enliven their debates by siding with whoever was in a minority. And it so happened that the outrageous Hans frequently found himself in a minority. In any event (the professor ended by reassuring himself) Sophie had continued to grant him preferential, even honorific treatment, confirming him as the incontestable authority in the salon and the starting point for any debate.

Frau Pietzine might have suspected something amid her giggles and embroidery, yes. But she was far too enthralled by the arrival of this young guest, too amused by the novelty, to go against the tide. As for Herr Levin, who respected and feared Professor Mietter in almost equal measure, in some inadmissible part of his prudent self he was glad of Hans's presence. Not because he agreed with his opinions, but because of the destabilising effect they had on the unshakeable self-assurance of the professor, who was so partial to criticising Herr Levin's own contributions. Álvaro had sided with Hans from the start, and delayed the discussion of any differences they might have for the privacy of the Central Tavern. He did so not only out of loyalty but out of convenience—he had never met anyone as like-minded in Wandernburg, and had felt less lonely since Hans arrived. And Frau Levin? Frau Levin was silent, although she wrinkled her brow thinking who knew what.

That afternoon there were magnolias in the drawing room. After they had taken tea, instead of shutting himself in his study as usual, Herr Gottlieb had stayed on to talk with the two of them. After chatting for a while about nothing in particular, Sophie had suddenly retired to her room. She hadn't done so because she was upset with Hans or annoyed at her father's intrusiveness. Quite the contrary, she had understood that if she wanted Hans's visits to continue unimpeded she must allow her father to keep up his friendship with him. Neither of the two men was able to fathom this simple strategy, and so her father chewed his pipe contentedly and stared at Hans, and Hans coughed disappointedly and stared at Herr Gottlieb.

During their hour-and-a-half-long conversation, accompanied by a bottle of brandy Bertold brought, Herr Gottlieb confided in Hans his concern about the forthcoming betrothal dinners. Luckily, he explained, the first of these would be held at the house of the bride to be. Imagine what a calamity it would have been for me, Herr Gottlieb told him, if the Wilderhauses—the Wilderhauses no less!—had received us first in their mansion, and then we—perish the thought!—had returned the honour here in this house. I tell you, I scarcely sleep a wink—scarcely a wink!—just thinking about the menu, what can one offer a Wilderhaus, you understand? Naturally we will be eating in the dining room rather than in here—a little more brandy my friend? Not even a drop?—Anyway, as I was saying, this week we will prepare the room, but will that be enough? I've already asked Petra—do you know Petra? And her daughter?—A fine woman, Petra, when we first employed her she was the best cook of her generation, why do I say was? No, yes, she still is, only things have changed, you know, we no longer entertain like we once did, times change, my friend! And this house, this house, well, anyway, there it is, but we're all so nervous! No, Sophie isn't, Sophie is never nervous, although I have to confess—are you sure you won't have another drop?—I have to confess I find it difficult to stay calm, and what would you think of chicken consommé, noodles with cinnamon, a joint of roast meat, and to follow I don't know, a compote, some meringues, what would you—and champagne, champagne to finish off obviously, but what about with the dinner?—Do you know what wines are served these days in Berlin, you'll ask around? That's good of you, I'd be most grateful. You know it's a great relief talking to you. Don't you think beef would be best?

And I swear, Hans told the organ grinder later on that same evening, it took a supreme effort for me to stay calm while he was talking to me about that accursed dinner. Sophie went to her room, and her father spent two hours telling me about the Wilderhaus family, could things be any worse? The organ grinder, who had been listening, his gaze wandering as he played with Franz's muzzle, finally spoke, only to say something completely bewildering: And you say there were flowers? Yes, yes, Hans said wearily. What flowers were they? What does that matter? replied Hans, why should you care? What were they? the old man insisted. I think, Hans relented, they were magnolias. Magnolias! the old man brightened up, are you sure? I think so, said Hans, puzzled. Magnolias, said the organ grinder, signify perseverance, she's telling you not to give up. And since when do they mean that? Since for ever, the old man smiled, where have you been living? In that case, said Hans, should I say something to her, declare my feelings? No, the old man said, you have to wait, don't be hasty, she's not asking you to do anything, she needs time. She needs time to consider, but knowing you are still there, do you see? She needs to decide the time of her love, you have no control over it. You must persevere but also wait. Do peasants twist their sunflowers to face the sun? Well. You can't twist magnolias either.

The dawn mist floated in and out of the cave's entrance. Hans and the organ grinder had stayed awake all night. They had just sat down side by side to look at the pinewoods, the river, the white earth. The fire warmed their backs. Hans was fascinated by the organ grinder's silent attention as he contemplated the landscape, sometimes for hours. Hans looked at the old man out of the corner of his eye. The old man looked at the snow-covered scenery. The empty landscape observed itself.

It observed itself weighed down by hardened mud, the long-established frosts, the compacted snow. The submerged pinewoods. The snapped-off branches. The bare tree trunks. In spite of everything, the Nulte went on flowing beneath the crust of ice, went on being the river of Wandernburg. The stark poplars swayed.

Can you hear? said the organ grinder.

Hear what? said Hans.

The cracking sound, said the organ grinder, the cracking

sound of the Nulte.

Honestly, said Hans, I don't think so.

There, said the organ grinder, a bit farther down.

I don't know, said Hans, well, a little. And is the river saying something?

It's saying, the old man whispered, I'm on my way. I'm nearly here.

What's nearly here? Hans asked.

Spring, the organ grinder replied, even though we can't see it, even though it's frozen, it is on its way. Stay another month. You can't leave here without seeing Wandernburg in spring.

Don't these frozen trees, this icy landscape, make you feel sad? Hans asked.

Sad? said the organ grinder, they give me hope. They're like a promise.

To the slow, steady rhythm of the handle, the days turned and turned, and Herr Gottlieb's long-awaited betrothal dinners took place. During the first of these, which was held in Stag Street beneath the chandelier that recalled better days in the dining room Hans had never seen, amid the cabinets filled with porcelain and Saxon china figurines, around the big, oblong table that had once seen many more guests, Rudi had presented Sophie with the engagement ring. Eight days later, on the eve of the second betrothal dinner, she had reciprocated by sending him her portrait enclosed in an oval-shaped silver medallion. The Wilderhaus family had behaved towards Herr Gottlieb in a correct if unenthusiastic manner, and were certainly willing to indulge their son Rudi if this wedding was really what he wanted. Neither Sophie nor her father had ever set foot inside Wilderhaus Hall, whose impressive facade they had only seen from King's Parade. Herr Gottlieb's first reaction as they walked around it was shock, followed by awe, then finally exhilaration.

Sophie held her chin up and remained silent during most of the dinner. Herr Gottlieb left the mansion feeling profoundly relieved. At last everything seemed to be going smoothly—after the desserts had been served, contrary to his expectations, the Wilderhauses raised few objections to his conditions and had agreed to the sum of her dowry.

Since their first tentative letters, Hans and Sophie had begun writing to each other almost every day, and by now Hans had become a frequent caller at the Gottlieb residence. He had achieved what he thought would be the most difficult aim— becoming Sophie's *friend*; and once he had, he felt disappointed. As had been their custom for some time, the two of them were taking tea in the drawing room. Herr Gottlieb had retired to his study and they were able to enjoy the luxury of gazing into each other's eyes. As the carpet soaked up the afternoon light, Sophie described in detail the dinner at Wilderhaus Hall. Hans responded to her narrative with a sour smile. Why is she telling me all this? he thought. To show she trusts me? To see how I will react, or to put me off? Even as she spoke to him in a relaxed tone, Sophie could not help wondering: Why does he listen so happily to all this? To show his friendship? So that I make the first move? Or is he distancing himself? Yet the more Sophie shared her misgivings about the opulence of Wilderhaus Hall, the more Hans thought she was trying to bring Rudi into the conversation, and the more he smiled out of self-protection. And the more he smiled, the more Sophie thought he was deliberately showing his aloofness, and so the more she persisted in giving him details. And in their own way, during this exchange, they both felt an uncertain happiness.

Imagine our amazement, Hans, Sophie went on, when half a dozen liveried footmen kept serving ice cream throughout the meal and offering us tea every fifteen minutes, then brought champagne, Scotch whisky and bottles of Riesling after dinner.

(I can imagine, Hans replied, how upsetting!) I swear I didn't know whom to greet first or how to address them, there must have been at least two uniformed coachmen, half a dozen servants, goodness knows how many chambermaids, and a kitchen staff the size of a small village (my, what indigestion! exclaimed Hans), seriously, I'm not used to so much etiquette, I wonder how anyone can feel truly at ease surrounded by so many people (oh well, said Hans, as with most things, you grow accustomed to it, you know), the only place where there's any privacy is in the gardens (the gard*ens*, he said, surprised), well, yes, there are two, one at the front and one at the back (of course, of course, Hans nodded), they were pretty, yes, but it sent a shiver up my spine when I realised one of them was full of graves, I'll wager you can't guess whose they were? (You have me on tenterhooks, he said.) The dogs'! Yes, you heard me, eleven dogs are buried there, the family's hunting dogs, and each has a headstone with its name inscribed (how very commendable, Hans said, to extend such treatment to their poor animals), I don't know, it all seems rather excessive to me, why would anyone need four billiard tables? (They certainly know how to keep themselves entertained! Hans said approvingly.) If they even play, because everything in that house looks unused, including the library, which incidentally is vast. I was able to leaf through a few old French volumes which I suspect no one has ever so much as glanced at. (And what about paintings? said Hans. Do they own many paintings, I imagine they must glance at them?) You seem in excellent spirits this afternoon, my friend, I'm delighted you are keen to know so much about my fiancé (I'm burning with curiosity, Fräulein, positively burning! said Hans, shifting in his seat), yes, indeed, they own many paintings, a large collection of Italian, French and Flemish masters they have acquired over the years from local convents. (What a magnificent investment! Hans exclaimed. And do they have a music room?) I'm afraid they do, a beautiful little room with gas lamps, and another marble-lined banqueting hall (yes, said Hans, marble is always best for banquets). May I offer you a herbal tea, Herr Hans, you seem a little on edge. Elsa dear, come here will you? I wasn't aware you knew so much about architecture, indeed, I was going to tell you about the English taps and drainpipes, but I'm not sure I should.

Hans arrived at the inn with a hunger on his skin and a hollow feeling in his chest. He had no inclination to go out, preferring to remain slumped on the old settee mulling over his conversation with Sophie. Lisa, who was still up, hastened to serve him what remained of the family's dinner. When he saw her approach with a plate and bowl in her hands, he was suddenly touched. Thank you Lisa, he said, you shouldn't have taken the trouble. There's no need to thank me, she replied, trying to look as if she couldn't care less, I'm only doing my duty. But the pinkish tinge to her cheeks suggested otherwise. In that case I'd like to thank you for doing your duty so well. Thank you, Lisa replied, without thinking. And, after she realised what she had said, she could not help smiling brightly.

Within minutes she was next to him on the sofa, sitting with her feet tucked under her. Where's your father? Hans asked. Asleep, Lisa replied. And your mother? Trying to put Thomas to bed, she said. And you? asked Hans. Aren't you sleepy? Not really, Lisa said, shaking her head. Then she added: What about you? Me? Hans replied, surprised. No, well, a little. Are you going up to your room, then? she asked. I think I will, he said. Do you need some more candles? Lisa said. I don't think so, replied Hans. Lisa stared at him with an intensity that was only possible from someone truly innocent or extremely artful. But Hans knew Lisa was still too young to be that artful. Good night then, Lisa said. Good night Lisa, said Hans. He stood up. She lowered her eyes and began picking at a hangnail.

When Hans was already on the stairs, Lisa's voice called him back. Aren't you going to tell me what you keep in your trunk? she asked, making patterns with her foot. Hans turned around, smiling. The whole world, he said.

Silence radiates, like concentric rings, from the centre of the market square towards the yellowish gloomy alleyways, from the capricious tip of the Tower of the Wind to the sloping contours of St Nicholas's Church, from the high doors to the railings round the graveyard, from the worn cobblestones to the dormant stench of the fields manured for spring, and beyond.

When the nightwatchman turns the corner of Wool Alley and enters narrow Prayer Street, when his cries dissolve into echoes ... *to go home, everyone!* ... *bell has chimed eight!* ... *your fire and your lamps* ... *to God! All praise!* ... and when his pole with the lantern at its tip is swallowed up by the night, then, as on other nights, a figure emerges from a narrow strip of shadow, the black brim of his hat poking out. His arms are thrust into the pockets of his long overcoat, his hands snug in a pair of thin gloves, his expectant fingers clasping a knife, a mask, a length of rope.

Opposite, there is the sound of light feet, of brisk heels coming down the alleyway. The gloves tense inside the overcoat, the brim of the hat tilts, the mask slips over the face, and the shadowy figure begins to move forward.

In Wandernburg a sandy moon turns full, a moon caught unawares, a moon with nowhere.

ALMOST A HEART

THE DAY SPRING CAME to call in Wandernburg, Frau Zeit woke up in an astonishingly good mood. She scurried about the house as if the light were an illustrious visitor whom she must wait upon. Herr Zeit stood behind the counter browsing through the *Thunderer*, an untouched cup of coffee in his hand, while his wife and daughter cleaned and oiled the pokers and fire tongs, before storing them in the backyard shed. From time to time, Lisa would gaze at the streaks of soot on her milk-white arm. Then her mother would hurry her along. Have you carded the mattress wool yet? she asked, fondly brushing a lock of the girl's hair from her face. Lisa wiped her forehead with the back of her hand and said: Only in number seven, mother. Is that all? said Frau Zeit, surprised. What about the other rooms? I was about to start on them when you called me, I came down to see what you wanted and after that there wasn't time. Don't worry, my love, the innkeeper's wife said, a rare smile appearing on her face, enhancing her good looks, you finish this, I'll go and see to them.

All that had hitherto been rattling bolts, half-closed shutters and darkened windows suddenly became a flurry of doors opening, shutters flung wide and gleaming windowpanes. Carpets, curtains and rugs unfurled like tongues from the inn windows, and from all the windows in the city. Young girls no longer walked with eyes lowered to the ground—they raised their heads as they passed by. They wore brightly coloured clothes and floppy straw hats with daises in them. The young men bobbed their heads at them, and inhaled an aroma of vanilla. Elsa turned into Old Cauldron Street. She was holding a parasol in one hand and in the other a mauve letter.

Hans was sitting on his trunk, shaving. Legs apart, he gazed into the little mirror propped up on the floor. He had not yet sloughed off his drowsiness and still felt startled at the way Lisa had burst into his room without knocking, or at least without him hearing her knock, in order to begin cleaning the room before he had time to get dressed. Hans yawned in front of the little mirror on the back of the watercolour. He remembered snippets of conversation from the salon the night before. The snuffbox Rudi had held out to him several times, whether as a sign of hospitality or contempt he could not tell. His disagreements with Professor Mietter, who never lost his patience. His own remarks, more vehement than he would have liked. Álvaro's resounding laugh. Sophie's furtive glances. The whispered jokes he had managed to share with her. The way in which …

There was a knock at the door.

He opened it to find Lisa standing there again. Instead of handing him the mauve letter, the girl stood gazing at his half-shaven chin, at the faint trace of down above his lips.

Hans sat down to read the letter without finishing shaving. He smiled when he opened it and saw that all it said was:

Why did you look at me in that way yesterday?

Hans dipped his quill in ink and sent Lisa to the Gottlieb residence with another letter which read succinctly:

In what *way?*

Sophie's response was:

You know in what *way. In that way you shouldn't.*

Hans felt a frisson as he replied:

How observant you are, my dear lady—I had no idea I was being so obvious.

Hiding the letters in her basket and keeping away from the busiest streets, Lisa would hurry back and forth between the inn and the Gottlieb residence. She would also try desperately to read the scrawls, to decipher some clue to their unfathomable code, some pattern, some telltale word. All she managed to determine was that their messages contained no numbers—this meant they weren't arranging a meeting. And Lisa was right, although only by chance—they usually wrote the times in words.

She knocked once more at the door of room seven and handed Hans another letter with the reply:

How observant you are, my dear sir—looks speak volumes.
Have a good day and do not to drink too much coffee. S

And so the morning passed, until he went out to meet Álvaro for luncheon. Before going into the Central Tavern, Hans went over to the corner where the organ grinder was playing. He listened to mazurkas, polonaises and allemandes. Franz seemed distracted by the new bustle in the square, but he wagged his tail to the rhythm of the dances. It was obvious from the half a dozen or so coins in the organ grinder's little dish that the gloomy Wandernburgers were delighted to have left winter behind. As was his custom, the old man winked at Hans, still continuing to turn the handle. Unwittingly copying the organ grinder's gesture, Hans responded with a circular wave of his hand that meant "we'll meet later". The old man nodded contentedly and glanced down at the dish, raising his eyebrows. Hans laughed, rubbing his hands together like someone contemplating a treasure trove. Franz's gently lolling tongue seemed to taste the sweetness of the noontime hour.

The organ grinder paused to sit down and eat the bread and bacon he had brought with him in his bag. While he and Franz were sharing their meal, Father Pigherzog stopped to watch them on his way back to church. Franz raised his head and gave an enquiring bark. My good man, Father Pigherzog said, bending over them, aren't you uncomfortable sprawled on the ground? If you have nowhere else to go, at the old folks' canteen we can offer you a meal at a table, it won't cost you a penny, my son. The organ grinder stopped munching and looked up at the priest in a puzzled way. Father Pigherzog stood there beaming, his hand clasped across his chest. When he had swallowed his mouthful of bacon, the organ grinder wiped the corners of his mouth with his sleeve and replied: Sir, I applaud your idea of a canteen and I hope it is a help for the old folks. With this, he took another bite. Sighing, Father Pigherzog continued on his way.

In the afternoon, Hans went back to the inn to change and find some warm clothing in order to accompany the organ grinder back to the cave. When he opened the door to his room he was not surprised to find a mauve letter at his feet— before going to lunch he had sent one of Novalis's poems to the Gottlieb residence, and Sophie did not like others to have the last word. He slowly unfolded the note. He saw there was another poem and smiled.

Dearest friend,

("Dearest"! Hans's heart leapt.)

Dearest friend, I reply to your Novalis poem with one of my favourite poems by Madame Mereau, I don't know whether you know her. I chose it because it speaks to us women readers, to all those who dream of another life in this life,

("Another life"? Hans paused. So is the life she has, the one she will soon have, the one that awaits her after this summer, not the life she longs for? In that case perhaps she? Perhaps it isn't? Enough, read on!)

of another life in this life, another world in this selfsame world, those who are gaining strength thanks to words such as these. I see this poem as a hymn to the small revolution in every book, to the power of every woman reader. And although you are a man, in this way I consider you an equal.

("An equal", no less! Hans thought, filled with joy. And then doubt cast a shadow over him—an equal "in this way", she says, but why not the other way? And what might that be? And why can't we be equals in that way too? I mean, could there be anything more or was "this" all there was? And between the two what does "dearest friend" mean? Am I more a "friend" than a "dear"? Oh, I can't read …)

And although you are a man, in this way I consider you an equal. For this reason I have copied out a few verses below, the ones I find most beautiful, in the hope that today or tomorrow you will respond with another poem.

(Aha! She's inviting me to reply—that's new. That is, she is allowing me the last word. Is that not a gift? A kind of surrender? Or am I reading too much into things as usual?)

Affectionately yours,
                    Sophie

(Mmm. "Affectionately". That doesn't sound very ... No, it doesn't. Yet she has written her name in full. She is offering herself, isn't she? As though she were saying: I am yours completely. I am Sophie, I am. Oh stop this nonsense! I'm going to take a bath. No, it's getting late. The old man will be waiting for me. It suddenly feels hot in here, doesn't it? Now, let's look at this poem. I'll reply tomorrow. Curses! Shall I look for something now? Better tomorrow.)

yours,
    Sophie

> *All these women at peace, not wasting time on war,*
> *Deeply aware of their intimate worth,*
> *Between them creating wave-like shapes,*
> *Summoned by the sign of the times,*
> *Have come to unfurl from a fantasy realm*
> *In spoken and written word, their unstoppable life;*
> *Better no one try to detain their surging strength*
> *Or they will find their way is blocked,*
> *Because all these women are announcing their awakening,*
> *The glad beginnings of their inner force.*

Beyond the path to the bridge, the light was thinning. The muted rays of the sun spread tiny tremors across the grass. Stretching away from the city, muffling its sounds, the fields were neither green nor golden. The windmill sails turned, scattering the afternoon. Carriages arrived on the main road. Birds flocked, organising the sky. Hans, the organ grinder and Franz had gone through High Gate and were approaching the River Nulte, which flowed brightly between the poplars showing their first new leaves. The mud on the path had hardened—the cartwheels turned more easily, Hans's boots threw up little clouds of dust that Franz sniffed over delightedly. Mixed with the heady scent of pollen and the heat of the paths, the countryside still gave off a smell of earth and manure, of fertiliser spread during the last ploughing. Beyond the hedges, labourers working late were hoeing weeds. Hans felt strange when he heard himself say: The countryside looks lovely. Didn't I tell you so? smiled the old man. And you haven't seen anything yet, just wait until summer. You'll see how Wandernburg grows on you.

When they arrived at the cave, Hans begged the old man to let him try playing the barrel organ for a moment. The old man was about to say no, but Hans's childlike tone won him over and all he could say was: Be careful, please, be careful. Hans focused on visualising the organ grinder's hand movement and tried to reproduce it with his own arm. During the first piece, the handle moved at an acceptable pace. The organ grinder clapped his hands, Hans gave a roar of laughter and Franz barked madly. But when, emboldened, Hans tried to pull on the handle to change the tune, there was a slight crack from the rolls inside the box. The old man leapt forwards, snatching Hans's hand away from the crank, and clutched the instrument to him like someone protecting his young. Hans, my friend, he said falteringly, I'm sorry, really, but no.

I'm going to tell you a secret, said the old man. When the barrel organ is playing and the lid is down, I like to pretend it isn't the keys making the sounds, but the people the songs describe. I pretend they are the ones singing, laughing, weeping, dancing up and down between the strings. And that way I play better. Because I tell you Hans, when I close the lid there's life in there. Almost a heart. And when everything goes quiet again, I hear the sounds of the barrel organ so clearly that for a moment I think I'm still playing. The music is here, in my head, and I don't have to do a thing. You see, in the end, what matters is listening, not playing. If you listen you will always hear music.

We all have music inside us, even those who walk through the square without even noticing me. The sound of instruments serves that purpose, it brings that music back. Sometimes, when I arrive in the square and begin turning the handle, I feel as if I had just woken up in the very place I was dreaming about. Thank goodness for Franz, he helps me realise if I'm playing asleep or awake, for as soon as the barrel organ starts churning I swear Franz pricks up his ears and lifts up his head. He's very partial to music, above all the minuets, he loves the minuets, he's a rather classical dog.

They had gone outside to watch the sunset. Wrapped in woollen blankets, they had sat like a pair of sentries at the cave entrance. Through the poplar trees, in the gaps between the trunks, the light formed into red knots. The organ grinder fell silent for a long moment, but suddenly he went on talking as if there had been no pause: And what are sounds? he said. They are, they are like flowers within flowers, something inside something. And what is inside a sound? I mean, where does the sound of the sound come from? I've no idea. Michele Bacigalupo—you remember Michele?—he used to say that with each sound we make we are giving back to the air everything it gives us. What does that mean? I'm not really sure either. I think music is always there, do you see, music plays itself and instruments try to attract it, to coax it down to earth. How strange, Hans said, I have a similar idea about poetry, only horizontally. (Horizontally? the old man said, looking puzzled.) I think poetry is like the wind you enjoy listening to, which comes and goes and belongs to no one, whispering to anyone who passes by. But I don't think the sound of words comes from the sky. I imagine it more like a stagecoach traveling to different places. That's why I believe in traveling, do you see? (Franz, said the organ grinder, stop that, stop biting his boots!) Yes, stop that, Franz. Deep down, people who travel are musicians or poets because they are looking for sounds. I understand, said the organ grinder, but I don't see the need to travel in order to find sounds, can't you also be very still, attentive, like Franz when he senses someone coming, and wait for sounds to arrive? My dear organ grinder, Hans said, placing an arm around his shoulder, we're back to the same idea—should we leave or stay, be still or keep moving? Well, the organ grinder grinned, at least you agree we haven't budged from that point. You win! said Hans.

They had fallen silent, shoulder-to-shoulder, absorbing the closing phrase of evening. Through the breaks in the pine trees beyond they could see the windmills. Hans heard the old man mumbling. Wait, wait, I don't think so, said the organ grinder, I don't think so (you don't think what? asked Hans), sorry, I don't think it's true (what's not true? Hans persisted), about being stuck at one point. I said the idea is always the same and that's true. But we also like to reflect on it, turn it over in our minds, like those windmills. So maybe we aren't so stuck after all. I was looking at the windmills, and suddenly I thought, are they moving or not? And I didn't know. What do you think?

In the midst of the crowd in the streets around the market square, Frau Pietzine was watching the Christs, Virgins, Mary Magdalenes go by, and with each new step of sorrows and tears she realised she felt better, a sense of comfort pulsed through her, this shared piety absolved her for something she perhaps had not done. With each beat—boom!—of the drums, with each beat—boom!—she clasped her rosary beads and—boom!—half-closed her eyes. Every Maundy Thursday— boom!—Frau Pietzine would venture out with heavy heart to see—boom!—the processions and recall—boom!—with sadness, all the other Thursdays—boom!—when her husband— boom!—would escort her to the stand opposite the town hall. It was no doubt loneliness—boom!—that had changed the meaning—boom!—of that crowd for ever—before it had been a kind of landscape, a distant backdrop—boom!—which she could ignore provided her faith and prayers were sincere, but for the last few years—boom!—Frau Pietzine would hurl herself into the crowd—boom!—letting it engulf her, and discover in its murmur—boom!—a frantic companionship. When she remembered—boom!—the touch of her deceased husband's bony fingers—boom!—Frau Pietzine instinctively sought the frail hand of her youngest son in order—boom!—to clasp it in hers, offering the protection she could now only give—boom!—but never again receive. God give you health and strength, my beloved son—boom!—Frau Pietzine muttered, and no one could have denied—boom!—that hers was the most sincere prayer of all those uttered—boom!—that whole week in Wandernburg.

On the far side of the square, on the corner of Archway and King's Parade, the Levins were also watching the processions at a distance from the main crowd. Mortified by her husband's indifference, Frau Levin did her best to counteract the impression they might be giving to those beside them, by standing bolt upright in an uncomfortably rigid posture that suggested rapt attention. Worst of all, she thought, was not her husband's radical ideas. It was the smirk on his face that betrayed his differences and, in the end, his contempt. A contempt which, due to his pride, condemned them to the most humiliating margins of Wandernburg society. Why would her husband not yield even an inch, if only for the sake of appearances? If his beliefs were as solid as he maintained, why this insistence on having nothing to do with popular religious conventions? Were they not mere conventions, poppycock, expediencies as he kept saying? Why, then, did he continue to repudiate them? Herr Levin, in the meantime, wearing the same fixed smile, was thinking the exact opposite—of the humiliation of having to accompany his wife year in, year out, as a gesture of goodwill, to see this grotesque display of opportunistic penitence and sham religious devotion. Herr Levin was equally if not more dismayed by the dreadful, jarring bands—each time he heard the trumpets' piercing, metallic blast—tara-tara!—his nose wrinkled instinctively. What is the point, he said to himself, of pretending we are what we are not? Tara! And what was the point of converting to something else—tara-tara!—if at all events they, the others, would never accept them as one of their own? Tara! If we came here to suffer exile, to grow and return—tara-tara!—what meaning was there in trying to escape fate? Tara! This was precisely the thing that most angered Herr Levin about his wife's behaviour—tara-tara! How could she be so naive as to imagine they would accept her if she obeyed their rules? Tara! And if she were to obey anyone, wasn't it more reasonable that she should do as he said? Tara-tara! Besides, reflected Herr Levin, the idea of God—tara!—is not reached through theatre. If all these people devoted the Easter week to studying theology—tara-tara!—astronomy or even arithmetic, they would be closer to faith than they were now—tara!—or did these bigots really believe all would be revealed to them one fine day, just because? Tara-tara! I hope, Frau Levin thought at that very moment, we shall be going to church today at any rate—tara! I hope, her husband thought simultaneously, that on top of everything else she's not planning to attend Mass. Tara-tara!

Not far from the Levins, Hans stood craning his neck, exasperated and curious. Even though he detested crowds, he had been forced to join in because every street in the city centre, including the street where the inn was, had been besieged since early that morning. He had been woken up by blaring bugles, and, after trying to ignore the din or bury himself in a book, had gone downstairs to have a look. How peaceful it must be in the cave now, he reflected, smiling to himself. As he weaved his way between elbows, wide-brimmed hats and parasols, he had the impression of witnessing a dual spectacle—the faithful taking part in the procession and the neighbours who had come out to watch them. No matter how much that gregarious display seemed to him like a mixture of the Inquisition and pagan spring worship, he had to admit he found it fascinating. After watching the most celebrated floats go by, Hans was in no doubt—the most ornate of all, the one that had stood out as it rolled down Border Street, had been the carriage belonging to His Excellency Mayor Ratztrinker, with its exquisite lines, folding hood and towering driver's seat upholstered in velvet.

Hans turned round and found himself face to face with Father Pigherzog, with whom he had exchanged no more than a few words outside the church in those early days when he had been following the Gottliebs. Ah, how he yearned to see Sophie. Happily, her salon was the following day. Father Pigherzog spoke to him first. Well, smiled the priest, what do you think of Wandernburg's famous Easter processions? Are they not extraordinary? You took the words out of my mouth, Father, Hans replied. Is it not astonishing? the priest went on, I would go so far as to say that such popular zeal, such a fervent display of spirituality is unique in all Germany. If I may be permitted to give my opinion as a novice, Hans said, I'm not sure spirituality is what brings this crowd onto the street. I feared as much, Father Pigherzog sighed, you are a materialist. You are mistaken, Father, Hans said, I believe in all kinds of unseen powers. Unseen and of this earth. Well, the priest shrugged, I only hope you are at peace with your impoverished notions. All I ask is that one day you consider how alone we would be without the Heavens to protect us. Indeed, Father, replied Hans, alone at last!

At last we are alone, Father, Frau Pietzine whispered through the grille in the confessional. I am so in need of your advice! What is ailing you, my child? came Father Pigherzog's voice. It's, she said, well, all the rest you know, but this is about time,

Father, do you understand? More than anything it is about time. (Try to be a little more specific, my child, whispered Father Pigherzog's voice.) It's nothing definite, moments, times when I fear everything is in vain. (Nothing is in vain, my child.) This morning, for instance, my youngest son gave me his hand and I squeezed it hard and it felt so small and defenceless, Father! And then I was afraid, afraid of my son's frailty, and of my own, do you understand, Father? Because I realised that neither I nor anyone can protect him from the trials of this life, from the suffering that awaits him. (The Lord can do so, my child.) Of course, He can do so, but how can I explain, there are things not even God, but only a mother should do for her children. (I see no contradiction in this, you are a mother and a child and He is the Father whose children procreate in his name.) Oh Father, you explain everything so well! Do you see why I need your advice? If only you had known me when my faith was strong, in the bloom of youth! When I was unassailed by doubt, all innocence and devotion to God. But then I met my deceased husband, may the Lord keep him in His glory, oh woe is me! (He is resting in eternal peace now and can hear us.) May the angels take notice of you, Father, and we were betrothed immediately, and I gave him four children, thanks be to the Lord, Father, and without a moment's pleasure. (God bless you, my child.)

The children filed through the entrance to St Nicholas's Church in two columns, one of boys and one of girls. They walked down the side aisles and past the transept until they reached the apse, where Father Pigherzog, at the high altar, was waiting to bless their Easter offerings. The smallest children's gaucheness, their mixture of nervous silence and stifled giggles, brought a sunny contrast to the gloomy interior. One by one, holding small bouquets of boxwood, they approached the altar laden with sweets, egg-shaped candies, coloured ribbons, garlands and miniature toys. Their bright faces clouded with fear as Father Pigherzog loomed over them. This was not the case for Lisa Zeit, who held out her brass ring with an absent expression, and who only appeared flustered when she thought the priest had stared at her chapped fingers before blessing the ring. Lisa had not thought seriously about God since she was nine years old, but as she curtsied and stepped back, she could not help wondering why God had given her such smooth skin only to let her hands be ruined. On the opposite side of the apse, in the boys' column, Thomas Zeit awaited his turn with a miniature lead soldier in an oval box. Just as he reached the altar, Thomas pressed his legs together and began wriggling—he had suddenly felt an overwhelming urge to let out one of his small explosions. Don't you dare, he ordered himself, staring hard at his offering—the diminutive soldier inside an Easter egg, musket shouldered, in uniform and campaign boots, cap tilted to one side in an attitude of weary anticipation, as though he wished he could fire or surrender once and for all.

The deacon stammered his way through the Epistle, and the choir sang the Gradual. Frau Pietzine sang along, her bosom swelling. Father Pigherzog finished blessing the incense, recited the *Munda cor meum* and began reading the Gospel in the calming voice Frau Pietzine loved so much—he was such a wise, simple man who was dedicated to his calling. But what might hers be? she wondered. What should it be now? How many sins would she commit not because of straying voluntarily from the path, but because she was lost? And why the devil did these new shoes of hers pinch her feet so? Oh forgive me, Hail Mary! Father Pigherzog had begun his sermon and was cautioning his flock against the dangers of the mechanical rationalism of our day that could so easily lead to a vulgar form of atheism, a life without God, turning men's souls into mere merchandise. Life, brothers and sisters, insisted Father Pigherzog, is not a transaction or an act of convenience. Living, my brothers is to act without looking, to look only into our own conscience, honouring with sanctity the … (Why, dear God, Frau Pietzine lamented, why did I buy them, however pretty they are, when I knew they were too small? It serves you right for being avaricious, how right Father Pigherzog is!) … much less the wretched materialism that holds sway, yes, holds sway over our families, our jobs, even our newspapers. Ah, my brothers, those newspapers! Those scurrilous pamphlets! We do not say reading is sinful in itself, nor that … (Praise the Lord, Frau Pietzine thought, relieved, in that case romances are …) … But tell me now, to *what* kind of reading do we refer? Does the complete freedom so vigorously demanded by some necessarily mean the impunity of the word, sin in print, heresies for purchase? … (But the romances I read are loaned to me, Frau Pietzine thought, justifying herself) … than decency? Can entertainment be said to be as worthy as virtue?

Suscipe sancte Pater, they prayed, offering the bread and wine, which the deacon nearly spilt over the sides of the chalice. *Offerimus tibi, Domine*, Father Pigherzog intoned, glaring at the deacon out of the corner of his eye. And the incense floated up, dispersed and was gone. While the choir finished chanting the offertory, the priest washed his hands intoning the lavabo. Frau Pietzine adored watching Father Pigherzog as he washed his hands—he had the purest, most trustworthy, comforting hands of any man (well, she corrected herself, not exactly a man, or at least not in that sense, he was more than a man, or less, or both?) she had ever known (known and touched, but in the pure sense of the word). This was why her favourite parts of Mass were the Eucharist, the lavabo and above all Communion—receiving Communion from the hand of Father Pigherzog (who had just said *Orate, fratres*) was like exchanging lies for truth, the taste of flesh for the crystal waters of the spirit. The priest recited the final prayer and said:

Per omnia saecula saeculorum. And the choir said: Amen.

The bread came apart like cotton wool. *Pax Domini sit semper vobiscum*—how easily Father Pigherzog broke the bread! After the Agnus Dei, the priest kissed the deacon and the deacon hoped Father Pigherzog had forgiven him for having almost spilt the wine. When the priest wet his rough lips in the blood, Frau Pietzine's breathless bosom shuddered as the moment of Communion approached—it was she who had asked Father Pigherzog to allow the parishioners to receive Communion. The priest took the host plate from the altar boy, holding it between his second and third fingers, holy, pure, learned fingers! *Libera nos*, and when it was time for the words *da propitious*, he crossed himself and held the plate beneath the host. The altar boy uncovered the chalice, bowed, and the priest took the host, broke it in two, obliging wafer, nimble fingers, *Per eundem*, and half of it fell gently onto the plate while the other broke into pieces, weightless specks, *Qui tecum, per omnia*. With what infinite care and grace, oh Lord, did Father Pigherzog make the sign of the cross three times with the half he was holding in his right hand, *Pax Domini*, above the chalice. As he dipped the morsel into the chalice, *Haec commixtio*, rubbing his fingers together in order to purify them, Frau Pietzine's eyes rolled up.

Back in the sacristy, Father Pigherzog slumped into his armchair with a sigh. When he saw the sacristan standing before him as though waiting to receive his next orders, the priest waved his arm to dismiss him. If the boy were as bright as he was obedient, he thought to himself, we would be in the presence of one of the chosen. Father Pigherzog plucked the volume entitled *Notes on the State of Souls* from a pile of reading matter, and placed it in his lap. He opened it at the last entry, reread a few paragraphs, dipped his quill in the ink pot and wrote the date in fine Roman numerals. He raised his eyes searching for the right words.

*... whose attendance at prayer has failed to lead her away from certain worldly interests. As a relatively young woman of xxxxxxxx healthy appearance, it is to be hoped the aforementioned Frau Pietzine will change her life. In order to do this it is essential for her to devote more time to the nourishing duties of motherhood, and, above all, not to let her mind stray so much. As for her dedication to prayer, she gives herself to it with such zeal that on occasion it seems (*caeli remissione*) *she is trying to convince God of something rather than praying to Him. It should be noted that, within her limitations, she is excellently disposed towards listening. Express disapproval of her attire at subsequent meetings.*

... in such a way that, as far as I can gather from her account, the closer she comes to the Roman Catholic faith, the more her husband, A N Levin, abandons himself to outlandish studies of the Kabbala, Palestino-Alexandrian doctrines and God knows what else besides. Every sin finds the absolution it seeks, but complacency is a different kettle of fish. I refer briefly, as an example, to some of the many heresies with which Frau Levin's spouse attempts to confuse his wife, clouding her understanding of the Scriptures. Taking random quotations such as "We speak the wisdom of God in a mystery" out of their doctrinal context and distorting them by relating them arbitrarily to others such as "But God has revealed them unto us by the Spirit" (1 Corinthians 2:7–10), which the foolish man reads as a mysterious conclusion, arguing that Paul understood the need to interpret the sacred principles of Christianity as a coded language inasmuch as "the letter killeth but the spirit giveth life" (2 Corinthians 3:6) and that Paul himself told the converts and initiates that divine wisdom could not be imparted (1 Corinthians 3:2). According to his deviant interpretation, this implies that biblical studies should be based upon Samosatenian treatises and Leovigildian readings, as though the Word of God were a mere introduction to other unrelated words or parables. Consider the degree of apostasy in these considerations, and take into account the known inclination of the circumcised towards the language of doubt and paradox. Strongly advise Frau Levin, for the sake of her nascent faith, to frequent other places and people at least for

the time being.

... for, in his case, his immaculate manners and attire are but the outward manifestation of the richness of his soul. After questioning him about his illustrious parents' impression after the betrothal dinners, the aforementioned Von Wilderhaus the younger replied, with customary discretion and graciousness, that they had found Herr Gottlieb's residence pleasant and simple, avoiding any allusion to their host's financial difficulties. In contrast to his fiancée, we have no objections to this virtuous gentleman. With the exception of his habit of taking snuff, a trifle at all events.

... his unspeakable desire to revel in xxxxxxxx repugnant images, over which he shows no hint of remorse nor yet of frailty. Continued use of hair shirt appears not to have diminished his aberrant appetites. Warn seminarists so that they take all necessary precautions with him. Try immersion in ice-cold water and castor-oil concoctions.

... extremely satisfactory, inasmuch as not only has he found employment, but he continues to learn to read and write. Such exemplary cases as his nourish the souls of those who are acquainted with them and recompense the difficulties of our tireless mission.

... and his wife's forgiveness, which shows an encouraging change in both their attitudes. Besides the sufferings endured by the good woman, who has recovered from her bruises, special mention should be made of the supreme torment undergone by the paterfamilias, whose conscience will act as a guiding light. Space out confessions as harmony is restored to the household.

... consider it appropriate to include an addendum to the last quarterly accounts of lands given in concession by the Holy Mother Church, as well as to update Your Excellency, whose hands I kiss and whose humble servant I remain, on the progress of contributions. Having previously informed Your Excellency that these had diminished by seventeen per cent from an average of half a thaler per parishioner to the current eight groschen per parishioner at Sunday Mass, thus amounting to an overall reduction in the parish revenue of twenty-two ducats gross, I am relieved *today to be able to report that this tendency was reversed at the end of March, thanks to the pious influence of the religious holidays, and, dare I say, to our humble yet tireless labours, which Your Excellency in his benevolence will doubtless recognise with generosity when in his xxxxxxx infallible judgement he deems it opportune and necessary, as has always been the case. Special mention should be made of the inestimable goodwill of the noble Herr Rudolph P von Wilderhaus and the most excellent Ratztrinker family, whose regular donations of alms and stipends have also continued to increase, giving the lie to malicious rumours about an alleged rapprochement with Lutheran sects in Berlin, and demonstrating once more their unequivocal devotion to the Holy Mother Church that watches over us all. And lastly I come to a list, revised only yesterday, of families in arrears, and peasants who have failed to pay their tithes. I have written out the sums for Your Excellency in descending order of the amounts owed, a more efficient method, if I may say so, than the one hitherto employed of writing them out in alphabetical order …*

Every Friday, five minutes before making his entrance into the salon, which he had begun attending more regularly since his formal betrothal to Sophie, Rudi Wilderhaus would send ahead a footman, who would barge into the drawing room carrying an enormous bouquet of white flowers. A whiff of expectation filled the air, of hope about to be fulfilled. Rudi knew how to manipulate this to perfection, waiting with theatrical timing before rapping with the left door knocker and deploring the state of the roads or the growing amount of traffic. Bertold bowed fulsomely, relieved Rudi of his cape, while the scar on his lip stretched as far as it would go: Welcome, Herr Wilderhaus, oh, no, you're not late at all, the others have only just arrived, yes, of course, Fräulein Sophie was delighted with the flowers, Herr Wilderhaus, you know I'm entirely at your disposition and *always* will be in this or any other residence, Herr Wilderhaus, as you may see fit.

Besides the flowers, that afternoon Rudi had brought with
him a gilt cameo. Hans liked to think Frau Pietzine and Frau
Levin were more impressed with it than Sophie, for whom it
was destined. During the first hour of debate, Rudi would make
an effort to take part, interposing brief or at any rate agreeable comments. After that his contributions would gradually
diminish amid discreet yawns, which Rudi ably camouflaged
thanks to his snuffbox, turning his boredom into an expression
of contemplation. The only thing he kept up all evening (and
this hurt Hans more than anything else) were the admiring
glances he directed at his fiancée, so distinct from the rather
regal manner with which he contemplated the other guests.
Each time Rudi made an affectionate gesture towards her,
Hans looked for a space in the bustle of the room, from which
he could watch Sophie in the round mirror on the far wall. And
although he would invariably discover her eyes smiling back
at him, he saw none of the irony he had hoped for in them.
In the confusion of Hans's emotions, on Fridays Sophie was
two different women. One was the delightful accomplice with
whom he exchanged furtive whispers. The other, duplicated in
the mirror, the perfect hostess, the mistress of her secrets who
not only accepted Rudi's attentions but returned them. This
behaviour, which Hans found so contradictory, was the only
honourable way Sophie had of being coherent—Hans was
her friend, perhaps her closest friend now, and she was not
prepared to renounce this connection between them, this frisson which so thrilled her, and to which, of course! she had and
would continue to have every right, whatever her civil status;
yet Rudi was to be her husband—as of October she would be
living with him, and she was loath to make him jealous or to
foolishly ignore the important commitment they had made.
Not to mention her poor father, who had for so many years

put the happiness of others before his own, and whom she had no intention of mortifying by showing Rudi less affection than circumstance demanded.

Aside from this, did she love Rudi? Had she grown accustomed to loving him? Well, perhaps. Not completely. Was she naive enough to believe all women were madly in love when they married? When it came down to it, wasn't marriage a social convention, an amalgam of family interests? In which case, what obligation did she have to feel, or convince herself she felt, a consuming passion? In the same way pleasure and love could clearly exist separately, despite what her priggish friends believed, could love and marriage coincide or not depending on each case? Would she live like every other silly young woman waiting for a ridiculous Prince Charming to come along? Precisely because marriage was an artificial institution, was it not hypocritical to imagine that every wedding should take place in the throes of a mutual passion? Rudi loved her, and this to her seemed a good place to start if he were to respect her wishes and not ride roughshod over her, as had happened to so many of her friends. As for her, well, she loved him in part, but in part she did not, not yet. But time, according to popular wisdom, could heal all. And if Rudi went on treating her with the same consideration, naturally he would end up winning all her wifely respect. Which, in view of everything, was a good start!

But much of this reasoning escaped Hans, who, in his anguish, could only conceive simple questions—if she doesn't truly love him then why the devil is she marrying him? And if she does, then why do I feel she feels something else? As for her fiancé, how did he behave? That was the most uncomfortable part— notwithstanding his natural arrogance, his hunched shoulders and the unbearable squeaking of his patent-leather pumps, Rudi was surprisingly courteous to him. Surprisingly? Perhaps this was an exaggeration. Rudi, who was no philosopher, was no fool either—he was aware Sophie had forged a friendship with Hans that went beyond the civilities of the salon. And, knowing his fiancée's rebellious spirit, he realised it was far more dangerous to question that friendship or to show his dislike for Hans than to be polite towards him. Rudi was perfectly aware that, provided he played his cards right, he had and always would have the upper hand over any opponent—after all, he was a Wilderhaus.

Don't talk to me about von Weber, Professor Mietter said, banging a teaspoon against his cup, von Weber is nothing compared to Beethoven! Ahem, insisted Herr Levin, I am not suggesting he is, Professor, but surely you must agree opera was never Beethoven's forte. A single movement of his—may God rest his soul!—is worth more than all the librettos, scores, stage sets, even the entire orchestra of your von Weber's operas put together! Beethoven's music has the ability to soothe men's souls. Do you know why? Because Beethoven knew how to suffer. If the listener has also suffered, he feels a bond with Beethoven's music. Alternatively, if he is happy then listening to it makes him feel relieved. Rudi, my dear, what do you think? asked Sophie, keen for her fiancé to give his musical opinion. What do I think about Beethoven? Rudi faltered. No, replied Sophie, about von Weber. I see, Rudi prevaricated. Well, I won't be the one to deny his merits. Von Weber is not bad, not bad, of course. Hans tried to catch Sophie's eye in the mirror, but she avoided him and ordered Elsa to bring more canapés. Rudi made an effort, adding: Mozart is the one I like. Do you know his opera *The Magic Flute*? (Vaguely, Hans hastened to agree, with sly courtesy.) Well, I saw it performed recently and, well, it is, it has, without doubt it is a most original work, don't you agree Sophie darling? Although I haven't much time, I find going to the opera exceedingly agreeable (how could he even think of saying *exceedingly*? thought Hans), indeed, my father and I have two annual season tickets for the Berlin Opera House. Also, and I mention this in case any of you are interested, I have a box at L'Opéra, *une vraie merveille*! Don't you think we ought to go, beloved? What? declared Frau Pietzine, her eyes lighting up. A box at L'Opéra, and you say it so casually? Madame, Rudi replied, tugging his lapels, one word from you and I shall place a carriage at your disposal. Ahem, if I may be so bold as to ask, said Herr Levin, the price of the season ticket is? … Ah, replied Rudi, let me think, I never remember these things, I don't believe it is very expensive, provided one uses it! (Rudi concluded with a guffaw that caused Sophie to turn to Elsa once more to tell her that the jellies were watery. How could Petra have put so much water in the jelly!) L'Opéra, yes, the professor murmured, realising he hadn't spoken for some minutes. Herr Mietter, said Rudi, if you ever want a box at L'Opéra, I have friends who could offer you one for little more than a florin. You are very kind, Herr Wilderhaus, replied the professor, however, on my occasional trips to Paris I usually go to L'Opéra already. Do you really? Rudi smiled, somewhat put out. How interesting, a magnificent building, is it not? Indeed, Herr Wilderhaus, the professor said, and as you so rightly say, it isn't easy to find seats in a box. It so happens an old friend of mine, an exiled Argentinian general, lives there and gets me tickets. He is a rather sad man, he doesn't seem like an army officer, his only aim in life is to educate his daughter. (Very commendable, very commendable, Herr Gottlieb applauded.) Argentinian? said Álvaro, I have always wanted to travel to the Río de la Plata, has anyone ever been there? Hans was about to nod, but thought better of it and remained silent. Whatever for? asked Rudi, it is so far away! Indeed, said Professor Mietter, these Argentinians are very restless, they are everywhere at the moment. They have a penchant for Europe and seem to speak several languages. They talk incessantly about their own country, but never stay there.

What a shame, said Álvaro, that there isn't a good theatre in Wandernburg. Quite, Sophie agreed. Bah! said Professor Mietter. You only have to travel a short distance. I wish we had operas in Wandernburg! Frau Pietzine sighed. Incidentally, Monsieur *Urquiho*, are you not an enthusiast of Spanish operetta? More or less, Madame, replied Álvaro, more or less. Ahem, in my humble opinion, Herr Levin reflected, theatre is superfluous. I beg your pardon? Professor Mietter said, astonished. Well, explained Herr Levin, I think actors do on stage more or less what the audience does at home, that is, they pretend. Whenever I go to a farce I think to myself: Why I am paying to see this, when all I need do is look behind closed doors! In that case, Sophie said, delighted by Herr Levin's quirky sense of humour, at least the theatre shows us how to behave, that is, how to pretend. For me, Álvaro joined in, theatre doesn't reflect real life, it ridicules it. I think theatre allows people to transform themselves, said Hans, on stage men can be women and slaves can be kings. My idea, declared Professor Mietter, and here we must agree with Schiller, is that theatre constructs public models to educate audiences. The aim of theatre is to depict opposing forces and to demonstrate convincingly that good prevails. And what about Shakespeare, my dear Professor? Sophie ventured. He is brilliant because he portrays evil in a convincing manner, his plays attempt to explain wickedness. Shakespeare, Mademoiselle, replied Professor Mietter, censures evil in the opposite manner. I adore operetta, said Frau Pietzine, the costumes are delightful, and, I confess, I have a weakness for anything with animals in it.

Frau Pietzine seemed to be overcome by an attack of cultural enthusiasm. She nodded violently, making her necklaces quiver. She laughed euphorically at Álvaro's comments, with which she tended to agree. She questioned Hans about every country, opening her eyes wide and fluttering her eyelashes. She clasped

Sophie's hands and exclaimed: What a clever girl! Have you ever seen such a thing! Or she admired Rudi's elegance despite his silence. All in all, it was probable that hours of lonely sobbing awaited Frau Pietzine when she returned home. Now, at her insistence, the conversation had turned to romances and historical novels. Everyone there (including Herr Gottlieb, who had just wound up the clock and said goodnight before retiring to his study with Rudi to discuss some details of the dowry) declared they had read one or more of Walter Scott's novels. This great Scotsman, asserted Herr Levin, is far more than a simple novelist. (Fair enough, said Álvaro, but what is so simple about being a novelist?) Ahem, he is a painter, a poet! Álvaro, who was the only one who had read him in English, said that in Great Britain people would queue to buy his books, and that the translations he had seen, the Spanish ones in any case, were truly atrocious and all copied from the French. Frau Pietzine thought it unnecessary to be able to read English in order to understand the knights of old, and that, notwithstanding certain excesses typical of those benighted times, she wished modern life had preserved the colour, loyalty and chivalry of Scott's stories. Then, for the first time Professor Mietter and Hans agreed on something, and they stared at one another in bewilderment—neither of them liked Walter Scott in the slightest. The professor said he lacked historical accuracy and credibility. Hans accused the author of being a reactionary, and affirmed that a single ironical verse by Robert Burns was worth more than any of Scott's moralising novels. You really don't find them charming? said Frau Pietzine with surprise. Those melancholy landscapes! Those noble bandits! Those fiery passions and ferocious battles! What gallantry and emotion, what fearless exploits! Life, my friends, is becoming more and more dull, don't you think? Madame, said Álvaro, I see that gallant knights turn your head. Beaming, Frau Pietzine seized

Sophie's hand and replied: I am not the only one. My dear, let us leave these learned gentlemen with all their knowledge, I am sure you as a woman understand—is there anything more heart-rending than these heroines who are prepared to sacrifice everything for love, for their one true love, who will endure anything rather than renounce their feelings? Where can we find such loyalty today? My dear friend, replied Sophie, you know how much I value your opinion, yet I confess all these tragic women alarm me. Writers and readers love heroines, but they must be dead ones. And the wretched creatures are forced to sacrifice themselves hither and thither. Could we not have heroines who are a little happier? Frau Pietzine blinked a few times, but was soon smiling dreamily once more. Of course, my dear girl, of course, even so, aren't they marvellous? I mean, is it human to remain unmoved when the Knights Templar discover the terrible curse of the chalice in *The Secret of the Clashing Sword*? Or by the heart-rending final cry in *The Unrepentant Temptress*? Or when the old king reveals the truth to his son in *Sir Highwolf in the Nameless Tower*? Can anyone who has a heart not tremble when reading of the vengeance in *Hindu Passion on the Cliff Edge* or the fire in the castle in *Rhythm's Last Stand*? Your trouble, Madam, Álvaro sympathised, is that you are too big-hearted.

The problem is, Professor Mietter declared, too many books are published. Everyone these days believes they can write a novel. As an old man (you exaggerate, Professor, don't be so coquettish, remarked Sophie), oh well, more or less, what funny ideas you have, *mein liebes Fräulein*, thank you, but as a relatively old man I can still recall the time when a book was a rare adventure, and I don't mean the kind the knights of old embarked upon! The adventure was getting hold of a real book. In those days, each one was a treasure and we expected it to yield important knowledge, something conclusive. Nowadays people prefer buying a book to understanding it, as though by purchasing books one appropriated their content. I, on the other hand. Excuse me, Professor, Herr Levin interrupted, don't you think it was far worse before than it is now, because almost no one could read? And, ahem, let's not forget that if we are to have good bookshops, good translations, reprints of the classics, and so on, we need readers who like to purchase books. The market, the market! the professor declared, don't come to me singing the praises of the …

Just then Sophie sought Hans's image in the round mirror and noticed he looked pensive. She turned to him, reading his eyes, and concluded he had something to say on the matter. Monsieur Hans, Sophie said encouragingly, calming the debate between the professor and Herr Levin, you haven't spoken for a while, and we are beginning to be alarmed by all this silence. So, if you please, explain to us why you dislike historical novels? Hans sighed.

Let's see, he began, it isn't so much that I dislike them. In my view Walter Scott's romances, not to mention those of his imitators, are a fraud. Not for being historical, but because they are anti-historical. I am passionate about history, which is why I regret the current trend for historical novels. I have nothing against the genre, but it is rarely done justice. I believe the past should not be a distraction, but a laboratory in which to analyse the present. These romances usually portray the past either as a rural idyll or a fake hell. And in both cases the author is being dishonest. I mistrust books that imply the past was much nobler, when even the author wouldn't go back there if he could. I equally mistrust books that try to convince us the past was worse in every respect, as this is usually a way of detracting from present injustices. What I mean is, and excuse me for sermonising, the present is also historical. As for the plots, I find them superficial. Full of action yet empty of meaning, because they do not interpret that period nor the origins of this one. They are not really historical at all. Romances use the past as a backdrop instead of as a starting point for reflection. For example, their plots rarely link passion and politics, or culture and feeling. Of what use is it to me to know exactly how a prince dressed if I know nothing of how it felt to be a prince? And what about the timelessness of these romances? Or are we to believe history changes while love stays the same? Not to mention the style, oh dear, the style of these historical novels! With all due respect, I have difficulty understanding why these adventure stories continue to be told as though nothing else had been written since the romances of the age of chivalry. Doesn't language evolve, doesn't it have its own history? But I've talked too much again. I beg you to forgive me.

On the contrary, dear Monsieur Hans, Sophie smiled, what do the rest of you think?

The afternoon light shone through the lace curtains, filling the room with lemons. Everything around the windows sparkled. Sophie ensconced herself in a brightly lit armchair, as though she had sat down on the sun. Hans was opposite her smiling, his leg crossed at right angles, stroking his ankle. Herr Gottlieb, who was now accustomed to Hans's presence in the house, was working in his study. Sophie had told Elsa not to disturb them and she was resting up on the second floor. From time to time Bertold would appear to ask if they needed anything, or to keep an eye on them, or both. Hans felt happy—Sophie and he had just had lunch together for the first time. They now exchanged confidences daily, and, if they were unable to meet, they sent notes back and forth to one another between Stag Street and Old Cauldron Street. Occasionally, Hans had the impression that Sophie was oddly close, that a gesture or a word would be enough to shatter the distance between them, while at other times he thought she would never lose control.

It was he who was unsure, who appeared to vacillate, perhaps because he was free to stay or to leave, to keep trying or to give up. Sophie seemed perfectly conscious of the boundaries imposed by her circumstances and she moved within them without ever overstepping the mark, like a ballerina dancing along the edge of a line.

She was laughing as she told him about her education as a child—she laughed because it didn't amuse her in the slightest. I never went to school, Sophie said, there you have a perfect excuse for my bad behaviour. It is true that at home everything was at my disposal, they wanted to turn me into everything I'm afraid I have become. They began by teaching me writing, arithmetic and singing. When I was six they hired a French governess whom I adored, but who I now suspect was a very unhappy woman. In her own way she was, or tried to be, the mother I never had. She would read *Les Magasins des enfants* and the tales of Madame Le-Prince to me, and she always insisted on perfect manners, *toujours en français naturellement.* The poor woman never tired of showing me how to drink tea properly, how to play the piano without mussing up my hair, the exact way to hold my skirts when I was in a hurry, things like that. Don't laugh, silly! You don't even know how to sit on a chair properly! Just look at you! For a girl like me who preferred rolling in the snow and capering about, training like that would have been an ordeal had I not swiftly learnt that good manners were a way not of being good but of being bad without anyone noticing. When I saw that children who lied more openly were more severely punished, I resigned myself to all these lessons in etiquette. When I was nine I became quite a nuisance and my father hired an English tutor who taught me English language and culture. At that time, please stop laughing, will you, I would cut off locks of my hair if I forgot my lessons. Later, almost an adolescent, a professor of grammar, Latin and theology taught me. You're the pedant!

Look who's talking! Theology was awful, so I pretended it was a Latin class. I can't really blame my father—he had a peculiar daughter and he did everything he could to please her without abandoning his own principles. That's why I respect him, however old-fashioned ... No, thank you, Bertold, I already told you we don't need anything, you can go ... The time came when I grew bored of private tutors and insisted on going to university. Each time I brought up the subject, my father would say to me: My child, you know very well that as your father I've always been careful to provide you with the best education, I've never prevented you from reading books other girls are forbidden from reading, etc etc. But to send you to university, to allow you to mix with all those students, to lead the same life as they do—do you realise what you are asking? And he lectured me on the privileged education he had given me, which after all was true enough. I kept telling him I didn't want any more privileges, that I was fed up with being an exception and that all I wanted was to study the way other people did, etc. Anyway, I don't wish to complain too much. And so I limited myself to regular visits to Wandernburg public library. To be honest, I never completely accepted not being able to study at Halle University. No, no, you're very kind, it's too late, and besides it would be impossible. It just would, Hans. Even so, you know, I sometimes imagine I'm far away from here, I fantasise about unknown places, new faces, foreign languages. But I immediately come down to earth with a bump, and realise I'll never leave here. Do you honestly not know why? Because everything keeps me here! My father, my betrothal, convention, my childhood, doubt, you know the kind of thing, fear, apathy, everything. There are always too many forces, like magnets, pulling at people born in a city like Wandernburg. I am different? Well, thank you from the bottom of my heart, you are truly kind, but don't be so sure. I may think differently from the people here, but I'm not convinced I *am* different; in any case I sometimes have my doubts. No, listen. Seriously. There is something that unites me with the others, that unites all of us Wandernburgers—a feeling of fatality. When we close our eyes and say the word *home* we cannot help but think of here, do you understand? Yes, I might be deluding myself. I could listen to you talk of your travels and envisage the whole wide world. But deep down, *Dieu sait pourquoi*, as my governess used to say, I know I'll never leave Wandernburg. If our grandparents and our parents were unable to leave, and despite their denials I know they tried, why should we succeed? So as to change our fate? Hans, my dear Hans! The moment you're off guard you seem like an optimist.

There it was, at last—a glimpse of something deeper. Although Sophie was skilled at using irony to protect herself, Hans realised she had opened up to him a little. He decided to keep pulling on this thread by asking her questions. The tea had gone cold. Sophie did not ring for Bertold.

My mother? Sophie went on. From what I've been told she was rather pretty, and, like all women from here, domestically minded, fond of saving on clothes and staying at home. Well, that is my impression, my father has never described her to me like that. When I was a child and I asked people about her, they would say "Your mother was a great beauty!" so I ended up assuming no one considered her particularly intelligent. Her maiden name was Bodenlieb, which is a shame, because I far prefer her surname to that of my father. I'm afraid, had we known each other, she would have been a much better mother than I would a daughter. I imagine her as gentle, compliant, full of feminine virtues like Goethe's heroines, do you remember? "Women should learn to serve from an early age, for it is their destiny"—how much we can learn from our masters! I for one don't intend to spend my days with flour up to my elbows. (You have no need, ventured Hans, your skin is already like flour.)

Is that meant to be a cheap compliment, Herr Hans? Let's call it a description. And stop chuckling, you seem far too friendly!

And yet, Hans ventured once more, your beloved Professor Mietter approves highly of such domestic virtues. If you'll allow me to be honest with you, Sophie, I find your admiration for him rather odd. I saw you give him your album the other day for him to write out one of his poems (don't fret, jealous one, she purred, I'll give it to you, too, so you may write one of yours), no, that isn't why I mention it (no, no, Sophie laughed, of course not), seriously, I don't write, I translate. Besides, I would never write a single verse in your album. (Oh, wouldn't you? And why not?) Because such albums are for showing to others, and what I would like to write in yours no one may read.

Sophie lowered her eyes, and for the first time she seemed uncomfortable. She quickly shrugged off her unease—she despised feeling embarrassed, because it gave the other person the initiative. Hans savoured this moment, tried to memorise its essence, the way it had occurred.

I have great respect for Professor Mietter, said Sophie, recovering her composure, because regardless of his conservative views he is, or at least he was until you arrived, the only person I know with whom it is possible to discuss poetry, music or philosophers. Whether we agree or not, I enjoy listening to him and I learn a lot. And I value that more than any differences we might have. It is thanks to the professor, Hans, that the salon has become what it is. I know you dislike him, and I wouldn't like to think this is because he is the only person there who is your equal. If he didn't come the others probably wouldn't come either. Everyone here admires him and reads his articles in the *Thunderer*. He is by far the most cultured person in Wandernburg, and I can't afford the luxury of rejecting his conversation. In addition, as I was unable to attend university, it is a privilege for me to include a professor at my salon. If all that were not enough, my father holds the professor in high esteem, and sees in him a kind of guarantor that nothing untoward will happen in the salon. How could I not appreciate him? We also play duets with him on the cello, and you, dear Hans, can't even play the harmonica.

Frau Gottlieb, Hans smiled, I confess your eloquence would be reason enough for any man, Professor Mietter included, to lose his head.

Sophie stared at him, blinking, as if she had forgotten something.

Touché, Hans thought, that makes two hits.

Well, she parried, and what about you? You also went to university, and I think it thoroughly ill-mannered of you not to have regaled me with stories of your student days in Jena. True, said Hans, with the unease that always assailed him whenever he was questioned about his past. Well, there isn't much to tell, I began studying philology when (philology? Sophie said, bewildered. Didn't you say philosophy), no, no, philology, I always wanted to be a translator, which is why I studied philology (at Jena, wasn't it? said Sophie), yes, at Jena, between 1811 and 1814. Those were years of great conflict. I felt a mixture of utter political disillusionment and a continued allegiance to certain ideals. The question I kept asking myself then, and which I still ask myself, was—how the devil could we go from the French Revolution to the dictatorship of Metternich? (A sad question, said Sophie.) Or, more generally, how the devil had Europe gone from the *Déclaration des droits de l'homme et du citoyen* to the Holy Alliance? I remember Fichte had just published his *Addresses to the German Nation* and Hegel his *Phenomenology of Mind*, as though they had both had the foreboding that Germany was about to undergo a change. Soon afterwards, the resistance to Napoleon began, funnily enough just as Schelling's *Of Human Freedom* and Goethe's *Elective Affinities* were published, do you realise I've always wondered how far history influences the titles

of books. But they all, starting with Goethe, went on support-
ing the alliance with Napoleon. They saw him as a hero who
had dared wage war on feudalism and its archaic laws (get to
the point, Sophie implored, get to the point), no, you'll see I'm
not digressing, I'm reminding you of this because the French
troops once more occupied the northern territories, and in the
meantime there were more reforms, academic freedoms, equal
taxation, the abolition of serfdom, many things, and then (and
then? Sophie said, impatiently. You went to university), exactly,
I went to university, and, well, it was a confusing time. In Jena
(yes, yes, tell me about Jena) the memory of the poetic circle
lived on, all those revolutionaries who were either dead, had
stopped writing or had renounced their beliefs. We students
inherited what was left of their legacy, let's say, but also the
reactionary turn that events were about to take. And so we
were chasing something that had already gone. I don't mean to
sound melodramatic, but that's what it's been like my whole life.

Sophie looked at Hans. Hans looked at Sophie. Sophie said
things to him with her eyes. Perhaps Hans translated them.

Bah! he said. I'll go on. In that situation, most of us knew we
would become nomads, constantly searching, never completely
in one place. We would spend hours in the university archive—
a dust-filled corridor lined with shelves from floor to ceiling.
It was much better than going to lectures, it was like going on
a journey, getting lost and accidentally discovering marvels.
On one of the top shelves, whether to protect or hide them I
don't know, I found some copies of the Schlegels' magazine,
Athenaeum. They were very dog-eared and we fought over them.
These were rich yet meagre pickings, six editions, three years,
nothing. Holding these journals was like clutching the remains
of a shipwreck, we still believed a magazine could change our
lives! (But wasn't that true? said Sophie.) I don't know, you
tell me, are we already jaded? Or were we naive? (Mmm, let

me think, perhaps both things are true?) Our generation was
a borderline, we were the last to study before Metternich's
repression began, but we were also the first to lose faith in the
Revolution. We didn't know which to fear more—occupation
or liberation. Support for Napoleon dwindled as he started
losing battles. (And you, what were you doing?) Me? I was
preparing for my final exams when Napoleon retreated and
the accursed Congress of Vienna was set up. When I finished
university, France had to apologise even for the good things
it had done, while we, the so-called victors, had the dreadful
restoration foisted on us, and, well, you know the rest. The old
regime came back to defend the old order, and that was that.
I remember student demonstrations and movements calling
for unity, which of course never came about. It was one thing
for the monarchies to unite, but quite another for the people
to unite, wasn't it? Then came the decrees, the repression, the
religious censorship, in short, all that shit, if you'll forgive my
language. (don't offend me, sir, by assuming I would take offence
at the word *shit* when used appropriately), well, you know what
I mean. Suddenly, the interests of the nation officially turned
against every principle of the Revolution, as though we had
never collaborated with Napoleon, never written the eulogies
we wrote about him, never signed the treaties we signed. The
funniest thing is that it was the Spanish then the Russians who
weakened the emperor, who had marched through Germany
without anyone batting an eyelid. (All right, but how did things
end for you at the university, what was it like? Sophie insisted.)
It was strange, we read Hegel's essays, the Brothers Grimm,
a book about Goethe's patriotic work, imagine! Suddenly we
had no idea what to think of the fatherland. Quite frankly, I'm
surprised the country's youth did not go mad. Or perhaps it
did? And then there was the final irony—the great Schlegel,
the young freethinker of Jena, became press secretary to the

regime. I saw all my heroes surrender, and I could not help wondering, when will my turn come?

Unclasping her fingers, Sophie asked: Is that why you travel constantly? In order to keep starting again all the time? Staring at Sophie's fingers, Hans smiled and said nothing.

Bertold (during his comings and goings in the corridor, or his pretence at coming and going) chose that moment to enter the room. Hans and Sophie looked around them. The sun had stopped streaming through the windows, a few shreds of light clung to the balcony railings. They had a sudden feeling of frustrated intimacy, as though, unthinkingly, they had fallen asleep without managing to touch each other. They had said many things and had told each other nothing. Fräulein, shall I light some candles? No thank you, Sophie replied, we're fine as we are. Shall I bring more tea? No thank you, Bertold, Sophie repeated, you can go now. In that case … Bertold said, without moving.

And, in that case, he was obliged finally to leave the room.

The moment they were alone, with the same urgency as the fading light, Sophie uncrossed her legs and sat up straight in her chair. Listen, she said, we've spent hours talking of politics and I don't even know where you were born. I know nothing about your family, your childhood. We're supposed to be friends.

Caught by two opposing forces, one driving him forward to be closer to her, the other forcing him to withdraw in order to protect himself, Hans was paralysed. Forgive me, he said, I'm not used to speaking about that. Firstly because where a person is from is purely accidental, we are the place we find ourselves in. (Perfect, she sighed, more philosophy, and secondly?) And secondly, my dear Sophie, because there are certain things, which, were I to reveal them, no one would believe.

Sophie sank back in her chair. Vexed, she said: I think that's unfair. You know my house, my father, things about me. And yet I scarcely know anything about you. I don't even know why you want to go to Dessau, or wherever it is you're going. If that's the way you want it, so be it.

No, no, Hans hastened to explain, that's not true, of course you know me. You know very well who I am. You know what I think, you share my tastes, you understand my responses. And besides, you nearly always guess what I'm feeling. Is it possible to know anyone better than that? But, Sophie insisted, is there something unspeakable, something that might shock me? Because even if there was, Hans, I swear I'd rather know about it. I'm here with you, he said, how could you hope for anything better? So that's how much you trust me, she murmured, folding her arms. My confidant is hiding the truth from me.

Hans watched Sophie withdraw completely. And he knew he had no choice but to lose all restraint. In a fit of recklessness, considering they could be seen from the corridor, and even though they could hear Herr Gottlieb in his study, he rose from his chair and grasped Sophie by the shoulders (she sat, arms still folded, gazing up at him in bewilderment) and declared: Sophie. Listen. Believe me. I've been traveling a long time, and I've never, never … I trust you. I do. And more.

More? Sophie asked, in a less hostile tone, still with her arms crossed, trying to hide the thrill she felt at suddenly having her shoulders grasped, at feeling Hans touch her for the first time, and also trying to hide the fact that she had not resisted as she ought. She was unsure whether to unfold her arms, aware that leaving them folded was a protection against any sudden impulses. Her own, not those of Hans.

I just want to be certain, Sophie said, that you are being honest with me.

Once Hans realised she had decided to stay, he loosened his grip very slowly and sighed. I believe in being honest, too.

But sometimes honesty requires us to remain silent. Love, for example ...

Sophie started when she heard this word, and looked at her arms, as though unsure of what to do with them. She immediately realised Hans had gone back to theorising, and felt a mixture of relief and regret.

... Love, he went on, which is the highest expression of trust between two people, is founded upon a lie. Those who love one another, even though all through their lives they have lied or secretly changed, are suddenly supposed to love someone else without knowing who the other really is. To me this is the greatest lie of all—to assume that it is absolute, sacred, a duty, as if those of us who love (and here, safe inside his theorising, Hans contemplated her open lips) were not relative, impure, unpredictable. That is why I ask you, Sophie, would it not be more profoundly honest to love from this starting point?

Nobody, she whispered, has ever spoken to me like that about love. And I, he whispered, have never met anyone who cared to listen.

Beyond the enclosed fields, towards the empty south-east, amid dozens of tired windmills, where the River Nulte's waters grew more turbid, the red chimneys of Wandernburg's textile mill loomed. Even before sunrise, the boilers had stirred and the noises of the mill had started up—the sloshing of the wool-rinsing machines, the cracking of the carders, the whirring of the Spinning Marys, the tapping of the meters, the rumble of coal in Steaming Eleanor's belly.

Lamberg wiped his brow with his forearm. His breath mingled with the steam from the machine. He was used to rising at the crack of dawn, the arduousness of his job didn't bother him, he had learnt to breathe with his mouth shut. But he couldn't bear the effect on his eyes. They itched like the devil; he could feel the smuts circulating under his eyelids, although he knew rubbing them would only make it worse. Sometimes, while he was watching Steaming Eleanor's engines from his platform, Lamberg would fantasise about gouging his eyes out. Whenever this urge came over him, he would close his eyelids, grit his teeth and put more effort in each of his gestures. Lamberg's smooth, bulging right arm would pull levers and turn taps.

Lamberg! yelled Foreman Körten. Have you finished with that? Not yet! Lamberg cried out, leaning over the platform, ten more minutes! Foreman Körten muttered and moved on between the tanks of hot water, soapy bleach, potash and bicarbonate, his hair blowing about in the blasts of air drying the tufts of wrung wool, stopping next to the wool carder who oversaw the combs. Günter! said the foreman, How much fine have we got? As you can see, Günter replied, no more than a couple of pounds for every three or four of half-blood, five or six of quarter-blood, not to mention a lot more low-quarter. It's not good enough! the foreman complained. How long is it since you checked the combs? I check them every morning, sir, replied Günter. That's what they all say, grunted the foreman, and this is the result!

Lamberg opened and closed his eyes as if he were trying to trap something with his eyelids. He yelled at the stoker to stop. He halted the inductor, unblocked the hubs, filled the mixers, straightened the funnels and belts, shouted again at the stoker, then started up Steaming Eleanor's pump. The sound, that rushing noise which echoed in Lamberg's ears each night before he fell asleep, crescendoed until it took off. The vapour condensed in the air. The cylinders heated up. The pump whistled and the wheels began turning until they reached full speed. Lamberg contemplated the machine, feeling as though he were watching the workings of his own body. The valves opened, the bobbins rattled, the pistons shunted, the tubes juddered, the regulator roared, the cogs creaked, the wheels spun round.

The machine operators came down and formed a circle. The circle was made up of men, women and children. It was lunchtime, yet no one was eating. Except for the children, who munched their bread and cold sausage. They were all silent, heads pointing towards the same place in the midst of the circle, where one of the workers was speaking in hushed tones and gesticulating furiously. Lamberg listened, nodded and pressed his eyelids together. Fellow workers! declared the man in the middle. We must act tomorrow, we can wait no longer. The situation will never change unless we use force. The bosses have their methods, and we have ours. In England, comrades, machines have been wrecked, mills burned to the ground. We propose more peaceful means, at least for the time being. But we mustn't let ourselves be bullied. There are men working here who were promised contracts seven years ago. There are children of men working here who are paid in food. And wives who work a full day and receive a quarter day's wage instead of half. The delegates have discussed this at the assembly and we carried the vote, but now we want to hear from our comrades. Every man and woman here has a voice. There are five minutes left before the return to work. We'll open the session to objections and criticisms and after that we'll put the measure to the vote. Agreed? Good. We're all agreed. Now is the time to speak up. Do we strike tomorrow or not? No objections, criticisms or questions? Nothing?

Come in, Flamberg, said Herr Gelding. Come in, take a seat. Let's see if you and I can reach an agreement. And I'm sure we will reach an agreement. I'll go straight to the point, because neither of us like to waste time, do we Flamberg? You're aware that yesterday, and I'm not saying you had any part in it, there was an attempt, let's call it that, an attempt to strike at the mill. That is, in plain language, an attempt on the part of some workers to abandon their posts. Isn't that so? Good. And you must

be aware that Foreman Körten was verbally and even physically
threatened. You must also know that the foreman attempted to
reason with the rebellious employees, isn't that so, Flamberg?
To persuade them to go back to their posts, in exchange for
overlooking the disturbing incident. And you know that were
it not for the intervention of the police, we would be having
this discussion at Foreman Körten's funeral. Good. My first
thought, then, is this, Flamberg. Notwithstanding the arduous
nature of the work, which no one denies has its problems, like
all work, have you ever seen an employee beaten or threatened
in this mill, of which I'm proud to be the owner? You needn't be
afraid to answer. Have you ever witnessed such a thing? Good.
As you can see I'm not even considering this from my position
of authority as the owner, but rather from one of pure and
simple logic. Now tell me, do you think that, apart from these
crimes of violence, which will be duly dealt with by the law, do
you believe that irresponsibly abandoning one's post is any way
to obtain concessions from the company, from me, or for that
matter that from Foreman Körten? Excellent. I can see you're
no fool. I thought as much, which is why I summoned you,
Flamberg. I like an observant employee. And you, Flamberg,
are clearly observant. My next question, Flamberg, for as you
see I only summoned you to ask you some questions, is simply
this—do you believe in solving problems through dialogue?
Tell me, do you? Of course you do! So do I, Flamberg, so do
I. And it is precisely because a handful of sensible employees
knew how to engage in dialogue like civilised people instead
of behaving like animals that the mill has agreed to these wage
increases and a week's annual holiday. Now, pay close attention, Flamberg. If, as you have seen, through civilised dialogue
we have achieved these improvements for our employees, for
employees like you who do an honest job, and who now receive
a bigger wage and more time off, in the midst of an industrial

boom, Flamberg!—if all that has been achieved through dialogue and with due respect to the mill authorities, don't you think the troublemakers deserve to be punished, not by me, not even by Foreman Körten, but by their fellow employees, whose conditions have improved thanks to the very dialogue these troublemakers were attempting to prevent? Think about it. I'm not here to think for you. Who was harming whom? Let's be clear. And it isn't, wait, let me finish my question, it isn't only the employees and the labourers who would have lost out because of this silly mutiny, oh Flamberg! Let's open our eyes! If this business does well, if our mill thrives, then the families of all its employees will eat. And so will the swarms of children. Do you think I like to see them working the machines, Flamberg? No, neither you nor I like to see them working the machines. But what happens is their mothers come to me begging, insisting, weeping. And I agree to help them, because a mother's love sways us more than any other consideration. I don't know about you, you're still young, but, myself, I'm a family man. And what of the peasants, Flamberg? What will become of them if the wool is not worked on? To whom will they sell it? And the tenant farmers? And the landowners? Do you see that by insisting on protecting two or three rebels, we are putting the lives of hundreds and hundreds of families at risk, what am I saying, those of an entire city? Do you see that? Thousands of people's lives in our hands, Flamberg! The mere thought is enough to make one shudder, isn't it? But in order that our mill thrive and we can meet all these people's needs, you will appreciate that a boss needs trustworthy employees, responsible employees like you, and that he must rid himself of those who do not perform their duties rigorously. Put yourself in my shoes, any boss has the right to assume that today's troublemakers and idlers will endanger the future of the company. And this cannot be allowed. Which is why, Flamberg, if I knew exactly who these people were who had breached our rules, I would be able to be as just as I would like and punish only the guilty ones. But if I don't know who they are, Flamberg, and I'm no mind reader—can you read minds, Flamberg? No, neither can I—well, if I don't know who they are, then I may have to commit an injustice by dismissing one or more employees, or perhaps everyone, simply in order to be sure of dismissing the leaders of yesterday's mutiny. Do you imagine I want that? I don't want that. Do you want that? You don't either. Once more we are in agreement. And so, I put it to you, and this is my last question, wouldn't it be simpler, far simpler, to remove the two or three rotten apples from the barrel and carry on with the harvest? Or should the innocent pay for the sins of the guilty? Have you read Genesis, Flamberg? I'm glad we had this little chat.

Time to go home, everyone! The church bell has chimed eight, watch over your fire and your lamps, praise be to God! All praise! The nightwatchman's lantern hovers for a moment at the entrance to Wool Alley, crosses from left to right and carries on down Jesus Lane. Then the masked figure's brimmed hat appears once more and he continues on his way, like an evil shadow emerging from the wall. Farther ahead, different, more delicate footsteps are heading towards Prayer Street and the lights of the city centre. The masked figure quickens his pace without breaking into a run. The number of paving stones between his resolute steps and the more delicate ones is diminishing. The mud on the street is soft from the afternoon rain. Two, now three, paving stones nearer. Four paving stones closer and the masked figure can make out the folds of his victim's robe—excellent attire for a party, but not for running. An occasional street lamp lights up a small pair of hands clasping the edges of the dress, trying to lift it off the ground. Five, six paving stones closer and now they are both running. The victim leaps as though over puddles, she is fleeing with a desperate elegance she now curses, forced on her by the corsets and crinoline petticoats beneath her ample skirts. The masked figure, shoulders moving rhythmically, is gaining on his victim without needing to take his hands out of his pockets. In his pockets is a fine pair of gloves, a knife and a piece of rope. The young girl cries for help, no nightwatch-man in the surrounding streets will hear her cry after the eight o'clock round. But a passer-by, especially in spring, might. The masked figure is aware of this, and on the final stretch, only a few paving stones away from her, he reaches out a long arm. Almost within his grasp, the young girl turns and sees the mask.

Hey, old man, take a look at this toad, said Reichardt. The organ grinder glanced over to where Reichardt was pointing at an enormous toad. It had a puffed-up throat, sagging gullet and huge back legs. The slimy animal looks like a green cow, said Reichardt. Alerted by the two men's gestures, Franz im-mediately went over and stood motionless in front of the toad. The toad croaked, Franz's hind legs tensed, and Reichardt and the organ grinder burst out laughing. Are you feeling peckish, old man? asked Reichardt. A little, answered the organ grinder, I didn't have any lunch. Reichardt pressed his toothless mouth close to the organ grinder's ear: Why don't we roast it? he said. The organ grinder looked at him aghast, then licked his lips. Have you any more firewood? Reichardt asked. Franz gave a growl that was more wary than aggressive. The toad throbbed, alert as a sumo wrestler.

About time, lads! Reichardt cried as he saw Hans and Álvaro arrive carrying a cheese, two big loaves of bread and two bottles wrapped in brown paper. They said hello and sat down next to Lamberg, who was relaxing on his back, hands clasped behind his neck. We're late, Hans said grinning, because Álvaro gets very talkative when he's in a tavern. We're late, Álvaro parried, knocking Hans's beret off, because his lordship doesn't possess a watch. Sorry, organ grinder, said Hans, what's that smell? Toad's turd! Reichardt replied, slicing into the cheese. What? said Álvaro, thinking he had misheard Reichardt's gruff voice. And you'll be next, said Reichardt, pointing the knife threateningly at Franz. The dog flattened its ears and scurried over to the organ grinder's side for protection.

The bottles in the grass shone in the evening sun. A warm breeze stirred the fragrances of the pinewoods. The River Nulte tinkled as it raced along. Lamberg had been more talkative than usual. So, Hans asked, did the police break up the strike? No, no, replied Lamberg, they came later, the strike had already ended. (Who ended it? asked Hans.) I don't know, I don't know really, actually not everyone was sure of following it through, some only wanted a few days' holiday and a better wage, well, we all wanted that. (And what about those who attacked the foreman? said Hans.) That was only a small group, mostly the strike organisers. (But you supported the strike, didn't you? said Hans.) Yes, well, sort of. (That Körten is a bastard! said Reichardt. You should have thumped him as well!) I don't know, suddenly we got scared, because that wasn't the plan, and then the police arrived. (But why did the strike stop before they arrived? asked Hans.) Oh, I think a few of the strikers made an agreement. (With Gelding?, Álvaro asked. Behind the delegates' backs?) Possibly, I don't really know, I think they went to the boss's office to speak to him and when they came out again they'd reached an agreement about the wages. It was around that time the police arrived. Then we left and … (I'm sorry, Álvaro interrupted, but what happened to the delegates?) The delegates? Well, they were dismissed, they were all dismissed. (And didn't anyone stand up for them? said Álvaro.) Yes, of course, we tried, but it was impossible. It was a case of them or us. And there were only five of them, and us was everyone else at the mill, do you see? That's what happened. That's all I know. No one likes anyone being dismissed.

Lamberg's eyes were very red and he was scraping at the ground with a twig. Hans remained silent. He glanced at Álvaro out of the corner of his eye. That Gelding is a bastard, sighed Álvaro. I've got to go home, said Lamberg standing up. But it's Sunday today, said Reichardt, stay a bit longer and we'll walk back together. That's why I'm going, replied Lamberg, because it's Sunday. I need to sleep. I need to sleep a lot.

When Lamberg disappeared through the pine trees, Reichardt looked at Hans and Álvaro, spat a gob of wine-stained spittle and grumbled: You've scared the lad off. He's got enough troubles. Don't talk to him any more about politics or any of that stuff and nonsense. I'd like to see you two as wool workers. All I'm saying, protested Álvaro, is if they fought back a little, all the mill workers, starting with Lamberg, would have better lives. Forty years ago there was a revolution in France and the working people rose up. Then came Napoleon, who, however much of a dictator, put an end to privilege and redistributed land. Instead, what do we have now? For your information, Reichardt replied, your bloody Napoleon was worse than the clergy, doling out more titles than ever in exchange for this or that. We never had so many counts and barons, and that went for the whole of Saxony. Things have never changed for us—the same infernal drudgery, working the land and paying taxes. That's the reality. The rest is politics and stuff and nonsense, a lot of stuff and nonsense. You're right, said Hans pensively, but since the end of the Revolution, and I think this is what Álvaro is referring to, there has only been one solution for Europe, the same one as always. We don't want Napoleon back, we want the promise there seemed to be then, do you see? The feeling that it was possible to change the old order. That's the problem as I see it—all the countries in Europe have agreed not to change anything.

I hope the French keep chopping each other's heads off until there aren't any left, they already came here and we don't need them. Look, Álvaro said, not so long ago in Spain there was a French-style constitution, and this constitution proposed selling off land, like that owned by your bosses, and handing it over to peasants like you. More stuff and nonsense! Reichardt said. Do you suppose the ones who draw up these constitutions know anything about the land? I'm old now and I don't give a damn, but I'll tell you why your infernal revolution never reached the countryside—because we peasants didn't start it ourselves. The wealthy families used us, they took over, then forgot about us. No one told the French peasants what would happen afterwards, no one explained their rights, or taught them how to organise themselves. You make me laugh with your revolution! Anyway, for God's sake, you're a businessman! (That's neither here nor there, Álvaro protested, you can be what you want and have the ideas you have.) What do you mean neither here nor there! Of course it is! I'm sick of all your sanctimonious speechifying! Your Revolution didn't stop the peasants here bowing and scraping to the landowners out of fear. In case you didn't know, the year after Paris, the peasants here in Saxony mutinied. And do you know what many of them did? They kept on calling the bloody slave-drivers we were rebelling against *sir*! The revolution was a farce. And do you know something else? I won't believe in any revolution that isn't started by those who do all the work, not all the talking. That is if I live to see another, which I doubt.

Reichardt turned away, his gaze fixed on the river. Upset by his response, Álvaro took his time in replying: All right, but surely you can't deny your situation improved somewhat under Napoleonic law. It gave you freedom and the right to acquire land. Oh yes, of course, Reichardt said, turning back, how generous to *give us* our freedom. But tell me, lad, once we were free, how were we meant to pay for a blasted acre of land? Look, when I was a boy, I saw with my own eyes people surrendering to the French without a fight. I saw French soldiers march into Wandernburg one afternoon, and the next morning they were helping washerwomen hang out their linen, do you understand? Shit, I'll never forget those blue uniforms, the posture of those grenadiers, sitting bolt upright in their saddles, how we admired their blasted uniforms! And I remember their muskets, how they'd get twisted up in the sheets. The young girls smiled at them, sang songs in French as they washed their linen and looked at the soldiers in a way that … Anyhow, I don't know why they needed their muskets. Well, the girls used to slip messages into the barrels. Sometimes the soldiers would accidentally step on a sheet and the girls would look at the boot print and laugh, and go back to the river and you wouldn't see hide nor hair of the girls or the soldiers until evening. It was bloody unbelievable. Everyone trusted them. I still know some French words, damn it! Some nights I have weird dreams and wake up with words like *botte* or *peur* or *faim* ringing in my ears, and I get a lump in my throat. And do you know what happened then? Do you? They betrayed us. They used us all. And when we began to demand what rightfully was ours, the princes allied with the French sent in more troops, more guns, and that was that. They attacked us, fired at us, accused us of not wanting to work. They told us if we didn't go back out to the fields they'd shoot us. Oh, and while they were at it, they raped our women. You can't learn that from reading books and newspapers. Revolutions! Look at the calluses on my hands, lily-liver.

Oh my God, breathed Álvaro. The organ grinder handed him his bottle. Franz suddenly barked, as if he had remembered something.

Álvaro, Hans said, as he let the dog nip his hand, we can't deny that the Revolution betrayed all its principles. Liberty was turned into empire, equality was confined to the middle class, and fraternity ended in war. All right, said Álvaro, then we're left only with its principles. *Those* principles. And I'm still waiting for a revolution, a real one. Revolutions don't come about through waiting, said Hans, you have to make them happen. You don't say, replied Álvaro, offended. Why don't you start one, then, if you're so clever? Because I no longer believe in revolutions, replied Hans. If you've stopped believing in your own ideals, muttered Álvaro, that's your business.

Hush, my friends, the organ grinder said raising his hand, they're making a nest up there.

They all listened as if transported to the twittering among the branches, the rustle of weaving, the occasional flap of wings. Hans was surprised he hadn't heard them before. And gazing at the organ grinder, whose head was tilted towards the pine trees, he said to himself: That man thinks with his ears. But, on thinking this, Hans stopped hearing the birds.

Have you read the news about this terrible case, ahem, of the masked attacker in the *Thunderer*? remarked Herr Levin, plunging the teaspoon into his teacup. Good God, don't even mention it, said Frau Pietzine, this is the third time they have printed it, apparently there have been several attacks, always by the same perpetrator, a masked man, who, who—saints preserve us!—violates his victims before releasing them, and the worst of it is the police know nothing, or so people say, really, it's dreadful to think the streets are no longer safe. It is obvious these events terrify you, *meine Dame*, Professor Mietter said mockingly, for you have retained every detail. Incidentally—Herr Gottlieb's whiskers leant forward—speaking of the *Thunderer*, congratulations on your poem last Sunday, Professor, I found it particularly brilliant. (Hans remembered the poem, which he had read in the paper while having lunch—declamatory tone, long symmetrical verses, forced rhymes.) My daughter and I agreed, you know how much we both admire you. Professor Mietter gave him a look of perfect surprise, as though he had no clue what he was talking about, and then pretended suddenly to remember. Heavens, that, really, it was nothing, said the professor, waving his hands in the air (as if to say, thought Hans, "my self-admiration is even greater").

As the discussion continued, Hans questioned his own state of mind. In an attempt to be honest, he had to admit his reservations towards Professor Mietter might be motivated by envy, or more precisely, by jealousy that Herr Gottlieb had included Sophie in his praise of the professor's poem. Although (Hans thought, consoling himself on the one hand while on the other feeling ashamed of himself for doing so) perhaps Herr Gottlieb had only said this in order to make his remark sound more polite. Could Sophie really admire poems such as those of Professor Mietter? Not knowing where to direct his dismay, Hans noticed that Rudi looked completely distracted, and almost instinctively, he said vengefully: And what about you, dear Herr Wilderhaus, did you appreciate the poem as much as we did? Rudi looked up from his teacup, glanced about with a startled air, and, sitting up straight, replied: Regrettably on this occasion I am unable to share my impressions, for there are days when I do not have time even to browse the newspapers.

Naturally, Professor Mietter said, straightening his wig, I don't mean to excuse these atrocities, but tell me, have you seen the way some young women dress nowadays? How much more can they reveal? At this rate, there will be no more dressmakers! Sophie (who that afternoon, Hans could not stop noticing, was wearing an elegant, low-cut, pearl-grey dress and a fine coral necklace, because when the salon was over she was going to spend the evening with some of Rudi's friends) raised an eyebrow and said: Professor, I am sure I must have misheard you, could you explain what you meant by that remark? Mademoiselle, said

Professor Mietter, it was only a joke, there is no need to make a drama out of it. You are quite right, Sophie smiled disdainfully, the victims provide us with quite enough drama. (Take that, Mietter! Hans thought gleefully. And once again he said to himself: Of course she couldn't like that poem.)

Given that there are no witnesses, suggested Herr Levin, we cannot rule out the possibility that this masked man might be a kind of collective myth, that is, ahem, a pretext to justify, as it were, shameful indiscretions. I must admit, said Professor Mietter, your idea is an ingenious one; in any event it would explain why the police have not yet. arrested anyone, and the increase in the number of cases being reported. Gentlemen, Sophie said folding her arms, both of you seem to me to be rather carried away this afternoon! *Liebes Fräulein*, Professor Mietter said, adjusting his spectacle frames, I hope we have not given you the wrong impression, rest assured I consider myself a most fervent admirer of the fair sex. Is that so, Professor? Sophie replied, clasping her coral necklace. And in what way do you admire us? I have the feeling this debate could prove most informative. Well, Professor Mietter said, taking a deep breath, in my opinion women, cultured women that is, are on a higher spiritual plane. Unlike so many uncouth men we encounter in our daily lives, such women appear to be untouched by vulgar things. (Even when they wish to be touched by them? remarked Sophie. My child, Herr Gottlieb chided her.) Believe me, Mademoiselle, no man of honour would dare underestimate the highest destiny that is the lot of every mother, to be the pillar of her family, a source of filial love, a focus of harmony and, why not say it, all that beautifies our homes—do such merits strike you as trifling? (Let us say, she replied, that with a little effort I could think of a few more.) My impulsive friend, I'm afraid you insist on misunderstanding me. I do not mean to argue that men are superior to women, almost the contrary.

I am simply saying that men possess certain innate abilities in some areas, just as women undeniably possess them in many others. That is why the roles some women writers challenge today are no more than the result of the application of logic, the product of centuries of human relationships. (How reassuring, Sophie said, to know that science sanctions our domestic chores.) These are not my words, but those of the distinguished moral philosopher Hannah More, whose works I should add I have read with interest, and who I imagine, being a woman herself, cannot be charged with militating against her own sex. (You would be surprised, dear Professor, how relentlessly some of my friends cultivate their misogyny. And speaking of British women moralists, have you by any chance read Mary Wollstonecraft? I can recommend a good translation.) I cannot say I have, my dear, but in any case there is no need—I'm perfectly able to read in English.

The clock struck ten. Herr Gottlieb and Rudi Wilderhaus rose to their feet as one. Seeing Rudi stand up with him, Herr Gottlieb paused—should he go first and wind up the clock as always, thus turning his back on his illustrious guest, or should he wait for Rudi to make the first move? As Rudi in turn waited courteously for the head of the household to take the initiative, there was a moment of comical embarrassment. Rudi himself put an end to this by offering his arm to Sophie from a distance and announcing in a commanding voice: Shall we go my dear? She made as if to get up, settled back in her seat then finally stood up. Perhaps, Sophie said, we might stay another half-hour and then ... Rudi smiled beneficently with the perfect understanding of one who regrets that the answer is no, spread his arms in a gesture of helplessness, and replied: You can see, my love, how late it is already. Sophie pursed her lips, and for a moment Hans thought they were going to show her dismay—he concentrated on them, on their shapely hesitation, willing them to pout. But

Sophie's sensible mouth formed into a proud smile, and she pronounced to her guests: My dear friends, please be good enough to excuse our hurry, which, as I announced earlier, forces us to bring our gathering to an early end. I promise I shall make it up to you next Friday by prolonging our salon into the early hours, and, your appetites and my dear father permitting, by offering you a more substantial dinner. My dear girl! declared Frau Pietzine, setting aside her needlework. Pray don't be late on our account! Then, with a hint of sadness Hans in some way found moving, Frau Pietzine added: And above all enjoy yourself! Enjoy yourself to the full!

The guests stood to bid the couple goodbye. Rudi Wilderhaus contemplated them loftily as though they had all remained seated. Herr Gottlieb embraced his daughter and whispered to her all the questions to which he already knew the answers—was she taking a coat, was the coach ready, should he accompany her to the door, did she love her father as much as he did her.

They all said goodbye to one another as they walked down the corridor. Elsa and Bertold moved among the guests distributing coats, shawls, gloves and hats. Herr Gottlieb brought up the rear of the entourage, as though discreetly sweeping them out.

Hans strode off, stamping his heels irritably into the ground. He had only gone a few paces when someone took hold of his arm. It was Álvaro, who smiled at him. Come on, he said, I expect you could do with a few beers. Hans shook his head and told him he didn't feel like drinking. A moment later they were walking down Stag Street, arms around each other's shoulders.

In the opposite direction from that in which the two friends were walking, a carriage with a sleek body and upholstered seats was about to turn into Border Street on its way to the western side of Wandernburg, where gas lamps illuminated the wide avenues lined with columned facades and acacia trees. A lemony odour pervaded the carriage, emanating from the velvet upholstery and from Rudi's neck. His manner was quite different from half-an-hour earlier—he was no longer distant, but joyful; his eyes exuded tenderness, not aloofness. Sophie's hand lay limp, cold, between her fiancé's purple gloves. Rudi Wilderhaus's illustrious head bobbed to the rhythm of the galloping white steeds. Above them, sitting upright on the driver's seat, the coachman looked to either side, bewildered, and thought: That's odd, I could have sworn this avenue was shorter.

Meanwhile, silence had descended on the Gottlieb residence, that melancholy stillness places have after everyone has left. Herr Gottlieb had ordered the turning out of the lights, and was sleeping, or trying to sleep. Bertold and Elsa had retired to their rooms. Bertold lay on his back snoring, half undressed, one leg dangling off the bed. From behind Elsa's closed door, however, came a glimmer of light and the sound of slow scribbling, the rustle of the pages of a tattered English dictionary, which no one, not even Sophie, knew Elsa possessed. In the kitchen were stacks of plates, teacups precariously balanced on top of one another, spoons stuck to plates, forks with meringue in their tines, greasy knives. Petra scrubbed her forearms by the light of a petrol lamp, while making sure her daughter ate every last noodle in her soup bowl and grain of rice on her plate. She herself hardly ate anything. She had seen so much food that evening, had kneaded, baked and fried to the point where the mere thought of eating made her feel sick. And yet, despite the dour expression etched on her slack, mistrustful face, despite the weariness ingrained in her skin, which, like the flour caked on her nails, would never rub off, Petra felt a smile on her lips—today there were leftover cakes and jelly, and so her girl would enjoy the finest pudding. Always someone else's pudding, scraps her daughter could innocently enjoy, but which could never taste sweet to her.

No sooner had Rudi Wilderhaus's carriage pulled up in front

of his hosts' residence than a pair of liveried footmen opened the doors, then stepped aside and stood stiffly on either side of the carriage. A third footman poked his head into the carriage and examined the inside, before stretching out a deep-cuffed arm that hovered at the level of Sophie's chest. Thank you, she said, placing her foot on the small step, I think I can manage by myself.

With an earnestness that kindly souls considered elegant, and spiteful ones attributed to plebeian insecurity, Sophie greeted all of Rudi's young friends, some of whom she had already met. Rudi thought his fiancée's self-assurance among strangers admirable, that mixture of haughtiness in her manner and gentleness in her gestures, that special something which in his eyes made her complex and eternally mysterious. These evenings had an ambivalent effect on Sophie—she was able to enjoy them because she found it easy to distance herself from her surroundings, to observe that luxurious milieu with irony, and yet this was what her life would be in only a few months time. Rudi's attentiveness irritated her, while at the same time she felt a guilty sense of gratitude. Each time he praised her in front of his friends she twisted a fold in her dress.

Besides dancing, skating and playing cards, Rudi's friends shared one other trait—without exception they all had revenues of at least a thousand ducats, which irrevocably set them apart. Or, in a worst-case scenario, at least until their annual incomes took a downturn. As she crossed an entrance hall as big as her house, Sophie was dazzled by the cascading chandeliers, the trail of white tables and the glinting tableware. She felt giddy as she contemplated quivering jellied fruits in their Saxony baskets, rows of exotic vegetables, spirals of sauces, mounds of meringues, walls of nougat, pyramids of fruit, fountains of almonds, mosaics of oysters, oceans of fish and cauldrons of wine. And in the centre, an absurd, glorious cake in the shape of a mountain range with avalanches of cream, chocolate covered peaks, cabins made of Lubëck marzipan, pine trees made with real greenery, sleighs fashioned from cashew nuts and drawn by dogs made of candied sugar with skiers of jellied fruit, each sporting a hat, goggles, ski sticks and a coat of arms across his chest.

About a league from there, the organ grinder suddenly opened his eyes and, feeling for his dog's back, murmured: Hey, Franz, aren't you hungry?

The following Tuesday, the same carriage carried the same passengers to the eastern side of the city. Rudi and Sophie were on their way to the Apollo Theatre, at the other end of Black Horse Avenue, at a distance from the centre of Wandernburg. Tuesday evenings at the Apollo Theatre were reserved exclusively for the landed gentry and their personal guests. Sophie liked going dancing there, although not so much on those days, because the ambience was too formal, and besides she could not meet her friends. In defence of these Tuesdays, she had to confess that Rudi was an extremely good dancer. With his face powder and dab of rouge, his carefully unbuttoned frock coat, his white-satin cravat and waistcoat with gold chain threaded through its buttonhole, puffing out his chest and raising his heavy shoulders, Rudi seemed like a caricature of himself—a mixture of lightness and manly strength, a rugged charm.

During their ride to the Apollo, Rudi had done what Sophie had been dreading for some time—he mentioned Hans. He had done so without histrionics, as though in passing, as one might gaze momentarily through a window. Rudi had been to the Gottliebs' residence that afternoon, and, for the second time that week, had found her taking tea with him in the drawing room. Two things had displeased Rudi: Sophie's laughter as he walked down the corridor, a laughter, how could he describe it (descriptions were not Rudi Wilderhaus's forte), so self-conscious, as if building on earlier jokes, and Hans's reflex of leaping to his feet as soon as Rudi appeared in the drawing room, a reflex that was too swift, a reflex of denial. Of course, none of this mattered in the slightest. Nor did this stranger. Nor did his know-all air. Nor did his flowing locks.

It seems, Rudi had said as the coach moved off with a jolt, you enjoy very cordial relations with Herr Hans. Do I? Sophie had said, offhandedly, I don't know, possibly, he seems like an interesting gentleman, I don't know him terribly well. At least he reads, which cannot be said for a lot of people. Tell me, Rudi had resumed after a calculated pause, what do you talk about, books? Who? Sophie had replied. Ah yes, well, occasionally we talk about poetry while taking tea, it amuses me. And so, Rudi had nodded, as though giving his complete consent, Herr Hans amuses you. No, my love, Sophie had said, talking about poetry amuses me, not Herr Hans. You seem a little anxious, did you have a bad shoot this morning?

The carriage stopped in front of the Apollo Theatre; Rudi hurriedly clambered down from the carriage and offered Sophie his arm. Unusually, this time she accepted. He stared at her enraptured and said: Your dress looks like a second skin. It makes you glow. It fits your waist to perfection. It enhances your shoulders. It makes you look immeasurably beautiful. You'll be the belle of the ball. It is very kind of you to say so, my dear, Sophie replied, perhaps I have overstepped the mark, then. Rudi took her arm, beaming. At the foot of the steps, the couple passed Mayor Ratztrinker, on his way down with a woman who was not his wife. His Excellency looked down his nose, bowed to Rudi, and swept on his way. At the ornate entrance to the theatre, Rudi brought his lips close to Sophie's ear and whispered: Tonight, my love, you are going to dance the best allemande of your life. Then night threw open the doors and the couple were swallowed up by the dazzling lights.

It's Tuesday already! Herr Zeit affirmed when he saw Hans leaving the inn, tomorrow is another day! Accustomed to the innkeeper's unsolicited remarks, which to begin with had struck him as banal, but were now beginning to sound enigmatic, Hans replied: How right you are. Herr Zeit, who was wearing striped pyjamas, the tight cord of his threadbare dressing gown digging into his belly, asked whether Hans had dined. He told him not to worry. Herr Zeit gave a snort and turned on his heel. A hand on the doorknob, Hans stood watching the innkeeper shuffle down the passageway in his checked slippers. At the far end the door to the Zeits' apartment opened, and the dimly lit figure of his wife appeared in the doorway. Frau Zeit was holding an oil lamp and had on the flimsy flannel garment she called her kimono. I'm coming, I'm coming, he muttered. His wife shrugged a shoulder and swung her hips to one side to let him pass. Then Hans closed the door.

Hey, Lamberg, the organ grinder said, don't go yet, you haven't told us your dream. It's late, said Lamberg, I have to go to bed. In that case, the old man smiled, tell us what you're going to dream when you've gone.

On many evenings, as they sat round the fire at the cave mouth, the organ grinder would ask each of his friends to relate their dreams. As he listened, he would remain silent, nodding his head, as though he had already dreamt them or guessed their meaning, which even so he never revealed. Instead of having dreams, the organ grinder preferred to say he *saw* dreams, and he enjoyed telling them his own, which Hans suspected were too outlandish or too perfectly narrated to be true. But this didn't matter, for his favourite evenings in the cave were beginning to be these ones when they relived their dreams.

Sometimes, Lamberg said, sitting down again, I dream that the Steaming Eleanor (the what? Reichardt exclaimed), the machine at the mill, my machine, I dream she starts to turn faster and faster until the platform begins to shake and I fall into her jaws. And then what happens? said the organ grinder. Nothing, that's it, said Lamberg, then I wake up and I can't get back to sleep. But you have to go with it, said the organ grinder, try going with it until the end, it isn't good to wake up halfway through a bad dream. When I wake up, Lamberg said shaking his head, I try to forget my dreams as quickly as possible, I dream horrible things sometimes, things I can't believe I'm doing in the dream. Maybe, suggested Hans, they're things you think about when you're awake and they come back to you when you're asleep. I doubt it, the organ grinder said, dreams have nothing to do with our waking state, on the contrary (why on the contrary? said Hans), I mean, for me dreaming is like being *more* awake, don't you see? And sometimes when you wake up, your dreams stay asleep. There are things you only know when you're asleep. Maybe what you say is true, organ grinder, said Lamberg, but I don't want to know anything about my dreams. There's no need to be afraid, said the organ grinder, try to concentrate, don't wake yourself up, just concentrate on the images and if they're not good, speak to them. Is that what you do? asked Hans. Yes, replied the old man, and I always wake up happy. The first thing I do when I wake up, said Reichardt, is to count my teeth with my tongue to see if they're all still there.

I don't sleep much, Hans confessed, and I often have the same dream. (What's that? asked the organ grinder.) It's foolish, I dream I'm crossing a very long suspension bridge, and just as I'm about to reach the other side the end of the bridge begins to give way in front of me, so I turn round and try to run back to the other side, and that's it. (But do you get there or not? asked Lamberg, his eyes wide open.) That's the thing, I've no idea because I always wake up before reaching the end or falling. (And what's below the bridge, Hans? asked the organ grinder.) Below it? I've never thought about that, I couldn't tell you to be honest. (Do you see? said the organ grinder. That's the question, that's what you need to find out, if you know what's below you can be sure the bridge won't give way.) What an imaginative lot you are, Reichardt said, belching quietly, I hardly ever dream, when I wake up my mind is empty. (Perhaps that's because you're dreaming of your beer tankard, quipped Hans.) Maybe it's your head, I'm dreaming about the inside of your head without knowing!

What? Álvaro said, surprised. You don't know the Apollo Theatre, where do you go of an evening? I go to a cave, replied Hans.

An hour later, having lost their way twice and ended up where they had started a couple of times, Álvaro and Hans found themselves standing in front of the Apollo Theatre. Good grief, what appalling taste, Hans said contemplating the overly ornate friezes. Well, said Álvaro, they were copied from the Redoutensaal in Vienna, but it's not bad for Wandernburg. Come on, let's go in.

Indeed, it was not bad for Wandernburg. The large rectangular dance floor was thronged with couples and groups. Some dancers wore masks, which was only legally allowed inside the Apollo Theatre. At the far end of the room, an imperial marble staircase led from the dance floor up to the surrounding galleries occupied by private tables and a small orchestra. The orchestra was playing a lively polonaise without bothering to discriminate between the loud and soft notes. Reaching from the galleries up to the ceilings were huge windows with square panes, classical mouldings, Doric friezes and imitation capitals. Enormous gaslit chandeliers in the shape of vine leaves hung between each window. Álvaro and Hans left their coats in the cloakroom and made their way slowly inside.

Hans hated dance halls, but at the same time they fascinated him, precisely because he never went to them. The crowd was a floating perfume, a shifting blot. In the light from the gas lamps, the ladies' arms and shoulders seemed separate from their dresses. The rows of dancers twirled and untwirled like threads round a bobbin. Dresses and jackets touched, brushed against one another, merged. Heads glided, hats passed one another like birds, fans fluttered of their own accord. Hans saw a glass of punch float by, and tapped Álvaro on the back, pointing towards the refreshment tables. Walking ahead, Álvaro gestured to him to go over and he would follow shortly. Hans veered towards the side tables, narrowly avoiding being ensnared in the middle of a quadrille. Trying his best not to collide with anyone, his eyes on his feet rather than on faces, he freed himself from the tangle. Just as he was reaching his objective, he raised his head and saw her.

He saw her, and she was smiling at him.

Her décolletage was ample as a map. A map tracing the splendours of her neck, the outline of her veins, the contours of her collarbones. Collarbones that resembled a necklace.

Hello, said Sophie, are you dancing or watching?

Watching, he replied. Or conversing. May I have the pleasure of this conversation?

They asked for two glasses of punch and clinked glasses, drifting towards a quieter corner of the room. Hans was finding it hard to direct his gaze any higher than her collarbones, and he scolded himself, afraid of seeming like an idiot. He had never seen Sophie Gottlieb dressed for a ball, he hadn't needed to in order to desire her skin, her smell, her touch; now he wondered what would become of him after seeing her in this gown. She noticed Hans's embarrassment. She felt flattered and pretended, of course, to disapprove of the way he was looking at her. To be honest, Hans said, longing to say something else, I never expected to find you in a place like this. Really? Sophie laughed. Do you imagine Dante and Aristotle are my sole amusements? And why ever not? Hans said. I'm sure even they would want to dance with you. Aristotle and Dante might, retorted Sophie, but apparently you wouldn't, do you really not like dancing? Not much, Hans admitted, and I'm rather bad at it. I see, she said handing him her glass. Men never like anything they aren't good at. But have no fear, we can talk. Between dances. Will you excuse me?

And Sophie fluttered her eyelashes, and joined a line that had begun a quadrille, leaving Hans holding a glass of punch in each hand.

Sophie danced as fluently as she spoke, and in an identical style—not overly mannered but elegant. She was charming to watch because she appeared to dance as though there were far more interesting things on her mind than to charm those watching her. From time to time, she would pause in front of a partner, lean forward to listen to what he had to say, then laugh softly before continuing to twirl. Hans wished he was beside her, dancing instead of thinking. But he had never been capable of overcoming his feeling of clumsiness and frustration the moment he moved his feet. Whenever he tried to dance he had the impression of an army of doubles jerking around him, multiplying as through a prism, showing him how ridiculous he looked. It became impossible for him to differentiate between his clumsiness and his embarrassment, and these feelings fed off one another until he finally fled to the side of the dance floor for safety. Watching Sophie and her friends, admiring their harmonious crossovers, he thought the difference might be that men tended to come apart when they danced, whereas women came together, uniting their minds and bodies. Noticing that Sophie kept stealing him glances as she danced, Hans could feel her getting closer. He knew it was too late for him to turn tail and run like he did on the bridge in his dream. He looked down at what was below and saw his feet, and then he felt awkward and joyful and helpless.

The orchestra paused for a break, the dancers applauded. As the couples, squares and rows broke up, Hans spotted Álvaro, whom he had lost sight of, in a clear space on the dance floor. He was talking to a young woman who had her back turned, and whom Hans thought he recognised. She seemed to be listening attentively even as she tapped her foot on the floor. She turned slightly and Hans glimpsed her in profile. It was Elsa. He tried in vain to hear what Álvaro was saying. Suddenly, Sophie came over to resume their conversation. Her collarbones moved in rhythm with her still panting breath. Once or twice, Hans imagined he saw Sophie sneak a glance at the patch of bare flesh between the top button of his shirt (which owing to the heat he had just undone) and the knot in his cravat.

A moment later, Elsa walked discreetly over to them. She greeted Hans with a nod, reminded Sophie of the time, then whispered something in her ear. Sophie nodded and took her by the arm. She allowed Hans to kiss her hand, although she withdrew it immediately. Suddenly adopting a serious air (That irresistible air Sophie has, thought Hans, when she returns to reality) and took her leave. Shall we meet again tomorrow? she asked. Yes, of course, he replied, at the salon. No, said Sophie walking away, I mean afterwards, here. Hans nodded without thinking.

Someone tapped him on the back.

Where's my drink? Álvaro chuckled, I've been waiting ages for it!

I grant you we have been waiting for it a long time, said Hans, but once there are no more borders and we have a customs union, why any need for a single centre, a headquarters? I am all in favour of unification, but not centralisation. How naive, retorted Professor Mietter, that's a utopia, especially in a nation as fragmented as ours. On the contrary, Hans insisted, our tradition of decentralisation makes federalism easier, think about it, the same laws and policies could govern each region without any of them yielding to a central power. That regional sacrifice, said Professor Mietter, if indeed it is a sacrifice, would be a lesser evil for the good of the fatherland. Nowadays, sighed Hans, everyone wants unification, and Germany is swarming with patriots. The odd thing is that the French invaders and not the patriots began this unification, *on est patriote ou on ne l'est pas*, Professor! My dear friends, interposed Álvaro, if you will allow me to say something about your country ... (But Monsieur *Urquiho*, Sophie protested, this is your country, too!) Well, yes, in a sense, you are right, no matter, what I wanted to say is that I agree with Hans, because in my country, forgive me, in Spain, similar ironies exist. For instance, whether the purists like it or not, if Spain had been more centralised, Joseph Bonaparte would have easily controlled the whole country, do you see? (Not entirely, to tell the truth, Professor Mietter said.) Yes, it was precisely this autonomy of the provinces that saved us from complete defeat, because there are many fronts, not just one. Each region was fighting for a common territory, but they almost did so entirely separately. And so you could say Spain's federalist spirit saved her national sovereignty. Ironic, isn't it? I don't know.

I maintain, said Herr Levin, raising a finger and clearing his throat, that if the Prussian leadership or the parliamentary-reform groups, ahem, stopped appealing so much to the national spirit and sought a united customs union once and for all, these questions would be far easier to resolve. Customs and commerce, gentlemen, that is the heart of the matter. Monsieur

Levin, Professor Mietter said, removing his spectacles and glaring at him, do you mean to reduce the entire national dispute to a question of commerce? Herr Levin was speechless for a moment, lowered his eyes, shook his head, and said almost in a whisper: Yes.

What I'm saying, Hans went on, is that Germany, like other countries, continues dreaming of things that aren't to be, and this is exhausting. The good old failed empire, the Lutheran rebellion converted into an orthodoxy (that's your opinion, Professor Mietter muttered with a frown), forgive me, but it's true, Napoleon's betrayal, the utopia at Jena, etc etc. Who knows what comes next, but that doesn't matter. It's as if we can only write history from a position of regret. And look where it gets us.

Increasingly, when Hans defended the ideas he had always believed in, he felt he was doing so in the name of a single cause—in the name of Sophie. Rather than, or as well as, out of a dialectical vanity, which of course he also possessed, Hans argued with such passion because he knew Sophie was in agreement with him. And each time he spoke, he felt he was arguing on behalf of that agreement, pushing it elsewhere, far away from there.

But Rudi began making his presence felt. Not with full knowledge of the facts, for nothing could really fluster him—after all he was a Wilderhaus, but rather instinctively guarding against the intruder. Occasionally he would glance sideways at the round mirror hanging above the fireplace, and although he was too slow to glimpse any exchanges between Hans and Sophie, like a billiard ball arriving after the two others have cannoned off each other, he was aware now with whom he must disagree during the discussions, and what direction his interventions should take. He would do this in his own language, naturally, not in the tiresome one favoured by academics or the pretentious one used by pedants. He wouldn't argue a particular point, for arguments were unpredictable and could always be refuted. No, he would speak from a place where he felt at ease, where he was unassailable—from his own social position. He was himself. He was Rudi Wilderhaus. Why, then, for God's sake, why did he sometimes feel so afraid?

Rudi decided to take advantage of the thoughtful silence that had descended on the room in order to make his move. He may have held few cards in that game, but those he had were of great value. And so he played his hand. His aim was not to offer his point of view, but to sweep away with a single gesture any possible interest in those of the others. And he knew a great deal more about gestures than anyone there—he had been trained in them. Rudi took advantage of the pause, which was beginning to undermine the intensity of the debate, in order to bring forward his usual brief meeting with Herr Gottlieb in the study. He slowly rose to his feet, waiting until he had attained his full height before tugging on his waistcoat and declaring in his best speaking voice: Politics, politics! Frankly I hardly find these discussions thrilling. They are at risk, how shall I put it, of becoming tedious, and in the end predictable. Do our happiness or our aspirations depend on the opinions of a chancellor or the proposals of a minister? Well, be that as it may, dear ladies, distinguished gentlemen, I must leave you in order to attend to some affairs. As always, it has been a pleasurable and most interesting evening. Herr Gottlieb, before I leave, when you are ready …

Herr Gottlieb hurriedly raised his whiskers, took Rudi's arm and asked if he would accompany him to his study for a brandy. Hans watched them turn to leave together and could think of no brilliant rejoinder or witty remark. And, perhaps for the first time, it occurred to him that Rudi Wilderhaus was cleverer than he had thought. He had the urge to go out onto the balcony or lock himself in the bathroom. But then Álvaro came to his rescue.

Rudi had just turned his back on them. Álvaro uncrossed his leg, and, clearing his throat, called out: Herr Wilderhaus, pardon me, Herr Wilderhaus. Rudi wheeled round and gazed at him absent-mindedly. Pardon me, Herr Wilderhaus, Álvaro said again, smiling, how most impolite of us not to respond to an interesting point you made. You asked whether people's happiness or aspirations could depend on the decisions of politicians who happen to be in power. Allow me to give what you may think a predictable answer—yes, they can, if one does not own a thousand hectares of land.

When Herr Gottlieb returned to the drawing room and sat down to fill his pipe, Professor Mietter was discussing public displays of religion with Hans. The professor agreed that the restoration had brought about an excess of public religiosity, but in his view this needed to be addressed by a return to the critical roots of the Reformation. Hans maintained that Europe had missed a remarkable opportunity to give secular education a boost. (As he pronounced the word *secular*, Hans glanced at Herr Gottlieb and shrugged beatifically as though he had said the word *spiritual*. Sophie turned away stifling a laugh—this man was imitating her wiles.) I am hardly surprised, Professor Mietter said, bearing in mind Bonaparte's repression of religion. When my parents were young, there were a good many Protestants, who had their own place of worship, the Alta church, here in Wandernburg. The church stopped offering services when the Lutherans fled Wandernburg because of the prince's fanaticism. The same thing happened here as in Munich; people were up in arms if a Protestant bell rang on Good Friday. Professor, Herr Gottlieb said, forgive me, but you know that at other times the opposite was true. God knows I regret what happened to your good parents, but let us not forget we Catholics have also endured persecution. Ahem, Herr Levin broke in, on the subject

of persecution, it must be said that the children of Moses ...
Gentlemen, Sophie smiled, giving Hans a sidelong glance, let
us all agree we have persecuted one another equally and leave
it at that. Will no one try a cake?

The festivals in Wandernburg today, Professor Mietter said
swallowing a morsel of cake, masquerade as religious but in
fact they are profane. They are a feast for the senses and, if I
may say so, encourage wanton behaviour. Faith ends with such
festivals and carnival begins. Professor, said Hans, wouldn't
you agree that true faith has never been exactly widespread?
Perhaps some princes have a real interest in Lutheranism. But
I don't suppose they'd be against appropriating the Church's
lands either. You are incapable, said Professor Mietter, of seeing beyond the most naive materialism. Luther laid bare his
times. He made the Vatican look like fools. He uncovered
their lies. He held a mirror up to their faces. That is why they
declared him an apostate and excommunicated him. These are
real events. My dear Professor, said Herr Levin, far be it from
me to defend Roman Catholic dogma, which, as you know, is
not my passion in life. But let us accept that this was no simple
rebellion, and that notwithstanding the Church's abuses, the
Reformation was, ahem, excellent business for the northern
princes. Remember that Luther himself advised them to wipe
out the peasants who had rebelled in allegiance with his ideas.
These are also real events. You interpret them, said Professor
Mietter, from a very personal point of view. As we all do, said
Hans. Isn't that what you call *libre examen*?

Frau Pietzine was following the conversation with increasing unease, as though each argument were endangering her
own convictions. She thought of her adored father confessor, clutched her necklace and said: Professor, why don't you
discuss these matters with Father Pigherzog? He is an erudite
man, like yourself, a sensitive man who would do anything for

his parishioners. Although you follow different doctrines, I am sure you would find it interesting. (That man, dear lady, said the professor, is a bureaucrat, a seller of indulgences.) Don't be unjust towards Father Pigherzog! He is a true comfort and a guide to many of his parishioners. I agree, Herr Gottlieb nodded, speaking of which, my child, how long is it since you confessed? (Oh Father, sighed Sophie, as if I had the time!) Well, one of these Sundays. (Remember our agreement, she said, I go to Mass with you on Sundays and you stop insisting.) I know, my child, but just for once, occasionally, it wouldn't … (Oh Father! said Sophie brightly. Your pipe is blocked, shall I fetch you some fresh tobacco?)

Staring down at his whiskers, which appeared to be giving off smoke, Herr Gottlieb murmured: Bertold, tobacco.

Hans became absorbed for a while watching Sophie's restless hands and waiting for her lips to purse slightly when she made a comment. Hearing Herr Levin mention Kant, he turned his attention back to the conversation and waited his turn to speak. On the subject of religion, Hans said with a shrug, I simply follow Kant's example. I doubt I shall ever understand the mysteries of the divine, and in the meantime there are many more unresolved matters here on earth. (Once again, Herr Hans, said Professor Mietter disapprovingly, you reduce human knowledge to the empirical, you are incapable of abstract thought, you haven't gone beyond Hume.) On the contrary, Professor, on the contrary, I would say I expand it, empirical thought seems to me infinite! And I believe when little old reason ceases to bow to a superior power, it comes up against the biggest unknown of all—how to understand the world without any help from the divine, is this what you mean by limiting knowledge? (And I say to you, replied Professor Mietter, that if we dispense with the divine, our reason is left empty-handed.) That depends, I didn't say I was opposed to any form of divinity.

For me divinity is our two feet on the ground, don't you see? (An interesting thought, ventured Herr Levin, but what of the higher emotions? Do we not explore the world through them? To what realm does a heartfelt prayer or a Bach cantata belong? Do Bach's cantatas have their feet on the ground, or ...)

If you'll allow me, said Sophie, joining in the debate, I don't see why higher emotions cannot also spring from reason, why they need to be separated. For example? asked Herr Levin. For example in chess, Hans agreed, his eyes fixed on Sophie's moist lips, isn't it possible to be moved by the inexorability of a checkmate? I mean, don't you consider that thinking to the limits of our possibility ennobles our spirit? I don't know, Sophie said very slowly staring at Hans's chin, if I'm able to play chess.

Sophie opened her lips to cool them. Hans's mind was no longer on Kant, although it was occupied with empirical knowledge.

The other members of the salon resumed their conversation about national religiosity. Professor Mietter railed against the Council of Trent. Herr Gottlieb spoke of an understanding between the different creeds. Herr Levin referred to the influence of Semitic studies and astronomy. Frau Pietzine extolled the Eucharist. Sophie tried to moderate the discussion, giving everyone a chance to speak, and doing her best to weave together the different themes. Álvaro and Hans whispered to each other, heads together. Gentlemen, gentlemen, Sophie said in a tone of light-hearted reprimand, pray do not leave us out of your reflections, they give every indication of being fascinating. As a matter of fact, Álvaro smiled, we weren't engaged in any great discussion, you are already familiar with our religious limitations.

Álvaro looked around him and saw that everyone was staring at him in silence. Very well, he said clearing his throat, a moment ago I was saying to Hans that countries that failed to undergo their own Reformation, such as Spain, Italy and Portugal, were obliged, as it were, to come up with a home-grown

alternative—anticlericalism. What else were we to do, take
Communion every Sunday, absolve our sins, and support the
Inquisition? However, out of self-respect, we Spanish anticleri-
calists ended up rejecting every kind of religious manifestation.
What worries me is that one day we may no longer be able
to enjoy St John, St Teresa or St Augustine. And I think you
Germans had an easier time of it, you had Luther, Bach and
Lessing who acted as partial counterweights. For over half a
century all we have had is Father Feijóo, may he rest in peace.
You Germans invented the Reformation, and we Spaniards the
Counter-Reformation, you split into two and we drove the other
half out, just think what a difference (ahem, quite, said Herr
Levin, but remember there weren't two halves but three thirds,
in the old Spain there were at least three religions, not forgetting the Toledo School, all those Christians, Jews and Muslims
translating, ahem, as I mentioned before, works of astronomy
and theology, naturally, not to mention Juan Hispalense, who),
yes, yes, but that was centuries ago and since then there has been
nothing, absolutely nothing. For centuries Spanish Catholicism
has refused to cohabit with any other creeds or denominations,
making it almost impossible to think seriously about God. You
Germans on the other hand are capable of looking Christianity
straight in the face and giving it a piece of your mind; you can
dialogue with it without worshipping it or detesting it completely,
you can even try to understand its reasons, and I admire you
for that! (Bravo! said Professor Mietter sardonically, you speak
like a Protestant!) I, on the other hand, cannot—I see a crucifix
and my blood begins to boil. And then I am no longer capable
of listening or of understanding a word, despite having been
educated by monks. But perhaps German secularism is more
logical. (Ah, said Herr Levin, incidentally, speaking of Lessing,
let me tell you that besides being admirably logical he was an
infamous anti-Semite. Being persecuted for his ideas did not

prevent him turning his back on a persecuted people. Deep down, that is typically Jewish. Let go of my arm, will you dear.)

Frau Levin murmured a few words into her husband's ear, Professor Mietter remarked on the difference between secularism and being non-religious, Frau Pietzine asked him what the difference was, and everyone went back to talking at once. Sophie did her best to order the debate, and, as she smiled and calmed this or that guest, she tried to eavesdrop on Álvaro and Hans who were once more whispering to each other, heads together. The whispers she was unable to hear at that moment went as follows: (... Yes, Álvaro, I'm not saying it isn't, just that the Reformation also created a misunderstanding, do you see? There are numerous churches here all springing from the same damned branch. People here may have accustomed, or resigned, themselves to a certain coexistence, but it is because of these religious differences that many think they look to other religions for a solution, and ... Have you noticed the way Frau Pietzine is fondling her necklace? She looks as if she's playing with herself ... Shh! You idiot, they can hear us! ... But do you see what I mean, Hans? Yes, I see, what I'm saying is that here a discontented Catholic might be tempted by Protestantism, or vice versa, and consequently, yes, now you mention it, she is fondling her necklace as if ... Anyway, that means both churches lose out, yet religion always triumphs. For the Spaniards on the other hand, albeit by dint of atrocities, things are much clearer, look at you ... Ah, Hans, how much happier foreigners always seem, don't they? You can say that again! That necklace is making me nervous ...)

Álvaro and Hans laughed. As the laughter made their heads pull apart, Sophie was able to pour them some tea without appearing intrusive. Hans understood that she was rebuking them not for whispering in private, but because they were excluding her from their reprehensible conversation, which was the sort she preferred. Hans explained in hushed tones as she filled their cups and her neckline gave slightly: We were talking discreetly about the necessity of God's non-existence so as not to offend your father. Álvaro added sardonically: I hope we haven't offended you either. Well, Sophie replied, I had moments of devoutness in my teens. And then? asked Hans. And then, gentlemen, Sophie grinned, straightening up, I made a full recovery. A recovery, my child? Herr Gottlieb enquired, pricking up his whiskers. From my migraines, Father! She wheeled round. Do you remember my dreadful migraines?

Well, gentlemen? Professor Mietter said, under the impression the two men had been criticising him. In short, Professor, said Hans, we think Catholicism and Protestantism are based on equivalent sources of authority—one cites an infallible institution, and the other an irrefutable book. Sophie tried to make the professor feel he wasn't under attack—Don Quixote also set great store by the latter. Yes, replied Álvaro, but he was shrewd enough to find a shield-bearer who had never read a novel in his life.

Their hands clasped in the air, first position, then raised in an arch above the head, while his other hand slips round her waist, second position, until their arms are in line with one another and he puts one foot forward as though testing the ground, and she withdraws as if to say "wait", third position, but suddenly she relents, some strands of hair work loose, and she brings her legs together, waiting for him to bend forward and take—How tortuous, thought Hans, who can do that?—take one of her hands over his shoulder and the other at waist level, fourth position, so that he is now bending down virtually tied into a knot, and for a moment she has him in her power, trapped from behind, as long as he doesn't stand up, fifth position, but now he straightens up—How did he do that? thought Hans. Where did he put his arms?—forming a perfect ring by looping his forearm inside hers, so that they are facing one another again, their hands intertwined as in a lovers' toast, my glass is your glass (Hans gripped his glass uneasily), until finally, sixth position, they have turned full circle and the embrace is complete, he places his arm round her neck and his hand under her arm (He touched her! The swine is touching her!) and she drags her heel backwards while her partner slides his leg forward and remains motionless, proud, balancing on one foot, the toe of his shoe touching the infernal dance floor in the Apollo Theatre—Sophie had just danced an allemande with a man Hans did not know.

He breathed in and plucked up his courage. Before walking towards Sophie, he repeated the words several times over in his head so he would become accustomed to them, so they wouldn't sound humiliating. Sophie pretended she hadn't seen him approaching her from the side—she adopted an absent-minded look, but in the meantime centred the neck of her dress and smoothed the rebellious curl, which instead of forming a bass clef on her cheek was intent on tickling her earlobe. Sophie started, pretended to start, when Hans touched her shoulder as someone might tentatively ring a door bell thinking "Please let there be someone at home". My dear Hans, declared Sophie, how delightful to see you here, I thought you wouldn't come, I had almost forgotten about you.

Hans ran over the sentence again and then, eyes half-closed, pronounced it out loud. His own voice seemed to boom in his ears. Teach me to dance, he said. I came here so you would teach me to dance. Sophie's eyes lit up, her lips flushed and her curl sprang out of place. Arms akimbo, she squeezed her waist, it felt ticklish. She replied: Why didn't you ask me before, silly?

She led him to the least crowded part of the dance floor. I'll begin by teaching you the basic steps, she said, so that at least you stop moving like a duck. Don't be offended, I've always liked ducks. The steps are the same in almost every dance, and once you've mastered them we can try a minuet, which is the most suitable dance for us, remember your partner is a respectable young woman about to be married! No, don't worry, it doesn't bother me, on the contrary, I'm only reminding you because when I start to dance I'm the one who sometimes forgets about my engagement and being respectable. What? Yes, I can imagine, all right, well, it was a joke.

Hans felt embarrassed by these exercises and asked Sophie if she would teach him the minuet straight away. Are you sure? she said, looking down at his feet. Hans nodded gravely. Sophie agreed, and as the orchestra had just started playing a complicated quadrille, she began explaining the minuet close, very close, to his ear. She told him it was quite a slow dance in three-four time, that the couple didn't have to twirl, that it was French, that is to say elegant but not very lively, that it was already going out of fashion, although people still danced it, particularly married couples of a certain age. (Are you teaching me a dance for old people? said Hans. No, Sophie giggled, I'm showing you the only dance you'll be able to manage tonight without falling over.) And she went on describing close, very close to his ear, the different steps. She took him by the arm, and, moving back slightly, told him about the "Z" on the floor, the man's right hand, the couple's left hands, about the last but one step and the final sequence of "Zs" before the dancers raise their arms and end saluting one another from opposite corners. (All very chaste, for real ladies and real gentlemen, that's why we young couples no longer want to dance it.)

How am I doing? asked Hans, bent almost double. Sophie did not answer. Not because she didn't want to, but because she was laughing so much. Although the other couples were busy dancing, and the crowd was more taken up with its own affairs and merrymaking, to Hans it seemed as if everyone were staring at him. Why am I making such a fool of myself? he wondered, not realising that only those who ask themselves this are making fools of themselves. Moved by Hans's clumsiness, Sophie decided to give up on the minuet and begin at the beginning, with the basic steps. Hans raised no objections this time, because among other things, besides feeling ridiculous, the infernal minuet had kept their bodies too far apart.

What did Sophie smell of? She smelt of rose water. Not of heady perfumes. Not of pungent lavenders or jasmines. But of translucent petals, of tranquil rose. Of self-possessed beauty. Yes, and, underneath, of almond milk. Of a neck you never wanted to stop … Pay attention Hans! Hans said to himself, and Sophie spoke close to his ear. And he longed to dance, but not in that way, not there.

All right, said Sophie, let's try it once more. Legs straight, that's right. Heels together. Now, feet in line and pointing out (feet in line? You do realise I'm a biped, Hans laughed), come on silly, if only you looked like a biped! Now, legs apart, more or less the length of a foot (whose foot? Hans whispered. Mine or yours, yours are so small and pretty and), shh! Listen, no, closer together, perfect, now cross them over, what do you mean what? Your feet! Yes yours! Cross your right foot like that over your left, more or less at the level of your ankle (Sophie, declared Hans, you'll have to pick me up off the floor), you're doing very well, don't be like that! *Quite* well anyway, now the salute, do you see? The lady bends forward once she is in position. (I can't hear you Sophie, why are you so far away?) Because that is how this part goes, can you hear me now? Good, so, the lady stands legs apart, bends her knees and lowers her head. Don't stand there gaping at me, it's your turn! Now, the gentleman … (Do you mean me? Are you sure? In that case why are you laughing, Fräulein Gottlieb?) Hans, please, enough! Carry on, transfer your weight to one foot, no, the one in front, and the one behind moves into the fourth position, do you remember? (What? Is this the fourth position already?) Shh, you rogue! Now transfer your weight to the other foot and then return it to the other, no wait! Return it to the first position (ah, then I think I'll stay still until you come back), now bend your head, let your body follow, there, you see, that wasn't so difficult, now lower your arms slowly. (Actually, I think I'd better keep them up, I surrender, help, Herr Gottlieb, take your daughter in hand! Father Pigherzog forgive her! Professor Mietter write a review! …)

Hans didn't learn the basic steps, he couldn't find his rhythm or his coordination, he didn't understand the minuet, but that night he learnt to love dancing. As he watched each of Sophie's quick, alternating steps, Hans was able to enjoy the crossing of her shoes, the brushing together of her ankles, the movement of her legs, the sway of her hips. And, depending on how close he was, he also noticed the different pressure she applied with her hands. So that, rather than focusing on her instructions, which in any event he was incapable of carrying out, Hans tried to follow the movement of Sophie's clothes, the way her gown folded and unfolded, the inner creaking of her corset, which pulsed beneath each movement, constraining the appetite. And unless Hans was much mistaken, he was not the only one whose arms were trembling.

The three of them, Sophie, Hans and Elsa, left late, and joined the queue waiting for a carriage in front of the Apollo Theatre. Sophie and Hans walked side by side, talking. Elsa lagged behind, pensive. Hans noticed his face felt cold, his brow clammy; he was sweating, his lungs burned and his throat was hoarse. But more strongly than any other sensation, he felt a liquid euphoria in his muscles, a kind of certainty. Had he been drinking? Yes, on top of everything else he had been drinking.

After quite a long wait, they managed to secure a landau.

Hans insisted on paying for all three of them, and immediately calculated that at this rate his savings would last him another two or three weeks. The coachman was unwilling to leave one of the four places unoccupied and insisted they cram together on one side so he could accommodate another couple on the opposite seat. Sophie allowed Hans to help her up—their fingers touched, exchanging imprints before separating. The carriage tilted and creaked in weary acceptance as Sophie placed her foot on the small step.

Elsa was solemn; her head turned towards the window, she maintained a discreet yet awkward silence. Hans sat on the other side of Sophie, who rode in the middle, smiling and brushing the side of Hans's tight breeches as he sat beside her. The jolting tipped the seat from one side to the other, throwing the passengers on top of one another. Elsa clung for dear life to the door, but there was too much of a crush. Didn't the carriage move an awful lot! What dreadful suspension! What bumpy roads! Hans sat with his leg pressed slightly against the side of the carriage so he was pushed towards the middle. Sophie sighed sedately, sat still and let herself be squeezed. From time to time, because the carriage hit a pothole or swerved suddenly, Hans would tread on Sophie's foot or Sophie would tread on Hans's foot, and one would apologise to the other, who would hasten to say it didn't matter, it was quite all right, it was only natural with five people traveling in one landau. But these apologies were so effusive that sometimes the one stepped upon would step on the other, and the expressions of regret would fly back and forth together with an arm, a leg, a hip. And they would knock against each other once more—How clumsy of me! No, it was my fault—and their laughter flowed. Hans's breeches grew taut. The window beside him was steaming up. Beneath Sophie's ample skirts, among the folds of her petticoat, wrapped in white muslin stockings, her thighs clenched, tighter and tighter.

Hans was not a man in whom instinct and intellect diverged. On the contrary, the greater his carnal desire, the more voracious his appetite for debate. This particularly intrigued Sophie. The men who had flirted with her before had either done so by stifling their urges in order to discuss books (a tactic that roused her interest, but ended by exasperating her), or they had thrust all literary interest aside in order to concentrate solely on their immediate desires (a forcefulness that did not displease her, but of which she grew quickly tired). Rudi had been infinitely patient in his courtship, which had proved necessary not in order to break down any resistance, but to convince her. Sophie thought she understood the rather limited methods of male conquest, which was inclined to separate (mind or body) rather than unite, and to divide time (speech—preamble, desire—discourse) rather than synchronise it. Hans, on the other hand, seemed to speak to her and desire her simultaneously. He encircled her with his questions, inflamed her with words. This was what the daily letters they sent one another were like. It was how Sophie knew that the passion with which he spoke about Greece one moment and vehemently asked her opinion the next was no preamble but the onslaught itself, desire as thought. Hans's attitude in debate was as earthy as could be. And in his general reflections Sophie could not help but glimpse the suggestion of an intimate proposal.

As was their custom every Friday at ten o'clock sharp, Herr Gottlieb and Rudi had just withdrawn to the study to take a glass of brandy and talk as father-in-law and son-in-law to be, each convinced that these private meetings strengthened the engagement. In the meantime, as was his custom every Friday at one minute past ten, Hans's opinions suddenly became bolder, his gestures more passionate.

Will you tell us what exactly you have against the ancient gods? Professor Mietter said, irritated. Me, said Hans, nothing at all, although I doubt they are of any use in explaining the world to us now. Myth, Professor Mietter pronounced, recalling his lessons in Graeco-Roman culture, will always be useful in our understanding of reality. Provided, Hans pointed out, those myths are transformed. The ancient gods seem remote to today's readers. For all their Olympian prestige, Juno and Zeus no longer evoke in us an immediate response. (And after uttering the words *evoke in us an immediate response*, Hans stared at Sophie's hands as though he'd been referring to them.) I don't dispute that the Graeco-Latin gods were able to personify the spirit of their times, but do they personify ours? I may study them, even learn to love them (and on saying this, Hans gazed once more at Sophie's fingers, which became startled and began moving among the teacups like a tangle of legs fleeing a hurricane), and yet I don't feel capable of identifying with those divine beings, do you? Well, replied Herr Levin, that depends, we are talking about allegories, not about representations, and besides, those who read them have also changed, in which case, ahem. True, said Hans, but surely myths also age? Of course they don't! bridled Professor Mietter. Not even a little, Professor? Sophie rallied. What annoys me, Hans resumed, is that when we fail to understand modern tastes we plagiarise the past, we insist on familiar forms. (And on saying the words *familiar forms*, Hans glanced at the precise place on the mirror where Sophie's head was floating above the outline of her collarbones.) Show me a single living soul in Berlin, Paris or London who can say he honestly likes triglyphs or identifies with Doric capitals? I trust, retorted Professor Mietter, you are at least generous enough to consider me a living soul, *gnädiger* Hans. And since we are on the subject of triglyphs and capitals, allow me to make an observation about modern tastes. Do you know why we are incapable today of building the great edifices of the past? It is very simple, because our forebears were men of great principles. We *modern* men only have opinions. Opinions and doubts, nothing more. But building a cathedral, my good fellow, requires more than stones, it requires powerful ideas. An idea, at least an idea of the divine. Today's architecture, like today's literature, philosophy and art, is one of opinions. And so we gradually become eclipsed. Unfortunately, if I may say so, much to the satisfaction of educated men like yourself.

Hans (who had only been half-listening to the professor's disquisitions while gazing dreamily at Sophie, who would shrug her shoulders occasionally as though abandoning herself to an embrace) said nothing, acknowledging the professor's comment. Even though he disagreed with his arguments, they were solid and imposing like the cathedrals he lamented. He tried to think of a rebuttal, but the discussion moved on, and by the time he had finally collected his thoughts, it was too late for him to air them. Professor Mietter smiled placidly. As he leant over his teacup, the reflection of his powdered wig floated in his tea like a jellyfish.

It was nearly midnight and the debate was still in full flow. Sophie, greatly entertained by Hans's and the professor's disagreements (and perhaps excited too by the growing tightness between her buttocks and her petticoats), did her best to keep the professor happy and to stir up Hans, whose passionate rejoinders filled her with she did not know what. They were now discussing poetic style. Professor Mietter was arguing that a knowledge of tradition was necessary to good poetry. Herr Levin agreed, although in his comments he implied almost the opposite. Hans wrinkled his brow. Álvaro watched him and let out an occasional booming laugh. Frau Pietzine, uninterested in the turn the conversation had taken, had taken her leave, claiming she needed to get up early. Some poets, said Professor Mietter, with the aim of appearing modern, give no importance at all to what their poems are saying. As if this had nothing to do with poetry, or as if they considered themselves far deeper than their readers. They try to show off with form in order to cover up their hollowness and then claim they are *exploring*. But the fact is they would be utterly incapable of writing a simple text or describing an object convincingly. You are not wrong, remarked Hans, but we need to know what we understand by *convincingly*. Yes, the reader has to believe what is written. But what each reader is able to believe also depends on his imagination, not merely on language. And what about clarity? insisted Professor Mietter. Does the effort of correcting or honing a poem matter, or can it be left a complete jumble? Of course it does, said Hans, and by making that effort a poet can attempt to see in the darkness instead of skirting round it. You are simplifying the notion of clarity, replied the professor, perhaps because you equate evocativeness with vagueness. Regretfully, a common mistake in poetry. I am talking to you about precision. Young poets on the whole lack precision. They consider it commonplace and prefer to perform pirouettes. Only when they are older do they begin to appreciate restraint, nuance. There is nothing tiresome, much less easy about it, do you understand? We quite understand, said Hans, it is what academics call correctness, and some of us others term the fear of making a mistake.

Fear of making a mistake, Hans had said, probing Sophie's shape, her luminosity, her eyes. And she, rather than avoid his gaze or busy herself with some object on the table, had stood up straight and replied: Yet fear of making a mistake, Monsieur Hans, is also the prerogative of poets.

My dear Professor, said Álvaro smiling, you remind me of Don Ignacio de Luzán's lawyer. I don't know this *Lutsan*, said Professor Mietter. There is no need, Álvaro quipped, you are his Saxon counterpart! Instinctively taking offence, Professor Mietter said: I don't know how you say this in Spanish, Herr *Urquiho*, but allow me to tell you the French expression for what some of you appear to be defending—*culte de la pose*. Listen, Professor, resumed Hans, still agitated after his and Sophie's recent exchange of glances, it is true there is a surfeit of rhetorical poetry. But the way to avoid this is not by following convention, but by refusing to conform. Rebelliousness may be aesthetically naive, but to me nonconformism is essential. And the problem with good taste is that it conforms. It doesn't conform, Professor Mietter objected, it *renounces*. It renounces clever ideas, innovation for its own sake. The best way to be original, as I said before, is to learn from the Classics. Yes, replied Hans, but the Classics themselves were daring! What was once brilliantly daring is now called harmonious, proper, etc … I am not against the Classics, Professor, far from it! I am against imitation. Your beloved ancient poets weren't copying anyone, so why should we? In the end every imitation is a betrayal of the original. Obviously, Professor Mietter sighed, the great works bore Herr Hans, they are too slight for a mind as inventive as his. And yet since Aristotle, Herr Levin pointed out, raising a finger, the norms have always been the basis of all art. I disagree, said Hans. So, Professor Mietter almost snapped, now our young writer doesn't think norms are necessary either? Not necessary, said Hans, unavoidable. The literary norms that interest me aren't the necessary ones, which are imposed, but the unavoidable ones, that is the ones each of us encounter in the act of writing. The former are dictated by prejudice, the latter by personal experience. You forget, the professor pointed out, that all personal experience feeds on collective traditions, shared principles that have survived thanks to. I haven't forgotten, Hans cut in, because that is also unavoidable. But being aware of those principles is one thing, and perpetuating them is another. I find it far more pleasurable to disobey them, to attempt to change them.

(Change principles? Disobey them? *Pleasurable*? Sophie mused as she held out a tray of canapés to Frau Levin.)

I am not suggesting changing one set of norms for another, Hans went on. Have no fear, Professor, my literary ideal is not to see young writers tear down the old norms and replace them with their own dogmas. My aim would be to steer clear of all previous definitions, to regard style as an eternal search, don't you see? You say this now, ventured Professor Mietter, because we are in a period of transition. When things become clearer you will see how this misguided impulse of yours was transitional. The thing is, for me, Hans said, raising his voice, all poets are transitional, because poetry is in constant motion.

(Suddenly, Álvaro, distracted by the continuous movement of Elsa's foot, began once more to pay attention to the discussion. Whenever his friend became involved in a debate about literature, he tried to listen, because he knew it was the only way Hans had of talking about himself. That fellow needs his head examining, thought Álvaro, he makes a living from translating and he needs translating himself.)

Be that as it may, Professor Mietter was saying in the meantime, but not all taste is relative, or perhaps you don't believe some taste is more worthy of respect? That, I regret to tell you, shows a lack of judgement. Or is sheer demagoguery. Naturally, no one denies that taste can be discerning or ignorant, said Hans. Relativity does not mean an end to criteria, it merely contrasts different criteria. If you will allow me to make a political parallel, Professor, it is a matter of avoiding the centralisation of taste. Since I hope literature will remain a republic, I prefer a federalism of aesthetics. And yet, young man—Professor Mietter gave a forced laugh—like the monarchist ideal, aesthetics obey a natural hierarchy and are not subject to the whims of a sovereign taste. And a good poet, as a subject of his art, must learn to respect the nature of things. It is the same for any artist, once he has matured. A painter, for instance, has a landscape before him. He may vary the colours, play with the light, experiment with texture, do whatever he likes. Yet the most honest approach would be to overcome his vanity and immerse himself in the reality he is contemplating, surrender to it, attempt to paint what he sees at that very moment. Naturally this implies a great sacrifice and a supreme technical challenge. Consequently many will choose to paint this landscape as best they can, or in the simplest way possible, claiming it was intentional. That is how things are today. And apparently you approve.

Turning away in frustration, Hans's eye fell once more upon the painting hanging next to the old family portraits, the copies of Titian, the still-lifes and the hunting scenes. It showed the back view of a figure walking in a snow-covered forest, lost or perhaps leaving somewhere. Noticing his interest in the painting, Sophie explained: We don't know whom it is by, my grandfather left it to us and the signature is illegible. It's wonderful, Hans said smiling, and since we are on the subject, Professor, let us compare the figure in the snow with, I don't know, one of the other paintings, with that one, yes, no, the one next to it, the hunting scene. Well now, academic poets suffer from the same problem as second-rate landscape artists—they give too much importance to observing nature, respecting forms, and it turns out these *realist* landscapes are based on a hundred similar paintings or theories of painting rather than on the landscape itself! I think if a painter looks at nature without any preconceptions it can seem far stranger than any of those supposedly faithful reproductions. To me a patch of fog seems more real than a precise outline. I do not defend imagination because I find reality uninteresting; on the contrary I want to know how far that reality can take us, how deeply we are able to fathom a landscape. Consider for a moment which painter is more of a realist, the one who paints outlines or the one who paints blotches? The poet who avoids ambiguity or who reveals the chaos of language?

Herr Hans, Professor Mietter replied coolly, you are confusing technique with subject matter. Or style with poetics. Irrespective of whether you like the snowscape and I prefer others—not the hunting scene, naturally—you are not playing fair, because that painting is ghastly, irrespective of our individual taste, the function of art is to examine the world, not the artist. Ah! Hans countered gleefully, but *objective* observers forget they are part of the very world they are studying! People's emotions play a part in reality, they give it shape! You are contradicting yourself, Professor Mietter protested. That is fortunate, Professor, that is fortunate, Hans replied, contradictions help create the landscape. If you will, Professor Mietter sighed, yet you repeatedly contradict yourself. You defend what is rational and what is mysterious in the same breath. You find norms too restrictive, yet you like exhaustive criticism. It is impossible to know what your principles are. Pray forgive me, said Hans, an orthodoxy such as yours is not within reach of all of us. In my view contradiction is sincere, it links extremes which examined in isolation are incomprehensible. Moreover, obscurity or mystery seem to me most reasonable for a writer, because faced with them his reason must work harder. Am I contradicting myself? I don't know, I abide by Schlegel when he says: "Poetry is a discourse that proposes its own laws, and its elements are free citizens who must give their opinion in order for an agreement to be reached". How curious, said Professor Mietter mockingly, that a rebel such as you should turn so readily to the Enlightenment.

Gentlemen, gentlemen, Sophie decided to intervene, it is twenty minutes before midnight, and I assume that my father and Monsieur Wilderhaus will come out of the study at any moment to say goodnight. Let us tone down the debate, I suggest we drink a toast, Elsa my dear, could you bring the liqueur? … So that we can await them, glasses raised. As for you, Monsieur

Hans (Sophie said at last, relaxing the tension in her thighs, unaware that her expression betrayed her preferences), I beg you, calm your temperament a little and clink glasses with the professor. That is what I like to see, gentlemen. Why, deep down you are as alike as two peas in a pod!

The Levins took advantage of the lull to leave. Álvaro, unusually, followed suit. Hans understood the reason for his early departure and he flashed him a wink of gratitude that only Elsa, the quick-witted Elsa noticed—by leaving the gathering together with the two other guests, Álvaro was trying to force Professor Mietter's departure in order to leave his friend alone with Sophie. However, the professor did not stir, but settled back in his chair as if to show he had all night ahead of him.

The sweet flow of liqueur relaxed the debate, but not its focus. The professor gave his best smile, which was small and sceptical, before continuing to play off classical and modern authors, insisting that a study of tradition was the only way towards a renaissance of national literature. He cited Goethe as an example, preaching that his return to classicism was a lesson in wisdom. Hans, while inventing any excuse to brush his hand against Sophie's (reaching for a napkin, putting down his glass of liqueur, nudging a candlestick), stuck to his guns, alternately objecting and clapping Professor Mietter gently on the shoulder, a gesture to which the professor responded with the face of someone sucking on a lemon. On the subject of a renaissance of German literature, Hans argued that with regard to respecting national traditions Goethe, thank God, was a perfect example of the opposite, for all he had done was to assimilate foreign authors. Sophie was careful to prevent any friction (except between her and Hans's hands), employing a strategy that often proved successful—mitigating Hans's opinions by summarising them for him. This kept both men happy—the professor because he presumed Sophie disapproved of Hans's forcefulness and was attempting to show him the tone he ought to adopt when speaking to the professor; and Hans, who understood that by choosing to explain his point of view to the professor, she was taking his side.

My dear, excellent Professor, said Sophie, I don't believe Monsieur Hans means to renounce our great masters, which as you say would be unjust, but to go a step further. Not to forget young Werther's suicide, as it were, but to encourage him to live. So, Professor Mietter said with surprise, don't you admire Werther for dying of love like every other young lady your age? Sophie replied, lowering her tone when she noticed Hans staring at her intently: If you want my honest opinion, I think the poor man takes his life so he doesn't have to love a real woman. He prefers to torment himself rather than act out of true desire. (How can she say this when that idiot of a husband-to-be is at the far end of the corridor and she has made no effort to stop the marriage, to admit to herself she does not love him, to rub her leg against mine yet again under the table?) Werther's decision never moved me, dear Professor, because I find the moral of the story, in the end, repressive. (What about you? Hans thought jealously. What about you!) I prefer Schlegel's *Lucinde* or *The Flowering of Sentiment* by Madame Mereau, which Perthes has published and which is extremely interesting. I find any everyday scene between Albert and Nanette, or Lucinde and Julius, more admirable than Werther finally pulling the trigger. (Then why, Schlegel be damned, don't you bring your thigh a little closer?) An artificial passion, agreed the professor, it is typical—Werther shot himself while his author went on holiday. In any case, Goethe was still very young. (Or already far ahead of his time! thought Hans, but he did not say so because he thought her thigh had moved closer.)

And what about the *Roman Elegies*, Mademoiselle? asked Professor Mietter, a Faustian look on his face. Ah, replied Sophie,

I find the *Elegies* extraordinary, there, you see, reason and passion aren't in opposition, tradition and, well, pleasure coexist, what do you think, Herr Hans? I find the poems at once masterful and intolerable. Why intolerable? she asked. Because the *Elegies*, said Hans, do not celebrate antiquity, or Rome, or even love. In fact they celebrate a much older, obsolete idea—that of the home. Please! protested the professor, don't be childish! What Goethe did in Italy was to finish Werther off, to show that his previous torments were senseless. Or are you going to tell us now that Goethe was a coward for running off with a tavern wench instead of joining the revolutionaries? On the contrary! On the contrary! replied Hans. That was the only brave thing he ever did! Calm yourselves, please, gentlemen, Sophie implored. As for *Elective Affinities* (she began saying when she suddenly heard a door opening at the far end of the corridor and the two voices approaching), I confess the ending was not to my taste either. Mademoiselle Gottlieb (smiling mischievously, Hans pretended to be shocked), the man she loves is married! Yes, yes, of course (Sophie went on, unnerved by the approach of her father's footsteps, the creak of Rudi's patent-leather shoes, the feeling Hans was pressing her to say too much), but once again the character has to sacrifice his feelings, why in so many novels does moral duty oppose? (Rudi walked into the drawing room followed by Herr Gottlieb's pipe.) Father! My darling! We missed you both, what is the reason for these long private talks? Have you so many things to say to Rudi behind my back? (Hans, instinctively, pushed his chair away from the table and folded his hands.)

On the way to the front door, while Herr Gottlieb and Rudi were saying goodbye to the professor, Hans took the opportunity to exchange a few words with Sophie. I was intrigued (he whispered, casting a sidelong glance at Rudi) by your defence of feeling in the face of marital duty. I am not sure you are in the best position to make such an argument. Sophie pulled a face. Then she lifted her chin and replied coldly: Be very careful, Herr Hans, not to confuse literary criticism with impertinence.

With this she turned on her heel and went to join in saying goodnight to Professor Mietter. She took her fiancé's arm, and did not speak to Hans again until Herr Gottlieb bade them goodbye and closed the door.

The afternoon sun waned indecisively. Leaden clouds hung in the sky, stirring like curtains trapped in a door, until a strong gust shifted them. The organ grinder narrowed his eyes and gazed at the horizon. He moved his hand in front of his face, delighting in the flickering shapes, the light passing between his fingers. The spring evenings were still timid in Wandernburg. Suddenly he found Hans even more so, as they sat facing the pinewood and he described to him in hushed tones, without looking at him, events of that Friday.

I really put my foot in it this time, said Hans. I don't know why I said that to her, I suppose I was trying to provoke her or something, to get a rise out of her, I don't know! It was incredibly stupid of me, what could the poor girl do with her father and that other fellow there? How could I think such a? How conceited of me to? Did I expect her to say yes and fall into my arms? Incredibly, incredibly stupid! (No, Hans, the old man remarked, you were simply impatient, stop tormenting yourself.) Yes, but now I think I've scared her away, I forced her to react and she seems to have done so by distancing herself, understandably (but how long is it since she last spoke to you? said the old man), not very long, in fact, three or four days, the thing is, I know this sounds foolish, but before that we would write to one another every day, so you see this silence must mean something (yes, of course, replied the old man, it means she's keeping silent. Not that she's never going to speak to you again, maybe she's thinking about what to say to you), I envy you your optimism, organ grinder, I think I put my foot in it and got my just desserts. (And why don't you write to her?) Me? Now? After what happened? (Yes and no, that is, write to her yes, but not straight away, wait a few more days, when she stops being annoyed I'm sure she'll start worrying that you aren't talking to her either, and then if you write apologising you'll see how glad she is.) Do you think so? (Yes, now stop fretting and look, bring your hand up, see how it looks like the clouds are passing through your fingers?)

Reichardt came to see if they had anything to eat in the cave. Although the organ grinder only had a few potatoes, dumplings and some fruit, he invited him to supper. Hans offered to fetch provisions from the inn and bring them back in a tilbury. The organ grinder refused. You came here today to talk, didn't you? he said. Friends talk, you needn't always bring gifts. On hearing his master, Franz gave an abrupt bark, which sounded like a hungry clarification.

No, Reichardt explained to Hans as he munched a potato, previously I was employed on several estates; you stayed on until they threw you out or you found a better-paid job. The trouble is now—any more dumplings? Thanks—none of the estate managers will hire me full-time, they say I'm too old. So every week I go to the market square touting for work, I talk to the farmers who are there selling produce and if I'm lucky they offer me a day's labour, or more, weeding, tilling, sowing, you know. The worst thing isn't when you stand there waiting to be hired and they look at you as if you were a dried up turd, it's ending the day wondering if you'll get any more work. I feel healthy, bah, I manage, I'm still strong enough to shift heavy sacks, the thing is you're out there surrounded by other labour-ers and you say to yourself: Is this my last day? I don't mean here on earth, I couldn't care less about that, when I die, well, it'll be good riddance, an end to all my problems! The thing is finishing a day's work and remembering how hard it was to get hired and thinking next time will be even harder. Working in the fields does my back in but I like it, why do anything else if that's what I've always done? Hey, are there any apples left? Pity. On top of that, those bastards see you're a bit past it and sometimes they don't pay you in money, which is better because you can save it, they pay you in leftover produce, it's true, Hans, it's true, but what can you do? Tell them to hire someone else, tell them to stick their vegetables up their stingy arses? So you accept whatever they give you, thank them, stuff it in your bag and go home. Where do I live? Over by the cornfields in one of those mud huts with the other labourers. No, of course I don't, not even an acre! The land belongs to the Church, but since they don't use it they let us live there and charge a tribute per hut. I swear on my eight good teeth these bloody tithes will be the death of us, apart from the priests we pay a tax to the landowners, the principality and I don't know what else. No, the farmers don't own the land either, they're tenants and pay the landowners a tithe for the harvest and for the livestock, you see? The same old families, the Trakls, the Wilderhauses, the Rumenigges, the Ratztrinkers' cousins, they're all the same. Who me? Leave here? Never. Well, when I was a youngster I thought of looking for work elsewhere, at the port in Danzig or in some factory up north. But in the end, you know it's not so easy to leave Wandernburg. Besides, this is my home, isn't it? I shouldn't have to leave, they're the bastards, I shouldn't have to go looking in some other bloody place. Do you know how Herr Wilderhaus used to treat us, Hans? No, not him, the father. Because, I don't know if you've seen him, now he looks like a rheumatic old man, but you should have seen the bastard before, son of a whore! In those days he'd show up in the fields whenever he felt like it and say: "Harness four horses,

I'm going to the ball." And we'd reply: "Sire, we're harvesting the grain and it's nearly dark." And he'd say: "I don't give a turd if it's late or blowing a gale! I told you, I'm going to the ball, now harness four horses. Besides, the grain is mine and you'll harvest it when I say so." That's how he spoke, rolling his *rrrr*s like a brute, ha*rrrr*mess fou*rrrr* ho*rrrr*ses this instant, and those of us who had to do it hu*rrrr*ied, how we hu*rrrr*ied to do that bastard's bidding! No, no, Herr Wilderhaus was a kitten in comparison to some of them! Do you know what old Rumenigge did to the daughters of the, bah, what's the difference, he's dead now, to hell with him. And so we saddled up the horses and d*rrrr*ove him to the ball. Which I'm sure you've guessed was no ball, although we had to swear on our lives that we would always call it d*rrrr*iving him to the ball! Grapes, thanks, Franz, you rogue, I can see you! I know. You're right there. Well, don't be too sorry about it, Hans, because that's not the worst thing. What's worse by far for a man my age is wishing things hadn't changed, do you understand, because nowadays there's less and less need for labourers, one man can do the work of five and the farmers prefer young men because they say we older men don't know how to work the machines. Machines, they say! I was already tilling these fields with my eyes shut before they'd even taken a shit in them! In the old days we let them lie fallow for three years, we didn't have all that irrigation and fertilisers and things. Now they rotate the crops, alternating cereal with hay and God knows what. And anything left over they throw away, just like that, they throw it away! Otherwise prices will go down, they say. That is, yes, the new machines are very intelligent, very well thought out my eye. And I say: What's to become of us? If I'm no good for working in the fields, what am I good for? Take the English planting and sowing machines. A lot of farmers make you use them now, they say this thing can plant and cover the seeds simultaneously, that it saves time. It saves time? The earth has its own time. I've never needed a machine to show me where to make a furrow or where the thistle root is, how to walk between the ridges, what colour ripe grain is, the way corn ears smell when the harvest is bad, none of that. Isn't this the same soil my father and grandfather worked? Haven't I been tilling and sowing here for fifty years? Who's telling me I don't know how any more? Where do they want me to go?

Reichardt stopped talking and gazed out towards the darkening fields.

As the weather grew warmer, shadows and figures began popping up in the corridors of the inn. Hans would meet them on the stairs. He didn't know who they were, he didn't know their names, he never spoke to them, but their elusive presence made him feel accompanied. Frau Zeit seemed suddenly thinner and her movements had acquired the invisible force of the breeze when it blows in through the window. After breakfast, for which Hans was seldom up in time, Lisa went off carrying a basket piled with dirty linen to wash in the unfrozen river. Herr Zeit had begun rising a little earlier—he would eat breakfast with his family then invariably go out on some errand, as though the sun were a long-awaited pretext. He would walk Thomas to school and come back for lunch. It was obvious from the glassy look in his eyes that he had stopped off at more than one tavern.

Good morning! It's Wednesday, already! Herr Zeit greeted Hans as he walked past reception. Did you sleep well? Me? said Hans. Yes, quite well, why? We're not used to seeing you up before midday, the innkeeper said, grinning mysteriously. Actually, said Hans, I came down to ask whether the postman had brought anything for me. For you? the innkeeper asked in surprise. No, nothing. Are you sure? said Hans, looking worried. Absolutely, the innkeeper replied trying to hold in his belly to seem more plausible. But he did come today, didn't he? Hans insisted, I mean, the post from Leipzig comes on Wednesdays, doesn't it? Certainly, said Herr Zeit, the mail coach from Leipzig arrived this morning and drove straight past the door without stopping. Hans sighed. His shoulders sank. Then he regained his composure, took a deep breath, and left the inn bidding them good day.

At a quarter to four in the afternoon, fifteen minutes earlier than the arranged hour, Hans had knocked at the door to the Gottlieb residence and Bertold had accompanied him into the drawing room. Hans had asked whether the master of the house was at home so that he could pay his respects, and Bertold had replied that unfortunately he had gone out calling and would be back late. After a few minutes of fretful waiting, Hans wondered whether Sophie was getting ready in her bedroom or whether she was inflicting a small revenge on him. However, as soon as the long hand of the clock struck four, he heard the swish of Sophie's skirt at the other end of the corridor. Hans leapt to his feet, sat down on the sofa, then stood up again. Good afternoon, Sophie said entering the room, may it be stated for the record that you are the one who is unpunctual.

Burying his nose in his teacup and peering over its rim, Hans studied Sophie more closely and realised that this time her expression was untranslatable—was she offended or on guard? Was that smile of hers sardonic or amused? Hans folded his legs, she unfolded hers. He clasped his hands on his knee, she unclasped hers, resting them in her lap. Hans frowned, as though about to speak, she raised her eyebrows as though preparing to listen. So, you read … Hans ventured. Yes, Sophie replied, I read your letter, which is why I asked you to come here. In any case, he continued, well, I'd like to take the opportunity, as we are here, to apologise once again for the way I spoke to you the other evening, I honestly didn't mean, I assure you, at no time did I imagine, that it, it wasn't my. Don't trouble yourself, she interrupted, you already explained all that in your letter. And are you still angry with me? he said.

Angry? Sophie repeated, and her question reverberated like a tuning fork. She glanced about, making sure neither Elsa nor Bertold were in the room. Then she did something so swift that Hans was only able to see it clearly in his memory, rather than when it actually happened:

Sophie leant forward.

She remained erect, poised.

She bent her body over the low table.

She brought her face close to his.

She collided with his lips.

She offered him her warm, determined tongue, which disarranged his mouth.

Swift, undulating.

She withdrew her face.

She tilted backwards.

She settled back in her chair, gazing at him unruffled.

Hans's reply was a stammer. His mouth was awash with flavours. His blood was on fire. Sophie's manner scarcely helped dispel his disbelief—she was watching him, completely serene, as though for a moment he had let his fantasies carry him away, and on resuming their conversation had discovered everything in its place, including Sophie, who was sitting still listening to him. What was most excruciating and delicious was how long their silence lasted. Sophie gave no sign of adding anything. Hans thought of a hundred words and they all dissolved on his tongue. That kiss didn't seem to accept any commentary.

Are you sorry? Hans finally managed to say. Because I'd quite understand, believe me, I mean, if it was just a sudden whim, I promise I'll pretend it never happened, you needn't worry, I don't mind, you know, these things, well they're normal between friends, they can happen to anyone, can't they?

Sophie's eyes narrowed, as she shrugged off the flood of unnecessary comments, still savouring the earlier silence. She gave a slow smile. And then she hurled herself at Hans in order to kiss him again, only this time much more violently, deeply and lingeringly. She bit his lip, he clasped her neck.

When they drew apart, Hans could see the strange expression on Sophie's face, and thought she was worried someone might surprise them.

But it wasn't concern that made Sophie look like that. It was the sweet ache in her groin.

At first glance Café Europa was just another reflection in the string of shop windows in Glass Walk, the place where all the city's glaziers were crammed together. Anyone walking down the narrow street had the impression they were being mesmerised, for each shop window was reflected in the ones opposite, and on a sunny day they became so superimposed it was difficult to be sure which door to walk through. Or at least that was Hans's experience whenever he went to Glass Walk to have a cup of hot chocolate, wake himself up with an umpteenth coffee or browse the newspapers.

Café Europa was the only place in Wandernburg, where, besides the skimpy pages of the *Thunderer*, one could read above all the French press, as well as the broadsheets from Berlin, Munich, Dresden and Hamburg. On his first visit there, Hans was surprised to discover among the magazine racks the cultural supplement of the *Morning News* and even an issue of the *Jena Literary Review*. As occasional out-of-date issues of the *Gazette* or the *Daily Bulletin* would arrive from Madrid, Álvaro was in the habit of going there to do his weekly business accounts. The moment he opened a newspaper from his native country he would begin railing against King Ferdinand or censorship. Even so he would continue to devour them with an avidity Hans found strange and moving in equal measure—his friend couldn't leave Wandernburg, yet he had never left Spain either. During the afternoons they spent reading in the café, Álvaro would bring Hans cuttings from *Spanish Pastimes* and other publications written by exiles in London that he received. He passed the time comparing news items and gesticulating furiously while his coffee grew cold.

That Saturday, they were sitting at one of Café Europa's round marble tables conversing in the soft glow of the oil lamps. At the other end of the room two billiard tables shone dimly beneath a halo of smoke. Álvaro had folded his newspaper and was once again telling Hans that he was behaving oddly, by turns elated and anxious. The fact is he was right. Apart from the organ grinder, Hans had spoken to no one about what had happened at the Gottliebs' house on Wednesday afternoon. Not even to Sophie herself. Nor had he spoken of her most recent letters, replete with double entendres and insinuations. Hans sensed he had no need to explain his excitement to Álvaro, and that somehow he had known what was happening from the start. As for what was making him anxious, Hans decided to be frank.

I'm embarrassed to tell you this, Hans admitted, but the fact is I'm running out of money. (Really? Álvaro was surprised. Why didn't you say so?) I told you, I was embarrassed, and I didn't want to think too much about it either, I suppose I was hoping for a stroke of luck. Up until now I always did things in the same way—I worked, saved and traveled until I ran out of funds, then I started all over again. But things changed since I came here, I stayed longer than I should, I've been careless with money, and now I can't expect that (of course you can, dear fellow! Álvaro protested, dropping his cup into its saucer. How much do you need?) No, truly, I'm grateful, but a loan won't solve my problem. (What will then?) A piece of good news. Yes, don't pull that face, I've been waiting for it for days. If it arrives, all will be well. If not, then, within eight or ten days at most I'll positively have to go to Dessau, talk to Herr Lyotard and look for work there. (At least let me tide you over! What are friends for!) Friends, my dear Urquijo, are there to listen, which is what you've been doing and, believe me, that's enough of a help. I'm relieved to have got it off my chest. But now I beg you let's not talk about it any more, and don't insist on lending me money—if my situation doesn't change, I shan't be able to pay you back, and if it does then I won't need it.) *Cabrón*, muttered Álvaro, patting him on the back, how well you pronounce my Basque surname! Rather better, Hans grinned, than your pronunciation of our German names. Álvaro gave one of his booming laughs. Then he straightened up in his chair and said with a solemn air: Just let me ask you one question, how much do you have left? How much? Hans sighed, gazed up at the ceiling, appeared to calculate among the rafters, and quoted a sum. Not one thaler more? exclaimed Álvaro, alarmed. Are you sure? What about the inn? Don't worry, said Hans, next week is paid for, we'll see if it's my last. And changing the subject: Do you dare to beat me at billiards again?

That evening, while they were dining together at the Central Tavern, two big lemon-scented hands alighted on their backs. They turned to discover Rudi Wilderhaus's closely shaven chin. Forgive me, gentlemen, he said, if I didn't greet you before. On the contrary, said Hans stiffly, we are the ones who apologise for not having seen you. That's only natural, replied Rudi, my table is at the back. I always reserve that one because it's the quietest, why do people always crowd around the entrance? There isn't a learned man in all Germany who can tell you, but there it is, gentlemen, they won't walk more than a few paces!

With this, Rudi began to laugh, closing one eye and watching Hans and Álvaro through the other to see if they were joining in. The two men exchanged glances, gave a few forced sniggers, and then, on seeing Rudi's ludicrous expression, suffered a genuine fit of laughter. In any case, gentlemen, Rudi said gesturing towards the table at the other end of the tavern, I'd be pleased if you'd agree to join us. They turned around and could make out the glowing cigars of Herr Gelding and his partners.

What a pleasant surprise, Herr Gelding said in greeting. Gentlemen, I believe you already know Herr *Urquiho*, who represents our distributors in London. Herr *Urquiho*, I can't remember if I've introduced you to Herr Klinsman, ah yes, I pointed him out to you, I thought as much, and what about Herr Voeller? But do have a seat, please, have a seat, our distinguished Herr Wilderhaus here has just been telling us that you and he attend the same salon, who would have thought it! By Jove, a literary salon, why, Herr *Urquiho*, you really are a dark horse.

In the middle of the table was roast chicken on a platter, together with a dish of seasoned endives and a bowl of strawberries. *Prost!* Herr Gelding belched, picking up a strawberry between thumb and forefinger and dipping it in his tankard of beer. Herr Gelding's remarks seemed to amuse Rudi, although he wrinkled his brow with each belch. Soon the others at the table, including Álvaro, began talking business. Rudi and Hans remained silent, sizing each other up like opponents across a chessboard. (Bah! one of Herr Gelding's partners suddenly exclaimed. Don't talk to me about Varnhagen, he's only good for charging in advance and paying late!) The more affable Rudi was towards him, the more uneasy Hans became—why did he insist on smiling at him when they had never liked each other? Why did Rudi refresh his tankard as soon as it was half-empty? Was he trying to make him drunk? Did he know something, did he want to know something? (Don't go all charitable on me Herr *Urquiho*, please! Herr Gelding chuckled. At this rate the labourers will be better off than us, mark my words, my grandfather was a labourer so I know what I'm talking about, things were far tougher in those days! So don't come to me with that, we need men, do you hear, men, but all their sons have trades now, they learn to read and write!) In spite of everything, from a sense of male pride of which Hans deep down felt ashamed, he drank all the beer he was served, as though refusing would not only be churlish but would give Rudi a reason to mistrust him. As the alcohol began slowly to permeate his consciousness, Hans had the impression that his memories were also liquid sloshing round in a tankard, a frothy substance splashing at the rim, and that his secrets could be viewed through a glass. (Let's be clear, said one of Herr Gelding's partners, everyone deserves respect, just so long as we the management are respected, everyone wants their say without even having an income of a hundred ducats.) Now Rudi was speaking to him, speaking to him earnestly, too earnestly, and his hand was creeping over his shoulder, like a spider, thought Hans. (That's a good one! Herr Gelding belched as he brought his hand down on the table.) Rudi placed his hand on Hans's shoulder and began talking to him about horses and hunting. (Don't even think about it! one of Herr Gelding's partners declared. While prices continue to go down it's best not to raise one's expectations.) He spoke in a soft voice and told him he was also a traveler and how much he appreciated men of the world, that he already knew half of Europe and soon he would see the rest, God and my health permitting, said Rudi, soon I'll see the other half with my wife Sophie, and it'll give us great pleasure to write to you, she tells me that as well as being a good friend you are an excellent letter writer, an admirable quality, I like men who appreciate the value of words.

At midnight, alone once more, Hans and Álvaro zigzagged down Potter's Lane. They were headed for the Picaro Tavern, where on Saturdays young women would dance without any of the affectations of the Apollo Theatre, to the strains of a small orchestra. Hey, you, Hans spluttered, how can you tolerate them? Who? said Álvaro. Oh them, it's very simple, my dear, very simple—I never mix business with pleasure; that's something I learnt in England. Before I knew that I was a little nobler and a lot poorer, *if you see what I mean*! And I'm telling you, Hans said distractedly, we've gone past it, seriously, isn't it farther back? In that other street, I mean. No, replied Álvaro, how can it be back there? Just follow me, come on! I swear, Hans went on, whenever those men open their mouths it makes me long for the cave. Your organ grinder is a strange bird, said Álvaro, sometimes he talks as if he knows everything, and other times I look at him and he seems like a poor old man in a cave. The organ grinder knows everything, replied Hans, don't ask me how, but he does. It's very odd, insisted Álvaro, I don't know where he gets it from, have you ever seen him read? Does he have any books in the cave? Never, replied Hans, he never reads, he has no time for books or newspapers. When he isn't playing his barrel organ, he's gazing at the landscape. When I'm with him I feel a little stupid, as if I'd read everything without having read anything, sorry, did I tread on your foot? Are you sure we're going the right way?

The Picaro Tavern was a place where no sooner people entered than the rhythm of the polka and the smell of sweat invited them to relax and cast their cares aside. Anyone who crossed its threshold with a heavy gait left with a spring in his step, wondering what had come over him. The clientele was mixed, everyone except the aristocracy, who preferred more discreet establishments farther from the centre, where they paid much more money to do the same things. On the chalkboard hanging next to a warped mirror, a message (complete with misspellings) announced: "The Picaro Tavern welcomes not ladies and gentlemen, but men and women." The police never interfered with the tavern's activities, provided it closed at three in the morning, held no parties during religious holidays and, in accordance with the Rules Governing Public Places of Free Admission in Wandernburg, its patrons did not wear masks. It was not uncommon after suppertime to find off-duty policemen in the tavern.

As they stepped through the tavern doors, an image of the organ grinder gazing through his fingers at the sun flashed though Hans's mind. He grinned drunkenly and missed him foolishly, as though he had not seen him in years. He thought instantly: Tomorrow I'll go to see him. They descended into the gloomy Picaro Tavern, looking for a place to sit. Suddenly, Hans thought he recognised somebody's back—a stocky figure, hunched over, muscles tensed as though suffering from cramp. The figure instinctively wheeled round and faced him—it was Lamberg, wearing an old mask that covered his eyes and half his brow. Opposite him, at a safe distance, a waiter was trying to persuade him to take it off. Lamberg appeared not to hear him. His arms hung at his sides, tensed, as though pushing down on a spring. For a moment, Hans thought Lamberg was going to tip up a chair or punch the waiter. But all he did was to stagger, tear off his mask, walk over to Hans and embrace him wholeheartedly. His face stank of stale alcohol, his back was rigid. After flashing Hans a look of relief, the waiter disappeared among the dancers. What were you doing wearing that mask? Álvaro asked, coming over. Lamberg slowly raised his head from Hans's shoulder, and said: I just wanted it to be Carnival. With that, he burst into tears for a few moments. He soon calmed down and remained silent, expressionless. Come on, Hans said, we'll buy you a drink.

They approached the bar and ordered three schnapps from the same waiter who had been arguing with Lamberg. The waiter looked at him askance, but Lamberg seemed to be concentrating on something on the ceiling. While the waiter was pouring out their drinks, a candle dropped from one of the cast iron wagon-wheel chandeliers above the bar straight onto his shirt, setting his sleeve alight. The waiter leapt into the air and began flailing his arm about. The bottle of schnapps spilt onto the bar. The customers standing nearby turned their heads. Álvaro and Hans yelled. Someone ran over with a siphon to spray the waiter, who was glaring at Lamberg with a mixture of loathing and bewilderment. Lamberg was still silent, his eyes fixed on the waiter's shirt.

The cave dissolved the remains of the heat like a stomach digesting soup. During the past few weeks the interior had offered a welcome contrast to the heat of midday and a buffer against the night air, which was still chilly. The organ grinder had lit two tallow candles and was examining the inside of his barrel organ. The strings, in groups of three, were looped around screws, the loops worn by the passage of time. The organ grinder adjusted the strings with a key, his bony hand turning it clockwise. Above the screws, written in pencil in the unsteady hand of an infant or one palsied with age, were the notes A, B, C, D ...

Hans was also spelling something out—his last meeting with Sophie at the salon on Friday. He was relaying all the details to the organ grinder, and although nothing was certain (even his next visit to the Gottlieb salon), these uncertainties seemed to diminish when he talked to the old man, as though every tuned string were an eventuality foretold, a doubt resolved. Since their snatched kiss that day, Sophie had been as discreet towards him in person as she had been audacious in her letters. They had not seen one another alone since then, which far from seeming to Hans a bad sign, suggested something was afoot. What flowers were in the house? the organ grinder asked, glancing up with a pin between his lips. What flowers? Spikenards, I think. Spikenards?—the organ grinder gave a start—Are you sure? I think so, replied Hans, they were white and pungent, they must have been spikenards, why, what does it mean? It means, the old man said, smiling as he lowered the lid, pleasure, pleasure and danger.

The moon was growing bigger and as round as a peephole in a door. Although at that moment, as Franz was lifting his leg on a pine tree, no one in the whole of Wandernburg was gazing at it, just as no one was gazing at the clock on the Tower of the Wind, or noticing it looked like the moon with clock hands. On the outskirts, however, Hans and the organ grinder were sitting contemplating the night from the entrance to the cave. Before he met the organ grinder, Hans had never spent so much time gazing at the sky. Now he had grown accustomed to this calm activity that brought them together without the need to talk or do anything. The stars were few and spaced out, like a spray of salt. The two men looked at them in very different ways. Hans's expression before the vastness of the universe suggested restlessness, choice, an uncertain future. The organ grinder saw in the horizon a shelter, a protective boundary, an undivided present.

Hans murmured:

> *The stars and the night*
> *Make the wine of life*
> *Let's drink without strife*
> *Till like them we are light.*

What was that? asked the organ grinder. It's by Novalis, replied Hans. And who's he? said the old man. Him? said Hans with a grin. He's just a friend of mine. Ah, said the organ grinder, why don't you bring him along one evening?

Back in his room, despite having walked from the cave at a brisk pace, Hans was unable to fall asleep. Eels of sweat wriggled down his back. His body felt tense. Lying face-up, shirtless, he could hear every sound of the night, the roof beams, the furniture. His feet stirred restlessly. He was breathing through his mouth. Suddenly, he threw back the covers. His hand moved down to his groin. His member was stiff. He cast off the rest of his clothes. He felt the coolness of the air on his testicles and an ardent pressure at the tip of his manhood. He gripped his member and began pulling at it, pulling it almost resentfully. The skin responded like red elastic. A wave of intensity spread up from his groin. Hans bent his knees. His hand swelled. His blood was pulsating. His abdomen clenched. Everything flowed from below upwards. Hans was quaking. It had to come out. Now.

Behind the lace curtains, a breeze rippled through the half-open window. It was already late but Sophie's bedside light was still on. The room gave off a smell of oil—from the thick oil lamp, and from the almond odour of her skin. The clutter of hairbrushes, combs and powders on the dressing table was a sign of recent disquiet. A damp sponge lay on the side of the washstand, whose lower shelf housed a small pitcher, facecloths, aromatic water, a soap dish and two towels, one of which had been used moments before. To the left of the bed on an oval rug sat two small slippers, one on top of the other. To the right, a silk nightgown lay in a tangle on the floor. Sophie let one arm dangle from under the orange-coloured eiderdown, the other writhed beneath the covers. Her lips kept going dry and she had to lick them. She felt an invisible needle pricking her thighs, the tip of her breasts. She lifted her forefinger and thumb to her mouth, once, twice, she moistened them with her tongue. Then she went down again restraining, containing, enduring her sense of urgency. As the fingers slid down she left a trail of saliva from her mouth to her chin, her chin to her throat, from the hollow between her collarbones to her breast, from her breast to the bottom of her ribcage, from her there to her navel, and along the faint outline of her pubic hair to the rim of her clitoris. Its folds opened. The contractions radiated from the inside out. A darting hummingbird finger insisted and insisted. Sophie yielded to herself. She felt an emptiness inside an emptiness.

Hans sent her a billet in which he called her *Fräulein Fräulein*, and Sophie wrote back with the heading *Dear Silly-Billy*. He signed his letters *Respectfully, your future abductor* and she ended hers with the words *Until never, at seven o'clock, at my house.* He sent her a comb in an envelope with a note that said: *So that my memory is never far from your thoughts.* She replied by sending a lock of her hair wrapped in tissue paper with the words: *So you may see that your wish has been fulfilled.* They had tea together almost every afternoon and took the precaution, but also the risk, of including Herr Gottlieb in their conversations—it is easier to hide what is plainly visible. They derived a perverse pleasure from using the polite form of "you" while staring at one another like lovers. Sophie did not know, or did not want to know, what might happen. But she did know that while what had to happen was happening, what she wanted was not to think. She was officially betrothed, and did not intend to renege on any of her commitments, but that would be after the summer, and what did that matter now?

That Tuesday Hans had got up in two distinct moods. Much to his surprise he had woken early of his own accord. He had hummed a tune as he took a bath and shaved in front of the watercolour. Suddenly, however, he had found himself staring out of the window like someone recalling an accident. Seated on his trunk, he had steeled himself to do the sums he had been avoiding, and had concluded silently: Two, three at the most if I stop eating out. Afterwards, full of anticipation and trepidation, he had gone downstairs and looked enquiringly at Herr Zeit. The innkeeper had shrugged and sighed: No letter today, if it arrives I'll let you know.

He had spent the morning reading, and had lunched in the kitchen before going to the market square to see the organ grinder. He had gone without coffee to economise. Later on, he had called at the Gottlieb residence, but Sophie had just left with Rudi. After supper, not yet sleepy enough, he had gone for a night-time stroll down winding, unfamiliar streets, through High Gate, and along the path to the bridge and the pinewood. And, almost unwittingly, he found himself in front of the cave. Franz had greeted him with excited barks. The old man hadn't been sleeping, or claimed he hadn't. I brought you some cheese, Hans explained. Thank you, my lad, the old man had said, is anything the matter? No, Hans had replied, I don't know, I just came to bring you some cheese. The organ grinder had given him a bony embrace, cupped his face in his grimy hands and said: Tell me about it.

The following morning, bright and early, a loud clatter of hooves came to a halt outside the inn. The postman's horn surprised Herr Zeit, his razor halfway down one lathered cheek— two dark drops fell onto the towel draped around his neck. The innkeeper muttered a few curses in a thick Wandernburg dialect. When the horn sounded a second time, he thrust out his belly indignantly, sighed and called to his daughter. Go and see what he wants, he grunted, and wake up that sleepyhead in number seven. When Lisa opened the door, the postman stared at her with annoyance, and, without dismounting, threw her a sealed envelope he had taken out of his saddlebag. All around, upstairs and down, like street lights in the daytime, heads peered out of windows.

Lisa raced down the second-floor corridor, stopping just before she collided with Hans, who was still in his nightshirt and a woollen dressing gown. Hans smiled and said good morning. Lisa stared at Hans's cared-for teeth. She shivered when she saw his unshaven chin, covered in black dots, and without knowing why felt foolish. Will you give me the letter, Lisa? said Hans. The what? she replied. Oh yes, sorry.

Hans tore open the envelope and his eyes sped to the end of the letter. Before he had even finished reading it through, he had let it fall to the ground and was dressing as fast as he could.

After floating from side to side to the floor, the letter had come to rest next to the legs of a chair. The light from the window fell across half the page. On the part in the light, between a colophon featuring a bird and the heading, printed in capitals were the words:

BROCKHAUS BOOKS, LEIPZIG.

As at every lunchtime, the air in the Central Tavern was beginning to thicken with the smell of cooking oil and working men's clothes. For the first time in months, Hans had a feeling of benign compassion towards the Wandernburgers filling the establishment. So, you're staying? Álvaro rejoiced, clinking tankards with Hans. Hans nodded, beaming, his lips moist with beer. What a pity, *niño*! chuckled Álvaro. I was looking forward to seeing the back of you!

In the middle of April, when his savings had first shown signs of running low, Hans had written to the editors at Brockhaus offering his services as a reader and translator. He had enclosed an exhaustive (and partially invented) curriculum vitae and a few publications. In the inflated list of his talents, Hans had claimed to be able to translate into German, with varying degrees of competence depending on the case, any European language of literary significance. Despite his repeated exaggerations about his professional experience, this was not far from the truth. Hans proposed writing detailed reports on authors or books the publishing house might be interested in translating, prologues to their anthologies of foreign poetry, as well as translations of essays and poems for their magazine *Atlas*. And also, perhaps, if the publisher was interested, bringing out an anthology of European poets encompassing a broad range of languages and countries. Although their reply had taken a long time to arrive, to the point where Hans had begun to fear that some of the fictitious additions to his curriculum might have been uncovered, in the end it was encouraging—the publisher had recently lost two of his collaborators (one deceased, the other dismissed) and were indeed looking for a reliable reader and a more or less permanent translator. They agreed to employ him at once as a salaried assistant on their magazine *Atlas*. They also took him on as a reader for a one-month trial period. And they acknowledged his idea about a future anthology of European poetry, although they could give no assurances. The best news of all, given Hans's financial situation, was the inclusion in their acceptance letter of two urgent commissions, one generously remunerated (the other, in the editor's words, should be submitted without payment "as a sign of mutual goodwill"). As soon as he had received the reply, before going out to meet Álvaro at the Central Tavern, Hans had sat down to write two letters: the first, shorter one, was to Brockhaus, in the most casual tone possible, accepting his conditions; the second, a garbled, exhilarated note to Sophie giving her the good news. Afterwards, he had gone downstairs to reception and announced to the innkeeper: My dear Herr Zeit, I should like to speak to you for a moment about business. Following twenty minutes of calculation, recalculation, mutual haggling and theatrical protestations from the innkeeper, Hans had succeeded in reaching a new agreement for the monthly price of his lodgings plus one meal a day. (Two? Out of the question! Impossible! Do you have any idea, Herr Hans, how much the price of food has shot up! do you want to ruin me? Two meals, out of the question! Impossible!)

While Hans was finalising his agreement with the innkeeper, Sophie was shutting herself in her room so she could read the note she had just received. Lying face down on the orange taffeta eiderdown, ankles folded in the air, she couldn't help giving a cry of joy when she reached the part that said: ... *therefore, if all goes well, you will have no choice but to suffer my presence in Wandernburg for the time being.* On hearing her mistress, Elsa burst into the room to see what the matter was. Concealing the letter under a cushion, Sophie sat up nonchalantly and replied: Nothing at all, why? I thought I heard Miss cry out, said Elsa, puzzled. My dear, said Sophie, is it impossible to sneeze in this house without creating a scandal?

That very afternoon, after lunching with Álvaro and downing three black coffees in a row, Hans went back to his room, bounding up the stairs two at a time. He flung open the door. His eyes fixed on his trunk, he strode across the room. On the oak table were three thick volumes, some carbon paper and an ink pot with a closed lid. Hans knelt beside the trunk. He tried shifting it, confirming how heavy it was. He heaved a sigh. He ran his fingers along its curved top, then unfastened its locks and clasps one by one. Inside, stacks of books lay in disarray from all his travels. The first volumes he saw were his old Greek dictionary, a manual of Italian verbs, a slim book of poems by Novalis, and a dog-eared guide to French grammar.

Hans posted his manuscripts to Leipzig each week, back and forth, like the wind. The publisher remunerated his work with a money order Hans cashed at the Bank of Wandernburg, a square-shaped building of somewhat ostentatious neoclassical design at the end of Ducat Street. Each morning, spectral yellow carriages would depart from there escorted by a police guard. Establishing a work routine in Wandernburg felt at once strange and natural to Hans. The place still felt alien to him, as though he had only just arrived there, and was preparing to leave. And yet there were times when, wandering down an alleyway or crossing the market square, Hans would look up, and an unexpected feeling of harmony would overwhelm him—he liked the pointed towers, he was drawn in by the maze of curves and inclines. Then he would quicken his pace, trying to shake off this uncomfortable nesting instinct by telling himself no, he knew perfectly well he wouldn't stay long, remembering the hundreds of cities he had visited.

He would invariably rise at noon and go out to have a bite at the tavern, and, if he had time, meet Álvaro for a coffee (or three) at Café Europa, where they would sit browsing the newspapers and conversing, always about the same old thing, always about something else. Excepting Fridays, when he went to the salon, he would spend his afternoons in the Wandernburg public library or translating at the inn. Sometimes, usually on Sundays, Hans would go to the market square to listen to the organ grinder, and if he saw his dish was empty, he would wait for someone to stop and then begin dropping coins into it with theatrical zeal—coins the organ grinder invariably gave him back in the evening, the moment he arrived. Hans would have supper at the inn, translate or read for a while in his room and then head for the cave, where he would remain until dawn. And Sophie? Hans saw little of her and he never stopped seeing her—aside from the long Friday evenings, they would both improvise momentary meetings, arranged teas, casual encounters in the city centre, any excuse to see each other for a few moments. And then, of course, there were the letters, which traveled back and forth like the post, like the wind, like bilingual words in dictionaries, from Stag Street to Old Cauldron Street, and vice versa.

The Wandernburg public library, like most libraries, was ugly but loveable, inadequate yet indispensable. It was run by a plump young woman, who would laugh for no reason when consulted about anything, and who spent the day reading, an open book clutched in her hands, which looked like paper pulp. The library was also an ideal place to meet Sophie, who often went there to read books deemed unsuitable to be seen in the house. Besides candles, shelves and dust, the library was also home to a large collection of magazines, specialist almanacs, romances, travel, history and pedagogy, regional newspapers as well as every single back copy of Wandernburg's local newspaper.

The *Thunderer* consisted of four sheets of convoluted grammar and bombastic language. It reported almost exclusively on local news, recording in unbelievable detail precise minutes of municipal meetings, verbatim transcriptions of Mayor Ratztrinker's speeches, including repetitions, hesitations and mistakes, readers' complaints about the state of a municipal flower bed, a stretch of road, a street lamp, exhaustive notices about the wealthy Wandernburg families (including the Wilderhauses), their illnesses, accidents, obituaries, death notices, funerals, births, marriages or receptions. There was also a section covering important news from neighbouring villages and, every now and then, an event of international importance—a coronation, a war, an armistice. The newspaper also boasted a financial section that gave information on the price of farm produce and wool (Hans was shocked to discover that Herr Gelding wrote monthly articles on the subject), the nation's stock-market index, as well as those of Paris and London. Every Sunday, underneath the heated sermon of a certain Reverend Weiss and a list of the week's religious services, there was a poem or literary review by Professor Mietter, whom the newspaper introduced in the heading above his contribution as, "Herr Doktor G L Mietter, a leading light of literature, a keen but impartial critic for our readers, an unrivalled bastion of good taste".

Hans lamented the dearth of poetry on the shelves of the

Wandernburg public library, but was overjoyed when he discovered nine volumes of Rotteck's *Universal History*, which he consulted frequently, as well as the helpful encyclopaedia *Konversationslexikon*, edited coincidentally by Brockhaus. One afternoon, while he was climbing a stepladder to reach one of Rotteck's volumes, Hans glimpsed a plump, dark-haired figure. Even though he could only see her from behind, he was in no doubt from the way she was chattering away to the librarian that this was Frau Pietzine. She would often drop in in order to stay abreast of the latest recommendations from the *Goddess of the Rhine* or the *Poetess of Swabia*, and to devour the latest editions of the *High Society Chronicle*, *Modern Trends* or *Remarkable Women*.

Another day, as Hans watched her condescendingly, Frau Pietzine came up to him and whispered in his ear, in a conspiratorial voice that left him wondering: I bumped into Elsa on the street and she told me Sophie would be here within the hour. Hans closed his book and looked at her, as though demanding an explanation. But Frau Pietzine simply repeated: Within the hour. And vanished between the rows of shelves.

Lisa came back smelling of river. She came back with a burning brow and frozen arms, with mud from the riverbank on the hem of her dress, with the weariness of the river. She pushed the inn door closed with her foot, dropped the basket of laundry and pulled off her headscarf with a sigh. She called her mother twice. There was no reply. She went to the yard, quickly hung out the laundry, then wandered about the house—her father wasn't there either and Thomas was still at school. She washed her face, tidied her hair and went upstairs.

She knocked on the door, and before Hans could say Come in, walked into the room. She saw him hunched over the table surrounded by piles of open books, holding a quill. Lisa contemplated the raised lectern, Hans's hasty writing, open-mouthed ink pot. There was something about those symbols, those printed characters that fascinated her, even though she couldn't understand them, or perhaps because she couldn't understand them. And above all there was something magical about the way Hans would spend hours immersed in these books, caught up in his own quiet fervour. He looked like a different person when he was reading, his face changed, he seemed distant but contented, like people when they sing. Her father also read, mostly newspapers, but it wasn't the same—he turned the pages without ever immersing himself, like someone who goes down to the river, dips a toe in the water, then turns round. Hans's way of reading was different. Hans was, what was Hans doing? What was it that held his attention? If throwing herself into books could change her that much then she wanted to learn, too.

Hello, Hans said, what is it? How are you? Lisa asked. I'm very well, thank you, I'm working, he replied, what is it? I just wanted to see how you were, said Lisa, and to fetch your dirty laundry. My laundry? said Hans. Yes, said Lisa, examining the room, where do you keep it? Doesn't your mother see to that? Hans said, rising from his chair. My mother, replied Lisa, beginning to walk round the table, hasn't got time to see to everything, so I have to help her, you see, that's why I came up, where do you keep your dirty laundry? Well, Hans paused, I don't know, look here, are you sure your mother told you to? Aha! she exclaimed. It's under the bed! Do you think that's the proper place to keep clothes? Leave it, Lisa, please, said Hans, there's really no need, honestly!

Hans went over to try to take the basket away from her.

Look here, said Hans, you shouldn't have to, please let go of that basket! (It's my job, said Lisa, what does it matter?) Quite, Lisa, it doesn't matter, honestly, I'll take it down to the yard (the yard? she said. You can't do the washing in the yard, you have to go to the river), all right, then I'll go to the river. (You?

Lisa scoffed. You couldn't wash out a single stain!) Give it to me! (Let go of that sleeve, will you, she insisted, brushing his finger.) Listen, Lisa, look here (all right, but let go), it's just, I think … (Will you let go, then?) Yes, no! Wait, listen, you should be studying, don't you see? Studying at school, let go of the basket, you should …

In that case, why don't you teach me? Lisa paused.

I beg your pardon? Hans took the basket.

Teach me, said Lisa, to read those books you're reading, you keep saying I should, I should, then teach me (but I, well, he stammered, that is, your family), I don't think it can be that difficult, I know plenty of stupid people who can read. Give me back that basket will you? That's better, thank you. We'll start tomorrow, shall we? You must excuse me now. My mother will be back any minute and we've lots to do. I'll leave you in peace. Until tomorrow, then.

Lisa went down the stairs with a grin on her lips and butterflies in her stomach. She tidied the kitchen before leaving to fetch Thomas from school. On her way, she bumped into Frau Zeit, who was hurrying home to get the tea ready. You're late, said her mother, I don't like your little brother having to wait at the gates. I've been doing laundry, she replied, and I cleaned the kitchen. Very good, her mother said, but you're still late. I'm on time, said Lisa. And if you keep answering back you'll be even later, Frau Zeit said finally. While you're about it, child, take your brother to the square until his tea's ready, you know what he gets like at home. But mother, Lisa groaned. And she watched Frau Zeit as she began walking away.

In the market square, Thomas was playing blind man's buff with some other children next to the baroque fountain. Lisa watched over them with a mixture of exasperation and envy, as though she were losing an intrinsic part of herself in the game, and at the same time something new was preventing her from joining in. Her brother was running around blindfolded, arms outstretched. Suddenly he stopped, stuck out his hip and let out one, two, three little explosions. Thomas! his sister bawled. The other children roared with laughter. Thomas went on searching. He caught one of his friends, hurled himself at the lad, groped his face, stomach and tiny prick before shouting out his name. The others came running to make fun of the captured boy. They formed a circle, scaring the pigeons away, a few punches flew and the blindfold changed owners. Lisa found herself smiling. The children might seem rather silly, but they were having a lot of fun. When had she last played blind man's buff? A long time ago. Well, not that long. Only last year. And why had she stopped playing? Because it was no longer appropriate, she was too grown-up to play those games. Was she really? Yes. Well, more or less. For a moment Lisa felt the urge to run around like her brother, to play with him and caper about. She was on the point of doing so when her heart leapt—Hans had appeared at the other side of the square and was heading towards her. Was he coming towards her? Of course he was. Or was he? For Hans had veered off, where was he going? He stopped in front of an old man with a beard, a beggar playing an instrument resting on a cart. Hans bent down, dropped some coins into his dish and—amazing!—stroked the black dog accompanying the old man. Only then did Hans turn round and acknowledge Lisa. She waved in a deliberately desultory manner. Then she turned her back and shouted to her brother: Thomas! For God's sake, stop playing the fool, come along, it's getting late!

The following day at noon, Lisa went to Hans again and finally persuaded him to give her secret reading lessons. They agreed to meet twice a week, at more or less the same hour—when Hans got up, while her father was out sampling a few beers and her mother was busy in the kitchen. Half-an-hour of class— according to her calculations, that was the longest Lisa could be out of her parents' sight without them becoming suspicious. Half-an-hour with her head buried in a book. Half-an-hour reading, becoming someone else. Half-an-hour alone with him. Hans bought her an exercise book and a pencil. He kept them in his trunk so that no one would see them.

From that day on, Lisa began memorising the alphabet, learning the syllables, forming words with a swiftness and eagerness that never ceased to amaze Hans. Seeing her contort her hand to trace the symbols, hearing her delicious attempts to pronounce diphthongs, Hans was overcome with true emotion (an emotion mixed with another, darker frisson) and a sense that all was not lost. Lisa applied herself to her studies with an almost furious determination. The only thing she did as she cleaned, sewed and washed the laundry was repeat the strange alphabet over and over to herself. In the evenings, as soon as her parents had gone to bed (or when their panting stopped after the rhythmic creaking), Lisa would light an oil lamp, put it close to her bed, and copy out the letters with her brother's pencils. Her homework had to be good, better than good. Too much depended on it—her self-esteem, her future, the threat of being punished by her parents, Hans's opinion of her.

One afternoon, while writing a report on a book, Hans became distracted by the noises in the house. This distraction was partly because he had found the work frankly tedious, and partly because Thomas's excited voice echoing through the corridor on his return from school was difficult to ignore. He stretched and left his room to go to downstairs and have a coffee. When Thomas saw him come down, he did the same as always—greet him cheerfully, do four or five acrobatic turns, and grin mischievously before running off in search of other amusements. As he watched Thomas run off, Hans felt forlorn—there is nothing more difficult to capture than a child's attention when he is playing, he reflected. Holding his cup to his lips, he puzzled over why an adult was primed for the hatred of another adult, but not for a child's indifference. Thomas's wandering gaze, which delighted in things only to forget them instantaneously, the restless eyes with which he viewed the world, were they enamoured of everything or did they retain nothing?

Thomas enjoyed picking his nose as thoroughly as possible, as though hoping to find some buried treasure deep inside his nostrils. He didn't do this using just one finger, but by forming a relentless pincer with his thumb and forefinger (the thumb tunnelling inside while the forefinger acted as a support). He did his homework in the same way, with a look of bemusement and scorn. Or rather, that was how he contemplated it, without writing a single word in his exercise book. Since Hans had begun spending more time at the inn translating, he had been able to observe Thomas's habits more closely, and to discover how little interest he had in studying. Because he liked the boy, and perhaps also to disguise the fact that he was helping Lisa, he would occasionally give Thomas a hand with his homework.

Thomas's school curriculum consisted of reciting aloud, hand-writing, arithmetic and above all Bible studies. Hans learnt that his fellow pupils were artisans, peasants and Jews—in other words he attended a municipal school. The week before, Thomas had misbehaved or so his teacher had thought, and had made him write out the slogan: "Patience, piety, purpose" a hundred times, as well as inflecting the three nouns through their different cases. The teacher had surprised Thomas ex-changing shameful drawings with another boy. He had caned them both for a quarter of an hour in front of the class. He had told them it was for their own good and they must learn to face the consequences of their actions. On discovering what had happened, Herr Zeit had gone to the teacher to apologise. The teacher had reminded him that unless the same discipline they attempted to inculcate at school were maintained in the

home, all their efforts would be in vain. In agreement with
the school's methods, Herr Zeit, furious, had gone home and
caned his son for another quarter of an hour while listing all
the sacrifices they, his parents, had made for him.

Hans had tried to give the boy reasons to study, but Thomas,
with a mixture of naivety and common sense, had refuted his
arguments one by one. What's the *use* of reading? he would
protest, digging his elbows into his schoolbook. It's useful for
everything, Hans would insist, for anything you might want to do.
But I don't want to do anything, the boy had retorted. Then
you'll need to know even more if you want to go through life
doing nothing, Hans had said, grinning. There are only three
ways of learning, Thomas—through experience, listening and
reading. But as children are prevented from doing practically
everything, including listening to grown-ups' conversations, the
only way to learn is to read, do you understand? Well, Thomas
had said grudgingly, but what about writing, what's the use of
writing? Hans had responded with amusement: So you can do
what mummies do. Mummies? the boy had gaped at him with
astonishment. In ancient Egypt, Hans had explained, oh, and
while we're on the subject, if you can find Egypt for me on a
map I'll give you a bag of sweets, *that's* what maps are for, too! In
Ancient Egypt they would write the names of the gods because
they knew words outlast statues, buildings, even the mummies
themselves. Stuff and nonsense! Thomas had protested. How
can a word last longer than a bit of stone! Stones are hard and
words are not. And anyway, look, pencil is easy to rub out, see?
… You're right, Hans had admitted, although I don't suppose
you or I will ever be able to build a castle or a pyramid; it takes
a very long time, lots of money and thousands of people. But
you and I on our own, do you see? can write *pyramid* or *castle*
without anyone's help. Stuff and nonsense! Thomas repeated,
picking his nose. But a moment later, as Hans began to walk

off, he had stopped him and asked: Hey, what sort of life did those mummies have?

Excuse me, Frau Zeit said, entering the parlour, I'd like a word.

Hans, who hadn't finished his coffee yet, gestured towards the sofa. Suddenly, the light began to wane. The afternoon was dissolving into the cauldron.

No, thank you, said the innkeeper's wife, I prefer to stand. Well, I'll get straight to the point, as I'm sure you have work to do and so have I. I wanted to talk to you about Thomas. About Thomas's lessons. I gather you've been helping him out with his homework and teaching him who knows what else. I'm grateful to you for taking the trouble. But my son doesn't need a private tutor. And if he did, rest assured we'd hire one. Thomas goes to a good school where he receives a proper education. Neither his father nor I enjoyed that privilege. Thomas complains of being bored at school and I'm not surprised, bearing in mind the sweets you give him and the games you propose that distract him from his homework. No, you listen to me for a moment. I know you mean well. And as I said, I'm grateful. But my son's education is the responsibility of his parents and his teachers. And not of strangers lodging at the inn. Have I made myself clear? Good. I'm glad to hear it. No, that doesn't matter. And, if I may say so it's none of your business either. For that reason, as Thomas's mother, I'm asking you not to teach Thomas anything, especially things that are of no use to him at school. As I said, I appreciate your good intentions. Now appreciate mine. Good afternoon. Let me know what time you want supper.

Before going out into the corridor, Frau Zeit added: Oh, I forgot. My husband says you're using too much oil and he can't keep filling the lamp. Tell your husband, said Hans solemnly, I need the lamp in order to work because tallow candles are a strain on the eyes, and I'll pay him each week for the oil I use. Good afternoon.

When Hans was alone with his cup of cold coffee, he made two decisions—that night he would not dine at the inn and, come hell or high water, Lisa would continue to receive lessons from a stranger.

Always watched over, ever closer to the high temperatures of summer, Hans and Sophie had gone on an outing. Elsa and Álvaro had gone with them. The four of them had hired a calèche and followed the main road to the banks of the River Nulte. Sophie was wearing an almost transparent shawl and a white bonnet with a flowered ribbon at the neck and a brim from beneath which her nose peeped out mischievously whenever she looked at Hans. Less sensibly dressed for the weather, Hans was sporting a simply absurd felt cap and a fine waistcoat. (Still in a waistcoat? she had remarked scathingly when she saw how overdressed he was for May.) They strolled through fields full of burgeoning colours in search of a suitable patch of shade. Spike aloft, Sophie's parasol swung this way and that, succumbed, rested on her shoulder as they spoke. Elsa and Álvaro walked behind them, almost in silence.

They chose a spot beside the river and spread out a checked blanket on the grass. The poplar trees along the banks of the Nulte were in full leaf and the reeds were beginning to poke through the water. A few bands of sunlight filtered through the branches making a bridge between the two banks. They sat in a semicircle—the two women folding their legs so they were sitting on their heels, the two men clasping their arms round their knees. They laid the food out on the blanket. They ate and drank, alternately talking and letting the river speak. After dessert, Álvaro asked the others if he might, as he explained in not very correct German, "take a flagrantly Spanish siesta". Elsa dug out some magazines she had brought along and sat beneath the perfumed shade of a lime tree;

none of the others noticed that, except for the first one, all the magazines were in English. For a moment Sophie and Hans were alone, or at least far enough away from the others to be out of earshot.

Sophie told Hans that Rudi Wilderhaus wrote to her every day and had begun addressing her as *my beloved future wife*, a liberty he had hitherto, as became the formal nature of their engagement, not seen fit to take. What are his letters like? Hans asked, wracked with torment. They are—Sophie paused—polite (but she was thinking *banal*), and solicitous (but she was thinking *pedantic*). You must be very happy, said Hans. Yes, she said, very. Then everything is going well, he said, I'm glad, I'm glad. I can't complain, Sophie added, because Rudi is very discreet and he doesn't pester me. He never comes to the house more than once or twice a week, and he scarcely complains when I go out dancing with my friends. How thoughtful of him! exclaimed Hans. How very thoughtful! Moreover ... she began, her eyes narrowing. Moreover? he came closer. Moreover, Sophie continued, he does his utmost to behave like a gentleman, a perfect gentleman, if you see my meaning! Aha, Hans began fidgeting. But Sophie said no more. Aha, said Hans, growing more and more agitated, by a *perfect* gentleman you mean ... too much of a gentleman? What a relief it is, Sophie smiled, to be able to talk to someone who is low-minded. And so, ventured Hans, do you think it's a good thing? I mean, do you greatly value such ... gentlemanliness? You should know, she replied, showing her profile under the brim of her hat. I'm afraid, as my father says, I'm a practical girl.

Hans swallowed hard. Everything felt inevitable and flowing, just like the river.

Hot and heavy, evening falls over the fields. The flock of sheep flees the encroaching shadow as if it were scorched grass. The air smells peculiar; it moistens their misshapen muzzles. The sheep parade their unease. A chorus of bleats interrogates the horizon.

The librarian makes sure the door is locked and leaves the building. She has stayed on after closing time to catalogue the new stock. She begins walking, her woollen coat draped over her shoulders. The librarian is looking forward to kicking off her shoes as soon as she gets home. She looks up at the sky and notices the closeness of the air, as if it were going to rain.

The flock hears the distant bark of sheepdogs. They begin running instantly, to be on the safe side, as though anticipating danger. The barking stops and they come to a halt. The sheep prick up their ears. Then mistrust gives way to meekness, and they resume their slow chewing.

The librarian walks past St Nicholas's Church, and turns left into Jesus Lane. She could take a less solitary way home, but it is farther, she is already tired, and her feet are aching too much. Each footstep sends a shooting pain through her heels, the sound reverberates in her head. The echoes stop. What was that? Did she hear something? No, it was nothing. The librarian resumes walking, a little more hurriedly.

The dogs head home, and with them the shepherd. They have herded the sheep into a line and are taking them towards the River Nulte. When the first sheep glimpses the riverbank, it stops in its tracks and tries to back away. Then the shepherd commands his dogs, the dogs bark at the sheep and the sheep begin crossing the river. Their legs plunge into the water, breaking up the reflection of the trees, their wool gets wet.

The librarian's heels clatter on the uneven paving, slipping on the traces of mud. A fine rain has begun to fall or so she thinks—her face is not dry. Not wanting to look behind her, the librarian feels for her keys in the pocket of her coat.

The first sheep sees the shepherd coming towards it and

freezes. Its leg muscles quiver. It takes two, three, four steps without knowing where to go. The shepherd lunges forward, hunched over. Moving its plump sturdy body, the sheep tries to flee. It scurries clumsily, thrusting its head forward as if it were a dead weight.

The church bells begin chiming with a thunderous clang. Keeping close to the wall, the librarian looks back. Now she knows she is being followed. She quickens her pace, trying not to stumble, trying not to think. Her heels, the bells, the masked figure's footsteps behind.

The sheep is dragged over to the dip. The shepherd thrusts its head under the stream of water. The sheep struggles to get away. The shepherd strengthens his grip. He has to rub the sheep down, and he has to do it quickly.

The masked figure has caught up with the librarian, who finds herself trapped between the wall and a still unlit street lamp. She wants to throw her head back and cry out, but she can't.

The shepherd begins rubbing the sheep's flank vigorously with the water from the fountain, washing away the chaff and dust and excrement and the grease the animal secretes, the oily film that sticks to the wool and has to be rubbed, pulled, scrubbed away.

She can't throw her head back and cry out because the masked figure has grabbed her from behind and is holding a knife to her neck, covering her mouth with his gloved hand, and has begun groping her with slippery urgency, panting behind his mask.

He ropes the animal's legs together and grabs the shears, the honed metal. The rope tightens and the sheep's flank goes into a spasm, seems about to explode, to leave its skin behind from so much writhing.

He binds her wrists with a piece of rope, grapples with her until he manages to cram a handkerchief into her mouth. The rope tightens, cutting into her flesh. The masked figure leans against the street lamp to steady himself, keeping the librarian with her back to him, her face pressed against the wall.

The wool closest to the skin resists the shears. The sheep's lip curls with fright, baring its teeth. The shepherd works with both hands, his fingers trembling from the effort. The sheep's mouth opens, letting out a more piercing bleat that resounds in waves. The shears become caught up in the twists of wool. The sheep's teeth grind resignedly.

The librarian screams with the handkerchief crammed in her mouth, the knife digging into but not breaking the skin on her neck. The masked figure works away, emitting short grunts. The librarian's heavy thighs stay clenched.

The sheep's eyes bulge, filling with an amber liquid. Wide open with fright, crazed, unseeing, the sheep's eyes swallow up the light.

The librarian's coat lies tangled on the ground.

The wool begins forming a mound.

In a nearby alley, moving off into the distance, the nightwatchman's cry can be heard: *Watch over your fire and your lamps. Praise be to God! All praise!*

Lieutenant Gluck was dictating to Lieutenant Gluck, who was taking notes. The two Lieutenant Glucks had been assigned to investigate the increasingly alarming case of the masked attacker. The two men got on badly but they loved each other—they were father and son. The father had held the rank of lieutenant for years. He had reached a state of calm contentment, and no longer aspired to any higher position. The younger Gluck had recently made lieutenant, although his rank would not become official until the next annual review of police promotions. He had his sights set even higher, and was occasionally exasperated by his father's lack of ambition. The veteran Lieutenant Gluck was proud of his son's meteoric rise, and yet this removal of the professional hierarchy between them gave him cause for concern on a personal level—he didn't wish to make too much out of it, but lately he had the feeling that his son disagreed with nearly all of his observations and flouted his orders, more out of defiance than conviction.

Lieutenants Gluck and Gluck were in one of the offices in Wandernburg's central police station, at the end of Spur Street. The room smelt musty, and the tiny window at the back was no bigger than a cell window. Lieutenant Gluck was leaning back in his chair, his heels resting on the edge of a desk full of woodworm. In the meantime, Lieutenant Gluck was pacing around his father's chair taking notes. The older Gluck liked to run through all the facts in his mind in order to have a picture of the whole, before making any conjectures. His son preferred to investigate every possibility, analysing each clue as he went along, pulling on every thread to see where it might lead. Son, Lieutenant Gluck raised his head, will you keep still for five minutes? Sometimes a little calm is necessary in order to concentrate. I already told you, father, replied Lieutenant Gluck, I think better when I'm moving. But it's the mind, not the body, that has to be agile, protested Lieutenant Gluck. It's a wonder you can tell them apart, Lieutenant Gluck retorted, vexed. Sub-lieutenant! declared Lieutenant Gluck, removing his feet from the desk. Show some respect and keep still, that's an order! And I'm warning you it applies to both things equally *whether or not you can tell them apart!* The son stopped pacing. Lieutenant Gluck announced solemnly: Is that clear, Sub-lieutenant? Yes, replied the son grudgingly. Yes, what, Sub-lieutenant? said the father. Yes, Lieutenant, said Lieutenant Gluck. Good, said the father, settling back in his chair, satisfied, in that case let's continue.

We know, Lieutenant Gluck resumed while his son took notes, that the attacker's modus operandi has remained un-changed since the first attack, that is to say—in addition to the aforementioned carnival mask, the provenance of which we are attempting to determine, and the knife and the handkerchief he uses to silence his victims and the rope with which he ties their wrists, the attacker invariably strikes, according to all the witness statements to date—I'm not going too fast am I? All right, son, all right, I was only asking! Now, where was I? Oh yes—the attacker strikes in the vicinity of St Nicholas's Church, more precisely in Wool Alley or Jesus Lane and other side streets off Archway. He doubtless chooses said streets because not only are they poorly lit and isolated, but because they enable him to lie in wait unseen by his victims, or rather by the women, intercepting them as they enter, or dragging them in as they walk past. To the best of our knowledge, the subject has never struck before seven o'clock in the evening or after ten o'clock at night. Therefore we can deduce (we can deduce, his son interrupted, stopping writing, that the attacker is well acquainted with the city's habits, that is, he knows what time he is likely to find a victim in those streets, and more importantly he knows what time the policemen stop patrolling and the routes the nightwatchmen take), just so, just so, yes, and not only that (not only that what? his son said, looking up from his notebook), not only that, but we can, indeed we must, deduce from it the hours the attacker himself keeps. We might also suppose that he strikes relatively early because the next day he has to rise early for reasons of work, family or obligations of a different nature ... (Go on, said Lieutenant Gluck.) Nothing, just that we should keep it in mind. If the subject is indeed familiar with police patrol times and the nightwatchmen's itinerary, this would narrow down the suspect's profile, whereas if his criminal routine is governed by familial responsibilities, then our search should include other types of profile (I can see no other reason for the criminal rising early except to go to work, reflected his son). Really? Why is that? (Quite simply, replied Lieutenant Gluck, because so far the criminal's victims have all been young women, it follows he must be quick and agile, and of working age.) Hold on, we can't be so sure about that, because it's precisely the younger women who wear the kinds of garments that make running more difficult. What I mean is, if we take into account his victims' clothing, the subject hasn't needed to be fast on his feet. Patient, more like, I'd say. Anyway, have you got all that down, son? Good, excellent. How about a small beer? Don't look at me like that, look at the time. We're off duty!

When Lisa handed him the envelope, he felt the same pang of excitement he always felt when he received one of Sophie's letters. As he sat down to read, his brow wrinkled—this wasn't Sophie's notepaper or her writing. Inside the envelope Hans discovered an ominous surprise. A white visiting card, substantial and stiff to the touch, embossed with heraldic insignia and military crosses. The card, he read, was that of Herr Rudi P von Wilderhaus, the younger.

The letter, polite but to the point, was an invitation to dear Herr Hans, with whom he had not yet had the opportunity to converse as quietly as he would have liked, to accompany him on a shoot the following day at dawn, assuming that he had no previous engagements and that he enjoyed fresh air and nature. So that, if Herr Hans saw fit to honour him with his company, he would pick him up in his carriage at six-thirty sharp. And with this, he ended the letter, sincerely yours, etc.

After weighing up for a moment the possible inconveniences of accepting this strange invitation against the possibly even greater ones of refusing it, Hans sent a note to Wilderhaus Hall (taking care that it sounded neither overly aloof nor overly enthusiastic) thanking Rudi kindly for his generous invitation, which he accepted with pleasure, in the meantime bidding him goodbye until the morrow, etc, with my sincerest gratitude.

Hans's first thought was: What does Rudi really want? And his second: My God, I have to get up at the crack of dawn. Followed by: What boots shall I wear? He had never cared for hunting. Or rather, he had an instinctive loathing for it. And yet he knew he should go. Not simply out of courtesy, but in order to wheedle information out of Rudi about his betrothal to Sophie, and to gauge how suspicious he was, if at all. Because of the hour, his apprehension or both, Hans was unable to sleep a wink, and the lordly clip-clop of hooves found him wide-awake, standing at the window.

Rudi greeted him from the top of a long shooting brake drawn by four black horses. The driver's seat towered aloft, and from behind a caged partition the dogs barked at the dawn. Rudi had pinned to his lapel an eight-pointed star with a falcon at its centre and an inscription that read: *Vigilando ascendimus*. He had on baggy breeches tucked into slender knee-length boots. Hans found them distasteful, yet felt ridiculous when he glimpsed his own as he clambered onto the carriage. Did you sleep well, Herr Hans? You look tired. Rudi's face shone like polished marble. Oh, extremely well, replied Hans, indeed, I slept so soundly I confess I had difficulty waking up. Did you? smiled Rudi. I did indeed, smiled Hans.

As Rudi's shooting brake sped north through the countryside along dirt roads Hans had never before been on, dawn burst on the scene, lighting everything as if catapulted into the air. Rudi appeared calm, or at least sure of himself. He spoke little and only about trivial matters. Occasionally, he would stare fixedly at Hans with an ominously friendly expression. Isn't it beautiful? he said, pointing at the woods. Then he would become absorbed in the landscape and inhale deeply. Only when he noticed Rudi's burly chest rising and falling did Hans realise he was scarcely breathing himself.

They descended from the vehicle and Rudi ordered the driver

and the footman to wait there until they returned. Hans, who had been interpreting Rudi's every gesture since their first greeting, was even more alarmed by this command—what did *until they returned* mean exactly? That they'd be a long time, that he didn't know how long they'd be, or that the driver and the servant weren't to go looking for them however long they took? Rudi slung his gun over his shoulder. He offered Hans another and quickly nodded his head.

They made their way into the wood. The dogs followed, sniffing the damp ground. Rudi walked forward, shoulders hunched, back straight. The weight of the gun clearly didn't hinder him in the slightest. Hans, on the other hand, was not sure which shoulder to carry it on. He had only handled a gun three or four times in his life, and on each occasion he had felt an awkward mixture of power and guilt. They walked in virtual silence for fifteen or twenty minutes. They came to a place that to Hans seemed identical to all the others. Rudi halted, lifted a finger to his lips and began noiselessly loading his gun. He did this with ceremonial slowness or with almost rehearsed precision, as though he were giving a demonstration. Each of Rudi's fingers moved with a dexterity that could not fail to produce admiration or panic. His expression was relaxed, almost indifferent to the weapon he was caressing. And yet, as soon as he took aim with his gun, Rudi was transformed. His features hardened. His jaw tensed. His gaze was that of a predator. The dogs shot forward like barking missiles as the gunpowder exploded. While the bloodhounds went to retrieve the prey, Rudi recovered his graceful indolence, smiled amiably, and said: Now your turn, my friend. Hans refused the invitation as politely as possible, and said that he was quite happy simply to accompany Rudi. In order to learn? Rudi enquired. Just as an observer, Hans explained. Ah, I see, Rudi replied, reloading his gun, but remember that by watching you are also taking part in the shoot.

Rudi hunted partridge, quail and rabbit. His quarry plummeted from the sky, crumpled as it attempted to flee, was blown from its hole. The dogs scurried back and forth excitedly. A string of dead animals hung upside down from Rudi's belt. He was an undeniably excellent marksman—he rarely missed and when he did it was out of carelessness rather than incompetence. As the morning went on, he kept insisting Hans try a shot, but Hans would refuse with a nervous gesture that seemed to bolster Rudi's confidence. Rudi's real ammunition, reflected Hans, was not the deafening cartridges flying through the air before falling to the ground, but his knowledge that he wasn't the fearful one. Rudi gradually fired less and laughed more—it seemed what he liked about hunting was not shooting but being *able* to shoot.

Yes, more than likely Rudi had brought him shooting to impress him, to assert his authority on his own territory. But precisely because this territory was not his, Hans preferred to relinquish any claim to it from the outset rather than entering into a futile contest. He thought that by leaving Rudi to shoot on his own, to show off unrivalled, his fervour would burn itself out and his eagerness to triumph would gradually subside until he realised no one but the partridge, quail and rabbit had been defeated, because, when all the shots had been fired, Hans would still be looking him in the eye without having pulled the trigger. Hans was fully aware that his pacifism was an attempt to match up to Rudi. And, like Rudi, he was trying to do so on his own territory.

Hans was prepared to keep up his passive resistance at all costs in order not to give up an iota of rage to Rudi. This was his strategy, and he intended to follow it calmly and with complete cynicism to the end. What Hans hadn't foreseen was what actually happened—as the sun rose high above the thicket, Rudi's strength began to wane forlornly. Without uttering a word his shots became spaced out, his pace slowed, his reflexes slackened. Finally, he stopped shooting altogether, his shoulders drooped and he sat down on a rock, leaning on his gun butt as if it were a cane. The barking stopped. The air grew calm. Strings of birds sailed across the sky once more. Ill at ease, Hans sat down opposite him at a prudent distance. Rudi raised his head, and for the first time Hans was able to look into his eyes—his gaze was one of firm memories and uncertain future. Rudi sighed. He let his head drop, and sat examining the furrows in the ground. Then he smiled with a disarming tenderness that (against his will) Hans found touching. Do you think, said Rudi, that Sophie loves me as much as I love her?

And suddenly Rudi began to talk openly and at length about his feelings. His broad back seemed to hunch slightly. Hans had the impression Rudi was talking to him in a beseeching tone. That he was speaking about Sophie as if Hans were his confidant, or Rudi wished he were. In a few gushing moments, which to Hans felt like hours, Rudi told him how he had met Sophie, confessed how long he had waited for her, how often he had refused to take no for an answer. He felt inside the folds of his garments, unfastened two horsehair buttons and showed Hans his treasure—an oval medallion containing a miniature of Sophie. Hans read the inscription engraved on the back, too affectionate to have been mere pretence. He felt a tightening in his chest as he contemplated Sophie's smile. Her portrait was painted on ivory (Ivory, Hans thought, more from jealousy than political conviction, imported by the British colonists in India, the imperialist pig!) and the glass was domed, like the mirror opposite the fireplace at the Gottlieb residence. Hans noticed that because of a defect in the glass, a tiny air bubble, one of Sophie's eyes looked slightly bigger than the other, wider open, as if in warning. Rudi carried on talking excitedly about the wedding in October, about the dowry agreed on by the two families, the forthcoming preparations. Unsure of how to respond to such directness, Hans softened and was on the point of lowering his guard. Had he misjudged his rival? But then Rudi made an ambiguous remark in passing, which put him back on the defensive: Besides, Rudi said, you're a close friend of hers, you must understand my feelings and be aware of hers.

You must understand my feelings and be aware of hers, Rudi had said. (What exactly did he mean by this? Hans wondered, was he referring to Hans's conversations with Sophie? Did he want to know what she had told him, was he asking him to be disloyal? Or was he insinuating that Hans had become *too* close to his fiancée?) I'm being completely honest with you, Rudi continued, because I know I can trust you in this matter. (Was Rudi a master of irony? Was he capable of subjecting him to such subtle torture? Was he speaking out of deliberate malice or with the innocence of the cuckold?) Sometimes, you see, I worry that Sophie might be too sophisticated for a man such as me. Let's be honest, I haven't had much time for study due to my obligations (what was this—a fit of humility or a defiant display of mockery?) In short, I needn't describe her to you (why needn't he, why?) but for me one of her attractions is that way she has of remaining slightly aloof (she might well be aloof with you, you fool!) and, how should I say, just a little wild (well, we agree on that) not to mention her beauty, I don't know what you think. (And now what should he do—agree or turn a deaf ear? What would rouse a jealous man's suspicions more—another man praising his fiancée or maintaining a stubborn silence?) And do you know what else I like about her? The way she smiles. That's what I most like about her. Knowing a woman's smile is important, isn't it? Because a man aspires to make his wife happy, and when people are happy they smile a lot. And if Sophie and I are going to be very happy together, it's important for me to like her smile.

Hans felt the urge to spit in Rudi's face or to embrace him.

As he reached the end of his declarations, Rudi gave Hans

a glimpse of the true source of his anxiety. Contrary to Hans's initial fear, what most troubled him about his betrothal to Sophie was not the appearance of a rival (a possibility he appeared to exclude out of ignorance or conceit) but the doubts that a woman as self-possessed and difficult to please as her could instil in a man such as he.

At that moment, Hans at last *saw* Rudi. And he understood his torment. And he pitied him. This betrothal might to some degree have been born of convenience—but not on his part. For Rudi it was a consequence of having fallen in love. And for this reason, sensing Hans had affinities with Sophie that were inaccessible to him, the powerful Rudi Wilderhaus was seeking his help, almost unwittingly. For a moment Hans was able to put himself in Rudi's place, to glimpse the weakness behind his show of strength, to put his finger on the trigger of his fears. And yet, seeing Rudi suffer, he knew he could never be loyal to him, and would never be his friend. And he felt wretched and jubilant, filled with cruel delight, more traitorous than ever, and truer to his desire.

He inhaled the intoxicating morning breeze, held it in his lungs like someone smoking pungent tobacco, breathed out slowly. He walked over to Rudi and without looking him in the eye said: Pass me that gun.

I dare not call this a reply, Sophie, for these hasty lines scarcely honour your radiant letter. Yet I am aware of how soon we forget feelings (not a complete but a gentle, imperceptible forgetting, like an unremembered tune you still hear as a murmur in the background). That is why I wanted to reply urgently, now, this instant. In fact, your letter is impossible to match. Were I to take the time necessary to write the reply you deserve, I would first have to overcome the turmoil your letter has caused me. And if I write to you while under its influence, as I am doing, I will not do justice to its loftiness. If I think about it, your letter can only be replied to with music.

But I have to say something, if only in prose. And it is this, and I don't know what else. I remember you each day with an overpowering feeling of complicity. An inexplicable complicity that seems to come from somewhere beyond, from many things we haven't experienced. It is curious. The last few times we have met, I have felt a strong desire finally to xxxxxxx sleep with you. And yet I notice a feeling between us of afterwards—not only the tension of two people who have never touched, but also (and this is what is so strange) the calm intimacy of those who have slept together. And I do not mean, the devil take me, platonically.

And between the before and the after, between the having and the not having slept together, there is this peculiar happiness. Sophie, I can't think of you without grinning foolishly. That is the good thing.

The good thing is you exist.

Yours, Hans.

I have chosen this moment to write to you because it has suddenly begun to rain, and on hearing the insistence of those playful raindrops and seeing how everything became more faint, I felt an irresistible urge to speak to you. But today there is no salon, nor any credible excuse for me to leave the house. What there is, is an arch of floating clouds that pass from me to you, or from you to me, I wouldn't know which way they are going. How are you today, you bad boy? What are you translating? I translate what I imagine you would say to me if we could see one another. I also read some of my beloved Duecento poets. Il corso delle cose è sempre sinuoso …

I wish I could converse with you a moment, dear Hans. I love addressing you using formal language, I feel deliciously nervous when I speak to you like that in front of others. I wish I could see you right now and that you were here beside me. Not so that we could sleep together (how reckless of you to say such things to me in a letter? What if someone read them? Don't you know we young ladies like to be a little more reticent, if

not in our desires, then at least in our words? I love your impulsiveness)
but in order to stroll along the path to the bridge and to walk beside the
river and lose ourselves in the fields.

I send you a kiss of rain, which has just stopped. Has it reached you?
Is it refreshing? And, with my kiss, a question. What is the origin of
beauty? Do you know? It sounds a little pretentious, I know, but it is a
serious question. What is its origin?

S

We shall meet. With or without proper excuses, we shall meet. And in
the meantime, yes—let us savour this waiting, which the ancients praised
so much. Nowadays everything seems so much more rushed than it did in
olden times, does it not? To me, patience is a kind of mysterious flower.
A flower all of us, unknowingly, have clasped in our hands. You are
teaching me how to pull out its petals, and so forgive me if I crumple it
without meaning to.

I am not complaining, though—you sent me a kiss, or so you said.

Xxxx xxxx Sophie, Sophie Gottlieb, I don't know why my language
goes all awry when I write to you. Never has stammering felt so satisfy-
ing. I don't know what I would do first if I were alone with you. Ah,
but you say I shouldn't write such things in a letter. In that case, it
gives me great pleasure to tell you in writing that I would do everything
that is unmentionable to you … So you see I am repeating what I said,
and enjoying it.

You asked me (and you say it is a serious question—of course it is!)
what is the origin of beauty. After thinking about it for a long time, I
would say it comes from transience and joy. I am almost certain of it.
Or perhaps an image would help—beauty originates from the tremors
of the bridge between tingling and truth. When that bridge trembles, it
means something important is crossing it.

I hear your footsteps. The bridge is trembling.

H

Hans, darling Hans, it upsets me a little to think that the other night, during our precious few hours together in the salon, I was unable to do anything but pretend. Luckily, the next day your beautiful flower arrived with the girl from the inn, thank you so much, again. I slipped it like a treasure between the pages of my album, and there it was this morning until my nosy father saw it peeping out and asked if Rudi had sent it (of course!) and said it had wilted and I should throw it away, because Rudi would be sending me many more. My father doesn't like things to wilt.

Elsa has just come into the room. I must leave you now, I shall take this opportunity to give her my letter. But no, I am not leaving you. Un bacio all' italiana e spero ansiosamente di rivederti presto, amore.

S

You were right, Sophie, cuore—*anticipation is a joy when you imagine the person you are waiting for will come. Anticipation is a kind of child. Only, unlike in parenthood, we nurture it before it bears fruit. Now I know. You are Ithaca. You are the journey.*

Did I tell you that when I imagine you I can't see you clearly, like in those portraits of people smiling in profile. I always see you in constant movement, a little blurred. In my imagination you are always on the move, doing lots of things, all of them marvellous, without you even realising it. And I see myself xxxxxxx traipsing in your wake, slowly catching up with you.

Beware of so much Italian fervour, it can be very dangerous in spring. If you persist I shall have to ask for your help with some of my translations. As an antidote to this agitation I suggest a dose of French relativism, tout au juste milieu, *as Professor Mietter is fond of saying, mixed with a few drops of German rationality. One has to be prudent. If I come into contact with your ear I intend to nibble it without asking your permission. That's a promise.*

Your very own, Hans.

If doors had voices, that afternoon Hans's seemed to have changed its tone; it didn't scream at him in the same way when he went to open it. Or so he would imagine later, after Sophie had left.

He played the clown in order not to show how nervous he was. Fräulein Gottlieb! he said stepping aside, what an honour, what a surprise! Bodenlieb, smiled Sophie, call me Bodenlieb. That's the name I gave the gentleman downstairs.

The moment Sophie set foot in the room, Hans saw the floor, the walls, the furniture from a different perspective, as though he were hanging from the rafters. I should have tidied up a little. Please excuse the mess, he said. Well, she said, glancing about, it's not bad for a bachelor.

They took turns stammering. They looked at one another anxiously, as if saying: Calm down.

Hans brought her a chair, took his time offering her tea, and tripped over twice. Sophie was curious about his trunk, leafed through a few books, admired the watercolour with the little mirror on the back, laughed at the tin bathtub. Although she didn't care about the trunk or the books or the picture or the bathtub.

They spoke of this and that, yet they still hadn't really said anything. At least, not until Sophie stood up and announced: Elsa will be waiting for me at seven o'clock in the market square. She's visiting a friend. Shall we make the most of our time? Or are we going to spend all afternoon chatting?

She let her hair down like a river breaking its banks. The water flowed over Hans. He swallowed hard. Without saying anything, he pulled the shutters to and lit some candles. Only then did they kiss, tasting the words in each other's mouth.

Sophie's slender hands read rather than caressed. She noticed Hans was trying not to be rough with her and was moved—she didn't need this gentle treatment. He found her body looser than

he'd anticipated. He noticed how she led him on, how sophisticated and un-childlike her responses were. Sophie thought
him supple without being strong. She guessed at rather than
glimpsed the muscles beneath his slender frame. They began
to undress, with all the awkwardness of people who are not
performing. Their skins gave off a not altogether clean smell.
Their desire opened like a valve.

Hans had perched on the edge of the bed. Sophie stood
looking at him, hands behind her back, fumbling with the last
laces. As he sat waiting, shoulders sloped, back hunched, a few
unbecoming folds pushed their way in around his midriff. The
insides of her thighs had a hollowed out droopiness to them.
Hans's toes were rather stubby. Sophie had rough patches on
her elbows. A few misplaced hairs sprouted from Hans's navel.
As Sophie's dress loosened, it revealed slightly sagging breasts,
veins that seemed to radiate from nipples scored with tiny
stretch marks.

And every new imperfection they discovered in each other
made them more real, more desirable to one another.

As she slipped off her petticoat, her stockings, her corset,
Hans saw Sophie's flesh bared in the light of the flickering
candles. He saw the light waver, bend over the wicks, quiver.
The candle flames shone into the contours of her skin, then
withdrew. Sophie was naked.

After so much waiting, so many distractions, Hans finally
saw her whole body. And something strange happened to him.
Instead of being able to dwell on every fold as he had dreamt
of for a hundred nights, instead of patiently contemplating her
body until he felt he had understood and assimilated it, Hans
became blinded from an excess of looking. He was so anxious
to take in every part of her, however much he cast his eyes over
her skin he only managed to become confused, his eyes clogging
up with shapes. He thought he had just made a discovery—eyes

also have an appetite. And if they are too greedy, they become clouded. And so his eyes became clouded as they moved from her feet to her shoulders, her hips to her breasts, her smile to her pubis, without being able to unite the images in one single one, without being able to determine the whole. Like words without syntax, like children learning Latin, like when you jump from one painting to another and a riot of colours forms on the inside of your eyelids. Hans looked at Sophie's body and did not understand what he was seeing. His vision stammered and his lips blinked, his mouth clouded over and his eyes watered. And so he decided to touch everything he was unable to see. He moved closer, clasped hold of her and felt that his senses had reunited, that action had prevailed over mystery. Now that there was no distance between them, he was able to grasp the real and imagined essence of Sophie, who trembled without a trace of fear and sighed without a trace of romanticism.

What did Sophie see of him? Nothing, everything. She looked without looking. Focusing on any detail. She read his ribs to accumulate evidence. And she concentrated on smelling him, soaking him up, becoming one with him. At first she did not try, like Hans, to make a whole out of the parts—she was content to assume he was there, undivided, she surrendered to the feeling that she was possessing him and therefore giving herself. She took in the immensity of Hans, all at once, encircling him. And, of course, she also touched him, part by part. But each part was a whole in itself, a place of arrival. She held him and let him go, took hold of him again, like learning to talk, or opening a map, like when light fills a space. It resembled a collapse. Accepting to be lost and discovering that she already knew this place, this well, this path. And so Sophie did not look at Hans—she remembered him. And as she came to him and he came to her, she knew if she closed her eyes she would see him always.

From the first mutual frisson, they both knew that yes. Yes because yes.

As they swayed, not gently or cautiously now, Hans turned his head and discovered that Sophie had turned the watercolour round so the mirror was facing the room. He was fascinated to see that only part of them fitted within its tiny frame. He looked at his image sideways on, trying to recognise them in the fragmented figures in the mirror, astonished that the naked torso pressing against a hip was him, that the arched back, hands plunged into the mattress, was Sophie. At exactly the same moment she had noticed the play of shadows their bodies cast on the opposite wall in the distended light of the candles—the two of them mutating, thickening or diluting, growing or shrinking like ink on a blotter. She wondered if he, too, was contemplating their shapes. Hans in the meantime was wondering if she had noticed the scene in the mirror.

At the end of everything, or at the start of something new, a cadenced silence enveloped them. Wrapped around each other like scrawled handwriting, their bodies almost hanging half out of bed, Hans and Sophie were gripped by an intense feeling of imminence. They waited quietly, each certain the other would whisper the truth, some kind of truth. They hung there as if they were on a motionless swing. All they could hear was their own breathing and the sputter of candles. Hans felt torn yet strangely at ease—he had the urge to talk and was brimming with silence. He felt at peace in this contradiction, as though opposing currents were pulling him by the arms, keeping him afloat. She said nothing either.

They looked at one another again before getting dressed. At last Sophie spoke: I love your knee, she said, leaning forward and running her tongue over it. Hans felt a flush of shame go up his leg and turn to joy when it reached his head. All of a sudden he noticed Sophie's thigh. The part of her thigh that had an elongated blemish as if drawn by a pencil on it. And I love your mark, he replied. I hate my mark, she said, covering her leg. But Hans insisted: Your mark enhances you, you're lucky to have it.

A few moments later, Sophie was running towards the baroque fountain, where Elsa was waiting for her, worrying about Herr Gottlieb's strict timekeeping.

THE GREAT HANDLE

A HONEYED LIGHT SPREAD OVER the countryside at rest. To the south of Wandernburg, fields of corn ripe for harvesting shimmered lazily. Each ear made its choice, catching hold of the wind that fluttered like a kite. Warm, sweet, expectant grain. A cloudless, limpid sky. Colours dripped onto the cornfield, dotting it with purple thistles and gaudy poppies. Melting under the unruly sun. The waters of the Nulte flowing between the poplars were scarcely deep enough now for washing clothes, for wading into or sustaining the green of its banks. In this blazing afternoon the labourers toiled. High above them all, as sharply defined as a dome, the sun beat down on the landscape, forging its shapes.

Lying at the cave mouth, Franz half-closed his eyes and sniffed the wind as it changed. Listened to the cicadas. Scratched his ear. Drooled thinking of a piece of meat …

(The meat his master and friends were roasting. The meat. Roasting. He was thirsty but didn't feel like getting up. Getting up to go and drink from the river. He wouldn't go now. He'd go after he'd eaten the meat. The meat. Would he go now? It was hot. Not as hot as before. Less. His ear itched. His master had raised his voice. What was going on? But his master had looked at him. Nothing was going on. No danger. They were all fine. His master and his friends. The one who always stroked him and the one who never stroked him and the one who had a strong smell and the one who came sometimes, on a horse. They were all fine. What a relief. It wasn't as hot. Less hot. It was getting dark. The one who never stroked him scared him a little because he didn't stroke him and he looked straight at him as if he were going to kick him. But he didn't kick him. He was his master's friend. His ear. The river. And the meat? Wait. His master didn't like him to eat the food before it went on the fire. He would feed him bits of meat after. Not before. He didn't like it. That sudden voice? Who had shouted? The voice belonged to him. The one who came sometimes. The one who came on a horse.)

… Álvaro let out one of his loud guffaws. The organ grinder's ideas amused him in a certain way. He still didn't fully understand his friend Hans's fascination with the old man, who mostly kept quiet and seemed to confuse austerity with not bathing very often. Although, as Álvaro began to get to know him better, he had to admit that when the old man did open his mouth, that mouth with its matted whiskers and every other tooth missing, what he said made sense. He gave the impression of being half-asleep, or daydreaming, until suddenly he would say something that, besides the typical Wandernburg naivety, revealed a keen awareness and an astonishing memory. Perhaps the most remarkable thing about the organ grinder was the impression he gave of being completely at peace with the past, as though he had already known happiness and expected nothing more from life. Quite the opposite of Hans, who suffered from a feeling of perpetual anxiety, as though waiting for some news that never came. The organ grinder almost never said anything Álvaro was expecting, and Hans invariably greeted his utterances with a warm smile. For a moment it occurred to Álvaro he might be jealous of the old man in some way. But as soon as the thought popped into his head, the same way a counter drops into the palm of your hand, he dismissed the idea as absurd. Him, jealous! Of that penniless old man! And on top of that because of Hans! Hadn't he better go easy on the wine?

Besides, Hans was saying, they've just inaugurated a new railway line at Saint-Étienne. Where's that? belched Reichardt. In France, said Hans, about two hundred miles from Marseille, an interesting place, have you been to France? No, and I haven't been to your fat aunt's house either, replied Reichardt. Marseille, you say? Lamberg added. I'd like to go there, to see the sea. There's no need to go to bloody France to see the sea, lad! said Reichardt. Or did the French invent the sea too! They didn't invent it, grinned Hans, but they call it *mer*, which you can't deny sounds a lot better than *Meer*. It sounds the same, exactly the same! Reichardt protested. Don't split hairs, Hans, said Álvaro, it sounds very similar. No, no, Hans insisted, say it, listen, carefully, the Spanish *mar* isn't bad either. For all I care the French can take their *mer*, growled Reichardt, and piss it into the mouths of their *mères*! The four others laughed, and Reichardt, pleased with his retort, went over to the organ grinder to see how the meat was cooking. Well, said Lamberg, pensively, what does it matter how it sounds, it's the same word, isn't it? It means the same, it refers to the same thing. But if it sounds different, insisted Hans, then the meaning changes, doesn't it organ grinder? Hair-splitting, I say, simple hair-splitting! Álvaro repeated, clapping him on the back. What's more, Hans went on, words refer to things, but they also create them, which is why every language not only has its own sounds but its own things. You're quite right, Álvaro conceded. All right, but what about the train? Lamberg said impatiently. Ah, Hans resumed, the Saint-Étienne line. Who has traveled by train? asked Lamberg. Álvaro and Hans were alone in raising their hands. And where did you go? he said, pointing at Álvaro. It was in England, replied Álvaro, where there are lots of trains: Darlington, Liverpool, Stockton, Manchester. And what's it like? Lamberg asked, agog. Like riding a horse! Reichardt exclaimed from over by the fire. Except softer on the arse! I don't know, said Álvaro, noisy. And enjoyable? Lamberg insisted. I suppose so, replied Álvaro, I was there on business. Lamberg, said Hans, do you know the most enjoyable thing about traveling by train? Not the places you see, but the people you meet, because there are so many of them, it's, imagine a hundred stagecoaches end to end filled with different people (rich people, only rich people travel! said Reichardt), and because trains can cross long distances, people come from many different places, even from other countries, that's the thing I most enjoy about trains, it's like being in a lot of different countries at the same time, do you see? As if the countries themselves were moving.

Well, in Spain, Álvaro said, munching on a chicken leg, we always like using the last but one invention, so we'll have to wait until they come up with something new, like diving on wheels or taking to the air with pedals, before we get the train. What about boats? asked Lamberg. Has anyone been on a steamboat? What about farts? said Reichardt. Has anyone gone home propelled by their own farts? Listen, why do you want to know about these things? You're not going anywhere, just like the rest of us. You don't know that, replied Lamberg. You do, declared Reichardt, you know it as well as I do. Steamboats, my friend, are marvellous things, said Hans, traveling on them is like, I don't know, like traveling by land and sea at the same time, like moving across water on a train, and the water behind you forms into two furrows, like two train tracks, but they immediately vanish and the water becomes smooth and you look at it and wonder: Which way did we come? And when you go up on deck, Lamberg, you feel as if you're flying, your hair gets messed up, your clothes balloon out, I hope you manage to go on one. (Ha! belched Reichardt, you'll be lucky!) I don't see why not, if you save up some money you could take a trip (do you really think so? said Lamberg sceptically), there's a steamer from Berlin to Charlottenburg which isn't very expensive, and another to Potsdam, which isn't very far either, in fact they have them all along the Rhine, and the Danube and the Elbe. Actually, I was thinking of traveling to Dessau by boat myself, you know, but I changed my mind at the last moment and, well, here I am. And here you'll stay, said Reichardt, no one ever leaves here, whether by their own farts or by steamer, do they old man? I don't know, the organ grinder said, feeding the last scraps of chicken to Franz, everything goes so fast these days. No one used to consider traveling more than twenty miles in one day. Maybe that's why young people are less attached to places, because it's too easy to leave them. They want to see the world. It stands to reason. In the end, Reichardt, it's not that you and I are unable to go anywhere, is it? It's that we don't want to. We like where we are, we're lucky.

Night tightened around the pinewood. Franz was playing with the empty bottles, pushing them along with his nose—the moon's reflection shimmered inside them like a tiny ship. The fire had gone out, but they hadn't noticed, the cheap wine warming their bellies. Except for the dog, each was drunk in his own way. Álvaro had just burst into tears all of a sudden. Hans, taken aback, crawled over to him. Álvaro, who usually avoided embraces, and always maintained the self-assured look other men admired him so much for, laid his head on Hans's shoulder. In garbled German mixed with slurred Spanish, Álvaro spoke of Ulrike, the train journeys they had taken together, the damp Wandernburg weather that had killed her, the terrible German winters, how much better the weather was in Andalusia, the dry climate in Granada that would have cured her, how every night before he fell asleep he could hear her faint voice, how mourning never ever ended.

Álvaro went quiet. He tried to smile. He straightened his hair and clothes, rising to his feet as though nothing had happened. Gentlemen, he said, if you'll excuse me, I think it's time I left.

Lamberg asked him if he could drop him off at the mill on the way, as it was a long walk. Álvaro said he would and saddled his horse. The sound of hooves vanished into the night.

Was Wandernburg the same? Or besides shifting furtively did it change appearance? Did it have a definitive shape or was it a blank space, a kind of map that hadn't been filled in? Could these wide, busy, light-filled streets be the same silent, cold and gloomy ones of a month or two ago? As he walked down Old Cauldron Street, Hans gazed in amazement at the gardens filled with barefoot children, at the flowering window boxes, the traveling musicians, the sweaty faces of the water-sellers hawking their cool water, sun-filled terraces where the pitchers seemed about to brim over with light. Sitting at one of the tables drinking a glass of iced lemonade was Lisa Zeit, who, when she saw Hans, moistened her lips, sat up straight and shrugged a shoulder in greeting, a gesture Hans found as exaggerated as it was heart-warming. Or that is what he thought, then said to himself he should have thought—simply heart-warming. Slumped opposite Lisa, Thomas was wolfing down a fruit sorbet. Hans waved to them and continued on his way. He crossed the sun-baked market square, walked through the impatient crowd gathered round the baroque fountain to fill their pots, winked knowingly at the organ grinder, and turned into Stag Street. Today, Hans thought, glancing about in a surprised manner, the streets seem just as I remembered them.

The last two Fridays, the salon at the Gottlieb residence had migrated to the courtyard, where the shade brought a pleasant breeze and a fountain burbled. The salon-goers sat in garden chairs around a table laden with food, polished fruit and ice-cold drinks. Although everyone had applauded the move outside, neither Elsa nor Bertold seemed very happy with the new arrangement, and spent all their time running up and down the steps to the house fetching and carrying trays, cups, jugs and cutlery. As was her custom, Elsa masked her displeasure by wearing a serious expression all the guests admired, mistaking it for conscientiousness. Bertold adopted two different faces, like the two halves of his harelip. Inside the confines of the yard, his mouth broke into a broad smile and his eyes twinkled good-naturedly; as soon as he stepped through the arch leading from the patio to the passage, he grimaced and began making sarcastic remarks and mimicking the speech of his master and his guests under his breath. Of everyone except Rudi Wilderhaus, whom he only dared mock when alone in his room.

That Friday, the Levins had been unable to attend the gathering because of a family engagement. And, as usually happens with those absent, they became the main focus of conversation. Although Sophie made polite efforts to change the subject, Frau Pietzine and Professor Mietter formed a rare alliance and, each in their own way, refused to move on to another topic. But don't you think she suffers? Frau Pietzine insisted, waving her fan more vigorously, isn't he a cold, aloof sort of husband? (My dear, Sophie said softly, slowing her own fan, there are many different types of marriage, and theirs …) Yes, yes, of course, I don't deny that, and naturally it is her affair! But a good husband, my dear girl—as our esteemed Herr Wilderhaus well knows!—should show affection towards his wife, be attentive at all times, make her feel (safe? Sophie smiled, brushing her fan against her lips), yes, precisely, my dear, you took the words right out of my mouth! Hans cleared his throat sarcastically and shot Sophie a sidelong glance. Rudi shot them both a sidelong glance, and cleared his own throat much more forcefully, at which Hans and Sophie immediately looked away. But Monsieur Levin, said Álvaro, seems like a respectful man to me, and you can't deny he is an excellent contributor to the salon. In a way, yes, Professor Mietter acknowledged, sucking a grape, Monsieur Levin is a good listener and his views, well, they are somewhat original shall we say. I understand he is a commercial broker and a mathematician, which is commendable. Unfortunately, despite being a self-taught and doubtless tireless reader, he lacks academic guidance. I agree that he is an interesting man, beyond his Judaism. Professor, Sophie said, folding her fan, at times your sense of humour is overwhelming. Frau Pietzine gave a nervous titter. A little more jelly, if you please, Mademoiselle, Professor Mietter said, pushing his plate forward with two fingers.

In order to change the subject, or to give Rudi the opportunity to shine, Herr Gottlieb asked his future son-in-law aloud about the state of the family lands. Grasping Herr Gottlieb's intentions, Rudi instantly put on a perfectly reluctant expression, as though the subject were loathsome to him. He waved his hands about, minimising the importance of his affairs and casually scaring off a couple of flies. He mentioned new crop fields, meadows and woods, cattle, sugar mills, breweries, distilleries and manufacturing plants. At one point in his inventory, he commented that the peasants were losing their traditional skills. They behave more and more like mercenaries, he said, as if they are working for you but they could be working anywhere. And couldn't they indeed be working anywhere, Herr Wilderhaus? declared Hans. Unfortunately for them, Rudi shrugged, I suppose they could, believe me when I tell you the old corporations were much more effective, they may have been stricter but they provided the day labourers with a home, whereas now they fill their mouths with talk of rights, roam up and down the country and end up in the big cities, lost and defenceless. Don't worry too much about them, said Álvaro sarcastically, I think they'd be happy if someone paid them a decent wage. Dignity, said Rudi, does not depend on pay. Until recently the peasants knew where they stood, and that they could trust the landowners. And that, Monsieur *Urquiho*, can be worth its weight in gold. Don't you think, dearest? I think, Sophie said, biting her lip, that my opinion on the subject is neither here nor there, business doesn't concern me. Quite, quite! said Herr Gottlieb, smiling with relief.

As soon as the corn had turned a burning yellow, a flaming yellow; before the ripened grain grew hard, at the precise moment when it began to glow inside and turn a coppery red; when the sunlight seemed almost chewable, ready for the harvest; in the anxious season, the mating, rutting season; when the sheep had lost their woollen coats and wandered the fields skinny and wounded looking, the lovers too cast off their clothes. Hans and Sophie would go on day trips to the countryside and remain alone thanks to the connivance of Elsa, who would leave Sophie halfway, stepping out of the coach to go and see her own lover, who was waiting for her at his house, to the south-east. The two women would meet again at the end of the afternoon and return home together.

Her face peeping out from under the circle of shade of her green parasol, seeing the fields pass by to the swaying of the landau, Sophie watched the harvesters at work. She contemplated their bent backs as they scythed, back and forth like pendulums. Yet she was thinking of Elsa, who seemed to be deliberately avoiding her gaze from the seat opposite. She trusted Elsa's loyalty, she had proved she was discreet and Sophie was sure she wouldn't betray her secret. Besides, Sophie thought, trying to put her own mind at rest, her meetings with Hans allowed Elsa a few hours off work to delight in love. To delight in pleasure, plain and simple, as every woman deserved, regardless of her situation or her station. What harm was there in that? In Sophie's opinion, none. But what did her maid think? Why did Elsa seem to obey her without really approving of what she was doing? How could a young, intelligent girl like Elsa judge her behaviour from a conventional moral standpoint? But more to the point, why did she, Sophie, care so much? Did she perhaps share Elsa's misgivings? Sophie was aware of being perfectly capable of deceiving her father, Rudi, everyone, but she didn't mean to deceive herself. And yet, if she closed her eyes and inhaled the mid-day breeze, nothing mattered very much compared to Hans's and her impetuous behaviour, which would carry on until she knew not when, as long as the summer allowed.

The carriage pulled up so that Elsa could get out. Seeing the sun on Sophie's face, she said: Fräulein, I implore you, keep covered, otherwise your father will notice and ask me what we get up to in the country. But I want to take the sun, replied Sophie, and I don't see why we girls always have to stay out of it. Tell that to your father, said Elsa, I don't make the rules. Sophie realised Elsa was in no mood for games. She leant forward and took her arm. Listen, Elsa, she whispered in her ear, you understand how much this means to me, don't you? And you understand how important it is to maintain absolute secrecy. Of course, Fräulein, Elsa nodded solemnly, you needn't remind me, have no fear. But you do understand, Sophie insisted. I understand nothing, I see nothing, I hear nothing. It's part of my job. That, replied Sophie, is what worries me, you understand everything, and I have no idea what you think. Don't worry, Elsa concluded, rest assured, my lips are sealed. I know, I know, breathed Sophie, but you do understand, don't you? I mean, besides being, well, my accomplice on these outings, it occurs to me you would do the same, and that's why you understand me. Fräulein, said Elsa, my job is not to understand your decisions but to do your bidding. Yes, yes, Sophie became impatient, but apart from that, Elsa, can you not put yourself in my shoes and feel what I feel, see what I see? Elsa lowered her eyes, then she looked straight at Sophie and said: Do you want my sincere opinion, Fräulein? I do, I do, said Sophie. If I were in your shoes, replied Elsa, I wouldn't bother asking my maid what she thinks, if you see what I mean. I see only too well, Sophie said with a sigh. Six o'clock back here, then? said Elsa. Yes, said Sophie, no, we'd better make it five-thirty. I'm dining out with Herr Wilderhaus tonight. I'll be here, said Elsa climbing down from the carriage. I'll see you then, Sophie said, sitting back in her seat, take care, take care.

The green parasol was propped up against the tree. The lovers' ankles were entwined. Her hiked-up skirts lay in folds about her thighs. His unbuttoned trousers were rucked around his ankles. Beneath the shade of the tree, as always when they spent a few hours together, they alternated moments of exhilarated conversation and long stretches of shared silence—aware of how much they could say to one another, remaining quiet did not bother them. They liked to think without speaking, each withdrawing into the other. They listened to the ebb and flow of their silence. Sophie sat up, fixed the ribbons in her hair, and reached for her parasol. Hans turned his head to look at her from below, still with the taste of her saliva, her sweat, her brackish sex at the back of his throat. She gazed at the countryside and turned the little ivory handle just as the sun turned among the treetops, as the wind turned, stirring the appetite, as the distant carriage wheels on the main road turned, as the cogs in the Tower of the Wind in the market square turned, as the organ grinder's handle, small, pivotal, turned and turned in its corner.

Hans was daydreaming and Sophie watched over him with a smile, trying to imagine what he was thinking. He also smiled and reached out to pinch her breast. He was thinking of her unruly breasts jiggling when she gave herself to him, of the violent way she clawed him, bit his face, sat astride him and shook him. He was thinking of the almost brutal honesty of Sophie's responses, of her surprising physical strength. Contrary to what he had imagined, she was not content to lie back submissively and let him decide everything—she satisfied her desire as naturally as a pitcher being poured. Hans felt embarrassed to admit it, but to begin with Sophie's sexual skills had intimidated him. Remembering his naive assumptions about her inexperience, Hans began to chuckle. She joined in without knowing what they were laughing about, then kissed him and said: What? Nothing, nothing, he said, it's silly, I was thinking about your, bah, about our, so you weren't a. Hans, my love, Sophie interrupted, pressing two fingers to his lips, I'm going to ask you this just once—don't try to resemble my father in any way at all! But I'm not saying there's anything wrong with it, Hans insisted, on the contrary! I simply wasn't expecting it, I mean, well, have you had many experiences with men, then? Sophie shrugged coquettishly and said: What would you like me to answer? That's not what I mean, he tried to explain, don't misunderstand me, it's just that, from the way you look, I expected you to be more … More what? Sophie arched her eyebrows. I don't know, said Hans, more innocent, I suppose. Now you know, she smiled, are you disappointed? No, no, he said, I'm surprised. Well, she said, shaking her skirts, before your surprise wears off, my love, try to keep it a firm secret, because I've always enjoyed a spotless reputation among the upper classes and suitable lovers among the lower classes. Why the lower classes? asked Hans. I'm surprised you ask, replied Sophie, firstly because of a natural attraction and secondly, you silly man, because coachmen, craftsmen and peasants are highly unlikely to gossip to the aristocracy. And if they did, no one would believe them. The truth is, your average nobleman is more puritanical than the man in the street. Don't look at me like that. And do you know why?

Because the aristocracy have such an easy life they end up underestimating pleasure. Respectable men are more fearful of a revolution in the bedroom than they are of political strife. Would you mind fanning me? I'm a little flushed.

One afternoon, while they were chatting in Hans's room, Sophie began leafing through the books and papers on the table. He showed her some magazines containing his translations, and a couple of poetry books for which he had written the prologues. They sat down next to the lighted oil lamp and read through the bilingual versions of the poems together, unable to resist the temptation to suggest alternative versions to the published texts. Sophie expressed three or four tentative objections to Hans, which he found surprisingly perceptive. They continued commenting on the poems until Hans had the idea that instead of spending time correcting what had already been published, Sophie could help him translate a couple of English poems he had to send off urgently to the *Atlas*. The *Atlas*? Sophie said eagerly, but I read all their issues in the library! They set to work, and despite Sophie insisting English was not her forte, Hans was delighted at the way she reformulated the sentences, the adjectives she chose, and her ability to take judicious liberties—she was like a child playing with her toys. Seeing Sophie's excitement as she reread the texts, her delight as she pondered the more challenging passages or recited the verses aloud under her breath, Hans had an idea that filled him with desire and enthusiasm.

A few days later, Hans sent her a note asking her to find any excuse to come to see him immediately. Not long after, Sophie appeared with Elsa at the inn, and while her maid waited downstairs playing with Thomas, she went up to his room. The moment Hans saw her come in, he gave her a kiss and told her to sit down and close her eyes. When Sophie opened them again, she found the proofs from the *Atlas* on her lap. When she saw her name printed under the translations next to that of Hans, she dropped the pages as if they were on fire. But Hans, you didn't, you shouldn't have! she stammered, with a mixture of delight and disquiet. Why not? he grinned, you translated almost half the verses! But, how? she said. Ah, it was easy, replied Hans, I wrote to the publisher and told them the translations were co-authored, it was only fair wasn't it? Are you saying you wish I hadn't? Sophie kept shaking her head and protesting, even as she began removing her underskirt until she was sitting astride Hans, pinning him to his chair. They rose up and down, clasping one another with wild gestures, without making a sound. When they were still again, the first thing Sophie did was to smooth out her skirt and pick up the proofs from the floor. Hans offered her some water.

Think about it properly, said Hans, if we translated together, not occasionally but officially, we could have a wonderful summer. We would enjoy reading and working together, and it would give us the perfect excuse to see one another here. We already agreed we have to act naturally so as not to arouse suspicion. If we insist on being secretive we'll end up looking as though we had something to hide. We share the same tastes in books as we do in bed, it's the perfect plan! Sophie made a gesture of partial surrender, before replying: I know, and I agree about the need for less secrecy, I don't know what will happen, but this way is better. As for my father, we'll have to see, I don't even want to think about that now. Rudi will agree, because I'll try, if I explain it to him in such a way, well, anyway—he'll agree. But to be completely honest, I'm not so sure about myself, about my abilities and what Brockhaus might think, Brockhaus, no less! (Don't say that, protested Hans, they see what they see, your translations, and they know they're good, and that's all they care about.) Yes, well, maybe you're right, and I appreciate your belief in me,

maybe you have more faith in me than I have in myself, but try
to understand, Hans, it isn't only that, there's all the rest, oh, I
don't know whether a man can understand! I also worry that
while the publishers judge you solely on your translations, they
judge me first and foremost as a woman translator, it's a small
difference but a terrible one, how can I be sure they will read my
work without bias, when not only am I young but I'm a woman?
Or that they'll they take me seriously? Or worse still, how do I
know they won't make allowances for me? (My love, said Hans,
you're complicating things unnecessarily, it's really quite simple,
if they like what you do they'll accept it and if they don't they
won't, as for making allowances—you're right, I'll ask them to
split the payment, to send me half and the other half to you, that
way you'll be in no doubt.) No, no, Hans, I won't hear of it! (Of
course, of course.) I mean it, please. (Too bad, princess!) Look,
this is crazy, I'm a young lady of means, but what will you do?
How can you survive on half the money? (I've managed to put
aside a few thalers, and besides, it wouldn't be half the money
because the two of us could translate almost twice as much, if
we split the work between us my earnings would be more or less
the same.) Hans, Hans, you're impossible, quite impossible and
I love you and no doubt I'll live to regret it, in short, I refuse to
argue with you over money, I don't know, let's assume you are
right, but in any case I'm sorry, I'll only agree on condition I
receive no payment for our translations, besides, my father would
never give his consent, believe me, he'll take enough convincing
as it is—imagine, a daughter of his, engaged to a Wilderhaus,
working! As though he couldn't afford to keep me! No, it will be
much simpler if I present this to him as a kind of literary pastime,
a form of education, do you see? Then perhaps he'll agree and
everything will turn out all right, and I will come here every
afternoon and talk Latin to you and decline all your verbs for
you and (hey!) and squeeze this thing here, and (Sophie, Elsa is

waiting for you downstairs) and give it a good bite (oh, oh, oh) and we can work in any tongue you like.

Herr Gottlieb pulled his moustache, curled it and wound it round his finger. He put his pipe down on the open magazine and shook his head in dismay. But my child, couldn't you have consulted me first? How could you do such a thing without even telling me, we've been through this before! Oh, God help us. But Father, Sophie purred, why are you so annoyed? Are you really so upset about your daughter amusing herself with a few harmless poems? You know perfectly well I've never prevented you reading or studying anything, replied Herr Gottlieb, that isn't what upsets me, what I thoroughly object to is you and Herr Hans (I and Herr Hans what, Father? Sophie said jauntily), well, this literary collaboration, as you call it, but my dear girl, do you think it decent for a young woman of your standing to associate herself with the publishing world? Father, smiled Sophie, you say *the publishing world* as though you were describing some criminal activity! Try to understand, I implore you, or are you suggesting a girl like me should stay at home reciting Children, Cooking, Church? Do you expect me even before I am married to devote myself entirely to cooking and giving you grandchildren? Please darling Papa, please, I know you'll say yes! All I ask, sighed Herr Gottlieb, pacifying his snake-like whiskers, is that you give some consideration to these matters. If that's your only objection, Sophie said with as much truthfulness as irony, then have no fear—I think of nothing else but the wedding these days. Be honest with me, my child, Herr Gottlieb beseeched her, aren't you happy at the prospect of starting a good family? That depends, she replied, if you refer to it as an inevitable duty, then perhaps not, Father, but if you mean it as a possibility, then, yes, I suppose I am, but is it really necessary to discuss that now? Tell me, Herr Gottlieb insisted, doesn't Rudi show you daily that he loves you? Father, Sophie took a gamble, it's getting late, I have to go and translate now, and I'm serious—if you try to stop me, if you forbid me to pursue this literary collaboration with Herr Hans, I'll lock myself in my room and translate anyway, I suppose you can't stop me from doing that, I'll lock myself in every afternoon, and do nothing but sleep, eat and translate until my wedding day! I'll grow pale, wretched and ugly, and the day I marry everyone will ask why I look so miserable on such a happy occasion and you'll feel ashamed to have such a, such a, such an ugly daughter, dear, darling Papa, be nice! My fate is in your hands, if you insist, I shan't go outside all summer, and that way you'll be happy, and in the end, Father, I'll also be happy because I'll have been a dutiful daughter and obeyed your orders. Child, Herr Gottlieb said falteringly, don't speak to me like that, you're being unfair (rest assured I'll obey your orders, Sophie said, pursing her lips), now you can't say that I (I trust you to be fair, Father, Sophie simpered, lowering her head), child, child! Be reasonable, I implore you! (I'm simply awaiting your verdict, whatever you decide will be for my own good.) But Sophie, if you would at least, I'm not trying to stop you! You know I always (I know, I know, and I'm eternally grateful, she said, fluttering her eyelashes), in that case, is there really no other solution? (Oh, Father, you're so understanding! Sophie tinkled, throwing her arms around him.) Child, dear child … (Not as dear as you are to me!) Very well, very well, but, wouldn't you at least consider translating with him here at home, what have you against that? Why do you have to do it at that godforsaken inn? (Oh, Father, I already told you, we would be distracted here, there are too many people, Bertold, Elsa, visitors, my friends, and besides, Father, Hans has a whole library at the inn, not to mention a pile of useful papers and dictionaries, everything we need for translating, imagine how cumbersome it would be to transport all that here every afternoon, let's be practical

Father, isn't that what you've always taught me?) Very well, very well! You're impossible! But there's one condition which I absolutely insist upon! (What is that, Papa?) Elsa must go with you every afternoon, and you must come back here together at the same time before it grows dark. (How tiresome, Father, are you sure? Sophie said, barely able to conceal her glee, do you really think it necessary for poor Elsa to watch over me all day long? Is this the trust you show your own daughter?) No, no, not another word! Either you translate at the inn with Elsa or you stay here and I won't hear another word about it! (How stern you are when you want to be! All those hours with strict Elsa! Very well, it will be as you wish, Father dear, a kiss and I bid you good afternoon.)

Reichardt lifted up his tricorn hat and wiped his brow with his forearm. He glanced about—he was the only harvester in his row who had stopped. It was hours since they'd paused for a break, yet the others kept toiling as though it were nothing. Did they never tire? Or were they trying to impress the foreman? Because it was impossible they didn't feel the slightest twinge, the same stabbing pain he felt in his shoulders from wielding the scythe all day long, the stiffness in his hips from turning to and fro all the time. It wouldn't be the end of the world, the corn wouldn't go up in smoke if they sat down for a moment to rest their legs. Reichardt waited for the foreman to look the other way before laying down his scythe. The calluses on his hands were stinging, although nothing hurt as much as his damned hips. He closed his eyes and took a deep breath, trying to recover his strength. Then the sound of metal scraping the ground, like a clash of swords, grew louder. As a youngster that sound had sent shivers down his spine. He had ended up becoming accustomed to it, had even grown to like it. Doubtless it still set the novices' teeth on edge as they scythed. Not his.

He was hardened. Not old, experienced. And he wasn't even tired. He only needed a short rest, that was all. Five minutes. Nothing. There was a time when he didn't need to stop either, but he wasn't as good with a scythe as he used to be. In fact, it didn't take as much strength as some muscly brutes thought. It was enough to know exactly where to cut the corn. If you cut very high, it would be too short and the foreman would shout at you. And if you cut too close to the ground, it was much more tiring and almost no one noticed the difference. Not to mention how some of them held the scythe! The clumsy oafs! No one could outstrip him where experience was concerned. Not even the foreman. So they thought they could tell him how to harvest corn? Working the land had its own time, like everything else. If you wanted to do a proper job, that is. And he wanted to do a proper job. That was why he needed five minutes, five bloody minutes' rest.

Facing into the hazy sun, against the light, the day labourers moved forward as one, heads down, scything the horizon.

Behind them, the women stooped to pick up the corn and tie it into sheaves. After that the labourers would stack the bundles on the ox-cart and transport them to the barns. Reichardt always tried to be chosen to drive the carts because it was less arduous than scything. But this time it was the foreman who came up behind him, tapped him on the shoulder and said: You. Reichardt wheeled round and gave him the most fresh-faced look he could muster in a bid to hide his weariness. Good work, eh? Reichardt said, splaying his arms and forcing a smile. More or less, replied the foreman. Listen, you've been around a long time, haven't you? Reichardt stared intently at the foreman, sharpening his wits, trying to determine whether the remark was a criticism or a sign of trust. More or less, he said, echoing the foreman's tone. I need a favour, the foreman said. At your service, Reichardt smiled, relieved, I was about to go on scything, but if there's something else needs doing ... I want you to go to the barn this instant, the foreman nodded, pick out the best grain you can find and take it in a horse-cart to Wilderhaus Hall. Of course, sir, said Reichardt, consider it done! Good, said the foreman, turning on his heel. Oh, sir, Reichardt called him back, excuse me sir. What is it? said the foreman, with the expression of someone whose time is being wasted. Nothing, sir, sorry sir, I just wondered, well, will I be paid? What for?—The foreman looked surprised—For going there and coming back? Of course not, old man, this is a favour, not a job, and I'm sure you'll carry it out in good faith, or am I mistaken? No, of course not, sir, Reichardt replied, lowering his head, I was just asking because, well, I do what I'm asked, naturally, only the law says that all transportation ... The foreman cut him short with a loud guffaw: I see you have friends in Parliament, I'll keep it in mind, I'll keep it in mind. Now fetch the cart, old man, go on, get a move on! And remember a horse-cart, not an ox-cart.

Having at last obtained Herr Gottlieb's permission, and under Elsa's supposedly watchful eye, the two of them met at the inn after lunch three times a week to work. Before leaving the house, Sophie took the precaution of having coffee with her father and chatting to him for a while to put him in a good mood. They discussed their relatives, various other families, the wedding preparations, or some anecdote from Sophie's childhood that might move Herr Gottlieb. At about three in the afternoon, Sophie would plant a kiss on her father's brow and casually take her leave. She and Elsa would walk to Old Cauldron Street together. They would enter the inn, and, after a prudent amount of time had passed, Elsa would leave again. After making sure no one was following her, she would take a carriage to her own rendezvous. The agreement with Herr

Gottlieb was to be home without fail before the nightwatchman finished his seven o'clock round. Elsa and Sophie would meet at exactly seven-thirty at the fountain. They chose to meet there because it was more likely to arouse suspicions if Elsa were always to return to the inn at the same time and always alone. Aware they were being observed, rather than dissembling they preferred to act as naturally as possible, which was the only way to forestall any rumours. And we can be thankful it's summer, Sophie had said, otherwise I'd have to be home much sooner.

During the four hours they spent alone three times a week, Hans and Sophie alternated between books and bed, bed and books, exploring one another in words and reading one another's bodies. Thus, inadvertently, they developed a shared language, rewriting what they read, translating one another mutually. The more they worked together, the more similarities they discovered between love and translation, understanding a person and translating a text, retelling a poem in a different language and putting into words what the other was feeling. Both exercises were as happy as they were incomplete—doubts always remained, words that needed changing, missed nuances. They were both aware of the impossibility of achieving transparency as lovers and as translators. Cultural, political, biographical and sexual differences acted as a filter. The more they tried to counter them, the greater the dangers, obstacles, misunderstandings. And yet at the same time the bridges between the languages, between them, became broader and broader.

Sophie discovered she had similar feelings when she made love to Hans as when she was translating. She thought she knew exactly what she wanted, what she desired. But then her certainties began to melt away, leaving fervent, conflicting intuitions to which she surrendered without worrying about the result. Later she would experience a strange fleeting lucidity, sudden bursts of light that would enable her to discover what she had been searching for—a definitive meaning, the precise feeling, the exact words. Then she would close her eyes and feel she was about to embrace an enormous sphere, to wrap her arms around it, to understand. Then, just as she was reaching the heights and was preparing to write or to speak to Hans from up there, the idea would unravel and the sphere would slip from her grasp, shattering into a thousand pieces. And although Sophie knew that no trembling emotion, no poem could be rendered in other words, because its totality was unattainable, her only wish was to begin again.

Hans's aim, which coincided in part with his publisher's weekly assignment, was to work on the modern European poets, always with the idea in mind of an improbable anthology, over which, for commercial reasons, Brockhaus was still hesitating. How many countries are we talking about here? his editor had asked him in a letter. As many as possible, Hans had responded, without really thinking. Begin by sending a sample, the editor had replied with probable irony, then we'll talk. Even so, Hans was convinced that in the end, with a little patience and with Sophie's help, this volume would one day come into being.

How can we speak about free trade, Hans pronounced as he lay next to Sophie, of a customs union and all that implies, without considering a free exchange of literature? We should be translating as many foreign books as possible, publishing them, reclaiming the literature of other countries and taking it to the classroom! That's what I told Brockhaus. And what did he say? Sophie asked, nibbling his nipple. Hans shrugged and stroked her back: He told me, yes, all in good time, and not to get agitated. But in such exchanges, said Sophie, it's important that the more powerful countries don't impose their literature on everyone else, don't you think? Absolutely, replied Hans, plunging his hand between Sophie's buttocks, and besides, powerful countries have a lot to learn from smaller countries, which are usually more open and curious, that is to say, more knowledgeable. You're the curious one! Sophie sighed, allowing Hans's probing fingers in and lying back. That, Hans grinned, must be because you're so open and you know what's what.

Refreshed and dressed, they were at the desk preparing to resume working when Hans began telling Sophie about a review he had read of the French adaptation of *Tasso* in which Goethe hailed the beginning of a new universal literature. He may be conservative in his political ideas, but you have to hand it to the old man, he's years ahead of everyone else in his literary thinking. A *Weltliteratur*! He was one of the first to defend French culture after the fall of Bonaparte, and he always describes poetry as the homeland of the poet, regardless of where he is from and what he writes. Goethe is a little like Faust, don't you think? And who wouldn't like to be a little like Goethe—to be a ceaseless reader, a polyglot, to know about every country and study every period in history. Hans rummaged in his trunk, found the article, and handed it to Sophie. Where did you get all your magazines from? she asked, attempting to see inside his trunk. I have them sent to me, he replied, hastily shutting the lid. An era of universal literature is approaching, Sophie read aloud, and each one of us should contribute to its formation. Yes, Hans nodded excitedly, the only way to build a German literature is by challenging it, comparing it, mixing it with foreign literatures. Anything else would be tantamount to locking the door and throwing the key into the sea. I recently read an article on this very subject by a fellow called Mazzini, why don't we translate it together next week, your Italian is better than mine. Mazzini was writing about Europe, but it seems to me that is only the beginning. For instance, Oriental literature is in fashion now, but soon it could be the turn of the Americas. And who knows, one day it might be necessary to go there in order to learn about ourselves. I'm thinking about sailing for America one of these days—listen! What if you came with me? What if we? What if we started working, Hans? Sophie interrupted, caressing him, it'll soon be five o'clock. Yes, yes, Hans said, coming back down to earth, forgive me. After searching through the disarray in his room, he placed several books and a handful of folios on the table. So, it's the turn of the English today, said Sophie, leafing through the various books. *Indeed, my dear*, sighed Hans in English, *and I must actually confess that it is urgent.*

There were two assignments for Brockhaus—a complete revision of an anthology of new English poets which the publisher wasn't happy with and which had been out of print for two years, and a translation of the main excerpts of the preface to *Lyrical Ballads*, which would be included as an appendix. They did a quick first reading in order to highlight the most problematic passages and lighten their work the following day. The method they used was simple—Sophie, who without a shadow of a doubt recited poetry better than Hans, would read the original poem aloud, pausing after each verse so that the rhythm of the stanza could unfold and settle, then go on to the next, like building a house of cards. In the meantime, Hans would go over the translated version, crossing out words, underlining any imprecisions, and noting down alternatives for discussion later. He was accustomed to working alone, and at first he had found it difficult to concentrate because Sophie's melodious voice, her pauses and inflections, made him feel an unexpected frisson. Slowly he began to enjoy this feeling that transported him from a foreign language to his lover's body. And he sensed Sophie was similarly aware of the sensual effect of this approach—she enjoyed holding back, modulating the tension between the discipline of work and the distraction of her desires. Indeed, it was from this electrifying struggle, which heightened their senses and sharpened their intelligence, that some of their best ideas were born. After several translation sessions, they both had become used to desiring one another as they worked, and had understood that their search for different words was another way of connecting, of shortening the distance between their two mouths.

They revised the versions of Byron's poems. These were somewhat mechanical although mostly accurate, because the translator had been careful to choose the simplest passages. It's strange, said Hans, Byron was at his most rhetorical, his most academic when he was at his least restrained. Perhaps, suggested Sophie, because he sometimes frightened himself with what he was saying.

They decided, however, to alter all the translations of Shelley, which they found stylised and filled with a stodgy pathos. Hans suggested eliminating all the adjectives and translating what was left. Sophie said she admired *Hymn to Intellectual Beauty*, which in her opinion refuted all attempts to separate the Enlightenment and the Romantics:

> *Thou messenger of sympathies*
> *That wax and wane in lovers' eyes—*
> *Thou, that to human thought art nourishment,*
> *Like darkness to a dying flame!*

Do you see? said Sophie, breathlessly, the darkness brings the flame to life! Mystery is the essence of this poem, but Shelley wrote it in order to bring light to the intellect. And this "human thought", untouched by emotion or love, is at once nourished by beauty, isn't it wonderful? Stop, Hans laughed, you're too convincing, I'm going to end up liking Shelley.

When they reached Coleridge, they concentrated above all on rewriting *Kubla Khan*, which was the only poem everyone knew:

> *In Xanadu did Kubla Khan*

A stately pleasure dome decree:
Where Alph, the sacred river, ran
Through caverns measureless to man
Down to a sunless sea.

The funny thing is *Kubla Khan* is far from being Coleridge's best poem, remarked Hans. But, as you know, it's the myth that counts, people don't expect poets to produce great works but to behave like great poets. And it occurred to the crafty Coleridge to tell people a three-hundred-line poem had come to him during an opium-induced slumber, and that when he awoke he recalled it word for word, an unrivalled work of genius! And so he began to copy it all down, but the poor man was interrupted and his poem remained unfinished, with only the few verses you can see ... So you don't believe him, said Sophie. I'd believe anything of a poet, smiled Hans, provided nothing he tells me is true. In that case, she argued, the poem wasn't unfinished, it continued in Coleridge's own narrative, in the tale he told about the dream, so that where the poem, or rather the dream, ends, the other tale begins, the one that begins when he wakes up. I get it! Hans declared, brushing her ankle under the table. In fact, Sophie went on, offering Hans her other ankle, the most romantic part of the poem is its explanation. You're right, Hans said growing excited once more, and what do think of the last line? "And drunk the milk of paradise"—all those *k*s at the end, such a struggle to drink some nectar! As if paradise were choking you! If you think about it for a moment, you realise the best Romantic poets never evoke paradise, only its impossibility. (When he had finished talking about Coleridge, Hans noticed with a touch of sadness that Sophie's ankle had moved away from his.)

Comparing styles, Sophie said, as she leafed through the

book, there seem to be two distinct approaches in English poetry—the grandiloquent and passionate, like Shelley and Byron, and the more serene but more modern one of Coleridge or Wordsworth. And where would that put Keats? Hans asked, indicating his poems. In both, Sophie hesitated, or neither. I agree, said Hans, that Byron or Shelley, however good they are, could never be modern like Wordsworth. He attempts to approximate speech when he writes, which in poetry is a cardinal sin. And as we know, literature only evolves through sinning (do you really think so? she smiled mischievously), yes, of course, I mean, when Wordsworth says in the Preface, wait, look, here, when Wordsworth says the language of prose can be perfectly adapted to poetry, that there is no real difference between well-written prose and the language of poetry, what is he doing? Debasing poetry? On the contrary, it seems to me he is enriching the possibilities of prose. And more importantly, he is associating poetry with everyday speech, with events in life that aren't necessarily sublime. Wordsworth takes poetry off its pedestal and broadens its scope.

I understand, Sophie said, taking the book from him, it sounds very convincing. But if poetry takes on too much of an everyday quality, how are we to differentiate between a well-written and a badly written poem? That, replied Hans, is Wordsworth's most difficult dilemma, which I suppose is why he tackled it early on in his Preface, pass me the book, please, look, here: "The first volume of these poems, blah blah blah, was published as an experiment, which, I hoped, might be of some use to ascertain, how far, by fitting to metrical arrangement a selection of the real language of men ..." (Ah, said Sophie sarcastically, and the language of women remains a mystery.) Well, all right: "to ascertain, how far, by fitting to metrical arrangement a selection of the real language of people ..." (how kind of you, Sophie broke in) "... in a state of vivid sensation that sort of pleasure and that quantity of pleasure may be imparted, which a poet may rationally endeavour to impart." Notice that Wordsworth refers to it as an *experiment*, there is nothing perfunctory about it, especially since he is referring to a *selection* of everyday speech, which is where the poet's talent comes into play, and that such everyday moments must coincide with a state of vivid emotion. If these premises are adopted, Wordsworth's experiment could never result in vulgarity. It would be different were someone to follow the simplest part of his advice and ignore the rest. Most notably, just a moment, let's see, I underlined it somewhere, where is it? Ah, here—most notably the part where he says "and, at the same time, to throw over them a certain colouring of imagination, whereby ordinary things should be presented to the mind in an unusual aspect", this is most interesting don't you think? And then further down: "chiefly, as regards the manner in which we associate ideas in a state of excitement", meaning, to delve into everyday emotions, to order them and translate them into everyday language, not forgetting the capacity our imagination has to associate images and ideas. Do you see how old-fashioned Byron seems by comparison?

I'm not trying to defend Byron or Shelley, Sophie mused, I just think that in order to judge a poet's style one must take into account the rhetoric of his forebears. I mean, rhetoric is like a pendulum, isn't it? There are periods when everyday speech and writing seem to be in conflict, such as in the works of Milton or Shakespeare, until that exclusively poetic language becomes mannered, giving way, so to speak, to Pope, and then poetry moves closer to speech again, as in some of Coleridge's or Wordsworth's poems. It strikes me that the swings of the pendulum have their propitious moments, and that a poet with a good ear should know at what point the pendulum is with regard to the poetry in his language. Hans said with admiration: We must include that idea in the introduction. Yes, Sophie went on, I see it like a set of scales, and perhaps Wordsworth is right, and now is one of those moments. Hans agreed: We could do with a dose of it here in Germany. We are constantly seeking purity, which is regrettable. And in my view poetry that seeks purity becomes puritanical, true lyricism is the opposite, how can I describe it? It is pure impure emotion. That's what I like about modern English poetry, its impurities. However lofty, it never loses faith in the value of immediate reality, as in "the fancy cannot cheat so well". That's why (Hans went on, skipping forward through the pages of the book) I left Keats, my favourite, until last. I was very keen for us to translate him together, beginning with *Ode to a Nightingale*. A simple nightingale would never satisfy a German poet, he'd have to hear the cosmos or at the very least a gigantic mountain.

Sophie had just finished reading the last words of *Ode to a Nightingale*. Hans remained silent for a few moments, eyes half-closed, savouring the possible sound of those words in a different tongue. Then he asked Sophie to read the last verse again more slowly. "Forlorn!" she began reading again softly. "The very word is like a bell to toll me back from thee to my sole self …" Hans simultaneously copied out his translation, which she read immediately afterwards.

Sophie reread the final verse. She noted down *fades* next to *vanishes* (I think it's more powerful, she said, crossing her leg), she wrote down *has flown* next to *has gone* (we lose a rhyme, she explained, slipping off a shoe, but we gain in accuracy, because music flies like a bird) and *submerged* instead of *interred* (it fits better with the stream, she explained, letting her other shoe fall to the floor). But if the song is *submerged*, Hans protested gazing at her feet, we sacrifice the idea of the nightingale not just flying away, but in some way dying in the poem. I see, Sophie replied, moistening her lips, what about *buried*, which sounds more terrible? Possibly, said Hans chewing his lip. Sophie read aloud the different versions. I like it, she nodded, standing up, although the poet seems pleased the dream has ended, as if by bidding the nightingale farewell he had vanquished it—farewell! Fly away! I've awoken, you can no longer deceive me, I know that nothing is eternal. True, Hans grinned, seeing what she was driving at, but don't you think Keats was saying the same thing? I'm not sure, Sophie said, standing in front of him, I thought he was sad that the nightingale's spell has been broken. The question is, Hans said, rising from the table, whether when he writes: "the fancy cannot cheat so well", he means: what a pity the dream can't deceive us for ever! Or is it his pride speaking: you can't fool me now!—like someone suddenly seeing the light. Exactly! Sophie said, running her hands over Hans's thighs, doesn't the same apply to "deceiving elf"? Is he writing with longing or regret? It seems to me, Hans said, spreading his legs, that Keats was saying farewell to his dreams, he was sick and knew what awaited him, he no longer had time for certain things, he wanted to come down to earth, to be as real as possible, I assume that's what happens when you have tuberculosis. Perhaps, said Sophie, her hand reaching his upper thigh, and yet what a beautiful and ambiguous poem! Precisely because he knew he hadn't long to live, I think, Keats was struggling to create a voice that would outlast his own, a means to fly away with the nightingale, as though the nightingale itself were poetry, don't you think? "Thou wast not born for death, immortal Bird!"—a bird that sings for all eternity. Do you know what? Hans said, unfastening his belt, I think both interpretations are right, Keats must have thought: How wonderful it would be to live in an imaginary world where death doesn't exist and one can sing for all eternity! Why not shield oneself from pain with this fantasy? Even as he was thinking: Yet each day I feel more pain, my condition is deteriorating, and when I sing blood pours from my mouth, how can I believe nightingales live for ever? Farewell, let them fly away, I'll spend what remains of my life down here.

A melancholy silence descended on the room—it was a quarter to seven in the evening, and the sun's rays were almost horizontal.

What remains of my life down here, Sophie echoed, kneeling.

For reasons of social discretion and because it was his personal retreat, Hans had scarcely talked to Sophie about the organ grinder or his cave. The first time he had mentioned his friend to her, Sophie had taken a moment to realise he was referring to the scruffy old man who played a battered barrel organ in the market square, a black dog at his feet. What? That old man? she had said in astonishment. What's so special about him? He's been there for years. Noticing that Hans had bridled slightly, Sophie began to insist on a formal introduction. Initially, he had resisted, partly out of a sense of shame (a shame that made him bitterly unhappy) and partly because he was afraid he couldn't bear it if, like everyone else, she were to look down her nose at him. After a while, faced with Sophie's pleas, Hans decided to take the plunge. In fact, for months he had been eager and reluctant to introduce her to the organ grinder. Apart from Álvaro, the organ grinder was his only friend in Wandernburg, and it was only natural he should introduce Sophie to him. Besides, as things stood, the old man knew virtually all there was to know about her. And so, at twelve o'clock one balmy Wednesday in July, Hans arranged the meeting and crossed his fingers. Sophie would arrive accompanied by Elsa just before lunch, on the pretext of having gone out to purchase some cotton thread and angora buttons at a haberdasher's.

The market square was bustling with children on their way home from school, women flaunting colourful frocks that billowed in the breeze, and men piling in to taverns. The Tower of the Wind cast a tall shadow over the cobblestones, its twin towers pointing skywards, as though about to pierce the skin of time and fly off like arrows. Hans waited anxiously and played with Franz, who was trying to bite the toe of his boot. Of the three coins in the organ grinder's dish, two were from Hans. When Hans recognised the familiar green parasol floating through the crowd, he turned to the old man and asked if he would play an allemande. The organ grinder nodded and began turning the handle, but suddenly he lifted his head and said: A waltz would be better. Why a waltz? asked Hans. Don't be such an innocent, because it's more daring, of course!

Sophie, Elsa, announced Hans ceremoniously, this is my good friend, the organ grinder. The old man bowed, clasped Elsa's hand between two fingers, brushed it with his lips and said: Charmed, I'm sure. He repeated the same gesture with Sophie, and added: I've been looking forward to meeting you, Fräulein, I've heard a great deal about you, all of which I can see was true. Seeing Hans become uneasy, the organ grinder explained: Your family has always enjoyed great prestige in this city. Perplexed by the old man's graciousness, which seemed so at odds with his appearance, Sophie handed her parasol to Elsa, leant forward and replied: The pleasure is ours, sir, and I confess that of late I have been hearing even more flattering things about you.

A silence descended, which Hans found uncomfortable, Sophie intriguing and the organ grinder utterly delightful. They all exchanged glances, smiled and looked at the ground at a loss for words. Hans gave a nervous cough. Then the organ grinder clicked his tongue, exhaled noisily and declared: Good heavens, where are my manners, a thousand pardons, ladies, this creature sprawled on the floor here is Franz, my protector, Franz get up and say hello to these young ladies. Hans raised a hand to his face and thought: This can only end badly. But Sophie, utterly enchanted by the old man, stooped to stroke

Franz, who sprang to his feet. Delighted to meet you, Herr Franz, said Sophie. Franz gazed at her with moist eyes, wrinkled his brown eyebrows and laid back down. He's a well-bred dog, but he likes to conserve his energy, explained the organ grinder.

Sophie, Hans and the organ grinder stood casually chatting a moment longer, before saying goodbye. The old man concluded by solemnly inviting her to his cave. My humble cave, he stated, which is wonderfully cool in the summer. Sophie bade him farewell, promising to come. Hans had a suspicion she would be true to her word. As she turned to leave, taking Elsa's arm, Hans studied Sophie's face—he knew she had enjoyed herself and that, in some way, the organ grinder had fascinated her.

The filthy old man with the barrel organ pointed towards the dog. Sophie bent down to stroke the animal and looked contented. Elsa stood watching, motionless. Hans, who also happened to be there, made a strange gesture with his hand. What were they saying to each other? Rudi Wilderhaus was observing the scene through the windows of the Central Tavern. He couldn't hear them or fully make sense of the situation. She was with Elsa, yes, but why were they dallying? And what were they talking about to Hans and that filthy old man?

Laughter broke out over by the bar. One of Rudi's young companions placed a hand on his shoulder as he sat gazing through the window, his back to them. Hey, Wilderhaus, said the young aristocrat, aren't you bothered by your fiancée associating with strange men? How can you accept her frequenting a common inn? My fiancée, Rudi replied, swinging round, associates with whom she pleases, because, unlike yours, she's no fool. As for Sophie's visits to the inn, her father and I are fully aware of them; she goes there to indulge in one of her favourite pastimes, which is literary translation.

Rudi's friends shot each other glances, stifled guffaws, raised their tankards: Your health, Wilderhaus! said one. I drink to your fiancée's literary endeavours! Rudi clinked his tankard and retorted: And I drink to your descendants carrying on the family tradition of ignorance. All but the toastee laughed. Rudi turned once more to the window. He saw the two women taking their leave of Hans and the filthy old man, before continuing on their way. He thought he detected a smile on Sophie's face. When he rested his elbows on the bar, he looked solemn, though apparently unruffled. Seriously, Wilderhaus, one of the others ventured, don't you think it's a bit much? Oughtn't you to intervene just to be on the safe side, if only as a matter of decency? Sophie's decency is beyond reproach, Rudi said lifting his chin. I told you, I trust her implicitly, and I trust myself even more. Of course, of course, the other man said, but be honest, don't you feel just a little jealous? Rudi remained silent for a moment. He gave a long sigh, slammed down his tankard and growled: Who do you think you're talking to, numbskull! Do you imagine for one moment that I'm intimidated by a lowly scribbler from God knows where, with no family, no estate, no refinement? Do you expect me to feel even remotely jealous of an ignorant commoner who lodges at an inn? What infuriates me are not Sophie's outlandish pastimes, which she has always pursued and quite rightfully, it's the disgraceful insinuations of people like you. The mere fact that you think I should be concerned about this is humiliating and offensive to me. I therefore demand that you retract your vile remarks this instant, or that you repeat them to me while brandishing the weapon of your choice. And the same goes for the rest of you.

The other man lowered his head and stammered an apology. His friends hastily did likewise. The group fell silent. Rudi Wilderhaus gestured to the waiter, left a few coins on the bar, and walked out without saying goodbye.

Each time Professor Mietter parted his taut lips to speak, the water fountain in the patio became clearly audible again—the other salon-goers dutifully stopped talking and waited for his opinion, fingers clasped. Hans could not help being impressed by the professor's authority, although he remained somewhat perplexed by it. The professor never grew excitable in an attempt to impose his arguments—he delivered them unhurriedly while the others appeared to take notes in silence. Herr Gottlieb would nod his head in solemn interest. Sophie would smile rather ambiguously. And Hans, who was beginning to understand Sophie's gestures, suspected that these long, ecstatic smiles were a sign that she disagreed completely.

Aware of Hans and Sophie's literary collaboration, Professor Mietter began by expressing his concern that she might be neglecting other important matters for a girl her age whose marriage was only months away. Upon hearing this, Herr Gottlieb uttered a cry that left his whiskers quivering like a pair of darts that have just hit their target. Then, almost imploringly, he said: That is precisely what I say to her, yet she refuses listen to reason. Frau Pietzine agreed with the professor. But on seeing Sophie frown, she added: Well, I dare say there's no harm in it. Frau Levin shifted her fan from one hand to the other, shaking her head disapprovingly. Her husband cleared his throat, pensively. Hans, who wanted to give Sophie a look of encouragement, felt sure Rudi was watching him and, regretting the absence of the round mirror in the drawing room, spiked a slice of orange sprinkled with cinnamon. Encouraged by this protective advice, Sophie resolved not to waste time trying to defend herself, but instead to use humour—the only thing Professor Mietter didn't understand, and which undermined her father's authority. How right you are, gentlemen, I wish I'd never translated a single verse, I've been so naive! But I promise you, as of tomorrow, what am I saying, as of today! I shall study only moral treatises and cookery books.

Were it not for Frau Pietzine's quick laugh, Hans could have sworn Herr Gottlieb and Professor Mietter were about to take her seriously. Sophie used this opportunity to ask her guests what they would like to drink, and stood up to go and give Elsa instructions. By the time she returned to her seat, the conversation had turned to the practical scope of translation. With scholarly serenity, Professor Mietter was questioning the legitimacy of translations of poetry. Hans, who had scarcely slept a wink and felt his eyelids drooping, was disagreeing with him rather tactlessly.

Don't get me wrong, young man, the professor was saying, I have nothing against the admirable efforts of those who endeavour to translate poetry. God forbid, on the contrary. But strictly speaking, if we leave aside good intentions and study the topic more methodically, you must all agree, as discerning readers of poetry, that each poem possesses an untransmissible essence, a distinctive sound, precise forms and connotations that are impossible to adapt to another language with a similar perfection. It would be quite another thing, of course, to renounce the overly ambitious task of translating the poem and instead offer the reader a kind of guide, a literal transcription of the words that would enable him to penetrate the original, which is what really counts. But these are no longer translations in the literary sense to which you were referring, which, dare I say it, seems to me an impossible undertaking from the very outset.

(As he listened to the professor's arguments, Hans reflected that everything he said was applicable to the field of the emotions—in short, someone who disbelieved in the possibilities of translation was sceptical of love. This man, Hans reflected unkindly, was linguistically born to solitude. Or, all things considered, to marriage. All of a sudden Rudi choked on his drink, and for a moment Hans was unsure if he had been thinking aloud unawares.)

Professor Mietter continued holding forth about fidelity to the original text, and respecting the author's words. Hans raised a finger and, to his astonishment, the professor instantly fell silent, yielding him the floor with a polite gesture. The professor's judicious mouth gobbled a piece of pineapple in syrup.

I understand your argument, Hans said rather uneasily, but I think being faithful is a contradiction (Rudi turned towards him and gave him a significant stare: Now what are we talking about? thought Hans), because the moment another text emerges, faithfulness is no longer achievable, the poem has been transformed, it has become a different poem. We have to take as a given the impossibility of rewriting anything literally, not even a single word. Some translators are wary of this transformation, seeing it as a betrayal rather than a variation. But if it is well done, if the job of interpretation gives the right result, the text may even be improved, or at least become another poem as worthy as its predecessor. And I would go further—I think it is the translator's duty to offer the reader an *authentic* poem in his own language precisely in order to remain faithful to the poetic nature of the original. Of course, this requires the translator to tread a delicate path between the liberties he takes and a true, or rather an honest, understanding of the text. That is the risk, and perhaps the hardest part of all. The fact is I see no alternative but to assume that risk. And let us not deceive ourselves—even an original poem has no single interpretation, to read a poem is also to translate it, we can never be completely sure of what a poem is saying even in our own language. As I see it, a translation is not made up of an authorial voice and one that obeys it, rather it is more akin to a meeting of two literary wills. In the end there is always a third person—isn't there?—who is a third discordant voice, which turns out to be that of the reader (but what are we really talking about here? Hans thought to himself), and if that reader could really understand the original, as you are suggesting, then, rather than a useful guide, translations would be almost superfluous.

Aha, said Professor Mietter. Ahem, that depends, asserted Herr Levin. Possibly, acknowledged Álvaro. I'm not sure, wavered Sophie. How confusing, sighed Frau Pietzine. Snuff, anyone? proposed Rudi. Goodness, it's hot, commented Gottlieb.

Look, the professor said, clearing his throat, given your penchant for getting lost in metaphor, I shall try to be as clear as possible. Poetry is obviously a universal form of artistic expression. However, in each of its particular manifestations, poetry is a cultural, national art, and as such, by definition, impossible to translate. And shall I tell you why? Perhaps you are familiar with Hamann, who rightly emphasises the inseparability of language and thought. I do not think something abstract and then translate it into my own language. I think directly in that language, because of it, through it. This is why no thought is translatable, at most it is adaptable. Are you with me? Good. If this applies to all disciplines, imagine how extreme the problem becomes in poetry, which is the language of emotions. Bear in mind, since you brought up the emotions earlier, that it is far easier to think in a foreign language than to feel in it (that, said Álvaro raising his head, is very true), and from this one can deduce that any feeling expressed in another language cannot be the same feeling, not even a variant of it. At best it can be *inspired* by another feeling. Call this an exchange, an influence or what you will. But, I beg you, do not call it translation.

Very well, said Hans, finding himself in the awkward position of having to contest a solid argument, very well, Professor, let us go step by step. You maintain that to translate feeling is more difficult than to translate thought. I am not sure in what measure it is possible to conceive of an idea as being divorced from emotion, or emotion devoid of any ideas. This would be my first objection, that you seem to take for granted the existence of pure emotion as if it came from nowhere and were self-contained. In my humble understanding, emotions are not only generated by a specific language, they also arise from cultural exchanges, from prior exposure to other languages, from national and foreign connotations. This is the heterogeneous basis of our thoughts, feelings and writings. In order to avoid getting lost in metaphor and upsetting you, I shall try to give you a concrete example, Professor. Does Goethe feel in German on the one hand and on the other speak six languages? Or rather, as an individual who speaks and reads several different languages, does Goethe feel in a specific way that is peculiar to him and which in this case expresses itself in the German language? Isn't his broad cultural knowledge a current that is channelled, *translated* into his mother tongue? And by the same token, are the translations of Goethe's own poems into other languages not simply one more link in an infinite chain of interpretations? Who are we to decide which is the original, the first link? Furthermore, Professor, allow me to say that even if translation were an impossible dialogue, culturally speaking it would be the most necessary one. Renouncing this dialogue would lead to the worst form of nationalism, not to say to esotericism. After separating the poetry of each country, the next step would be to decide which came first and which was superior to the rest. And so this is not simply a question of grammar and philology but of principles.

Sophie clicked her tongue—her smooth, expressive, darting tongue. Herr Levin? she said, noticing him drumming his fingers on the table.

Indeed, ahem, said Herr Levin I would like, I mean, I think we have ignored an important point in this discussion, or something I consider has a certain bearing. For translation is not simply an individual process, is it? It is also a process that depends on the community in which it is being done. That is, a translator translates for others, or rather with others, and communities change with history. Doesn't every author, book and text have a history of the ways in which it has been read? And this history forms part of the work itself. What I'm saying is, ahem, how are we to separate the collective readings of the Classics from the Classics themselves? In my opinion translations belong to this kind of rereading, every translator is also a product of his time, of the period when he wrote his translation. No book remains exactly the same throughout time, the readers of each period change it, don't they? And the same goes for translations, each period needs to retranslate its literature. Ahem, I don't mean to go on.

You are quite right, said Hans. (Do you really think so? stammered Herr Levin.) A work doesn't begin and end with its author, it forms part of a much broader group, a kind of writing collective that includes translators. Translation is neither a betrayal nor a substitute, it is another contribution, a further push to something that is already in motion, like when someone jumps into a moving carriage. And as you say, dear Herr Levin, every text continues to be translated over time by readers of its mother tongue. Each German reader of Goethe understands, misunderstands, interprets and over-interprets each word, there is no transparency between a book and its reader, there will always be some peculiarity that gives rise to a second text, a new reading. That is why, if you'll forgive my insistence, no good translation can ever distort the translated work—it simply exaggerates the mechanisms of reading itself.

Sophistry, demagoguery! protested Professor Mietter, with all your insistence on communities, are you trying to deny the influence of national culture? The nation is important even when translating a text, gentlemen. The French, for instance, have always appropriated texts rather than try to translate them, which is why they built an empire. A French translator will seldom attempt to stay close to the foreign mentality of the author he is translating, but will instead try to adapt the work to fit his own mentality. Aristotle in the French, for example, appears French. This approach undoubtedly has its merits, and yet it also shows that the real Aristotle is and can only be written in Greek. (Yes, argued Hans, but however hard a French translator tries to approximate Aristotle to his own way of thinking, don't you think the outcome will resemble neither the original Greek nor a French philosopher? And won't this French translation of Aristotle for ever change French philosophy and what you refer to as its national mentality?) Ah, young people, young people, how they love to answer back! This elderly gentleman deserves a rest, now, my dear, is there any more raspberry jelly?

(Raspberries! Hans thought suddenly, like someone opening a window. Sophie's sex tastes just like raspberries—raspberries to begin with, and afterwards lemons.)

Raspberries, yes! Rudi declared, stirring from his bored stupor, a capital idea, Professor Mietter! Elsa, *liebe Jungfer*, would you? …

(There's something strange going on here, Hans said to himself, glancing anxiously at Sophie, who flashed him a look of desire. There's something decidedly peculiar going on here, Hans repeated to himself, or didn't I get enough sleep last night, or what?)

Raspberries! exclaimed Frau Pietzine. Heaps of raspberries!

(No, I didn't get enough sleep, Hans said to himself, I stayed translating into the small hours, and it was late, late, very late when I went to bed.)

Heaps of raspberries! Frau Pietzine howled ecstatically. And Frau Levin joined in, dropping her fan and lifting up her skirts: Just like Sophie's sex!

(Wait a moment, what? Hans said to himself, what the? …)

Herr Hans, said Sophie.

(What the? …)

Herr Hans! Sophie repeated, giggling.

What! asked Hans, his eyes opening with a jerk.

We rather suspect, Sophie said with amusement, that you were enjoying a little nap, Herr Hans. Hans sat up in his chair and noticed a crick in his neck. He glanced around him—the other guests were looking at him, amused. Ladies and gentlemen, Hans stammered groggily, I'm terribly, terribly sorry. On the contrary, said Sophie, it shows you feel at home in our courtyard. You see, last night, Hans tried to rouse himself, last night I, er, I translated, ah, translation! Forgive me, So, er, Mademoiselle Gottlieb, but how long was I asleep? Not very long, said Álvaro, unable to stifle a chuckle, a few minutes, about as long as it took Professor Mietter to answer you! Professor, said Hans, sitting up straight, please forgive this mishap, which owes nothing to your reply and everything to my tiredness, I have an accumulation of work and last night … Oh, the professor said, waving his hands disdainfully, don't worry, don't worry—we *translated* it in accordance with your theories as a form of cultural exchange with Herr *Urquiho*.

The other salon-goers burst out laughing. Hans joined in, forcing a smile. He felt a hissing in his ears, his eyes smarted and he had a slight taste of raspberries in his mouth.

As evening closed in, Elsa and Bertold brought down four candles to the yard and spread them out along the folding table. The conversation became filled with shadows and glistening profiles. Before taking his leave at the customary hour, Herr Gottlieb placed a fleshy hand on Hans's shoulder. My dear Herr Gottlieb, said Hans, rising from his chair. Herr Gottlieb lowered his pipe, drew his bushy whiskers near, and whispered discreetly: Would you be so kind as to accompany me to my study for a moment? Fearing the worst, Hans said of course, it would be an honour. Sophie watched the two men leave out of the corner of her eye.

They climbed the steps together and walked down the icy tunnel of the corridor, which always seemed to remain at the same temperature. Although since the beginning of his friendship with Sophie he had taken the precaution to continue visiting Herr Gottlieb on his own, Hans had never been invited into the mysterious room where Herr Gottlieb would withdraw for hours. Bertold opened the door for them, went ahead, and lit a couple of oil lamps before disappearing. Hans's attention was immediately drawn to the shelves lined with leather-bound volumes. Next he glanced at the desk made of dark wood, the leather armchair and the bronze inkstand containing an inkwell, quill pens, a penknife and a bell to ring for the servants. On one side of the desk was a framed photograph of a pale-faced young woman. The lamps were placed so that that the whole room was plunged into a purposeful gloom, forcing the visitor to tread more cautiously, almost with trepidation. Herr Gottlieb sat down in his chair, gesturing to Hans to sit down opposite him, and poured two generous glasses of brandy. Hans swallowed hard.

You see, my friend, said Herr Gottlieb, I would like to be frank with you. I know I can trust you, because we have got on from the very first and you have always seemed to me a responsible and perceptive young man. I have been observing this literary collaboration between you and my daughter for some weeks now. Don't get me wrong, knowing my daughter as I do, I find nothing surprising about her interest in translating and seeing her work published in these magazines, indeed I would describe it as yet another of her countless whims. I understand her need to begin freeing herself from her father's authority, and also, to some degree, to establish her independence in the eyes of her future husband. Sophie has ever been thus, since she was a child. I'm afraid Herr Wilderhaus knows it only too well and, thank Heaven, loves her all the same. However, my dear Hans, I cannot help wondering how appropriate it is for a young woman about to marry to be working, let us say, at such close quarters with a bachelor like yourself. I assure you I have no objection to you personally, on the contrary I like to think you and I have developed a certain friendship, correct me if I'm wrong, good, I'm glad you agree. I am relieved to be able to tell you all this, because, you see, I am concerned as a father, and also as your friend. What do you say, dear fellow?

The brandy thickened.

Your feet, Sophie commanded, your feet, too. Hans hated his feet. Sophie adored them. She adored his rough heels, his rather stubby toes. Come on, show me, she urged as she undressed, and he obeyed with the awkward excitement of one allowing the last of his modesty to be trampled. Sophie raised her arms to strip off another garment, revealing her underarm hair. Hans, embarrassed, contented, removed his socks as one might peel a piece of fruit.

Hans lay on his back awaiting Sophie's manoeuvres, which she would draw out, prolonging these moments when she felt he was in some way at her mercy. She liked it when Hans showed his eagerness, called out her name, implored her. And not because she didn't share his urgency, but because she felt a violent symmetry, a harmonious tension in possessing him before being possessed. Sophie lay on her side, and studied Hans's testicles. She saw their heaviness, their blemishes, their tight pores and wrinkled darkness. The lines and furrows reminded her of a map with its maze of rivers, paths, promontories and valleys. She imagined traveling over these testicles made of earth, exploring their seed. She brought her mouth close to them, closed her eyes and began to lick them, to moisten their folds, soften them. Sophie's wandering tongue reached his anus. She moved the tip of it close to the orifice, then paused. Opening her eyes she looked up at

Hans. He silently consented, covering his face with his forearm. Sophie raised his legs, which seemed light or put up no resistance despite the puzzled look on their owner's face. Hans feared Sophie's nails might hurt him, but out of the corner of his eye he saw her drag the washstand over and soap her hands. First she circled the orifice, probing its mysteries. Then she discovered its softness, the hair around the fissure. Then a soapy finger slipped inside. Then his flesh opened to her.

Sophie enjoyed watching the muscles along Hans's back go taut as he moved on top of her as if he were climbing. She liked feeling his weight, that mixture of protection and aggression, of freedom and suffocation. She could read his exertions, his spasms, his pauses in the skin on his back. She lay back, felt close to the edge of something, and gripped Hans's arms, which were flanking her, throbbing, straining, scarcely able to hold themselves up. She gripped them as someone might clasp a railing to prevent themselves falling, she pushed against them, tried to make them give way, felt every muscle, then suddenly began laughing without knowing why. She went into the tunnel of laughter, searching for an end that might be a beginning. Hans pressed hard, but held back his climax and closed his eyes—in the darkness he saw a double helix of light turning on itself, almonds within almonds, as though fingerprints were being etched on the inside of his eyelids.

She rolled around, spun on herself like an axle—now astride Hans, sitting on his urgency, sinking into position, she had the impression of being the one penetrating him with her own member. Hans's sex was no longer his, or hers, it was an intermediary. She pressed her hands against his chest, she felt she was bathing in a river, thrashing, diving, swimming. Beneath, drowned, saved, Hans watched her writhe, testing the resilience of the wooden bed frame. He thought they might hear the creaking downstairs. He thought Herr Zeit might realise what they were doing. He thought Frau Zeit might be on the stairs. He thought Lisa might be loitering in the passageway. He thought they shouldn't be doing this and he didn't care. He stopped thinking in a flash, and Sophie dragged him with her. Hans groped in the air, lost control, and found her breasts. They both rolled downhill together.

She washed, humming to herself beside the washbasin. She washed between her legs, freshened her underarms, dabbed her neck and cheeks with perfume. She asked Hans to help tighten her corset. He took the opportunity to remove a few pubic hairs that had stuck to her back. She straightened her skirts, carefully smoothed out her crinolines. Then she went over to the tiny mirror to straighten her hair and refresh her make-up. After this agile performance, Sophie wheeled round and Hans gazed at her in admiration—in ten brief minutes, she was once more Fräulein Gottlieb.

Sophie sat down at the desk, folded her legs and said dreamily: Shall we go over what we did on Monday or move on to something else?

With the broiling heat of July, with burning skins and exhausted fans, the summer began in Wandernburg. The more well-to-do families chose a spa or headed for their country houses on the banks of the Nulte. The young people preferred to travel to the Rhine to enjoy the nightlife of Bonn or Cologne. The summer holidays had begun, although few people went away—the majority of Wandernburgers stayed behind, spending the days in the shade of their gardens. A few families were content to go on day trips, cramped and uncomfortable in carriages, but happy because the sun was in the zenith. Craftsmen laid down their tools, shut up shop and slept with the windows closed. Children gambolled in parks or squares, suddenly faced with what seemed like eternal freedom.

Farther south, in the fields, shepherds watched idly over their flocks. Sheep shorn of their fleeces meandered around with a melancholy air, feeling cheated or possibly ridiculous. Those on heat bleated shrilly and allowed the vigorous rams to mount them, discharging from their vulvas a liquid as viscous as the summer air, while the castrated rams, plumper and more lethargic, looked on with disdain. To the west of the fields, like a moored ship, the textile mill billowed smoke. Inside, Lamberg, bathed in sweat, stood on his platform, closed his smarting eyes and thought of his week's holiday in August as one might go over the words of a prayer. Outside, in the surrounding cornfields, the peasants were slowly preparing for the next sowing, heralding the stealthy arrival of autumn, which to everyone else seemed like a vain threat.

And the organ grinder? The organ grinder fanned himself with old newspapers, bathed in the river, and blew on Franz's ears.

Herr Gottlieb had of late been spending a great deal more time than usual in his study. He had given orders not to be disturbed and had been going over his accounts again and again. Sophie had risen that morning to find her father wearing the same shirt as the day before and not looking rested. They ate breakfast in silence to the sound of sipping, the scrape of cutlery and the crunch of toast, until Herr Gottlieb pushed his cup aside, cleared his throat and said: I've been thinking, my child, I've been thinking about this summer, and I've decided, well, why do the same thing every year, I mean, we're perfectly happy here in the city, aren't we, my child, and besides this summer isn't as hot, you seem content to be here, and, well, it's of little consequence, but the prices of spas this season are sky-high. Not that we can't afford it, but this kind of sharp practice makes me cross, what right have they to double their prices from one year to the next? It's not good enough, no indeed. What about the summer cottage,

Father? asked Sophie. Herr Gottlieb pretended to look puzzled, as though she had alluded to some long forgotten detail. Then he replied: Oh, didn't I tell you? I thought I had. Anyway, the fact is I sold it a few months ago. Why are you looking at me like that? There's nothing strange about it, the opportunity to sell arose, and I thought, well, as you are soon to be married and we needed a considerable dowry, that is, a sum befitting such an occasion, didn't we? And besides, I wanted to …

(Herr Gottlieb continued giving her explanations, but Sophie had stopped listening. All she could think of was that now she would be able to spend a whole summer with Hans. A whole summer! She hadn't wanted to tell Hans, but for weeks she had been fearing the moment when her father announced the date of their departure, as he did every August. She could scarcely contain her glee at such good fortune. This really was news. She had to tell him at once, she had to write and tell him.)

… And so, my child, Herr Gottlieb said at last, I'm sure we shall enjoy a very pleasant summer and that this decision is for the best, vis-à-vis your wedding and your future. Although, I repeat, if you'd been looking forward to going away, I could still see if. No, I won't hear of it! Sophie interrupted. No, Father, no. Naturally, I can't deny I'm a little disappointed we aren't going away as usual. But the most important thing is you've reached a considered decision, and I trust your reasons implicitly and, as ever, place myself blindly in your hands. Are you sure, my child? said Herr Gottlieb. Yes, Father, completely, she nodded, putting on a stoical air. My dear Sophie, her father rejoiced, I knew you'd understand! Come over here and give me a kiss, my darling, my darling.

My darling, my darling, you won't believe this, I'm so happy …

Sophie stopped writing, went to check that her door was closed properly and lay down again on her orange eiderdown.

… in fact, I already noticed when we went away on holiday last summer, that for the first time ever we spent the whole journey facing away from the horses. My father told me it was because all the forward-facing seats were taken, but it struck me as odd, and while we were traveling I saw several coaches with empty seats. My father only tells half the story and everyone at home seems nervous. What does it matter, I'm happy. I'm staying here, my love, to translate for us. And with any luck, a little extra luck, Rudi will soon be off on holiday and everything will be easier, amore d'estate, estate d'amore …

Elsa knocked on the study door—she did it so timidly that she had to repeat the gesture three times before Herr Gottlieb looked up from the portrait of the pale young woman, cleared his throat and replied. This was only the second time since Elsa had been in his employ that Herr Gottlieb had called her to his study. The first occasion had been prompted by Gladys, the chambermaid, threatening to resign unless she was granted a weekend off every month.

Come in, my dear, come in, Herr Gottlieb said, topping up his brandy glass, how are you, my girl? Everything shipshape? Busy today? Good, good, I'm glad to hear it. Now, you know how much I value your efficiency and your sense of responsibility, without you this house would be a shambles! In short, I've always known I could depend on your cooperation, isn't that so, my dear? Good, very good. You'll be wondering why I haven't rung for Bertold, but, you see, I can't ask him about this delicate matter because it concerns Sophie, and naturally I wouldn't want this conversation to leave this room, especially with the wedding drawing near, and not a word of it to Sophie, either, you know how difficult she gets when something displeases her, do I make myself clear? Good. You see, it's about these strolls and excursions you take with Sophie and, and well, these sessions, these work sessions with Herr Hans. As you always go with them, I was wondering whether the two of them, that is, if you have ever, in passing, noticed anything—don't look so worried, my dear, rest assured this isn't an interrogation, as I see it we are simply having an informal chat, aren't we? The head of the house sometimes needs to reassure himself that everything is going according to plan, that is all. Yes, of course, my dear, I don't doubt that if you had noticed anything ... Only, you see, sometimes people talk, and such gossip might reach ... Naturally, our family is above reproach, you needn't remind me of that, what I'm asking you, Elsa, and please consider this a friendly suggestion if you will, is to increase your vigilance and to take care that ... Yes, precisely. Well then, that's settled.

No sooner had Elsa stepped into the kitchen than Bertold began asking her what she had been talking about to Herr Gottlieb. Nothing in particular, she replied. Don't give me that, Bertold said, grabbing her arm, do you take me for fool? You said it, Elsa retorted, pulling her arm free, and if you don't believe me, then don't ask. Oh, pardon me! he exclaimed, Miss Elsa doesn't like to be questioned! Especially because it would mean an end to her strolls and outings to the countryside! What's coming to an end is my patience, so leave me in peace, Bertold, I have to go out to do the shopping. Did you hear that, Petra! he said, turning to the cook. Do you think it's fair her gallivanting all over the place with Fräulein Gottlieb while we rot away indoors all day? On the other side of the marble-topped table, beneath the five service bells connected to the five rooms their employers could ring from, Petra raised her head, stopped chopping tomatoes, and said: I couldn't care less what anyone does, this isn't my family, it's my job. Yes, Petra, Bertold replied, but it's still unjust! The only justice, Petra said, slicing through another tomato, would be if my daughter didn't have to peel potatoes for a living.

Elsa and Bertold carried on bickering as they descended the stairs. Why all the secrecy? he insisted, don't you trust me any more? I trust you as much as you trust me, she snapped. But Elsa, my sweet, he whispered, don't you remember when we used to spend the whole night together, what's the matter, why won't you tell me things any more? Yes, I remember perfectly, she replied, and that's why I prefer not to talk to you, because I know what you're like. And are they good those memories of yours? he said, clasping her waist. No worse and no better than any others, Elsa said, wriggling free. Bitch! he cried. Lackey! she retorted. I'm a lackey, said Bertold, furious, you call me a lackey when all you do is obey your mistress! You daren't even breathe without her permission! You're mistaken, as usual, she said, pausing before the front door. No, he said, I'm not mistaken—you should be loyal to Herr Gottlieb, but instead you trot around after your little friend even though she doesn't pay our wages. I'm paid to wait on her, said Elsa, and besides, Fräulein Gottlieb isn't my friend, and she never will be. In that case why do her bidding? said Bertold. Why accompany her to that inn when you know it could bring dishonour on the Wilderhaus family and leave us all in the street? What do you do at the inn, Elsa? Why won't you tell me what Herr Gottlieb said to you? Aha, she chuckled, so that's it, you're worried about the honour of the Wilderhaus family! I can see where your loyalties lie! What are you hoping for, you fool, that he'll give you a job as butler, or present you with a carriage, perhaps? I'm saving up, said Bertold, what's wrong with that? Nothing, said Elsa, I'm saving up, too. Look, he said, try to understand, Elsa, I need more money, and if the wedding falls through then I'm off, I want a better life, I don't know, to open my own shop. I understand perfectly, she said, you're the one who doesn't understand, I also want to do better for myself, to get married. Is that what you're saving up for? he asked, narrowing his eyes, displaying his scar. Maybe I am and maybe I'm not, Elsa said opening the front door. Who is he, tell me? demanded Bertold. No one, she said stepping outside. Wait, Elsa! he shouted after her, Wait, come back here! You never tell me anything! Bitch! And for your information, I don't remember our nights together either!

The sacristan found Father Pigherzog eating a leg of cold chicken and drinking the altar wine. Father, he said awkwardly, it's nearly time. Yes, yes, the priest said with his mouth full, I'll be with you in a minute. Forgive me, Father, the sacristan said hesitantly, shouldn't we be fasting? Ha! Father Pigherzog licked his lips. You still have much to learn about doctrine! Tell me, didn't the apostles receive Communion from Christ himself after a big supper? Hadn't they sated themselves with food and wine? Do you believe a genuinely pure spirit is determined by a mouthful more or less of food? Do we not partake of Christ's flesh when we eat the bread at any feast? The sacristan stammered an apology and began laying out the alb and the amice. Wait, my son, said Father Pigherzog, come here and wash my fingers, please.

Frau Pietzine leant forward and put her lips close to the grille in the confessional. Her rosary swung out from her chest and rattled against the partition.

Beloved Father, she murmured, it's a good thing you received me, and I thank you from the bottom of my heart, it's been too long since my last confession and I have to commune tomorrow, immediately, as soon as possible. Daughter, Father Pigherzog's voice said on the other side of the grille, I'm not the only priest to whom you can confess, if you were in such a hurry there is always Father Kleist. Oh no, Father, never! Frau Pietzine insisted. Very well, daughter, very well, Father Pigherzog said, trying not to sound smug, I am at your service.

Frau Pietzine confessed for twenty minutes, continually

gasping and covering her mouth with her fan. Father Pigherzog remained silent, although from time to time he could be heard fidgeting in his seat and breathing in a slightly laboured manner. When Frau Pietzine had finished, the priest took a deep breath and said: I can see how greatly you suffer, daughter. And you are of course right to confess with such fervour, for it calms the soul. However, we must endeavour not to fall into immoderation when confessing. It is also necessary to make room for atonement, in order to arouse our feeling of guilt and to offer our tears to Jesus. (I will, I will, I will, Frau Pietzine said contritely.) I absolve you, daughter—follow this instruction and say ten Our Fathers and six Hail Marys. (Amen, amen, amen, she agreed.) Now listen, daughter, there is another small matter to which I wish to draw your attention (I'm all ears, Father), and this is nothing other than the somewhat ostentatious dresses you have begun to wear, even though you ought still to be in semi-mourning. (Father, Frau Pietzine said, pulling up her décolletage, my husband passed away more than five years ago!) Five years ago, indeed, and what is five years, daughter, compared to a whole marriage? Compared to the vicissitudes of eternal life your deceased husband is currently experiencing? Five years, you say—is not death eternally present in our lives? (You are right, you are right, you are right, but, please, try to understand, I implore you—it may sound frivolous, but clothes are a solace to me, one of my few amusements, I purchase fabrics, choose colours and styles, yet I am constantly grieving, if not I wouldn't need to distract myself with such trifles.) I understand, daughter, but that doesn't mean I approve, these dresses, are, well, they are ... (Tell me, Father, with all due respect to your holy condition, have you never been tempted to try on new clothes? A suit? The odd overcoat?) Me? Never, daughter. What fancies. I was very young when I was ordained and have always felt quite at home in a humble habit.

Seeing her agitated state, Father Pigherzog considered it best to administer Holy Communion to Frau Pietzine there and then, outside of Mass. He summoned the altar boy and asked him to prepare the altar.

... in so far as her will to repent is still weaker than her devotion. Having warned her about the lack of moderation of her attire, the aforementioned Frau H J Pietzine showed a degree of obstinacy that bears out our negative prognostications. In addition, she would be well advised to forgo reading sacrilegious tales of Knights Templar and to concentrate on more pious texts. Insist more upon this point.

... turning finally to set before Your Excellency, whose hands I kiss most fervently and whose loyal servant I remain, the state of the quarterly accounts for the lands rented on behalf of the church. In general terms, after a meticulous examination of contributions made during the second quarter, we are able to confirm with comparative regret that the tendency to growth in the Holy Easter period failed to continue through to the end of spring. I say with comparative regret, because, even as we continue to suffer from the shortages, of which Your Excellency has already been made aware, the news is perhaps not all bad, for thanks to the assistance of Our Lord, the provider of all things, and xxxxx xxxxx perhaps also in an infinitesimal way to our own humble work, I am pleased to inform Your Excellency that the collection for Sunday Mass has almost reached ten groschen—only two less than the average number of thalers at the end of the previous quarter.

What are we translating today? Sophie asked as she got dressed. Ah, Mademoiselle Gottlieb, Hans replied, buttoning up his shirt, *nous avons de bonnes choses aujourd'hui!* But first let me show you something, come here.

Hans crouched beside his trunk. He rummaged around in it and pulled out a few old editions of the magazines *Frankreich* and *Deutschland* which he handed Sophie. Where did you get these? she asked, surprised. Truthfully? he grinned. From the public library. What! cried Sophie. You didn't! I did, I stole them, Hans confessed, I know it's wrong, but I couldn't help myself. Hans … she chided him. But no one ever reads them, he excused himself, clasping her round the waist, on the contrary, they're frowned upon nowadays for promoting Franco-German dialogue, I was amazed when I found them, believe me, it'll be fifty years before anyone notices they're missing. Thief, Sophie growled, letting him embrace her. No, said Hans, not a thief, a collector!

They turned in circles as they held one another, and Sophie came to a stop beside the open trunk. She tried discreetly to take in as much as she could—a few scattered notebooks, objects of indeterminate usage, heaps of jumbled papers, piles of books of unusual colours and with strange bindings she had never seen before. When Hans turned to pour himself a glass of water Sophie began rifling through the books in the trunk. What's this? she said, holding up a volume. That? he replied. Victor Hugo's *Cromwell*. Yes, she said, but where did you get it? Ah, it was sent to me, why? Oh, nothing, Sophie said, bemused, just that it says it was published in Paris by Ambroise Dupont in … Yes, yes, he cut in, plucking the book from her hand, a recent publication with a very interesting preface, Brockhaus sent it to me, they may translate it next year. Shall we begin working, my love? It's getting late.

They sat on opposite sides of the desk, each with a quill and with an inkwell in the middle. The job consisted of making a small selection of the most contemporary French poets. Hans and Sophie exchanged books and magazines (odd copies of *Le Conservateur littéraire*, *Globe*, *Annales* or *La Minerve*) and they noted down the authors they most liked. This young man is right, she remarked, underlining the prologue to *New Odes*, it makes no sense to classify authors as either classical or Romantic, what would Goethe be for example? A rather Romantic classicist? Or Hugo, for that matter, who is a Romantic among classicists, what do you think? I agree, said Hans, I suppose the Romantics are restless classicists. What saddens me about Hugo or this other fellow, Lamartine, is that they should be so young and yet be staunch monarchists and Christians, Chateaubriand seems to have infected everyone! Quite, Sophie laughed, and the more they declaim the more they seem to encounter God along the way. Hugo is good, isn't he? Hans said, leafing through one of his works. He seems more aware than the others, and yet there is something, how can I describe it, something irritating about him, isn't there? Sophie thought for a moment: He sounds as if he takes himself terribly seriously. Exactly! said Hans, moreover he is the son of one of Napoleon's generals and calls himself a viscount, so you can just imagine, all that *grandeur perdue*, and oh woe is me! Do you know what, she said, it seems to me modern French poetry has a rather pathetic air for that very reason, you can tell it was written after the fall of an empire. Write that down! Hans said brushing her shoulder with the feather end of his quill.

They finally chose Hugo, Vigny, Lamartine and, at Hans's request, a young, virtually unpublished poet called Gérard de Nerval. He proposed they each translate two poets and then correct one another's versions. She suggested they read the finished drafts aloud to see how they sounded.

Hans raised his head, laid down his quill and said: I like Nerval a lot, he writes as if he were half-asleep. Moreover his German is excellent and he spends his time traveling, and do you know what else, he's a translator, he just translated *Faust*, and Goethe says his French version is better than the original. The poem I'm going to read you isn't in this little volume, I found it in the latest copy of *Muse parisienne* and it's my favourite:

THE HALT

The carriage halts and we step down,
Slip between two houses in the town
Dazed from the noise of horses, road and whips,
Eyes tired from looking, and aching hips.

Then all at once, silent and green,
A lilac-covered vale is seen,
A stream midst poplars making play,
And road and clatter seem far away.

Stretched in the grass our lives we feel;
The fresh-mown hay makes senses reel,
Minds are blank as we gaze heavenward,
Alas! Until we hear the shout: "All aboard."

Very you, she nodded thoughtfully, very you. The question would be—is the voice at the end simply the cry of the coachman? Or is the traveler hearing his destiny because he is unable to remain in the place where he is happy? Sophie lowered her head and continued translating.

Presently, her foot sought out Hans's foot. Ready! she declared. Actually I have a soft spot for this little poem by Hugo. I'll start with the first three verses, which are the only ones I'm more or less happy with:

WISH

If I could be the leaf
Spinning on the wings of wind

Or floating on rapid waters
Or that the eye follows in a dream

Still green I would gladly fall,
Freeing myself from my branch
To the morning breeze
Or the stream of evening.

Far beyond the rushing flood,
Far beyond the dark forest,
Far beyond the deep abyss,
I would escape, swift as I could.

Bravo! said Hans, although I see your leaf doesn't wish to stay where it is either! Yes, replied Sophie, but unlike your traveler the leaf isn't free, it is trapped in its birthplace, and longs to fly away before it withers.

They worked on two more poems and when it was nearing six o'clock they took a break. They decided to correct their drafts the next day and to leave Vigny and Lamartine for the following week. Then Hans went over to the trunk, searched for a couple of volumes with dark bindings and gave Sophie an impish look as he handed them to her. She read the names—Theophile de Viau, Saint-Amant, Saint-Évremond. Aren't these the … she said, surprised. Yes! Hans nodded, the old French libertines. And are we going to translate them? asked Sophie. Yes, we are, he said. But aren't they banned? she said. Indeed, he grinned, but there's a very simple way round that. Because they appear in the official censorship list under their noms de plume, I have managed to convince Brockhaus to publish them under their given names—Marc-Antoine Girard and Charles Marguetel. We will call it something innocuous such as *Amusements*, and, being ignoramuses, the censors won't notice a thing. And if by any chance they do, we will claim we had no idea these eminent men of letters were the selfsame libertines. That won't work with de Viau because he never used a nom de plume, but since his *Libertine Ballads* were published anonymously over two hundred years ago, we will keep them anonymous and wash our hands of the matter. I don't know if it will work, but we won't have to take responsibility. The publisher knows how to deal with that kind of thing. The idea of translating them excites me, they did as much for the French Revolution as Voltaire, Montesquieu or Rousseau. Listen, listen:

ON THE RESURRECTION

Then came the happy day, if we believe in history,
When the Creator, crowned as he was in glory,
Cheated his own death and defeated Hell.
Friend, if you believe that, you're a donkey's arse,
We nailed him there with our eyes wide open—
When he returned to life, he was all alone!

That de Viau was a terror, Sophie chuckled, Father Pigherzog would love that! Further on he turns serious, said Hans:

Why all these bells and all these masses?
Do you think you can revive the dead?
Let us rather wisely share the news
That the soul dies with the head.

Sophie ran over to sit on his lap. Well, my libertine, she said, her skirts enveloping his legs, why not leave poetry until tomorrow and do something for our mortal flesh?

We have to do something, said Elsa, her leg rocking beneath

her dress. The doors of the Central Tavern creaked, and Álvaro turned to see who was coming in. Even though he knew they were unlikely to bump into anyone he knew there, he felt jumpy—he seldom met Elsa in public places. We have to do something, I tell you, she insisted, I can't go on living like this, in that house, Fräulein Sophie makes me cover up for her almost every day, I can't stand that idiot Bertold, and Herr Gottlieb is drinking more and more (Elsa, darling, said Álvaro, your position in the Gottlieb residence isn't as bad as all that, I assure you I know many houses where). Nonsense! A servant is a servant! Don't you see? (Of course I do, said Álvaro, all I'm saying is that Herr Gottlieb pays you a decent wage and.) Decent? Decent according to whom? (All right, Álvaro said, lowering his voice, I'm sorry, but they treat you with respect, don't they?) You call that respect? Don't make me laugh! Look, do you want to know how I learnt to read? Do you? Well, I'll tell you. Before I went to the Gottliebs, my mother packed me off to work for the Saittemberg family, do you know them? Yes, well, them. Anyway, it may surprise you to know that I taught myself to read aged fourteen thanks to the love letters Silke Saittemberg received from her paramour. Fräulein Silke would give them me to hide under my mattress because she knew it was the only place her father would never find them. Yes, my dear, I learnt to read from those letters, and that wasn't all, I also learnt that we servants live off the masters' leftovers, we thrive on their scraps, Álvaro, and a servant has to take every opportunity, like I did with Fräulein Silke's love letters. I would read them at night, copy them out word for word and use them to study grammar with the help of a book I stole from Herr Saittemberg's library.

Wait a moment, wait a moment, said Álvaro, do you read Sophie's letters, too? She bowed her head and stirred her luke-warm coffee. Elsa, answer me, do you read them? Yes, Elsa confessed, but I'd never show them to anyone else, I swear! I only read them out of curiosity, and habit (Elsa, Elsa, my girl, he said clasping her hand, you know that's wrong), we all do things knowing they're wrong, look, Álvaro, I'm only doing what they do, taking advantage of my position. Think of Fräulein Silke's letters, if I'd been discreet, as you would probably have advised, I'd be nearly illiterate now. (You're right, said Álvaro, what I'm trying to say is that Sophie values you and you'd have difficulty finding that elsewhere.) I don't plan to go elsewhere to carry on doing the same thing! And my love, don't fool yourself, you should know better at your age, Fräulein Sophie is kind, I have no complaints about the way she treats me, but I'd feel a lot more comfortable if she stopped pretending we're friends, because we aren't. I'm her maid. Her servant. I wait on her. I help her to dress. I listen to her. What more does she want? Must I love her too? (You're a hard one, said Álvaro.) Not with you (really? he grinned), no. I just want us to live together, to begin another life. (Don't be in such a hurry, Elsa.) But time is racing by! And if you'll forgive me for saying so, my love, you have less time than I do. (If you think I'm so old, why do you like me?) Because I like my men like that, old!

Elsa finished her cold coffee. Why don't we go away? Don't pull a face, not for ever, just on a trip, we could go to England, I've never been to England. (That's impossible, he murmured, letting go of her hand, I mean, not for the time being at least.) Why not, tell me, why not, explain to me, be truthful, I implore you, are you ashamed to be in love with a servant, is that it? (Of course not, Elsa, he said, clasping her hand once more, how can you even think that!) Why then? Because we mustn't be seen together? Who are we hiding from? (And what about now, here, aren't we being seen together?) Oh come, come, you know perfectly well your rich friends never frequent this tavern. (What? What are you saying? Do you want us to meet in the

Central Tavern next time or in Café Europa or wherever you like, is that what you want?) No, my love, I don't want to meet you in a tavern or anywhere else, what I want is to be free, not to hide any longer, to leave that house once and for all, that's what I want. I want to do other things. I'm not young any more (you look younger than ever to me. And lovelier), don't flatter me. Oh don't flatter me.

Tell me, she said, letting him kiss her hand, what is England like? (Big, Álvaro said with a sigh, and complicated.) Well I want some complication in my life. In any case, I've started studying English. Seriously! Why are you laughing, silly? Don't you believe me? Don't you … *no* … *believe me not?* she said, partly in English. And for your information … *know you now that I* … that I don't intend spending the rest of my life like this! … *being a* … (*A maid*, smiled Álvaro, the word is *maid*, Elsa, I don't believe it!) Well you'd better believe it, silly, *maid* you say? Well, being a *maid*, then, anyway my love, dear *dear*, start getting used to the idea, and I don't know why you're so surprised. If you can learn to speak German, I don't see why I can't learn English, or Spanish even. (Of course you can, I believe you're capable of anything, and besides I like it Elsa, I like it.) Do you? … *Mucho bien!* Because I've seen a Spanish grammar at the house too. In a few months I'll be giving you lessons in your own language!

Elsa, he said, I love you, you know that. You'd better! she said, rubbing her leg against his calf and revealing a stockinged ankle.

Lisa clutched the pencil clumsily in her delicate but chafed hands. The pencil wobbled, turning on itself in search of an angle, a thrust. Hans glanced at Lisa's fresh face and saw her wrinkle her brow, screw up her eyes, push the tip of her tongue out of the corner of her mouth. Lisa was concentrating so much, reflected Hans, that she did not even notice him—there was only an interminable line, a sluggish pencil, a pair of burning eyes and an unsteady hand. Everything else had vanished. Lisa's powers of concentration never ceased to amaze him. Up until ten minutes ago she had been running back and forth to the market, hastily scrubbing floors, sewing incessantly, as she would soon go back to doing until evening. And yet now, sitting at Hans's desk, staring intently at her writing, she looked like a schoolgirl who spent her whole time in a classroom. Considering how little time they had for lessons, half-an-hour twice weekly, she had made remarkable progress. She made few mistakes, and if she did, she would be the one to scold herself and impose minor punishments from which an astonished Hans tried to dissuade her. If I get that verb wrong once more, Lisa had said the week before, I'll burn myself with the candle flame, how will I ever do anything in life if I can't even conjugate the verb *to do*! Hans had tried to encourage her by explaining that the verb *to do* behaved erratically, and therefore it was logical that she got in a muddle with the different tenses. Lisa had insisted this was no excuse, because her behaviour was also erratic, sometimes she did things one way and sometimes another, so she oughtn't to get into such a muddle.

Hans became distracted as he remembered this exchange. When he looked again at Lisa's exercise book, he raised his eyebrows—she had completed the table of verbs in the present and past tense; furthermore, of her own accord, Lisa had added the verb *to finish* in the column for the verb *to do*. When you do things, she said, you have to be able to finish them, don't you?

As Lisa was reading back with laborious pride the sentences Hans had just dictated to her in the present and past tense, a roar came from the floor beneath. Lisa immediately dropped her pencil and leapt to her feet in terror. Herr Zeit was shouting his daughter's name as he lumbered up the stairs. Lisa closed her exercise book, said goodbye to Hans with a swift kiss on the cheek (a kiss, which, on the other hand, Hans reflected, proved she wasn't very scared), ran across the corridor and hid in one of the other rooms. Hans stood behind his door listening—when Herr Zeit found her, she pretended she had been changing the sheets up on the second floor. But her father refused to be placated, he had come up in a terrible rage.

Wretched girl! he bellowed. Where did you get this? Lisa looked down at his hands and recoiled in horror—it was her new make-up. Where did you get it? Herr Zeit repeated, you don't have money for this! He seized his daughter by the hair and dragged her from the room.

Frau Pietzine turns into Archway. She has spent the afternoon in church, meditating. This has made her late and she needs a carriage. There are no empty ones in the market square, so she must either wait there, or try her luck at the stand on the north side. When she hears the bell in the clock tower strike seven-thirty, Frau Pietzine pauses. She thinks about how neglectful of her motherly duties she has been of late, and how much her children hate having to eat their supper with the servant. And so she walks back the way she came, making her way to the stand on the north side, taking short cuts through the side alleys.

Once inside their apartment, the innkeeper slams the door, releases his daughter and looks around for a bag. When she sees her father hurl her make-up and perfumes into it, Lisa begins to cry. Herr Zeit bears down on her, fist raised. How did you pay for this filth? he bawls. With the change from the shopping? Have you been robbing your own family? Answer me, you wretched girl, is this how you make your father happy?

The masked figure hears the sound of Frau Pietzine's hurrying shoes behind him as she turns into Wool Alley. As it is not quite dark yet, instead of waiting for her, he walks on, hands in pockets, careful not to make any strange movements, even quickening his pace slightly in order to get farther ahead. It would be rash to do anything before they reached the bend in Jesus Lane.

What's more, Herr Zeit screamed, it isn't right for a young girl, a girl like you, to be perfuming herself! As well as giving the money back to your mother, I forbid you to bring another bottle of perfume into this house. That's the last time you disobey me, the last, do you hear me! Do you hear me!

Backed into the dark corner in Jesus Lane, the shadow tilts his hat, puts on his mask and checks he has all his tools. The sound of heels draws closer and closer. The mask moves at cheek level—the masked man is smiling. He is very lucky. For several weeks he has been avoiding the side streets as a precaution. Policemen have been patrolling the neighbourhood, he has seen them when he has been walking through without his mask. He has even greeted them with a polite nod. But for a few days now the police have stopped patrolling, and this is the first evening he has gone out wearing his long coat and black-brimmed hat. Fewer and fewer women walk out alone after seven o'clock.

Biting her lips until they bleed, Lisa shuts herself in her room and blockades the door from inside. She lies on her bed, presses her face into the pillow and tries to ignore the stinging in her arms, back and buttocks. She struggles to stifle the sobs she feels neither her father nor her mother deserve to wring from her. She must stop crying like a child and learn to weep like a young lady—soundlessly, without gasping or snivelling, letting the tears roll down her cheeks dispassionately, as though she were thinking about something quite different. Groping around, she finds one of her old rag dolls. She sits up, holds it before her eyes and stares intently at it. Then she notices a seam unravelling between the doll's arms and chest.

The first thing she sees when she comes round the corner is the blade. For a split second Frau Pietzine is so startled by the knife close to her neck she forgets to scream. When she does try to cry out, someone has already stopped her mouth with a handkerchief.

Herr Zeit is still haranguing Lisa from the other side of the door. Lisa doesn't listen, she doesn't want to listen to him, she concentrates on her old rag doll and the hole in its chest. As the pounding on the door continues, Lisa begins to pull at the loose threads. She pulls harder and harder, watching the doll's chest gradually unravelling. She experiences a searing joy, a bitter sense of superiority, and begins making the hole bigger, ripping apart the doll's chest.

Frau Pietzine's dress tears slightly. She thrashes her legs about, waves her arms, then suddenly freezes as she feels the knife prick the side of her neck. She lies motionless, gasping, as though waiting for two different guillotines to drop. She does not begin to pray then. She thinks first of her children, then of the supper, and then of death. She feels no remorse, but that she is being punished. At the first touch of cold air on her legs, she begins to pray silently.

Lisa tears the doll in two and probes its entrails. Does it hold some hidden secret? What is it hiding? But she finds nothing of interest inside her beloved doll. Pieces of thread, cloth and cotton wool, nothing. On the other side of the door, trying to force the handle, her father is shouting her name.

In a final gesture of resistance, Frau Pietzine tenses her thighs and presses her arms to her sides—she has discovered a brute strength she didn't know existed. The masked man gives a start. He freezes for a moment. He falters—this is the first time he has known the victim. He is on the point of letting her go. Withdrawing. But it feels too late to stop now. Besides, he is excited. Very excited. And deep down it is this unexpected element that thrills him. And so, in order to ease his struggle, the masked man finally pulls off a glove, releasing a faint smell of lard. As she lies doubled up, a shiver of panic coursing through her, Frau Pietzine thinks she recognises the hand, or that it is in some way familiar. Afterwards she thinks she is mistaken. She thinks she is hallucinating, having a terrible nightmare from which she will awake, that everything is spinning very fast, that the pain is filtering through a crack. Then she has the impression of slipping down a steep slope, and that nothing will matter to her any longer.

Herr Zeit bursts angrily into the room and remains motionless for a moment—his daughter Lisa is holding the rag doll's torn off head, smiling absently, as if he weren't standing there brandishing a leather strap.

As Frau Levin sat down and noticed the empty chair, she asked after Frau Pietzine. Over time she had grown to respect her, and, underneath all their differences, suspected they had much in common—Frau Pietzine's compulsive chatter was nothing more than a manifestation of the same paralysing shyness she suffered from, and widowhood had plunged her into a state of solitude with which she, a married woman of many years, was only too familiar.

As she poured the first serving of tea, Sophie informed her guests she had received a note from Frau Pietzine, who was indisposed and excused herself from attending that Friday. When Sophie stopped next to Hans and leant over to fill his cup, she had the impression that he had raised his shoulder in order to brush against her breast. Although Rudi had his head turned and was talking to her father, Sophie decided to caution Hans by letting a few drops of tea splash into his saucer. Hans sat up with a start and whispered: Oh, never mind, Mademoiselle, never mind. Elsa and Bertold brought trays laden with bowls of consommé and fruit compote. There was a sound of scraping chairs and clinking spoons. Álvaro tried to catch Elsa's eye, but she avoided him. Hans attempted to strike up a conversation with Rudi. He responded amiably and began regaling Hans with stories of his latest hunting expedition. Seeing them chatting together, Sophie gave a sigh of relief. Elsa left the garden. Álvaro rose to his feet and said he needed to go up to the bathroom.

After a scholarly tribute to Schiller from Professor Mietter (which earned him the praise of both Herr Levin and Herr Gottlieb), Hans said without thinking: Schiller studied for the priesthood and ended up being a doctor! For your information, young man, Professor Mietter replied sharply (at which Hans looked at him almost with gratitude, because he was bored), Schiller was one of our most eminent men, the only man equal to Goethe, he spent his life writing in defence of freedom and strove to fight disease, working until the day he died, I don't see why you should find that amusing! I can see, said Hans with a grin, you would prefer us all to be serious. All right. Hölderlin, who was Schiller's disciple, says that philosophy is the hospital of the poet, and I agree with him there. Schiller died ill, and still philosophising. This seems to me worthy of the greatest respect. What I don't understand is why Schiller wrote odes to happiness in his youth, and then spent his life admonishing young poets, who, incidentally, were better than he. That is your view, protested Professor Mietter. No, said Hans, that is the view of poetry. Don't be so conceited! Professor Mietter rebuked him, folding his arms. Sophie interceded gently: Do go on, Professor. Well, he nodded, straightening his wig, let us see. Schiller was merely pointing out the basic rules of art to the young poets, he was not censuring them, but reminding them of the need to study these rules. In doing so he was merely following the *Critique of Judgement*, and, if I remember rightly, Monsieur Hans has defended Kant on more than one occasion. Sophie turned to Hans, amused: Do you have anything to say, dear Hans? Hans, who had decided to remain silent to avoid generating further tension, saw the congratulatory pat Rudi gave Professor Mietter, his mocking smile, the haughty way he inhaled his snuff, and, fixing his eyes on Sophie, he replied: Our inestimable professor claims that Schiller followed Kant. True. Yet Kant was an independent critic, because he established his own norms. Thus, to obey Kant is to betray him. Do any of you truly believe we can speak of a universal judgement, an objective aesthetic, an inadequate use of beauty? What the devil does that mean? What was Schiller so afraid of? If it was the differences between the social classes then I understand, because those are imposed (Rudi, my love, Sophie distracted him, how do you find the compote?) but to say there can be no different aesthetics, to propose a consensus on taste is grotesque! Or should we create a law governing taste? Hasn't Metternich given us enough laws already? Holding his pince-nez on his nose Professor Mietter countered: You are confusing censorship with rules. All freedom, whether in art or in society, requires order. And true fear derives from the denial of this self-evident fact. All right, replied Hans, waving his cup so that his tea spilt over into the saucer, but that order can never be permanent. As Kant said, that would be a return to infancy. The surrender of reason, the death of *räsonieren*. You have clearly misread Schiller, Professor Mietter concluded with a shrug. Perhaps, said Hans, and until the law takes it away from me, I assume I can still enjoy that privilege.

Calm yourselves, gentlemen, insisted Sophie, here our greatest privilege is to disagree without losing our manners. Well said, my child, Herr Gottlieb said approvingly, twirling the tip of his moustache around one finger, and incidentally, if our guests are in agreement, I would like to propose that next Friday, by way of closing this salon for the summer, we read a few passages from one of Schiller's plays. (Rudi looked at Hans and gave a snigger.) I might add that although we are no experts, we are particularly fond of Schiller in this house, and. (Dear father-in-law, Rudi interrupted, where will you have the pleasure of taking your summer holidays?) What? Where? Ah, well, we shall find somewhere! You know what August is like, dear son-in-law, people everywhere! We are waiting to hear from various friends before we make any plans (very wise, nodded Rudi, very wise), or—who knows!—we might simply stay here and relax, when you get to my age the crowds at the spas become a bore. (Forgive me, ahem, Herr Levin picked up the conversation, and which work of his do you prefer?) Which work? Ah, yes, I beg your pardon, well, of course one perhaps hasn't read Schiller's entire works, I don't know, how about *William Tell*? (An excellent choice in my view, father, said Sophie, if everyone else agrees …)

An excellent choice, Professor Mietter declared, if I may say so, I only wish today's young playwrights would see it! They might learn how to write good theatre instead of writing theatrically. An exemplary work, seconded Herr Levin, isn't it, dear? Frau Levin nodded dully. *William Tell*, yes, of course, Rudi said doubtfully. The only good thing about it (Hans whispered to Álvaro, who had taken his time coming back from the bathroom) is that the tyrant dies. Álvaro let out a guffaw and glanced sideways at Elsa.

When it was past midnight, the guests began to say their farewells amidst the oil lanterns in the courtyard. Herr Gottlieb, having retired to his study, came back down to bid them goodnight and to keep an eye on his daughter. The first to leave were the Levins and Rudi Wilderhaus, who offered them a lift in his carriage. Sophie drew Rudi aside, let him kiss the back of her hand and replied yes to her fiancé when he alluded to an engagement the following day. Although Hans pricked up his ears, this was all he heard. Professor Mietter was the next to leave. I trust, said the professor, that at least *William Tell* will be to your liking, Herr Hans. Do not worry, Professor, Hans replied, with a broad grin, I am relatively easy to please. Hans's intention had been to infuriate him, but instead the professor walked over to Hans, placed a hand on his shoulder and retorted: Young man, you are still impetuous, and I quite understand.

Sophie, Álvaro and Hans stayed behind talking in the coolness of the yard. Herr Gottlieb hovered around them pretending to give orders to the servants.

When Sophie had persuaded her father to go to bed, they remained alone with Elsa, who seemed unusually disposed to stay awake. Amid laughter brought on by fruit liqueur, Sophie confessed: What I least like about Schiller is the fear of pleasure expressed in his ideas, as though sensuality were a betrayal of intellect. Keep your voice down, my girl, Hans jested. I mean it, said Sophie, this is what depresses me about Schiller and the school of respectable scholars. Emotion to them is like a geometric equation, "thus far, no further, perfect, we must not give way to rhetoric", and the worst thing is, they call this being noble. In short, with all due respect to the gentlemen present, they are altogether too masculine. Well, said Álvaro, masculinity doesn't seem like such a bad thing to me. Hans placed an arm around him, and declared: *Viva España!* The others laughed, even Elsa. Seeing her standing in a corner, Sophie invited her to sit with them and poured her some of the leftover port. Álvaro said: *Prost!* Elsa replied spontaneously: *Salud!* Had they been sober, Hans and Sophie would have been surprised.

They lingered in the doorway, chatting in raised voices before saying goodbye. Occasionally, Sophie would whisper: Shh! then carry on shouting. I have a confession to make, said Hans, the sad truth is that I think Schiller's essays are excellent, but I refuse to give that pompous Mietter the pleasure of admitting it. I knew it! Sophie rejoiced, perhaps you haven't realised, but when the professor isn't there, you repeat his arguments. I know, I know, replied Hans, and do you know what the worst thing is? I only argue with him to prevent him convincing me, because sometimes what he says seems very true. Álvaro peered into the street and declaimed: *"Everyone dreams of what they are, but none understands! What is life? A frenzy! What is life? An illusion! A shadow, a fiction!"* Hans clambered onto his back, howling: Hush, Calderón!

Leaning against the confessional, Frau Pietzine was sobbing so much she could scarcely speak. She had locked herself in the house refusing to see anyone, afflicted with fevers and migraines. Finally, that morning she had left the house, attended Mass and after that confession. She had not mentioned, nor did she ever intend to, what had happened in Jesus Lane. She had convinced herself that, beyond any shame, scandal or cruel gossip, recounting her experience would have meant accepting that it was really true. And she was determined to keep quiet until she had banished those few dreadful moments from her memory. She knew the havoc fever could wreak on the mind, the false imaginings it could produce, the phantom pains, the ghastly hallucinations. Why couldn't this, like so many other things in her life, simply be a terrible nightmare?

Noticing she was more agitated than usual, Father Pigherzog questioned Frau Pietzine more carefully. My daughter, he calmed her, you must not torment yourself so, sin dwells in all of us, and it is best to accept our guilt. But Father, she sobbed, if this vale of tears is but transitory why go on living? Our Creator demands that we live and honour him before going to join him, the priest explained. But where is he? cried Frau Pietzine. Where is our Creator when we are suffering? My daughter, said Father Pigherzog, today your pain is different, open your heart and tell me everything, everything, in order to unburden yourself.

... said stranger, to whom we have referred on prior occasions, who is undoubtedly a harmful influence on Fräulein Gottlieb (already somewhat

fickle in the observation of her duties), and who, if my experience is anything to go by, is in danger of compromising her imminent union with the illustrious Herr Wilderhaus the younger, a God-fearing man and a perfect husband. After several failed attempts I can confirm the impossibility of having a reasonable discussion with the aforementioned individual—he is a lost soul, xxxxxx imo serio irascor. *God willing he will leave and take his Voltaire with him before it is too late …*

While Father Pigherzog began filling the pages of *Notes on the State of Souls* with his elegant handwriting, Frau Pietzine left the church with a sense of complete emptiness—as though an inner part of her had come permanently unstuck, or as though a cracked corner had finally snapped off. Always, ever since she was a child, she had feared life would bring her more suffering than joy. Now she realised the meaning of all her anxieties—it was a sinister message, but one she now fully understood. Thenceforth, her existence would be a mere conduit to eternal life, and her children the sole reason for remaining as that conduit. As she stepped out of St Nicholas's Church, eyes fixed to the ground, Frau Pietzine paused to contemplate the grains of rice from that morning's wedding scattered over the steps like a mysterious symbol.

Frau Pietzine walked away from the church's twisted towers towards the market square, avoiding Archway. This was the same street Elsa had just avoided, knowing how keenly Father Pigherzog and his faithful informant, the sacristan, spied on the passers-by. She had just left Sophie at the inn and, face half-obscured beneath her parasol, was hurrying to find a carriage to take her to the country. Frau Pietzine was walking at a slow pace, lost in thought, clasping the brim of her sun hat between gloved fingers. The two women bumped into one another in front of the coach stop—Elsa almost knocked her over. Frau Pietzine looked up, took off her hat and stared at the young girl in bewilderment. Switching her parasol to her other hand and discovering Frau Pietzine's sad, painted face, Elsa opened her eyes wide, murmured an apology and continued on her way in a hurry.

Why hadn't Frau Pietzine spoken? Or had she been so absent-minded she hadn't even recognised her? I hope so, Elsa thought anxiously as she stepped into the carriage, because that foolish chatterbox is the greatest busybody in Wandernburg.

A few yards away from her, staring into space, Frau Pietzine understood everything, and, unmindful of the passengers ahead of her in the queue, she said to herself: I hope they are happy.

In a corner of the square, echoing quietly, the organ grinder turned the handle.

Clothes, that paradoxical pleasure—one loves to see them on and cannot wait to take them off. Sophie's corset constrained her eager breasts, the surprises of her belly, the arch of her back, pressed against her flesh, making her impatient. Hans undid knots, peeled off layers, unfastened girdles. Meanwhile she pushed aside collars, defeated buttons, pulled his linen breeches down. He undressed her in a hurry. She enjoyed pretending not to be in one.

Recovering their breath, Hans and Sophie contemplated the tangled landscape of clothes on the floor. They looked at one another, smiled, kissed the tips of each other's tongues. He jumped up to gather their clothes and draped them over the back of a chair—like someone repacking luggage, after sex he was in the habit of carefully folding his high-waisted jacket, his linen shirt, his satin cravat. Sophie, who preferred to see a riot of clothing, to savour the vision of those torn-off garments, sat up and said: What are you afraid of, my love? Hans stopped what he was doing. Me? he replied, turning his head. Nothing, why? In that case, she asked, gazing at Hans's buttocks, why are you so concerned about untidy clothes? He blinked several

times, let his shirt fall to the floor, and said: It seems to me you
are the translator here.

She would smile—why not? The moment she entered the courtyard and the others stood up and came over to greet her, Frau
Pietzine decided she would carry on as before. Since she no
longer expected anything from life why not laugh instead of
crying? She had been in her room for a whole week without
speaking to a soul, and now she had returned to society and to
the salon, she realised it made no difference—she would always
be alone. Like an act of personal revenge rather than out of
simple good manners, she began frantically greeting everyone,
talking loudly and laughing at every joke. Yet it wasn't like
before. Now she was aware that she was play-acting.

We missed you last Friday, my dear, declared Frau Levin!
Please, sit down next to me, try these delicious cakes, how did
you say you are feeling? Oh, much improved, replied Frau
Pietzine, it was nothing, my dear, a few silly fainting fits, you
know certain things happen when you get to our age! Frau Levin
whispered into her ear: Oh but I, that is, you and I, are still
too young for *that*! Mmm, Frau Pietzine replied mysteriously.
Mmm! echoed Frau Levin, I quite agree! And the two women
laughed and embraced, content to be talking at cross-purposes.

No one could accuse Herr Levin of being long-winded, but
that afternoon he was eloquent. At times he even dominated
the conversation. Hans listened with surprise, and reflected
about the unexpected loquacity of quiet men. Quiet men have
much to say, particularly when they are not talking. There are
many types of quiet man. The avaricious type, who keeps his
opinions to himself only to air them wittily and at great length
when alone. The resigned type, who is so convinced of having
nothing to say that it never occurs to him to open his mouth.
The mischievous type, whose takes great pleasure in the curiosity

his silence inspires in others. The impotent type, who wishes to speak yet never finds the right moment, and who is, in effect, a frustrated conversationalist. The austere type, who is not even tempted to confess his thoughts to himself. And finally the cautious type, which was perhaps the case of Herr Levin. Herr Levin had learnt to keep quiet when others voiced their opinions in order not to cause any awkwardness. His habit of silence might have proved terribly tiresome for him, were it not for the advantage it gave him of knowing others' thoughts whilst they remained ignorant of his. And although he made no concrete use of this advantage, it seemed to him that this parsimonious use of speech was a form of moral capital which sooner or later would bring him dividends.

However, that evening Herr Levin was holding forth without moderation or caution, almost with abandon. Someone had touched on his favourite subject, interpretations of the Bible. He had mentioned the seven astral spheres, Ezekiel's wheel, and thereafter he was unable to contain himself. Sophie, marvelling at this phenomenon, did her best to cut off the others so as to prolong his outburst. And yet, my dear Professor, Herr Levin argued, by calling himself *the Gate*, Jesus was clearly saying: You must open the gates, open them! That is, Christian teachings about love of God and of thy neighbour had a clear theosophical basis, ahem, what I mean is this wasn't simple emotion but love in the Greek sense, or *agape*, an appreciation of the supreme truth of human experience, which belongs to us all equally, or to no one, in as much as all beings are made in the image of the one and should therefore act as one, should they not? Ahem. Upon close reading, the dynamic, centripetal, essentially creative nature of the divinity becomes clear, and in that sense, if I may be blunt, the heavenly bodies could be said to be copulating in the sky. All things copulate with one another and all is as it should be. Creation, my friends, is nothing more than an act of mutual fecundation ... (Please, dear! interjected Frau Levin. These metaphors! But her reproach had the opposite effect—when she dared to disagree with her husband her ultimate submissiveness towards him became more evident. Professor Mietter looked at Herr Levin with an expression of contained horror, as though the ringlets of his wig were being singed. Each time the word *copulate* echoed round the yard, Hans and Sophie gave each other mischievous sidelong glances and tried to be solicitous towards Rudi, asking if he was hot, passing him a jug of something or smiling amiably at him) ... and nature behaves like a living, volatile, organism. It is an infinite and infinitely subordinated cycle, that is, individual organisms are like tranquil pools which disturb the main current in order to intensify it. That is why there is no such thing as death, each individual is born of another being. The same applies to thought. Thought is also a force that evolves by feeding off everything, assimilating opposition. That is the law of the comet and the comet tail—they appear to be two separate entities but in fact one is the consequence of the other. Everything revolves in a circle of heat and this whole is the primordial oneness, the single living entity. The rest is appearance, pure reaction, ahem.

When Herr Levin's spinning, thermal and centripetal energy appeared to abate, Sophie allowed herself to bring up a name she had for some time wanted to introduce in her salon. Refresh yourself, Herr Levin, try some of this tea from India we just received, I hope you like it, and, while we are on the subject of religion, have any of you read Schleiermacher by any chance? I hear he is a theologian who concerns himself with worldly affairs. Never heard of him, said Frau Pietzine, but I would very much like to try some of your Indian tea. Schleiermacher? Professor Mietter shrugged, bah. Tea from India, you say? Rudi perked up, from Jaipur or Madras? I'm not sure, Herr Gottlieb replied, relighting his pipe, I think it is from Calcutta. Herr Hans, Sophie continued, disheartened, what do you think? And I am not referring to the tea. I think Schleiermacher is a brave author, replied Hans, although he lacked the courage of his convictions. If, as he claimed, religion belongs in the realm of the emotions, the next step would be to acknowledge that the essence of God is subjective, that is, if you'll forgive me for saying so, he feeds on human emotion. Don't you think, Álvaro, that would have been more revolutionary than Descartes? For if reason itself depends on the existence of God then religion becomes irrefutable. However, if religion is born of the emotions ... Herr Hans, Sophie grinned, contented, are you suggesting that a feeling cannot be reasonable? No, no, Hans said, blushing, I mean to say that some of Schleiermacher's ideas were progressive and others reactionary, you need look no further than Schlegel to see how *feeling* took over. Schleiermacher began by saying "more education, less religion" and went on to declare that religion was the essence of humanity, what a pity! To have come so far only to lose his nerve! Attention, young man, said Professor Mietter, atheism can be the biggest expression of cowardice, "what I do not understand cannot exist" is hardly the bravest of slogans. Ahem, if you'll permit me—Herr Levin joined the conversation once more after finishing his tea—I am prepared, Herr Hans, to accept the idea of the cowardliness of Catholicism, by which, dear Herr Gottlieb, dear friends, you must understand I do not mean Catholics themselves but the religious orthodoxy which, ahem, in some way aims to oppress its devotees. I can accept that, but I do not agree about the rest. There is no cowardice in divine thought, on the contrary it takes great courage to launch oneself into that abyss, because we cannot know what form it takes. Indeed, that is why, ahem, I insist that divinity is dynamic in essence and the heavenly bodies copulate in the sky.

Frau Levin set her cup down on its saucer and declared: There you go again with your talk of copulation! You have a fixation, my Lord, a fixation!

Speaking of dynamic nature, said Frau Pietzine, a bitter taste in her mouth, where are you all planning to spend your holidays?

Nowhere very exciting, Rudi replied smoothing down his lapels, you know the kind of thing, a few days here, a few days there, I imagine my parents and I will go to Baden in August. (In Baden, Frau Levin said, her eyes opening wide, at the spa?) Naturally, dear lady, what else is there to do in Baden? A frightfully boring place! And from there we will spend a few days at our small country mansion near Magdeburg, it doesn't have many rooms, but ... Incidentally, my Sophie (*My Sophie!* Hans recoiled), if you would reconsider the invitation, there's a pretty little garden which you (I thank you from the bottom of my heart, Rudi dear, but why this impatience? You know how I feel—I will gladly go there, but only after the wedding), yes, yes of course, I was only suggesting ... (Good! Hans muttered under his breath.)

As for us, explained Herr Gottlieb, we shall find somewhere, my daughter is fond of surprises, aren't you my dear? Indeed, only the other day I was telling our friends how tiresome it is to travel anywhere these days, people are in such a hurry, the wheels of a carriage don't seem fast enough, no sooner do they get in than they want to get out again, the faster we go the faster we want to go! I suppose travel has gone out of fashion, the new fashion is *to arrive*. I couldn't agree more, said Professor Mietter, and when I see the speed at which we travel I fear for the mental health of passengers, and this isn't me, it is the doctors who say this, the less human our method of transport, the more perilous it is for our nerves, this obsession with speed is absurd! Travelers today want to anticipate everything, the exact time of arrival, they want to avoid all surprises. *Alles klar*, carry on, full steam ahead and no more argument! But what will they think about when there is no more uncertainty? (About where to go, said Hans, just as they do now.) Yes, but what about the ritual, the excitement of departure? (I assure you, said Álvaro, that on the platform at Liverpool station the passengers become more excited than at Mass.)

Before the courtyard grew dark and the lamps were lit, the guests proceeded with the promised reading from Schiller's *William Tell*. They agreed to an informal performance of the first scene and the last, and a couple of scenes from the middle. The allocation of parts was interesting. Someone suggested Rudi play the influential Baron Attinghausen, or if not, his nephew. However, he refused both and elected the role of Conrado Baumgarten, a man of the people. Álvaro jested: You must tell us how it feels! Álvaro, who had never actually read the work, was given the role of Ruodi the fisherman, and Hans was asked to read the part of the hunter Werni so that he and Álvaro would appear together in the final scene. Herr Levin was the victim of another little whim, and, without even proffering an *ahem*, asked if he could play Baron Attinghausen's nephew, Ulrico de Rudenz. Everyone agreed that the young heiress, Berta de Bruneck, would be a perfect role for Sophie. After some insistence, Sophie managed to persuade Herr Gottlieb to play William Tell, as a tribute to paternal love. Frau Levin, who was hiding her face behind her fan, smiled nervously when, amid applause, she was allotted the part of William Tell's wife, Hedwigia. Does Hedwigia have many lines? she asked, flustered, and Sophie put her mind at rest by explaining that none of these scenes had more than five or six lines. As for the bloodthirsty, tyrannical Governor Geszler, no one volunteered to play him. Even Professor Mietter, who rejected Hans's barbed suggestion, insisting that instead of acting he would provide a cello accompaniment to give the performance atmosphere. After some discussion, and since Geszler was crucial to one scene, Frau Pietzine requested to speak, and, with an expression of infinite weariness, said: What does it matter, I will play him. Finally the professor, who, as well as taking charge of the music, had designated himself director, declared as he leafed through the pages of his copy: One moment, we have forgotten Pastor Kuoni, who has a couple of lines in the first scene. Herr Gottlieb instantly gestured to Bertold, and with a sigh of resignation the servant received a copy of the play. We will need at least one village woman as well, added the professor. The salon goers turned towards Elsa, who to begin with seemed quite willing. However, when she learnt the woman's name, she dug her heels in: Ermengarda! Not in your wildest dreams, not with a name like that! Sophie volunteered to read the village woman's lines, and the distribution of roles was complete.

ACT I, SCENE 1

   ... RUDI *[in a loud booming voice]*: Quick, quick, they are at my heels! The governor's guards are after me, and if they catch me I am a dead man.

   ÁLVARO *[exaggerating a look of surprise]*: Why are they after you?

   RUDI *[more authoritative, less imploring than was called for]*: Save me first and then I will tell you.

   HANS *[with a fine delivery, although casting unwarranted sidelong glances at Berta, that is at Sophie]*: You are bleeding, what happened?

   RUDI *[also turning towards Sophie]*: The emperor's ball at Rossberg ...

   BERTOLD *[reluctantly, his feet aching]*: Is Wo ... Er, is Wolfenschieszen after you?

RUDI [*imitating the gesture of someone raising a sword*]: No, he will do no more harm; I have killed him.

ALL [*not quite as one*]: God forgive you! What have you done?

RUDI [*with authentic fury*]: That which all free men would have done in my place. I have rightfully taken revenge on the man who insulted my honour and that of my wife.

BERTOLD [*exaggerating the intonation of the question; Hans suddenly begins to take notice*]: The ball was an insult to your honour?

RUDI [*staring intently at Hans*]: God and my axe have put an end to his wicked intentions.

HANS [*swallowing hard*]: Did you … split his skull open with an axe?

ACT V, SCENE 3

ALL [*Frau Levin's voice is scarcely audible; Frau Pietzine roars even though she isn't supposed to; Herr Gottlieb greets them, honoured*]: Long live Tell the hunter, the liberator!

SOPHIE [*with perfect intonation*]: Friends, confederates, admit into your alliance the happy woman who was the first to find refuge in the land of freedom. I entrust myself to your strong arms, will you defend my rights and protect me as your fellow citizen?

ELSA [*convinced at the last moment by the professor, responding in the name of all the villagers*]: Yes, we will protect you with our possessions and our blood.

SOPHIE [*suddenly distracted, without knowing why*]: Very well, I will marry this youth. A free woman will wed a free man.

HERR LEVIN: And I, ahem, grant freedom to all my serfs.

Professor Mietter plays a long note on the cello, letting it fade into a diminuendo. There is a brief silence. Applause, congratulations. They all embrace one another and begin their cheerful farewells, wishing each other a good summer. Sophie bids her guests goodbye one at a time, although suddenly she seems preoccupied. When it comes to Rudi's turn, he kisses her hand effusively and declares: When the summer is over, my love, it will give me great joy to return to this salon as your legitimate husband. The curtain of night has fallen. A lamp goes out.

What flowers were on the table? asked the organ grinder. Acacias, replied Hans, acacias. How do you know? asked Lamberg. On hearing Lamberg's voice, Franz put his tail between his legs. I didn't know, Hans said, I asked the maid. That's good, very good, the organ grinder grinned, taking another swig of wine, acacias mean hidden love.

After wolfing down his supper, Lamberg stood up. Leaving already? Reichardt objected, but it's Sunday tomorrow! I know, said Lamberg, but I'm tired, I have to go back. There's still some wine left, Reichardt tempted him, and I mean to polish off your share. You're welcome to it, said Lamberg, rubbing his eyes.

Lamberg walked past the mills, skirted round the factory buildings, crossed the mud track where the workers' lodgings were crowded. He groped his way up the stairs—the creak of steps merged with the snoring coming from the dormitories. As he passed the rows of doors, Lamberg checked who was asleep and who had gone to the city to enjoy their night off. He was glad to see the rooms adjoining his were empty.

He tiptoed inside. A smell of underarms pervaded the room. He could make out Günter's sleeping figure. At the foot of the straw pallet stood a bottle of grain alcohol and two glasses of water containing floating candles. Lamberg smiled in the gloom—it amused him that his room-mate, a burly, bearded, rough fellow, couldn't go to sleep in the dark. Lamberg moved closer to Günter. He watched him as he slept, lying naked on his front, the sheet rumpled between his thighs. He was breathing through his mouth. A film of sweat glistened on his shoulder blades, sculpting them. Illuminated by the sputtering candles, Günter's downy hair appeared orange, like splashes of lava. All of him seemed to pulsate placidly, except for his buttocks—his buttocks tensed then relaxed, as though in his dream Günter were making a physical effort. Lamberg went over to his own bunk, undressed quietly, lay face down, eyes open. He knew he wouldn't be able to sleep. In summer with both men's bodies sweating the temperature in the room became unbearable. It occurred to Lamberg he ought to have stopped off at the Picaro Tavern for a while to have a few drinks and enjoy himself. But then he heard Günter's hoarse drowsy voice. Is that you? Lamberg smiled, turned his head and said: Yes, were you asleep? No, no, Günter replied turning over and stretching his arms, I was waiting for you. Lamberg sat down on the edge of Günter's bunk. He brought his lips close to his red beard and spoke softly in his ear: Tell me, what were you dreaming about? Nothing, said Günter, I told you, I was waiting for you. Are you sure? Lamberg said, wiping the sweat off Günter's broad chest with his hand. Günter grabbed his wrist, squeezing it until he winced. Lamberg let Günter pull him close. He found Günter's mouth and licked his liquor-smelling tongue. Günter folded his knees. Lamberg saw his member stiff on his belly. His lips moved round it, disturbing his pubic hair, then lingering at his hips and the muscles on his abdomen. Günter let out a different groan, almost an entreaty. Lamberg lifted Günter's member from his belly, leant forward, and with bloodshot eyes, sucked the tip as if it were a strawberry.

They leafed through Quevedo's poems while they were waiting for Álvaro. Hans and Sophie had asked him to help them out with the Spanish translations. His imminent arrival inhibited them, and they smiled nervously, not daring to touch one another. What time did he say he was coming? she asked. At half-past three, he replied, and I'm surprised because he's very punctual.

Fifteen minutes later there was knock at the door of room number seven. Álvaro greeted them in Spanish, humorously imitating his friend's Saxon burr, and apologised for his tardiness. Is Elsa downstairs? Sophie asked. Álvaro replied uneasily: Who? Elsa? Ah, yes, yes, I saw her there, why? Sophie explained: I don't know what's got into her today, she's been very curt with me, and she made up all kinds of excuses not to accompany me, and rather than go off in a coach as she usually does she has stayed downstairs. Well, Álvaro cleared his throat, servants aren't what they used to be, you know.

We've got Quevedo, Hans read out, Lope de Vega, St John, Garcilaso … And what about Góngora? asked Álvaro. I think we'll leave Góngora out, replied Hans, he's untranslatable. But, Sophie said, according to you poetry is always translatable. It is, it is, Hans grinned, except for Góngora. And you're able to read him in Spanish? Álvaro looked surprised. Well, said Hans, more or less, I have a few of his books in my trunk. How many languages do you know? insisted Álvaro. A few, replied Hans. And where did you learn them? Álvaro asked. Let's just say on my travels, replied Hans. Then he went over to his trunk and rummaged around in it before extracting a weighty volume, which he brought back to the desk. Álvaro examined it with interest. Its title was *Dictionary of the Spanish and English Languages, Wherein the Words Are Correctly Explained, Agreeably to Their Different Meanings*, compiled by Henry Neuman and printed in London in 1823. It contained a vast number of terms pertaining to the arts, sciences, business and navigation. This gem, explained Hans, has helped me out of a tight corner on more than one occasion.

We still have no modern Spanish poets in our European anthology, can you recommend any? Don't worry, Álvaro laughed, in Spain all the modern poets died out with the baroque era. In that case, said Sophie, I'd like to include Juana Inés de la Cruz, who I understand lived in colonial Mexico and was widely read in Spain. I have read some of her sonnets, where is that old edition from Madrid? Could you pass it to me, Hans, thank you, now, let me see, this one, for instance. This isn't yet another chivalrous knight praising his beloved, one of those absent maidens that have nothing to say throughout the entire poem, here it is she who speaks. It is a courtly sonnet, very serious and very ironical. Here, read it:

> *To whoe'er is heartless I give my heart,*
> *The one who gives his heart I heartless leave,*
> *Plight constant troth to whoe'er mistreats me,*
> *Disdain the one who offers constant love,*
>
> *Whoe'er I beseech fondly I a diamond find,*
> *Am diamond myself to any fond approach,*
> *Triumphant wish to hail whoe'er would slay me*
> *And slay the one who would see me triumph.*
>
> *The one I reward sees the fading of my desire,*
> *Whoe'er I implore sets me on fire*
> *In either way I unhappy find myself.*

If you are going to translate this, Álvaro remarked, you have to take great care with the word *diamante*, it's a play on words— *di-amante*, someone precious yet hard, impervious to love. Of course, Sophie said, looking up from the book, I hadn't thought of that! And look at the end. The poem begins tragically and ends so pragmatically. After all that strife, the lady chooses between causing pain or suffering. And she decides torment and self-denial are not for her:

> *But then for sport I choose*
> *The one I love not, to labour in vain,*
> *And to whoe'er loves me not, am all aflame.*

Of course, Sophie went on excitedly, the ideal would be reciprocity, but Juana Inés warns us if there has to be a victim it won't be her. A seventeenth-century Mexican nun! If only my friends could read her! (We will translate it, Hans laughed, and you can give it to them as they come out of church on Sunday.) It is so different from any other love sonnets! Like these ones by Garcilaso, for example, they are wonderful, so subtle, and yet they have the same dreadful essential idea behind them—I love you provided you remain silent, you are perfect because I scarcely know you, nor do I need to:

> *Inscribed on my soul is your face*
> *And whenever I wish to write of you …*

If I'm not wrong, said Sophie pointing to the page with her slender finger, the poet has such a clear image in his soul of his beloved that he has no need to see or even to speak to her—he already knows everything he intends to say about her, it is engraved within him (oh, come now, please, come now! Álvaro protested), and that is why he goes on to admit, correct me if I'm wrong, my dear, that he prefers to contemplate this image of his beloved when he is alone:

> *… you alone inscribed it there; I read*
> *It so alone I withdraw from you …*

We have to assume that in order to inspire this poem, Sophie continued, she must have possessed amazing qualities. And yet when he is interpreting them, the poet *avoids* her, isn't this because he is protecting himself? Or hiding, so his beloved doesn't get in the way? That is, he writes the poem on his own, with his eyes closed, and reads it to himself! (Hans, implored Álvaro, stop her, say something! She's tearing our classics apart! Hans shrugged and gave a sigh.) And further on, look, another beautiful, rather suspect verse: "my soul has moulded you in its image". Why should anyone be moulded?

With the aid of Álvaro, a couple of dictionaries and a Spanish grammar, they worked on poems by Quevedo, Juana Inés, Garcilaso, and St John of the Cross. They began by making observations, then discussed their meaning and finally translated a first draft. Álvaro's German was almost perfect, but he couldn't follow metre. If either Hans or Sophie weren't sure of a meaning, they would ask Álvaro to translate it as literally as possible, then try to adapt the rhymes and metres. Álvaro enjoyed watching them trade syllables and stresses, as if they had a metronome in their mouth. They seemed to him similar, happy and faintly ridiculous. When they took too long, Álvaro wondered why if they already knew what they were going to say it mattered so much how they said it. A strange pastime, he thought, and a strange way to love. But he said nothing to them (about love or poetry) and waited for them to decide.

They took a break. Hans asked Frau Zeit to bring them up a jug of lemonade. While they chatted, Sophie spoke of the differences she found between her language and Álvaro's. It's the opposite of what I expected, she said, metre in German or English poetry resembles a dance, while in Spanish it is like a military march. In German poetry the dancer marks the rhythm until he decides to turn round and go on to the next verse, regardless of how many steps he takes. It is more spoken, more from the lungs, isn't it? Spanish verse is beautiful and yet there is something rigid about it, something imposed that doesn't seem to originate from speech, one has to count both accents and syllables, it's almost Pythagorean. I imagine it requires great technical skill, perhaps that is why Spanish poetry can seem as rhetorical as French poetry. It must be so difficult to sound informal in your language, Álvaro, while observing metre! I suppose so, Álvaro shrugged, I don't know much about verse. Although I have to say I think Spanish grammar is much more flexible, more fluid, shall we say, than German grammar. I feel like I'm banging a drum when I speak German and English, b-boom! B-boom! First–second! Subject–verb! You can never stray far from the path of the sentence, maybe this is why your German reasoning is so convincing; your language doesn't allow any improvisation in mid-flow, you have to think before you speak in order to respect the word order. Whilst, as you see, Spanish grammar is like Spanish politics! Everything happens willy-nilly, by jerks. Ulrike always said I was more imaginative and less clear-headed when we spoke in Spanish. *Ich weiß nicht*, it's possible.

And yet it is far more difficult to translate a rhyming poem from Spanish into German than it is the other way round, isn't it? Assonant rhymes are easy to achieve in Spanish and they have a *ring* to them. In German, on the other hand, because of all our different vowel sounds and the endless consonants, ach! Assonance is more difficult and the rhymes are weak. What I find tedious about the Spanish language, said Álvaro, is all the long adverbs—*larguísimamente largos, coño!*—and how bad it is at joining nouns together. In English or German, two or three things can become one thing, one new thing, whereas we are as purist about language as we are about religion, each thing is what it is, and if you want something else you have to use another word. And yet, replied Hans, as you were saying earlier, Castilian grammar, do you say Castilian or Spanish? (Oof! Álvaro sighed. That is

an extremely tedious subject, I don't mind, whatever you like.)
Well, in your language grammar allows you to play with words
as if they were riddles, and this is immediately noticeable in poetry. Sentences in German are constructed like ships, out of big
heavy sections. How funny! remarked Sophie, Álvaro eulogising
German and Hans going into raptures over Spanish! What's so
odd about that, Miss Wandenburger, said Hans, doesn't everyone
aspire to being a little more of a foreigner?

They went back to work after finishing the jug of lemonade.
They had left Álvaro's favourite poem for last. After looking
up the meaning of the words *antaños* and *huirse*, Sophie asked
Álvaro to read Quevedo's sonnet aloud.

ON THE BREVITY OF LIVING
AND THE NOTHINGNESS OF HAVING LIVED

"Is life there?" No reply is given
Despite all the years I have lived!
Fortune all my days has gnawed,
My madness steals away the hours.

Unable to know how or where
My health and years have fled!
Life gone missing, the living past endures,
And every calamity presses round.

Yesterday's no more; tomorrow is not yet,
Today is leaving in all haste,
I am a was, a will be, and a weary is.

Today, tomorrow, yesterday, I shape
Shroud and swaddling clothes, and remain
Present successions of the dead.

I don't know what moves me more, Sophie gulped, the way time passes so swiftly in the poem or the poet's despair over the time that he has left. Wait, said Hans, am I right in thinking this poem is divided into two? (Well done, Álvaro said sarcastically, quartets and tercets!) Very funny. The title suggests the poem will be about the fleeting nature of time, how quickly we grow old. And the quartets are about that. Yet the tercets say almost exactly the opposite, here a different voice appears to be speaking, the voice of a person who is tired of life, an old man for whom the end is dragging on, why is that? I'd never thought of that, said Álvaro, surprised, and I know the poem off by heart. You never thought of it precisely because you know it off by heart. I've had an idea, Sophie said pensively, perhaps the key to this is in that peculiar "soy un *fue*", that is, why isn't it "soy un *fui*"? What if, after reminiscing in the quartets, the old man, fearful of time, is able to contemplate the whole of his life, and he distances himself so much from his memories that he sees them as though he were another person, he becomes detached from himself and a second voice is born, the one we hear in the tercets. *Bravo!* declared Hans. You're both crazy, Álvaro said, surreptitiously rereading the poem. Now that you mention it, said Hans, I can think of another turn of the screw—after turning into someone else who contemplates his own life, the old man continues along the path towards death, and when he stumbles on it, or at least catches sight of it, he arrives full circle, encountering the child he was, his own beginning. Then, in the final tercet, yesterday, today and tomorrow merge into one. In that case, Sophie added, let me suggest an optimistic ending—once he has encountered his beginning, the circle closing could be construed as a kind of eternity. That would explain the "present successions of the dead". *Present*, do you see, because he is still alive!

Quevedo, Quevedo! Álvaro exclaimed. Come back to life, defend yourself!

Hans and Sophie looked at one another. They were no longer thinking of Quevedo, all they could see was a succession of present moments.

In the end, at the behest of his parents, Rudi had no choice but to leave Wandernburg. They wished him to spend the holidays with them at Baden, where each summer the family rented a section of the spa, and then at their country mansion in the environs of Magdeburg, where the Wilderhauses owned land, which it was necessary to supervise occasionally. Rudi said goodbye to Sophie solemnly, insisting once again that she go with him. And once again she politely refused, citing her need to keep her father company, as well as the zealous care with which Herr Gottlieb was preparing for the wedding. You do know, my love, Rudi had said before giving her a last snuff-flavoured kiss, that even if you came with me, I would never dream of disrespecting you before our wedding day. I know, I know, she had said, blinking, and responding to his kiss more passionately than usual, that's what I love about you, my darling, but let's be patient, that way we'll enjoy our reward even more.

And so, having made a hundred promises, and with a vague sense of unease, Rudi embarked on his last summer holiday as a bachelor. The day of his departure, he had a manservant deliver an emphatic love letter to Sophie, in which he swore he would write to her daily and would return at the very latest at the start of the shooting season. She replied to him immediately with a briefer letter, which she addressed to the spa, so that Rudi would read it on his arrival at Baden. But before that she scrawled a few lines on her violet notepaper.

My love, my mischievous love—the faster time passes, the more I seem to leave my mark on things, as though the depth of my footprint depended on the speed at which I am going. Even as my actions excite and scare me, I feel indifferent to their consequences. Is it possible to experience all those things at once? Yes, as more than one person. The Sophie who has just said goodbye to Rudi feels relieved, and yet she pities him, too, and feels sorry in spite of herself. That Sophie is walking a tightrope so as to give the appearance at home that everything is normal when in fact it is most irregular, so as not to rouse Father's suspicions about something that is deeply suspect. Yet the Sophie who writes to you is like a swirling current running hot and cold. When she needs to lie or to dissemble, she possesses a self-assurance that scares me, and that somehow I admire, because I never thought her capable of it. And yet as soon as she sees you or thinks about seeing you, the current boils over, it rages with a strange urgency. Then nothing else matters, all obligations, all suffering can wait until tomorrow; anything to avoid the unbearable torment of not seeing you now. And from where I am now the future seems like a useless, beautiful mountain. I am down in the valley, lying naked in the shadows, talking to you. E non abbiamo più.

At least until September, while everyone is away on holiday, it will be easier for us to meet. It is simply a question of keeping up appearances outside your room, which is our world. I want to enjoy these days, which of course entails taking a certain amount of risk. Calling on my father's acquaintances is beginning to grate on my nerves. It is exhausting having to weigh every word, every opinion. It is exasperating having to dress up. It is hateful that the library is closed. My friends bore me to tears. When we aren't discussing eligible young men, we talk about dresses, and vice versa. But discussing Dante with them would be worse! Did I tell you how much I love you? Well, just in case.

I shall see you tomorrow. What a long wait! I found a book of Calderón's poems in the house, I thought it could be of some use. By the way, when are you going to show me your famous organ grinder's cave?

The most multilingual, melodious kiss from your

S

... and a tendency to leave your mark on things, you say. I know that feeling—like stepping back into the impression left by a pleasurable experience. But there is also the other side of the coin. We leave our mark on things, and things leave their mark on us. These past days, Sophie, I know very well, that wherever we may be, they have left their mark on us and there is nothing we can do to change that. I don't know xxxxxx how long it will all last either, and for now I don't care. Today it is thus, we both agree, and with you it is always today.

Even so, my darling, will you allow me to say, until tomorrow?

All my love

H

At the windows dawn broke insistently and night fell gently. The light expanded, blistering. One by one, without anyone realising they had gone, the city authorities abandoned Wandernburg. Mayor Ratztrinker took his family to the landscaped country estate he had just purchased from Herr Gelding. One Friday, around mid-morning, the councillors abandoned the town hall. And, in what one of the journalists at the *Thunderer* would later refer to as a "scandalous" coincidence, on that same day, six underage girls suddenly ran away from home.

For Lieutenants Gluck and Gluck, however, there was no repose. They discussed the different possibilities, made renewed searches of the alleyways where the masked man usually perpetrated his deeds, returned to the office to compare notes. The son insisted there were now only three possible suspects. The father, more cautious, thought there were four. Let's question them, Lieutenant Gluck said with irritation, and put a stop to this once and for all! Not so fast, son, his father said, holding him back, let's not be hasty. If we start questioning suspects, the culprit will probably take off the next day. We have to wait a little longer, we can't make any mistakes. We need him to make another move. And when we're absolutely sure, we won't question anyone, we'll simply get a warrant from the superintendent and arrest him. You're not as quick as you used to be, Dad! Lieutenant Gluck protested. Sub-lieutenant, I order you to be calm, replied Lieutenant Gluck.

Rumours. Rumours passing from mouth to mouth, from window to window, from name to name, rumours resounding like a changing melody, propagating like weeds. In a small city words are expansive, viscous, they belong to no one and to everyone. The good people of Wandernburg wanted to know who, where, what, when and how. And in order to find out who was who, they all gave the appearance of being what they were not.

The rumours had gradually ballooned, spreading from street to street, from door to door. Everyone was talking about the same thing and they all fell silent as one.

Sophie was gazing out of the window. She had been lying quietly, curled up on her orange silk eiderdown for some time. Her eyes were glassy, her eyelids puffy, the tip of her nose red as if she had caught the sun. At the foot of the bed lay a scrapbook, a discarded mirror, and a bundle of folios with a quill pen on top. She wasn't sure what she ought to do, although she knew what she wanted to do. She didn't want an eternity, just a little more time. She breathed in slowly, rubbed her nose. She tidied the papers, folded them and slipped them into an envelope then rang for Elsa.

When Elsa came into the bedroom, she held out the sealed envelope. Could you post this for me, my dear? she said. I'll do it first thing tomorrow, Miss, said Elsa, when I go out to do the shopping. No, no, said Sophie, go now. But I've got to lay the table for lunch, Elsa protested. It doesn't matter, said Sophie, standing up, I'll see to the table while you go to the postbox. Elsa sighed: You know your father doesn't like you doing the. That's an order, now go, Sophie interrupted her sharply. And on seeing Elsa pull a face because she was not accustomed to being spoken to in that tone, she added: Please. Elsa shrugged, took the envelope and left the room, puzzled by all this hurry to post another letter to master Rudi. When the bedroom door closed once more, Sophie went over to her dressing table. She applied a brisk layer of make-up to hide her puffy eyes. She added some rouge. She gave her hair a half-hearted comb, then hurried downstairs to her father's study.

... convinced that, after much deliberation, such an important event should coincide with Christmas as well as with another joyous celebration, for it was during that festive season (do you recall, my love?) that you proposed to me. Bear in mind, too, that there are still a few minor organisational details which need resolving, and which, with a little extra time, I will be able to oversee myself. I know you understand my reasons, and I thank you with all my heart. It is going to be wonderful!

Your letter arrived on Thursday, and as always it was a delight. I really do think you should read poetry from time to time, because, despite your objections, I insist you have something of the poet in you, and then we could enjoy sharing some of the books I would like you to read. Will you do that, my love? Have a good rest in that beautiful spa (where, of course, we will be going together next summer), take care of your charming parents, and please send them my fondest regards. Don't play too much at cards, I know you, and beware of Fräulein Hensel, the shy ones are the worst! From what you have told me, I don't think I like her very much. But of course you may invite her to spend a few days at Magdeburg, silly, you know you needn't ask my permission about that kind of thing. And it isn't that I am not jealous, as you said in your letter—I detest telling people what to do with their free time as much as I detest them telling me what to do with mine.

A kiss from your "elusive little diurnal moon" (what a wonderful metaphor, my darling Rudi!) and thank you so much for the gemstone necklace, I don't know how to show my gratitude for such a gift. I miss

you dreadfully, too. Until the next letter, your
S

What! Herr Gottlieb roared, you did what? Without consulting me? Is this some sort of bad joke? Or have you gone mad? There's nothing mad about it, Father, whispered Sophie, it's only a slight change, that's all, just a few weeks, and besides, December is a much nicer time of year than October. But we were all set to begin the final preparations! her father growled, flinging his pipe across the desk (it struck the brandy bottle and clanged like a bell). I know, Father, I know, she insisted, that's why I thought now was the moment to tell Rudi about it, before we started organising everything. And have you considered what the Wilderhauses will think of us, you foolish girl? said Herr Gottlieb, twirling his whiskers. Or what Rudi will think? Don't worry, Father, Rudi will agree, I promise you, I already suggested a slight postponement in my last letter. You did what—Herr Gottlieb became incensed—and what did he say? Tell me his exact words or I shall read the letter myself! He said he wasn't keen on the idea, said Sophie, but that if I was sure and if there was no other way … Heaven help me! said Herr Gottlieb in despair. One of these days you will be the death of me! Don't say that, Father, she stammered. Well I am saying it! her father shouted, oh, and as for the fair tonight, don't you dare mention it to me, do you hear, you're not going and that's final! Do you understand? Whatever you say, Father, Sophie nodded. Now leave! he said at last. Leave me alone, go!

Wandernburg's summer fair was like any other provincial celebration—its pretensions to grandeur gave it a pathetic, touchingly ridiculous air. The little paper lanterns hanging in the small park opposite the Hill of Sighs brightened the already moonlit night. There was a youth orchestra, plaster pilasters encircling a dance floor, brightly coloured garlands and trestle tables with drinks. Hans asked for a fruit cocktail, and scanned the crowd once more, surprised not to see Sophie—this was a perfect opportunity for them to go off into the park together, as they had agreed. While he was talking to Hans, Álvaro was watching Elsa's movements out of the corner of his eye. She had a very solemn face and had remained talking to Bertold without giving him the pleasure of a dance. All of a sudden, behind Elsa, Álvaro spied Lamberg's hunched figure roaming the dance floor. Look, he said to Hans, pointing at Lamberg, he's been circling round like that with his glass for about an hour now, and he still hasn't danced with anyone! Poor Lamberg, said Hans, let's go over and say hello, maybe that will cheer him up a bit.

Lamberg seemed pleased to see them, yet he hardly said a word, and shook his head in irritation when they suggested he approach a girl with golden ringlets who was staring insistently at him, stroking the folds in her dress. They soon lost sight of him, and Álvaro went over to Elsa. Hans decided to join in their conversation to see if he could discover something about Sophie. But before Hans had a chance to ask, Elsa, who had been expressly requested to notify Hans of her absence, observed absent-mindedly how pretty the festival was, and what a shame Fräulein Sophie was indisposed.

Perfumed without her father's permission, and with her hair scraped up to reveal her neck, Lisa Zeit crossed the dance floor beaming, her eyes fixed on Hans's back. What she found most attractive about him were his flowing locks, inappropriate for a man of his age, and his deep, rather solemn voice when he was teaching her grammar. He wasn't overly tall, but more importantly, he had good posture. She also liked the fact that some mornings he didn't shave. Lisa had managed to persuade her father to let her go to the fair with her friends, provided she

was home no later than eleven o'clock. She had flown into a
tantrum, insisting the evening would only just be starting then,
and had locked herself in her room sobbing until, at last, after
tea, she had got ready to go out as though nothing had happened. Before she left, Herr Zeit had repeated his instructions
and, when he went to kiss her forehead, had given her permission
to stay out until eleven-thirty, but not a minute later.

Hans felt a hand touch his shoulder and wheeled round in
anticipation. Although in a flash he replaced his grimace of
disappointment with an amiable smile, Lisa noticed the gesture, and anyway she felt her new dress and high-heeled shoes
deserved a little more than mere amiability. Hans looked at
the dress—he acknowledged that it flattered her budding figure, but it was too formal for his taste, and touchingly vulgar.
The clear purpose of Lisa's dress, hairstyle and perfume was,
he reflected, to make her look older at any cost. Yet this very
eagerness, which emphasised the grace of her arms and the
curve of her waist, only served to show Lisa's true age, and her
need to dress up like a woman because she was still a girl. Good
evening, Fräulein, Hans smiled. Lisa thought: That's better,
he's smiling. Good evening, Herr Hans, she replied, I thought
we might bump into each other here, knowing what late hours
you keep. Hans replied, a little uneasily: It's quite a surprise to
see you here, knowing what an early bird you are. Ah, sighed
Lisa, habits change, people change, time passes so quickly, don't
you think? Yes, said Hans, you can't imagine how quickly. Well,
she declared, glancing about significantly, I came here hoping
to meet my girlfriends, but I don't see them anywhere, what a
shame, I was sure they'd come, their parents must have kept
them in, they're nearly a year younger than I am, you know.
Tell me, Hans said, attempting to sidetrack her, how is your
homework going? Are you still struggling with the subjunctive?
We're not in class now are we, Hans? Lisa retorted. I'm sorry, he

said, I didn't mean it like that, I just wondered how you were. Then why not ask me, silly, she laughed, just say "How are you, Lisa?" and I'll tell you, and we can have a normal conversation.

Hans went to fetch Lisa the cocktail she had asked for, and instructed the waiter to add only a drop of alcohol to the glass. When Lisa tasted the drink and said it tasted nice but strong, Hans smiled and felt vaguely relieved. Lisa spoke in a very loud voice, moved her shoulders about a lot and was beside herself with joy. Every now and then Hans looked for Álvaro but couldn't see him. Their hesitant conversation slowed to a halt until they fell silent. Lisa glanced over at the orchestra as though she had only just noticed it and said: Wouldn't it be terribly polite of you to ask me for a dance? To be honest, Hans croaked, it would be more polite if I didn't. Lisa's face turned pale, she thought she might faint and nearly dropped her drink. She felt a sharp pain in her stomach, as if she had eaten glass, and she pressed her rosy lips together, stifling her tears. Hans saw her gesture and thought how beautiful she looked. I'm really sorry, he muttered. It's all right, she replied in a faint whisper, and anyway it doesn't matter, I've just seen a friend. Have fun, he said. Don't worry, I will, she said wheeling round. Lisa, Hans stopped her, you do understand, don't you? Perfectly, she said, walking away, you're free to dance with who ever you like, goodbye, see you sometime.

As soon as she was lost in the crowd, Lisa ran from the park, clutching her dress in one hand like a jilted princess.

During their initial sessions, Hans and Sophie couldn't decide whether to do the translations first and then make love, or to begin their lovemaking and move on, less excited, to the books. To begin with, Sophie was in favour of putting off jumping into bed, not out of any lack of desire, but because she enjoyed Hans's agitation, and because they both had the impression that being in a state of sexual anticipation made them more sensitive to the allusions and ideas in the poems. Hans had at first favoured sex as a preamble to reading, not only because of the urgency that assailed him when he was alone with Sophie, but also because he was convinced the blissful, floating state they found themselves in after their lovemaking was conducive to understanding the nuances of a poem.

As the afternoons went on, however, they began improvising the order in which they conducted matters. They never made any explicit decision—simply when they greeted and their tongues intertwined, each gauged the other's preference and opted for whatever felt most urgent. The fact of not establishing any other routine within their work routine kept them on their toes, habituated but not quite knowing. This alternating was also sexual—sometimes Sophie was dominant, and Hans felt scared and in awe of her almost brutal impulses; on other occasions she enjoyed slipping beneath his body, letting herself be rocked, out then in, slow then fast, in a kind of deep repose, which also satisfied her.

Now, for instance, they were leaning against the rickety headboard shoulder to shoulder, leafing through a novel. It was uncomfortable, the blazing light shone through the window casting a shadow over the page, forcing them to twist and turn in order to be able to read. They didn't care—their muscles retained the suppleness of recently satisfied desire. Sophie and Hans were fulfilling a promise they had made to each other a while ago, of rereading Schlegel's *Lucinde* together. Occasionally they would stop to have discussions that grew out of the novel itself.

Do you know something? he said. I have the feeling right now that we two are as one. As one? she asked, turning her head and resting it on his shoulder. I don't mean when two people are or believe they are one person, Hans explained. (What a dreadful thought, gasped Sophie, like being only half a person.) Quite! And that's not the same as being two people at the same time, is it? Two as one. Here, now, you and I seem completely harmonious, and yet at the same time I feel each of us is both more strongly ourselves, does that make sense? If I tell you that I feel the same, Sophie laughed, will I always have to agree with you?

But, said Sophie, caressing his knee, aren't you afraid that we fell in love because it was forbidden? I don't know, Hans said, I don't think about it, it would complicate things too much, how can we know what we would feel if we were able to see each other normally? And what the devil would seeing each other *normally* be? No, I only think about how much I like being with you. And what do you like best about it? she asked. I don't know, the fact that we can be ourselves, we don't have to pretend. Mmm, Sophie hesitated, isn't that rather a lot of *being*? What I like best is that we can be the other if we want—you can be a sweet young girl who opens herself to me, or I a vigorous man who forces you to embrace me. You've been reading too much of the younger Schlegel! he laughed. Never enough to forget his older brother, my dear, she retorted.

"At first nothing attracted him or made such a powerful impression on him", Sophie read aloud "as the realisation that Lucinde was similar or identical to him in character and spirit; with each day he began to discover new differences. Yet even these differences were founded upon a deeper similarity, and the more each of their personalities developed, the more versatile and exhilarating their love became". You see? For me this is one of the most important passages in the novel. And yet we are still so far away from this, can you imagine legions of narrators reflecting about the changes in themselves because the women they love have changed? And what have you to say of this? Hans remarked, look, this part here where he compares himself to lovers who feel they don't belong in the world, who feel detached from everything because of their love, and he says: "We are not thus. All that we loved before, we love more. The meaning of the world has become clear to us", to me this vision is admirable, love not as a way of fleeing but of discovering the world. This means a new society would begin by reinventing love. Quite right, said Sophie, although Schlegel also has his contradictions, remember the chapter we read just now, let me see? I think it was in this one, there was something, wait, which I found rather shocking, and I don't mean that nonsense about women being the purest of all creatures, I won't even mention that, ah, here it is: "The loftier a man becomes, the more he resembles a plant, the most moral and beautiful of all the forms that nature takes". Surely it's the other way round, surely we must question the roots of things, challenge what is considered natural, there are times, for instance, when in order to blossom a woman must defy nature. And besides, plants also evolve, like people they adapt to their environment, their needs change. And why shouldn't novels evolve, too; *Lucinde* has a hybrid rather than a pure nature. Prologue! Hans cheered, we want a prologue from you for the new edition. Don't flatter me, please! she protested. Well, flatter me, but without me realising it.

Did you know that Schlegel wanted to write a sequel to his story? Sophie said, poking at Hans's sex with her finger. Apparently he planned to continue the story from Lucinde's point of view rather than that of Julius. It is odd that she scarcely has a voice in the novel. Sometimes I think that if Schlegel had written the second part of *Lucinde*, his life, and perhaps ours, would have been different. But didn't his wife, Dorothea, publish a novel at the same time? Hans asked, pinching her stomach. Yes, replied Sophie, and despite writing about a young girl who wishes to defy her family and see the world, the book was finally entitled *Florentin*, after its peripatetic young hero. They say Dorothea also planned to write a sequel called *Camilla*, a woman's story narrated by a woman. She never finished it. Silence. That's the story of literature.

The thing is, said Hans, trying to lead her on, *Lucinde* is about marriage isn't it? Absolutely not, Sophie hastened to reply, it's about the union of two people in love. Yes, he insisted, but the characters who love one another are husband and wife. My sweet, she said, disappointed, your brain becomes a little confused when it comes to men and women. This novel is about love, a different kind of love, and the fact that it happens within a marriage is simply to make the passion more natural, to give it an everyday feel. Some of us women readers, you know, are fed up with tragic love affairs and impossible desires, that's why I think Schlegel was right to place his story in the ordinary setting of a marriage. Call me curious, Hans ventured, but can the same be said of your marriage?

Sophie stood up without saying a word. She crouched over the chamber pot and, for a few moments, all that could be heard was the wistful trickle of urine. She went back and perched on the edge of the bed, her back to Hans. He feared she was more offended than he'd expected, but just when he was about to offer an apology, she murmured: I've postponed the wedding. What? Hans gave a start. She repeated the words in an identical voice. Hans felt bewildered, ecstatic, terrified. How long for? he probed. Until December, she replied, until Christmas. He knew he mustn't speak. Sophie sat for a long time, naked on the edge of the bed, listening to the sound of her own breathing. At last she turned around and lay down again, her head resting on Hans's belly, and, having casually discovered the cobwebs in the rafters, she began to talk.

After listening to her, Hans thought the time had come to pose the obvious but awkward question he had been carefully avoiding. He did not want any ties, nor was he asking for any. But that fact was since he had met Sophie he felt strangely rooted, and he looked on with astonishment as his stay in Wandernburg lengthened. And given that he was still there, perhaps carrying on behaving as if he had just arrived was a mark of weakness, not of freedom. Sophie, he said gently, how could you have become engaged to Rudi? Why are you still with him?

Sophie was aware that Hans was not in the habit of asking this type of question, and she decided to be relatively frank with him. Look, she said, I'm not in love with Rudi, and I won't try to pretend I am either to you or to myself because that would be pointless. But I never resisted the marriage. Rudi adores me and I am increasingly fond of him. This is less than I had hoped for, but a lot more than many women can boast. And, well, fantasy aside, such a marriage secures any woman's future; it will make my father happy and solve our financial worries. Not that I sought Rudi out, to begin with I had no interest in him. But my father began inviting him to the house more frequently, and then he joined our salon. One day he confessed he was in love with me and told me that was the only reason for his coming to the house (I can't blame him for that, thought Hans), I didn't take it very seriously, but he swore he would keep coming until I began to love him or refused him entry, which of course I would never have done. And time continued to go by, sometimes it can be as simple as that, can't it? I never said yes or no to him, I accepted his flattery, my father begged me to consider his proposal, and I thought about the needs of my family, and the fact that in any event I had never fallen in love with anyone. I was attracted to a lot of men, certainly, and would meet with them in secret, but I admired none of them. They didn't seem sufficiently sensitive or intelligent, I suppose that was my youthful vanity. Finally I decided that if I weren't going to love a man I'd do better to marry one who was rich and kind. You may think this conform-ist, but I prefer to call it pragmatism. Rudi has promised that, providing I bear him children and am a good wife, he will never try to prevent me from studying or pursuing my music or traveling. (But couldn't you aspire to a different sort of marriage? said Hans.) I'm not chasing dreams, I want reality, we women too often confuse love and expectation. At any rate, Rudi is young and handsome. (Is he, really?) Of course he is, are you blind? And although he might seem dull to you, he respects my tastes, he is tolerant with me, and he couldn't have been more persistent. (Tell me, how did Master Wilderhaus woo you?) Well, you can imagine, he showered me with gifts, took me out to dinner, that sort of thing, but above all he wrote to me. His letters were so passionate I almost envied him, I wanted to be in love the way he was, to be in love with his love. He told me how he saw me, and it was strange, because the more qualities he found in me the less I recognised myself in his descriptions. I swear, I even began to refer to his letters in order to know how I should behave, don't look at me like that, Hans! It didn't bother me, I knew perfectly well that when a man portrays his beloved he is portraying his desires. Now please let's drop the subject and enjoy the news. I'm not getting married until December and that's what matters.

What matters, Elsa said standing beside the carriage, is what happens later, you understand, she has a future and she shouldn't throw everything away. But don't you think they get along very well? Álvaro said, restraining her. I don't think anything, Elsa replied, gesturing to the driver to wait, he's your friend so of course you'd say that. One fine day he'll go back where he came from, and my mistress will have to pick up the pieces. I doubt it, said Álvaro, besides, like I said, it's nobody's concern but theirs. You're wrong, said Elsa, this concerns a whole family, not to mention those of us working for them. How funny, said Álvaro, suddenly you sound as if you cared about their family.

Elsa leant forward, gave him a swift kiss and said: I must go,

I'll arrive late at the fountain.

Steps, we're off, position yourself, together, turn, faster, more lively, cross over, step back, together again, waist, hand, very good, legs closer together, one-two, one-two-three, much better, don't forget the arms, wait, not like that, too late now, more lively, shoulders, clumsy you! I love it, heels and stop, cross over and we change, not too fast, your foot with mine, I'm waiting, are you following? Up, lean forward, turn, wait, what are you doing? ... Hey, where are you going?

Decidedly, the waltz was not made for Hans.

The dancers at the Apollo Theatre saw him leave the floor in mid-dance, and watched Sophie follow him, unable to stop laughing. Earlier, they had seen them join in a square dance, and more than one had noticed that she, an impeccable dancer and a rather sensible young woman, had been distracted by the young stranger's whispers and had lost her rhythm in a most unladylike fashion. Hans and Sophie ran up the marble staircase, crossed the gallery and sat down at an empty table, opposite some gaslit chandeliers in the form of grapevines. Never had Sophie acted so boldly, so openly, in public. And never had she felt so indifferent to what others might think—the summer was one big dance floor and she intended to enjoy herself on it until it was closed. And even as her situation became increasingly vulnerable, her feelings gave her a sense of invulnerability.

Impelled by the waltz and in high spirits from the punch, Sophie told Hans about Rudi's most recent letter. After putting up some resistance, Rudi had accepted postponing the wedding, and even seemed persuaded the new date was more appropriate for such a momentous event. Aside from that, reassured by the eloquence with which Sophie had striven to imbue her letters, he declared himself to be as much in love with her as ever and proud of his fiancée's organisational skills, which ensured the success of the ceremony. This was all true, but it wasn't the whole truth—Rudi had been sensitive of late, alternating between a tone of injured pride and one of emotional entreaty. For a few days he had stopped sending her gifts through the post, but when he saw that Sophie made no mention of it, he had regretted his retaliatory act and had redoubled his stream of offerings. She knew Rudi well and could imagine how much pain he was in. And for this reason, in the same way that she regretted being unable to reveal to Rudi her true state of mind, she also lamented being unable to tell Hans how much Rudi was suffering—each man was a moral intruder in the other's eyes.

No, Hans, my love, I am not as generous as you think nor do I give myself to you freely—whatever you take from me you have already given me, and when I return to you it is because everything has the power to flow back and forth between us, like an echo. When I think of you, when I give myself to you, I feel I am going to meet myself, and this makes me stronger and more serene. Serenity also comes from being able to give back exactly what you receive. What a selfish kind of generosity!

Good night, my happiness. Touch one of your toes and pretend it was my playful hand. Your

S

Sophie, my delicious Sophie, what a wonderful idea—whatever you take from me you have already given to me. I have been reflecting about it all day, and I think your idea, which, like all true ideas, is more of an experience, elevates our love to a higher plane—that of individualism in its truest sense. Lovers in the classical tradition promise they will always remain the same, but with you I have learnt to change my plans for the good. I am not talking about freeing the one you love out of self-righteous altruism. This is about the certainty that your breadth is my horizon.

After each brief parting, after that tranquil repossession of ourselves separately, I feel ready to embark upon a sweeter conquest of ourselves together.

With you, love from

H

The smoke from the tables formed a halo round Álvaro's hat, crept round its brim like a ghost along a cornice, then, rising up its crown, finally disappeared with a shimmer among the oil lamps. Café Europa had filled up suddenly, as though the customers had been waiting for a signal to storm the doors. Álvaro had been over some of the company budgets, had ordered a cup of hot chocolate and was presently leafing through an out-of-date copy of the *Daily Clarion*. Hans was on his sixth coffee of the day, and was absent-mindedly contemplating the vagaries of the smoke. Álvaro had just said goodbye to Elsa and Hans had arrived fresh from his tryst with Sophie. Neither of them had ever mentioned these parallel encounters, not out of mistrust but out of discretion. Whatever became of his affair with Elsa, Álvaro reflected, it would have few repercussions. The situation with Sophie was different, much more delicate. And he wasn't sure which was more helpful to Hans—continuing to hold his tongue or speaking up once and for all.

Have you seen this? Álvaro said, deciding to dissemble, and picking up another newspaper. Have you seen the *Manchester Guardian*? He opened it and spread out a double page that overlapped the table. Hans leant forward and read the caption—in Frankfurt they had just celebrated the anniversary of Metternich's naming as chancellor. King Francis of Austria, King Frederick William of Prussia, Tsar Nicolas, King George of England and King Charles of Spain had all attended. Hans shrugged. Have you seen these speeches? Álvaro went on. Listen to this: "His Imperial Majesty"—referring to King

Francis—"emphasised his continuing achievements"—he means Metternich—"a result of his unstinting zeal"—zeal! They can say that again—"his political astuteness and the courage with which he has devoted himself to safeguarding the established order"—it's nothing if not accurate!—"and the triumph of law over the chaos wrought by those who aim to disturb the peace both within and beyond our borders". Well, it goes on like that, and then: "His Majesty Frederick William III of Prussia praised Metternich's career, extolled the Assembly's work, and warned of the need to increase the room for manoeuvre of the German states"—what a nerve! And then, listen: "At all times in a spirit of friendship and cooperation"— how touching! "His Majesty King George IV underlined the importance of the Quadruple Alliance, which strengthens the economic and trade agreements between the states regardless of religious differences". Ah, they're so English, the English! But there's more, listen to what ... Sorry, interrupted Hans, may I? Álvaro handed over the newspaper, raising his arms in a gesture of innocence. Hans read in silence:

Finally Prince Metternich took the floor, ending his speech to the applause of the Parliament: "The word freedom has no value as a point of departure, but rather as an end worth fighting for. It is the word 'order' that designates the point of departure. Admirers of today's press wish to dignify it with the title of representative of public opinion, although it merely publishes the views of its journalists. Do these same demagogues even recognise the aforesaid function, that of representing public opinion, in the consensual declarations of our governments? Public opinion is a powerful force in every sense. Like religion, it penetrates where administrative measures cannot. Underestimating the power of the press would be as perilous as underestimating the value of moral principles. Posterity would never understand if we responded with silence to our opponents' protests. The fall of empires depends on the spread of unbelief. That is why religious belief continues to be not only the highest virtue, but the greatest of powers. And therefore a decline in religion would also bring about a decline in the power of our nations.

Hans sighed.

By the way, Álvaro continued to dissemble, how is the organ grinder? Last night I had supper with him, said Hans, he's the same as always, he sings to himself and sleeps like a baby. Sometimes he coughs. I succeeded in buying him a new shirt and threatened to give him a bath. What did he say to that? asked Álvaro. He thinks cleanliness is overrated, replied Hans, that it depends on guilt and he is at peace with his conscience. Hans and Álvaro both laughed, but then suddenly Hans went quiet. Álvaro asked him how the translations were going and he said they were going well, he mentioned three or four poets and fell silent quiet again. Then Álvaro thought Hans might be anticipating another question and he resolved to bring up the subject. He was poised to open his mouth when there was a collision of billiard balls, followed by victorious cheers.

Listen, Álvaro said at last looking straight at him, you are aware of the trouble you're getting into, aren't you? Hans gave a sigh, more of relief than unease. A smile flickered over his lips. Then he looked down, contemplated the dregs of his coffee, shrugged and said: It's out of my control now. And I don't want to control it. Álvaro nodded. After a measured pause, he went on: What about Sophie? Sophie, replied Hans, has more courage than both of us together. And the wedding? said Álvaro. I suppose it'll have to go ahead, murmured Hans, Sophie doesn't need saving, only loving. But do you seriously love her? asked Álvaro. So seriously, said Hans, that I know very well I mustn't obstruct this wedding. And afterwards? said Álvaro. Afterwards, replied Hans, I've no idea. We'll either continue seeing each other … Or? Álvaro pressed him. Or I'll leave for

Dessau, concluded Hans, where Herr Lyotard is expecting me.

Álvaro's hat continued to smoke, as if it was on fire. They did not notice when a fly landed on the brim. The fly liked it. It stayed there.

Tell me something, Álvaro said, if you're so in love with Sophie, how can you stand her being with another man while she's with you? Because while she's with me, Hans grinned, she's not with anyone else. Yes, but you're not the only one, said Álvaro, and when you really love. The truth is, Hans interrupted, we're never the only ones. Everyone is or thinks about being with others. Come now, said Álvaro, you don't fool me, don't pretend you aren't jealous when you think of her and Rudi together! (The fly began crawling over the hat, rubbing its tiny legs on the shiny fabric.) I'm not saying I never feel jealous, replied Hans, only that my jealousy doesn't depend on what she does. One can be eaten up with jealous imaginings. But aren't you afraid of losing her? Álvaro insisted, that she'll choose someone else, Rudi or some other man? Of course! said Hans. I just doubt I could prevent that by being the only man she sleeps with, do you see? I'd even go so far as to say one is more likely to lose a woman if one tries to stop her meeting other men. And what if she meets someone else and falls for him, Álvaro argued. There's always that danger, Hans admitted, but frustrated curiosity is an even greater peril. We can become obsessed with someone we've never touched precisely because we've never touched them. That's why I always mistrust faithful women, don't laugh, they're capable of idealising another man so much it becomes impossible for them not to fall in love with him. Don't relationships between faithful couples fail? And how many marriages survive thanks to lovers? I'm still not sure, sighed Álvaro, if you're pulling my leg, or if you genuinely believe this. My dear fellow, replied Hans, I do believe you're becoming conservative in your old age! Álvaro shook his head: This is the young man in you speaking. When you're young you enjoy playing with ambiguity. But as you grow older you stop being certain of almost everything, and you cling like a leech to the few things you know—the one you love, your family, your territory. I'm not as young as you think, replied Hans, and, aside from Sophie, I'm no longer certain of anything. And what about her, does she share your ideas? asked Álvaro. Oh, very much so! Hans chuckled. And besides … Besides what? Álvaro enquired, leaning closer. (The fly's tiny wings quivered, threatened to take off.) And besides, Hans whispered, that way she'll give me more pleasure, she can teach me what she learns with others. Oh, please! Álvaro exclaimed. Now you're being cynical! No, no, Hans bridled, it's impossible to be cynical when you're in love. And I'm more in love with Sophie than I've ever been with anyone. How can I explain, for me there's nothing more beautiful than feeling chosen, do you understand? Anyway, either report me to Father Pigherzog or buy me another coffee, it's your turn. Coffee, no, said Álvaro, whisky. Waiter! Two whiskies, please! Both for this gentleman!

It was then they saw the fly.

What do we have to translate today, she asked slipping back into her white stockings. The Italians, he said, and the Portuguese. But first look at this.

Hans searched through his trunk and passed Sophie a copy of *Atlas*. In the centre pages was a selection of a young French poet they had translated together. And, underneath the heading, an introductory note accredited to Sophie. What's this? she said, surprised. When did I write this? You didn't, he replied, you said it. That day, I wrote down your ideas, copied them out, and sent them off together with the poems. And as you can see, the publishers of the magazine thought it was brilliant. *C'est la vie, mademoiselle Bodenlieb.*

We can do nothing with Camões, said Hans, because he's already published and the translations are good. Have you heard of Bocage? You haven't? He has no reason to envy the greats. I've jotted down some queries, there are a few verses I don't quite understand, what does *pejo* mean exactly, and *capir*? We have this (Hans handed Sophie a small, thick volume: *A Pocket Dictionary of Italian, Spanish, Portuguese and German Languages*, published in London in 1799), have a look at the poems.

> *Hark Marilia to the shepherds' pipes,*
> *Their merry lilt, their happy sounds!*
> *How the Tagus smiles! And can you hear*
> *The breezes dancing among the flowers?*
>
> *See how in their playful love*
> *They invite our most ardent kisses!*
> *Look how innocent from plant to plant*
> *The idling butterflies splash their colour!*
>
> *Over in yonder bush waits the nightingale,*
> *While amongst its leaves hovers a bee*
> *Or suddenly buzzes through the stirring air!*
>
> *Such a happy landscape, so clear a morn!*
> *And yet if in seeing this I saw not thee,*
> *Worse than death it would seem to me.*

Yes, said Sophie, I think "breezes" works better than "zephyrs". What about the butterflies, asked Hans, is "floating" better than "idling"? No, no, said Sophie, "idling" is better, because it gives the impression they take their time going from flower to flower, and inadvertently show us their colours.

Sophie worked in silence, head down. She went over the

different versions, copied them out and consulted the dictionary. Hans became caught up watching her, so serious and concentrated, the long fingers of her right hand stained with ink, and he found her terribly beautiful. He tried to go back to the draft of the sonnet he had translated, but something buzzed in his ears like Bocage's bee. Then he said: How is Rudi? Sophie looked up; Hans didn't mention him very often, for which she was grateful, and she was surprised. Well, said Sophie, he is all right, he seems to have calmed down. On Monday I received a jet bracelet and a mother-of-pearl comb, so I suppose all is well.

> *Importunate reason, pursue me not;*
> *Your harsh voice whispers in vain*
> *If with terms of love or force of gentleness*
> *You rule not, nor contrast, nor soften;*
>
> *If you attack the mortal instead of giving succour*
> *If (knowing the disease) you offer no cure,*
> *Let me linger in my madness;*
> *Importunate reason, pursue me not;*
>
> *Your aim, your wish is to corrupt my soul*
> *With jealousy, make me victim of the one*
> *Who fickle I discern in others' arms—*
>
> *You wish me to abandon my love*
> *To accuse and scorn her, while my desire*
> *Is to bite, go mad, to die for her.*

You've done a perfect job, Sophie smiled.

They finished the jug of lemonade Lisa had brought, and moved on to the Italians. In my view, said Hans, Leopardi is

the best of the new poets, although he's still very young. I also
proposed a few articles by Mazzini to the magazine, but the
editor thought them too scandalous and said this wasn't a good
time to publish them, but going back to what we were saying, I
found these poems by Leopardi in the *Gazzetta della Nuova Lira*.
Tell me which you prefer.

Sophie read them and chose *Song of Ancient Fables* and *Saturday
in the Village*, which reminded her of weekends in Wandernburg
when she was a child. Hans suggested *Song for Italy* because, he
said, he liked poems that spoke with disenchantment about the
fatherland, whatever that happened to be.

> *I see oh Italy! the walls, the arches,*
> *The columns and the images,*
> *The lonely towers of our ancestors;*
> *And yet I nowhere see the glory*
> *Or the iron and the laurels that once bedecked*
> *Our forefathers. Today, prostrate,*
> *Your forehead bare, and bare*
> *Your breast, you stare back at us.*

In Leopardi there seem to be two kinds of nostalgia, Hans
asserted, I prefer the personal one. I see what you mean, she
said, his historical nostalgia sounds imposed; the other is much
more physical, as though it came from real experience. Here for
instance:

> *The young maid comes in from the fields*
> *As the sun is setting o'er the land*
> *Carrying her load of hay; while in her hand*
> *She bears a bunch of roses and violets,*
> *To use on the morrow as is her wont*
> *For a day of celebration,*

As decoration on her bosom and her hair.
On the steps with her neighbours
The old woman sits and spins,
Facing the sky where the day is fading,
Telling stories of the happy times ...

Isn't it moving? said Sophie, the way the young girl with the posy and the old lady spinning meet fleetingly in the street? The girl must be in love, because she has brought a posy from the fields, which she will take to tomorrow's fair. Yet for the old lady there is no tomorrow, what she sees is the close of day, and she waits for nightfall, spinning. I can just see her watching the girl pass by, smiling, then turning to one of her neighbours and saying: When I was a young girl ... Anyway, shall we go over it again? No, no, replied Hans, it's fine as it is.

... O playful boy, your flowering youth
Is like a day full of delights,
A calm and cloudless sky,
Herald of the celebration of your life.
Enjoy, my child, the sweet state
Of this happy season.
I say no more; but if perchance
That celebration tarries, fear thee not.

I much prefer this tone! Hans said, excitedly, it sounds far more authentic! The best thing when tackling important themes is to pretend to be discussing very simple things.

In front of the watercolour's reverse side, Sophie combed her hair slowly, as one weighing up the day. Arms and legs crossed, still excited, Hans contemplated her from the bed in the very way he had said important subjects should not be considered—with solemnity. He didn't know why Sophie's meticulous, wistful way of dressing moved him so, as if those exquisite gestures of withdrawal encompassed a miniature farewell.

You are my good fortune, you know, Hans whispered. She stopped combing her hair, turned and said: I know what you mean, my love, the same thing happens to me, I get up each morning, I remember I'm going to see you, and I feel the urge to give thanks. But then I come to my senses and say to myself, no, this wasn't good fortune, it was an act of boldness, *our* boldness. You could have left and you stayed. I could have ignored you and I did the exact opposite. All of this was intentional, magically intentional. (You sound like the old man, said Hans.) What old man? (The organ grinder, of course, who else?) Ah, speaking of which, when (yes, yes, soon), in fact, do you know, sometimes I think we haven't been fortunate. I mean, we could have met somewhere else or later on. Sometimes I try to imagine what it would be like to live in other times, maybe things would be easier for us then.

Hans said: Sophie, my love, other times will come, and they won't be *so* different from now. Is that a prophecy? she asked, laughing.

That same morning, before Sophie came to translate Bocage and Leopardi, Hans had got up early to say goodbye to Álvaro, who was traveling to London on business and to see his relatives. They met at the Café Europa. Álvaro congratulated Hans for being only ten minutes late. After breakfast (a hot chocolate and an anisette for Álvaro and a coffee followed by another coffee for Hans) they walked towards the carriage rank, where Álvaro's manservant was waiting for them, luggage ready, beside the coach. As they passed the twisted towers of St Nicholas's Church, Álvaro crossed himself and muttered: Please, Lord, let them fall down on my return.

As the carriage loomed, the two friends looked at one

another as if they had only just realised one of them was leaving. Hans had the uncomfortable impression of swapping places. Álvaro smiled uneasily, trying to calm himself and trying to understand why he remained troubled. They didn't know what to say, how to embrace each other. I'll miss you, Hans shouted at last to the head poking out of the side of the carriage. I-it's o-only t-two w-weeks! replied Álvaro's head amid jolts.

As Frau Zeit had predicted months before, at that time of year, the inn, incredibly, had almost no vacancies. Two fair-haired young girls moved quietly about, helping lay the tables and do the laundry. The majority of guests were distant relatives, or friends of distant relatives of the Wandernburgers who had remained in the city for the summer. Hans, unaccustomed, would occasionally cross them on the stairs, and it would take him a moment to recover from the shock and return their greeting. That morning, the Zeits were expecting some of their own relatives, who were coming to spend a few days with them, and who would be obliged to spread out between the innkeeper's lodgings and the only vacant room, number three. The very room Lisa would hide away in to do her homework.

Cousins, nephews and nieces, uncles piled rowdily into the inn. Some were stout and sluggish like Herr Zeit, others slender and jumpy, like Lisa. Stationed in the doorway, Frau Zeit welcomed them one by one, gave them each a perfunctory kiss and gently ushered them inside. However, as soon as she spied cousin Lottar, she wiped her hands on her apron and stepped forward to greet him.

Lisa saw Lottar walk in, drop his luggage and approach her with his arms outstretched. Aware that her mother was watching her, Lisa gave a little cry and rushed to embrace him. But while she was greeting her second cousin, whose eyes slid down as he clutched her waist, she glanced over to the light streaming in through the doorway.

From the other end of the inn, a nasal voice belonging to one of the Zeit family members suddenly rang out: Come here will you, please, dear, your son won't stop ... Little Thomas keeps ... he keeps giving little ... Can you hear me, dear?

Bumping his belly against the belly of his brother, Herr Zeit declared: It's August already! Who would have thought it?

In a corner of the kitchen, Frau Zeit was speaking to her daughter in hushed tones: Is that clear? If you behave in that manner cousin Lottar will never like you (I don't want cousin Lottar to like me, said Lisa), well you'll have to. He's a doctor's son. He's respectable. He's not a bad man. It's enough that he noticed you. So not another word and be nicer to him, do you hear? Answer me, Lisa, answer me!

Lisa marched out of the kitchen, her mother behind her. At that moment, Hans, who had just returned and was looking around surprised by all the commotion, almost walked headlong into Lisa. She paused to straighten her hair and smile at him. Then she turned and shouted at her mother: If you'd ever been in love you wouldn't speak to me like that! Frau Zeit stopped in her tracks, bewildered. What, she stammered, what on earth are you talking about? Lisa disappeared down the corridor. Having no one else to speak to, the innkeeper's wife looked at Hans and exclaimed: Heavens! What a girl! Do you understand her?

Lisa spent the rest of the day shut away in her room and refused to have lunch. Frau Zeit explained to cousin Lottar that Lisa was indisposed. Cousin Lottar nodded ambiguously and said this was perfectly natural, because Lisa had grown a lot since last summer and was no longer a child.

A few minutes before five o'clock, Lisa voluntarily came out of her confinement and walked into the kitchen wearing a nonchalant expression that made her mother even more infuriated. Without saying a word, she helped prepare the lemonade, and when it was time hurried to take it upstairs herself to room number seven.

Before knocking at the door, Lisa eavesdropped outside. Hans's deep, rather serious voice, was reciting sweet words:

> *... you wish me to abandon my love,*
> *to accuse and scorn her, while my desire*
> *is to bite, go mad, to die for her.*

As usual, Lisa knocked on the door twice without waiting to be told to enter. For this reason, she was able to hear the reply of that stuck-up prig who came there almost every afternoon: You've done a perfect job! That was scant praise for a man like Hans.

She walked in deliberately slowly, holding the jug; the sun from the window shredded the lemon pulp, setting off explosions of light. Turned towards her, smiling, the adorable Hans sat holding a piece of paper covered in jottings. Opposite him, the prig sat upright, her hair dishevelled, stupidly clutching a quill. Lisa moved forward. The room was a complete mess. There were open books strewn everywhere, the water jug was filthy, and, to top it all, the prig had clumsily allowed her beautiful peach shawl, which she didn't deserve, to fall to the floor. Even poor Hans's bed was unmade—if the chambermaids weren't more careful she would tell her mother. Lisa glanced at the bedclothes, becoming absorbed in them for a moment until Hans gave a slight cough. Then she carried on walking as if she had never stopped. She went over to them, leant over to fill their glasses, placed the jug on the table and walked out closing the door roughly.

It is night now. The noises, the voices, the scrape of furniture have long ceased. The sound of the cricket emerging from silence floats through the air. The inn is a pool of darkness, scarcely interrupted by the oil lamps on the ground floor. The dining room is deserted, the stove cold. There are no stirrings on the first floor either. No light illuminates the stairs. Yet, somewhere along the corridor on the second floor, the flame of an oil lamp flickers slowly. Lisa is walking barefoot, on tiptoe, as though the ground were covered in prickles, balancing so as not to spill anything from the plate, aware it might give her away the next day. Lisa's icy feet reach the end of the passageway and stop at the door to room number seven. This is when her hands begin shaking and she fears she may tip up the plate or make some other blunder. Her pointed breast swells beneath her nightdress, holds the air for a moment, then hollows out again. She can hear herself breathing. She counts the breaths. One. Two. Three. Now or never.

As Lisa turns the handle slowly and pushes open the door, the oil lamp casts an intense glow over her hand, illuminating her knuckles, light seems to flow from her fingers. Hans hasn't noticed yet, for he is no longer reading but forgetting, repeating in a dream the words of the book he was reading until a moment ago. On a chair beside the bed, the flame in the oil lamp flickers. Hans is lying on his back wearing only a pair of short white pants. The open book rests on his chest. Lisa gazes at Hans's long legs, his big feet spread out. She approaches the bed. She crouches down and places the candle in its plate on the floor. When she stands up again, Lisa's heart misses a beat—Hans's eyes are shining now, staring at her with an intensity that startles her.

Half propped up, Hans contemplates Lisa equally alarmed. He looks at her high, pointed shoulders. He looks at her dark figure through her backlit nightdress. He looks at her downy thighs, those slender thighs now leaning timidly against his bed. Is he still asleep? No, he knows perfectly well that he is wide awake. Lisa's left shoulder strap begins to give way, it falls. Hans tries to think of the number thirteen. Is it a high or a low number? Her shoulders are high, her collarbones, too. He is having difficulty concentrating. Lisa carries on undressing like a sleepwalker, as if she were alone. Is it a high or a low number? That depends on what and when. Lisa's skin and hair smell of warm oil. Hans lies still. He isn't doing anything, he is blameless. He glimpses a nipple, like a new sun. Yet he can't help telling himself that there comes a moment when lying still is no less of an action than moving. Thirteen, is it a lot or a little? Lisa's fingertips are at once rough and delicate. These fingers explore his chest. Life is wretched, wretched. Choking with emotion, with conflicting desires, Hans manages to lift his arm and clasp Lisa's wrist. The wrist rebels at first. Then loses its resolve. Lisa withdraws her hand, puts her nightdress back on. She refuses to look Hans in the eye or let him hold her chin, which moves from left to right, quivering like the wick of the oil lamp. Finally Lisa's chin surrenders, he cups it in both hands, she consents to look at him, showing him her tear-stained cheeks. They say nothing. Before moving away from the bed, Lisa instinctively kisses him on the mouth and he does nothing to stop her. Lisa's breath smells of caramel.

When the door closes, Hans remains on his back, motionless, his pulse racing. His brow is bathed in a cold sweat, his skin is burning. He tries to think for a moment. Tries to convince himself he did the right thing, to pat himself on the back. Yet he seriously suspects that if Lisa had insisted a little more, if she had prolonged that kiss, he would have gone along with her, collaborated even. Life is wretched, wretched. He leaps out of bed, treading on the book that has fallen on the floor, he rushes over to the jug, wets his head a few times, does not feel the coolness of the water.

The first thing Álvaro did on arriving back from his trip was to drop in at Old Cauldron Street. He climbed the stairs without speaking to Herr Zeit, who gazed at him sleepily from behind his desk. Álvaro had a bad feeling when there was no reply from number seven. When Lisa told him Hans had just gone out, he heaved a sigh of relief. He set off for the market square and, seeing that the organ grinder had already left, took a tilbury to the cave. There he found the three of them, Hans, the old man and Franz, singing a Neapolitan song to the strains of the barrel organ—the old man gave a low croaky rendering, Hans tried to sing along without knowing the words, and the dog barked and growled, showing an uncanny sense of rhythm.

On their way to Café Europa, Álvaro confessed, in the nonchalant tone men sometimes adopt when revealing their feelings to another man: For a moment I thought you'd left. Why? asked Hans. It's hard to explain, replied Álvaro, whenever I spend time with my relatives speaking in my own language, I feel as if Wandernburg no longer exists or has disappeared off the map, do you know what I mean? As though each day it were drifting farther away, and then I begin to think my friends are no longer there, or that they were perhaps a figment of my imagination. Álvaro, dear Álvaro, Hans laughed, I can't decide whether you're a fantasist or just plain sentimental. Is there a difference? Álvaro grinned.

Hans stopped dead amid the criss-cross of reflections in Glass Walk. Just a moment, he said, but, but wasn't the café over there, opposite the. Bah, Álvaro shrugged, it's always the same story. Just keep walking, it'll turn up.

They played billiards, talked about London and browsed the foreign press. In the *Gazette*, Álvaro read an article about the revolt in Catalonia. Banners showing King Ferdinand dangling by his feet were waved, the unrest spread to Manresa, Vich, Cervera. The peasants joined the uprising backed by some dissident army members. That is good news isn't it? remarked Hans. More or less, Álvaro said, it reeks of Carlism to me, I hope they don't try to topple a traitor and crown an imbecile. What exactly is Carlism? asked Hans. Oof, sighed Álvaro, that's what we Spaniards would like to know. Well, if you have the time I'll try to explain it to you. Although the Carlists themselves would be hard pressed to do that.

Hans listened with astonishment to Álvaro's account of modern Spanish politics. And, as his friend had warned, it wasn't easy to understand. That is, Álvaro summed up, the bastard Ferdinand plots against his traitorous father, is tried and absolved, and later on his father abdicates in favour of him, so far so good? Napoleon kidnaps them both, blackmails Ferdinand into returning the crown to his father, and his father hands it over to Napoleon's brother. Aren't we the limit! Ferdinand gives up his freedom, or rather he gives banquets at his castle until the war of independence is over. The bastard Ferdinand plays the martyr, and, as always, the people welcome him as if he were the Messiah. Bonaparte recognises Ferdinand as the bastard King of Spain, the republican constitution is torn up and the restoration begins, right? The bastard king accords an amnesty, some of us return and he reluctantly accepts the Constitution of Cádiz, which as you can imagine wasn't upheld for very long. (I understand, nodded Hans, more or less, and what did you do after that?) For a while I thought of staying in Spain, but things didn't look good and Ulrike wasn't convinced either, our life was already elsewhere, and, besides, we planned to raise a German family, which we never did. Wait, I'll have the same again. My God, if you existed! We leave again, the liberal era is soon over, and in '21 there's a revolt in Barcelona. I try to go and join it, but when my coach reaches the Pyrenees we are told the uprising is being put down, and at that point, I admit, I turned around and went back to Wandernburg. Do you know the thing I most regret in life, besides not having had a child with Ulrike? Not having pressed on that day. (Don't talk nonsense, said Hans, what could you have done?) How should I know! I could have given them money, fired a few shots, anything! (Although I know you have, I find it hard to imagine you shooting someone.) Don't be so shocked, there are times when violence is the only way of getting justice (I doubt it, Hans disagreed, folding his arms), doubting it or fearing it, my friend, doesn't make it any less true.

Yes, the same again, thank you, where were we? Álvaro resumed. Ah, yes '23. We could see it coming, Metternich and Frederick William had already tried it out in Italy. The hundred thousand bastard sons of Saint Louis arrived, fully armed, you see! To lend Ferdinand a helping hand, and that was the end of the constitution and of everything else. The Holy Alliance occupied Spain more completely than Bonaparte ever had, they persecuted half the population, the Inquisition was revived and so, my friend, my country returned to its favourite place—the past. That is Spain for you, Hans, an eternal merry-go-round. *Scheiße!* Do you like Goya? So do I, have you by any chance seen a painting called *Allegory of the City of Madrid*? Well, no matter. In this painting is a medallion with a portrait of Joseph Bonaparte. Like many other Enlightenment figures, Goya had sworn loyalty to him, but when Madrid is liberated from the French, Goya replaces the head of Joseph Bonaparte with the word *constitution*, what do you think of that? And when the French take back the city, he repaints the head. After the final victory, Don Francisco Goya did not hesitate to replace it once more with the word *constitution*, but wait! In 1815 he covers the word up with a portrait of that bastard Ferdinand, whose head remains there until the Liberal Triennium. After that the constitution is reinstated in the painting until '23, and so on. You see what a merry-go-round Spain is! In my view Goya is the greatest genius in all of Europe, and that painting is the supreme expression of Spanish history (I wasn't aware Goya was so calculating), no, Hans, he wasn't calculating, half of Spain was doing the same thing, waiting to see who the victors were in order to save their own skins. Some people did it for their children's sake, others to safeguard their positions, I'm sure I would have done the same for Ulrike. It's as simple as that. And in the end what did we others do? We left.

Here's to the other Spain, Álvaro said, emptying his tankard, which they always destroy. It happened with the Catholic monarchs, and then the Counter-Reformation, it went on happening for three centuries, it happened again in 1814, and then again in 1823, who knows when it will happen next. A country as conservative and as monarchist as Spain can only breed cynical rebels, and cynical rebels can only end up being punished by the fatherland (the fatherland doesn't exist, said Hans, you blame everything on the fatherland! But it's patriots, not the fatherland, who do the punishing), no, no, you're wrong, of course it exists, that's why it causes us so much grief. (Well, in that case, from a purely patriotic standpoint did you grieve over the loss of Spain's colonies?) Did I? On the contrary! I rejoiced! It was high time we gave up the pretence of empire and focused on our own disasters. And the same goes for the Turks in Athens. I was delighted by poor Riego's actions, he was a true patriot! A Freemason, a Francophile and a Spanish general (what did he do? Tell me), well, instead of going to defend Spain's colonies in the Americas, he revolted, demanded the reinstatement of the Constitution of Cádiz and led the movement into Galicia and Catalonia. Perfect! Why attack the Americas? I doubt Bolívar will treat his people any worse than our Viceroys did (perhaps not, but let's wait and see what the national oligarchies do after independence), ah, that's a different matter, I think they'd be well advised to unite. (You see, empires are real, fatherlands aren't!) You're an obstinate soul, aren't you? (So, what happened to the general?) Who? You mean General Riego? Nothing, he was executed to loud applause in a pretty square in Madrid.

In honour of Sophie's visit, the organ grinder had decorated the entrance to the cave with a row of geometric shapes cut out of newspapers, hanging from the clothesline. Lamberg and Reichardt had helped him dust off the largest rocks and he had improvised some seating out of burlap sacks stuffed with wool. In order to create some atmospheric lighting, he had placed the open umbrella in front of a row of candles. He had arranged the earthenware tumblers, the plates, the bottles and tin mugs neatly on two trays, each on a straw chair. Outside were several little piles of wood and kindling to light the fire for the tea. Between them they had managed to give Franz a bath in the river; he had put up a struggle and growled throughout while Lamberg held him in his vice-like grip. In the middle of the cave, the barrel organ stood on its rug like an arbitrary statue or humble effigy—the organ grinder had changed the barrel for one containing the most lively dances. Although the plan was to have a simple picnic on the grass, the organ grinder knew how much this visit meant to Hans, and he wanted to make a good impression on Sophie. Do you think it's too gloomy? he asked Reichardt, pointing to the umbrella. Reichardt rubbed his nose, made a sound like a blocked drain, and said: It's fine so long as we can see her cleavage.

As she stooped to enter the cave, Sophie's expression divided into two moments, as though half of her had preceded the other half. In one sense she had expected better, and in another worse. She found it awful and touching, as inhospitable as any grotto and yet believable as a dwelling. It took her a few moments to adjust to the dirt, to move in such a way as not to soil her dress without letting it show. Once she had overcome her awkwardness, she began to feel at home in the coolness of the cave, and, to Reichardt's delight, bobbed delightfully when she accepted her first cup of tea. Elsa reacted differently. She took one look inside the cave, pulled a face, and elected to remain outside helping Álvaro prepare the tea.

Once the tablecloth and the food were spread out, the picnic turned out to be agreeably eccentric. Elsa and Sophie held their little tin mugs as if they were china teacups, sipped their tea slowly, and munched modest mouthfuls, fingers in front of their lips. Reichardt wolfed down everything in sight, spilling crumbs all over the place and belching, admittedly less explosively than usual considering there were ladies present. Lamberg said nothing, his cheeks bulging with lumps of bread as he ate. Álvaro spoke more loudly than Elsa would have liked, guffawed prodigiously, egging the excited Franz into the middle of the tablecloth, from which his master shooed him away gently so that he would not step on the ladies' skirts. The organ grinder was a silently attentive host, intervening here and there, giving the impression of accompanying everyone while scarcely uttering a word. Sophie, who noticed his behaviour immediately, admired the harmonious atmosphere the old man had managed to create amid this diverse group of picnickers whilst passing almost unnoticed. Hans, who had been worried she would disapprove of the cave or his friends' appearance, breathed a sigh of relief. And, were it not for who he was and for his age, he could have sworn the organ grinder was flirting with her a little.

Once they had finished their tea, the organ grinder proposed a round of dreams. Hans explained the ritual to Sophie who seemed to think it a delightful diversion. As no one elected to start, the organ grinder recounted the first dream. Last night, he said, I dreamt about a group of fellows eating soup in a tavern. The table was in darkness except for one or two red faces. Suddenly one of the men hurls a spoonful of soup into the air, the soup flies out of the dream then lands back into the spoon as if it were a die. Then the man drinks it and says: Six. And the same occurs with each spoonful. That, Álvaro surmised, means you wanted some luck. Don't talk rot, said Reichardt, it means he wanted something to eat! The last interesting dream I had, said Hans, was a week ago. I dreamt I was on an island. But this was a strange island because it wasn't surrounded by sea. What, no water at all? Lamberg asked curiously. No, replied Hans, no sea, no water, nothing. The island was surrounded by an enormous void. So, how did you know it was an island? said Lamberg. Good question, said Hans, and I don't know how, I just knew it was an island. And I wanted to leave, I wanted to leave for some other islands I could see in the distance. But it was impossible, I didn't know how to get to them and I became scared. Then I began running round in circles, like a headless chicken, until the island gradually began sinking. And I had to choose between leaping into the void and going down with my island. So what did you do, for Christ's sake? Reichardt asked. I woke up, Hans grinned. Good! the organ grinder said approvingly, very good! And what about you, ladies, haven't you any dreams to offer us? Elsa shook her head and lowered her eyes. Sophie looked at him a little embarrassed and said: I don't know, well, I never dream much, last night, this is silly, but last night …

After the end of the round, Sophie told them a fable she remembered reading as a child. What if the dreams of those who love one another are woven together as they sleep by silken threads, she said, threads that move the characters in their dreams from above like puppets, controlling their fantasies so that when they wake up they are thinking of one another? What rot! Reichardt barked. I believe it, Hans rallied. I don't, said Lamberg. What if the threads get tangled and you wake up thinking about the wrong person, Álvaro jested. Elsa looked at him, disconcerted. The organ grinder, who had been nodding thoughtfully, declared suddenly: Like a great handle, you mean? The handle of dreams! Yes, Sophie smiled, that's exactly it.

Hans had slipped away for a moment in order to relieve himself amid the pine trees, when he heard Sophie call his name. He stood waiting for her, kissing her neck as she arrived. Hans, my love, she said, breathless from running, your old man is wonderful, a real character! We must bring him to the salon so that everyone can see him. No, not to the salon, he said. Why? Sophie asked, are you ashamed of people meeting him? Of course not, Hans said earnestly, lying, but the organ grinder isn't a fairground attraction. He's my friend. He's a wise old man. He likes a quiet life. Well, she said, returning his kiss, there's no need to get annoyed, just promise me we'll come here again. Elsa doesn't like it, said Hans. I know, she nodded, she's ill at ease, although I'm not sure that that's due to the cave. You mean … Hans probed. Him, of course, Sophie replied laughing.

That night, the interminable wall Hans dreamt of was the same one Sophie saw herself scaling, daunted by how tall it was and surprised at being naked, without knowing what awaited her on the other side. Above the wall, the branch of a hollow tree trembled beneath Álvaro's weight. He lay curled up in an awkward ball, balancing precariously. At the foot of the hollow tree, Elsa was burying a violin in the hole in which the organ grinder sat playing dice with a man with no face, swathed in black wool.

What are we translating today? Sophie asked as she came in. Realising she was in the mood for work, Hans struggled to ignore the erection in his breeches. This effort excited her, for she had arrived in a state of desire and felt like tormenting him a little. But Hans's self-restraint was such that Sophie ended up thinking he preferred to work.

That afternoon they weren't going to translate. At any rate not from one language into another—a certain Mr Walker had written to Hans on behalf of the *European Review* asking him for an essay on contemporary German poetry. The fee was good and they paid half up front, which was rare. Hans had accepted without a second thought. He suggested to Sophie that they write the essay together. Walker says he'd like us to include a woman poet, he explained. You can tell Herr Walker, she retorted, that our best poets will be included on their own merits, thank you very much.

Sophie began writing down a list of names: I would mention Jean Paul, Karoline von Günderrode, the Schlegel brothers, Dorothea, of course, and Madame Mereau. We could also talk about the lays of von Arnim—doesn't he have a castle near here?—and those of Clemens Brentano. Not forgetting his sister Bettina's delightful ones (I haven't read any of them, confessed Hans), too bad, Monsieur, because there's a most enlightening one by her which ends:

If your girl is faithful, who can tell?
Although she begs the Heavens
For your love to stay close by
If your girl is faithful, who can tell?

Included! Hans declared laughing. And what do you think of Brentano and von Arnim? she asked. To be honest, he sighed, they remind me of those students who go around with a guitar, a bandoleer and a German leather jacket, smelling flowers and singing about medieval exploits. And yet if you were a medieval princess, I wouldn't even be able to speak to you. I'd be a commoner who obeys his liege lord and dies from the plague. That's the reality of it. Reality, said Sophie, is many things at the same time. In poetry you can be here and there, in the present and in the past, in a castle or at a university. All right, said Hans, all I'm saying is that if we could see what the past was really like we would be speechless with horror.

Another thing that irritates me about that idiot von Arnim, is his hatred of France—what are we to do, burn half the books in our libraries? But don't you think it's a good thing to rescue popular poetry? said Sophie. If there were anything popular about poetry, replied Hans, the people would be reading it in the street. Oh let me guess, the dear fellow wished to capture the essence of popular poetry without the people realising it! Isn't that a French tradition? My dear, said Sophie, smiling, politics blinkers you, and you are being unfair on von Arnim. He's one of Germany's most underrated poets. If he is virtually unknown it isn't simply because people don't read poetry, it's because he's a more difficult poet than he appears, filled with death and darkness. In addition, he is detested by his Catholic friends for being a Protestant, and by the fanatical Protestants for having Catholic friends. You won't find any cheap patriotism in *The Youth's Magic Horn.* In the authors, perhaps, but not in the texts. You never know what the soldiers are fighting for in his war songs, only that they are scared, they die, they are in love and they long to go home. I used to love the sentry's song when I was a girl:

No my boy, don't be sad,
And let me await you
In the rose garden
Among the green clover ...

I'll not go to the green clover!
I'm obliged to stay here
In the garden of weapons,
Weighed down with halberds.

If you fight, may God help you! ...
Everything always depends

On the will of God!
Who believes such a thing?

The one who does is far away,
He is the one giving battle!
He is a king! A king!
Halt! Who goes there? Stand back! …

Who was singing there? Who was it?
Only the poor sentinel
Singing at midnight.
Midnight! Sentinel!

All right, all right, said Hans, included!

Well, said Sophie, drawing a line under her list, those are my choices, what about yours? I'd start, replied Hans, with the Jena poets, of course. I admire their way of life as well as their work, isn't that part of what poetry is? A way of living a different life. There are poets who seem sure of their roots, which may be a tradition, a genre, a country—no matter. I like the wandering poets, the ones who are not rooted anywhere. That's where the younger of the Schlegel brothers and the poets of the *Athenaeum* come in, they wrote in a fragmented way, they weren't looking for a system, or didn't believe they'd ever find one, they were continually searching. I'd like to include Tieck, because he describes his library as though it were the world and he a wanderer. And Hölderlin, because, in spite of everything, his poetry shows us we can't be gods, much less Greeks.

Hans felt another erection—this often happened when he indulged in an excess of literary criticism with Sophie.

Ah, he smiled, I've left the best until last—Novalis (your Novalis lived in a dream world, too, Sophie contended), true, except it wasn't fantasy that interested him, but rather the unknown.

His mysticism was, shall we say, practical. A mysticism through which to explore the present. (I understand, she said, but I'm surprised, wasn't he a religious poet?) No, exactly, that's the point! I think Novalis was like Hölderlin, his hymns describe the impossibility of overcoming the earthly condition, when he says "I feel in my depths, a divine weariness", his weariness is worldly, his disillusionment is rational. (Yes, she said, but he also wrote: "Who, without the promise of the skies could bear the earth and all its lies?" How do you explain that? How can you understand Novalis without heaven?) You're right, I disagree with him there. (Then why all the interest in Novalis, you, the atheist? Didn't your poet compose canticles to the Holy Virgin and even write a treatise on Christianity?) Touché, touché, Novalis fascinates me because I don't quite accept him, I have to struggle with him in order to admire him. And since I never quite succeed, I constantly go back to him. I don't think anyone should completely agree with a poet of genius, unless he also believes himself a genius. Don't laugh! The question is—why must spirituality be the exclusive preserve of believers? Why should we atheists relinquish the unknown? My ideal as a reader, for we all have one don't we? Would be to read Novalis without the idea of God. (Do you really think he can exist if you take away his religiosity?) Novalis used religion as a lever (Hans, my love, you're the strangest critic I've ever met. I think religiosity in art can be moving, look at sacred music), precisely, and why are we atheists stirred by religious music? Because we transcend it, or rather we bring it down to earth. And music makes this possible because it has no dogma, it takes the form of a passion, nothing more. One last thing and then I promise I'll be quiet, bear in mind that Novalis wrote his best poems after he lost his love, who died very young. Who knows what wonderful earthly poems he might have composed to a love who was still alive. In contrast (in contrast? Sophie echoed, sitting astride him), er, in contrast I have you on top of me.

Hans and Sophie lay, half-undressed, gazing at the ceiling, at the gentle progress of the spiders' webs. He was breathing noisily and rubbing the tips of his toes together. She smelt faintly of violet water, and the stronger, damper odour of another flower. Sophie sat up, kissed his foot, told him she had to leave, and got up to drink water from the jug. The semen Hans had spilt over her thighs began to trickle down her legs as she walked. When she stepped over their discarded clothes, a drop fell onto an open-mouthed shoe.

(Before he met Sophie, Hans hated his feet, or he thought he hated them—they were hopeless at dancing, rather stubby and the slightest touch made them recoil. He felt they were guilty, but of what he did not know. Guilty of being the way they were, averse to being shoeless, getting cold at night. That afternoon when Sophie bared his feet for the first time, she studied them at length and gave them her simple blessing: I like your feet, she said. And she planted a kiss on the tip of his big toe. Nothing more. It is the small things in life that change you, reflected Hans. A man who has walked as much as you shouldn't be ashamed of his feet, it would be churlish. From that moment on, Hans began walking barefoot around the room.

Hans and Sophie had decided to go on an outing to the country rather than stay inside working. The day was too splendid, too fragrant. Elsa gladly agreed to the change of plan as it allowed her to go to the market square duly accompanied and without the risk of arousing suspicion. Even so, she asked to take a separate carriage in order to conceal her lover's identity, which, in any event, Hans and Sophie had known for a while.

Half-an-hour before going out, as he did every afternoon when he was expecting Sophie, Hans bathed his feet in warm water, salts and essential oils. He soaked them in the tin tub. He stirred the water with his ankles, let it ripple through his splayed toes, he massaged them, perceiving, as though for the first time, that they were ticklish. As he explored the wet soles of his feet, he noticed himself becoming excited, and experienced a delicious feeling of urgency and calm. He sat for a moment in the tub, closed his eyes. He emerged naked and went to shave in the front of the painting. Over the washbasin, he rubbed his face, hands and forearms with water, pounce and soap. He didn't dry himself immediately. He thought about masturbating but didn't, partly so he wouldn't be late and partly as a sweet form of punishment. He used a soft towel to dry his body and a new sponge for his face. He dressed, pulled on his shoes with a sense of regret.

Although no longer high, the Nulte seemed satisfied with its slender line. Its blue-green waters flowed gently by. Hans and Sophie touched each other beneath their clothes; they spoke of everything, of nothing. In the shade of a poplar tree, they watched the light play over the cornfields. Sophie's fingers grew longer, became entangled. Hans's shoes were hot. The balmy air shimmered, circled through their arms. The poplars were good, steadfast. She felt a ball unravelling in her belly. He felt as if a branch were springing up from between his legs.

It's a hiatus, isn't it? Hans whispered, the summer, I mean. As if the rest of the year were the text and the summer were a separate clause, an additional comment. Yes, replied Sophie, pensive, and do you know what it says? "I am fleeting." It's curious, said Hans, I feel as if time has stopped, but at the same time I'm aware of how fast it is going. Is that what being in love is? she said, looking at him. I suppose so, he smiled. Sometimes, said Sophie, it feels strange not to think about the future, as though it were never going to happen. Don't worry, said Hans, the future doesn't think about us much either. But what about afterwards? she asked, when the summer is over?

The light was beginning to fade, casting a shadow on the meadow towards the east. Both had to go back to the city, but neither stirred. Evening was gradually closing in on them. And the light, in sympathy, lingered on.)

She was fastening her corset while Hans was opening his trunk. Today, he said, I'd like us to translate a young Russian poet I recommended to Brockhaus. But Hans, do you know any Russian, she asked? Me? he replied. Only the Cyrillic alphabet and a few dozen words. Well then? Sophie said, surprised. Ah, Hans chuckled, I told them you were fluent. We'll translate using a third language, don't worry. We have an original edition here—look: Александр Сергеевич Пушкин—a French translation, and an English one, and this nice Russian-German dictionary, what do you reckon?

They selected a few poems from the translations they had. They copied out the English and French versions, placing each stanza in a separate table. They checked each word in the dictionary in order to make sure they had understood the literal meaning of the original, then noted down the different meanings next to each table.

Do you know what? Sophie said playfully, this Pushkin's adulterous loves are more believable than his spiritual ones. That's typical of you, Bodenlieb! said Hans, looking over the draft they had just done:

Dorida's long tresses hold me in thrall,
As does her blue-tinged gaze at the ball;
When yesterday I left, her charms
Enchanted me as I looked on her arms,
Every impulse leading me to more,
My desire sated as ne'er before.
But suddenly in the bitter gloom
Strange features filled the room;

A secret sadness made me start,
Another name was in my heart.

After Sophie had left, Hans reread the drafts of their translations. His head began to grow heavy, his muscles went slack and his cheek settled on the desk where it was warmed by the oil lamp. Before sitting up straight again, he had a strange fleeting nightmare—he dreamt he was going from one language to another like someone running through a line of sheets hung out to dry. Each time he encountered a language, his face became wet and he thought he had woken up in his mother tongue, until he got to the next sheet and realised his mistake. Still running, he began talking to himself, and could clearly visualise the language he was speaking—he was able to contemplate the words he was uttering, their structures, their inflexions, yet he always arrived too late. The moment he came close to understanding the language in which he was dreaming, he felt something slap him in the face, and he woke up in the next language. Hans ran like a madman, arriving once, a hundred times too late to perceive these languages, until suddenly he understood he had really woken up. Looming before his eyes he saw a huge oil lamp and a great mound of papers. He noticed, as he sat up, that one of his cheeks was burning. Then, with a sense of relief he began a train of thought, and for a moment he contemplated in amazement the logic of his own language, its familiar shape, its miraculous harmony.

Listen, the organ grinder implored, is this really necessary? Are you sure? (Hans looked at him reprovingly and nodded several times.) All right, all right, let's do it.

Slowly, clumsily, as if with each garment he were peeling off a whole year, the old man finally took off his tattered shirt, his linen breeches and his worsted shoes. Just so you know, he added, as a last protest, I'm only doing this to please you. Separated from the organ grinder's dry flaccid skin, the garments curled up into a stinking ball. The earth appeared to swallow them up.

Barefoot, his trousers rolled up to his knees, Hans took the old man by the arm in order to help him into the river. He watched as he immersed himself bit by bit—his paper-thin ankles, his unsteady legs, his sagging buttocks, his hunched back. At last all Hans could see was the organ grinder's dishevelled white head as he turned and beamed at him, mouth wide open, and began swimming like a child, arms thrashing in the water. Hey, it's not so cold! the old man shouted. Won't you join me? Thanks, said Hans, but I take my bath when I get up in the morning! *Every* morning! Bah! cried the organ grinder. Old wives' tales! Princes bathe in scented water and die young!

Hans watched with repulsion and fascination the ripples of grime dissolving around the organ grinder's body. He splashed his arms about in them playfully: Look! the old man laughed, pointing at the grey and brown lumps. It's attracted the fish! Yes, thought Hans, there was something repulsive and yet honest about such an attachment to dirt. There was an obscure integrity about the old man's lack of hygiene, or rather his lack of shame, a kind of truth. Some time ago, the organ grinder had said something ridiculous and at the same time true—perfumes were a deception, they wanted to be something else. Perhaps. Although Hans loved perfumes.

He helped the old man out of river and draped a towel around his bony shoulders. His knees were knocking, more from the shock of the water than from its temperature. As he rubbed himself down with the towel, the organ grinder began fiddling with his dripping testicles. Hans could not help glancing at them out of the corner of his eye, and at his tiny shrivelled penis. The organ grinder noticed this at once and he laughed good-naturedly. He was laughing at Hans, at himself, at his penis and at the river. Hey, he said, do you fiddle with yourself much? Hans looked the other way. Don't be embarrassed, the old man said, I shan't tell anyone. Do you fiddle with yourself much, then? No, yes, replied Hans, well, no more than is usual. You might find this strange, the organ grinder said, but from time to time—whoosh!—so do I! Do you know what I think about when I fiddle with myself? I think about a woman with no clothes on, dancing a waltz. A young woman, who smiles at me. I think Franz knows, because every time—whoosh!—the scoundrel starts barking as if someone had come in.

They ate lunch together, talking then falling silent for a while. Hans spoke of Sophie and the dreaded end of the summer. Next month everything will change, he said. But, *kof, kof,* coughed the old man, everything is always changing, there's nothing wrong with that. I know, sighed Hans, but sometimes things change for the worse. By the way, what's that cough you have? Cough? said the organ grinder. What cough? *Kof. That* cough, said Hans. Is it from the water? No, the old man shrugged, it's from before, don't worry, maybe it's the first sign of autumn, but, tell me, do you love her? Do you really love her? Yes, replied Hans. How can you be so sure so soon? the old man asked. Hans reflected for a moment then said: Because I admire her. Ah, well, the old man smiled. *Kof.*

Two sun-drenched days later, the organ grinder's cough went away and he said he felt better than a brand-new organ string. Concerned about the old man's diet and the state of his clothes, Hans resolved to find him work through Sophie's friends. He remembered the old man saying that in the summer people always asked him to play at some dance or other, but he wasn't aware that he had received any such commissions that year.

Lisa knocked at the door and handed him a violet note without looking him in the eye. Hans thanked her and reminded her that the following day they had a lesson. She said "Yes, I know", and disappeared down the corridor. Hans stood watching her, reflecting about the unfairness of age, how it came too slowly for some and too fast for others. He forgot all about the matter as soon as he sat down to read the letter:

My love, good news—a close friend (well, not that close), Fräulein von Pogwisch, is having a ball on Saturday and I've convinced her how much more original it would be if she hired a "real" itinerant musician instead of the customary quartet. I know this may seem a rather silly argument, but if you knew Fräulein von Pogwisch you would understand perfectly. The reason I thought of her is because, although her family have a good income, they aren't exactly wealthy, and her parents will be only too happy to save some money under the pretext of being original. Do you approve of the idea, my love? I feel happy. Did you notice how light it was this morning? Or were you fast asleep? I love you to pieces, your

S

The following Saturday, as agreed, Hans went to the end of Bridge Walk at six-thirty sharp to fetch the organ grinder. And Franz—the one condition the old man had insisted upon when accepting the job was that his dog be allowed to accompany them to the Pogwisch residence. Hans had hired a dogcart so Franz would feel at home. Hans's face broke into a smile when he glimpsed the two of them walking down the path. Obeying his instructions, the old man had put on his only new shirt, a more or less presentable pair of breeches, and his best shoes. As he approached the cart, Hans saw that he had even combed his hair and trimmed his beard. Somewhat nervous, the organ grinder heaved himself into his seat, not allowing the driver to touch his barrel organ. I can manage, he said, I can manage. At that moment Franz gave two short barks, and Hans had the feeling he was repeating his master's words. When the horses pulling the dogcart broke into a gallop, the organ grinder glanced about him, suddenly taken aback. How wonderful! he said. Do you know I can't even remember the last time I rode in a carriage.

As I told you, my dear, Fräulein Kirchen was saying to Sophie, she's always been such a good girl, what a terrible thing! And in the meantime the police do nothing, if they had their way, well, what do they care? Of course until something happens to the police chief's daughter if you think they're going to catch this masked attacker you've got another think coming! But, Sophie asked, when did this happen? Sometime yesterday afternoon, it seems, replied Fräulein Kirchen, near to ... Good heavens! Do you see what I see, my dear? What on earth does Fanny think she's wearing? She's getting worse lately, has she lost her taste or her senses? Did I tell you what she said to Ottilie when they were having tea at ...

Sophie heard a murmuring near the door and walked out into the hallway. She saw Fräulein von Pogwisch waving her arms about in front of Hans and behind him, at a slight distance, the old man and the dog waiting beside the barrel organ. What's the matter, my dear? Sophie asked. Nothing really, replied Fräulein von Pogwisch, I was just telling the gentleman and the musician that if they expect to bring that mongrel in here, the least they could do is to give it a bath first. My dear young lady, the organ grinder said, doffing the hat Hans had forced him to put on, I assure you that my dog, which is far from being a mongrel and extremely well-behaved, will do what he's told and stay by the door. In that case, replied Fräulein von Pogwisch, please tie him up. Believe me, the old man smiled, that really isn't necessary—Franz only misbehaves when he's tied up.

Seeing the organ grinder enter the room, everyone present turned as one to look at him. The old man paused, bobbed his head and walked on pushing his little cart. Hans and Sophie accompanied him to the corner of the room Fräulein von Pogwisch had set aside for him, and offered him a glass of wine before he began. Thank you, my dears, the old man said earnestly, but I never drink when I'm working otherwise I lose my rhythm. Very professional! Sophie said, winking at Hans as she went over to greet a friend.

At eight o'clock sharp, most of the guests had arrived and were keen for the dance to begin. The lady of the house signalled to Sophie. She in turn signalled to Hans, Hans looked at the organ grinder, and the old man lowered his head, inhaled, closed his eyes and slowly began to turn the handle.

Despite the suspicious glances the guests gave the old man as they passed close to him, the first two or three dances went down well. Above all the first, a popular polonaise which the old man had been canny enough to play at a faster pace than usual on account of the guests' youthful exuberance. The rows of couples began dancing around the room, laughing as they changed places. Hans heaved a sigh of relief, and for a moment he thought everything would go smoothly. Little by little, however, the dance began to lose steam. By the third tune, several couples began to leave the dance floor muttering. In the two that followed, the complaints became audible. At the sixth or seventh, the dance floor was all but deserted. Before the organ grinder could start up with his next tune, Fräulein von Pogwisch marched over crossly and ordered him to stop. The instrument quivered like an animal suffering from cold.

Hans and Sophie did their best to calm Fräulein von Pogwisch and the more irate among the guests. I say, what's going on! one of them piped up. Whose idea was it to play minuets, anyway? What about some waltzes? another one demanded indignantly. Where are the waltzes! Well, added another, if the idea was to send us to sleep it's been a great success! Which century does that thing belong to? cried another. Which century! We should invite my great-grandmother! Another one declared: My great-grandmother! Tell me, a voice rang out from the back of the room, where did you find this clown? Which poorhouse did you drag him out of?

Hans pushed his way through and found the organ grinder backed into his corner clutching his barrel organ, unable to move.

They crossed the room amid disdainful whispers, mocking laughter and jeers. The organ grinder followed behind with that detached air that made him seem at once fragile and unassailable. As they were reaching the hallway, they heard a voice from inside shout: What a relief! Here's a pianoforte! Come here, Ralph! Ralph! Come and play us a lively tune!

Walking through the door was like plunging into a fountain of cool water. Night had fallen and the air was laced with the sound of crickets. Seeing them emerge, Franz pricked up his ears, lowered his tail and frowned. A moment later, Sophie appeared. She stopped Hans, clasping his hands and bringing them up to her cheeks. She closed her eyes in a gesture of deep regret and sighed: I don't think it was a good idea to choose this house, it's my fault. No, Hans replied stroking one of her ringlets, it wasn't your fault and it wasn't your idea either. Sophie went over to the organ grinder, gave him a long embrace and told him she was sorry. I'm the one who is sorry for playing your friends tunes from thirty years ago, replied the old man. I think I'm no longer …

At that moment, Fräulein von Pogwisch appeared in the doorway. She contemplated Hans sharply, looked scornfully at Sophie, and finally her gaze settled on the organ grinder as one encountering a peculiar rock in her path. I've come to pay you for your concert, announced Fräulein von Pogwisch. She placed a few coins on top of the barrel organ and made as if to leave. I should think so, Hans said angrily, especially as you were the one who cut it short. I wouldn't dream of taking your money, Madame, said the organ grinder (the only trace of irony Hans was able to detect in his words was his use of *Madame*—the hostess was still a young woman), I couldn't accept payment because I haven't done my job, people pay me for playing, but I have never charged anything for not playing. Good evening, Madame, I apologise for the inconvenience.

Will you please explain why you didn't accept? Hans rebuked him on the way back, that money was yours, you earned it! You did the best you could! Dignity is one thing, pride another. You, Franz, and the barrel organ all need the money and you weren't stealing it from anyone. Now it turns out you went through all that for nothing. Ah, no, replied the organ grinder, forgive me, but you're wrong, it wasn't for nothing—it was lovely riding in this elegant carriage.

(Whenever I am menstruating, Sophie had reflected as she climbed the stairs at the inn, a strange thing happens to me. On the one hand I feel, or in theory I know, I'm more of a woman than ever. Yet on the other hand it stops me, limits my fulfilment. For example, I imagine Hans will want to make love as soon as I get upstairs, or that's what I like to imagine. And I know I will, too, and I won't stop feeling awkward, like an intruder in my own body. In any event I'll end up feeling guilty, which I detest. Guilty about what? It's hard to be open when nature dictates one thing and one's conscience another. But is it really a dictate? Or is it a wonderful possibility, which I'm free to refuse? The fact is today I have cramps, I feel sick, I have a pain shooting down from my waist, and I haven't felt like eating all day. I'd like to tell Hans all this, but I'm not sure he'd understand or that I'd be able to explain it to him even ...)

Lying face up, clasping his back between her calves, Sophie

said: Don't pull out this time, then.

The smell of blood hindered them at first and then finally made them lose all inhibition—they shared its stains, soiling themselves in the act of lovemaking.

She was embarrassed at him seeing her bleed onto his sheets, but she felt this sight united them or obliterated a secret. Suddenly it seemed natural and profoundly true—now, when he spilt his seed inside her, they would be brought together by a common desire *not* to conceive, to unleash together a pleasure that began and ended completely with itself. If the past is like a father, its true offspring would be this absolute present, not the future. (This idea struck her as she reached the edges of orgasm, interrupting her thoughts.)

They spoke in hushed voices, naked. Sophie's loins were soaked in blood and Hans's pubic hairs were matted, solidified. Their features expressed the intensity and repose of those still in the aftermath of pleasure. They listened to one another breathing, wiggled their feet, stretched their limbs. How delicious, he said, not having to pull out. Mmm, she said. Or did you not enjoy it? he asked, concerned. No, it isn't that, she replied, I don't know how to describe it, I loved it and at the same it scared me, do you understand? I'm not sure, he said, turning to look at her. You see, Sophie said sitting up, I've always been afraid of being a mother. Don't get me wrong, I want to have children. I just don't want to be a mother. Is it possible to be both a selfish girl and a doting mother? What can you do when you want to be both things? Oh, my love, so many stupid things go through my head, the discomforts of pregnancy, gaining weight, my skin losing its smoothness, physical pain. I suppose I don't know how to be a strong woman. On the contrary, Hans said, embracing her, only a strong woman admits these things.

Sophie spoke of her need for independence, of Rudi's plans to have a family, of what her fiancé's buttocks felt like through his breeches, of what she imagined her sex life with him would be like, of the most curved penises she'd seen, of her curiosity about semen, of her monthly curse. And then in the same breath, incongruously, she began talking about Kant. According to Kant, Sophie said, killing an illegitimate child is less of a crime than being unfaithful. Pure reason, my eye! He says it would be better not to know of the existence of such a child, because legally he should never have existed. An adulterous relationship is a fictitious love. An illegitimate child is a non-existent being and therefore ending its life shouldn't be a problem. This is what Kant says. And so our morality, Herr pretty bottom, becomes a negation of life. The morality we are taught is aimed at restricting life not helping us to understand it.

Kant and menstruation, Hans reflected, why ever not?

"The drama of this most recent and shocking attack," Lieutenant Gluck was reading from the third edition of the *Thunderer*, "is thought to have taken place on Friday in close proximity to the area where the assailant usually operates; that is, as our well-informed readers will already be aware, in the narrow pedestrian streets leading from the above-mentioned Wool Alley as far as Archway. Although the identity of the latest victim has not been officially revealed, reliable sources have informed this newspaper that the young woman's initials are A I S, that she is twenty-eight, and that she is a native of Wandernburg. As before, the lack of any eyewitnesses precludes the elaboration of any new theories over and above those already mentioned in previous cases. We would like to believe that the local police force and the special constabulary might be roused from their baffling inactivity and shameless ineptitude. At least this is the hope in the hearts of Wandernburg's imperilled young women, whose fears we have tirelessly reported in these pages. Lest the sole clues on the files of the above-mentioned forces of order be those already in the public domain, this newspaper is in a position to confirm with near certainty that the masked culprit is a relatively tall, stocky man, thirty to forty years of age. It only remains for us to wait with resigned impatience for …"

This is shameful! Lieutenant Gluck protested, hurling the newspaper onto the office desk. Reliable sources, for Heaven's sake! Those fools have no idea what they're talking about, and to crown it all they have the nerve to try to teach us how to do our job! Don't upset yourself, son, Lieutenant Gluck remarked impassively, as a matter of fact these articles suit our purposes—if the culprit reads them he'll feel safer, and that's better for us. I prefer him not to know that we're almost on to him. Now, forget about the press and tell me, did you copy out the draft report? Good, excellent, and the marks on the wrist were identical? Identical, replied Lieutenant Gluck, he definitely prefers to use fine cord, which indicates that he's not a particularly strong man. And what did the latest victim say about the smell? his father asked. She seems adamant that it was lard, said Lieutenant Gluck. Yes, but what sort of lard? She isn't sure, his son explained, she said she was in no position to notice that sort of detail at a time like that, but she thinks it could have been bear fat. And does the victim cook? Asked Lieutenant Gluck. I beg your pardon, Father? said Lieutenant Gluck, puzzled. I asked you, his father said, whether the victim is in the habit of cooking or whether she has servants who cook for her. As you'll appreciate, said his son, the woman's domestic arrangements didn't enter into the interrogation. This isn't a matter of domestic arrangements, Lieutenant Gluck corrected him, on the contrary, it is of vital importance—if the girl is in the habit of frying, she'll know the difference between pig lard and bear fat, for example. And if she confirms this detail, then we are down to two suspects.

So, go and ask for her to be summoned to make another statement, please. And while you're doing that, I'll go to the Central Tavern and reserve a table. You know how busy it gets at this time of day.

With no pressing assignments from the publisher, with September closing in and the days growing shorter, that afternoon Hans and Sophie decided to go for a walk. They strolled as far as the banks of the Nulte, avoiding the main pathway and taking a narrower trail that led from the south-eastern edge of Wandernburg out into the countryside. They sat down beside the river. They kissed each other with longing but didn't make love. Then they fell quiet, reading the waves.

Suddenly there was a sound of splashing and the lines of water were erased. They looked up and saw some swans flying past in formation. Hans watched them with delight—their harmonious whiteness felt like a small gift to him. Sophie, however, contemplated them with a feeling of unease—on the shifting surface of the water, the swans looked deformed, broken. A wing there, a whorl of water here, farther away half a head. A detached beak, a patch of sunlight, two ridiculous webbed feet. How easily and swiftly beauty can be undone, Sophie thought.

Sophie stood up and the afternoon appeared to teeter. The sun had begun to melt behind the vast landscape, its bright light eclipsing the outline of the poplar trees. Seen from the ground where Hans was still sitting, five-sixths of the day was sky. Sophie's back looked bigger, it had a slippery, zest-like sheen. She was surveying the horizon, and as she moved her arms, the rays of light traversed her sleeves. The two of them found it hard to look at one another—both were thinking more or less the same thing.

Isn't it beautiful? Sophie said, her back to him, pointing at the blazing grass. Yes, beautiful, replied Hans. Don't you think this light is special? she asked. That too, he answered. And the hill, she said, have you noticed the way the hill glows? I have, he nodded. Rudi wrote to me, Sophie announced without changing the tone of her voice, he says he's coming back soon. And the cornfields, said Hans, have you seen them? Of course, replied Sophie, they're the same colour as my eiderdown! I've never seen your eiderdown, said Hans, is it really that colour? Yes, well, almost, she shrugged, it's a little darker. And when is Rudi coming back? he asked. A little darker, said Sophie, yet somehow brighter. Ah, that's better, said Hans. In a couple of weeks, Sophie sighed, I don't think he'll stay away longer than that. That shade of orange, he resumed, only looks good in big rooms, is your room big? Neither big nor small, she replied, cosy. Couldn't he stay longer in that accursed country house of his? asked Hans. Can't you convince him, make up some story, delay him a while? Sophie wheeled round, gazed at him with trembling eyes, and exclaimed: What the devil do you want me to say to him? An orange eiderdown, said Hans, tracing circles with a dry twig, it's a little bold, to be honest, if the room isn't all that spacious or there's no adjacent window.

Auntie, said little Wilhemine, what are spiders' webs for? Sophie looked round at her niece, puzzled. Elsa and Hans laughed.

Little Wilhemine had come to spend a few days in Wandernburg with her grandfather and her aunt. Much to Herr Gottlieb's dismay, her father had not come with her, and had sent a servant instead. While the little girl scampered in the field, closely monitored by the servant, Hans and Sophie moved a few yards away in order to talk in private.

Do you know Dresden? he asked. I've been there a few times to see my brother, she replied. And do you like it? he said. It's an improvement on Wandernburg, she sighed, although it has a rather neglected air. Like all Napoleonic cities, said Hans.

The best thing is the Elbe, said Sophie, observing the Nulte, a real river, and those bridges, those arches! It needs a bigger theatre, Hans asserted. Don't tell me you've been to Dresden as well? she said, surprised.

Auntie, auntie, Wilhemine insisted, running towards to them, what are spiders' webs for? Why do you ask, my love? asked Sophie, stroking her hair. There's a butterfly in that tree, the girl said, pointing, it's caught in a cobweb and can't get free. Ah, smiled Sophie, now I understand, poor butterfly! It's very pretty, and it's trapped, repeated the child. Shall we rescue it? Sophie proposed, approaching the tree. Yes, the child replied solemnly. That's my girl! her aunt said approvingly, lifting her up. Let go of it, nasty spider!

Forgive me for asking, Hans whispered as Wilhemine strained to reach the spider's web with a twig, but why didn't you tell her? Tell her what? Sophie turned to him, without letting go of her niece. I'm asking you why you didn't tell her the truth. And what is the truth, may I ask? said Sophie. That however ugly the spider's appearance, he replied, it isn't bad, it's simply trying to survive. And it does this by spinning webs. That everything follows a cycle, even the beautiful butterfly. It's another law of nature. If she were my niece, I would have explained that to her. But she isn't your niece, Sophie bridled, and besides, teaching her to protect what is beautiful, however fragile or ephemeral, is also part of learning. That's another law of nature, Herr know-it-all. And I don't see why scepticism will teach her more wisdom than compassion. All right, all right, Hans backed down, don't get angry. I'm not angry, said Sophie, it makes me sad.

At that moment the child's twig pierced the spider's web and hit the tree trunk, causing the spider to fall and crushing the butterfly.

A sharp shower crumpled the grass, its needles pricking the

grateful earth. They sat in silence watching from inside the cave, as though the storm were a monologue or a guest who dared not venture inside. Álvaro and Hans were sharing a bottle of wine. Lamberg and Reichardt were vying over a piece of cheese. At the back of the cave, surrounded by candles, bending over the open barrel organ and squinting in concentration, the organ grinder was adjusting the workings with a spanner. How goes it, organ grinder? Hans asked. Better, replied the old man, raising his head, much better, some of the strings are worn out, I'm thinking of dropping in at Herr Ricordi's store to buy some new ones. The other day at the dance, you know, I thought some of the low notes sounded off-key, do you think perhaps that's why they didn't like my music? Young people today have a good ear, they go to the conservatoire, they study piano, don't they? That could explain it.

Even as the organ grinder closed the lid of his instrument, the storm outside began to subside, the rain fell more slowly, lost its fury. The pinewood hung there, trickling green. The grass shook itself off, blowing hard. Excellent! the organ grinder said joyously. If it doesn't get cold, we can make a campfire tonight and sleep in the open air. Good idea, Reichardt agreed spitting out a plum stone, I've brought my blanket, and besides there's plenty more wine.

The clouds floated away to the east like washed linen hung out on a line. A ribbon of light fell through the cave entrance. Heavy with the last breath of summer, the afternoon had an overpowering smell. Just as well I didn't bring an umbrella, said Álvaro. It's hot all of a sudden, isn't it? said Hans. What peculiar weather. Lamberg frowned, blinked hard then murmured: I don't like it when the weather's good, I prefer storms. What nonsense is this, lad? Reichardt asked. It's true, said Lamberg, I don't like it, people think they have to be cheerful when the weather's good, as soon as the sun comes out they behave like idiots.

The night was warm. Lamberg lit the fire, staring intently at the flames—each time he moved, Franz would put his tail between his legs. They roasted a few sardines and finished off the bottles. They sang songs, spoke ramblingly, confided their secrets to one another, told a few white lies. Álvaro confessed he was in a state over Elsa, and Hans pretended to be surprised as he listened to the details. Later on, the organ grinder allotted them all turns and they each recounted a dream. Álvaro suspected Hans had made his up. The organ grinder said he liked Lamberg's so much he would try to have the same dream himself that night. Lamberg took off his shoes, placed his feet closer to the fire, and heaved a sigh. Are you staying? the old man asked. It's Saturday, Lamberg replied without opening his eyes. Reichardt got out his blanket before also settling down. Álvaro rose to his feet and announced he was going home. The gallop of his horse floated among the sound of the crickets. Hans and the organ grinder stayed awake talking in hushed tones, their whispering gradually becoming more sporadic, less coherent. Soon, only the fire's crackle and the sound of snoring could be heard around the cave.

Snores, crackles, crickets, birds. The stars look like sparkling dust. The organ grinder has fallen asleep with his mouth so wide open that a toad could seek shelter in it. Lamberg is breathing through his nose, jaw clenched like a vice. Franz has crawled under his master's blanket and only the tip of his tail is poking out. Depending who you are, Hans thinks, sleeping under the stars makes you feel exposed or invulnerable. It is still early for him. Surrounded by slumbering people, he feels like an impostor and attempts to fall asleep himself. He has tried concentrating on his own breathing, counting the fire's tiny explosions, making out the soughing sounds of the pinewood, watching the position of his companions, and even imagining what they're dreaming about. But he doesn't fall asleep. It is because of this, a quirk of fate he will later regret, that he is able quietly to spy on Reichardt's actions. Reichardt's blanket stirs, he sits up, pulls his shirt down, glances about several times (when his turn comes, Hans closes his eyes) and rises to his feet without a sound. His face is changed. In the light of the fire, his wrinkles harden and his lips set in a grimace of weariness, of loathing. Before taking a step forward, Reichardt makes sure the others are sleeping. He stares so intently at Franz's tail, poking out from beneath the blanket, that Hans thinks he will do something to it. He collects his belongings, ties a knot in his blanket and begins to gather up everything he can lay his hands on—Lamberg's sandals, the organ grinder's hat and empty bottles, the remainder of the food, Hans's unknotted scarf, the coins in his frock-coat pockets. When he feels Reichardt's hand groping his ribs, he can't help jerking slightly, enough to make Reichardt pause, withdraw his hand, and look up at Hans's face. Then he discovers his watchful eyes. The two men fix each other's gaze. Reichardt is holding the coins in the palm of his hand. Hans is unable to utter a word. Instead of moving away, Reichardt continues to stare at him, making no attempt to justify himself. Hans can't work out whether this hesitation is a plea or a threat. At first he thinks he sees surprise on Reichardt's face, then he thinks it is contempt. Finally he opens his eyes wide, focuses properly and decides it is a look of shame—Reichardt is capable of stealing from his friends, but perhaps not with one of them watching him.

Embarrassed and more taken aback than Reichardt himself, Hans does something he had not intended, something that takes Reichardt by surprise and which relieves and saddens him in equal measure—he closes his eyes once more. With a mixture of shame, gratitude and resentment, Reichardt resumes what he was doing. He takes Hans's cap, adds it to his spoils, and runs off down the path.

SOMBRE CHORDS

THROUGH THE WINDOWPANES, the sky resembled a piece of paper held up to a lamp. A tiresome drizzle persisted. For a few days now Hans and Sophie had said goodbye half-an-hour earlier—the days were growing shorter.

Leaving already? Hans asked, touching her nipple like someone pressing a bell. Sophie nodded and began hurriedly getting dressed. Wait a moment, he said, I want to tell you something. She turned, arched her eyebrows and went on dressing.

Look, said Hans, the publisher thinks, that is, he's written to me to say it might be a good idea if we revised the French libertines a little, you remember, the poems by de Viau, Saint Amant? (If we revised them? Sophie asked, stopping in the middle of rolling up her stocking, *a good idea*? What do you mean?) Yes, I mean, or rather Brockhaus means, that because of the problems they've had in recent years, they suggest we. (Suggest or demand?) Well, that depends on how you look at it, they're asking us to do our utmost to avoid alerting the censors. Apparently they were cautioned last month about one of the translations we sent. (What? Which one?) I'm not sure, they didn't say exactly, you've read the libertines' texts, but the fact is now it seems the publishers are worrying they might seize their book list, do you see? It's just a question of, I don't know, of toning them down a little, without relinquishing the. (Wait a moment, wait a moment, didn't you say that by signing them with the authors' pseudonyms the censors wouldn't realise they were banned authors?) And they haven't, my love, they haven't realised, but apparently the censor raised an objection when approving the galleys, the publisher explained this wasn't their usual man, who is on our side and who lets everything through, he was unwell and the idiot replacing him says there are at least fifteen pages that are unprintable unless we, do you follow? That's what Brockhaus said, unless we're artful enough to revise certain passages, and …

Sophie, by now fully dressed, stood with arms akimbo. Hans stared at the floor without finishing his sentence.

Listen, he ventured, I don't like the idea any more than you, but if we want to see the libertines in print we have no choice but to (but then, she objected, they'd no longer be libertines), yes, yes they would, they'd be libertines published against the odds, as libertine as possible in times of censorship, it's that or nothing, it would be worse to withdraw the whole translation (frankly, she sighed, I don't know if it would be worse or more honourable), all right, all right. Do you know how many threats were issued to the magazine *Ibis*? And do you know what happened to the periodical *Literarisches Morgenblatt*? They stopped publication several times, Brockhaus changed its name, it was banned again, and it went on like that for years, the publisher ended up losing a huge amount of money and tens of thousands of sales, it's only natural they should try to avoid problems, this is part of the world of literature, too, Sophie, it isn't simply about visiting libraries, there's also this other side, of fighting against the elements. (I see, then let's refuse to make any changes and allow them to commission someone else to do the translation, that way we aren't preventing the publishers from printing the book, nor are we colluding with the censors.) But we've almost finished the texts! How can we throw away so many hours of work! (I don't like it either, but I'd rather sacrifice our work than our dignity.) My love, all I ask is that you look at it from another perspective, censorship is unavoidable but also stupid, if we rewrite the most sensitive verses we can say the same thing in a subtler way, we could even use this opportunity to improve the translation (I can't believe you're suggesting we comply with such a command), I don't intend to comply with it, but to manipulate it at our whim. (Translation and manipulation are two different things wouldn't you say?) You know perfectly well I detest this situation as much as you, but if we really believe in our. (But my love, it is precisely because I believe in it, in our translation, that I refuse to delete a single comma!) I agree, in an ideal world, but the reality is different, wouldn't it be more courageous to accept that reality and fight it from within in order to publish as much of the original text as possible? (You talk to me about fighting! Why don't we pick a real fight by refusing to be trampled on? Write to the publisher and tell him …) That's not fighting, Sophie, it's giving in, trust me, this has happened many times before. (What? You've done this before? Is that how you work? Hans, I don't recognise you, I honestly don't recognise you!) Yes, no! That is, occasionally, but in my own fashion, I've never made an author say anything he hasn't already said or couldn't have said, I swear to you, but, how can I explain, instead of getting angry and doing nothing, I've tried to find inventive ways around it, using ambiguity, do you understand? It's a question of strategy (it's a question of principles, retorted Sophie).

Hans fell into an irritated silence. He looked at Sophie who was gathering up her things to leave, and said: It's very obvious you don't earn a living by translating, nor Rudi, for that matter.

Hans saw Sophie's fingers tighten around the door handle, her gentle knuckles tensing. Sophie released the handle. She slowly buttoned her gloves and responded, still facing the door: Do as you please, Hans. After all, as you've been kind enough to remind me, you're the professional and I'm only an amateur. I wonder whether a professional needs the help of an amateur. Good day.

My love—I don't know which of us was right. But I do know that this translation, like all the others, belongs to both of us. And although I may have given a different impression, yesterday's discussion was my clumsy way of consulting you.

I have written to Brockhaus saying we won't change the text, and if they wish to publish the book would they please find another translator.

Would you do me the honour of continuing to work with me, Fräulein Bodenlieb, and of making me a better translator?

Libertine bites from your

H

Dear professional libertine, I am not sure either which of us was right, although I am glad we agree on the main point—if we are working together the decision should be taken jointly.

I know how difficult it was for you to send that letter to your publisher. I see in it an act of love. And, since I have the honour of being your assistant translator, it would be unfair of me to interpret it any other way. Thank you.

Ah, what bites I have in store for you

S

Rudi's shoulders, Hans reflected looking at them, had, so to speak, come back bearing a heavier load after the holidays. And the tone in which he spoke to Hans in the salon was not the same either—the words he used hadn't changed, but there was a nasality about his voice, an air of restraint each time he turned to him and said for instance "Good night, how nice to see you again" or "Herr Hans, would you pass the sugar bowl?" How could he describe it, Hans kept thinking, it was as though Rudi were studying Hans's every gesture, his every response, through a magnifying glass. He tried to ignore all these nuances and even attempted to appear more amiable, to wipe away any possible trace of guilt from his demeanour. Yet there Rudi was, every Friday, breathing down his neck, pressing his hand in an overly vigorous manner when he greeted him. Regardless of everything, with some difficulty, order reigned once more in the lives of both families—the Wilderhauses had reinstalled themselves in their sumptuous mansion on King's Parade, Rudi had opened the hunting season and at the Gottlieb residence preparations had resumed for what would undoubtedly be the wedding of the year in Wandernburg.

From the frame on the desk, a pale-faced woman stared into the distance, beyond Herr Gottlieb's watery eyes, which were contemplating the photograph as though hoping it would utter a word, a whisper, anything, as he held onto his sixth glass of brandy. As far as Bertold could tell from having spent the past few weeks posted outside his study door, Herr Gottlieb spent entire afternoons doing little else but opening and closing draw-ers. The previous evening, Bertold noticed that his master had suffered a curious memory lapse that was most unlike him—he had not wound the clock at ten o'clock sharp, but had left it until almost twenty minutes later. In addition, that same morning Herr Gottlieb had not risen bright and early, as was his custom, and at midday, had burst into the kitchen and yelled at Petra on account of something to do with black olives.

After eavesdropping for a few moments, Bertold rapped gently on the door. A grunt came from within. The servant entered, chin on chest. Sir, stammered Bertold, er, I came, well, to tell you you're expected at the Grass residence, sir, and that yesterday they sent another polite reminder, that's all sir, the carriage is ready whenever you are. (The Grass residence? Herr Gottlieb declared, lifting his head turtle-like. Those fools? And since when am I obliged to call on fools simply because they send me their pretentious visiting card? Is that what you came for, is that why you are bothering me?) Oh, no, sir, I didn't mean to trouble you, it's just that, if I may be so bold, sir, you haven't been out of the house for days, and frankly, we are beginning be concerned for your health, sir, indeed, the other night you were imprudent enough to (imprudent? Herr Gottlieb flashed angrily. Who's being imprudent, me or you!?) Er, I mean, you didn't take the precaution of instructing me to accompany you on your evening stroll, exposing yourself to God knows what dangers, and I'm not sure whether you were even warmly enough dressed, sir, which is why I took the liberty this afternoon of preparing the carriage, and moreover (you may go, Bertold, thank you, Herr Gottlieb said, waving him away).

Bertold took two steps back, and, concealing his displeasure, lifted his chin in the air and said: There's one other thing I came to tell you, sir. Bertold spoke in a calm, outwardly respectful voice while endowing his words with an insidious, almost reproachful tone, as though deep down, rather than doing Herr Gottlieb's bidding, he were attempting to warn him that it was time he pulled himself together for both their sakes. One of the Wilderhauses' servants, Bertold resumed, after a calculated pause, has just delivered a card announcing Herr Rudi's arrival. What! Herr Gottlieb snapped, and you're telling me this now! Why the devil didn't you say so before? I was about to, sir, replied Bertold, when you. Bah, interrupted Herr Gottlieb, pushing aside the bottle and straightening his lapels as he sat up, stop wasting time, go and tell Petra to prepare something to eat and a tray of Indian tea, why the devil didn't you tell me this before! When did his servant say he was coming? Within the hour, Bertold said, standing to attention. Then take this away, Herr Gottlieb ordered, gesturing towards the bottle, and help me get dressed.

The creak of patent leather stopped in front of the study. The sound of someone clearing his throat could clearly be heard. Rudi Wilderhaus's right shoe rubbed against the left leg of his breeches as though it had paused suddenly in the middle of a procession. Dense, almost visible, the particles of his lemony perfume dispersed before the door. There followed three sharp raps—Rudi knew that one knock at a door betrays unease, two knocks sound obsequious, but that three always sound resolute.

On the other side of the door, Herr Gottlieb also cleared his throat, neither man aware that they were performing the same gesture. Herr Gottlieb was about to stand up and open the door when he instinctively realised that any remaining strength he possessed ought to be deployed there, in the centre of his own office, without stirring from his leather armchair. Yes, enter, he said in an overly high-pitched voice that failed to sound nonchalant. Rudi strode in with deliberate abruptness, rather like a husband arriving home earlier than expected and walking over garments strewn all over the floor. They hurried through the polite greetings, made a few of the usual noises and went straight to the point.

This is why I'm asking you, dear father-in-law, said Rudi, and for the moment let us refer to these as mere questions, how can you permit your daughter to go on working with that man, and to top it all, in that filthy inn! And why do you go on receiving him in this respectable home? Herr Gottlieb replied with as much aplomb as he could muster: This gentleman continues to visit my home, which you correctly refer to as *respectable*, because there is no valid reason why Herr Hans should not continue to attend my daughter's salon. Were it otherwise, dear son-in-law, wouldn't I have already taken the necessary steps? Wouldn't I have categorically prohibited him from coming here? Wouldn't I have punished Sophie? The fact that I have failed to take any such steps is precisely because they are unjustified. What I'm trying to say, my dear Rudi … Or do you have convincing reasons? Well, do you? You say you've heard rumours, *rumours*! Now tell me, do you doubt my daughter's honour, the honour of your future wife? For, so long as her virtue is without blemish, no one will be prohibited from entering this house. Anything else would be tantamount to recognising these sinister slanders, which in the name of my own decency I refuse even to consider.

Rudi detected a mixture of severity and alarm in Herr Gottlieb's eyes. Plunging a little deeper into his liquid gaze, which was struggling to defy him, swimming in his moist entreaties, he understood that Herr Gottlieb was not defending Hans, he was simply behaving like a true gentleman.

I, dear son-in-law, Herr Gottlieb resumed, tugging on his moustache as he might a bootlace, can vouch one hundred per cent for my daughter, her honour and her good name. However, in your place, if, as Sophie's soon-to-be husband, I harboured the slightest doubt I would put a stop to it immediately. With the utmost discretion, naturally. I mean, if such were the case. Because, needless to say, it is not.

Rudi smiled tersely and replied: Of course not, my dear Herr Gottlieb, of course not. This is simply a question, how can I say, of the norms of acceptable behaviour. But you have set my mind at rest. God be with you.

The inn had been slowly emptying. The early morning sounds of doors opening and closing, of feet on the stairs, of noises in the corridor, had ceased. The creak of wooden floors was different, hollow. The windows seemed smaller, the light from them shrunken. Dawn had an insipid feel, and there was a brooding echo to Frau Zeit's slow passage through the empty rooms, as if she were expecting the departed guests to somehow reappear. A pile of firewood had begun to form in the lean-to in the backyard, the tongs appeared gleaming in the hearth, the wool blankets had reappeared on the beds. The postman's gallop scarcely slowed before the entrance, and the only packages he left were for the guest in room number seven. Silence had settled once more over the inn, and yet Hans, who had spent the whole summer lamenting the early morning noises disrupting his repose, was still unable to sleep properly. He would fall asleep for a few hours, then suddenly, inexplicably, he would begin to toss and turn, kept awake by the expectation of comings and goings that never materialised. Until that morning, after getting up and turning the watercolour round in order to shave, he looked at the dark shadows under his eyes, the stubble on his chin, and he understood the reason for his unrest. It wasn't merely the deserted atmosphere of places once people had departed. It was above all the aftermath of that emptiness—with the arrival of autumn, he had stopped being an observer at the inn and had become a protagonist. He had become accustomed to studying the anonymous guests, to guessing at their lives from their faces, to imagining their futures. And now, all of a sudden, he was once more the focus of his own gaze. Hans closed the razor, ran his tongue behind his lips, checked the sides of his face and turned the mirror back to the wall.

Contrary to his nocturnal habits, Hans spent the morning translating. At noon, he went down and devoured a bowl of Frau Zeit's thick vegetable stew. Afterwards, he went back up to his room to change his clothes and put on some scent—today was Friday. He left the inn winking at Lisa (who initially pretended to turn away) and walked towards Café Europa to have his fourth coffee of the day with Álvaro. As usual he arrived late, despite having left in good time—he had to circle Glass Alley half a dozen times, and swore to his friend he couldn't for the life of him find the side street he usually took. The two men exchanged confidences, grumbled about the same things, and began strolling in the direction of Stag Street. As they stood in front of the doors to the Gottlieb residence, Hans remarked: Look, I'm sorry, this must seem stupid, but wasn't the swallow door knocker on the right, and the lion's head on the left? What?

Álvaro said, surprised. The swallow on the? Hans, did you sleep all right? The fact is I didn't, he replied.

As they entered from the icy corridor, they discovered Sophie sitting at the piano, and her father, Rudi and Professor Mietter all applauding. Hans thought she looked pale as she smiled at him, concerned. Would you give us latecomers the pleasure of an encore, dear friend? Hans said in greeting. As you already know, Rudi replied sharply, *"Paganini non ripete"*. Paganini, declared Álvaro, is a violinist. Rudi took offence: And what has that to do with anything, Herr *Urquiho*. Hans slipped over to the windows. The blue curtains seemed heavier. Through a gap in the shutters he glimpsed a misty corner of the market square and the question mark of the Tower of the Wind. Hans sensed Sophie's eyes on his back, but he decided to be careful and carried on staring out of the window until the others arrived. In the meantime, Álvaro, Rudi and Professor Mietter discussed the aesthetic of the encore. Half-closing his eyes and listening carefully, Hans could distinguish Herr Gottlieb's gruff, tutorly murmur addressing his daughter, whose voice was scarcely audible. It's going to rain, thought Hans, and his observation was accompanied by one of Sophie's distinctive sighs (well-timed, drawn out, with a hint of playful irony). Suddenly Frau Pietzine's voice burst in, followed by that of Bertold, and a tinkle of cups and teaspoons rang out. When Hans turned round, he glimpsed Elsa's raised eyebrows as Álvaro flashed her a sidelong smile.

More tense than usual, although employing her usual strategic methods, Sophie clung to her role as organiser—it was her way of defending herself against the despondency that was beginning to haunt her, and above all, of protecting those few hours of subtle independence for which she had fought so hard. She stood up to greet the Levins, who had just walked in with that forced, rather unconvincing display of cheerfulness couples have when they have been arguing minutes before arriving at a party. Well, my dear friends, Sophie announced, now that we're all here, I'd like to propose that we keep the promise we made to Herr *Urquixo* last week of reading a few passages together from our beloved Calderón (marvellous, Álvaro beamed, marvellous), and I've taken the liberty of selecting a few scenes from *Life Is a Dream*, because I assumed everyone would be familiar with the work. (Rudi cleared his throat and helped himself to a pinch of snuff.) Is everyone agreed, then? There are, let me see, one, two, three, seven characters altogether, and we have two copies of *Life Is a Dream* here in the house, plus two more which I borrowed from the library. (Ah, Álvaro suddenly realised, we'll be reading it in German, then.) Naturally, *amigo*! How else? (Of course, Álvaro nodded, disappointed, I understand, but, *La vida es sueño* in German, ay!) View it as an informative exercise, it'll be as if you are hearing it for the first time (let's look at the translation, may I see a copy? Hans asked), here you are, don't get too professional about it now, Monsieur Hans! Well, if everyone is ready, we'll assign the roles. Any volunteers?

Everyone decided Rudi should play the part of Prince Segismundo, at which Hans clapped his hands ironically. Sophie asked Professor Mietter to read the part of King Basilio, and the professor, flushing with pride, made as if to hesitate before accepting. Hans was given the part of Astolfo, also a prince, though with fewer lines than Segismundo. Frau Pietzine seemed happy to personify Lady Rosaura. They had difficulty convincing Frau Levin to take on the timid role of Princess Estrella. Álvaro declared he was incapable of reciting Calderón in German and preferred to listen, and so Bertold had no choice but to accept the part of Fife the jester. (Seeing as it's only a play, thought Bertold, why the devil can't I play a prince or a king?) Herr Gottlieb was equally displeased at being given the role of old Clotaldo, although he limited himself to twirling his whiskers in protest. Herr Levin, who wasn't an admirer of Calderón, sat next to Álvaro to give the impression of an audience. Sophie acted as stage director, instructing everyone until at last the performance was ready to begin.

PROFESSOR MIETTER [*with affected unease*]:
  What was that?
RUDI [*in his element, looking at Hans, or perhaps not*]:
  It was nothing.
  I threw a man who wearied me
  From a balcony into the sea.
BERTOLD [*nodding unenthusiastically, and without an ounce of charm*]:
  Be aware—he is the King.

Hans, who is not in the scene, stops listening and stares at Sophie—in profile, very alert, she looks like a melancholy statue.

PROFESSOR MIETTER [*his wig all a-tremble and with such lofty indignation!*]:
  Greatly it grieves me, prince
  That when I have come to see you
  Thinking to find you restored,
  Having freed yourself from fates and stars,
  Instead I find you so severe
  That you on this occasion have committed
  A foul murder ...

The professor's earnestness and the stress he places on each inflection amuses Hans—the exceedingly Protestant professor has become quite Catholic. Álvaro catches his eye, they wink at one another:

  ... Whoever that has seen

The naked blade which
Struck a mortal wound
Can be without fear?

Elsa comes in with a tray of canapés halfway through the professor's speech; she wonders whether to carry on or to stop in order not to distract him; she almost loses her balance, catches herself, steadies the tray, sighs angrily. Álvaro watches her affectionately.

RUDI *[recalling suddenly, as he reads, a sad episode from his childhood]*:
  … that a father who against me
  Can act so cruelly
  And with such bitter spite
  Cast me from his side …

Mortified by Rudi's intonation, his insistence on leaving a long pause at the end of each verse thus breaking up the flow, Sophie gives up trying to direct him and instead her gaze rests on Hans's reflection. She thinks he looks handsome and tousled. When she rouses herself, the scene is nearly over and she affects a look of concentration.

PROFESSOR MIETTER *[very much at home, more admonishing than ever]*:
  … Although you know who you are,
  And are now freed from deception
  And find yourself in a place
  Where you stand above all,
  Heed this warning that I make—
  Be humble and be gentle
  Because perhaps this is a dream
  Even though you see yourself awake.

With exemplary professionalism, Professor Mietter makes as if to exit, as indicated in the original text. Hans watches his gestures and thinks that, all in all, the professor isn't a bad actor. He tries to imagine him in costume on a stage. He succeeds so well that for a moment his eyelids grow heavy. He startles himself in mid yawn.

RUDI:
    … I know now
    Who I am, and know I am
    Half-man, half-beast.

The first to applaud is Lady Rosaura, that is, Frau Pietzine. Álvaro and Frau Levin politely follow suit. Sophie gives a relieved smile, declaring: "And there, dear friends, our little production ends, congratulations."

As he kissed her, Hans realised there was tension in Sophie's mouth—her lips were pursed, her tongue was rigid, her teeth seemed reticent. Is something the matter? Hans asked, withdrawing his lips. She smiled, lowered her head and embraced him. He did not ask her again.

Sophie sat at the desk and looked at Hans in silence, as if to say it was his turn. He went to open the trunk, took out a book and handed it to her. Do you remember our essay on German poetry? said Hans, attempting to sound cheerful. The one we did for the *European Review*? Well, before we send it off I'd like to add another poet, see what you think, it arrived yesterday from Hamburg, *The Book of Songs* by Heinrich Heine, only just published, apparently it's a roaring success, I read a review of it in the magazine *Hermes*. Sophie opened the book and noticed its appearance. It didn't look to her like a new copy, but she said nothing—she had grown accustomed to Hans's bibliographical secrets. He seemed to notice her bewilderment and explained: The postal service is getting worse by the day, those clumsy postmen are so slapdash. So, what do you reckon? he asked.

(I'm not sure, she replied, he sounds awkward, as if he were sabotaging the seriousness of his own poems on purpose.) Yes! That's exactly what I like most about him. There's a poem in there, perhaps you saw it, about two French soldiers who return home after having been kept prisoner in Russia. Traveling through Germany they learn of Napoleon's defeat and begin to weep. The poem caught my attention because it dares to give the enemy a voice, and that is something we Germans would have appreciated in a French author when we were defeated. I believe that in today's poetry there is no place for half measures—either you aspire to being a Novalis or a Hölderlin, or you turn your back on heaven and try to be a Heine. (Wait a minute, Sophie said, slipping her finger between two pages, is this the poem you were talking about? *The Grenadiers?*) Yes, that's the one, shall we read it?

> *... the two soldiers weep together*
> *At the fateful news:*
> *"How they hurt!" says one,*
> *"How my wounds sting!"*
>
> *"I would like to die with you,"*
> *Says the second, "this is the end;*
> *But I have a wife and children,*
> *Who cannot live without me."*
>
> *"Wife, children? What matter?*
> *Something grieves me more;*
> *Let them live on charity,*
> *In chains lies my Emperor!"*

Reading it through again, she commented, I'm not convinced the poem is Bonapartist. They feel bound to spill their blood for

Napoleon and this allegiance is inhuman, like the first grena-
dier's impassioned response when his companion fears for his
family. You could be right, said Hans, I hadn't thought of it
that way. Perhaps the poem's strength is the way it avoids con-
demning either of the grenadiers, it simply offers two different
ways of understanding fate.

Her head leaning on Hans's shoulder, Sophie observed the
mineral response of her nipples—they were still hard, not out
of excitement now, but from the cold. My love, said Sophie,
isn't it time you lit the fire? You're right, said Hans sitting up,
it has got colder. The summer is over, she whispered. Not yet,
he whispered.

Listen, said Sophie, there's something I want to tell you.
(Hans handed her a shoe.) Oh, thank you, where was it? (Hans
gestured towards the space between bed and wall.) Anyway,
there's something I want to tell you and I don't know how.
(He shrugged, and smiled forlornly.) It's just that, my father is
becoming more and more nervous, he never stops drinking, the
Wilderhauses are growing impatient, and I'm doing my best
to keep up a pretence, but I don't see how I can keep them
at bay any longer. Rudi had a talk with me yesterday, he was
furious, we quarrelled, and I had difficulty calming him down,
I don't know how long for (and so? he said, closing his eyes),
and so, I was thinking, it might be a good idea, at least for a
while, to stop (to stop? he echoed), I mean, to stop translating
for a while, don't you think? Look at me, Hans! Just for a while,
until things settle down a little. (Aha, he breathed very slowly,
you mean that we should stop seeing each other completely.)
No, of course not! My love, I've already worked that out. (Ah,
how?) Look, it won't be so very different, we'll just have to be
more careful that's all, and perhaps see each other less, Elsa will
go on helping me, we can meet at least once a week, when Elsa
goes out on an errand I'll go with her, I'll come and see you

and she'll wait for me in the usual place at a reasonable time, I've worked out that we'll have a couple of hours to ourselves (if there's no other way). I don't think there is, not for the moment.

Halfway through the door, she turned and said: Do you know what annoys me? Not being able to finish our European anthology! Hans stuck his head out and replied: We'll finish it one day.

Lying open on the desk, a book reproduced some verses by Heine:

> *So much we felt for one another that*
> *We reached a perfect harmony.*
> *Often we played at being married*
> *Without suffering mishaps or quarrels.*
> *We played together, cried out for joy,*
> *Exchanged sweet kisses as we caressed.*
> *At length we decided, with childish pleasure,*
> *To play hide-and-seek in woods and fields.*
> *So well did we succeed in hiding*
> *That never again did we find each other.*

The pulp of the day was squeezed out over the countryside. From Bridge Walk Hans contemplated Wandernburg's misty domes, its pointed spires. The earth exuded a muddy smell of rain. The River Nulte shimmered in the distance. An occasional carriage shattered the calm of the main road. Hans lingered absent-mindedly for a moment, until he looked down and clicked his tongue—he had left the organ grinder's sheep's cheese behind at the inn.

The cave was cold inside. The surface of the rocks had a slimy sheen. Franz greeted him, sniffing timidly at his hands, as though sensing they ought to be carrying something. The organ grinder and Lamberg were gathering furze branches, old newspapers and kindling. Can I help? said Hans rubbing his arms. Yes, please, the old man replied, do me a favour, sit down and tell me what you dreamt last night, Lamberg hasn't dreamt anything for me for days. Hans scoured his memory and realised he couldn't recall a single recent dream; he would just have to make one up like he'd done so many times. That, the old man sighed as he stacked the firewood, is what most amused me about Reichardt, he always had a new dream to tell. Have you heard nothing? asked Lamberg. The labourers say they haven't seen him for a while. No, the old man said mournfully, nothing. Hans went over to help fan the flames. When the fire began to shine light on them, Hans noticed a circular blotch on Lamberg's neck—a wound or a bite mark. Lamberg caught him looking and turned up the collars of his wool coat.

Lamberg left early. He explained that tomorrow would be hard work, they were late with the autumn orders and there was a rumour going round the factory about more people being laid off. The organ grinder wrapped a scarf round his neck and accompanied him outside. A few moments later, seeing he hadn't come back, Hans wrapped up and went after him.

A fine drizzle was falling, next to nothing. He found the old man absorbed in watching the twilight. The clouds were trailing off, like burnt-out fireworks. This rain makes me nervous, said Hans standing next to him. It's always the same at this time of year, said the organ grinder, this is a clever rain, it tells us winter is coming and it takes care of the flowers. What flowers? Hans said, puzzled, observing the bald grass. There, there, the old man replied, pointing to some specks of colour among the tree trunks, the last flowers of autumn are much more beautiful than those of spring. And they fell silent, in their different ways, watching the light snap like an umbilical cord.

Hans left the Café Europa and peered down the narrow passage that was Glass Alley—if he wasn't mistaken, the third turning on the left should take him down to Potter's Lane, and from there into Ducat Street, where the Bank of Wandernburg was situated, which would lead him straight into the market square. That was right, and it was the shortest route. But where the devil was Potter's Lane? Was it the third on the left after Café Europa or before? If he was able to draw a mental map of the city centre from memory, why were his calculations so seldom correct? How could he …

Idiot! a coach driver screeched from his perch, where do you think you're going? Hans leapt backwards like a cat, flattening himself against the wall, and repeated the question to himself: Indeed, where did I think I was going? The wheels sped past, clipping his boots. When the coach disappeared from sight, at the end of the street, Hans was surprised to recognise the cobblestones of the market square.

Glancing up at the Tower of the Wind, he was pleased to see he was still in time to say hello to the organ grinder. He felt like listening to him play for a moment and then inviting him for a beer. They hadn't taken a stroll together for quite a while; lately they only met at the cave. At first he didn't notice—he walked on without glancing at the organ grinder's spot. And even when it was obvious he still carried on walking like he always did, as if he were listening to the music. Only when he was within yards of the edge of the square did he blink several times and stop in his tracks. For a moment he had the sensation that he was in the wrong place. Hans glanced up at the clock tower once more, he looked around bewildered—for the first time that year, the old man wasn't at his post during work hours.

Hans entered the cave uneasily. He found the organ grinder curled up in a ball on his straw pallet. He tried to smile at Hans. Hans touched his face. His brow was burning, his lips cold. His shoulders trembled and he kept rubbing his feet. A sharp cough punctuated each of his sentences. My head hurts, but, you know, *kof*, it's not my head, it's inside, *kof*. But, it's freezing in here, organ grinder, Hans said, breathing on his hands, why haven't you lit the fire? Oh, this is nothing, replied the old man, *kof*, last year was much worse, wasn't it Franz?

The bark and the cough rang out as one.

The following four mornings, Hans got up (moderately) early to bring the organ grinder breakfast and a few provisions. He forced him to drink broth, herbal infusions, and lemonade for his cold. He also brought him some warm clothes, which the old man only accepted on the condition that he would pay for them as soon as he could play again. As the old man sweated, his straw pallet grew limp, and his eyes lightened. It was impossible to convince him to see a doctor. Are you crazy? he had objected. With what they charge—*kof*—and with all their quackery? Hans had finally given up trying, in return for a promise he would obey all Hans's instructions. The first two days, the organ grinder let him have his way without any objection. He complied cheerfully, ate everything Hans brought, and slept for hours on end so that occasionally Franz would lick his beard just to see his eyelids flutter. On the third day, he threatened to get up. Listen, my dear Hans, he said without coughing, I know best how I am feeling. I thank you for all your attention from the bottom of my heart, but I'm fine, really, in the end this has been a rest, do you see? Old as I am, I should allow myself a holiday, that was my mistake, and I promise I'll dress warmly, I do, no, thanks, I've already had some, yes, it's marvellous, I'm going out for a while, let go of me! I'm not a child, really? Then I'll behave like one, it can't be helped, won't you let go? I don't believe this? Franz, bite one of his boots! Heavens, we are a stubborn pair aren't we, Hans?

Hans managed to keep him in bed until the fifth day. That morning, the colour having returned to his cheeks, the old man got up, pulled on his clothes, donned his bright-red, thick woollen beret and left the cave, calmly pushing his barrel organ.

After Sunday Mass, Father Pigherzog was conversing with the mayor beneath the portico of St Nicholas's Church. In order not to be overheard, the two men stood so close together that the mayor's pointed nose was almost prodding the priest's waxy chin. The mayor found this somewhat offensive, not simply on account of the priest's breath, but because the difference in height between the two men became glaringly conspicuous. Suddenly, something distracted the priest, and he turned towards the group of parishioners leaving the church. Failing to connect with the priest's ear, the word *thalers* slipped from beneath the mayor's oily whiskers, lingering for a moment, before dissolving like vapour.

Sophie was walking arm in arm with Herr Gottlieb towards Archway. Father Pigherzog turned his head, cleared his throat, and called out to her a couple of times. It was Herr Gottlieb, not she, who responded to the call. They approached the priest, Herr Gottlieb beaming, Sophie more solemn, while Mayor Ratztrinker took his leave, saying: We'll discuss this tomorrow. As he walked past Herr Gottlieb, the mayor doffed his hat. My child, the priest said, how glad I am to see you, you have been in my prayers of late. You're most kind, Sophie retorted, am I to understand that you didn't pray for me before? Good Father, Herr Gottlieb intervened, flustered, you know what a witty girl my daughter is. I certainly do, said Father Pigherzog, not to worry, not to worry, I've been praying for you my dear (the priest placed his hand on Sophie's), and for the happiness of your marriage, you know how highly I esteem the Wilderhaus family, and how proud I am to see that curious, studious child, do you remember, Herr Gottlieb? Now a fine young woman about to wed such a God-fearing, honourable and principled man. I thank you, Father, with all my heart, she said, although there are still two months to go before. That is precisely, the priest cut in, what I wished to discuss with you: I have been reflecting about the details of the liturgy, the *missa pro sponso et sponsa*, the arrangements for the holy space, because, well, as one of the participants I consider it advisable to leave nothing to chance, in view of the repercussions of. Yes, yes, of course, Herr Gottlieb hurriedly declared, we would be most grateful to receive your advice on all necessary matters, and I can assure you here and now—in fact haven't we already discussed this Sophie my dear?—I can assure you we never doubted for a moment about appointing you to officiate at the wedding, we were, how shall I put it, counting on it, indeed, we were about to ask you for a meeting in order to. Naturally, naturally, Father Pigherzog beamed, there is still plenty of time, I was merely reflecting, my child, that in order for the preparations to proceed smoothly, it might be a good idea if, for the time being, we resumed our old talks, what I mean is, although it is no longer your practice, since you are obliged to confess before taking the marriage oath, I would like you to know that I am willing to offer you guidance and prepare your soul for receiving this sacrament in peace. Mmm, thank you very much, Father, Sophie murmured glancing towards the street, I'll bear that in mind. I am sure, intervened Herr Gottlieb, the opportunity will arise, these will be very busy days! Although naturally your offer is most. The talks, Sophie broke in, turning to her father, will be with me. I do not feel you are at peace, said Father Pigherzog, is something worrying you, my child? You may confide in me, is there some reason why you are anxious? Are you afraid of anything in particular? One is always afraid, Father, she sighed, to live is to fear. Quite so, said the priest, which is why our Father is here to help us when we are most in need, you must not torment yourself, none of us is free from sin, and our redemption is His everlasting gift, for as you know, man is born a sinner. Tell me, Father, replied Sophie, if man is born a sinner, how can he know when he is sinning? And what about us women, what are we to do in the meantime?

What were you thinking! Herr Gottlieb hissed as they made their way towards Archway, how could you be so insolent! Why do you humiliate me like this? Have you taken leave of your senses? What's the matter with you? (Sophie was about to reply, when she encountered a pair of bloodshot eyes and a vaguely familiar, haggard-looking face—Lamberg turned away, embarrassed, then was about to stop to say hello when he noticed she was looking the other way, and he carried on walking stiffly.) Did you hear what I said, child? Are you listening to me? (Yes, I am, said Sophie, I'm forever listening to you.) Good, then do me the favour of responding when I talk to you, do you realise the way you're behaving towards him? (Who do you mean? she said uneasily.) Who do you think I mean? Rudi, of course, for heavens' sake! Are you listening or not? (Ah, she responded, I've already explained to him that everything is fine, that it's just nerves.) I don't care if it's nerves or whatever, but you mustn't give him this impression just now, you must be more considerate, affectionate, obliging. (Are you trying to make me into a good wife or a good actress?) Sophie Gottlieb! Now listen to me! You know I've never been in favour of that kind of thing, but I warn you, you are asking for a good hiding! I'm only reminding you, and God knows I shouldn't have to, that you cannot behave so coldly towards your fiancé and be so friendly towards that man, or do you imagine the guests at the salon haven't noticed? (Forgive me, what are you insinuating?) Naturally I am not insinuating anything! I am simply telling you, no, I am ordering you from now on to devote all your energy and time to what really matters, to your forthcoming marriage. (Even more time than I do? Sophie said, raising her voice. Haven't I already sacrificed what I most enjoyed doing? Haven't I already stopped working with Herr Hans in order to please you? What more do you want from me? Do you want me to stop thinking?)

What I like doing, *kof,* the organ grinder protested, is going out
to work, I can't stay here all day thinking. What you can't do,
Hans chided him in earnest, is wander round outside in this
condition. But I've only got a, *kof,* a cold! the old man insisted.
His words sounded distant, as if the layers of blankets Hans had
placed on top of him were muffling his voice.

Less than a week after his return to the square, the organ
grinder had been obliged once more to take to his bed. The
damp breeze and intermittent rain had given him a chill. His
cough was persistent now, it had gone onto his chest. His temperature would not go down. His bones ached. Hans would
wrap him in woolly layers, before helping him out his bed so he
could urinate. A dark liquid dripped feebly from his shrivelled
member, making a hole in the frost.

If Lamberg had entertained the possibility of stopping to greet
Sophie in Archway, this was because she had been unexpectedly friendly on the two or three occasions when they had met.
Lamberg had very clear ideas about Wandernburgers such as
the Gottliebs—their good name and their appearance meant
more to them than other people and their lives. He had always
mistrusted Sophie, and yet the unaffected way in which she had
behaved at the cave had made him reconsider. This was why it
hurt him so much that when he plucked up the courage to smile
and approach her she had walked straight past him. Would he
tell Hans when he reached the cave? No, what was the point,
he would only leap to her defence. What a fool I am, he said
to himself, striding angrily down Bridge Walk, I never learn.

Lamberg thought the organ grinder looked less pale than
the day before, but still poorly. When he saw Lamberg arrive,
the old man put down his spoon and tried to get out of bed.
Hans restrained him gently and pulled the covers back over

him. Álvaro, who had just arrived, handed Lamberg a bottle of schnapps. Lamberg declined with a brusque gesture that startled Franz. Never say no to schnapps, my lad, the organ grinder said, even dogs know that! Lamberg allowed himself to smile for the second time that day, sat down on the edge of the straw pallet and raised the bottle.

The fire blazed. Cold air wafted in and out. Álvaro's horse was gone. The schnapps was finished. And what about you? Lamberg asked, what did you dream about? This morning, the old man said, before I woke up, I dreamt of a lot of women standing in a row with their hands raised, and do you know the strangest thing? They were all wearing black, except one. Why do you think that was? Hans asked with interest. How should I know? the organ grinder replied, it was a dream!

Just as the poplars by the river had difficulty holding onto their leaves, and the waters of the Nulte began to ice over, and the streets became slippery, Sophie and Hans's resolve began to falter, to lose its momentum. Meeting alone was becoming more and more complex. The rumours were no longer a possibility or something to guard against, but a fixed routine that dogged them in every street, on every corner, behind every shutter. Elsa and Sophie would circle the inn, gradually approach the doorway, and glance about before slipping inside. Their random encounters grew briefer—the days were shorter and she and Elsa had to be home before nightfall. Some afternoons, because of the timing or the hurry, Elsa was unable to visit Álvaro, and this affected her mood and her willingness to make excuses for Sophie when she went out. Sophie did not always manage to keep her temper with her father or to behave affectionately towards her fiancé. And Hans could not stop thinking of Dessau. They even argued now some afternoons.

I didn't say I wanted to leave, replied Hans, tugging at the blankets. Before I met you I traveled all the time, and, well, I just wanted to know if, given the opportunity, you'd have the courage to follow me. Sophie sat up, pulled the blanket over to her side, and said: *Given the opportunity?* I must remind you I'm about to marry, and I can't leave my father all alone, not to mention subject him to such a scandal. Don't forget, I've told you many times—it's not so easy to escape from here. In the end, given the opportunity, you could as easily stay in Wandernburg in order to be with me as I could leave here in order to be with you, don't you think?

They said goodbye obliquely, without giving one another a last kiss, the way people do when they don't know when they will see each other again. In the doorway, he offered to accompany her to the baroque fountain. Leave together? Are you crazy? she said. There's already enough gossip, I'd better go alone as always. But it's different now, he insisted, the streets are darker and emptier, I could pretend to be walking behind you, just for a few minutes, if we cover our faces properly no one will recognise us. Listen, my love, she said, pulling on her gloves and folding her cashmere shawl into three, it's very kind of you, but I have to go.

Sophie peeps out into Old Cauldron Street. She looks to left and right, fastens her bonnet and sets off. The contrasting warmth of her cheeks and the chill air has the effect of slightly lowering her spirits. She imagines Elsa must be waiting for her, and quickens her pace. She can still feel a prickle of moisture between her legs. Although uncomfortable, the reminder makes her smile. A bitten moon climbs the sky.

Near the corner of Archway, installed in the shadows between the street lamps, the figure in the long coat hears a woman's shoes approach. He narrows his eyes, judges the distance, puts on his mask. When Sophie passes the corner, he waits a few moments before moving away from the wall. He begins walking at a slow pace. He leaves Jesus Lane and follows her. He walks behind her at a steady distance. Sophie hears or senses something moving behind her. She holds her breath and listens hard—all she can hear are her own alarmed footsteps. She walks on, nervously. She glances behind her. She sees no one. Even so, she quickens her pace. The masked figure gradually shortens the distance between them, taking great care his feet strike the ground in tandem with his victim's nervous steps. He estimates that twelve or fifteen strides will bring him close enough. Less than eight or ten, now. A few yards from the inescapable, Sophie has the happy idea of suddenly stopping in her tracks. Caught off guard, the masked figure cannot avoid taking a few more steps before coming to a halt. She clearly hears the echo of feet that aren't hers. Then she reacts. She drops everything—her parasol, her shawl, her ridiculous bag. She takes off. She runs as fast as her legs will carry her, screaming at the top of her voice. For a moment the masked figure hesitates—usually his victims attempt to flee when he is closer to them. Flustered, he gives chase, calculating how long he has until the end of the alley. After covering half the distance separating them, he doubts he will catch her before they come perilously close to the next street, which is more brightly lit. Still chasing her, he slows down. Sophie reaches Potter's Lane and turns into it, crying for help. The masked figure stops dead, turns round and runs off in the opposite direction, towards the darkness. Just then a nightwatchman blows his whistle and comes over brandishing his lamp.

The next morning, accompanied by Elsa, Sophie reported to the main police station in Wandernburg. A sleepy looking Hans arrived to offer moral support; he had just received her urgent message and had immediately made his way to the address on Spur Street. Amazingly, he had found it at the first attempt, following Sophie's hastily drawn map. Outside the police station,

Hans heard about the masked attacker's unsuccessful assault, and it was all he could do to stop himself from uttering the reproach he could anyway see in Sophie's startled expression. She had decided not to tell Rudi, and much less her father—it would have provided him with the necessary excuse to forbid her from leaving the house. When Sophie finished telling him about it, Hans embraced her recklessly, and she didn't stop him. Elsa gave a meaningful cough and they stepped away from one another. Before entering the police station, Sophie glanced at Hans's appearance and asked him to take off his beret. Didn't someone steal it? she whispered in his ear. Yes, he said putting it away, but I had a spare one. Where do you get them from? she asked, puzzled. They've been banned for years!

In here! a voice on the other side of the door cried out. The policeman who had accompanied them stood aside to allow Sophie, Elsa and Hans to enter the Chief Superintendent's office. The Chief Superintendent himself was a nondescript, flabby individual, utterly unremarkable except for one subtly terrifying trait—his teeth clacked as he spoke, as if his dentures lagged behind his words by a fraction of a second, or as if a voracious appetite caused him to devour what he was saying. He listened to Sophie's stammering, raised an arm to interrupt her, and ordered her to be taken into the adjoining office. And, teeth rattling, summoned Lieutenant Gluck and Sub-lieutenant Gluck.

Removing his cap in front of his superior, the younger Lieutenant Gluck corrected him in a hushed voice: Lieutenant, Chief Superintendent, sir, I'm a lieutenant now. The Chief Superintendent clacked an "Ah" and addressed Lieutenant Gluck's father: Lieutenant Gluck, you must be proud of Lieutenant Gluck. I am, Chief Superintendent, sir, his father nodded, I'm ever so proud of my so, of Sub, of Lieutenant Gluck, Chief Superintendent, sir, thank you, sir. Don't mention it,

Lieutenant, clacked the Chief Superintendent, I always take an interest in my men's progress. Speaking of which, how is the investigation coming along? Have we any strong suspects? People are nervous, politicians are beginning to ask questions. The young Lieutenant Gluck stepped forward to give his reply: We have, Chief Superintendent, sir. Is that so, Sub-lieutenant? his superior asked with interest. Lieutenant, Chief Superintendent, Lieutenant, the young man corrected him. Well, his father spoke up, best not to count our chickens, given the public disquiet the case has caused, it would be impossible to put right any mistakes. On the contrary, on the contrary! clacked the Chief Superintendent. The sooner we give them a culprit the sooner we can all relax. And in my view this is probably the work of a Jew. Do you think so, Chief Superintendent, sir? said Lieutenant Gluck, taken aback. Remember we already had a Jewish rapist nine years ago, the Chief Superintendent explained, we can't dismiss the possibility of this being another one. I see, Lieutenant Gluck said, that's a good theory, Chief Superintendent, sir, we'll bear it in mind. The Chief Superintendent gave one last clack: I hope you can wrap this up quickly, lieutenants, it has gone on long enough. You may go, *Vorwärts!*

No sooner had they left the main office than Lieutenant Gluck approached his son and told him: You mustn't speak to the Chief Superintendent like that, a sub-lieutenant isn't supposed to ... A lieutenant, insisted Lieutenant Gluck. A lieutenant isn't either, Lieutenant Gluck said, annoyed, and don't be so hasty. Whatever you say, Father, said Lieutenant Gluck. Lieutenant, call me Lieutenant, his father corrected him.

Lieutenant Gluck was questioning Sophie. His father remained silent, gazing out of the tiny window at the back of the room. The office, much smaller than that of the Chief Superintendent, had a musty odour. The young lieutenant was standing taking notes, and each time Sophie paused, he circled the woodworm-riddled desk. Is that all you can remember? he asked, hurling his quill into the inkwell. (The ink sloshed around in it, threatened to spill over the edges, gradually settled.) Are you absolutely certain you didn't notice anything else about your assailant? His hair? His skin colour? The size of his hands? Nothing? I already told you it was too dark, Sophie replied, and as you can imagine I was too busy running away to notice these things. What about smells, insisted the lieutenant, did you notice anything peculiar about the way he smelt, his breath, his sweat, anything? I wasn't close enough to him, she said, lowering her eyes and shaking her head, believe me, gentlemen, I wish I could be of more help. It's a pity, said the lieutenant. Pardon me, Hans interrupted, isn't there more we could do? How about if we kept watch at night pretending we are out strolling? I imagine you have a shortage of police officers, and there aren't many nightwatchmen around. My dear sir, replied the lieutenant, irritated, we've already or-ganised numerous special patrols to no effect. Repeating the exercise now would be of little use, the masked attacker never strikes two days, or even two weeks in a row. He's nothing if not patient. He attacks out of the blue, bides his time. He appears then disappears. As though into thin air. Sophie (separating two slender fingers she had been clasping together since the start of the interview, brushing them against the sleeves of her dress, running them along the edge of the desk) said with a lump in her throat: Well, I hope you catch him soon, gentlemen, I had a narrow escape last night, but perhaps next time I won't be so lucky, a few more seconds and, good God, I dread to think! Very well, Fräulein, sighed the lieutenant, we appreciate your assistance. You can go home now. We suggest you take extra care, and we're glad you're so quick on your feet. Well, Sophie murmured, standing up, I'm not that quick, just well informed. We women do read newspapers.

On hearing her last words, Lieutenant Gluck senior (who had

been gazing absent-mindedly out of the tiny window) swivelled round suddenly and said: Wait, wait, so when did you say you started running? Sophie almost jumped when she heard the other lieutenant's voice: What do you mean? I'm asking you, he explained, when exactly you started running away. You just said you weren't very quick. So why couldn't the masked attacker catch up with you?

Sophie sat down again and described the chase once more, this time mentioning the brief halt that had allowed her to discover she was being followed. Apparently excited, Lieutenant Gluck senior wanted to know why she had left out that detail in her previous account. Sophie told him she hadn't considered it important, and that anyway all the questions had referred to her would-be attacker, not to her. The lieutenant asked her to recall as precisely as she could their positions in the alleyway, and to calculate how far they were from one another when she dropped her things and began to run. After listening to her with his eyes closed, the lieutenant went on: Are you sure this was more or less the distance between you? And yet you say he couldn't catch up with you before reaching the next corner? Sophie nodded, pale-faced. Lieutenant Gluck glanced at Lieutenant Gluck, let the weight of his years slump into a chair and declared: Excellent, excellent! We've got him now, son. Fräulein, you are wonderful.

Draped in corners, folded on shelves, spread out over her orange eiderdown, piled on top of the dresser, arranged in boxes and according to size, the wedding trousseau swamped Sophie's bedroom. Elsa, whose task it had been for months to gather it together, was reading aloud from a list. Leaning against the doorjamb tugging the ends of his whiskers as though they were two pieces of string, Herr Gottlieb presided over the inventory. Sophie sat in a corner yawning discreetly.

Let's see, Elsa recapped, plain and patterned cotton and

silk stockings, petticoats, under-corsets, so far so good, now for the accessories, cuffs, bonnets, camisoles with lace trim, I think three dozen is enough, don't you, sir? What! replied Herr Gottlieb. Only three dozen? She should have at least four, what am I saying, make that six! (Father, Sophie broke in, don't be ridiculous, why spend all this money?) My beloved child, we are not here to scrimp and save but to do things properly, you deserve all this and much more! And remember, once you are a Wilderhaus, you will no longer have to worry about economising, well, six dozen then, Elsa, go on. As you wish, sir, Elsa intoned. White silk peignoirs for summer and dark moiré ones for winter, assorted camisoles, satin slippers, yes, that's right, brocade and damask sheets, organdy pillowcases (organdy for pillowcases? Why? declared Sophie), to give you sweet dreams, Miss, bedspreads, blankets, bath towels, hand towels, face towels, extra towels for guests, three, I mean six dozen, that's enough isn't it? We need each kind. (I tell you I don't need half of this, Sophie protested, it's absurd.) It pains me deeply, Herr Gottlieb chided, to hear you say such things when you know how many years your father has been saving up for this moment, and the hardships your mother endured, may God rest her soul, and how happy she would have been to see the luxury you will enjoy. All I want, my child, is to know you will never need for anything so that I may grow old peacefully in the sure knowledge that I have done my duty, is this so hard for you to understand? And your ingratitude, Sophie, is not the best way of repaying my efforts. Anything more, Elsa? (Thwarted, Sophie stopped protesting and fell silent.) Yes, Elsa resumed, three high-waisted jackets, an otter-skin coat, a sable stole, four new bonnets, two with feathers and two with flowers, is that enough, sir? I don't know, probably not, make it four of each just in case. As you wish, sir, Elsa intoned, and should Miss Sophie's name be stitched in white? Not stitched, embroidered,

Herr Gottlieb corrected, everything embroidered! (But I'm no good at embroidery, Father, Sophie reminded him.) Then Elsa will do it, damn it, that's what she is here for. Let's stop now, the guests will be arriving soon.

Halfway through the afternoon, Hans noticed the logs burning in the marble fireplace—he thought there were too few for such a big room. Glancing around, it occurred to him the candles looked less white and gave off a more unpleasant smell, which led him to deduce that they were made from a cheaper wax than the usual ones. Rudi Wilderhaus's patent-leather shoes creaked, his pointed shoulders tensed, and for a moment Hans imagined him as a two-branched candlestick. Only then did he hear Rudi's words, which he had stopped listening to a while ago: A little over two months, Rudi declared. Two months? said Frau Pietzine excitedly. They will go by in a flash! Rudi, beaming with satisfaction, seized Sophie's hand, which she gave up half-heartedly, and announced: We will spend our honeymoon in Paris. Oh, my dears, oh! Frau Pietzine declared, her excitement growing. Hans brushed against Álvaro's elbow. Álvaro whispered in his ear: *Coño*, that's original! Frau Pietzine perceived Hans's sardonic expression and raised her voice: My dear girl, men will never understand how much the ceremony means to us. Entering the church in white as the organ plays. Led down the aisle amid a cloud of incense. Watching out of the corner of our eye our friends and family gathered for this one occasion, smiling through their tears. Men cannot imagine how intensely we long for this moment from a young age. Yet years later, my dear, believe me, this ends up being the most important memory of our lives, the one we will recall in the minutest detail—the flower mosaics, the lighted candles, the children's choir singing, the priest's voice, the ring on the anxious finger, the holy blessing and most of all, isn't it so, Herr Gottlieb, the proud arm of our father. Hans tried to catch Sophie's eye in the mirror. She looked away, a vacant smile on her face.

Professor Mietter's echoing voice called him back to the discussion. What about you, Herr Hans? Do you agree with Pascal? Not knowing whether he was being sarcastic, Hans decided to reply: If that's what Pascal says, I have no objection. I believe Pascal also said almost no one knows how to live in the present. This applies equally to me, so please forgive my absent-mindedness. Sophie came to his aid: We were discussing whether or not Pascal was right in considering it dangerous to reveal the injustice of a law, given that people obey laws precisely because they believe them to be just. Ah, Hans thought on his feet, mmm, a profound idea, and a fallacious one perhaps, for many a just law has arisen as a result of people rebelling against unjust laws. Not necessarily, said Herr Levin, not necessarily. If you'll allow me, Álvaro asserted, I'd like to quote an idea of Pascal's which I find delightfully republican, "the power of kings is based on the folly of the people", I think this explains the question of law. God help us! Professor Mietter groaned, straightening his wig. Pascal deserves more than mere demagoguery!

Professor Mietter appeared hungry for debate, and exasperatingly dialectical. Imagine, Herr *Urquiho*, the professor said, only the other day I was looking through Tieck's translation of *Don Quixote*, which, to be honest, I don't think is much of an improvement on that of Bertuch (what? Hans countered. Bertuch even changed the title! Really? Álvaro was surprised, what did he call it? *Life and Miracles of the Wise Landowner Don Quixote*! replied Hans. Imagine how ghastly. And how mistaken, added Álvaro, because Alonso Quijano has no land to speak of, and he fails at almost every miracle he tries to create. The only miracle, Hans chuckled, was that Bertuch managed to teach himself Spanish by translating *Quixote*), perhaps, gentlemen, perhaps. In any event, you must admit it is amusing that a militant romantic such as Tieck should translate a book that

mocks all his own ideals. In my view, Soltau's is the most successful translation (too anachronistic, Hans disagreed), *alles klar*,
my compliments on being more meticulous than me, but going
back to what were we saying, while I was rereading *Quixote* the
other day, I thought: Is Don Quixote not a conservative at
the end of the day, a conservative in the best meaning of the
word? Why is he considered a revolutionary hero when what
he really wants is for history to stop and for the world to be
the way it was before, when what he really longs for is a return
to feudalism? (Ah, said Rudi, rousing himself and closing his
snuffbox, not for nothing did they call him a wise man!) In
contrast, gentlemen, I don't know what you think, but in my
opinion his most brilliant speech is the one about arms and
letters. (My dear professor, Hans laughed, I hope you won't
be disappointed to hear that we very nearly agree.) Heavens,
young man, what a welcome change! In this discourse, Don
Quixote refutes a separation, which unfortunately still holds
sway—physical strength on the one hand and intellectual prowess on the other. I would even venture to say that the thing has
worsened, because today the humanities themselves have been
divided into the arts on the one hand and the sciences on the
other, further evidence of the decline of the West. How can
feeling be separated from reason? And how can anyone deny
that a lack of physical fitness is an obstacle to understanding?
I for example read much better after doing physical exercise
(surely, Hans argued, Don Quixote wasn't referring to physical
so much as military strength), you are wrong, he was referring
to both, and moreover they are one and the same, war is as
necessary to the peace of nations as physical strength is to
the peace of the spirit. (You can't be serious, said Hans, wars
don't happen in order to bring peace, and physical strength
is seldom used to enhance the spirit. Well, Álvaro asserted, in
this instance the professor is right, in his speech about arms

and letters Don Quixote says as much, doesn't he, "the aim of weapons is to bring peace, and this peace signals the true end to war". That sounds like something the Holy Alliance would sign up to, Hans retorted.) Or Robespierre, Herr Hans, or Robespierre! (For your information, Professor, Hans replied angrily, I find Robespierre every bit as repellent as Metternich. What? exclaimed Álvaro, you can't be serious?) Gentlemen, you cannot imagine the pleasure it gives me to see the pair of you at odds. (My dear friends, Sophie intervened, please let's calm down, the whole purpose of these gatherings is to have different opinions, there would be no point to them otherwise. I beg you not to become agitated. As for this admirable speech, I'd like to remind you from my position of boundless ignorance that our hero from La Mancha, he who compares arms and letters, becomes a knight thanks to letters, not arms. And incidentally he does much more speaking than fighting, and wins arguments rather than battles. Elsa, my dear, would you bring the cakes?)

Ah, no, forgive me, the professor objected, when we speak of Calderón we speak of a poet rather than a playwright. It is enough to read the verse in his plays, which far outweighs the action. Furthermore, with all due respect, *lieber* Herr Gottlieb, for I am aware of your fondness for him, Calderón serves up his poetry with too liberal a sprinkling of holy allusions. Faith is one thing, religious zeal another. Good grief, Professor, declared Álvaro, how very Spanish you are this afternoon! As Spanish, retorted Professor Mietter, as the confusion to which I have just alluded. I shan't deny it, smiled Álvaro, I shan't deny it. My favourite of all the Catholic poets is Quevedo— he could be reactionary, but never overly pious. God! What sublime wickedness, if you'll pardon the expression. What exasperates me about Calderón are his religious plays, rich and poor as one in death, kings and their subjects joined in the afterlife! What would Sancho Panza have said of *The Great Theatre of the World*? My dear friend, the professor said solemnly, if anything makes us equal it is death. That is an inescapable truth, and a powerful idea for theatre—hearing what the dead would say if they knew what awaited them. Only by politicising philosophy can one question such a thing. Look, replied Álvaro, if life is a play, then Calderón forgot to describe what goes on behind the scenes. All that interest in the afterlife disguises what's going on here and now. Didn't Cervantes do the exact opposite in *Quixote*? He moved us by showing up everyday inequalities, injustices and corruption. By contrast the death of his character, what happens afterwards, is almost irrelevant. How can you say that, protested the professor, when Quijano recants on his deathbed! Quijano recants, said Álvaro, but not Don Quixote.

How fascinating, Frau Pietzine declared, I adore *Quixote*! I haven't read all of it, but some of the chapters are wonderful. And who do you prefer, as a Spanish reader, dear Monsieur *Urquiho*, Don Quixote or Sancho Panza? I hope I am not putting you on the spot! My dear lady, replied Álvaro, it is impossible to choose, the story needs them both, and neither character would make sense without the other. Don Quixote without Sancho would be an aimless old man who wouldn't last a week, and without him Sancho would be a plump little conformist without his curiosity, which is his greatest asset. I agree completely, commented Hans, except in one respect—the key to Don Quixote is that he has no aim: "He continued on his way"—do you remember?—"taking nothing save his beloved horse, believing that therein lay the true spirit of adventure". If there can be no knight without a squire bearer and vice versa, without Rocinante there would be no book. How fascinating, Frau Pietzine cooed, and what de-li-cious cakes! Sophie, my dear, my compliments to Petra. Ah, scoffed Rudi, a speck of snuff on the tip of his nose, a sensible remark at last!

After several days of running a temperature, coughing, and feeling nauseous, the organ grinder agreed to be seen by a doctor. Just so you know, *kof*, he had declared, I'm doing this to put yours and Franz's minds at rest. Hans gave him a scrub down for the occasion. His muscles sagged like pieces of string.

Doctor Müller arrived by coach. Hans waited for him at the end of Bridge Walk. The doctor alighted nervously and approached in little leaps, as though his feet were tied together at the ankles. Haven't we met before? asked the doctor. I don't think so, answered Hans, but who knows. How odd, said Doctor Müller, your face looks familiar. And even though I say so myself, I seldom forget a face. The opposite happens with me, said Hans, leading him through the pinewood, I'm constantly muddling people up.

They entered the cave. Without batting an eyelash, the doctor made straight for the organ grinder's straw pallet. He studied him with interest, nodded a couple of times, draped an enormous stethoscope round his neck (It's French, he explained), listened to the patient's chest and proclaimed: This old fellow is suffering from pemphigus. And what is that, doctor? Hans asked anxiously. Pemphigus, replied Müller, is a common ailment. Yes, but what is it? Hans insisted. Blisters, the doctor explained, skin blisters, in this case mostly on the hands. I imagine this fellow has worked a great deal with his hands, or so it seems to me at least. Quite so, said Hans, but what has that to do with his condition? You mean the fevers and the coughing? said Müller. Oh very little. Nothing, in fact. But as soon as I saw him I knew. Without a doubt. Pemphigus. But what about the other symptoms? Hans said impatiently. Doctor Müller digressed onto the subject of nervous ailments, boils, lingering colds, old age, bone disease. In brief, he concluded, nothing serious. Or perhaps it could be.

After examining the organ grinder more thoroughly, Doctor Müller prescribed aloe purgatives at eight-hour intervals. Six different chest ointments, one for every day except Sunday. Soothing morning enemas using a chicken's gut for easy application. Poultices in the afternoon, mustard plasters after supper. Pomeranian vinegar to be taken with each meal. Fenugreek poultices to aid digestion. Five grams of shredded lemon balm to reduce the nausea. Ten grams of decoction of horehound to ease minor coughing. Four small cups of juniper berry at the first sign of a convulsive coughing fit, followed by four more infusions of arnica and maidenhair fern to help bring up the phlegm once the fever has subsided. Mandrake root with crushed peppercorns as a tonic. Optional doses of snakeweed root if the patient's bowel movements become too frequent. And if he suffers any acute pains or thirst, a cocktail of lilies boiled in milk and schnapps. Finally, if all else should fail, vigorous rubbing with swallowwort leaves on the forehead and temples.

Isn't that rather a lot, Hans asked, jotting it all down. Doctor Müller bridled: Tell me, do you know the Reil method? Carus's experimental anatomy? Mesmer's animal fluids? Well, in that case, kindly place your trust in science. Hans sighed: I'm doing my best. Is there anything else? No, I don't think so, Doctor Müller replied wistfully, or perhaps there is, say a prayer or two for the patient, it's a small gesture and it can do no harm. I'm afraid I can't promise anything there, said Hans. I understand, the doctor smiled, don't worry, I'm not a very religious man myself. The thing is patients sometimes feel more relief from prayer than from the treatment.

The old man appeared to be sound asleep. Doctor Müller folded his French stethoscope and straightened up brusquely. Franz let out two barks. Well, said Müller, giving Franz a wide berth, mission accomplished, wouldn't you say? I'll be on my way, that is ... How much? asked Hans. For you, the doctor replied, five florins. The organ grinder opened one glassy eye, and, to their surprise, spoke up: Hans—*kof!*—don't give him a pfennig more than three thalers, do you hear!

Lately, each time Sophie went out she noticed people staring at her. Scrutinising her gestures. Comparing what they saw with what they had heard. Staring at her waist, for example. Gazing intently at her dress and her stomach, examining her from the side just in case. To begin with she wasn't sure. She found it hard to distinguish between outside speculation and her inner fears, between what others thought and her own doubts, and she tried to convince herself it wasn't true. Until one morning, a distant acquaintance had greeted her in a peculiar way; after saying good morning, she had narrowed her heavily made-up eyes and said: My dear, you look, how can I put it, as healthy as a horse, don't you agree? Fuller, more radiant, of course now-adays, as you know, they make women's clothes in such a way …

Back home, alarmed, Sophie had hurriedly weighed herself on the scales. She discovered she had not only gained no weight but had lost several pounds since the summer.

One afternoon after lunch, Elsa and Sophie went out under the pretext of making a few final purchases to complete her trousseau. At the end of Old Cauldron Street they bumped into Frau Pietzine. Frau Pietzine was friendly, although she wore a concerned expression that made Sophie feel ill at ease. Before saying goodbye she beckoned to Sophie with a silken finger. Elsa took two steps back and began watching the passing coaches.

All I ask is that you reflect on it, whispered Frau Pietzine, you wouldn't want to throw away something so full of promise, such a privileged future for a foolish passion. And don't look at me like that, I beg you, I am your friend. Perhaps you don't consider me a friend, but I am, and my advice as a friend is to try not to lose your head. My dear lady, Sophie replied coldly, you sound like your Father confessor. That's unfair of you! Frau Pietzine replied with unusual insistence, let us be frank for once, a difficult thing in this damnable city. Yes, damnable, and I know perfectly well you feel the same. I sympathise, my dear friend, a girl like you! With your temperament! How could I not sympathise? I'm not talking of sin, but of time—we lose our time over love, do you know why? Because we invest everything we have in it, all that it has taken half a lifetime to build up, in exchange for a fleeting reward. But after this passion has died we have to go on living—do you understand?—we have to go on living! In the end, all a woman has left are the things she sometimes rejects—family, friends, neighbours. Nothing else lasts. Remember that Sophie, we aren't young for ever. Everyone knows this, but we prefer not to think about it until it is too late. When we are young and happy we don't want to accept that our happiness is a product of youth and not of the rash decisions we take. But, mark my words, the day will dawn when you realise you have become old. And there is nothing you can do. And what you possess that day will be all that you possess until the end of your days. I shan't hold you up any longer, dear. Good afternoon.

Stretched out next to Hans, her brow wrinkled, a nipple poking above the blanket, Sophie broke the silence. Do you know what? she said. I bumped into Frau Pietzine on my way here, and she said some terrible things to me. The wretched woman is a busybody, replied Hans, don't pay her any attention. I shouldn't pay attention to most people, said Sophie, but it isn't so easy. We can't live as if no one else existed, Hans. Besides, I think Frau Pietzine meant well, I had the feeling she was trying to help me. She was misguided, but she wanted to help me. Yes, of course, he sighed, everyone wants to help you decide about your life, above all the Wilderhaus family with their son to the fore!

Sophie's belly, against which Hans had his ear pressed,

suddenly clenched. He heard her reply: How dare you criti-
cise someone who goes on loving me despite all the rumours?
You're always talking about leaving, and yet you speak of the
Wandernburgers as if they concerned you. Make up your mind!
Are you here or aren't you? I'm not criticising Rudi, said Hans,
defending himself, I'm worried about you. You know perfectly
well this marriage isn't what a woman like you needs. How do
you know? she said angrily. Or are you also going to tell me
what I ought to do? Who told you what I need? You did! He
shouted, you told me! Here in this room, in a thousand different
ways! Hans, she sighed, I went as far as to postpone my wedding for you. Don't talk to me as though I didn't know my own
feelings. Did you do it for me? he asked. Or was it for yourself,
for your own happiness?

Sophie did not answer. There was a pause. Suddenly Hans
heard himself say: Come with me to Dessau. What? she sat
up. You heard me, come with me, he repeated, I'm begging
you. But my love, said Sophie, I can't just leave. You mean
I'm not a good enough reason for you to leave, he said. I can't
understand why you expect so much of your lover and so little
of your husband. That's different, she said. I have no expectations of Rudi, but I have them of you, do you see? That's why
I'm asking you to do something, Hans, I'm asking you to stay.
I'm terrified you might leave tomorrow. What terrifies you is
not having the courage, he murmured. And what about you?
Sophie shouted, are you incredibly free or an incredible coward? What right have you to preach to me? Be a woman for
a moment, just for one moment, and you'll see how different
courage looks from here, you stupid man!

A folded piece of paper, papyrus-coloured rather than mauve,
written in haste. Hans read:

Dear heart—this is a message of possibilities, for I am no longer sure of anything. Will I write to you again? Will you write to me? Will we see one another? Will we stop seeing one another? Will I think about what I write? Or will I think as I write?

Until a moment ago, I wanted our next meeting, if we are to meet again, to be up to you, I wanted you to ask to see me after these long and lonely days. The reason for this, if indeed I was capable of reasoning, was that if I had asked, you would have come at my behest (you would have, wouldn't you?) and perhaps contrary to your misgivings, to our misgivings.

Yet it turns out this perfect reasoning has failed. Quite simply because between yesterday and today I realised that my desire to touch you, even if only for an hour, is stronger than everything else. To have you in the way that I want, however inappropriate or irresponsible. And I realised that if I kept my calm these past few days it was because deep down I believed you would come after me, that I wouldn't need to chase you. It wounds my pride to admit it. And yet the proudest part of us is our intelligence and mine was insulted by keeping up this charade. It is not so much my feelings that have imposed themselves (my feelings are in turmoil) but the facts. Naive creature, how could I have been so sure of myself? Why didn't I realise sooner that my treasured pride was also a token of my love for you? And how could I have assumed you would want to stay on here, unreservedly? I am comforted by the thought that my obstinacy in doing so was equal to yours when you assumed that, sooner or later, I would agree to follow you wherever you went.

Although I still believe in the intensity of things, in their fleetingness, it is only now, as the afternoon fades, that I have begun to assimilate the idea that you might be leaving. It isn't that now I know (I have always known) but that I feel it. And the idea feels unbearable. There is nothing more unbearable than experiencing in the flesh the suffering you have gone over a thousand times in your head. Perhaps tomorrow I will receive a message similar to this, a few lines asking me to go and see you. Or perhaps you will change you mind after reading this. Or perhaps neither of these things will happen, and the days will simply go by. Or (I tremble at the thought) perhaps when you read these words you will already be somewhere else. It is possible. As I said, this is a letter of possibilities.

I have nothing more to say. Or I have many more things to say, but in another place, at another time. If love is a possibility, I kiss you here or there, now or on another day.

Mistress of myself all of a sudden, that is to say yours

S

At noon the following day, a brief, lightly perfumed mauve note arrived, Hans read:

Your reply cheered me up. Reading it was like a sip of water in the middle of a desert. I also forgive you. We'll see each other at the inn from three o'clock until four-thirty. Not today. Better tomorrow, because the salon is the following day and it will be easier for me to find some excuse to go out on an errand. You are a naughty man. I shall reward you appropriately.—S

Sophie bit the air, ensconced on top of him, legs apart. More than making love, she was treading grapes. Each time her hips collided with Hans's stomach, she would propel herself higher in order to crash down with more force. Underneath the storm, at once overwhelmed and moved, Hans was scarcely able to resist the current dragging him to somewhere that was beyond them both, away from there, inside himself.

The fire in the hearth crackled and sparked. For a while Hans had been staring intently into the embers. Sophie was still, she had sucked up all of him. Hans looked away from the fire, turned his head and gazed at her. Is anything the matter, my love? he asked. No, she replied, I don't know whether I had an orgasm or a premonition.

Elsa had taken off all her clothes, Álvaro had not. Now he was fastening his belt, tucking his shirt into his breeches. She hurriedly finished dressing and tidied her hair. Álvaro had remained in a sluggish daze—his movements were dulled, even his speech. In contrast, Elsa seemed distracted, as though on the point of saying something. It made him uneasy to see her in this state after they made love, it cast a cloud over his satisfaction. Moreover he was aware that at these times she appeared more demanding about certain things and he was more obliging.

Listen, said Elsa, I'm going to try to speak plainly to you (Álvaro sighed, sat up straight on the sofa, made it clear he was paying attention), you claim, and I believe you, that before you went into business you were on the side of the working man (I was and still am, Álvaro clarified), yes, but you have money now (my fortunes have changed, not my ideals, he declared), well, whatever the case, you understand that better than I, but listen. In spite of what you say, I think you'd be a little ashamed if people saw us together. (What is this nonsense you are spouting?) Exactly what you are hearing, my precious. Out here in your country house we are equals, but back in the city I am what I am, and you are what you are. (Sorry, but you insult me. Have you still not realised that it's my widowhood that troubles me, not our social positions? That's what I am, a widower, is it so hard for you to grasp?) Oh Álvaro, of course not, but I don't think the present can ever offend the past. Isn't it time you forgot the past? I don't mean her, but her death? (I need more time, Elsa.) We have time, my love, but not an eternity! (I know, I know.) When will you let me go to England with you, for instance? (Soon, soon.) Do you really mean soon? (You know I do, my darling.) How am I to know! (*Do you speak English enough, princess?*) You lost me after the word *English*, but I am making headway. (*Nobody would deny it, my dear.*) Precisely, *nobody would* whatever it was you said, so, when are you taking me to England? (Soon, soon ...)

It's as if I'd been exiled twice, Álvaro said, staring into his tankard, first when I arrived here and then when I stayed on. That's how I feel, Hans, what more can I say? *Prost! Y salud.*

According to what Álvaro had just discovered, the Wandernburg authorities were trying to persuade Herr Gelding and his associates to consider changing their textile wholesaler. Herr Gelding had dismissed the idea, for the time being. Not out of loyalty to Álvaro, but because so long as their balance sheets continued to be extremely satisfactory, he saw no reason to alter their business arrangement. Apparently, an increasing number of voices within the town hall were, more or less overtly, beginning to make suggestions to anyone related to the textile mill. The more enthusiastic councillors referred to the initiative as "strategic action against ideological incompatibilities". Mayor Ratztrinker called it the "restoration of managerial cordiality". Herr Gelding preferred to call it "the boys getting in a strop".

Why don't you go back to London? asked Hans, clinking tankards with Álvaro. This is my home, replied Álvaro, and besides, I refuse to leave anywhere again because someone wishes to throw me out. But what if you went of your own accord, said Hans, wouldn't you be better off over there? Probably, Álvaro sighed, who doesn't want to live in London? The problem is this city, this damned city, I can't explain. One day I'll clear off.

It was past midnight. The chairs were resting upside down on the tables. At one half of the bar, a few locals drank up while a waiter wiped down the other half with a soiled cloth. Look at the paintings of the Congress of Vienna and what do you see? The same old thing! A group of stout gentlemen determining Europe's fate! Bureaucratic buffoons convening in order to stuff themselves silly and fix a date for the next meeting! A legion of noblemen admiring each other's rings while they sign in the name of their people! Crossing their flabby legs, buffing their shoes on the backs of their calves, and examining their neighbours' bellies as they belch discreetly! Hey, Hans said, pealing with laughter, you're worse than Goya. Amen! belched Álvaro.

Mark my words, said Álvaro, stumbling through the tavern door, something's going to happen here, it has to happen. Here wh-where? Hans stammered. You mean in the tavern? No, of course not! replied Álvaro. Here in Europe! Look out for the door, Hans said, grabbing his arm. Look out, Europe! Álvaro shouted, charging into the street. Hey, I'm fa-falling, said Hans. Europe could fall! She should hold on, *cojones*! cried Álvaro. Co-come on, Hans gasped, it's this way, Álvaro, you're tw-twisting my arm. Where are you going? said Álvaro, confused. Let's go and see the old man, Hans suggested. Now? said Álvaro, isn't it a bit far? N-nonsense, replied Hans, places are neither near nor far, it's all re-relative, if we st-start walking now we'll be there in no time, come on, follow me, what are you doing? Don't sit down, give me your arm, ge-get up.

Álvaro didn't reply. His face was buried in his hands, his shoulders were rising and falling.

All Souls' Day began on a harsh note, with gusts of wind that bent the branches of the trees as if to give them a fright. The sky was filled with leaden clouds. A smell of snow permeated the air. The cobbles were slippery underfoot, sprinkled with some murky substance. The horses whinnied more loudly than usual. The market square had filled up with shadows that passed one another in silence. At the top of the tower, the clock hands seemed weighed down by a pulley. The weathervane creaked erratically. The parishioners who had just left afternoon Mass walked along, backs to the square, heads lowered.

That afternoon Hans had gone out for a stroll, less for pleasure than because he felt restless—he had been trying to concentrate for hours, unable to translate a single sentence. His brain was a dicebox in which images, fears and the roots of words were being jiggled about. He was fretting over the difficulty of the text, the situation with Sophie and the organ grinder's health. He followed the stream of people climbing the Hill of Sighs until he found himself opposite the railings of Wandernburg Cemetery—a place he had never visited. He contemplated the sea of black headscarves, the long flowing coats, the lowered veils, the felt hats pulled down, the dark armbands, the shoes submerged in their own blackness and the rebellious contrast of floral offerings. Where did all these people come from? Why were Wandernburg's streets even more crowded on All Souls' Day than they were in spring?

At the entrance, a shabby beggar sat slumped against the wall. As they passed, the visitors stretched out their arms and dropped a few coins into his lap before hurrying on. This was the only day in the year when the beggar didn't need to speak to or look at his benefactors. He simply accepted their charity, eyelids half-closed, almost with indifference. Mourners are generous, reflected Hans—they hope to buy a little more time. Hans began rummaging through his pockets in front of the bundle of rags. It opened its eyes and grunted: How's the patient? Who, me? Hans started, I'm in perfect health, thank you, how about you? No, the beggar replied shaking his head irritated, not you, the organ grinder, is he any better? Ah, Hans said, surprised, well, sort of. When you see him, the beggar said, tell him his friend Olaf is waiting for him, don't forget, will you? Olaf from the square. Now move along, please, you're getting in the way of my customers.

Hans noticed that no one, absolutely no one in the whole of Wandernburg Cemetery allowed a hint of a smile to cross their faces, not even when they greeted one another. He found such consensus incredible. In a place like that, wasn't it as reasonable to weep or to laugh aloud out of pure astonishment, to laugh at the absurdity, the miracle of being alive? But those gathered there acted as if they were standing in front of mirrors rather than tombstones. Veils raised, the widows displayed their sorrow and practised the various overtures to falling into a faint. The men vigorously shook their umbrellas, flexed their shoulders, clenched their jaws. Fascinated by this spectacle, the children copied their parents as closely as they could. Each time a sob rang out, another louder one next to it ensued. Suddenly, amid the figures dressed in black, Hans made out Frau Pietzine's puffy, painted face. Seeing her entranced, busy murmuring her laments and dabbing her eyes beneath her veil, he did not dare disturb her, and walked on by.

Farther along the path, he stumbled on a strange sight—on an isolated knoll a man was dancing silently, eyes closed, around a grave bedecked with chrysanthemums. The dance was serene, old-fashioned. The painful memories etched onto the man's face were overlaid with an expression of profound gratitude. Hans walked away thinking his grief was perhaps the most genuine of all those he had witnessed.

Near the exit, as he was reading some of the names and dates on the tombstones, Hans almost tripped and fell onto a grave whose edges were concealed by weeds. A voice behind him cried out as if from nowhere: "Hey, careful with my lads." It was the gravedigger. Hans wheeled round and gazed at him curiously. He was surprised by his youth (why do we imagine gravediggers to be old?) and relative cheerfulness. A lot of work? Hans said, just for something to say. Don't you believe it, replied the gravedigger, it's the living that give us all the work. My lads—as I like to call them on account of it makes me more attached to them, see?—they don't give me much trouble, ha, ha! Forgive me for asking, said Hans. (No need to apologise, the gravedigger declared, am I that scary looking?) Of course, sorry, I mean, this is my first visit to the cemetery and I wondered whether many people come on normal days. Many, you say? the gravedigger laughed. No one comes! No one at all! People only come here once a year, on All Souls' Day. Well, said Hans, clapping him on the back (an amazingly firm back, hard as wood), I must be going, it's been a pleasure, good luck. Thanks, likewise, replied the gravedigger, if you ever need me you know where to find me. I hope I shan't be needing you, said Hans, no offence. It's only a question of time, ha, ha! The gravedigger raised his arm and waved goodbye.

The first thing Hans glimpsed through the railings was not Mayor Ratztrinker's exaggeratedly large hat, nor his fine silk socks, nor his velvet frock coat, it was his beak-like nose as he climbed out of his carriage. While the mayor's whiskers ventured into the open air, a servant folded back the hood. No sooner had His Excellency's foot touched the ground than a second servant handed him a wreath; the mayor clasped onto it as he would a funereal life belt. The cortège advanced slowly, accepting peoples' greetings. When they walked past Olaf, Mayor Ratztrinker gave one of the servants a sidelong glance, at which the servant showered the beggar with coins. Good afternoon, Your Excellency, Hans murmured as he passed him on the way out. The mayor stopped, handed the wreath to a servant, and doffed his hat, pausing a moment before returning the greeting. This struck Hans as suspicious. They exchanged pleasantries, remarked on the worsening weather, and before saying goodbye Mayor Ratztrinker took a step forward. He looked Hans up and down, gestured to his beret and said nonchalantly: Jacobins aren't welcome in Wandernburg. Neither are adulterers. Imagine what we think of Jacobin adulterers? The police, quite naturally, are concerned. Good afternoon.

He arrived at the cave as night fell. The organ grinder was

talking to Lamberg, who had brought him some supper. Hans sat down on a rock and patted Franz's side. You've arrived, *kof*, just in time, I was telling Lamberg about my dream last night. (And how are you feeling? asked Hans.) Me?—*kof*—fine, just fine, you sound like a mother! But listen, I dreamt, *kof*, I was alone in the woods and I was very cold, like I hadn't a stitch on, and then I began, *kof*, to shiver, and the more I shivered the more I sweated—funny, isn't it?—only instead of droplets, *kof*, instead of droplets of sweat, my body gave off sounds, you know? Like notes, and the breeze carried them through the woods, *kof*, and they started to sound familiar, and I went on shivering and giving off sounds until, *kof*, I began to recognise the tune coming from my body, and at that moment I woke up (because of the dream? asked Lamberg), no, no, *kof*, because I was hungry!

Hans burst out laughing. Then he grew very serious. The organ grinder stretched out his bony arm, beckoning him to come near, and asked cheerily: How is Olaf?

No, child, no, Father Pigherzog whispered into her ear as the bell in the round tower rattled out the midday chimes with a clang like coins dropping into the collection plate, calm yourself, child, in spite of everything it is best you tell no one, *nemo infirmitatis animi immunis*, I sympathise, we spoke about this the other day, do you remember? Yet no matter how great your suffering only you can free yourself from it, that is what makes us worthy of the Lord, the power to transform evil into good, and to forgive, of course not, my child, I am not saying the Lord wishes you to suffer so much, but that He wants you to love once your suffering is over, so that your reward will be much greater. That is why, my child, you must tell no one about what happened to you.

At the foot of the other tower, the pointed one, Frau Levin and

Sophie were moving their lips, nodding their heads, shrugging their shoulders, warding off the cold wind and clutching their hats. A few yards away, Mayor Ratztrinker and Herr Gottlieb removed their hats, although in the gloomy afternoon daylight it might, from a distance, have seemed as if they were doing the opposite—taking off the heads of their respective hats. After the farewells, His Excellency's last words hung thickly in the air, climbed the cracks in the tower, scaled the damp steps of autumn, edged between the flat clouds, dissolved little by little: "… and I'll say it again, Fräulein, you look positively radiant, there's nothing like a wedding to enhance a woman's beauty!"

Although it had lasted a matter of seconds, Frau Levin felt positively exalted by the mayor's greeting. The Gottliebs' presence had no doubt been a determining factor. Even so, this was the first time the mayor had deigned to address her, to utter her name. To acknowledge her as a respectable citizen and to accept her, finally, as a good Christian. For this reason, she was more determined than ever to do what she was about to do. What a neighbour of hers, who was a policeman, had been urging her to do for some time. Frau Levin waited for a group of carriages to pass before crossing Archway. She must hurry. In an hour's time she had to serve her husband lunch; he continued stubbornly to refuse to attend Mass, and she had been forced to lie to him in order to be able to go home later. Lying to her husband terrified her—she always had the impression he knew. But besides fear, that morning she felt the excitement of being useful, of really being useful to the authorities. Frau Levin glanced behind her, from side to side, making sure no one was watching her. She quickened her pace. She walked towards Spur Street. She was more determined now than ever.

Aha, the Chief Superintendent's teeth clacked. Are you taking note, sergeant? Carry on.

The words began to spill from Frau Levin's lips. She was

scarcely able to pause, to emerge from her trance when the Chief Superintendent rearranged his denture ready to pose another question. Some questions were easy to answer: Herr Hans's profession, Herr Hans's political leanings, Herr Hans's friends, arrival of books at Herr Hans's lodgings, Herr Hans's everyday habits, Herr Hans's dubious patriotism. Others were a little more tricky or ambiguous. And yet Frau Levin answered them without hesitation, supplying a wealth of detail, embellishing what she knew and inventing what she did not. After all she wasn't doing this only for herself—although he didn't know it, she was also doing it for the sake of her husband. Perhaps one day His Excellency the mayor would greet him, too.

The Chief Superintendent nodded, clacked his teeth, and made sure his officer was keeping pace in his note-taking with the hastily delivered statement. From time to time he raised his hand, made the Jewish bitch shut up and waited for a few moments before moving on to the next question.

When he had gathered more than enough information, the Superintendent raised both hands, and, without looking at the Jewess, said: Thank you for coming.

Herr Gottlieb stood at his desk finishing the inventory of his daughter's trousseau—family jewels, imported fans, kid gloves, fine-quality brushes, bottles of perfume, expensive sponges, ornate sweet dishes. As her father paused between items, Sophie would say "Yes" or "It's here", and he would murmur, "Correct" and resume going through the list.

As he closed the inventory book, Herr Gottlieb's face grew suddenly solemn. He placed his smoking pipe on the table, tugged on his waistcoat and stood to attention like a general about to embark on an important mission. He offered his daughter his hand, and led her along the chilly corridor. If Sophie were not mistaken they were going to her father's bedchamber—a room she had not set foot in for years.

A strip of light from the window reached across the room to the opposite wall—the rest was darkness. Herr Gottlieb walked slowly over to the vast mahogany wardrobe, pausing after each step. He turned the key twice, opened the heavy door and whispered his daughter's name three times. Then he thrust his arms into the wardrobe's depths and pulled out a trailing luminescence. Sophie recognised her deceased mother's wedding gown. It was a strangely ethereal garment. It appeared to be made of light. She studied the gown as her father handed it to her—the smooth feel of the satin, the tiny band of organdy around the waist, the airy netting on the skirt. Placing the dress in his daughter's arms as one passing an invisible ballerina, Herr Gottlieb said: This was your mother's favourite shade of white, egg white, the purest white of all, that of innocent hearts. If only she were here to help us! My child, my child, will you make me a grandfather soon? It pains me that you barely knew your own grandparents. I don't wish the same on my grandchildren. But go, child, try it on. I need to see how the dress suits you.

A quarter of an hour later, Sophie reappeared in her father's bedchamber wearing the gown. As soon as she had stepped into it she knew it would fit her. The three pearl buttons were perhaps a little tight at the back. The gold ribbon on the neckline was perhaps a little lower than it should be. And yet it was undoubtedly her size. Elsa had helped her into the old-fashioned corset that sculpted her waist, pushed up her bust, rounding off her subtle décolletage. She had donned a pair of embroidered silk stockings and wore satin-lined slippers adorned with ribbons. Before stepping out into the corridor, she had studied her reflection in the glass and had felt a strange tingling sensation, like a needle running down her spine.

A quarter of an hour later, when Sophie reappeared in her

father's bedchamber wearing the gown, Herr Gottlieb said nothing. He said nothing at first and looked at her, he looked through her, squinting the way short-sighted people do, focusing like those who are sightless. He stood motionless, his mind elsewhere, until abruptly he opened his eyes, dilated his pupils, parted his lips and said at last: It is perfect, my love, perfect.

Sophie hadn't heard her father call her *my love* for a long time, not since she was a child.

Then Herr Gottlieb said: Come here, my child, my precious, come closer, my love.

Sophie walked over to her father. She stopped two steps away from him. She stood motionless and let him embrace her.

You have your mother's shoulders, her father said.

Sophie felt slightly faint. The room was airless. The wedding gown was pressing her stomach. As were her father's arms.

You have your mother's waist, her father said.

The whole length of the white dress was reflected in the wardrobe mirror.

And you have your mother's skin, her father said.

The airlessness, the gown, the mirror.

As though emerging from a well, Sophie pushed herself away with her arms.

But I'm not like my mother, she said.

Herr Gottlieb's lips disappeared behind his whiskers. His face fell. His pupils contracted.

How young you are, child, he said, how terribly young (don't say that, Father, Sophie replied, don't talk as though you were already old), oh, but I am (no, Father, she insisted), you see, it isn't just about age, my child, it is also about loss, you have so much youth left in you because—how can I put this?—you still have the feeling of being whole, the unmistakable belief that this wholeness will never end. When you lose that, whatever age you are, you are old, do you understand? And I love you so very much.

Shortly afterwards Rudi's servants knocked at the door. His berlin was waiting in Stag Street.

Is something the matter, my dear? Rudi asked, removing a speck of snuff from his velvet frock coat with one finger. No, replied Sophie, rousing herself, nothing, why do you ask? For no particular reason, Rudi said, giving off a whiff of lemon scent, or perhaps because I've spent ages trying to decide on the wedding menu with you and you've hardly said a word. Oh, she said, you know I'm not very bothered about that kind of thing, honestly, you decide. Not very bothered, he stipulated, or not bothered in the slightest? Well, she retorted, is there a difference? Driver! shouted Rudi, rapping three times on the roof. Stop here!

Don't stop, she cried, or rather she thought. But Hans hesitated, as though he'd just remembered something. Something that removed him from the room, and, at the same time, allowed him to see it vividly. They were both there. He could see himself. She, too.

Lying across the bed, he on his side, legs hooked under hers, both were assailed by the same vision, the exact same one, without knowing it. They saw two L-shaped torsos submerged in water, as though they had discovered themselves fornicating with their own reflection, struggling to possess it and to be separate from it. As though, thrusting against each other, neither knew where one ended and the other began, and they were no longer sure if they were two or one. As though neither could decipher the other by contemplating him or her, by contemplating each other as they gave themselves to one another. When the frisson came and they cried out as one, the image disappeared. The water went still. The mirror dissolved. Their bodies grew cold.

After leaving the mansion for his daily coach ride, Rudi saw him, on the right-hand side of the pavement, a few yards from where King's Parade meets Border Street, strolling along. He saw him strolling along in his rabble-rouser's beret, his common frock coat, his sloppy cravat, walking with that irritatingly absent-minded yet insolent gait of his, partly nonchalant, partly self-conscious, much like his free-flowing hair, as though while behaving as he pleased he always knew he was being watched. Rudi saw him through the window, he felt his gorge rise and took a deep breath in an attempt to calm himself a little. He gave three short raps on the roof of the carriage, his body rocking with the rhythm of the braking vehicle, slid his buttocks along the length of velvet. He waited for the driver to open the coach door, gracefully thrust one hip forward and let his boot fall onto the folding steps. He descended them with a faint creak of patent leather, his bulky frame leaning back in order to compensate for the tilt of the carriage, and stepped onto the pavement without muddying his boots. He approached Hans from behind, marching in step with him for a few paces, took one long stride forward. He dug his pointed heel in the ground, steadied himself, and nimbly brought his ankles together. He stretched a gloved hand towards Hans, and prodded him on the shoulder. And when Hans wheeled round, without uttering a word, he gave him a resounding punch in the face.

Hans crumpled like a rag doll and lay sprawled over the pavement. He tried to get up. Rudi reached down, helped him to his feet and punched him again. Twice. Once with each fist. A fist for each cheek. Hans crashed to the ground once more. During this second fall, amid the shooting pain and the spray of blood from his face, he realised what was going on. As he lay on the ground he received six or seven swift, precise patent-leather kicks. He made no attempt to defend himself. It would have been futile in any case. Amid the hail of blows, he noticed Rudi wasn't trying to break his bones—he was aiming at the soft parts, mainly his stomach, avoiding his ribs. The kicking was astonishingly forceful yet measured, as though he were drumming a signal. Hans's response to the punishment was to try not to choke or to cry out. When the battering was over, besides a feeling of panic, a sour taste on his tongue and a ring of fire in his head, Hans experienced a humiliating pang of sympathy.

Somewhat agitated, Rudi examined his gloves to make sure they weren't soiled. He congratulated himself on having avoided Hans's nose and mouth—such blows turn the defeated opponent into a blatant victim, besides being unnecessarily messy. He steadied his hands, adjusted his sleeves so that they were even, raised his chin to its normal height. He realised he was missing his buckle hat, stooped to pick it up from the floor bending at the waist, blew on it gingerly. He placed it on his head, turned round, walked back to his carriage. He caught sight of a mounted policeman, waited for him to approach, signalled to his driver.

The Chief Superintendent looked at him with languid curiosity, as though the sight of Hans's wounds had woken him from a nap. His jaw dropped and his lips formed into something resembling a smile. Before he began to speak, his teeth clacked, emitting a sound of toppling dominos. The policeman who had arrested Hans stood in the doorway gazing at the ceiling. On it he counted six cracks, four candle stubs and three spiders spinning.

You, here again? clacked the Chief Superintendent. That was quick, you like a bit of fun.

The Chief Superintendent questioned him for half-an-hour. Hans went from being addressed politely as *"you"* to being called *"foreigner"*. When he mentioned Rudi, Hans was told no charges would be pressed because he had been defending his honour. He, on the other hand, would remain in custody for a few hours in order to make a statement about the incident and about his relationship to the offended party. The offended party? Hans said in astonishment. The Chief Superintendent, realising he was refusing to collaborate, ordered the foreigner to be thrown into the cells for the night in order to help him to collect his thoughts.

The cell itself was innocuous—it was more ugly than intimidating. A simple square plunged into darkness. It was no filthier than the organ grinder's den. It was, of course, cold. And above all damp, as if the walls had been smeared with a mixture of steam and urine. The pallet wasn't the worst he'd slept on either, although to be on the safe side, Hans decided to remove the mattress. The jailer guarding his cell was given to belching and had a queer sense of humour. He didn't seem concerned with the arrests or what went on in the police station. He only opened and closed the cell door. All the rest, he affirmed, was none of his business, nor did they pay him enough for him to worry about it. When Hans asked whether he might use the bucket as a seat, he replied shrugging his shoulders: Masturbate into it if you want. Then he added: That's what most people use it for. Hans let go of the bucket instantaneously and crouched as best he could.

To begin with Hans was surprised that the jailer insisted on bringing him supper. He even found his cruel jokes amusing. (If a man's to be condemned to death, he had said, it might as well be on a full stomach.) Hans wolfed down the salted bread, the slice of bacon and the sausage. Afterwards, he was surprised when the man diligently offered him a second loaf. He quickly understood the reason for all this generosity—the jailer had been ordered not to give him any water. Don't take this personally, he said, and don't complain, it could be worse. Did you really think we'd tie you up? Beat you? Hang you upside down by your feet? Don't be a fool. We save our strength here. Go thirsty for a day. Or sign the declaration and leave.

At midnight a bailiff woke him up tapping on the bars with a truncheon. In between gulps of water, which he made a point of spilling on purpose, the bailiff tried to persuade Hans to sign a declaration admitting to provocation and disturbing the peace in exchange for his immediate release. Each time Hans refused, the bailiff turned to the jailer and exclaimed: "Will you listen to that?"; "Well I never!"; "What's to be done?" To which the jailer replied: "They say he studied at Jena"; "A real scholar", and other such remarks. If Hans invoked justice or demanded a lawyer, the bailiff would guffaw: "A lawyer!" and the jailer would add: "Whatever next!"

Before leaving, annoyed at the stubbornness of the prisoner (who, deep down, was beginning to lose his nerve), the bailiff said: The law, you talk to me about justice? Let me remind you how justice works. Fritz Reuter spent two years in prison for waving a black, red and yellow flag. Arnold Ruge was sentenced to fifteen years on suspicion of belonging to subversive organisations. Several of your comrades took their own lives in prison. Others ask to do hard labour just so they can drink water or see the sun. In the Harz region mutilation is legal. It isn't the only place. And for your information, in this principality, the death penalty can be carried out with an axe. Peasants who steal are beheaded. People pay eight groats to watch. They're right. Some things are educational. Have I made myself understood? There's justice for you. Real justice, you son of a bitch. Have a good night.

The next morning, when he went to wake him, the jailer found Hans with his eyes wide open. A viscous light poured through the bars, like oily gravy. A very young sergeant took him to the Chief Superintendent, who hadn't changed his clothes, or was wearing similar ones. Have you calmed down, foreigner? the Chief Superintendent greeted him. Have you had time to think things over? Are you ready to sign? Nervous, battling with the fears that assailed him, Hans refused once more to sign the statement. The Chief Superintendent ordered him to be locked up again. Back in his cell, Hans sobbed in silence. Moments later, the jailer opened the bars and he was a free man. Hans left the police station bewildered. Álvaro was waiting for him on the corner of Spur Street. About time! he said. I was getting anxious. How did you persuade them to let me go? asked Hans. Simple, replied Álvaro, I paid your bail. Oh, said Hans, surprised, I had bail? It wasn't very much, said Álvaro, didn't they tell you? Three guesses! Hans sighed. Never mind, what did they say? I came here first thing, explained Álvaro, and they told me I had to wait because you were signing a statement.

They made their way dolefully down Potter's Lane, zigzagging towards Café Europa. Well, Álvaro said, patting him on the back, how do you feel? Fresh as a rose, *hombre*! declared Hans. They only wanted to frighten me. And did they succeed? Álvaro grinned. They did rather, replied Hans.

After his second coffee, Hans's sleepiness gave way to the keen alertness that overcomes anyone who hasn't slept all night. He told his friend about the beating on King's Parade, the Chief Superintendent's interrogation, his detention in the cell, what the bailiff had said. Does it hurt? Álvaro asked, pointing to his puffy cheek and red nose. Hans was about to reply when he caught sight of one of the billiard players on the tables at the back—over the sound of colliding balls, Rudi was smiling disdainfully at him. Look who's here, Hans whispered, glancing away and realising he did so with fear. Herr Imbecile, growled Álvaro, I'm going to tell him I'll be waiting for him at eight o'clock on the bridge, I'll give him honour! Don't play the hero, said Hans, have a herbal tea instead. Álvaro insisted: I'm going to challenge him, I tell you, and you ... Let go of my arm! Let go! Hans managed to calm his friend down. It wasn't very difficult—the last thing Álvaro needed was a feud with the Wilderhaus family. When they stood up to go, the waiter informed them Herr Wilderhaus had paid their bill.

As soon as Hans walked in, the innkeeper leapt with

unaccustomed agility from behind the reception desk. It's Thursday already! he said with a look of consternation. Clasping his belly as though he were lifting up a sack of potatoes, he added: A couple of policemen went up to your room this morning. (What? Hans said, alarmed. And you didn't stop them?) Listen, they had bayonets! I tried my best, but they insisted on searching your belongings (damn! Hans cried, raising his hands to his head), but I managed to ask Lisa to hide your trunk in number five, which is empty. No, there's no need to thank me, sir. You've always paid. And a guest is a guest.

Hans pelted up the stairs. On one of the landings he bumped into Thomas, who crouched like a cat, slipped between his legs, tugged at his breeches and took off down the stairs.

He walked into his room and glanced about. The chairs were upturned, the mattress half on the floor, his valise open and his clothes strewn everywhere, the bathtub had been moved, the papers on his desk rifled through, the logs pulled from the fire. He searched everything carefully, and discovered the policemen had taken nothing of any importance except for some money he had hidden in a sock inside his suitcase. The only real casualty was the watercolour, which he picked up off the floor, its mirror smashed to pieces. He went out into the corridor, made sure no one was there and slipped into the adjoining room—he was relieved to find his trunk under the bed behind some brooms and wash bowls Lisa had placed there as camouflage.

Later on, after a long bath, some lunch and a nap, Hans went out to hail a coach and make his way to the cave. Franz, who had spent the whole day skulking around the bed, greeted him with the enthusiasm of a sentry who sees the relief guard arrive. Hans found the organ grinder in a rather frail state. He had a temperature and his eyes looked sunken. My eyes hurt, the old man said, *kof*, and I feel dizzy, *kof*, like my ears are being pulled and I'm floating. Have you been on your own long?

asked Hans. I'm not on my own, the organ grinder said, Franz looks after me, *kof*, and Lamberg's been here, *kof*, he brought me some food. And do you feel any better? asked Hans. Come over here, the old man replied, *kof*, sit beside me for a while.

On Thursday afternoon Hans received a note on papyrus-brown paper. The message was succinct and the writing a little stiff for Sophie's hand. This, he reflected, meant she had written it against her will, or at least that she had forced herself to write what it said—that it was best if he didn't come to the salon the following day.

Before she signed off, however, Hans read the word *love*. And below her signature, a postscript:

PS I think I understand why there was no sequel to Lucinde.

Hans crumpled up the note and dressed to go out. He put on his beret, paused, took it off, put it on again, paused once more then finally flung it at the fireplace, cursing.

Bertold's scar spread incongruously, as though his lip were producing two separate smiles—a polite one and a scornful one. I'm sorry, she's not at home, Bertold announced, Fräulein Sophie is taking tea at the Wilderhaus residence, do you wish to leave a message? I wish to pay my respects to Herr Gottlieb, Hans replied almost without thinking.

Herr Gottlieb and Hans scrutinised one another. The one attempting to deduce the true reason for this surprise visit, the other to discover whether news of his arrest and the incident with Rudi had been made known. Neither managed to come to any definite conclusion, although both men were aware of a change—the normally hospitable Herr Gottlieb was offhand and irritable, while Hans appeared ill at ease, less elegant than usual. And those cuts on your cheek, Herr Hans? Herr Gottlieb asked, without giving away the faintest glimpse of a clue behind his whiskers. Cats, said Hans, my inn is full of cats. Yes, said Herr Gottlieb, cats are unpredictable creatures. Rather like men, said Hans. You are right there, sir, Herr Gottlieb nodded solemnly, you are certainly right there.

At no point was Hans requested to leave, yet he was offered no tea either. Hans began to take his leave, and Herr Gottlieb asked him to wait for a moment, went to his study and handed him a folded card embossed with sumptuous arabesques. We were obliged to personalise the invitations, said Herr Gottlieb, chewing his pipe, because of the number of guests. Hans read the names of the betrothed couple and felt a pang. As he walked through the corridor towards the hall, he noticed the jug Sophie used as a flower vase—it contained violets.

Hans left Stag Street and queued for a coach opposite the market square. While he was waiting he saw Herr Zeit walk past, belly atremble.

The innkeeper was scurrying along with difficulty—he was late fetching Thomas from Bible class. The sacristan greeted him from the steps. His son was cavorting in the doorway. As Herr Zeit began climbing the stair, the sacristan disappeared inside the gloomy sanctuary. Almost at once, Father Pigherzog reappeared in his place.

Good afternoon, may God be with you, said the priest, how is your wife? Good afternoon, Father, said Herr Zeit, in perfect health, thank you. I am glad, my son, I am glad, Father Pigherzog beamed, a healthy family is a blessing indeed. And now that you are here, I would like you to tell me about that guest of yours. Who? Him? Very well, replied the innkeeper, but there isn't much to tell. He goes to bed late and gets up at noon. He spends hours in his room reading. He's very quiet. Don't you know he is an unbeliever? said the priest. I don't know much, Father, Herr Zeit shrugged, and I'm getting old.

All I know are thalers and groats, if you follow me? Because I can hold them in my hand. I don't know whether Herr Hans is a heretic. If you say so, Father, then who am I to doubt your word? But no one can deny he pays on time.

The organ grinder had not sat up all day. His forehead was bathed in sweat. He had no appetite. When Hans arrived he perked up a little. Seeing his master move, Franz ran over to lick his beard. Violets, you say?—*kof*, the old man asked. A huge bunch, Hans confirmed. In that case, said the organ grinder, resting his head again, you needn't worry about her, *kof*, violets are the choice of a heart at peace with itself, do you know what I dreamt last night? It was a bit strange, *kof*, there was a crowd of men with no hands. And what were they doing? Hans asked, wiping the old man's brow. That's the strange part, he replied, they were waving at me!

The figure in the black-brimmed hat takes his long overcoat off the stand. He holds it up by the lapels for a moment, like a hunter examining his kill. He feels a vague unease, a sense of foreboding in his guts. He replaces the coat on the stand. As is his custom before going out, he stretches, flexing his arms and legs. Slow. Quick. Slow. Quick. He feels an erection stirring in his trousers. He takes off his hat. He looks around the darkened room for a cotton handkerchief. He has difficulty locating it—without his spectacles, which get in the way when he wears the mask, his vision is increasingly blurred. He discovers the handkerchief amongst the manuscripts of his latest poems. He unbuttons his breeches. He slips his hand inside his undergarments. He pulls out his member. He masturbates mechanically, his mind elsewhere. This is simply something he must do in order to remain calm and collected while he is waiting. It also avoids him wetting his sheets the next morning, which he finds deeply distasteful. He spills his seed into the centre of the handkerchief. He folds it meticulously. He dabs the tip of his member with the clean part. He buttons up his breeches. He drops the handkerchief into the laundry basket. He washes his hands using plenty of soap. He takes the opportunity to clip his fingernails. He refreshes his face with cold water to stimulate his reflexes. He perceives with disgust the faint aroma of bear fat emanating from his scalp. He applies scent to his bald pate. He gobbles up three tomato halves open on a plate. The invigorating effect of the tomatoes is considerable. He swills his mouth out. He washes his hands again. He goes back over to the coat stand. He ties his scarf. He puts on his hat again. He pulls on his coat. He checks the content of his pockets—the knife, the mask, the rope, the gloves. He exhales. He thinks of Fichte. He rubs his eyes. And he leaves the house paying no attention to the burning sensation in the pit of his stomach. As the door closes, a curly white wig rocks gently on one of the arms of the coat stand.

Herein! the Chief Superintendent clacked, opening the dispatch box and taking out an urgent communication a mounted policeman had just brought him.

Following a calculated pause of a few moments, as though their intention were to make the Chief Superintendent anxious, Lieutenants Gluck and Gluck entered his office. They walked slowly, thrilled to know that all eyes were upon them. They were escorted by two officers more heavily armed than usual. Between the two lieutenants and the two policemen, hands cuffed behind his back, pale and indifferent, was Professor Mietter.

Professor Mietter listened for half-an-hour to the two lieutenants' detailed report and the charges being brought against him. He responded to the Chief Superintendent's questions in monosyllables, scarcely batting an eyelid. His lips

seemed to tremble as if he were on the point of laughing. He
followed what his captors were saying as though in a trance.
He heard the young lieutenant say that at the prisoner's
dwelling (it took the professor a few moments to realise they
were talking about him, and their vulgar bureaucratic jargon
amused him—*the prisoner*) they had proceeded to confiscate,
among other incriminating items (*Items!* the professor scoffed.
How absurd!), a collection of Venetian masks and a set of
Prussian steel knives. He heard the older lieutenant (who, as
the professor noticed, spoke somewhat more correctly, adhering
to everyday speech and avoiding the excesses of bureaucratic
rhetoric) give a fairly precise account of his modus operandi
(although the officer hadn't used the phrase *modus operandi*,
and it was unlikely that Latin was one of his aptitudes). He
heard the young lieutenant enumerate (or rather justify in a
roundabout way) the difficulties that had slowed down the
elimination of the remaining suspects, the prisoner's continual
ruses and attempts to throw them off the scent (the professor
flashed his eyes ironically—some of the ruses mentioned had
never occurred to him). And he heard him explain that, after a
close comparison of the different attacks, they had noticed none
had taken place on a Friday, except on one occasion in August.
And it was this fact that had finally led them to the prisoner,
whose habits they had already begun studying, including his
attendance at the Gottlieb salon, which only stopped during
the summer holidays (yes, but wouldn't it have been even
more suspicious if I'd missed the odd Friday at the salon in
order to commit an assault? Mietter protested in silence). He
heard the older lieutenant assert that one reason why they
had doubted the professor's guilt was the masked man's agility
over the short distances, an agility that appeared in principle
to point to a younger man (I shall take this conundrum as a
compliment, the professor laughed sneeringly to himself). He

heard the young lieutenant remark on how the excellent physical condition of the aforementioned (*The aforementioned!* God help us!) had indeed surprised them, and how they had finally found out about his exercise regime and healthy eating habits. He heard the older lieutenant add that, as the investigation made headway, one small detail had proved decisive—the smell of grease, bear fat to be exact, which at least two of his victims had claimed to detect beneath their attacker's strong cologne. Up until that moment, the lieutenant went on, there had been various suspects. When we confirmed the use of bear grease, which is a remedy for baldness, we knew we were looking for a man who was unhappy about his baldness. (What a stupid tautology, the professor reasoned, what bald man is happy with his baldness?) And this man, Chief Superintendent, sir, never goes out without his wig. And so you could say, his vanity gave him away.

On hearing these last words, G L Mietter, Doctor of Philology, Honorary Member of the Berlin Society of the German Language and the Berlin Academy of Science, Emeritus Professor of the University of Berlin, tireless collaborator on the Gottingen *Almanac of the Muses* and chief literary critic on the *Thunderer*, did what no one, not even he, would have thought—he began sobbing uncontrollably.

Gentlemen, we've done an excellent job, declared the Chief Superintendent.

Congratulations, sir, said Gluck the younger, ironically.

The following day at noon, the other members of the Gottlieb salon were sent brief notes informing them the Friday meetings were suspended until further notice.

As he gobbled down a late breakfast at the Café Europa, Hans read with sleep-filled eyes a fervent article on the first page of the *Thunderer* that ended:

… of this shady individual whose Lutheran tendencies had on more than one occasion sown the seeds of suspicion among the local authorities, not least because of his suspected association with Anabaptist sects. Even his writings seemed to have fallen off in comparison to his earlier work, and while his previous merits remain unquestioned, the quality of his contributions—as our observant readers will have noticed—had become noticeably inferior. Given the deplorable circumstances, we now feel at liberty to reveal that for this and other reasons, our newspaper had long been considering relieving the professor of his Sunday column with the—as we see it—worthy intention of allowing fresh young voices to be heard, which is what our public deserves, and what our newspaper has always prided itself on providing. Yesterday's appalling turn of events has merely brought forward this imminent change fortuitously—wisdom would decree, there are times when the fate of scoundrels appears to be carved in stone. As newspapermen and as fathers, we welcome wholeheartedly this unexpected arrest. It is precisely what we have been demanding both actively and passively from this very tribune. By the same token we now have a duty to ask ourselves—is this case absolutely and unquestionably closed? Was the wretched culprit really acting alone? Is he, without a shadow of a doubt, the sole perpetrator of each of these attacks? Or could this be an official version designed to allay the population's fears? For such fears are indeed legitimate, and only when they have been properly laid to rest will we feel safe in our own homes. And moreover we are convinced that at this very moment our readers are mulling over similar concerns. We will provide a more in-depth analysis of the matter in tomorrow's edition.

November was growing cold, the organ grinder was burning up. Towards the middle of the month, Doctor Müller admitted that his patient was deteriorating—his bronchioles were closing up, his fevers were worse, and in the past few days he had suffered momentary losses of consciousness. Occasionally he would come round, utter three or four intelligible words, and close his eyes before plunging into a fitful sleep. Doctor Müller continued prescribing him with purges, balms, infusions, cataplasms and enemas. Yet he did so with less conviction (or at least so Hans thought), as one might read out a list of minerals. Faith is as powerful as any remedy, my friend, the doctor had assured him on his last visit. Do you believe that, doctor? Hans had said, removing the bedpan from between the old man's wizened legs. Absolutely, Müller had replied, science comes from the spirit. Be patient and have faith, your friend may still get better. And what if he goes on getting worse? Hans had asked. Doctor Müller had smiled, shrugged and folded his stethoscope.

The organ grinder's eyelids wriggled like a pair of caterpillars. They creased, puffed up, their crusty edges opening to reveal two eyeballs floating in liquid. For a moment his eyes turned in circles and were lost between blinks, until gradually he was able to focus. Franz gave his brow a cooling lick. Behind, at the back, far away, Hans greeted him with a wave of his hand. Hans stooped, crossed the pool of light and shadow separating them, and spoke into his ear. The doctor is coming, he whispered. What a shame, the old man gasped, I was thinking of going shopping. Then he remained silent, supine.

Hans watched him, not daring to touch him, breathing with him, following the air going in and out of his lungs, watching him give and receive light, suspended between each breath. He knelt down next to the old man, held him gently by the shoulders and said: Don't go.

The organ grinder opened his eyelids once more and replied slowly, without coughing: My dear Hans, I'm not going any-where, on the contrary, I shall soon be everywhere. Look at the countryside. Look at the leaves on the birch trees.

At which, he was wracked by a prolonged yet strangely calm coughing fit.

Hans gave him a handkerchief and turned to look at the

leaves. From inside the cave he could see only one birch tree, almost leafless. He gazed intently at its branches, at the dark fluttering leaves.

Hans, the old man called out. What? he replied. I'm going to ask you a favour, the old man said. I'm listening, Hans nodded. *Kof,* please speak to me using the familiar form of *you,* said the old man. All right, Hans grinned, carry on, I'm listening. That was all, thanks, the old man said. What? That was all, the old man repeated, *kof,* I just wanted you to address me informally. Hush, don't talk, whispered Hans, don't talk so much, be patient, you're going to get better. Yes, breathed the old man, just like that birch tree.

The wind outside whistled along the river. The branches in the pinewood were rattling. The air inside the organ grinder's lungs also crackled, it climbed up his trunk, sprouting branches. The pine trees pierced the mist. His chest scaled the branches.

Having overcome his sense of shame, or perhaps because he wanted to be as close to the old man as possible, Hans became curious. How does it feel? he whispered in his ear. The organ grinder seemed to like the question. You feel it, he said, smell it, touch it. And above all, *kof,* you hear it. You make your way in little by little, it's like swapping something with someone. But everything happens slowly, *kof,* ever so slowly, you start to recognise it, you see? It comes towards you, and you can hear it, as if dying were a, *kof,* I don't know, a sombre chord, it has high notes and low notes, you can hear them quite clearly, some rise, others fall, *kof,* they rise and fall, can't you hear them? Can't you hear them? Can't you? …

Doctor Müller cleared his throat twice. Hans wheeled round with a start. Müller doffed his hat. I thought you were never coming, said Hans, more in a tone of entreaty than reproach. Unfortunately, said the doctor, I have many other patients to attend. Hans remained silent and moved away from the old man. Doctor Müller knelt down next to the straw pallet, listened to his chest, took his temperature, placed a pill between his lips. His temperature is quite high, Müller announced, but he seems comfortable. How can he be comfortable, Doctor? Hans demurred. He's bathed in sweat and shivering. My dear sir, Doctor Müller said, rising to his feet, in my lifetime I've seen many men go through this, and I can assure you, rarely have I seen one who is suffering so little. Look. Take his wrist. His pulse is slow, remarkably slow considering how much difficulty he has breathing, it's as if he were sleeping, you see, ah, well, he has fallen asleep! It's the best thing for him. He needs rest, lots of rest. And now you must stop worrying, my good man, I've given him a sleeping pill. Get some rest yourself.

The week went by slowly, the hours dragged like mud. Health has a slippery quality—its swift passage is imperceptible. Illness on the other hand lingers, it delays time, which ironically is the thing it extinguishes. Slowly, inexorably, illness coursed through the organ grinder's body, anointing it with shadows. His limbs had grown emaciated. A translucent layer enfolded his bones. When his fever peaked, his hands shook even more, tracing indecipherable pictures in the air. And yet the old man seemed to be passing away with instinctive equanimity. When he was not exhausted after vomiting or drifting into unconsciousness, he would make an effort to sit up amid the filth of his straw pallet in order to gaze at something in the pinewood and beyond. At such times, Franz, who only left his side in order to scavenge for food or to defecate among the trees, pricked up his triangular ears and watched with him. Can you hear that, Franz? the organ grinder nodded, can you hear the wind?

Hans went to the cave at noon every day. He brought the old man lunch, made sure he drank liquids and stayed with him until nightfall. Depending on how strong he felt, they would talk or remain silent. The organ grinder slept a lot and complained very little. Hans felt he was more afraid than the sick man. Franz was also nervous—he kept up a continuous watch, letting out vaporous breaths through his nose, and one afternoon he had tried to bite Lamberg when he called at the cave. Some nights Hans had fallen asleep by the old man's bed, and had woken up shivering next to the embers. He would relight the fire before going back to the inn, crossing the bridge in darkness, as he had so many times that year. But those walks through the pitch-black countryside that had once seemed mysterious to him, with the flashes of excitement that come from wilfully exposing oneself to danger, now seemed long, tiring and reckless. As soon as he returned to his room, he pulled on as many layers of clothing as he could, collapsed onto his bed and fell into a deep sleep. He dragged himself out of bed at first light. Splashed his face with cold water, drank three cups of coffee in quick succession, wrote to Sophie and settled down to do some translation. He spent ages lost in thought, mumbling to himself as he pored over a book written in hostile, mysterious, unfathomable language.

One day he was late leaving the inn. When he saw how full each passing coach was, and the long queue waiting in the market square, he resolved to walk. Instead of taking the usual route along River Way, he took a short cut along a track that crossed the open fields and came out on the path to the pinewood. He set off, his mind blank. The wintry rain had turned the path to slush. The breeze, like a torn sack, fluttered feebly in all directions. Far off, the furrowed cornfields to the south appeared and disappeared from sight. A mottled light blurred the contours of the landscape. This was a day (reflected Hans) for painters, not ramblers. When he attempted to estimate how far he was from the pinewood, he realised he had lost his way.

He glimpsed the cornfields straight ahead of him and

managed to get his bearings. He walked towards them in order
to be sure of not straying. On the horizon he could see a row
of farm labourers stooped over the ground. As he approached
the edge of the field, Hans noticed the crooked figure of an
elderly labourer. He stopped to look at him.

Across the fence, a man looked up, trying to work out why
the devil the fellow with his hair flying in the wind was staring
so intently. For a split second (he convinced himself it wasn't
true) he thought the man was staring at him. The labourer spat
(it was all right for some, did the young dandy have nothing
better to do?) and bent down once more. (He had to work fast.
It was no joke. The Rumenigge's overseer was foaming at the
mouth. He had bawled at them for being two days late with the
ploughing. Had complained that some of the furrows were as
crooked as snakes. And had told them that as of the next day
their wage would be halved unless they made up the lost time.
The overseer was right, but if they ploughed more quickly it
would only make matters worse. And if they sowed the seed any
old how, the seedlings wouldn't have enough cover. How long
was it since the overseer had planted seed? If they hurried they
would sow badly. But if they didn't they'd be paid less. That
was the way things were today. Anyone who didn't work fast
was never hired again, like Reichardt. And why did the long-
haired idiot insist on staring?) Hiking up the sack once more
and clutching it under his left arm, the farm labourer thrust
his hand inside, scattering another handful of seed, trying to
trace a complete circle with his wrist (and how the devil was he
supposed to sow quickly when the wind was changing all the
time, making it impossible to scatter the seed?)

Hans moved away from the edge of the field still staring at
the line of peasants combing the ground with their hoes, dib-
bers and mattocks. While he strolled along, he tried to think
of how to say hoe, dibber and mattock in the languages he

thought he knew. And he wondered why his translations were so bad of late?

Once he found the path again, he quickened his pace, his mind on the medicines he had to administer to the organ grinder. Now that the old man's strength was waning, Hans fully realised how fragile his journey, his love, his stay in the city, his certainties were. And he knew, or he accepted, that he was not looking after his friend only out of loyalty—he was doing it above all for himself, so as not to take to the road once more, to cling to Wandernburg, to Sophie, to the happy days he had spent at the cave, to delay the moment when he would leave, as he had always left every place, every city, every country he had traveled through.

Near the bridge a flock of crows sailed across the grey clouds, fanning out among the branches of the trees, waiting for the seeds in the cornfields to be left unattended. One of the crows plummeted in such a straight line it looked as though someone had dropped a stone from one of the branches. Others followed, cawing noisily. Amid the riot of beaks Hans could see the purple entrails spilling from a sheep's open belly, a swirl of flies.

As he crouched beside the organ grinder, the old man opened his eyes and tried hard to smile. You've walked a long way, he said, stifling a cough, where did you go? How did you know? Hans said, surprised. You're a witch! Don't be silly, the old man said, your boots are muddy, very muddy. Ah, of course, grinned Hans, I took a short cut and got lost. I'm going to let you into a secret, said the organ grinder, *kof*, listen—do you know what you have to do in order not to get lost in Wandernburg? Always take the longest route.

Hans heard the sound of someone dismounting, and looked outside to see who it was. The air had congealed, the sun was drawing away from things. I thought I'd find you here, Álvaro said, embracing him. Hans could smell a mixture of horse's

mane and women's perfume on his shirt. How is he? asked
Álvaro. (Hans shrugged.) And your publisher? (Not terribly
pleased with me, said Hans, I'm late with all my work.) And
Sophie? (I wish I knew, said Hans.) Suddenly, the organ grinder
gave a cry and they went inside the cave. They found him talking in his sleep. Is he often delirious? asked Álvaro. Sometimes,
answered Hans, dabbing the old man's face, it depends, these
past days his temperature has gone up. Yesterday, he was so
feverish he wasn't himself at all. I think he's slightly better today.

Seeing his master was being looked after, Franz went out to
scavenge for food. His eyes filled with sky. The horizon raced.
The light scattered the clouds, like a torch spreading panic.

The fever raged and calmed, flared up and went cold, it climbed
the organ grinder's brow then yielded a little, letting him rest.
Hans was sleeping four hours a night and had asked his publisher for a week's grace.

Hey, Hans, the old man spluttered. Ah, Hans turned round,
you're awake? I'm always awake, replied the old man, *kof,* especially when I'm asleep. Hans wasn't sure if this was the fever
talking or if he was serious. Hey, guess what I dreamt about?
the organ grinder said. Something amazing, *kof,* I always say
that, but this is special, see what you think, I dreamt about a
man who had two backs. Hans stared at him with a mixture
of surprise and alarm. He tried to imagine the man with two
backs, to form a clear image of such a creature, until it made
him shudder. The man with two backs would spend his life
looking in two directions, leaving everywhere twice, or arriving
and leaving everywhere he went at the same time.

So, *kof,* tell me, said the organ grinder, do you think dreams
speak the truth? Who knows, said Hans trying to stop thinking
about the man with two backs, although Novalis said dreams
occur somewhere between the body and the soul, or at a moment

when body and soul are chemically joined. (I see, *kof*, said the old man, and does that mean dreams speak the truth?) Well, more or less. (Just as I thought, said the organ grinder, closing his eyes.)

Hey, Hans, said the organ grinder, opening his eyes, are you still there? (I am, I am, he replied, dabbing his brow with a damp cloth.) I'm bored, Hans, I haven't, *kof*, played my barrel organ for days, *kof*, how long has it been? If I can't, *kof*, if I can't play it I become bored, and so does he (Hans glanced at the back of the cave and couldn't help feeling a pang when he saw the bulky instrument a blanket draped over it), *kof*, that's what I regret most, Franz and I have no music, *kof*, we spend hours listening to the wind.

Kof, Hans, hey Hans, the old man woke up again, talk to me about something (what, for instance? asked Hans), anything, whatever comes into your head, you talk about lots of things (I don't know, he hesitated, you've caught me unprepared, let me see, I can't think of anything, actually I can), *kof*, I thought so! (I'll go on telling you about Novalis, the fellow I just mentioned, do you remember?) *Kof*, of course I do, I'm dying, not suffering from amnesia (you're not dying), yes, yes I am, go on. (Well, I've just remembered something he said about your favourite subject.) Barrel organs, *kof*? (No, no, dreams.) Ah, excellent. (I think he said that while we sleep the body digests the soul's perceptions, that is, a dream is like the stomach of the soul, do you see? Hey, organ grinder, are you awake?) Yes, *kof*, I'm thinking.

Hey, Hans, listen. (You're awake already, are you thirsty?) Yes, thanks, but tell me, so, *kof*, let's see if I've understood this properly, when the body has digested what the soul has eaten, yes? *Kof*, when there are no more dreams to digest we wake up hungry?

Kof, Hans, hey … (Yes?) I'm … (Thirsty? Do you want more water?) No thanks, no, not thirsty, *kof*, I'm afraid. (Afraid of dying?) No, not of dying, you die, and then it's over, *kof*, in a flash, I don't know if it's painful, *kof*, but I'm accustomed to physical pain, you see? No, I'm afraid for my barrel organ, Hans, my barrel organ, *kof, kof*, who will play the tunes? Come here, come closer. (What is it? What is it?) I want you to do something for me (anything you ask), *kof*, I want you to find out how to say *barrel organ* in as many different languages as you can, I'd like it very much if you could tell me the names, *kof*, I need to hear them, will you do that for me, Hans, will you do that for me?

Light seeped from the afternoons like milk from a broken jug. The first snows had come, settling on the branches. An icy wind whipped the countryside. The old man's coughing fits had given way to something altogether denser, deeper, inside his chest cavity. Hans had to sit right next to him in order to hear what he was saying. The lilt had gone from his voice, the air escaped from his lungs. He didn't speak so much as gasp. As soon as he saw Hans come in, he struggled to sit up. Do you have them? he breathed. Did you bring the names? Hans pushed aside the stale knot of sheets, straw, woollen covers. He sat down on the pallet. He clasped the old man's fleshless hand and fished his notebook out of his pocket.

You already know that as well as *Leierkasten*, Hans said, still holding his hand, we also call it a *Drehorgel*. (I've never liked that name, the organ grinder whispered, I prefer *Leierkasten*, that's what I've always called it.) And apart from that, where shall we begin? Let me see, well, for instance in Italian they call it *organetto di Barberia* (the name has humour, don't you think? said the organ grinder. It's a festive name), and it's very similar in French—*orgue de barbarie* (those Frenchmen! chuckled the organ grinder as Hans pronounced the words), the Dutch have lots of names for it, there's one similar to the one you don't like, I'd best leave that out, but there's another very simple one—*straatorgel*. (Excellent, yes, sir, the organ grinder said approvingly, that's exactly what it is, did you know the barrel organ originated there, in Holland?) No, I didn't, I thought we'd invented it, what others, *lirekasse* in Danish. (That's a good one, very good, it sounds like they copied it from us, doesn't it?) Possibly, or maybe we copied it from the Danes (impossible, impossible, the German barrel organs are older), well, shall I go on? In Swedish they say *positiv* (excellent, excellent), the Norwegians call it *fataorgan* (that sounds like a name for a bigger instrument), the Portuguese say *realejo* (unusual, but pretty), in Polish it's *katarynka* (wonderful! This one has a tinkle), and after that, well, the English have various names for it, according to its size and what it's used for, you know? (That's logical, the English are so pragmatic.) Let's see, for instance they call it a *barrel organ* (aha), also a *fair organ* (quite right), then there's another, *street organ* (good, good), and here's my favourite—*hurdy-gurdy* (oh yes! For children!) …

When Hans had finished telling him the names, the organ grinder remained lost in thought. Pretty, he nodded at last with a smile that grew weaker, they're very pretty, thank you, I feel much better now. A fleeting sense of relief seemed to relax his face. Almost immediately, the spasms made it tense up again.

He's stopped coughing, said Hans, is that a good sign? I'd say it was inevitable, replied Doctor Müller.

The organ grinder would gaze for hours glassy-eyed at the roof of the cave, or whimper in his sleep, before waking abruptly. Breathing appeared painful, as though instead of air he were inhaling a thick liquid. His ghostly voice was almost lost in his beard. It was difficult helping him to relieve himself. Washing half his body was an achievement. His limbs were greasy, his hair a matted lump, his skin covered in bites from bedbugs. He looked repulsive, beautiful in his own way, deserving of infinite love.

Kitted out with blankets and clothes from the inn, Hans had slept several nights at the cave—he had resolved to stay there until the end. Álvaro brought them a daily hamper of food. That morning Hans had also asked him to bring a book by Novalis. I need to commune with him, Hans had said. When his friend handed him the volume, Hans started—this wasn't the volume he'd asked for, which he had told him was lying on the desk, it was another he kept in the trunk (or at least so he thought). Had Álvaro discovered the key to his trunk? Had he rifled through its contents? What else had he seen? Hans looked straight at him. He couldn't tell. Nor did he ask.

Towards nightfall, against a backdrop of watery snow, Hans felt his eyelids begin to close. Soon afterwards, in the dark, he was awoken by a sound like a branch breaking. The snow had stopped. He fanned the flames, turned to the old man and discovered the source of the noise. It wasn't branches breaking, it was his lungs. He was groaning, his face straining. The cold air blew in through the mouth of the cave, yet it scarcely left the old man's mouth. What's the matter? Hans drew closer. What is it? Nothing, said the organ grinder, I'm nothing now, it feels like someone else is going.

Hey, organ grinder, Hans called out, are you still there? I don't know, the old man replied. What a fright! said Hans. For a moment I thought ... Soon, soon, groaned the organ grinder. Listen, Hans drew closer, there's something I want to ask you, that is, I don't want to, I have to, I'm sorry, but, where do you want to be buried? Me? replied the old man. Leave me here, please. What do you mean here? Where? Here, anywhere, replied the old man, spread out on the ground. What do you mean on the ground! Hans protested, don't you at least want a respectable burial! There's no need, thanks, said the old man, if you leave me on the ground the crows and vultures will eat my corpse, and if they bury me it'll be the maggots and the ants. What's the difference?

Hey, Hans, hey, whispered the organ grinder, are you asleep? No, no, Hans yawned, do you need anything? No, said the old man, I just wanted to ask you to tidy up the cave a bit when it happens.

The organ grinder had not spoken all day. He had stopped turning in his bed. He no longer groaned. He was silent and wide-awake. His features looked as if they were etched in charcoal. His expression was one of pain and apathy, like someone who prefers not to know what he knows. Next to him, alert, in darkness, Hans felt that this waiting was at once the ultimate loneliness and the closest companionship.

Suddenly, the old man began to pray softly. Hans looked at him, alarmed. That very morning, he had offered to fetch a priest, but the old man had refused. Without really knowing what to do, he kissed his grubby beard. He placed his mouth close to his ear and asked if he wanted a ceremony. The old man opened his stiff lips slightly, squeezed his wrist and said: This is the ceremony.

Franz came over and licked his master's fingers. Hans instinctively glanced towards the cave entrance, even though he knew no one would come: Álvaro had already been by with the hamper, Lamberg was at the factory, and he wasn't expecting Doctor Müller. The brutal simplicity of the moment took him by surprise. They were together, alone, and there would be nothing more. Not even a great pronouncement. The organ grinder had spoken many words of wisdom during his illness, and now, at the end, he was silent. He only looked at Hans, a brittle smile on his lips, clutching his hand, like a child about to make a courageous leap. Unable to bear the silence, Hans asked: A little more water, some wine, what would you like? The organ grinder moved his head almost imperceptibly and said: I'd like to breathe. Then he closed his eyelids, inhaled, and that was all.

Hans stared at him, incredulous. He did not weep yet. He remained motionless for a few moments, like someone who has broken a glass and dares not open his hand. Then, slowly, he stood up, forcing himself to be aware of every movement. He resolved not to look at the bed, not to break down completely until he had kept his promise. He went round the cave, tidying up, gathering the tools, picking things up from the floor. When he reached the barrel organ, he went weak at the knees. He paused, stepped away, approached once more and pulled off the blanket covering it. On the lid of the barrel organ he found a note weighted with a stone. The note was a scrawl that said: "Hans".

Franz poked his head out of the cave and barked. The wind had begun to blow hard.

THE WIND IS USEFUL

D RIZZLE MELTED THE FIRST big snowfall in Wandernburg. The fine spray didn't clean the streets so much as make them muddier—the earth on the roads, the flagstones were bordered with dirt, brown water filled the spaces between the cobbles. The days broke half-heartedly, as though hauled aloft by an inexpert arm. Chimneys darkened the clouds. Overcoats encumbered the shadows of passers-by.

Hans stopped in the middle of the market square. He turned his gaze towards the spot where the organ grinder used to stand. The space he had left was imperceptible, cavernous. Hans tried to look at the square the way the organ grinder had seen it, the way he himself had once seen it. He found it bleak and unappealing. He slipped his hands inside his frock-coat pockets, lowered his head, and kept on walking.

Despite having managed to catch up with some of his work, Hans had the impression he wasn't translating as well. He would spend whole afternoons shut in his room, devouring page after page, shifting words around, and he began to work better, and yet he did not enjoy it. And when he took a break, besides his meetings with Álvaro, he could find nothing to do, nowhere to go. It was impossible to see Sophie—Herr Gottlieb wouldn't let her out of his sight, and had imposed a strict curfew until the day of the wedding. She was only allowed to go out in a coach with Rudi, who would fetch her and deliver her home. All they had were their letters. Elsa cooperated with her usual mixture of displeasure and loyalty. Each time she went out on an errand, she would leave or collect a letter at the reception desk at the inn, and hurry away down the street.

Sophie's long, ardent letters left Hans on edge, torn between the desire to stay close to the one who sent them, and the despair at not being able to see her face. Sophie's face, which was growing ever more faint, which was becoming that of a stranger. In Hans's memory, flashes of her features, her profile, her different smiles appeared, which refused to meld into a complete image. And yet he did remember, with absolute clarity, her hands reaching out to him. Her hands and her voice. That voice he heard when he read her letters. Which spoke of everything except what was about to happen.

Hans's terse, anxious letters unsettled Sophie. He continued to write steadfastly, to show her his feelings, to be patient. And yet there was a sense of farewell in all the beautiful things he said to her, as though he had accepted they would never see one another again, as though each letter were a prelude to his departure. Did Hans say those things to her because he knew he was leaving? Or, on the contrary, did he say them because in spite of everything he had decided to stay? And if so what was he expecting? Why was he still in Wandernburg? She couldn't ask him this kind of thing in a letter. Or rather, they were not things that could be answered properly without being face to face. And what about her? What were her hopes? In the end, this was the most difficult question of all. As far as she could see, she could hope for nothing. Yet if she tried to be honest with herself, perhaps this unfamiliar resignation, this sadness to which she was becoming accustomed, still contained a measure of hope.

In their daily exchange of letters they did not limit themselves to declaring, or to concealing, their tumultuous emotions. They also made love in writing. And they did this as literally as they could. Some mornings, Hans woke up to a mauve note in which Sophie said simply: *I'm licking the tip. You open your eyes.* Or: *I'm*

sitting astride you. Good morning. Half asleep, Hans would respond:
I'm slipping three fingers inside you. I open my hand. Or: *I have just soaked
you, I'm sorry about your skirts.* Then he would masturbate and go
downstairs to breakfast.

Hans crossed the square, head lowered, hands in his frock-
coat pockets. When he was plagued by doubt, only walking
would calm him. Movement gave him the comforting feeling
he was leaving everything behind. So, was it time to move on?
Was this his fate? Or was he fleeing? Who was freer—those
who gradually accept they are beaten or those who insist on
staying behind in order to experience defeat? As he walked past
the ornate fountain, Hans's hat flew off and was blown a few
yards. The weathervane on the Tower of the Wind creaked this
way and that. Birds circled the steeple, they, too, transformed
into minutes.

Lisa squinted, wrinkled her nose, and breathed through her
mouth. The stench began to blend with the fumes of chlorine
and sodium. She tipped a couple of buckets of water into the
latrines and gave them a scrub before swilling them out again.
As soon as she had closed the doors, she exhaled abruptly and
kicked the buckets away. When she grudgingly went to pick
them up, she cut her knuckles on one of the sharp edges. Lisa
let out a cry, raised her fist to her mouth, and, just before licking her knuckles, she paused, and cursed. She went over to the
well to wash her hands. As she scrubbed them with soap, she
contemplated them in disgust—how could a man like Hans
ever like her if she had hands like this? The marks of the river
on her wrists, her chapped knuckles, her split nails, her flayed
fingertips. Men like Hans prefer stupid women who have hands
like princesses, women like Fräulein Gottlieb who probably
didn't even know how to fill a bucket from a well, assuming she
could even pick one up. Fräulein Gottlieb, who always smiled

at her falsely when they met on the stairs. Fräulein Gottlieb, who, had it not been for the dresses her father gave her, and the servants who did her hair, would be no better than she. Fräulein Gottlieb, who, incidentally, hadn't been coming to see Hans for how long was it now? They saw each other little and wrote to each other a lot. This, Lisa concluded, drying her hands, was a very good sign.

Lisa went into their apartment to put the starched laundry away. After making sure Thomas wasn't there, she spent a few moments freshening her face and combing her hair. She walked along the corridor humming to herself. In the dining room, the logs were crackling in the hearth, the cauldron was steaming. Herr Zeit was snoozing behind the counter. Lisa peeped into the kitchen. Her mother was busy stirring the broth and chopping up bacon while the potatoes roasted on the fire. Have you done all the ironing? Frau Zeit said without looking round. Lisa wondered how her mother always managed to sense her presence even though her back was turned. Yes, mother, answered Lisa, all of it. What about the latrines? I've done them, too, Lisa sighed. Very good, said the innkeeper's wife, now go and fill the. Sorry, mother, interrupted Lisa, are those vegetables for today? Yes, said Frau Zeit, why? Because, Lisa replied coolly as she reached for a ladle, Herr Hans asked me to bring him his lunch, then you can tell me what else, I'll just take up these two dishes and a slice of bread, and I'll be down at once, mother.

Lisa rested the tray on the floor. She knocked on Hans's door, and, as was her wont, walked in without waiting for a response. The room had a troubled odour. Lisa, who had a very strong sense of smell, was convinced that when a person was troubled their breath became foul and polluted the air. The fire in the hearth had almost burned down. Hans's crumpled clothes lay in a heap on a chair. The top of his dishevelled head peeped out from behind the lectern, between two mounds of books on his desk. The light filtering through the window scarcely illuminated the mass of papers, where the oil lamp and candles stood unlit.

I've brought you some food, Lisa announced cheerfully. How kind, thank you, murmured Hans. Shall I open the shutters a little? she suggested. As you like, he said. Lisa placed her hands on her hips and gazed at him, discouraged. You look tired, she said. Yes, I am, Hans replied, staring into the plate. Are you angry? she ventured. Me, angry? he replied, raising his head. With whom? With you? Lisa nodded glumly. Hans pushed the plate aside, stood up and went over to her. My dear girl, he said, cupping her face in his hands, how could I be angry with you? Now, at last, Hans had smiled at her. Lisa blinked, her eyes fixing on his warm hands, his splayed fingers, the gentle strength of his thumbs. Life should be like this, exactly like this, always. How wonderful it would be, she reflected, if I fainted right at this moment. She began to feel the blood draining from her head into her breasts, her stomach, her legs. She even thought Hans had moved his face ever so slightly closer, not much, just a little closer, to hers. Lisa! Frau Zeit's voice echoed up the stairs. Lisa, the oil lamps! Hans withdrew his hands from her face and stepped back. Lisa stood motionless. Her face twisted in an expression of loathing. I'm coming! she shouted as she left the room.

That evening Álvaro called at the inn, and forced Hans to dress and go out with him. Hans let himself be steered towards Potter's Lane. The noise inside the Picaro Tavern hurt his ears— everyone was laughing, getting drunk or groping one another openly. On the iron wheels hanging from the ceiling, only every other candle was lit—at that time of the evening, it was best not to see too clearly what the customers were doing. Hans stared into his tankard of beer as if it was a kaleidoscope. Not drinking? Álvaro asked, surprised. Yes, yes, Hans murmured, downing half his beer in one go. Álvaro made two or three stabs at conversation then placed his arm round Hans's shoulder. How long since you last saw her? he asked. Hans sighed, made the calculation in silence, and replied: Two and a half, nearly three weeks. Álvaro began nudging Hans's tankard with his own in an attempt to cheer him up. Hans, who had begun brooding again, had to respond to stop his beer from spilling. The golden liquid sloshed around the tankard, slopped against the rim, settled with a quiver.

The reddish liquid curled like a tongue, reflecting the carbide lamps as it whirled round, licked the rim of the glass then spilt violently over the lace tablecloth. Two servants instantly came over with damp cloths to clean the stain. Rudi righted his glass and screamed at the servants to close the dining-room doors and to leave them in peace.

Frozen in mid-mouthful, Sophie stared at Rudi through the tines of her fork. She had noticed him raise his voice more often during these past days than he had in a whole year. As soon as the dining room was quiet, he exclaimed: How dare you mention his name in my house! I'm sorry, she said, I didn't think the servants knew who he was. The servants know everything! replied Rudi. They always know everything! I said I'm sorry, Sophie repeated, looking away. How could you! Rudi yelled. That's what I want to know, how could you! My friends already tried to warn me, they told me about the rumours and I wouldn't listen! And do you know why, Sophie? Because I trusted you, I trusted you! Good God, what a betrayal, not to mention the scandal! How ungrateful can a woman be! No, don't let's talk in here! We'll go out into the garden!

Shivering in the damp garden, her eyelids puffy, her voice faltering, Sophie realised it was futile to go on denying it and at last she admitted the truth. And to her surprise, instead of getting angrier, Rudi calmed down as he listened. He became lost in thought, walking round the bushes like the bloodhound that has just dug up a bone. Sophie felt sorry for him as she watched him pace up and down. And, even as she cursed herself for it, she couldn't help feeling guilty. She had often promised herself that, come what may, she would never regret doing what she had done, of having the courage to follow her desires. Now everything was turning into a disaster—she had betrayed Rudi, her engagement was hanging by a thread, Hans appeared to be on the point of leaving, and to top it all, she was going against her principles and beginning to regret her audacious behaviour. Just then Rudi began speaking to her again. And how could you prefer him to me? he implored. Moved by Rudi's weakness, Sophie tried to soften the blow. It isn't that I prefer him, she whispered, it's a different feeling. Different? he said. In what way different? Are you fond of me and you love him? Do you love me and desire him? Tell me! Say something! Are you sure you want to go on talking about it? she asked. Haven't I said enough? I demand an explanation, he replied, I need to understand, aren't you supposed to be good with words? In that case explain it to me! Incapable of going on without wounding him further, Sophie preferred to remain silent. She was aware that men's rage requires an antagonist. And that if she avoided confrontation Rudi would be more lenient with her.

Half-an-hour later, still in the garden, the roles had begun to be reversed. Sophie felt in some way relieved now that her secret was out in the open and she had admitted her betrayal. And it was Rudi who, having made his accusations, felt suddenly defenceless. For several months she had been walking a tightrope, and, as she'd expected, she had ended up falling off. But now she could look at Rudi without any pretence. And she began to see that there was more strength in her honesty as an unfaithful woman than in her fiancé's angry indignation. His recriminations had given way to perplexity, and his perplexity to pain. I thought as much! he howled, stamping his feet. I tell you, I thought as much! You betrayed me! With that fop! And if you thought as much, she said, surprising herself with a show of conjugal pride, then why didn't you come back before? Why did you stay at your spa? How could you be so sure of yourself? Rudi stopped pacing. He stared at the ground and replied: No. I wasn't sure of myself. I've never been this in love with anyone. And I've never felt so unsure of myself as I have with you. Rudi! she sighed, biting her lip. In Baden, he went on, I was plagued with doubts. I doubted myself, you, everything. There were nights when I cried as I fretted over whether to go back to Wandernburg unannounced. But I tried to convince myself that I had to trust in you, in us. That I mustn't behave like the typical jealous husband a woman such as you would never aspire to marry. And in the end I decided to stay, in the hope you'd understand that my absence wasn't a sign that I didn't care, but the hardest test of my love.

Rudi uttered these last words with the cold clarity of a doctor diagnosing his own illness. Sophie did not speak. For a moment the two of them listened to the silence, the sporadic burble of the fountain. Until Rudi added: Unless this is an even harder test. I am still in love with you. As much as or more than ever. Good God! Sophie Gottlieb, look at me, listen to what I'm saying. I'm willing to forgive you, to forget everything, do you understand? I, too, am crazy and I'm still willing. We'll both deny it, we'll deny everything until he's gone, until all this has been forgotten. What do you say? Just give me a sign, do you hear? One simple sign and things between us will be as they were. As if nothing had happened, do you understand? Nothing. Ask of me whatever you will. Just ask.

Unable to open her mouth, Sophie was aware then that she

had never felt so much respect for Rudi nor had she loved him less.

His eyelids grew as heavy as bags full of clothing. Up in the rafters, the cobwebs expanded. Unable to stop even in sleep, their drowsy eyes kept moving left and right, deciphering the darkness.

He dreamt the floor was spinning on an axis, his body was a clock, the bed was a water wheel. He was moving without getting anywhere, space spun in spirals, traced a bull's eye, circles within circles. In the middle of it all a plughole awaited. A hand emerged from the water and waved about asking for help. And Hans was going to but he didn't, the ground was a sticky web, his legs turned to jelly, and suddenly he only had one hand.

He woke up like someone falling backwards. It was cold. The room was enveloped in a white glare. The bed felt peculiar. When he realised he had woken up with his feet on the pillow and his head at the bottom of the bed, he knew the time had come. He leapt to his feet, pulled on a wool overcoat, sat down to write two letters.

Elsa leant out of the window to see who was there and instantly went downstairs before Bertold could get to the door. She was surprised to see Lisa there so early—Hans's letters didn't usually arrive before breakfast. She concealed it down the front of her dress. She patted Lisa's head, gave her two aniseed balls, and closed the front door. Lisa walked to the market sucking one of them guiltily—when would she stop accepting sweets as if she were a child?

Sophie locked herself in her bedroom to read Hans's letter. She was unable to have any thoughts. All she could feel was a spasm coursing through her body, an emptiness in her veins. She bit down hard on her lip. She tried to distract herself by gazing out of the window. Then she rang for Elsa and told her to start inventing some excuse. That afternoon they were going out no matter what.

It was drizzling. It drizzled constantly now. Hans could scarcely believe that only a few months ago he was out walking in the dazzling sunshine. He was standing under one of the balconies. Waiting. His nose dripped as he counted the seconds. Reaching up to wipe it, he noticed a hazy blotch in the distance, and recognised Elsa's nervous walk among the umbrellas and horses. He thought of waving to her, but cautiously refrained. He was worried not to see Sophie. Suddenly Elsa gestured to him imperceptibly (a movement of her head, a click of her heels) before vanishing. Hans was alarmed, although Elsa instantly reappeared, as if nothing had happened, head held high, and a few yards behind Sophie appeared, unable to help staring at him intently. Elsa stopped, said something to Sophie and remained on the corner of Grinder's Alley. As Sophie approached him, hiding her face under her umbrella, Hans felt a hollow sensation in his gut. The same thing happened to Sophie as Hans's boots, frock coat and scarf loomed ever larger.

Thank goodness you came, said Hans. I had good reason to, Sophie replied, tilting her umbrella. They looked at one another strangely. He thought Sophie looked beautiful and a little tired, like an actress with dark shadows under her eyes. She thought Hans looked too thin and rather handsome with his dripping-wet hair. There was a moment's silence, as though they had met simply in order to gaze at one another. It was Sophie, accustomed to being practical as a defence, who spoke first. Elsa, she explained, will wait for five minutes on that corner. I thought it best for us to see each other here because it is a craftsman's quarter, a place friends of mine would never set foot in. Hans laughed and then immediately became serious. I've just sent my resignation to the publisher, he said in a hushed voice.

What about our European anthology? asked Sophie. I don't know, replied Hans, perhaps one day. Perhaps, she whispered. I also wanted to tell you that I told Brockhaus about you, I sent them some of your translations and poems, don't pull a face, they want to meet you. Hans, Sophie protested, who said you could? How many times have I—? Well, anyway, I'm grateful, I can't think about those things now. At least think about it, he insisted. I can manage by myself, she said. Are you very annoyed with me? asked Hans. Not at all, said Sophie, I understand, you have your life. Now I have to think about mine. But, aren't translating and writing part of your life, too? They are only my dreams, she replied.

On the corner of Grinder's Alley, Elsa folded her arms and looked at Sophie, shaking her head. Sophie raised her hand to tell her she was on her way.

Listen, Hans said quickly, I can't stay here any longer, I have to continue my journey, I need to move, to start again. I know, I know, she sighed, where will you go? To Dessau I suppose, he replied, you never know. I see, she said. Look at me, he said, please look at me—even though I know you can't, I'd like you to come with me. Sophie remained silent. Hans's eyes were flashing. Or can you? he insisted. We still have time! Would you come? With a sad but resolute look, Sophie replied: Don't you think it's better not to follow anyone? Hans shrugged his shoulders. Sophie smiled, tears in her eyes. Elsa crossed the street.

Farewells are so strange. There's something terrifying, deadly, about them, and yet they awaken a desperate urge to live. Perhaps farewells create new territories, or they send us back to the only territory that truly belongs to us, that of solitude. It is as though we needed to go back there from time to time, to draw a line and say: I came from here, this was me, what sort of person am I? I used to believe love would provide me with the answers. Our love has filled me with doubt. What sort of person am I? I don't know, I've never really known. I am alone with myself (I on the one side, she *on the other) and in a sense this has been possible because of being with you. Oh, my love, I'm afraid I'm not explaining myself well! I hope you can hear me even though you don't know what I'm saying. Wouldn't that be a kind of* greeting *in the* farewell? *And more than anything a lot of pain, of course. I'm making your head spin! (Good, that way I shall xxx xxxx xxxx be able to steal a few kisses while you ponder my words.) Hans, will I see you once more before you leave, even if only for a few moments? If I managed to get away once I can get away twice. Do you know what my father said when he saw me come in with ...*

... for farewells, as you say. I think that living is above all about greet-ing things deservingly, and saying farewell to them with the appropriate gratitude. I suspect no one has this ability.

Sophie, I'm going to make a confession. Xxxx xxxx xxx xxx xxx In the past, when I would go back to a place and meet up with old friends, I was the one who ended up saying farewell to everyone. Now, I don't know why, I feel as if it is the others who are saying farewell to me. I'm not sure if this is a good or a bad thing. We lose the fear of letting go of our baggage, but also the certainty that what is in them belongs to us.

My love (will I be able to keep calling you my love *in the future?), of course we'll meet. Even for a few moments. We'll find a way. There are so many things I'd like to say to you. In that sense writing is like being in love—there's never enough time to say what we want.*

You asked me whether I think about the old man. I think about him every day. And also (don't laugh) I worry about Franz. His dog, Franz, do you remember? I don't know where he is. I've looked everywhere, but I can't ...

... *convinced that people who stay in one place are more nostalgic than people who travel. What do you think? For those who are sedentary, time moves more slowly, leaving a trail, like that of a snail on the pages of a calendar. I think memory feeds on stillness. Those of us who stay feel nostalgia, and I know what I'm talking about. Nothing leaves me more wistful than going to see someone off, watching the carriage grow smaller until it vanishes. Then I turn around, and I feel like a stranger in my own city. I can't stop thinking about how I'll feel on my way to say farewell to you, my love, and I swear I don't think I am able. I don't even want to think about how I would see the things around me, how everything would look to me, when your carriage ...*

... *because I can't bear it either. I prefer it that way, too.*

You're right, people who travel are fleeing nostalgia. There's no time for memories when you are traveling. Your eyes brim. Your muscles ache. You haven't the strength or the attention for anything except keeping moving. Packing a bag doesn't make you more aware of changes, rather it compels you to postpone the past, and the present is taken up with concerns about the immediate. Time slides over the traveler's skin. (How is your skin? What does it smell of today? What colour stockings you are wearing?)

Yes, time slides over us. After a long journey, as though abundance produced amnesia, you think—is that it? Is that all? And where was I in all this? ...

He had imagined every possibility. That no one had read his note. That no one would open the door to him. That they would call the police. Insults would be hurled at him. He would be kicked down the steps. He had imagined every possibility, except this one—Herr Gottlieb would receive him without putting up any resistance.

Hans had resolved not to leave Wandernburg without saying goodbye to Herr Gottlieb, or without at least trying to. He felt, on the one hand, indebted to Sophie's father for all the hospitality and kindness he had shown him when he first arrived. And on the other, that sneaking out of the city like a fugitive would have been an admission of guilt that he refused to accept. Overcoming his awkwardness at the situation, his anger at Herr Gottlieb's tyrannical behaviour towards his daughter, and perhaps a secret sense of shame, he had sent a note asking to pay a visit to the house he had not set foot in for over a month, and had made his way towards Stag Street for the very last time. And yet now that he was in front of the door, staring at the swallow and lion's-head door knockers, everything looked different. What the devil was he doing there? Why should he endorse anyone's authority? How far could his visit be construed as an apology? And in the end, wasn't it an accursed apology? Just then, the door on the right swung open. Bertold reluctantly let him in and began mounting the stairs without waiting. Hans was almost compelled to run after him. Once in the hallway, Bertold avoided his eyes, and told him in a hushed voice that Herr Gottlieb was in his study. Hans ventured to ask whether Fräulein Gottlieb was at home. She's gone out, Bertold replied, turning on his heel.

Once more Hans experienced the dizziness of the corridor, its murky ceiling, its icy passage. Before stopping outside the study, he couldn't resist peering into the drawing room where he had spent so many Fridays—he saw the furniture lined up as in a museum, armchairs with their dust sheets, flowerless vases. The curtains blocked off the windows. The clock on the wall gave the wrong hour. The round mirror warped the empty hearth.

The study reeked of tobacco, sweat and brandy. Herr Gottlieb didn't appear hidden in the gloom so much as fused to it, a flattened image. When he moved the lamp to the middle of his desk, Hans noticed the maze of furrows on his face—how old was he? They didn't greet each other immediately. The dense silence exuded alcohol. The carpet exhaled dust. Hans waited for the first reproach, an angry gesture, a raised voice. But the head of the house didn't appear to be looking at him with genuine resentment—what most showed in his eyes, what they exuded, was dismay. Have a seat, he said at last. Hans positioned himself in the leather armchair opposite. Herr Gottlieb gestured to the bottle, Hans served himself a small brandy. More! Herr Gottlieb ordered. Hans poured out a little more, raised his glass, not knowing what to toast.

The conversation began like all decisive conversations—with something else. They commented on the awful news about Professor Mietter. Hans made an effort to look aggrieved. Herr Gottlieb expressed his astonishment and even the hope that this was a result of some dreadful calumny or of police bungling. He said this with such conviction that Hans realised this defeated host would never accept the idea that he had invited a rapist as well as an adulterer into his home. They discussed the cold spell. The merits of French brandy. How pretty sleighs were. Afterwards they fell silent. Then the real conversation began.

I came here, sir, Hans coughed, to say goodbye. I know, replied Herr Gottlieb, my daughter told me you were leaving. It is the only reason I agreed to see you. You see, Hans tried to explain, I blame myself for the problems my friendship with your daughter might have caused (no, no, Herr Gottlieb interrupted calmly, I don't think you do), believe me, it was never my intention, but when feelings, when feelings emerge, sometimes it's impossible, even inhuman, to foresee how far ... Don't even try it, Herr Gottlieb sighed, things happened the way they did. And I can't say I'm surprised.

Herr Gottlieb tried to relight his pipe. The cold, dry tobacco wouldn't catch. He didn't speak or look up until he had succeeded. With the smoke in his eyes once more, he resumed talking. His whiskers had an air of a bedraggled bird about them.

I feared this, Herr Gottlieb went on, I feared it from the beginning. The moment I saw the pair of you, my daughter and you, talking. I saw the disaster unfolding. There it was. And I could do nothing about it. I saw you talking and it was terrible. Sophie's face lit up. Her face lit up, and I felt a mixture of tenderness and pain. I fought it to the end, of course. To the bitter end, damn it. As a loving father and as a man of honour. But I already suspected it would do no good. I know my daughter well. She's, she's (Hans ventured: Fascinating and strong-willed), dear God, she certainly is! Much too strong-willed. At first I considered forbidding you to come to the house. Yes, don't be surprised. And I thought I'd do all I could to prevent you from meeting outside it. However, knowing my daughter, I told myself it would make matters worse. She would resist, quarrel with me, with the Wilderhauses, with everyone. And so I decided to cross my fingers and trust her to act sensibly. I thought that that way, without trying to force her, she would see reason and end up losing her infatuation with you. I knew that the more I stepped in the more she would turn it into some heroic passion. What I failed to predict was that the two of you would take it so far. Or that you would begin writing together, what a bright idea. Wait a moment, let me finish. And I had to grin and bear it. To keep up appearances. In front of my daughter, in front of Rudi, even in front of you. To act the fool. Those were agonising months. I can't tell you what thoughts went through my head, but believe me they were many and various. Then it occurred to me to make some enquiries about you.

Hans's blood went cold. It was as much as he could do not to spill his brandy. What sort of enquiries? he asked in the strange voice of someone straining to sound normal.

In Jena, Herr Gottlieb replied, gazing into the glistening circles of his drink. A few months ago, while we were making preparations for the wedding. When things had already started getting out of control, it occurred to me to write to Jena University to ask for your references. (And? was all Hans could say.) And the upshot of it was, of course, as you imagine—they had no record of anyone with your name studying there or obtaining a degree. That was all the information I needed (Herr Gottlieb, if I could just explain), you needn't, what difference does it make? (And why didn't you say anything to Sophie?) Well, actually I did. (What do you mean you told her? Hans was alarmed. And what did she say?) She said it was irrelevant. Irrelevant! And so we never mentioned the subject again. And now I see she didn't discuss it with you either. Sophie is a very headstrong girl. What more could I do? I sat here and waited. What followed, as you can see, has been a catastrophe. A complete catastrophe. (All I can say is how truly sorry I am.) No doubt you are. No doubt you are.

Herr Gottlieb stood up with difficulty. Hans was beginning to feel light-headed. Herr Gottlieb walked a few paces then paused beside the door—he had no intention of going into the corridor to see him out. Hans wasn't sure whether to improvise a few words of farewell or leave as quickly as possible. Herr Gottlieb decided for him. He placed a weary, darkened hand on Hans's shoulder, and, looking at him resentfully, he said: You're leaving my daughter on her own. I'm not sure I heard what you said, replied Hans. I said, Herr Gottlieb repeated, you're leaving my daughter all alone, you wretched impostor.

On his last afternoon in Wandernburg, Hans arranged to meet Sophie at the Café Europa. They sat at a table at the back and ordered hot chocolate. Elsa sat at a neighbouring table, jiggling her leg.

Hans spoke slowly but she noticed his voice was strangled, as if he were holding his nose. Sophie appeared calm, apart from her coral necklace, which Hans could see shaking above her neckline. He kept running his fingers through his hair. She fondled the cup, the saucer, the spoon.

So you've cancelled the wedding, said Hans. Sophie shrugged, her gaze wandering towards the ceiling. And your father? he asked. He must be furious. She nodded feebly, tried to smile and her mouth set in a fold. Everything is so strange, said Hans. Very strange, whispered Sophie.

A waiter walked between the tables holding a flaming taper. The candles inside the lamps lit up like cages that have reclaimed their birds. What time is it? asked Sophie. Hans felt his pockets. She glanced up at the clock on the wall. She looked back at Hans, blinked quickly, pursed her lips. She began to stand up. Elsa closed her book. Hans felt the weight of all the words he had not uttered. He listened very quickly in his mind to all the explanations he could have given her, the reasons why he had to go away. He imagined hurling himself at her. Kissing her in front of everybody. Dramatically knocking over the marble-topped table. Tearing her clothes off. He sat motionless. Sophie was leaving. Hans left a few coins beside their empty cups, stood up and followed her. The three of them filed towards the door. As Sophie crossed the threshold, Hans held her back by the arm. They stood facing one another on the far side of the doorway. A customer sitting by the window might have observed how Elsa, when she saw Hans's gesture, went on walking slowly without glancing back, book in hand, hair billowing beneath her scarf.

Hans and Sophie watched her go.

Sophie, he stammered, buttoning up his frock coat, I, you do understand that after all that has happened here I can't, that is, I couldn't. Shh, she replied, tying her shawl, it's all right. It's the best thing for us both. And it was worth it. Meeting you, said Hans, has been like a miracle for me. Hush, said Sophie kissing her forefinger, go. Miracles don't exist. You, too.

As they finished wrapping themselves in silence, like a pair of knights donning their armour, Sophie saw Hans weep openly for her. She doubted and was sure, she knew she was doing the most difficult thing, the right thing. What a stealthy man you are, she said, trying to make a joke of it, leaving exactly as you came. Yes, he said, catching hold of himself. No. I'm not leaving exactly as I came.

When Hans took his first step away from her, Sophie cried out: Wait. He wheeled round.

"Thank you."

"I was thinking of saying the same to you. Thank you."

Hans walked down Glass Alley. His shadow glided from one window to the next. Sophie stood watching him and her eyes felt cold. She was still aware of the pang in her gut she had been feeling since she arrived at the café, yet she felt strangely content.

She hurried down two streets until she caught up with Elsa. He strode towards the market square. Looked at from above, from a high balcony or a slit window in the Tower of the Wind, they might have seemed like two insignificant creatures, two flecks on the snow. Looked at from the ground, they were two people weighed down by life.

Hans walked into the inn, went upstairs and opened his trunk. He rummaged through his belongings in search of a long letter he had written the morning he decided to leave Wandernburg. He read through it, crossed out many words, added others. He thought of giving it to Álvaro, but was afraid he might read it. He slipped the letter into an envelope and went downstairs to look for Lisa.

He found her in the dining room, on her knees stoking the fire. She leapt up with a start, shook the hem of her skirt, and looked mournfully at Hans. Are you really leaving tomorrow? she asked. Yes, I am, he replied, stifling the urge to caress her.

You can't be, she said shaking her head. Yes, I can, he smiled. Then he added: Will you do one last thing for me? Anything you want, said Lisa. I need you, Hans explained, to deliver this envelope to the Gottlieb residence today. Is it very late, or do you still have time to go out? Lisa stuck her head into the yard to gauge the brightness of the afternoon, and replied proudly: Since it's today, I can. Excellent, said Hans, in that case listen to me. You must give this letter to the maid as usual. But it's very, very important that you tell her not to deliver it until after breakfast. That means she must keep it with her tonight and make sure no one sees it, is that clear? I'd be very grateful if you could go as soon as possible. I'm leaving tomorrow at dawn, and I may not see you again. You've no idea how important that envelope is to me, and how much I appreciate your help, dear Lisa.

Lisa took the envelope with a solemn air, tucked it between her skirt and blouse, sighed, and threw herself into Hans's arms. He managed to catch her in time to prevent her from falling flat on her face. Lisa considered herself embraced—she kissed the corner of Hans's mouth and declared: I'll tell my mother Thomas has left one of his schoolbooks behind and can't finish his homework without it. But what if Thomas finds out? Hans frowned, what if he tells your mother it's a lie? She gave the laugh of a heroine and retorted: And what do you suppose I'm going to steal from his room? You'll go far, he said, astonished. We'll see, Lisa said moving towards the door. Ah, and it might be a good thing if you kept the little scallywag amused for a while. He's playing in the corridor. Wish me luck.

Hans went to find Thomas, who was scrupulously dismembering and scrutinising a toy cart made of wood. What's that game you're playing? Hans asked. The boy held out a twisted axle and a torn-off wheel. Dear little Thomas, Hans said, kneeling down, you know I'm leaving tomorrow. What's that to me? the boy said, pinching his leg.

Lisa had scurried off towards Stag Street. She was clutching the envelope in one hand, and holding onto her hat with the other. She was reflecting on the importance of her mission, and how handsome Hans was, and how much he had always trusted her. Halfway there, however, something began to niggle away at her, then to upset her and finally to enrage her. She slowed her pace. She came to a sudden halt. She stared at the envelope. At Hans's flowing, expert writing. At the stupid name, Sophie, which she could now read with loathing. She looked for a lighted doorway. She sat down on the step, and without hesitating, opened the envelope, doing her best not to tear it. She read stumblingly the first few paragraphs. The sentences were terribly long and the writing difficult to decipher. She made out the odd sentence, a word here and there. She recognised many of the verbs and some of the nouns. She was unable to understand its content, but it was obviously a love letter to that stuck-up woman. A love letter from Hans, which she couldn't even read. Lisa leapt angrily to her feet. What was she doing? How could she have been such a fool? She ran back in the direction she had come. She reached Highgate. As soon as she glimpsed the water flowing beneath Bridge Walk, she tore the letter into little pieces and scattered them on the River Nulte.

Álvaro and Hans met at the Central Tavern to say their farewells. Neither spoke much—they looked at one another, smiled awkwardly, clinked tankards. A cold draught seeped through every crack in the walls, cancelling out the effect of the wood stoves. Outside, along the sides of the market square, the vendors were staying up to arrange their Christmas stalls with rattles, pumpernickel bread, stars, sugar sweets, baubles, flagons of wine, coloured candlesticks, marzipan, wreaths.

I shouldn't have come, Álvaro grumbled, last evenings are always terrible. Shall I get you another beer, you poor martyr? said Hans, clapping him on the back. Is this it, then? Álvaro insisted, you're really leaving? Yes, yes, replied Hans, why are you so surprised? I don't know, Álvaro shrugged, well, I am a little, I suppose I was hoping something might happen, I'm not sure what, anything, and that you'd end up staying. *Amigo mío*, Hans raised his tankard, I have to continue on my way. And, said Álvaro, raising his tankard in turn, you have to work on your Spanish accent. If you like, retorted Hans, we could discuss your German accent. Their brief burst of laughter ends abruptly. Anyway, sighed Álvaro, I've never seen anybody leave Wandernburg before. Not wishing to quibble, said Hans, but I'm still here, aren't I? Nobody, said Álvaro, astonished. Maybe, said Hans, I just loathe Christmas. And I loathe farewells, replied Álvaro, so, if you don't mind, I'd prefer not to be there tomorrow when your coach leaves.

They quit the tavern. They walked along, trying to talk about something else, anything else, until they reached the corner of Old Cauldron Street. Their eyes met. They took a deep breath. They nodded as one. They promised to write to one another. They took another deep breath. Hans stepped forward, arms outstretched, Álvaro withdrew. No, he said, I'd rather not. I mean it, I can't. It's bad enough having to go back to that accursed tavern tomorrow on my own. Let's pretend we're meeting tomorrow as usual. Really. Not another word. I'm going home. Goodnight. *Que descanses, hermano.*

Álvaro raised an arm, wheeled round, and hurried off along the street.

Hans splashed icy water on his face, making himself start. He shaved in front of the broken mirror on the back of the watercolour. He cut himself twice. He wanted to believe he had slept a little, even though he had the impression of having lain awake all night talking to himself in whispers.

He squashed in clothes, crammed in books, folded papers. He managed to close his luggage. He glanced about the room to make sure he had left nothing behind. Under the bed, covered in fluff, he made out a mass of fine fabric, which he assumed at first was a sock, but which turned out to be something completely unexpected—Lisa's nightdress. He placed the chairs in the corners of the room, lined up the candleholders, pushed the shutters to—the steamy windowpanes distorted the neighbouring rooftops. Hans took hold of his valise, the handles of his trunk and the rest of his belongings. The trunk seemed heavier than when he arrived. He didn't glance back to take a last look at the empty room. He walked out into the corridor, closing the door behind him.

Before reaching the stairs he almost tripped over a fir tree he couldn't remember having seen there the day before. He left his luggage on the landing. He went down to the ground floor where he found Frau Zeit in her skirts and apron, already hard at work. Will you be wanting breakfast? she asked, a bucket of greyish water at the end of each arm. Just coffee, thank you, replied Hans. What do you mean, just coffee? the innkeeper's wife scolded. You aren't going to travel on an empty stomach, I won't allow it, wait here. Frau Zeit set down the buckets (a pair of dirty cloths quivered like octopuses in the soapy water) and went into the kitchen. She came back bearing sausages, a wheel of cheese, a bowl covered with a cloth tied with string. Here, she commanded, and make sure you eat properly. My husband will be out in a moment to help you with your things.

Herr Zeit's face turned pink, swelled up, glistened, let out air like a balloon. As they went down the stairs, Hans had the impression that the innkeeper's belly, crushed by the heavy bundles and splaying over them, was adding to the weight of his luggage. They placed everything behind the counter. Herr Zeit collapsed onto a chair (the back quivered like a hammock) and opened up his accounts book. It's Monday already, he announced feebly. Hans handed him a linen bag containing some money. The innkeeper opened it and looked up at him, puzzled. There's some extra, Hans explained. There was no need, said Herr Zeit, but I'm not one to refuse. Tell me, Hans asked, is Lisa here? She's just gone out, replied the innkeeper, to take Thomas to school, is there something you want me to tell her? No, no, Hans hesitated, nothing.

To kill time until the coach arrived, he went out for one last stroll around Wandernburg. The streets smelt of mud, bread and urine. He could already hear the creaking bars of shop windows. The frost softened with the dawn. Hans wandered down Archway, past the church, around the market square, paused in a corner. He saw a beggar walk by, kicking his legs in the air to stretch them. He thought he recognised Olaf. He called out. The beggar looked at him—it wasn't Olaf. Excuse me, Hans said, do you remember the organ grinder who used to play here? What organ grinder, replied the beggar, continuing on his way.

Hans looked up at the clock on the Tower of the Wind. Slowly he made his way back to the inn. Only when he found himself standing in front of it did he realise with astonishment he hadn't got lost. A Christmas wreath was flapping on the door.

The wind is a rake, a pulley, a lever, the wind knows, it flattens the landscape, it blows everywhere and is everywhere a foreigner, it draws near, takes shape, runs in a ribbon around Wandernburg, it drops, surfs over rooftops, strips chimney stacks, buffets street lamps, scratches walls, it whistles along, whips up the snow, settles in doorways, rattles doors, the wind rolls, rotates, roams, it heads towards the market square, it is empty, the cobbles are slippery, the Christmas stalls are not finished, the water from the baroque fountain has almost iced over, the wind shakes and breaks it, suddenly it turns, accelerates, climbs as though up a ramp, reaches the top of the tower, the ground shrinks away, the eaves thrum, the tower doesn't move, but the time inside it does, the time which coughs in the clock, the wind plays with the weathervane making it point in a different direction, then spins round a few more times, shoots up, arches downwards onto a coach roof, slowing it slightly, bounces off and careens over the cobbles, buzzes behind the town hall, the market square was empty, or nearly empty, there was at least one dog, sniffing around between the stalls, a black-haired dog with triangular ears, a restless tail, an attentive nose, the wind strokes Franz's side, ruffles his tail, Franz lifts his head, his stomach rumbles, he keeps on walking, he leaves the square, sniffs at several doorways, scratches with his paws, finds a few titbits, some strips of fat, peel, rotten fruit, bones, he glances about more relaxed, roots around here and there, moves off, crosses Archway and as he passes St Nicholas's Church, passes its twisted facade, Franz stops and urinates copiously against it, the wall absorbs some of the urine, Franz continues on his way, turns the corner, disappears, the wind dries what's left of the urine, the wind scrapes the wall, spreads over the steps, reaches the portico, polishes the arches, creeps under the iron main door, skates up the central nave, makes the candle flames and lamp lights sputter, weaves through the lower aisles, tumbles over the benches, sends a shiver up the spines of the early risers, one of whom draws in her shoulders, raises a hand to her chest and clasps her rosary beads, Frau Pietzine moves her painted lips, she has shadows under her eyes, she prays and prays, another, more slender back repeats aloud the same prayers, Frau Levin intones them vigorously, masticates the words, the wind turns towards the altar, it blows round the crucifix and the candelabras, and makes the angels' toes go cold while on the other side of the altarpiece, in the sacristy, Father Pigherzog tightens his girdle and steps through the door, as the door to the sacristy opens the draught inside collides with the wind, and, as if driven back by a piston, the wind spins round, escapes under the door and dissolves in the open air, for a moment the wind in Wandernburg is still, the smoke from the chimneys rises vertically, the window panes rest, the clothes repose, until the wind gathers its various parts and grows in strength, skips once more up the steps, surges aloft, rises above the church, sharpens a spire, shakes the bell, flies over a few streets and begins to die down, to calm, it blows past balconies, drips with the water trickling from the flowerpots, forks into branches, one of which sweeps along the ground, ambles down Glass Alley, catches in horses' hooves, carriage wheels, legs, eludes the shop windows, invisible in their reflections, licks the entrance to Café Europa, imbibes the aroma of chocolate, pauses in the doorway, on the other side of which Álvaro is resting his elbows firmly on a copy of the *Gazette*, he hasn't slept, he's been sitting like that for a long time, without reading, staring absent-mindedly at the far wall, the wind goes on by, moves forward, at the next corner runs into its other parts, it churns, swells, crosses Old Cauldron Street, enters the inn through the yard, sweeps down the corridor, bursts into the Zeits' apartment, visits the children's room, scarcely disturbs Thomas's toys, discovers Lisa under her bed with a candle, secretly studying, spelling the words in her exercise book, on the other side of the room the firewood crackles, the wind flies up the chimney and out into the white sky, stretches like a piece of rubber over the city, leans against the other tower in the market square, coils around it like a rope, makes the weathervane spin, then crosses diagonally towards Stag Street, the knockers on the Gottlieb residence, lion and swallow, threaten to tap against

the hardwood, or they do tap imperceptibly, the sound travels
to the gallery, the coach houses, the frozen garden, a puff of
wind is carried up the stairs, where Herr Gottlieb is asleep or
does not want to get up, Bertold does not insist, Petra curses the
food she is cooking by the five chimes of the five bells of the
five rooms from which the servants can be called, on the top
floor, Elsa browses her English-grammar book half-heartedly,
she hasn't a lot to do these days, on the ground floor, the wall
clock waits for someone to wind it, everything in the drawing
room has a lifeless air, and yet the Prussian-blue curtains flutter,
twist, let themselves be ruffled by the gusts of wind blowing
through the gap in the windows not properly closed, these gusts
of wind scatter some of the ash from the marble fireplace, the
statues stand idle on the mantelpiece, the unused flower vases,
and to one side of the hearth, glimmering discreetly among
the family portraits, Titian reproductions, still lifes and hunting
scenes, is the painting of the traveler walking into the forest,
a snow-covered forest, a forest that resembles the pinewood
where the wind is also now blowing among the rocks on the
hill, the spindly poplars, the frozen band of the River Nulte,
thirty-two pointed pine cones, the mouth of an empty cave,
the wind invades everything and leaves behind everything, it
leaves behind the flat, milky-white fields, the planted cornfields,
the frozen pastures, the flock of sheep on the point of lambing
in the depths of winter, it leaves behind the fields where the
peasants are burying roots in the ground, the windmill sails, the
factory that tarnishes the air, the snow-covered paths, the main
road that passes to the east of Wandernburg, and on which
a few coaches are traveling to Berlin, or south to Leipzig, it
leaves behind Bridge Walk, where Sophie is standing with her
two valises, clinging on to her hat so that it doesn't blow off,
waiting for the next coach, her two valises filled with clothes,
papers and doubts, and farther away, much farther away, the

wind is also pulling along the coach that carries Hans, who is traveling wherever it may be, his trunk rattling on the roof rack, weighted down by canvas, ropes and snow, Hans, at whose feet sits a casket with a barrel organ inside, Hans who uses his sleeve to wipe the window, opens it, sticks his head out, and feels the wind welcoming him.